NEW AUSTRIAN ORDER

ORDER

L.D. Towers

Cataloging-in-Publication Data

Towers, L.D.
New Austrian Order / by L.D. Towers.
p. cm.
ISBN 978-0994910325
1. Germany--History--1933-1945--Fiction. 2. Nazis--Fiction. 3.
Intelligence officers--Fiction.
I. Title.

813.54--dc22

Acknowledgements...

There are two people without whom this book would never have been written:

Rachel White- my amazing editor, who has read this more than anyone should ever have to. I think the last edit almost did her in. Thank you, Rachel!

Secondly, Dietrich Pütter- who has taught me so much about the time in which he lived. Thank you for time, patience and amazing stories.

To my parents, Robin and Heather Towers- I know that having a WWII obsessed writer as a child makes for boring Sunday dinners! Thanks for your continued support! Every single car is for you, Dad!

To Joanne Pearson- I know that when I fall, you will be there to catch me... just as you did after the Camino. I don't have the words to describe my gratitude.

To my muse – This world exists because you helped create it.

To all those who helped me pick a cover, sat and listened to me ramble about where to split the monster, politely nodded and smiled while I pontificated on the Third Reich, who didn't tell me to shut up as I told the same story about Galiena for the sixth time and who were just there... Thank you!

To all the people online who have supported me! Thank you all!

Wehrmacht Ranks	SS Ranks	American Ranks
Soldat		
Grenadier	SS-Schütze	Private
Obergrenadier	SS-Oberschütze	Private 1st Class
Gefreiter	SS-Sturmmann	Corporal
Obergefreiter	SS-Rottenführer	
Stabsgefreiter		
Unteroffizier	SS-Unterscharführer	Sergeant
Unterfeldwebel	SS-Scharführer	Staff Sgt.
Fähnrich	SS-Junker	Officer Cadet
Feldwebel	SS-Oberscharführer	Technical Sgt.
Oberfeldwebel	SS-Hauptscharführer	Master Sgt.
Hauptfeldwebel	SS-Stabsscharführer	
Oberfähnrich	SS-Standartenjunker	Sr. Officer Cadet
	SS-Standartenoberjunker	
Stabsfeldwebel	SS-Sturmscharführer	Sergeant Major
Leutnant	SS-Untersturmführer	2nd Lieutenant
Oberleutnant	SS-Obersturmführer	1st Lieutenant
Hauptmann	SS-Hauptsturmführer	Captain
Major	SS-Sturmbannführer	Major
Oberstleutnant	SS-Obersturmbannführer	Lt. Colonel
Oberst	SS-Standartenführer	Colonel
	SS-Oberführer	
Generalmajor	SS-Brigadeführer	Brigadier General
Generalleutnant	SS-Gruppenführer	Major General
General der	SS-Obergruppenführer	Lieutenant General
Generaloberst	SS-Oberstgruppenführer	General
Generalfeldmarschall	Reichsführer-SS	General of the Army

Table of Comparative Ranks

September 12, 1937
Dearest Poppet,

I know that I have hurt you, and because of this you have left me. Nevertheless I am here, waiting for you to return, as I know you will. You belong to me and I am desolate without you. I miss you.
Eternally yours,
Meinrad

Chapter 1
February 10, 1938

The Pfalzgräfin von Steinberg zum Riesa held the limp hand of the man laying in the hospital bed. Galiena was rubenesque, with thick auburn hair braided in a knot at the back of head. Her large-brimmed hat was perched elegantly on her head and matched her violet suit perfectly. A wide velvet ribbon encircled her throat, pinned shut to one side with a broach; the long streamers trailing to the level of her waist. The ribbon looked out of place, as if it was to cover something.

"Come now, Rottenführer Lustig. You must get better! I know you must be upset to hear the Mercedes was irreparable, but don't let that deter you from consciousness!" Galiena urged the motionless figure.

"He is in a coma, Pfalzgräfin. He cannot hear you," Hauptsturmführer Eugen Freisler, the six foot five giant, rasped at her side. Immaculately turned out in his SS uniform and with his vocal cords shattered by gas in WWI, Eugen was a man much feared. Called the Höllenhund[1] by his enemies, Eugen was known to be ruthless to a fault. Galiena believed Eugen to be in his forties, but taking in his strangely unlined face, pure white hair and eyebrows, gauging Eugen's age was a difficult thing.

Eugen was the best friend and subordinate to Galiena's intended husband, Standartenfuhrer Doctor Hagen Kohl. Some had

---

[1] Hellhound

told her to fear Eugen, but strangely, she felt no fear of the man at all. Eugen was a monolith of a man, but she had seen a different side of him. Besides, she had her own nightmares, and she knew Eugen would protect her from them to his last breath.

Galiena turned to Eugen where he stood quietly at her back. Since the attack on Reichsführer-SS Heinrich Himmler's car just a week previous by a group assumed to be members of the army, Eugen had become her shadow; steps behind whenever she left the protection of her residence. Something had changed since she had become Hagen's fiancée. It was as if being claimed by the one man had made her the property of the other.

"But he must hear me! Just because he is asleep, doesn't mean he can't hear, Eugen! I refuse to believe he can't!" Galiena protested, before turning her gaze back to the stricken young man. Rottenführer Thilo Lustig was Hagen's driver and Eugen's nephew. He had been shot three times in the chest during the ambush. He was only alive because the bullets of the field machine guns had passed through the door of Hagen's Mercedes before entering Lustig, slowing down their path of destruction. Lustig had been using the Mercedes to push the Reichsführer's disabled Maybach out of the range of the attack at the time. The young man had not regained consciousness in the eight days since the battle.

Galiena did not know Lustig well; indeed she barely knew him at all. He was Hagen's chauffeur and the young SS man who delivered Hagen's letters to her. Galiena remembered how the shy soldier had been teased into demonstrating his ability to do one handed push-ups like his uncle and how he had once buried her in a snowball fight. Now he hovered between life and death and she wished she had taken the time to know him better. There had been too much death that day. The attack occurred just after the funeral of one of Hagen's officers, and eight of the Reichsführer's guards had perished defending them.

A pale hand inadvertently touched the ribbon at her throat. Underneath lay a finger-shaped burn; oozing and blistered, close to her jugular vein. The spent shell of a defender's gun had landed there and the searing heat of it had blistered. Still, she was very lucky for she had been protected in the footwell of the Maybach; Heinrich Himmler covering her with his person. Hagen, Eugen,

Himmler, and the brave Gruppenführer Wolff had all emerged unscathed.

A large paw descended on her shoulder, jolting her back to reality. "That is fanciful, Pfalzgräfin, but I do appreciate the gesture." The ruined voice dropped even lower. "Lustig is like my own son."

Galiena rested her cheek on the hand; she liked Eugen very much despite his terrifying voice and powerful body. He struck her as being a man lost. Arrested in development. He'd never moved past the Great War and it coloured all aspects of who he was.

"He will get better, Eugen. I know he will. I feel it," Galiena replied earnestly, trying to reassure the man with her eyes. "He just needs time. That is what the doctors say. Time. I'm sure they are right. Herr Himmler assured me that he sent his personal doctor to help Rottenführer Lustig."

"If he dies, my sister will have my guts for garters. Excuse the expression," gruffly said, but the hand squeezed her shoulder. Eugen touched her all the time now; her head, neck or back, in a way which was new to her. It was as if that was the only way the taciturn Bavarian could demonstrate his affection. Galiena didn't mind precisely; but it was foreign. In the cold world of the aristocracy, people didn't touch one another. The only person who had free reign of her body was her maid.

Galiena leaned her head back to gaze all the way up into Eugen's eyes; brilliant green like a cat's. "You are forgiven, Eugen."

"Very gracious of you, Your Serene Highness."

"My pleasure," she smiled up at him. He did not return the smile, but he did pat her shoulder slowly, almost absently. She stroked the hand in hers again, returning her attention to the invalid. "Come, Rottenführer Lustig! Fight harder! Just open your eyes! Please? You're too young to give up!"

"The Freisler blood is in him. We are hard to kill," Eugen told her flatly.

Galiena stood, and arranged the flowers she had brought. Her previous bouquet of a few days ago had faded and she relegated them to the trash. Hospitals were so dreary. Galiena walked over to the window and opened the drape to let in the feeble winter sunlight. The day was overcast but the sun kept trying to break through the clouds. "It is so dark in here. Who would want to wake up at all in this gloom?"

"The boy is asleep. I don't think it makes any difference," Eugen stated, his consternation evident.

Galiena glared back at him. "It makes all the difference in the world, Eugen. Put a plant in a closet and it dies. People must be the same way."

Eugen rolled his eyes and grunted. "His eyes are closed. He can't see the light."

"But he can feel light! Feel the sun on his skin," Galiena retorted hotly at his lack of understanding. It all seemed so simple to her. Feeling useless, she twisted her blue diamond engagement ring on her finger. It's newness still felt strange on her hand.

Eugen grunted again; he seemed to be fond of that noise. He moved closer to the bed and bowed his head in recognition. "Get better, boy. The Reichsführer wants to give you a medal. Hard thing to pin on a corpse."

Galiena walked to the other side of the bed. "Now that is encouraging," she replied dryly. "You would have me leaping out of a coma!"

"What am I supposed to say?"

She blinked at him. "What's in your heart!"

The huge man inhaled and slowly exhaled. "My heart? I don't have one."

Galiena laughed out loud. "I know it's there! I've seen it." She walked around the bed and took his arm.

"And you, Pfalzgräfin, do not know me as well as you think you do."

"That's possible, Hauptsturmführer Freisler!" She returned her gaze to Lustig. "You have to get better because Eugen tells me you love cars. I plan to order another for Hagen, and as his driver I think you should help me pick it!"

"You are not going to buy Hagen another car." Eugen stated, all but issuing an order.

The young woman rounded fearlessly on the SS officer. "Indeed I am, Eugen!" Galiena had bought the bright red Mercedes to replace Hagen's previous car which she had destroyed in a collision the night they met.

"He won't like it if you do," Eugen cautioned her.

Herr Doom and Gloom could get so tiresome when he was being demanding. "Stuff and nonsense, Eugen. I have the money. If I want to buy a fleet of the silly things, I can." As Galiena was heiress to one of Germany's great fortunes, money meant little to her.

"You shouldn't do it!" A pointy finger thrust its way under her nose.

She slanted Eugen an amused look. "Do not think, Eugen Freisler, to tell me what I can and cannot do! The consequences would be dangerous and potentially very expensive."

"I can believe that, Your Serene Highness," the man muttered under his breath.

"I do so hate it when you use my title, Eugen. I really do." Galiena was a Pfalzgräfin, or Countess Palatine, an independent ruler with a title going back to the first Holy Roman Emperor. In essence they were princes who used a different title. Her family once ruled a swath of Germany, but had lost their independence during the Napoleonic Wars. They still controlled vast tracts of land, and the family corporation, an international conglomerate, made them an economic powerhouse. Galiena was a pragmatic woman when it came to her title. She didn't believe an accident of birth made her better than other people. Once upon a time, she could have been accused of the sin of republicanism.

"I am not going to discuss this with you again, Pfalzgräfin. I am not calling you by your name." This had become a long standing issue between Eugen and Galiena. The times he used her name were few and far between, and only in times of danger or duress. It seemed a point of honour for the man, and Galiena found it incomprehensible that he could be so free with his hands on her person and not use her Christian name.

Galiena sighed, then moved away from Eugen and bent over Lustig to press her lips to the cold forehead. "Please recover, Rottenführer."

"Be a Freisler, Thilo Lustig. What are a couple of bullets to a Freisler? Heil Hitler." The man saluted crisply, his heels coming together with a snap.

Galiena turned and slowly walked out of the hospital room, Eugen looming behind her. "Do you think he looks better, Eugen?" she asked in a small voice.

"Don't know," the man paused. "You shouldn't have kissed him," he said finally.

She laughed and threw her eyes up to his. "You aren't serious, are you?"

"Of course I am. The only man you should kiss is Hagen," the Hauptsturmführer answered matter-of-factly.

"Oh Eugen! I've kissed you on the cheek. What's the difference?" Galiena drawled impudently.

"I don't count. I won't get confused. I know who you belong to." The great paw was on her shoulder again.

"How positively medieval, Eugen, and just a little bit insulting. I don't belong to anyone," Galiena spoke forcefully; her own independence something she was learning to treasure.

The rumbling laugh seemed to surround her. "As you wish it." Eugen seemed a little too amused by her statement.

"So who, pray tell, do I belong to?"

"In order? Hagen. Me. After that it gets more complicated."

She stopped in her tracks and challenged the man face on. "I belong to you, do I, Eugen? You want to claim me?"

Eugen simply shrugged. "I have to protect both of you. You belong to me. You belong to Hagen a different way. You are his wife." He screwed his face up thoughtfully, and then nodded to himself. "Yes. It will be much easier for me when we are married. Having the two of you in separate residences is getting tiresome."

"When we get married? That's the second time you have said that. Hagen and I are getting married, Eugen," Galiena informed him patiently.

The big man rolled his shoulders again. "I know that. But you get me, too. Not for the children part, of course; those you will have with Hagen," he patted her shoulder again, all seemingly correct in his world. "Though I'm looking quite forward to us all getting married. Enough of this, shall we go? We don't want you to be late for your lunch with the Reichsführer and Gruppenführer Wolff."

Galiena shook her head, somewhat mystified. Eugen was usually so quiet, and yet whenever he started to get chatty, the strangest things came out of his mouth. Eugen was simply Eugen. There was no explaining him. When she really thought about it, there was a certain veracity to his words.

They exited the building and entered a large Pullman Mercedes limousine bearing the pennant of the Commander in Chief of the Luftwaffe, Hermann Göring. Göring was Galiena's guardian and honorary uncle, a protégé of her dead father during the Great War. Galiena had fled to Göring's protection in September after her grandfather, the Pfalzgraf, brutalized her. A strangely deluded man, the Pfalzgraf seemed to believe that Galiena was his wife as well as his granddaughter. The day and night he claimed his marital rights were the darkest of her life, and something she was still unable to comprehend or think about. It was the night she escaped her grandfather that she crashed into Hagen, meeting the man who would so completely change her life.

Galiena had only seen her grandfather once since the attack, at a wedding not even a month ago. She had tried to shoot the old man in the parking lot of the chapel but the gun had misfired and now the Pfalzgraf was in the custody of the SS.

"You are upset," Eugen was studying her, his head cocked. The car slowly pulled away. "I did not upset you by saying Hagen and I owned you, did I? It was not meant badly."

Galiena's shaking hand made a negative gesture. "I was thinking about the Pfalzgraf," she breathed, trying to calm herself. The nightmare she knew Eugen would die protecting her from. Trying to push the memories back into the dark hole they came from. No man would ever touch her the same way again. She just hadn't come up with a way to articulate that to her future husband.

Eugen reached across the car and touched her gloved hand with his finger, tapping it impatiently. Of course, Eugen knew everything. If Hagen knew, Eugen knew. "Not a good thing to think about."

"No. Probably not," she agreed, but the spectre of Meinrad von Steinberg had reawakened in new ways. Her grandfather's business manager kept trying to contact her. Galiena knew she could only put him off for so long.

Eugen leaned toward her, his eyes intense. "He can't hurt you anymore. We won't let him hurt you. The SS looks after its own."

Galiena encased his big hand with her two. "Where is he, Eugen?"

The hard eyes assessed her. "I shouldn't tell you that, Pfalzgräfin. You might have a gun handy and hie off to kill him. That wouldn't make Hagen happy."

She laughed mirthlessly. "No. I can't kill him. Not now. I did so already, when I fired that gun. My mind is much clearer now, and I realise I am not done with him. I just want to know where he is."

He raised a pale brow under his cap. "He is in KZ[2] Buchenwald."

"Where is that?" Galiena pressed breathlessly.

"Near Weimar."

"Would you take me there, Eugen? If I asked you?" Galiena pleaded; suddenly vulnerable now that she had a name.

It was Eugen's turn to laugh; but this laugh was cold. "I would never take you to that place, or any other like it. Hagen would kill me for it, and Hagen would be right. You don't need to go near your grandfather and you certainly don't need to visit a KZ." He clenched his fist around her hand, firmly, but not painfully. "Put that right out of your mind."

How little the big man understood women. "Yes, Eugen," she responded with deceptive meekness. Eugen wasn't the only person who could help her with this. Galiena was not without deviousness or resources. "You didn't tell Hagen we were having lunch with the Reichsführer or Gruppenführer Wolff, did you?" Galiena changed the subject.

"No. I didn't. You asked me not to, and I didn't think it was relevant for him to know. You did say you were planning a surprise for his birthday." Eugen curled the corners of his lips up into what he considered a smile. It was only faintly different from his usual expression. "I think it's a good idea."

"I was surprised Herr Himmler agreed to meet with me so soon," Galiena remarked, wondering how this meeting would go. They had seen each other once since the ambush; the Reichsführer-SS had dropped in to visit her at the hospital. Under the direction of her her uncle, she had been kept at the famous Charité hospital for two days for observation. It had been a brief meeting, cut short when an infuriated Hermann Göring arrived; bristling and on the

---

[2] Konzentrationslager – Concentration camp

attack for the injuries received by Galiena while in Himmler's care. The famously frigid relationship between the two men did not need the strain and while Galiena had tried to explain to her uncle that the attack was hardly Himmler's fault, Göring still would have none of it.

"Hagen is his fair haired boy and he is very taken with you," Eugen added quickly. "It could be because he nearly got you killed. He would be very upset if you broke off your engagement with Hagen because of that. The Reichsführer was very pleased you agreed to marry Hagen."

"As if I would break with him," Galiena scoffed as she grinned back at Eugen; feeling the need to play. "Hagen's mine and I'm not letting him go."

Eugen glanced at her sharply, assessing her. "What do you mean by that?" He asked as the car came to a halt.

"Exactly as I said, Eugen," she patted his cheek. "I suppose that means I own you, too."

The SS man appeared faintly taken aback. "How do you figure, Pfalzgräfin?"

Galiena blinked at the man, her face a mask of innocence. "Didn't you just say that you and Hagen came as a matched set?" The driver of the limousine opened the door and she exited. "Coming Eugen?" she asked, walking into Horscher's, one of Berlin's premier restaurants.

Galiena surveyed the place. Horscher's was one of her favourite places to eat, and as she had invited the Reichsführer and Gruppenführer Wolff out to lunch today, she picked the locale. Galiena knew from a one-off comment of Hagen's that the Reichsführer was notoriously parsimonious when it came to luxuries for himself, so it pleased her to bring him to this place. She figured that the man probably deserved a dining experience.

The maître d' came up to her as soon as he saw her. "Pfalzgräfin von Steinberg! Such a pleasure to see you again. Are you dining with Feldmarschall Göring? I have not yet seen him though he is expected today."

"No. I am here with the Reichsführer-SS. Has he arrived yet?" Galiena answered the man as she allowed him to take her coat.

"Yes he has. I will take you to him immediately," the maître d' replied efficiently.

"Thank you. Please put lunch on my account," Galiena ordered. Göring had long established credit for Galiena here and conveniently the restaurant settled directly with her banker.

"Yes, Madame. If you would be so kind as to follow me."

"Do bring a bottle of my uncle's favourite champagne please and don't allow the bottle to stay empty," Galiena instructed and wrinkled her nose mischievously. She was escorted to a table which was decent, but not the best in the restaurant; certainly not one her uncle would be shown to. She hid a smile. Obviously the Reichsführer wasn't as beloved at Horscher's as other people were; but then who in Germany, barring the Fuhrer, was as well loved as Hermann Göring?

"Is that my little Leutnant-girl?" A slurred voice called out as she passed a table and Galiena turned around. A man was climbing unsteadily to his feet behind her, arms outstretched. It was General Ernst Udet, the famous fighter pilot and Great War ace. He was also Galiena's flight instructor and friend. She was somewhat surprised. It was only one thirty and Galiena had left him at eleven this morning from her lesson; how could he have become so drunk so quickly? General Udet was famous for his ability to carouse but this might be a record, even for him. Galiena was very fond of Udet and his lessons. It was true, some mornings when he arrived he was still awake and quite drunk from the night before, but even completely intoxicated he was the most gifted pilot in Germany. Udet was simply Udet. One got used to his idiosyncrasies. She spent at least two hours a day with him in the air, rain or shine. There was something to be said for having the country's premier pilot as a teacher.

Galiena affected an Oriental style bow. "Is that my esteemed master?"

Udet laughed and kissed her cheeks exuberantly. "It is! It is! How are you, my darling? What has it been? Three hours?"

"Something like that, yes!" Galiena giggled, towering over the shorter man.

"Too long. Yes. Too long. Come! Sit! Are you here to meet Göring?" His eyes seemed fantastically bright as his hands dropped to her waist. "We're dining together." Udet was usually more respectful of Galiena's personal space, though now he seemed so drunk he could barely stand.

"No. I am meeting others. Is my uncle coming here today?" Galiena asked with some concern. She didn't want her uncle to see her with Himmler, but if it happened, it couldn't be helped.

"Yes. I am in the soup, my dear. Getting chewed out by that bastard Erhard Milch. Pardon my language." Udet made a face. "Best defence against that bloody little Jew is the scotch defence. The more scotch you have the better defended you are! I think I drained a bottle in the car on the way over. Medicinal, you know."

"I didn't know General Milch was Jewish?" Galiena questioned the older man. It pained her to see Udet so wasted with drink. It was such a squander of a brilliant man.

"Bah! Göring fixed it so officially he isn't!" Udet narrowed his eyes and laid his finger alongside his nose. "But I know the truth! The man's father was a Jew, no matter what Göring says! What do they call them? U-boats? Well, that's what he is."

She laughed. "Master, I believe that Jewishness is matrilineal. Having only a Jewish father wouldn't make him a real Jew to other Jews."

"That's not what the law says. And I'm not Jew baiting. There are good ones, and bad ones, and that one is a first class rotter. Mark my words. He wants to tear my wings off and make me look bad to the big man." Udet finished with a pathetic desperation. "I'm not going to let that happen. No desk jockey is going to ruin my good name."

"I'm sure it's all a misunderstanding. You know uncle Hermann loves you! Best of luck and I will see you tomorrow!" Galiena smiled again and then squeezed his arm. "I must go join my party." Before I'm discovered by uncle Hermann. Curse my damned luck for coming here the same day as him, Galiena thought.

Udet's eyes searched around blearily. "Who you here with?" He slurred. "I don't see that fellow of yours."

"No. Hagen isn't here today. I am here with others. But I must dash," she said evasively, hating to do this to Udet.

"You always leave me. One of these days it might just hurt my feelings!" The man sat down with a decided lack of elegance.

11

"If Milch gets too hard on me I am coming to find you and stealing you away as consolation! Maybe take that plane up again to watch the sunset! We could fly to Tahiti! That would be a lark. Kiss the old Reich goodbye. No more being chained to a desk!"

"Not such a terrible idea!" Galiena blew a kiss to the little General. "You are always welcome wherever I am!" She continued behind the maître d', who had been waiting rather patiently in the aisle. They finished their journey to the table where Heinrich Himmler, the Reichsführer-SS, and Gruppenführer Karl Wolff were waiting. They were both eyeing Udet with looks of distaste. Himmler was a very pale, spare man with short dark hair and intelligent blue eyes, hidden behind a pince-nez. A triangular moustache rested on the top of his thin lips, and beneath them was his weak chin. Karl Wolff was a tall, sinewy man, with extraordinarily pale eyes and blond hair slicked straight back away from his face. There always seemed something kindly about Wolff, a gentleness which radiated from inside, yet Galiena had seen him with a machine gun in his hands, just as aggressive as his namesake. Wolff's fanatic loyalty to Himmler was well known; as Eugen was to Hagen, Wolff was to the Reichsführer-SS.

Both men stood up as she approached. Himmler walked around the table to kiss her on both cheeks. "My very dear Galiena! What a positive delight it is to see you looking so well." His mild Bavarian accent filled her ears as his lips brushed her skin. His gesture was perhaps overly forward if one based it on the length of their acquaintance; Galiena and Himmler had only met a few times, but their experiences together during the ambush had forced an intimacy on their relationship. Lying in a man's arms while bullets flew overhead would do that. He had been very careful to cover her with his body and protect her. On their rescue, he had begged the honour to consider her as his only sister and she had agreed, occasionally calling him brother in return.

"Heinrich! You flatter me," Galiena responded, batting her eyelashes at him. The intimacy could remain, as far as Galiena was concerned. Himmler was a powerful ally to have and a girl really couldn't have too many in this day and age.

"Never, Madame! Never!" The blue eyes sparkled with pleasure.

"Your Serene Highness," Wolff clicked his heels together and bowed to Galiena, formal as always.

She inclined her head, then moved over and embraced Wolff quickly. "Dear Gruppenführer Wolff!"

Wolff coloured bashfully. "How are you, Madame?"

Galiena sat down elegantly. "I am very well, but I have just been to see Rottenführer Lustig and he does not seem to be recovering. I fear he won't wake up."

Himmler and Wolff found their seats immediately and the Reichsführer studied her for a moment. "Yes. I had heard the young man was still in a coma. It is a terrible tragedy. So many good men lost or wounded. We will make the perpetrators pay for what they have done." There was a dreadful finality in his voice, and then it changed. "But enough of that. I see you are acquainted with General Udet?" He spat disapprovingly.

Galiena laughed dismissively. "How could I live in the house where I live and not, Heinrich?"

Himmler nodded in acknowledgement. "Indeed."

She felt the need to elucidate further. "But more than that, he is my flight instructor. We fly together every day."

Wolff raised his eyebrows. "You fly, Madame? You are a pilot?"

"Not as yet, but very soon I will take my pilot's test. I'm very nervous about it and General Udet is unable to take the time train me as he would like. I believe he is scouring the Luftwaffe to find someone he thinks is good enough to tutor me." She told the two men easily, for flying was both her distraction and her joy.

"How fascinating," Wolff sat back, gazing at her, a bemused expression on his face.

"General Udet has promised to let me take up a Stuka as soon as I am qualified. Then he says the real training will begin." Galiena smoothed her napkin in her lap as she evaluated the SS leaders for their reaction. Himmler was famously old fashioned about the roles of women.

"Surely the General must be joking," Himmler scoffed. "It's hardly seemly for a woman to be flying a bomber."

Sadly, he didn't disappoint her. "But you see, my dear Heinrich, to General Udet I am not a woman. I am the child of Rudiger von Steinberg." What a complete falsehood. Udet was more than aware of her femininity. "He thinks it's his sacred mission to ensure I am at least as good a pilot as my father was." She assessed the man opposite her. "He considers it a duty to my blood."

Himmler nodded very solemnly. "Yes. I had forgotten your father was a pilot. Then it is all understandable if it is in your blood; such things must be nurtured so they can be passed on."

Galiena studied Himmler under her lashes. His fixation with her ancestry was a trifle unnerving, but obviously could be used in her favour. "Besides there is nothing unnatural about female pilots! Look at Hanna Reitsch! Or Amelia Earhart for that matter!"

"Did Earhart not perish flying?" The Reichsführer-SS touched her hand. It seemed little larger than hers and just as delicate; not what one would describe as a masculine hand. "No. I'm sorry. I do not mean to degrade your accomplishments. They are not you, Galiena! You are special."

"I am no more special than any other woman, my dear brother," Galiena retorted lightly but firmly.

"Yes." Himmler paused, and his eyes took on a bright light. "Yes, you are. Very special indeed. You link us to the past, my dear Pfalzgräfin von Steinberg zum Riesa." The man drew out her title in an exceptionally pointed fashion and Galiena wondered what it was in aid of. "You are very special," he repeated again before he smiled at her; a genuine smile, not a practised one. "And because you are so special, we must indulge you in all things. King Heinrich would want us to indulge you," he added, with a glance at Wolff. "Don't you think so, Wolffschen?"

"Yes. I would agree," Wolff concurred, his face a strange mask.

"King Heinrich the Fowler, Galiena," Himmler added at her questioning eye. "He guides our order in all things. Our patron, as it were."

"He was a Saxon King, was he not?" Galiena asked, dredging through her memories of history class from school.

"Yes. He drove the Slavs out of Germany. We are rebuilding his tomb; it is one of my special projects. Speaking of, my dear, I have assigned two of my personal historians from the Ahenerbe Society[3] to completely chronicle your family as far back as they can. I have given them an unlimited budget to accomplish this task. If there is anything you can do to assist us, we would be extremely grateful," Himmler told her, encouragement shining from his eyes.

Galiena thought hard on this. "I would have to go back to Riesa to get the information." A chill went up her spine. Could she go there? Enter that place which had been her home and prison? The place where her Grandfather hurt her so badly?

Wolff leaned forward. "You have turned quite pale, Your Serene Highness."

Himmler's face twisted in concern. "I have not distressed you, have I?"

Galiena was saved from having to answer right away when the waiter came to take their orders. The men had obviously made their choice before Galiena arrived and she merely picked her favourite Krug vintage. The champagne also arrived, chilled and dripping in its ice bucket. "Thank you," Galiena said to the waiter.

"We did not order champagne," Himmler looked askance at the bottle.

"A member of the Göring household can't dine at Horscher's without champagne." Galiena replied with a small smile, desperately craving a drink.

"I normally don't partake of alcohol."

"You don't want to hurt my feelings do you, Heinrich?" Galiena flashed a winsome glance at Himmler. Alcohol had become her salvation in the last few months. Himmler's prudishness about drink could go to perdition.

"No. That would be ungentlemanly." Himmler nodded at the man, who opened the bottle.

They toasted each other and drank the ice cold champagne. The bubbles tickled Galiena's nose as she sipped. "Lovely as always," she whispered, her eyes rolling back into her head with pleasure.

"Now tell me, what did I say to upset you?" Himmler asked; his face gentle and paternal.

Galiena considered what she said very carefully. "I left the guardianship of my Grandfather under difficult circumstances, and

---

[3] Ancestral Heritage

I have not been to Riesa since I left last September. I am conflicted about returning."

Wolff's face showed his sympathy. "While I do not know the precise details of your flight, you can rest assured that neither the Reichsführer or myself would want you to return to a place which could cause you pain." There was a note of warning in his voice, but she didn't think it was for her. Wolff's eyes had moved over to Himmler's as he finished his sentence.

"Yes. Of course. If you are not able to assist us at this time, my men will still work on the project," Himmler hastened to assure her.

Galiena studied the bubbles in her glass, contemplating her next proposal. "You might be the person to ask, Heinrich. If somebody wanted to visit a prison inmate, how would they go about it?"

"I suppose they would apply to the commandant of the institution, but it would very much depend on the institution. Shall I assume the visitor is yourself?" Himmler asked directly, seeing through her with ease.

"Yes. It is me."

Now Wolff was studying her, dreadful certainty etched across his face. "What institution would you be interested in?"

"Konzentrationslager Buchenwald, I believe the name is," she replied deftly, for artifice would be useless at this juncture.

Himmler started to laugh. "And who, pray tell, do you know in Buchenwald? I can't imagine you could possibly know anyone in that place!"

Wolff shook his head curtly. "No, Your Serene Highness. I think that would be terribly ill advised. I cannot imagine Hagen would allow you to go there. Has he already denied this request?"

A brow slid up over the pince-nez. "Wolffschen! Have you been keeping secrets from me?"

"The Pfalzgraf von Steinberg is our guest at KZ Buchenwald on the request of the Minister President of Prussia and under the authority of Standartenführer Hagen Kohl," Wolff detailed the situation for his superior with brusque finality.

"And in answer to your question, Gruppenführer Wolff, Hagen has not denied me the request because I have not made it of him. I would not make it of him, because I have it on very good authority he wouldn't let me go." Galiena drew herself up to her full height in her chair. "But there are issues that I must address with my Grandfather before I can get married, and I would rather Hagen be kept ignorant of the situation. I would also prefer my uncle be kept ignorant as well."

Wolff tapped the table with a finger. "The last time you saw your grandfather, you tried to kill him, Madame. I can understand why Hagen would want to keep you as far from him as possible."

Himmler bobbed his head. "Ah, yes. Now I remember," He turned to Galiena. "Wolffschen does have an accurate reading of the situation."

Galiena turned to Himmler, hoping to manipulate him to her way of thinking. The tactic disgusted her as she did like Himmler, but this was business. "Partially it's a question of duty. I have been approached by my grandfather's business managers to assume the reins of the family Gessellschaft. I cannot do so without a letter expressing his wish that I do so. I was groomed to be his," she paused, her mouth going dry. Wife. That was what Meinrad von Steinberg groomed her to be. "Heir," she said at last, almost choking on the word. A quick gulp of champagne steadied her nerves and helped chase the demons away.

"What makes you so positive you could get that authority?" Himmler's face turned very shrewd.

"I know my grandfather. Or at least I did." Her voice trailed off as she thought on the night everything changed. "And I would be very grateful for any assistance rendered to me in the acquisition of that authority." She wondered how well the Reichsführer would respond to an appeal to his greed.

There was silence as the waiters came with their food, yet Himmler's eyes never left hers the entire time. Galiena could see the gears turning behind his gaze. Finally the staff departed, and Himmler spoke. "Why is this so important to you, Galiena? I can't imagine it is about finances." How did he manage to strip her bones clean with a sentence? Could the Reichsführer read her mind so well? Or was it something else? What did he know?

"You, yourself are the reason, Heinrich. Your talk of blood. My blood. I have a responsibility to my family. I was born to assume the mantle of First Lady of Riesa. My grandfather is incarcerated. My sister is incapacitated. There is no one else. What kind of creature would I be if I allowed my family properties, some of which have been in our care for over a thousand years, to crumble through neglect? What would I be leaving for my children? My grandfather could potentially live another ten or fifteen years. That is a very long time without someone at the helm," Galiena replied directly.

"You speak very elegantly, my sister." Himmler smoothed his napkin in his lap, his face carefully composed. "I shall look into the matter and consider it. One should never shirk one's duty. It is not the German way. You are a very lovely young woman and yet there is a gravity to you I had not sensed before. You have an understanding of the world and the way things work which is a credit to you." He touched Wolff on the arm. "I would appreciate it if you did not mention the Pfalzgräfin's request to Hagen. It need not concern him at this time."

Wolff looked askance at his superior. "As you wish."

Galiena picked up her fork and began eating. "I appreciate your devoting the time and effort to my problem. I understand that you are a very busy man and the problems of one woman must be far below your notice."

Himmler chuckled as he cut into his meat. "Now don't say that, my dear lady! We have bonded, Galiena. You are of my clan and I feel responsible for you. The problems of one are the problems of all in the SS!"

"How very Alexander Dumas, brother! All for one and one for all? I thought you were the Schutzstaffel, not the king's musketeers!" Galiena exclaimed, her lips curing up in a cheeky grin.

Wolff sipped his champagne. "You are beginning to understand, Your Serene Highness. We are very similar. The SS is a clan. A family. That is why we are so exacting in our standards. Only the best are allowed to join us or wear the black."

"And we really aren't all that different from the king's musketeers, only instead of a king, we have Adolf Hitler. He is our king," Himmler informed her proudly.

They ate and spoke long of trivialities. They told her more about the history of the SS, and Himmler explained his part in the Munich Putsch of 1923; how he had held the standard of the party on the barricades. He described his first meeting with Hagen Kohl, and she could sense very genuine affection for Hagen on behalf of both these men. It gladdened her to hear it. Her uncle hated Himmler with such passion, and while there had to be a reason, Galiena found it hard to see at a glance.

Over dessert she directed the conversation to her real purpose in bringing them here. "Have you gentlemen remembered that the sixteenth is Hagen's birthday?" she asked archly.

"Is it? I had forgotten." Himmler counted numbers on his hands. "I suppose it is, isn't it, Wolffschen."

"It's in your calendar," Wolff replied with a half smile. "You know my staff keeps track of all such things for you."

"Of course, Wolffschen. You always keep me on the ball." The Reichsführer turned his gaze back to Galiena. "You look like a young lady who is plotting."

"I would like to kidnap my beloved from his office on that day. He has been working far too hard and I have plans for him," Galiena replied with a devilish grin.

"How ominous sounding, your Serene Highness," Wolff deadpanned, his amusement evident.

"I made my uncle promise he would send me home from the Obersalzburg on the fifteenth, no matter what. We are leaving tomorrow to go visit the Fuhrer." Galiena tried to keep the dread from her voice, for the last person she wanted to visit was her uncle Fuhrer.

"Yes. We shall be flying up on the morning of the twelfth for a meeting. I am sure it is the same meeting Feldmarschall Göring is attending." Himmler raised an eyebrow at Galiena.

She laughed impishly at him. "No trying to steal my secrets, my brother. I am not so easily drawn out! Not even for family!"

"No. Of course not. But I am sure the meeting in question is no secret," he responded wryly, his body language betraying consternation.

"You could be correct," Galiena leaned over and batted her eyelashes at the Reichsführer and pouted theatrically, her voice breathy. "So may I have Hagen for the day?"

"You are relentless when you are after something, aren't you, Madame?" Himmler laughed at her, but at the same time a shy blush broke out across his cheeks. Was Himmler not used to the flirtatious wiles of a winsome female? Galiena was surprised. The man was married after all, though strangely enough, she had never met his wife who perennially kept to their countryside estate.

She touched his fingertips. "Of course I am, my dear Heinrich, but it is in my blood. How do you think my family ended up where it is today? It wasn't by practicing any kind of impulse restraint! I'm surprised the expression even exists in my vocabulary! No. Self moderation was never a von Steinberg family trait." The moment she said it, she felt a twist in her belly. No. None of the von Steinbergs she knew had too large a measure of self control.

Himmler was obviously trying to stifle another laugh, unaware of the ice in Galiena's gut. "How indeed? What blood you bring to my SS! How very formidable you are. Yes. I will make sure he is back in Berlin for his birthday. You may have him at your leisure."

Galiena pulled herself together and smiled dazzlingly at him. "Why thank you, my very dear Herr Reichsführer. You have made me the happiest girl in the entire Reich!" The breathy little girl voice flustered Himmler again.

Wolff raised a brow. "Until you want something else, I think."

"No, Gruppenführer Wolff. Nothing so visceral. I'm practicing a very special kind of tactics. I have an objective, and I am removing all the stumbling blocks my objective might throw in my way. It makes acquisition so much easier," Galiena sipped her champagne innocently, striking an angelic pose.

"That sounds like something my wife might say," Wolff replied archly with a shake of his head.

"Then I must be practicing for the future."

Chapter 2
February 11, 1938

Doctor Hagen Luitpold Kohl, Standartenführer in the SS and Oberst der Geheime Staatzpolizei or Gestapo, sat at his desk, his feet resting on the surface of the antique monstrosity. He thumbed through a very interesting file, but as this wasn't his first time through, he afforded himself the comfort and ease of his present position. He was meeting with the Reichsführer later on this material, and wanted to have as much committed to memory as possible before hand. That was the way he liked to work. Hagen was nothing if not methodical.

He ran a hand over his carefully pomaded, apricot coloured hair. It was an absent, habitual gesture. In truth, he was beginning to feel normal after all the excitement of the last several months. He had been chasing a group of traitors the length and breadth of Germany trying to prevent an assassination of the Fuhrer. In the end he had stopped an assault on Gestapo headquarters itself; not bad for a few months work. Now he felt at a loose end. He had been investigating officers in the Heer[4], but with the present upheavals in the armed forces, brought on by Adolf Hitler's assumption of direct command and the subsequent reorganization of the ranks, the Reichsführer-SS was changing Hagen's focus. That suited Hagen very well. Previous to the von Taschen case, he had been hounding the SA[5], culling truly foul individuals from the service. People who were criminals as well as men betraying the ideals of National Socialism. Men who were guilty of crimes ranging from extortion to murder. But recent events had lead him to believe that treason was not nearly so clear cut a crime. These traitors had been idealists; believing Hitler to be a tyrant and they loved Germany enough to put their lives on the line to remove him.

Hagen was a follower of National Socialism and a servant of Adolf Hitler. He had been a loyal member of the party since 1930, yet his focus was always the Schutzstaffel or SS. The SS had given him a purpose; an outlet for his love of his country and a way to help his Fatherland back on its feet. His friend, Heinrich

---

[4] Army
[5] Sturmabteilung

Himmler, had created something truly miraculous with his organisation. It was somewhere between a holy order and a knighthood; a devout, militant arm of the Party. Members of the Schutzstaffel were special, and it took extreme dedication to be admitted into the organization. The Schutzstaffel controlled so many different areas in the Reich: from police and prisons, to internal and external intelligence, and even several corporations. Its members had to ascribe to very strict codes of behaviour and in return enjoyed full protection from the civil laws of the Reich.

This file however; was not an example of one of the SS' finer moments. It was the Reichsführer's personal file on the murder of Austrian chancellor Dolfuss and the attempted putsch in 1934 by the Austrian SS. The attempt to take the Austrian government had been a disastrous and embarrassing failure. According to the report, the shooting of Dolfuss had been a mistake; the SS officers involved trying to keep the man and his bodyguards from fleeing. There had been a hail of gunfire and the only man wounded was the Chancellor. It had taken the man hours to die from the belly wound, and even in his mortally injured state, Dolfuss worked to bring about a peace between the members of the Putsch and his government. In the end, the putsch failed because Austrian SA, who didn't leave their barracks at the appointed time, betrayed the Austrian SS to the police.

Hagen felt his lip curl. He hated the SA with every fibre of his being. They were the dinosaurs of the Nazi party. Long ago they had served a purpose and now it was time for them to disappear into the night. The more he knew about them and their betrayals, the more he believed they should be eliminated. It was a fair thought. They seemed to think he should be eliminated too, given their numerous assaults on his life.

Hagen checked his watch; he was going to be late for his meeting if he didn't get moving. He dropped his feet from his desk with a thud and put the file back together. It was never good to keep Himmler waiting, no matter how in favour one was. As he scanned across his desk, his eyes fell across the shoe on his desk, a red scarf resting inside it. The piece of footwear belonged to Galiena, as did the scarf. The pearl grey shoe had been his first tie to her, falling off her foot when the medics had taken her from the scene of the car accident where they met. It was a symbol of her, and not something he could part with. He touched it every day; a ritual for him, calming him to have it near and helping him to focus his thoughts. Hagen supposed it was his obsession, or symbolized his obsession with her. The shoe on his desk reminded him of the prince in the Cinderella fairy tale. He had vowed months ago he would have the foot that fit the shoe, and now he did. She was within his grasp.

The scarf was a favour she had given him, thrown from an extremely low flying plane just before Christmas at the Carinhall. Hagen, who was an indifferent flyer, nearly had heart failure when the Great War triplane buzzed his car, upside down, no less. The pilot, General Ernst Udet, had taken a huge risk as far as Hagen was concerned, but the event convinced Galiena that she should learn to fly.

Hagen ran his finger along the toe of the shoe, feeling an almost sexual pleasure at the feel of the leather under his fingertips. No. Now was not the time. Tearing himself away, he placed Himmler's file in his briefcase before putting on his coat and hat to leave his office. The office of the Reichsführer-SS was not in this building, as Hagen was quartered in the Gestapo and SD Headquarters. The Main SS Hauptamt was the building next door, but the two were not internally connected. It was not a concern for Hagen. A moment of fresh air, even cold February air, would be welcome.

He nodded to Tilda Richter, his secretary, and strode off, his perfectly polished boots echoing in the halls. Hagen was tall and thin, having only filled out in his late twenties. He was one of those men who had spent their youth looking like a bean pole. The SS uniform was well designed and served to make him look broader, which pleased him. While he wasn't so vain as to be disturbed by his lack of bulk, sometimes Hagen wished he was a tad broader through the shoulder. Now the only place which seemed to get broader was around his middle, still he didn't have that problem as badly as some. Hermann Göring for example. Now there was a man who could definitely cut back on the whipped cream!

Hagen's mind drifted back to Galiena and her flying as he took the stairs at a sedate pace. Hagen didn't like her flying. Flying was inherently dangerous, especially in the fast little planes

23

General Udet was teaching her how to fly. When he had seen her two nights ago, she had burbled on about buying a little six seater for travelling, and a two seater for playing when she passed her flight-test. Now, Hagen didn't have a problem with commercial planes, and charter planes flown by professionals, but his fiancée flying some zippy little biplane did not make him happy. It wasn't the money, Lord knew, she had more than enough to do whatever she wanted, but Hagen hadn't courted Galiena to see her slam herself into the ground! Knowing Udet, he was probably encouraging her to do tricks already! Hermann Göring seemed to be encouraging this folly, so who was Hagen to say she couldn't fly? At least at this juncture. Perhaps when they were wed he could put his foot down. He might do that. Certainly when she was with child, the nonsense would stop!

The February air was bracing but the snow on the ground was filthy. Looking up at the dark grey clouds made Hagen suspect more snow was on the way. Not nice dry snow either, but wet snow. Mother Nature was preparing to unleash her worst on the city. The grounds of the buildings were not looking their most attractive, but such was the nature of winter. The walkway between the buildings was meticulously cleared of snow but that was to be expected. This was the SS Hauptamt, after all.

Hagen nodded at his acquaintance, Standartenführer Heinrich 'Gestapo' Müller, as they passed on the walkway. Gestapo Müller and Hagen worked well together and were polite to one another, but there was always something between them. Hagen was a highly educated man; he held a doctorate in German literature. Müller was a former Munich vice detective who had worked his way up through the ranks before being brought into the SS by Reinhard Heydrich. Hagen was known to be ruthless, but Müller was a step beyond. Cold, calculating and completely without morality when it suited him, Müller's penchant for physical brutality and torture were well known in the Gestapo. Müller thought nothing of beating a man to the edge of death to wring a confession from him, and Hagen could not look at Müller's coarse hands without thinking he could see dried blood on the skin. It was that image which always leapt to Hagen's mind whenever he saw the man. Blood crusted fingernails.

"Well, afternoon, Teufel! What brings you outside on this piss poor day?" Müller always called Hagen by his nickname, echoing their mutual master, Gruppenführer Reinhard Heydrich.

"Going to see the boss," Hagen nodded, aware Müller would know which one.

"Lucky you," Müller replied snidely. "But then you are the fair haired boy, aren't you?"

Hagen cocked a brow at Müller. "Is that what they're calling me?"

"Heydrich might have said it, yes, but then he is out of favour at the moment and he so hates competition," Müller snorted derisively. "Watch yourself. The RF might like you, but you don't want Heydrich to get jealous. He isn't above making your life difficult."

"I appreciate the warning, 'Stapo," Hagen said with sincerity, using Müller's nickname.

Müller shrugged gamely. "Easy for me to say, Teufel. I'm low on the riser too, right beside Heydrich over the von Fritsch fracas, but I wouldn't want to be in your shoes for all the factories in the Ruhr. Heydrich's still agitating over the von Fritsch inquiry and he's looking pretty damn stupid to all and sundry. By extension, so am I, but then I don't have a reputation for being infallible. I'm just one of Heydrich's lackeys. Then there's you. Nabbed von Taschen and his merry men, played the hero in that ambush, single-handedly saving the boss and the fair maiden. The RF is singing your praises from one end of the city to the other."

"It certainly wasn't single-handed," Hagen replied tartly. "There were a number of others, including Eugen Freisler, who played a far more active role than I did."

Müller leaned in conspiratorially. "And I also heard you made a late night rendezvous with the new C in C of the army on the night we were going to be stormed. With Göring, no less."

Hagen looked Müller directly in the eye. "I don't have the foggiest notion what you are talking about, 'Stapo." That information could hang Hagen if it became common knowledge. He had supplied SS interna to Hermann Göring and oath breakers weren't exactly popular in his organization.

The shorter man laughed; an ugly noise. "No. Of course you don't. But don't worry, Teufel! Heydrich doesn't know about it, and I am not going to tell him. He's gnawing on his liver enough these days, and that would only serve to bother him more. Heydrich isn't the only one with sources, you know."

"I appreciate your discretion in all matters, 'Stapo," Hagen nodded. Was this a warning? Müller had something on him because of his meeting with von Brauchitsch, and Müller wanted him to know it. That was for certain. But what did Müller want in return? A future consideration, perhaps? Perhaps it was an acknowledgement of Hagen's star being on the rise in the SS.

"I am capable of it, from time to time." Müller slapped Hagen in the shoulder. "But I shouldn't keep you. The RF hates to be kept waiting. We should go for drinks one night. Not this week, I'm a little busy hunting down the last of those ambushers. But soon. With Heydrich so on the outs, I don't think he's planning any of his debauches for the next while. Thank God."

"Will do, Müller. Good hunting." Hagen turned as Müller nodded and carried off in the other direction. Hagen entered the Hauptamt and took the stairs two at a time to the top floor. He checked his watch when he hit the last one. He had bare minutes to spare. He moved down the hall and breezed into Heinrich Himmler's outer office. One of Himmler's adjutants immediately took Hagen's hat and coat before bidding him to sit down. Hagen preferred to stand. He knew he was going to be sitting down again soon.

Gruppenführer Karl Wolff, Hagen's very close friend, came out of the inner office with a warm smile. "Hagen! Good to see you."

"Afternoon, Karl! How is business today?" Hagen raised both brows.

"Oh I think we're winning on most fronts. Can we get you anything? Coffee? Mineral water? Fruit juice?"

Hagen held up both hands. "No, thank you, Karl. I'm fine."

"Good to hear," Wolff nodded and turned to the adjutant. "The Reichsführer would like an orange juice; fresh, not canned, if you would see to it."

"Yes, Gruppenführer Wolff." The man leapt up right away.

Wolff watched the adjutant for half a beat and returned his gaze to his friend. "Well, Hagen? Coming?"

"Thank you." Hagen picked up his briefcase and followed Wolff into the office.

Himmler stood up from his desk and walked around to shake Hagen's hand. "Hagen. Excellent. How are you today?" The Reichsführer asked cordially.

"Very well, thank you," Hagen replied. Yes. He was in favour at the moment, but then he knew that. He was always in favour to some degree, but these days he really was teacher's pet, to use Müller's word. He was going to bask in it.

Himmler examined Hagen closely, his visage turning myopic in the process. "Always glad to hear it. Always glad to see you. You are looking well; more rested. That pleases me. You were looking like the very devil." Himmler moved over to the wing chairs at one end of his office, and motioned for Hagen to do the same. Wolff sat down on the couch.

"This last week has been on the quiet side," Hagen admitted, thinking of the truly blessed amount of sleep he had in the last few nights. "I suppose there is rest for the wicked after all."

"You aren't wicked, Hagen. You are the best we have." Himmler glanced over at his ever-present companion. "Wouldn't you agree, Wolffschen?"

"Absolutely," the Gruppenführer concurred.

Hagen looked from one man to the other. "If I was a woman, Herr Reichsführer, I would think you were trying to lure me onto the veranda for some mischief," he raised a brow.

Both men laughed. "Nothing nearly so nefarious, Hagen." Himmler flashed his perfect teeth in Hagen's direction. "Did you read that file I sent you?"

To business, to business. "I did. It was interesting, but not entirely new. I remember the situation from when it happened. But I am investigating the Heer. The file is about Austria. I fail to see why you sent it to me," Hagen spoke quietly.

"You must know that the von Fritsch affair has changed our situation with the military. Heydrich cocked the whole thing up, and we have to lay low." Wolff made a frustrated gesture with his hand.

"Yes. I would agree. The situation was not handled in an optimal manner." Hagen crossed one leg over the other, the polish of his boots gleaming. "It had been my intention to be very careful in my inquiries for the time being."

Himmler inclined his head, and gave Hagen an owlish look through his pince-nez as he came to his point. "I want you removed from the SD, Hagen. I intend to transfer you to my personal staff. I don't feel that Heydrich is using you to your full potential."

"With all due respect, Herr Reichsführer, I would prefer to remain where I am." Hagen felt real alarm. He was an investigator; it was what he loved to do. He didn't want Himmler to take that away and turn him into yet another prancing lackey. His SD sleeve diamond gave him a great deal of power. People feared it.

"No, Hagen. While I won't formally remove you from the unit, I believe it's useful to have you as a member, I am transferring you and your team into my staff to be my personal investigator. None of this inland/ausland nonsense. You are going to become my eyes, ears and nose where I need it. When and where I want answers, and more specifically the truth. These recent events with Heydrich have left me feeling that I can't trust him entirely," Himmler paused. "No. That's not it precisely, it's his apparatus. It's too big. I don't believe he has the control over his men and their efforts that he thinks he does. This recent disaster on the von Fritsch matter is case and point. They aren't being careful enough." The Reichsführer-SS held up a hand as if to stave off a comment. "Yes. I know. You tried to warn me, and I didn't listen. Well now I am listening."

"Aren't I of more use to you where I am?" Hagen responded quietly, cold fear griping at his guts. "Where I can keep an eye on Heydrich for you? That is why you transferred me into the SD in the first place, if I may respectfully remind you of that, Herr Reichsführer."

"No. I hadn't forgotten that, Hagen." Himmler took off his pince-nez and wiped the lenses with his handkerchief. "But you have been there almost four years now, and I think you would be better served coming over here with me. Get you out of Heydrich's claws and give you new challenges, for I'm told he'd dearly love to sink his claws into you."

Hagen glanced over at Wolff. "New challenges, Karl?"

Wolff laughed abruptly, his entire face lighting up. "You look so worried, Hagen."

The Reichsführer-SS joined in with his adjutant's mirth. "Yes he does, doesn't he?" He agreed with Wolff. "Not to worry, Hagen. I am not going to keep you from doing what you do best. You aren't joining my adjutant corps. Absolutely not. You are going to be my nose, as I said; attached to my staff so that no one can derail or appropriate you. You will report solely to me; Wolffschen in my absence. You will have special powers to investigate inside the SS or outside as I see fit. Complete powers. Your title will be Special Investigator to the Reichsführer-SS and Chief of the German Police. You will retain your rank of Oberst in the Gestapo to give you any arresting authority you require. You will not report to Heydrich, nor will you be under the orders of Müller, even though he will still rank you in the Gestapo. You will be completely independent, as will your department."

This almost seemed too good to be true. Complete independence of the system? Complete independence from Heydrich? His respect for Heydrich was in the toilet of late, so that was no true loss, yet this would probably make an open enemy out of the man. If he had been worried about spies from Heydrich before, he would be doubly on guard now. "Thank you for the confidence you have in me, Herr Reichsführer," Hagen said quietly. "I would be pleased to accept this position."

Himmler leaned back into his chair with satisfaction. "Excellent, Special Investigator Kohl. We will have to move your office into this building. On this floor, of course, so that I can have you closer to me. Get you out of that nest of adders over there too. Your men can attend to that while we are away."

Hagen blinked. "Away?"

"You will be accompanying the Reichsführer and me on tonight's train to the Berghof for the meeting between the Fuhrer and Chancellor von Schuschnigg tomorrow. I want you to make Austria your concern for the time being. We will be assuming the mantle of power in Austria shortly and I want you to observe at the conference. The Fuhrer will be making several demands of the Austrian Chancellor; demands the man won't be able to deliver. At that point, it will only be a matter of time before we take control. I have Heydrich making lists of all undesirables in the country. I think his man Schellenberg is on it now. But I know there is a great deal of bad feeling still over the Dolfuss affair and I want you assess the difficulties that will create for us. I don't want another problem like Dolfuss. I realise I should have paid far more attention at the time to what was going on, but I thought Gruppenführer Wittje was on top of the situation."

"The Order has been far better off since you cashiered Wittje out," Wolff grunted sourly under his breath.

"Absolutely. I agree. That was just one more of his crimes." Himmler placed his pince-nez back on his face and returned his gaze to Hagen.

"Why me, Herr Reichsführer?" He was fairly sure of the answer, but he wanted to hear it anyway.

"Because you don't lie to me and you don't tell me what I want to hear. Heydrich lied to me, and I don't quite trust him to give me information anymore. One thing you should be aware of, Hagen, I might have you run parallel investigations in the future against those of Heydrich, so I can be assured he is being truthful. I don't want and can't afford a repeat of the von Fritsch affair." Himmler inhaled and exhaled deeply, frustration evident on his face. "I believed him, and the egg is as much on my face as it is on Heydrich's. That doesn't make me happy."

Hagen inclined his head. "I thank you for your confidence."

Himmler pointed at Hagen, his finger very white against the background of his black uniform. "Heydrich may very well be a genius, Hagen. I would not dispute it. He's so damn logical all the time; and it's true, he is infrequently wrong. Yet he was this time and it has torn away a great deal of the buttressing I have done to build myself up with the party. Heydrich may be clever, but he needs me and he needs me to be powerful for him to enjoy the privileges he does. He has no standing with the old fighters in the party. You have far more than he does. Heydrich has no credit with the Fuhrer and if his mistakes cause me to stumble, or worse, fall, then he falls with me, only he falls faster and further. That is just the way it is." Himmler's eyes burned with a dreadful intensity. "I will take him down before he brings me down. I don't need him nearly as much as he needs me and I have given him too much carte blanche. The von Fritsch affair was an awakening for me."

"Here enters the Special Investigator for the Reichsführer-SS." Wolff spread his arms expansively.

"I feel like an insurance policy," Hagen chuckled, wondering if this would be the beginning of him or the end.

Himmler touched Hagen on the arm. "It's a two way street, Hagen. Heydrich is very jealous and you are quite the commodity these days."

Hagen felt like someone was walking on his grave. "You are the second person to give me that warning today."

"Am I? Who else is concerned about your welfare?" The brows raised behind the pince-nez.

"Gestapo Müller. He seemed to feel that being teacher's pet might be a little on the unhealthy side for me."

Wolff snorted. "Teacher's pet, hm? Now that is amusing. Very amusing. If they call you that, I wonder what they call me?"

"You've been teacher's pet for so long the rest of us don't even notice it anymore." Hagen grinned. "You're just the hand which holds the ruler."

"I would have rapped Heydrich's knuckles if I could have," Wolff grunted bitterly.

"I would ignore the jealousy of the plebes, Hagen. You are above them." Himmler nodded as much to himself as to his men. "But I shouldn't keep you long now, we can work on the file this evening. Our train leaves at eight, and you need to pack; both your private effects in your office and for the trip. I have put you in the office beside Wolffschen. Your rank is a little junior for the size, but you never know what's coming down the pike." Himmler's blue eyes sparkled briefly.

Hagen stood, knowing the interview was over. "Then I shall endeavour to prepare."

Himmler and Wolff also rose to their feet. "Glad you are happy about the change, Hagen. Not that you had much choice!" Wolff winked at Hagen rather uncharacteristically.

Himmler paused, apparently considering something. "Also, I would be appreciative if you would bring the official file on the Pfalzgräfin von Steinberg for me to review on the train. And I want everything, Hagen. No pruning before you give it to me." The finger was back in his face, making evasion difficult.

Hagen nodded slowly. He didn't want to share that file with Himmler, and he wondered where this was coming from. He knew she had lunch with Wolff and Himmler yesterday, but didn't know anything more than that. "As you wish, Herr Reichsführer. Is there a problem with Race and Settlement? Our marriage application?"

Himmler shook his head gamely. "Of course not, Hagen. She's a lovely girl. I am very fond of her, and I would never stop your union; I would just like to know a little more about her. The details of her relationship with her family," Himmler replied airily, but there was something in face which made Hagen suspicious.

"As you wish," Hagen repeated.

"It's nothing to concern yourself with, Hagen," Himmler assured him, again with that overly absent and exaggerated casualness. Why did it not make him feel better?

September 19, 1937
Dearest Poppet,

What have you done, Poppet? What have you allowed that foul Göring to do? I am no longer your guardian? What nonsense is this? What did you tell him? He has no right to interfere! I am most seriously displeased. We will discuss it when you return.
Eternally yours,
Meinrad

Chapter 3
February 12, 1938

Hermann Göring and Galiena arrived early at the Berghof. They were joining Adolf Hitler, Joachim von Ribbentrop, Frau von Ribbentrop, and Heinrich Himmler for breakfast to discuss the coming meeting. Galiena had been asked last night to play hostess for Hitler, as the ranking woman on the mountain. Göring had also intimated to her that Hitler was using her title to impress the Chancellor of Austria. She didn't mind particularly. Such things were second nature to her.

Galiena had dressed elegantly in a cobalt blue suit, a matching scarf about her neck and she wore the beautiful string of black pearls Hagen had given her for Christmas. The engagement ring he had given her winked on her finger, making her feel claimed. She certainly didn't mind.

Hermann Göring, natty in a double-breasted suit which,while exquisitely tailored did nothing to hide his enormous bulk, walked up the stairs beside her. His blue eyes glittered in the bright sunlight, accentuated by his black cashmere overcoat and fedora; his cheeks rosy from the cold. His shoes were polished and gleamed in the snow, completing the image of the aristocratic executive. "Well, Liebschen! Are you ready?" He slanted her an encouraging look.

"Completely. My handbag is full of witticisms and inane gossip." Galiena smiled at him, feeling far more trepidation at seeing the Fuhrer than entertaining his guests.

"I have no doubt you are more than up to this task. I haven't heard how many people von Schuschnigg is bringing up with him today, but can't be too many. I think our party is a little on the large side, but one can't hiccup internationally these days without Ribbentrop. As for Himmler; he has limpetted onto the Fuhrer, desperately trying to prove his worth. Which isn't much, I am afraid," Göring muttered under his breath

"Now uncle Hermann! You know I like Herr Himmler! It's not nice of you to be so derogatory of the people I like!" Galiena exclaimed with mock ferocity, poking her uncle in the shoulder before twining herself about his arm.

"Oh tosh, Galiena! You like everybody. That's what makes you such an angel!" Göring chuckled, leaning over to kiss her cheek.

The Pfalzgräfin rolled her eyes. "I do not! I don't like that SA man, Victor Lutz. Martin Bormann is a downright pig! Who else don't I like? Hm. I find Herr Hess a little on the odd side. His dietary ideas are a little strange, and if he gives me one more lecture on the vitamins I should be taking, I might just scream." Galiena ticked off each man on here fingertips.

"Hess is harmless," Göring winked at her. "And his diet seems to be keeping him a little trimmer than mine is keeping me." The man's tone was rather on the rueful side. "Perhaps I should indulge in his vitamins."

"And whose fault is that, oh Feldmarschall 'please bring me some more whipped cream' Göring?" She retorted pointedly, having walked in on one of her uncle's binges last night. "I heard you bellowing for Robert Kropp to get you a midnight snack! What would Emmy say? She would be terribly disappointed if she knew! You are supposed to be being good when you are away from her."

Göring shrugged unashamedly. "I would hate to feel that my darling is alone in her recent weight gain."

Galiena gave her uncle a dirty look. "She is pregnant, Herr Feldmarschall! What's your excuse?"

"I have my own personal vitamin C."

"And what, pray tell, is that? Champagne?"

The moon faced man broke into his famous smile. "Not as pedantic as Hess' and it never leads me astray!"

34

She couldn't help a pert reply. "Does it not?"

Göring didn't have to answer, for Adolf Hitler walked out of his house to great them on the terrace. The Fuhrer of Germany was also well dressed in a charcoal double-breasted suit. He spread his arms expansively. "Göring! Dear Galiena! Good morning! Good morning."

The men shook hands. "You seem in a fine mood this morning, mein Fuhrer!" Göring noted, relief crawling across his face.

"I'm pretending I didn't get up an hour early this morning." Hitler's lips twisted under his moustache. "You know better than anyone that mornings are not my best time. But von Schuschnigg will be here in two and a half hours, and I think it's smarter we have breakfast together this morning, just to have everyone on the same page. Mine." Hitler turned and kissed Galiena on both cheeks. "And how is my lovely hostess today?"

"Very well, uncle Fuhrer." Galiena used the strange greeting Hitler insisted she use with him; her flesh crawling at his touch. More than anyone else she'd met, the Fuhrer reminded her of Meinrad von Steinberg. Not in his manner, of course, for Hitler was a peasant, but in the burning will shining from his eyes.

The Fuhrer lifted her chin with his hand and he stared at her with those intense blue eyes of his. "I am glad to hear it, my dear Galiena. As soon as my baroque songbird disappeared last night, I missed her and I almost sent for her."

Hitler was obsessed with Galiena's ability to play the harpsichord. He had given her a beautiful instrument for Christmas and insisted she travel with it when she came to visit him. He made her play for a very long time last night. Galiena was very wary of the Fuhrer and his demands on her time and attention. She apparently reminded him of his dead niece, which she was told by others was not a good thing. His behaviour towards her ranged from extremely kind and solicitous to controlling; there was never any warning as to what she was going to receive when they met. Galiena had not yet told him of her engagement, and was planning to address the issue soon. Last night had been one of those strange nights where he demanded she play for him, but completely ignored her the rest of the time. Though when she ceased her playing and insisted she was too tired to go on, the man's eyes glittered with fury. There was no rhyme or reason to it. "I am complimented, uncle Fuhrer, that you are so entertained by my efforts," she responded weakly, not up for a struggle with the man this morning.

Hitler offered her his arm and she took it politely. "More than that, my dear girl. You play like an angel."

Galiena blushed, woman enough to enjoy the compliment. "You flatter me, uncle Fuhrer! Say no more or my head will swell like a balloon and then there will be no living with me!"

The Fuhrer chuckled and leaned in as if to share a special secret. "Yes. How like an artist. Artists flourish in obscurity, but fame causes them to change, and not for the better."

"There is no better acknowledgement than that of a charming patron!" This Hitler she liked; the charismatic host, the attentive gentleman. So different from the flipside.

"Charming patron, my dear? Now it is you who flatters me. Come. Let us go eat breakfast. You can commiserate with me on this terribly early morning." Hitler patted her hand and led her into the breakfast room on the other side of the house. "It is unseemly for duty to awaken me this early, but at least I am blessed by your very special companionship."

Himmler was standing talking with von Ribbentrop in the corner of the room near the window. Von Ribbentrop was a handsome older man with silvering hair and bright blue eyes. He had married very well to the Henkel's champagne heiress and bought the von in his name by paying an old baroness to adopt him. That certainly didn't make him an equal, as far as Galiena was concerned. The old peers were the old peers, and buying a peerage didn't make you a member of the club. Unfortunately, Galiena had a similar scheme in mind for Hagen, for an acquired von was better than no von at all.

Galiena's grandfather hated von Ribbentrop with every fibre of his being. Von Ribbentrop made several terrible gaffes as ambassador to England, a place very close to the von Steinberg family's heart. Both Galiena's mother and grandmother came from England and Galiena had spent many summers there. The Pfalzgraf had been an unofficial ambassador to England for the Kaiser, and when he had heard that Ribbentrop gave the Nazi salute to the king of England, the old man had almost blown a blood vessel. No.

Even Galiena, who worked very hard to not be a political entity, thought the man was either very blind or very foolish! They had met in England two years ago and the man had not impressed her; but he did cut a fine figure in his navy suit.

"Your Serene Highness," Von Ribbentrop bowed very low over her hand.

"Foreign Minister. Might I congratulate you on your new position?" Galiena offered pleasantly.

"Thank you, Pfalzgräfin," the man smiled at her.

"Frau von Ribbentrop." She shook hands with the other woman. A well educated and interesting lady, Galiena didn't hold the husband's sins against his wife.

"Your Serene Highness."

Galiena turned to Himmler, who looked dreadfully out of place in a brown three-piece suit. He looked so ordinary out of his uniform, like a modest clerk and she almost didn't recognise him. The colour he was wearing was terrible, and she wondered who had chosen it for him. If this was the best Frau Himmler could do, no wonder she was immured in the country.

Himmler came forward and kissed her on both cheeks. "My dear Galiena, it has been too long." He spoke her name quietly, as if he didn't want to share their intimacy with the rest of the room.

Galiena laughed, enjoying their little secret. "Such gallantry, Heinrich! Beware, or people will begin to confuse you with Doctor Goebbels!" She winked devilishly at him.

He drew back, a small hand raised to his chest. "Now you wound me, Pfalzgräfin!" His voice was louder and increased in formality. His eyes twinkled behind his pince-nez for a moment before he laughed out loud.

"Never, Herr Reichsführer! Never!" She would follow his lead. Yes. Some things weren't for public consumption.

Hitler stalked over. "Galiena! I did not know you were so well acquainted with my loyal Heinrich?" Göring appeared a little askance at their friendliness.

Himmler turned to Hitler. "The Pfalzgräfin has made me a very happy man. She has decided to join my clan, as I am sure you know?"

Hitler went very still, turning to stare at Göring and then Galiena. "What is this?"

Galiena wanted to tread on Himmler's foot, but resisted the urge. This wasn't the way she wanted Hitler to find out, but some things couldn't be helped. Ignoring the ice in the pit of her stomach, she held up her finger with Hagen's ring on it. "I have become engaged, uncle Fuhrer. Just a few days ago."

The eyes dropped to the ring, and then back to Göring. "What is this?" Hitler hissed through clenched teeth. He took Galiena's wrist in a vice like grip. "Who?"

"Standartenführer Doctor Hagen Kohl, uncle Fuhrer," Galiena breathed, surprised at the extent of the man's reaction. "The man who has been courting me for the last few months."

Hitler loomed over her, or so it felt despite their almost equal stature. "I was not consulted. You did not ask me about this." He swivelled his wild gaze between Himmler and Göring. "Why was I not consulted? I don't give my permission for this marriage," he growled finally.

Galiena felt her face go hot, and her eyes narrowed to slits. Who did this man think he was? There were only two people on this earth who had the right to deny her marriage; her Grandfather, who had given up his right by his actions, and the Prince of Prussia, deposed emperor of Germany and her liege lord. Who was Hitler to make such a pronouncement? "You what?" She asked flatly, the words glacial.

"I don't give my permission for you to wed. I don't wish you to marry." Hitler glared fiercely at Göring. "And I am very put out that this has been kept a secret from me."

Himmler looked from Göring to Hitler, obviously assessing the situation. "Mein Fuhrer, this was not a secret from you. I thought you were aware of the situation."

Galiena needed a moment to think, and she also felt it was time for a test of her place with the Fuhrer. "I'm suddenly feeling a trifle overcome, gentlemen. If you will permit me to withdraw." She turned on her heel and left the group, not giving them an instant to reply. She had to analyze every interaction she had ever had with Hitler. She needed to figure out the right way to bring him around. She was also on the verge of furious tears and would not give him the satisfaction of knowing he had upset her quite so much.

"Get back here!" Hitler thundered after her, but instead she closed the French doors into the small parlour behind her with a decided snap. She wasn't going to argue or beg Adolf Hitler in front of those other gentlemen. She walked over to the fireplace and stood by it, taking a deep shuddering breath to calm herself, knowing she only had a second or two. The Fuhrer was like her grandfather. He would respond to submission, but how to submit and still get what she wanted?

The door banged open behind her, and Hitler strode in, Göring trailing behind him. "Mein Fuhrer, really," Göring began weakly.

"Get out!" Hitler snarled ferociously. "And shut the door behind you!"

"Yes, mein Fuhrer!" Göring bowed his head and left the room.

"Turn around." Hitler ordered, walking over to her. She did as instructed, and realised she was staring him right in the eye. They glared at each other for several seconds. She was feeling every inch of her rank and title. Who was he to deny her? "What is this marriage nonsense?" Hitler demanded finally, his voice a fraction more civil.

"Doctor Kohl proposed and I have accepted, uncle Fuhrer," she whispered softly.

"No. I don't wish it." Hitler's eyes were incandescent. "I don't wish for you to marry. Not now. You aren't allowed to leave me! I'm not finished with you."

Galiena resisted the urge to take in a great breath. "Mein Fuhrer, I wish to marry Doctor Kohl."

The Fuhrer shook his head stubbornly. "No. I'm not finished with you, yet."

"You aren't finished with me, yet?" Why was she suddenly parroting him? "What do you mean?"

"Precisely that, Galiena." He raised a finger under her nose. "I forbid you to marry that man."

"Why?" Galiena pressed him for some reasonable answer. "Why are you doing this, mein Fuhrer?"

"Because you love me!" Hitler crossed his arms over his chest angrily. "Or at least I thought you did!" He snarled.

This felt uncomfortably familiar; shades of her grandfather. How had this happened? And how could she control this situation? First she had to control the fear blossoming in her chest, and then she had to think. Galiena stared into his eyes, plumbing their depths. They were angry, perhaps even furious, but they weren't insane. He was acting like a jealous lover, which he wasn't, never had been and never would be. She had to remind him of that. She had to remain calm if she were to win.

"Of course I love you, mein Fuhrer!" Galiena told him with what she hoped sounded like sincerity.

"Then how can you love me if you want to marry him?" Hitler ground out, his lips compressed into a tight line.

"Because I love you as a devoted servant loves her Fuhrer; and as a niece loves her beloved uncle," she answered him, trying not to choke on the words.

Hitler erupted swiftly. "That's not how it should be!"

Galiena bowed her head. "How could it be anything else, mein Fuhrer? You have told me from the very beginning that you are married to Germany. How could I possibly allow myself to love you in any other way?"

The Fuhrer turned on his heel and prowled into the center of the room. Then he turned back, clenching and unclenching his fists. "That shouldn't matter if you love me! You have hurt me beyond measure What have I done to deserve this absolute betrayal?"

She dropped to her knees, in a position of supplication. "I am sorry, mein Fuhrer. I did not mean to hurt you. I do love you! I do! You mean so very much to me."

Hitler stalked back over to the mantle. He stood, towering over her, obviously pleased by her submission. "Then how can you want to marry him?"

"Because I want to be married. I want to have children. It is my duty to my lands and family." She would take a page out of Himmler's book, and see if it worked. The word duty seemed to ring bells in Nazi skulls.

"I can't do that," Hitler frowned darkly. "I am resigned not to have children."

"And are you not equally resigned to having a wife, mein Fuhrer?" She lifted her chin to stare up at him with exaggerated innocence.

"I do not wish to wed. No," Hitler acknowledged reluctantly.

"Then how could I love you in that way?" Galiena pleaded, hoping her logic would have the desired effort.

"But if you marry him you will no longer have time for me." Hitler snapped back, the jealousy having returned.

"Nonsense, mein Fuhrer! I would have more. I must be careful of the time I spend with you now. I am an unmarried woman. You are an unmarried man. People are beginning to talk and I have my reputation to consider!" Her eyes slowly drifted down and to the side.

"Who is talking? Who is besmirching your name? What is this slander?" Hitler exploded, grabbing her by the shoulder. Hard.

Galiena flinched as his claw dug into her collarbone; the pressure and his nail digging into her flesh caused her to take in a sharp breath. "People talk, mein Fuhrer. I don't know who. I just know the talk is there. People have filthy minds." Unconsciously her fingers came up to protect the welt at her neck.

"You give me the names and I will have the people dealt with." He seemed to have little control over his hand in his anger, the grip tightening until it felt like her collarbone was about to snap.

Her mouth was dry as dust, each word an effort. "They are small people and don't matter; but it hurts me that I can't be with you as I would like to. You don't need to worry, uncle Fuhrer. If I marry Doctor Kohl, I will still be your baroque songbird. I will still come when you call. Nothing need ever change. You will still be my uncle Fuhrer. You will always be my uncle Fuhrer. How could any man ever replace you in my affections?" What more could she say to him?

Hitler gnawed on his knuckles as emotions played across his face. Abruptly releasing her, he turned and walked to the doors. Through the gap he opened Galiena could see her uncle and Himmler in the midst of a heated conversation; both men looking worried and angry. "Someone get me Kohl. I know I saw him earlier talking to Sepp. Go get him, Heinrich, and send him in here!" Hitler ordered heatedly before he slammed the doors shut. He moved into the center of the room and stared at her for what seemed like forever. "You are very beautiful there, Galiena. If I could draw the human body, I would want to draw you, but that is not where my artistic talents lie. I am an architect." His voice had returned to normal; jarring after the fury.

Galiena didn't know whether or not to answer him. "Thank you, mein Fuhrer." Her collarbone throbbed.

"That picture there over the mantle. It is one of mine."

It was a picture of the view of the mountains from the terrace, and seemed quite well rendered. It was a watercolour; hazy as all watercolours were. "It is lovely. You have an eye, uncle Fuhrer." Her knees were starting to ache, but she did not dare to get up. Instead she folded her hands in her lap and dropped her chin to her chest.

"Thank you, my dear. I appreciate beauty." She could feel his hot eyes on her.

There was a knock at the door. "Come!" Hitler barked.

Hagen entered, resplendent in his uniform, his hat under his arm. He raised his other arm and saluted. "Heil Hitler."

Hitler did not acknowledge Hagen but walked over to where Galiena was kneeling, and put his hand on her shoulder. His thumb found its way to its previous position, beating a tattoo on the wounded flesh. "So there he is. I will admit he cuts a fine figure."

Galiena didn't move. "Yes, mein Fuhrer."

Hitler's hand moved to direct her chin up toward him. "And do you love him, Galiena?"

She didn't know how to answer. She thought she was prepared for this question, but she wasn't. Yes. She was certainly infatuated with Hagen, but if she answered to the affirmative, would that set the now calm Hitler off again? She ventured a peek at Hagen. His face was a mask, impossibly cold. How much did he know about the situation here? How much had he guessed? Finally she just bit the bullet. "Yes," she breathed.

"As a woman loves a man?" Hitler pressed, twisting his thumb into her. The man must not have cut his nails in some time, for it felt like a chisel in her skin.

42

Suddenly not caring whether his action was in anger or a warning, Galiena nodded slowly. "Yes."

"The way you would have loved me, had I not confused you on the subject?" Hitler sighed. "No. Don't answer that. I know the answer. Of course, were I able to marry you and father your children, you would love me that way. Perhaps this tangle is my fault. How I hate these triangles." Hitler moved over to Hagen. He eyed Hagen from the tips of his toes to Hagen's outstretched hand. "Well, Kohl. What am I to do with you? I don't like rivals. No. I don't like them at all."

Hagen did not lower his arm. Hitler had not returned the salute. "My apologies, mein Fuhrer. It was not my intention to interfere."

Hitler crossed his arms over his chest, his head pulled up like a cobra. "I won't ask if you love her, for I imagine you do not. You love her connections and her fortune, I'm sure. But answer me this. Will you protect her?"

"Yes, mein Fuhrer," Hagen answered very simply.

Hitler inhaled and exhaled, before turning to face Galiena again. "I shall have to consider this. You may continue with your engagement, but do not set a date until I give you leave to do so. I must consider this. I am not happy, Galiena, but your arguments have moved me. This is more my fault than I realised and for that I apologize. I will let you know sooner, rather than later. Take a few moments to compose yourself, for then I expect you to join the rest of us for breakfast as planned. This has already taken up far too much of my time this morning."

"Thank you, uncle Fuhrer. Thank you so very much!" Galiena dropped her hands to her sides, her eyes filling with stress related tears. She didn't want to think about how Hitler's words about love to Hagen chilled her soul. Not that she didn't have those thoughts occasionally, but it was painful to hear them.

"Do not get your hopes up, Galiena. I am sorely displeased you did not ask my permission before you entered into this betrothal," Hitler paused, and then saluted to Hagen. "Heil." He spoke crisply before striding out through the door. He shut them in together.

Galiena closed her eyes with a sigh, her entire body slumping. She felt like a wrung out rag. Then she felt movement before her and opened her eyes to see two boots appear in her vision; his hand in front of her face. Galiena allowed him to help her to her feet, still not looking at him for she couldn't bear to see that cold mask. Hagen wrapped his arms around her and brought her against his hard chest. He was warm and his cologne intoxicated her. Galiena found herself sagging against him.

"I never want to see you down on your knees before any man again," he whispered frostily against her temple. "Nothing is worth debasing yourself like that."

Galiena lifted her face to his. Now he wasn't cold. He was angry. The imperious expression on his face made her want to slap him. "I did what I had to do, Hagen. I didn't have a large number of options." His anger made her made her furious and she roughly pulled out of his embrace. She turned her back to him and brushed the lint from her skirt.

He spun her around, his hands catching her in the place where Hitler had clutched at her, and she threw her forearm up, bashing his hand away. "What? I didn't hurt you!" he exclaimed crossly.

"You didn't, Doctor Kohl," Galiena hissed through her teeth to keep from screaming at him in her anger.

Hagen assessed her and slipped a finger into the draped neck of her blouse, moving the fabric aside. Revealed was a red welt, complete with a half-moon shaped indent which she knew would turn into a bruise. His eyes turned positively flinty. He inhaled as he traced around the place with his finger. "I'm sorry," he breathed finally, his pallor stark and bloodless against his uniform.

"It's nothing."

His hand was shaking as he moved his finger up her neck and along her jaw line to her hair. "I will never let another man hurt you again, Galiena," he rasped hoarsely. "On my honour I won't."

"You can't promise that, Hagen." Galiena stepped closer to him, dropping her forehead against his shoulder. In this instant, she couldn't bear to look at him. She felt something in her soul that hadn't been there before. A kernel of doubt about their future. "I thought you were mad at me."

"No. Not at you. Never at you. But I just about lost my composure when I saw you on your knees before him. But we shouldn't discuss this now." Hagen became more businesslike with every word. Colder. Bound by his duty, perhaps? "You need to have breakfast and I need to go do what I am here to do."

"Why are you here, Hagen?" she asked him.

"I'm here as aide to the Reichsführer," he replied blandly, propelling her towards the door.

"That's rather evasive," Galiena retorted.

"How very observant of you." Hagen stopped her at the door, with an unreadable expression on his face. His eyes had gone from their usual lavender grey to a more intense violet colour and Galiena knew that meant he was feeling his emotions strongly. "Were you telling the Fuhrer the truth?"

Galiena had a feeling she knew what he was angling for and she wasn't going to give it to him. Arrogant creature. "When?"

"When you told him you loved me as a woman loves a man?"

Galiena focused on her shoes and then over to his boots. She didn't want him to see the satisfaction she felt at his ever so casual question. "I was fighting to preserve our engagement, Hagen." She rested her hand on the doorknob.

"That's rather evasive," he echoed her words.

She pushed the doors open. "How very observant of you." Galiena smiled brilliantly back at him, her own eyes feeling dull in their sockets as she walked into the room. The Pfalzgräfin, a persona she put on like a cloak, engulfed her as she returned to the Fuhrer and his guests. Göring gave her a questioning look, and she winked at him. "Please forgive my outburst of earlier, gentlemen. Nerves at serving as the Fuhrer's hostess, no doubt."

Himmler touched her arm solicitously, bringing her to the table. "The Pfalzgräfin is quite recovered?"

"I am quite recovered. Yes." She sat down at her place.

"About time, Galiena." Hitler's lips twisted snidely as he sat down. "Then let us eat, for my guests will be arriving in two hours."

September 26, 1937
Dearest Poppet,

Another night, our night, has passed, and I am up here at your window waiting for you to come home to me. I am still angry, my Poppet, but not at you. Göring has confused you. You have such a gentle heart, and have never understood the lies people tell. You need me to look after you.
Eternally yours,
Meinrad

Chapter 4
February 12, 1938

Galiena excused herself from the breakfast table where the men were still talking and moved into the living room to inspect her harpsichord and warm up her hands. She had been informed that she was to play during the meeting of the two leaders, in an effort to lend a festive air. Given the words of the men at breakfast, there was going to be very little festive about this informal meeting. The men were so cold blooded about their intentions, and while she understood, even agreed that Austria should be rejoined with Germany, listening to the casual power brokering was chilling.

Galiena walked around the living room and sat at her Nicholas Blanchett harpsichord. Thankfully it was still in tune, as harpsichords could lose their sound with something as trivial as a change in temperature or humidity. She ran a finger along the ivory keys and then leafed through the music on the table nearby. Of course the Wagner was on the top. Completely unsuitable to the instrument at hand and boring to play, but absolutely the Fuhrer's favourite. Somehow the *Ride of the Valkyries* did not seem appropriate to the situation. She found some Bach in the pile, as well as some Chopin and Hayden. Hayden would be pleasant. One would think that whoever had chosen the sheet music would have noticed the difference between a harpsichord and a piano. Then Galiena laughed aloud. No. Hitler would have given an order and his orders were obeyed to the letter. What did something as minor as an instrument matter when he wanted Wagner? She noted that all the composers represented were either German or Austrian. That was all very well and fine, but out of sheer bloody-mindedness, she was going to play music from other countries. She sat and played a Chopin nocturne, which had a much different sound on the harpsichord. She should have chosen a dirge. That would be more in keeping with her mood.

Galiena closed her eyes and caressed the keys in another Chopin piece she knew from memory. The piano sonata became even more otherworldly on the harpsichord; even more a representation of what she felt inside. As always when she played, her entire being calmed. She was an extension of the instrument. She was the music. The tension flowed out, the world completely vanishing. It was the only time she ever felt at peace with her thoughts. She finished the piece and opened startled eyes when there was the sound of clapping. Himmler stood at the other end of the room, moving up to approach her when she opened her eyes.

The Reichsführer-SS inclined his head to acknowledge her skill. "We have been released from service for a moment while the Fuhrer prepares himself. I was attracted to your music. I am not disturbing you, am I?"

She cocked her head in return. "No. Not at all."

"Your music is extremely compelling." He rested his forearms at the end of the harpsichord as he continued. "I must apologize for my terrible faux pas of earlier. If I'd known your uncle hadn't informed the Fuhrer of your engagement, I would not have made so clumsy a statement, Galiena. Do forgive me."

Galiena had not expected an apology from the man, and smiled sadly at him. "There is nothing to forgive, Heinrich. You didn't know and it would have made sense for us to have informed the Fuhrer a week ago. I tried to tell him last night, but he was far too involved formulating today's plans."

"It was still not well done of me and I appreciate your understanding in the matter." He rubbed his palms together nervously.

"No, Herr Himmler. It is quite forgotten." The moment of formality slipped out as she stared into the obsidian depth of the keys before her.

"And what was the Fuhrer's eventual decision?" Himmler asked quietly but his eyes were probing.

"He sees the arrangement more clearly, and would like time to consider it. We are not to set a wedding date, but we aren't forbidden to see each other either. I am hopeful," she said dully, not feeling hopeful at all. "I'm positive that with reasonable arguments he can be brought around to our nuptials."

"That is good. Very good. I hope I have not done irreparable damage."

"No. I don't think you have. The scene today, I think I expected it, perhaps explaining my reticence to bring the subject up." Galiena rolled her shoulders, trying to dispel the returning tension.

He nodded and caressed a finger along the lip of the harpsichord, his eyes travelling along the painted fresco of nymphs and satyrs frolicking on the underside of the lid. "My dear Galiena, I have thought a great deal about your request of the other day, and I have a few questions for you."

"Then I shall try and answer to the best of my ability." Her hands folded deftly in her lap as she braced herself for a new onslaught. Could she not have a moment's peace today? Suddenly she ached for a drink and cursed that it was well before noon.

"I have read your file now and I have a more accurate reading of your relationship with your grandfather. Frankly, I am at a loss for why you would wish to see him." Himmler's words were spoken very gently as he slid closer to her.

"I believe I explained that over lunch," Galiena replied wearily, too tired to walk down this road again.

Himmler furrowed his brow. "And I believed you at the time. You presented a very well thought out argument, but that was before I completely understood the extent of your Grandfather's perfidy. I am not a foolish man, Galiena. Please don't treat me as such."

Galiena turned her head to watch the 1AH[6] sentry moving outside the window. "I don't think I can define it, Heinrich. I am getting married and I would like to notify my Grandfather of my

---

[6] leibstandarte Adolf Hitler - Hitler's personal guard

betrothal. I would ask his permission, even though it won't have any bearing on my actions if he denies my request."

"There must be more to it, my dear," he pressed her as he came to stand at her side.

"I would have answers from him. The answers I tried to get at Feldmarschall von Blomberg's wedding." The words slipped out as the barest whisper.

"I believe he gave you his reason." She could feel his breath against her ear as the Reichsführer leaned over her.

"Your files are very detailed, Herr Reichsführer," Galiena replied bitterly, unconsciously using Himmler's title. Would she ever stop feeling so invaded?

"I am sorry to address such a painful subject. Yes. They are. There were many witnesses to the event. The Pfalzgraf was very explicit in his ravings."

She shuddered, her entire body caught up in the reflex. "You have no comprehension just how explicit." Bile rose in her throat. It was simply too soon after her duel with Hitler to have this conversation.

Tentative hands unwound the scarf around her throat, then his thumbs began to rhythmically trace the hollows on either side of her neck, pressing almost into her spine. "Then why would you want to see him again? Why not let him rot?" Himmler continued his ministrations as he spoke and she found it strangely soothing. "Why this need to rock the boat, dear Galiena? I fail to see how pursuing this course can bring anything of merit to you."

Galiena inhaled deeply. "Because it isn't over yet. Not for me. I am not finished with him."

"I would hate for this to become an obsession for you, Madame. Let it go. Marry and leave him where he is." His fingers pressed into the base of her skull where her spine ended and rolled in firm circles at her hairline.

"I can't," she whispered brokenly, lost in the NB inscribed on the keyboard before her.

Himmler sighed, his hands stilling to rest gently on her shoulders. "I am doing an inspection of Buchenwald sometime in the second week of March; Wolffschen can appraise you of the correct date. If you arrange to be in Weimar that day, I will send someone to collect you when the inspection is over and bring you out to the camp. This is my engagement gift to you, Galiena, and my apology for today."

"Thank you, Heinrich." Galiena looked up at him, her coiffure pressed against his chest. "Words cannot express my gratitude." He smelled of cologne and faintly of cigars. She was reminded oh his protection in his car. She should have been afraid, but strangely she wasn't.

Himmler touched his finger just below the exposed burn on her throat, his face twisting. "I'm not doing you a service in this, so don't thank me. I do have a request, however."

"Yes?"

Himmler's finger completed a circuit around the burn, guilt tightening the skin around his eyes. "Before you do this, I wish you to return to Riesa and the scene of the crime. If you can do that for me, then I will take you to Buchenwald. In fairness, I will even make Hagen available to you on the day you choose to go." Himmler raised a brow.

There was a commotion as the door into the living room was opened and an SS officer stepped in. "Excuse me, your Serene Highness, Herr Reichsführer, but the Fuhrer sent me to collect you. The guests are approaching the Berghof."

"Thank you." Himmler dismissed the man before turning back to Galiena, his hands wrapping themselves in the scarf. In a moment he could have throttled her with it, had he wanted to.

"I agree to your terms, Heinrich," she said with absolute sincerity.

Very carefully, Himmler rewound the scarf about her neck; the action making Galiena feel extremely vulnerable. She shivered and he made a strange noise in the back of his throat before he spoke again. "There are those in the Reich with whom you would be a fool to let so close to this fragile column; Reinhard Heydrich and the Fuhrer for a start." There was a light tap on the ridge of her vertebrae as he continued wrapping the length of silk. Himmler's voice then dropped and took on a much stronger Bavarian accent. "But I, Galiena, am not amongst that number. My fascination with you is not base or physical in nature; such hungers don't attract me. Your place in my tapestry is far more spiritual. More important; for to me you are an artefact. You represent a direct unbroken link to the age of Germany's greatness and now my scientists tell me you are tied to one of the purest Celtic bloodlines in the British Isles? My sweet Galiena! You are my holy grail. The blood in your veins is as Aryan as I believe possible; perhaps even Atlantean." As he tucked the ends of the scarf underneath one another, she could feel his hands shaking.

"You're mad, Heinrich!" Galiena replied with far more confidence than she felt. Now the nervousness had changed, for Heinrich Himmler had just sung the same tune her Grandfather had spoken from the time Galiena was small. The purity of her blood was the reason Meinrad von Steinberg decided to rape her; to father a child who would conquer all of Germany in the name of the family. But how did Himmler know these things? The Pfalzgraf didn't discuss his theories of racial purity with just anyone, certainly no one who would share them with the Reichsführer-SS.

Himmler moved around her stool to lean against the corner of the harpsichord. He appeared amused by her heated words. "Am I, Galiena? I know you don't believe that. How could you be who you are and what you are, and not know of your inherent superiority?"

"I am well versed in the concepts of eugenics and theosophy, Herr Himmler, and I represent neither a superhuman nor a long lost tribe of magical humans," Galiena retorted sharply, moving to rise from the stool. "And I believe you've managed to disquiet me more than the Fuhrer, were such things possible."

He stayed her with a hand. "Your mother was of Kincaldie, was she not? My archaeologists have told me very interesting things about that place."

Galiena froze abruptly. "My mother was the daughter of the Duke of Candingmere, yes."

"Then how can you not believe me?" Himmler took her hand between his own. "That line has never lost its Atlantean blood. You know that. All you need do is look at your cousin."

Her breath hissed in through clenched teeth. Damn the man! How did he know so much about her? "The doctors say Dickey's affliction is a disease of genetics, as such, under the laws of eugenics, would he not be degenerate?"

The Reichsführer laughed at her, but not unkindly. "You are well versed in the terminology, aren't you, my dear girl? But in counterpoint, your very accomplished cousin proves that his genes are higher evolved than others. The instabilities of his health are a burden of the weaker genes bred into the line, not out of it. Take yourself, Galiena?" The siren voice continued, the bright blue eyes never leaving hers. She could tell that he believed this, it wasn't some web he was spinning, hoping she would say something foolish. "Look at the phenomenal result of the Kincaldie-Candingmere strain to that of von Steinberg? Intelligence. Beauty. Poise. Compassion. Wit. I could go on, but I don't need to. You are living proof of positive eugenics and theosophy; where hard science and faith meet."

Galiena tried to dispel his glamour, but to hear this man whom she trusted and respected repeat the same words from her past was almost too much. Her grandfather and his ancient cronies, she could disparage, but Himmler was a younger man; the foremost police officer in the Reich, and a very powerful entity in his own right. Even Dickey himself rattled on about the divine right of kings and how he and Galiena were born to rule. But what were Himmler's motivations in this? She felt her lips twist bitterly. "Then you do wish to mount me, don't you, Heinrich? You're no different from the rest, only like my Grandfather, you put a pseudo-scientific spin on your carnality!"

Himmler flushed at her clinically crude terminology, and made a sharp gesture with his hand. "No, Galiena. Not at all! I am entirely satisfied with where your natural inclination has taken you; in fact, I couldn't be more pleased with your choice. While I am Reichsführer-SS and Grandmaster of my order, my blood is not as pure as some, and it is my duty to improve at whatever cost, even at the expense of my own. That is the role of the constant gardener. As for Meinrad von Steinberg, how could I not consider him mad? He became so obsessed with the beauty of his ultimate and careful creation that he tried to pollute it with his own lesser strain. Even the ancients knew what a heinous crime inbreeding is." Himmler took her hand and brought it to her lips, brushing her knuckles. "And while the gardener repudiates the crime against the breed, the man abhors the brutality and injury perpetrated on so precious and special a sister."

Her composure crumpled as Himmler enfolded her in his arms. Could they not all leave her be? Men and their wasteful, selfish demands! "How do you know so much about us?" Galiena gasped.

Himmler's lips were soft against her forehead. "It is my business to know. As for the Kincaldie information, that family has a particular notoriety in certain circles. A scholar of mine has been researching that family for years, but I did not make the connection until last night on the train. I'm sure my man would give his eyeteeth for a few hours of your time."

The door to the room opened and Gruppenführer Sepp Dietrich, commander of the 1AH and Hitler's chief bodyguard poked his head in. "Herr Reichsführer, with all due respect, if you don't get your-" Sepp caught himself before certain profanity, "person outside, the Fuhrer is going to use you for target practice! And where's our Pfalzgräfin? Bloody woman's up and disappeared on me!" The man's irritation appeared to be extreme.

Himmler sighed in exasperation. Galiena knew that the two men did not like each other at all and while Sepp was technically underneath Himmler in the SS, his position as Hitler's personal guard gave him complete autonomy. "Dietrich, your powers of observation must be failing if you didn't notice the Pfalzgräfin's presence before you profaned her."

"What?" Sepp blinked.

Galiena poked Himmler in the shoulder. "Heel, Heinrich!" She winked conspiratorially at him as she pulled out of his embrace. Walking around the Reichsführer, she straightened her suit and addressed Sepp Dietrich. "My apologies, Sepp. I was tired from my late evening last night and Herr Himmler came in to chase my blue devils away. Any tardiness is entirely my fault."

Sepp stared at Himmler with a highly dubious expression. "I doubt he helped," he muttered before he inclined his head at Galiena. "I'm sorry for my profanity, Pfalzgräfin."

Galiena rolled her eyes. "Don't be. I can be as bloody minded as the next woman and am probably three times as difficult."

The Gruppenführer grinned wryly at her, his visage lightening up as he did so. "I know."

Himmler held his arm out to her without deigning to glance at Sepp. "And now, might I escort my very lovely hostess to her adoring public?" His tone of voice completely changed. Lighter. Jovial.

Galiena felt Sepp's scrutiny as she took Himmler's arm. What a day this was turning out to be. Any more surprises and she was going to keel over! "Thank you, Herr Himmler. Your assistance is most welcome." She buttressed herself from the inside and flashed him a dazzling smile.

Himmler appraised her with his eyes. "There! There is the woman my loyal Hagen finds so entrancing. You do claim a very special place in my affections." Was that for Sepp's benefit or hers?

Galiena was unsure how to respond. Himmler had completely returned to his usual self. Did two men lurk in that shell? "How so, Herr Himmler?" She watched him through her lashes flirtatiously.

"After our adventure together, I feel a particular responsibility for you. Hagen put your life in my hands and I feel that duty quite keenly still. You will never need to fear again, dear Pfalzgräfin, for I shall always be here to protect you." He led her from the room and Galiena was sure she heard a derisive snort out of Sepp Dietrich as they passed him. They walked into the entry hall of the Berghof and found the other gentlemen waiting for them. Himmler passed Galiena onto Hitler's arm, who laid his other hand on top of hers possessively. Göring, Himmler and von Ribbentrop followed them.

They walked onto the terrace as the two large Rolls Royce sedans pulled up to the stairway. Galiena glanced around the terrace and was completely astounded to notice that Hagen and Wolff were the two SS sentries at the top of the stairs. They stood at attention, facing each other on the top step, completely within earshot of the Fuhrer's party. Interesting. What was Hagen doing here?

The Austrians exited their car, and came up the steps. Galiena was fascinated by their reaction to the cordon of SS guards. Chancellor Kurt von Schuschnigg had a look on his face that, while subtle, seemed to be somewhere between fear and disgust. Walking beside him was Franz von Papen, former vice chancellor of Germany under Hindenberg and present Ambassador to Austria. Galiena had met him years ago with her Grandfather. A woman who Galiena suspected was von Schuschnigg's wife was on the man's other arm. There were more men behind, but she couldn't see them.

The men reached the top of the stairs, and Galiena was introduced to Kurt von Schuschnigg. The Chancellor of Austria was a charming man with silvering dark hair and bright eyes which were hidden behind thick horn rimmed glasses. His face was bland, but Galiena had the feeling the man was not pleased to be here. She gave him a soft, courtier's smile as Hitler introduced her. Schuschnigg seemed duly impressed with her title, and gallantly bowed over her hand, before moving to talk to her uncle. Galiena greeted Frau von Schuschnigg, and exchanged the usual trivialities. Franz von Papen asked to be remembered to her Grandfather and she assured the man she would as soon as she saw him. That would be the day! The Austrian foreign minister, Guido Schmidt, a man whose romantic exploits about Europe were not unknown to her, was also very pleasant. She did, however, have the strangest feeling that he knew what she looked like without her clothing. There was something decidedly rakish about him.

Then she heard a voice which wreathed her face in smiles. "Well if it isn't my sweet little Gallie!" The voice drawled elegantly. Frederick Graf von Reitersbach, pristinely turned out almost to the point of being foppish, stood before her. He was also one of Galiena's closest friends.

"Dearest Freffie!" She laughed as he kissed her very noisily on both cheeks. Then with a theatrical glance to make sure they weren't being examined too closely, which of course they were, he took her hand and kissed it up to the elbow.

"And how is my dearest sweetheart of a wife?" Freffie asked in his debonair way. "What are you doing here with such important people?"

As soon as he said it, Galiena's eyes flickered to Hagen, and wondered if this day could possibly get any worse. Her fiancé hadn't moved, or even blinked, but his face was suddenly bloodless. Her uncle had also heard the comment, as had Himmler, for they both sent shocked glances in her direction. It seemed there was the odd thing they didn't know about her! "Now Freffie, you know we aren't attached anymore, you silly thing!" She laughed thinly, staring at him pointedly.

He heaved a great sigh. "I know, sweetheart, but you were my first wife and the only one I shall ever have, so you'll always be wife to me! I regret letting you go almost hourly."

For the sake of the huge ears of the various people listening in, she stated the obvious to Freffie. "That was only a lark in Scotland, Freffie. You know that. We weren't even married! We were hand fasted. We jumped over a broom together!" Her teeth bared in a strained smile, she hissed quietly in English through clenched teeth. "And if you don't be quiet, I shall drive the heel of my Ferragamo right through the toe of your perfectly polished oxfords!"

Freffie responded in kind. "And scuff me, you demonic wench?" Then the man switched loudly back to German. "Yes, darling Gallie. Trust those damnably economical Scots to invent a trial marriage!" He wrapped his arm around hers. "Oh my very dear girl! How I have missed you! It has been far too long! You just upped and disappeared on us. I telephoned and the Grandpater tore an absolute strip from my rather delicate hide. Just ghastly, it was!"

Himmler's curiosity got the better of him and he came over. "My dear Pfalzgräfin," he said in a flat, unfriendly tone of voice as he took her other arm possessively. "Do introduce me." The look on his face as he examined the extravagantly turned out man reeked of distaste, but then, compared to Freffie, Himmler certainly looked below the salt.

Freffie surveyed Himmler with an amused condescension. Galiena had the real feeling these two men would never be friendly. Hopefully Hagen would like her friend once he was over his present upset. That was all she could hope for. "Herr Himmler, this is my very dear friend, His Illustrious Highness, Frederick Graf von Reitersbach. Freffie, this is Heinrich Himmler, the Reichsführer-SS, a very new friend of mine."

The men shook hands. "A pleasure, Herr Himmler," Freffie said, his words dripping with sarcasm. Himmler did obviously not enchant him, his refusal to use the man's title a pointed slight.

"Your Illustrious Highness." Barely perceptibly Himmler bowed his head. "And how are you connected to our Pfalzgräfin?"

Freffie chuckled, his arm snaking about Galiena's waist with easy familiarity. "All Uradel are cousins, Herr Himmler. We are so terribly inbred! But in our case, the Pfalzgräfin and I are bound by the fact that all half breeds need to stick together in this world." He raised Galiena's hand to his lips. "How I love every drop of your terribly polluted blood, Gallie!"

Himmler's pallor took on an indignant cast. "Half breeds, Herr Graf?"

Galiena stared up at Himmler placatingly. After their earlier conversation, she knew the Reichsführer would take her friend's words as a personal insult. "Herr Reichsführer, don't take any notice of Freffie. What he is saying is that we both have an English parent, which didn't serve us very well after the war." She glared at her friend. "And you! Don't be such an inflammatory beast!"

"I can't help it, sweetheart! I am a beast. I admit it, humbly and gratefully," the handsome Graf responded flippantly.

Curtly, Himmler bowed again. "I see." He most assuredly did not. "If you will excuse me, I must go join the Fuhrer."

Freffie waggled his fingers somewhat insultingly at Himmler. "Cheerio," he used the English word, before escorting Galiena inside. "It's roaringly splendid to see you, my love," he said in English.

Galiena responded in German; only polite given their host didn't speak English. "I would agree, dearest Freffie! But what are you doing here?" She took one last glance at Hagen, who had still not moved, and blew him a kiss.

"The same thing you are, sweetheart. I lend the legitimacy of the nobility. Old meets new, and I am the most adored man in Vienna! Everyone who knows me, loves me, and I know everyone. I was a charming and witty addition to the drive. I can defuse almost every situation. If I was as lovely as you I would rule the world." Freffie was never one for modesty.

"I see you, my dearest, but where is Wilhelm? I think this is the first time I have seen you without him in, well, since the pair of you started rubbing along together," Galiena asked after her friend's lover. Freffie's relationship with Wilhelm Ritter von Glass had so long been a part of her life it was no longer shocking.

Bellows could not have expelled such a quantity of air as Freffie's sigh. "It was thought not politic to bring him, these Nazis being what they are. Not very cosmopolitan, my dear! Well that

Göring isn't so bad, but the rest! Lord love you, Gallie! They would sniff out our relationship in no time. I miss my Wills, though. He's waiting down in Salzburg. He's probably going to find some boy he fancies more than me and leave me forever!"

"You always say that, Freffie, and I think it's solely for attention!" Galiena refused to give the man so much as an inch for she knew he would run with it. "You must come back up the mountain tomorrow and bring Wills with you! It's only a few hours from Salzburg and then I can tell all; and there is so much, Freff! I am staying with Hermann Göring, and he is completely unconcerned with my friends. I even have some new records from Dickey." She used a stage whisper. "Contraband, you know!"

He gazed down at her with his gentle eyes. "Yes, Gallie, I believe I can drag Wills over the border tomorrow. We have no fixed engagements and I am sure the Chancellor will free the lad and me for you. I would like to hear your story. You were the last person I was expecting to find on Adolf Hitler's mountain!" As usual, Galiena could smell alcohol on her friend's breath. Time of day meant very little to Freffie and his definition of sobriety was very broad.

They walked into the living room and Freffie sprawled on the 'Austrian' side of the room. Galiena sat at the harpsichord, playing softly. The men began with all the usual diplomatic language, testing each other and probing. They weren't friendly but cordial, drinks were offered; it almost seemed like a gathering of friends. Frau von Ribbentrop and Frau von Schuschnigg talked quietly on the other side of the harpsichord in two overstuffed wing chairs. It was all so prosaic; but Adolf Hitler and Kurt von Schuschnigg were not friends, nor were they political allies.

"What am I to do, Herr Chancellor, when the Austrian Nazi Party has been banned by your government? I take this as a grave insult to my people," Hitler said finally. "How dare you maintain the ban on my party?"

"The Austrian Nazi party is not beneficial to the people, Herr Chancellor, at least not in Austria," von Schuschnigg replied evenly. "They have caused riots and strikes against the government in the past. That is not good for the Austrian people."

"I am Austrian by birth, Herr Chancellor," Hitler spoke very flatly. "I would never allow a party I created to hurt my beloved homeland. Austria is very close to my heart."

"You presume to tell me that the Austrian Nazi party has never hurt Austria? By God, Herr Hitler! Need I remind you of the murder of Herr Chancellor Dolfuss by members of the Austrian SS? The putsch of '34?" Von Schuschnigg spat, losing his composure.

"The overzealousness of the Austrian SS in '34 was an unfortunate incident, but it had no connection to the Reich government. Those men were radicals and acted independently," Himmler voiced quietly. "Since that time there has been no further action by any appendage of the Schutzstaffel in your country."

"Unfortunate incident? Herr Himmler! Engelbert Dolfuss was my very good friend and he did not deserve to be shot down like an animal in his office!" Von Schuschnigg turned his fury on Himmler.

Göring spoke up. "No one regrets the unsanctioned murder of Chancellor Dolfuss more than I do, Herr Chancellor. You should know I also have strong ties to the Austrian nation, due to my family's intimate association with the Ritter von Epenstein. I would never wish to see anything happen in Austria which would hurt her; yet the Teutonic peoples must be united again."

"Yes," von Ribbentrop agreed vehemently. "There must be formal union between Germany and Austria! We must cast aside the villainous treaties of Paris and take our place in the world once more. Anschluss is the only way we can accomplish that. Germany is strong, but without Hungary, Austria is small and impoverished. The treaties of Paris weakened her and she needs German protection."

Guido Schmidt interjected himself into the conversation smoothly. "With Italian support we are not as weak as we appear, Herr von Ribbentrop."

From her place at the piano, Galiena could see the gleam of satisfaction in Hitler's eyes. "I would be very surprised to see Mussolini come to the defence of Austria. He has given me his assurance that he sees conflict between our two nations as an internal matter and not of interest to his country."

"Italy is Austria's ally!" The Austrian foreign minister returned.

Von Ribbentrop laughed grimly. "Is it?"

Von Papen spoke up, eyeing von Ribbentrop with distaste. "There is no need to be inflammatory, Herr von Ribbentrop."

"The German speaking peoples must unite, Herr Chancellor," Hitler reiterated in his turn. "Either peaceably, or by force, but it will happen. It is the mandate of this government to see it happen." The threat was naked for all to see.

"You wouldn't dare! The League of Nations would never allow it!" Von Schuschnigg exclaimed in defence.

Göring smirked. "Pah! The League of Nations!" He slapped his hand on his thigh. "Now there is a toothless lion!"

"Need I remind the Chancellor of Austria that Germany has not been a member of the League since 1933 and we do not fear its useless sanctions and boycotts? The League did nothing when my good friend Mussolini invaded Ethiopia. What makes you think it will stir if the German people reclaim their lost cousin Austria?" Hitler's words were mild but his eyes became very bright.

"They will see a German invasion of Austria as an act of aggression!" The Austrian Foreign minister retorted.

"We don't agree," Himmler countered, his voice barely above a whisper, yet carrying across the room. "The League of Nations has neither concern nor pity for those they consider to be the aggressors in the Great War. A war that Austria started and Germany bled for."

"You wouldn't invade my country!" The Austrian Chancellor inhaled deeply. "Tens of thousands would die on both sides!"

"You underestimate the skill of the modern German Wehrmacht. They have proven themselves very adept in the Spanish civil conflict. My Luftwaffe, in particular, has demonstrated very well that cities can be decimated and armies destroyed before the infantry need be put at risk," Göring stated blandly, leaning forward, and the iron in his voice chilled Galiena's soul. "How big is your air force, Chancellor von Schuschnigg?"

"I cannot and will not give in to you! This is extortion of the worst sort!"

Von Papen held a hand up to Göring. "What if we put it to the people? A referendum?"

"This is a very smart man, Herr von Schuschnigg. Perhaps you should step down and let him govern in Austria?" Hitler suggested dryly.

Von Schuschnigg's eyes were hard as agates. "Might I remind you that he's your ambassador?"

Hitler rolled his shoulders in a small shrug. "If an Austrian can rule Germany; a German who serves said Austrian can rule Austria."

Von Schuschnigg glared at his German counterpart. "Would it serve the interests of peace if I agreed to this referendum? Put it to the people?"

Hitler shook his head in the negative. "You are Chancellor, Herr von Schuschnigg. Make an executive decision to save your country the discomfort of invasion. Also I would have you agree to a few other points."

"And those would be?"

Göring spread his hands expansively. "Of course you would rescind the ban on the Austrian Nazi Party. I am sure they have learned their lesson and the riots will cease. Also you will appoint my friend Arthur Seyss-Inquart as Minister for the Interior. He's a moderate gentleman and will serve you well."

"I will put it to my cabinet." Von Schuschnigg bowed his head.

"And you will limit the activities of the criminal organisations known as the Fatherland Front and the New Austrian Order," Himmler added firmly in a tone which brooked no refusal.

"The Fatherland Front is a legitimate political party, Herr Himmler," Guido Schmidt rejoindered. "In fact, it is the only legal political party in Austria."

"I don't know of this New Austrian Order," von Schuschnigg replied, his face blank.

Freffie raised a languid hand. "It's a gentlemen's historical club. I have heard of it. Dressing up in robes in the middle of the night and ranting on about the mad monk, von List[7], and Austrian

---

[7] Guido von List – An Austrian occultist and mystic who wore monk's robes in his later life.

domination of Europe. Nationalist, you know. Frightful bore. Totally harmless." But there was something in his eyes, glittering at Galiena, which made her think there might be more to it.

"Not according to our information," Himmler addressed the fop coldly. "They are an armed and violent group."

"Not unlike the SA then?" von Schuschnigg snarled at the Reichsführer-SS.

Hitler also leaned forward. "I would not say such things were I in your position, Herr Chancellor." His finger danced in a chastising gesture.

Von Schuschnigg sighed, ignoring the insult. "I will do what I can to limit the groups you have specified. That is the best I can promise."

Göring smiled ferally, his lips pulled back to bare his teeth. "You can ban them, Herr Chancellor. You can have their members arrested. Use your secret police to break up their meetings. That might give you a suggestion of how you can limit them," he paused. "As you did with the Austrian Nazi Party."

Von Schuschnigg's eyes burned. "You go too far!"

"No, Herr Chancellor. Herr Göring only seeks to remind you of the powers at your disposal," Hitler said dismissively. "I don't believe there is a too far in this situation. It is the familial duty of a big brother to assist a smaller brother. That is how Germany views Austria. Germany's little brother, who needs aid."

"Austria doesn't want German interference in its affairs!" Guido Schmidt spoke hotly.

Himmler leaned back, crossing one leg over the other. "No, Herr Schmidt. You and your government don't want Germany's assistance in Austria's affairs. It is our belief the Austrian people feel differently. Our Fuhrer is a son of Austria, Mein Herr. He knows what is best for all the German-speaking peoples. He can bridge the gap between our two nations. Our governmental style is not so different from your own, Herr Chancellor. We are both Nationalist and Fascist, though you have muddied the waters by allowing Judeo-Christian influence into your government. The Fuhrer's way is better than your way."

"I refuse to agree," Von Schuschnigg muttered darkly.

"That is, of course, your prerogative, Herr Chancellor. This is merely a friendly discussion between the leaders of two nations," von Papen said, trying again to reduce the choler in the room. "In the end, we only want what is best for the people."

"Dolfuss wanted what was best for the people. I have done my best to continue his mission. This is not it, Herr Ambassador!" The Austrian Chancellor rounded on von Papen.

"Have you? How tremendously noble," Hitler spoke after a moment of pregnant silence. His words were sarcastic in their ordinariness. The pummelling of von Schuschnigg by the leaders of her nation made Galiena feel embarrassed. She understood that this was politics, but now she understood the words of her acquaintance, Doctor Goebbels, who tried to impress upon her just how dirty politics were. This was it, real and undiluted. She wished she had been spared the demonstration. Not that she didn't understand about business, but the business dealings she had seen her grandfather transact were not like this. She had never seen her Grandfather resort to this kind of heavy handed manoeuvring. Poor von Schuschnigg looked so pale. So defeated.

Galiena played on and noticed Freffie staring at her. His eyes were sad and it added to the heaviness in her heart; but as Himmler said today over breakfast, the ends justified the means. Germany and Austria would be better off as a single nation united against the world. Freffie had to see that; he was a smart man. The Austrians just didn't know how gifted a leader the Fuhrer was! No matter her strange relationship with him personally, the Fuhrer was a great and remarkable man in his capacity as leader and Chancellor. Germany was a magnificent creature now. Just as it should be! Its people were strong and proud! The economy was booming! Crime was at an absolute minimum! The things Germany could do for Austria. She had to keep that well and truly in mind. The things Germany could do for Austria!

"I feel I must give in to your demands, Herr Chancellor. In the interests of peace, I will put it to my cabinet at the end of April," von Schuschnigg said at last.

"Not good enough. The beginning of March," Göring countered with undue haste.

"That is far too soon!" von Schuschnigg retorted. "There is much to be considered, Feldmarschall Göring."

"Perhaps mid March would suffice?" von Papen suggested quietly.

Hitler looked at Göring. "I think the middle of March would be sufficient for our purposes. What do you think?"

"I suppose that would be acceptable, Mein Fuhrer," Göring agreed then he looked at von Schuschnigg. "But going to the cabinet will only be acceptable provided the people are allowed to vote their conscience," he said very pointedly.

"I would never interfere in the opinions of my government. It will be honestly administered."

"Excellent." Hitler stood and held out a hand to von Schuschnigg. "You have been a most reasonable opponent, Herr Chancellor."

The Austrian Chancellor also stood, his entire being defeated. "Thank you, Herr Chancellor."

"Come. Now that business is settled, let me show you around my home and my mountain, and then lunch before you drive back to Salzburg?" Hitler smiled benignly.

Von Schuschnigg shook his head. "I'm afraid I don't have the time. I have national policy to modify."

"Nonsense. You must stay. National policy can wait until this evening. Listen to our dear Pfalzgräfin von Steinberg play some more, and I would like to show off my home. It's my oasis, you know." Hitler took the man by the hand. "I would be offended if you left so soon," he said in a tone which suggested refusal would be very foolish.

Chapter 5
February 13, 1938

    Hagen walked into the Alpen Song, a small beer hall in the Austrian city of Salzburg; as always, Eugen was right behind him. They wore civilian clothing; their uniforms back home in Germany as they weren't in Austria in an official capacity. Of course they weren't. No. Hagen and Eugen were taking a day off, driving through the Austrian countryside. That they should just happen to bump into Oberführer Doctor Ernst Kaltenbrunner, head of the Austrian SS in this beer hall, well, that would be a complete coincidence.

    Hagen was well rested. He had driven the unmarked SS sedan the two-hour drive from Hitler's mountain to the city of Salzburg, and had reached a meditative state. He'd forgotten how much driving freed his mind, it was almost as if his brain rose above his body, scanning ahead along the road and yet free to process his thoughts. It helped that the drive was beautiful, and he left in plenty of time to enjoy it. He smiled to himself. Standartenführer Hagen Kohl. Tourist. What a very amusing thought! Thankfully his escort vehicle was not following them. Hagen was not worried about the SA following him here in the countryside, either the Austrian or the German one. No one knew about this meeting, and the SA certainly wasn't going to follow him from the Berghof.

    Hagen reached up to his face and pulled off his sunglasses, he didn't need them in this dim hole in the wall. Alpen Song indeed. What a completely inane name for an establishment, but then that was probably why Kaltenbrunner picked it. It was an innocuous place and as Hagen scanned the room he saw a giant of a man stand up from a table in the corner, beckoning to him.

    The man was massive; even bigger than Eugen and that was certainly saying something. He had to be almost seven feet tall. Terrible duelling scars carved through the man's cheeks, giving him a gruesome profile. Hagen walked over to the huge man, and held out his hand. "Doctor Kaltenbrunner?" he asked.

    The hand which took his was very strong, the fingers stained yellow from tobacco. "You must be Doctor Kohl?" The man's voice was melodious and gentle, but his teeth were ghastly. The man was positively snaggle-toothed, and the teeth he did have were terribly stained.

Hagen turned to introduce Eugen. "This is my friend, Herr Freisler."

"Good afternoon," Eugen said politely. There was a strange note in Eugen's voice, but then he wasn't used to people being bigger than he was. Hagen wondered if his friend was a little rattled.

"Please sit down. Join me." Kaltenbrunner indicated a chair, and folded his frame into a seat.

Hagen reached into his pocket, pulled out a letter of introduction from the Reichsführer-SS and passed it over to the Austrian. "I believe you are expecting this?"

Kaltenbrunner pulled a pocketknife from his coat and slit the envelope. He scanned through the letter carefully, before refolding it and putting it in his pocket. "So you speak with the voice of the Reichsführer, do you, Doctor Kohl? This note says I am to render you aid in any capacity to the very extent of my abilities. Then I shall do my best. I am an obedient servant of the SS."

"Thank you, Doctor Kaltenbrunner. I appreciate your assistance in this matter. Primarily this meeting is so that you can brief me on the situation here in Austria, in particular the atmosphere in relating to, shall we say, the marriage between our two nations. I am sure you are aware there was a meeting yesterday between the Fuhrer and Chancellor von Schuschnigg at the Berghof?" Hagen asked directly, cutting through the polite trivialities and pushing straight on to business.

"Yes. Of course I know that. We may be in Austria but we are kept up to date by the powers that be. I understand the ban against us will be lifted and there will be a vote in cabinet to decide whether Austria will join Germany. Provided the people vote yes as their conscience dictates, all will be well. " The man shifted in his seat, the musical tone of his voice strange and disquieting. "And it's about time. Von Schuschnigg has bled us dry with this ban, but we won't bow down before the government. If they thought they had riots before! We are more than ready to resume whatever force is necessary to bring down the government. You can assure Herr Himmler of that, Doctor Kohl." Kaltenbrunner offered cigarettes to Eugen and Hagen, who both demurred and then lit one himself.

A dark haired girl in a dirndl skirt came to the table, smiling at Eugen rather brazenly. "Might I get you gentlemen anything?"

"Come, Doctor Kohl, Herr Freisler! Let me buy you a beer. It's nice to see a face from the head office," Kaltenbrunner offered, his face open and encouraging.

Hagen spread his hands expansively. "We will have whatever you are having." Inwardly he winced. He hated beer. He tried to avoid it wherever possible, but he didn't want to offend Kaltenbrunner. He needed the man right now, and besides, Kaltenbrunner technically outranked him.

"Three beers, Fraulein, and don't get too much head on them." The Austrian ordered before the girl flounced off. "It is safe to talk here, Doctor Kohl. This place is one of ours. That's why I picked it. The owner is one of our members, but very quiet about it. We sometimes come here to do discrete planning away from the prying eyes of the Stormfront."

"That's von Schuschnigg's answer to the SS, is it not?" Hagen asked.

"A damn poor copy. They wear blue uniforms similar to your blacks, but what is underneath is cheap quality. Certainly not made of the sterner stuff as we are. They try and pretend to be elite soldiers and police but they don't have the training; their power stems only from the fact that they are legitimate and armed, whereas we have nowhere near the resources. But they will regret every time they sent our men to the concentration camps. I know our days of hiding from the police are over." Kaltenbrunner growled, his scarred, brutish face taking on a bestial quality.

Eugen gave Kaltenbrunner an amused glance. "How strange that sounds," he rumbled.

"You have no idea, Herr Freisler."

Eugen grunted sourly. "Oh I might, Doctor Kaltenbrunner. I joined the party in 1920. I understand the difficulties of unfriendly police."

Kaltenbrunner snorted angrily. "Just wait until we come out on top, Herr Freisler. Then I shall have my revenge on them for every night I spent in detention. Every time they beat me. We will show them." The lips turned up cruelly. "But what can I do for you gentlemen? How can I help you?"

"I am curious about the opposition to our organisation, Doctor Kaltenbrunner. The SD in Berlin is making lists of all those who are in opposition to our Fuhrer and his plans for Austria, but I want to have your assessment of the situation. You are the head of the Austrian SS," Hagen said quietly, finding the giant Austrian's thirst for vengeance distasteful. The vengeful made mistakes.

"We do have a problem, Doctor Kohl. One that began as more of an embarrassment then anything else, but now has become more sinister, the New Austrian Order. We suspect they are an ultra nationalist organization primarily made up from the upper classes and military officer corps. We don't know too much about who they are, and the demographical strata of our membership does not lend well into getting a spy into their sphere," Kaltenbrunner admitted. "The problem with being in a workers party means the nobility tend to view us with suspicion."

"I understand the problem, Doctor Kaltenbrunner, though that is a problem we have eliminated in Germany. The Reichsführer-SS has worked very hard to secure the support of the upper classes," Hagen told the other man.

"Then you have been very lucky. As for this New Austrian Order, we don't precisely know if they are for the government or just against us. We find it very difficult to gather any intelligence on them at all. As you know, the Fatherland Front, the only legal political party here, is a Catholic party, as well as being fascist in nature. It some ways it is very similar to Italy in that aspect. Both Dolfuss and Schuschnigg are or were very devout men. Of course they see the non-Christian aspects of the Nazi party as being heathen and therefore not to be allowed. From what we have gathered, the New Austrian Order straddles the two. From what we understand, they are not precisely Christian, but what else they are is a mystery," Kaltenbrunner paused as the girl came back with their beers. He paid her and she scuttled off. "But from the other tidbits we've heard, they may be trying to bring about the restoration of Archduke Otto von Hapsburg to the Imperial throne of Austria."

"So how have they been a problem to you?" Eugen asked, reaching into his pocket to pull out a pen and notepad.

"When it started, it was mostly harmless, just irritating. They took great delight in kidnapping our members. Men disappearing in the streets, only to wake up a week later in some other part of the country, usually near a border crossing with Germany with a note telling them to go where they are wanted, trip courtesy of the New Austrian Order," Kaltenbrunner sneered, before taking a deep swig of his beverage. He sighed lustily and wiped his face with the back of his hand. "That's good, that brew," he muttered.

"You are telling me they just kidnapped your men? The men weren't harmed in any way?" Hagen asked, unable to contain his disbelief. Were he the leader of this New Austrian Order, with all the advantages that the group seemed to have, he would use his power more, to affect greater harm on his adversary rather than relegate himself to childish pranks and silly games.

Kaltenbrunner was silent for a long moment, and then slammed his hand down onto the table. "No. Not harmed at all. Drugged to the gills, but not harmed. It was strange. Nothing was taken from them and they weren't hurt or beaten. As I said, it was irritating. In the last year they have become more aggressive. Meeting places of the party or ancillary organizations have been firebombed, particularly the offices of the German Gymnasts club, which is primarily a front for our organization. Always left behind is a letter stating that delousing was courtesy of the New Austrian Order," Kaltenbrunner growled. "Firebombs transcend nuisance."

Eugen sipped his beer. "Have there been any fatalities as yet?"

"Still not. They have remarkable timing or we have remarkable luck. We don't know which."

Hagen furrowed his brow. "So how do you know about their religious affiliations or lack thereof?"

"Some of our members have woken up in the middle of strange rites. Men in hooded robes going through the motions of complex ceremonies to drive the devils out of Austria. One was staked out naked in a pentacle star, his body inscribed with odd symbols while they chanted over him. Then he was drugged again and dropped off ten feet from the border in the middle of the night.

The guards at the crossing saw nothing, of course, which was strange given that one of them was secretly one of us. There is no rhyme or reason to it. Another man, a good, sober individual not given to fantasy, described a naked demon woman with hair like blood sitting above him on a throne."

Eugen glanced up, a hint of a grin on his face. "I fail to see how that could be a problem for a stalwart SS man. I can think of one or two ways to subdue a naked woman, even if she's ugly as a demon!"

Kaltenbrunner's eyes glittered suddenly. "Indeed! I've never let ugliness stop me and I certainly wouldn't take being tied up naked in front of a woman lying down." The brutish face gleamed in satisfaction at the statement.

Hagen rolled his eyes with a sigh. "I'm sure there were extenuating circumstances to the individual's lack of masculine fortitude as regards his feminine captor, but can we get back to the topic at hand?"

"We don't know when they are going to strike next, or where they get their intelligence about us. It is a mystery." Kaltenbrunner heaved his shoulders. "If we could just find out who they are, we could take steps. Drive them out of their holes or even denounce them to the authorities. The government doesn't like organizations which disturb the peace, and the irony of turning the NAO over to the government amuses me. Oh yes, and they robbed one of our offices. The treasury was delivered to an orphanage to aid those who were in greater need than us. They infiltrated one of our stores of weapons, and replaced all the guns with farm tools. Again the note. "You would be better served cultivating the land with your back rather than fertilizing it with our blood. A parable from the New Austrian Order. " Kaltenbrunner finished his cigarette and immediately lit another one.

"What makes you believe they are from the nobility?" Hagen continued his questioning, though his mind drifted to the thought of a particular noble he knew with hair like blood and what it would be like to be on his back, helpless before her. Damn. Where did that thought come from?

"Their notes. The handwriting isn't that of the uneducated. And some of the victims heard their captors talking. Very highbrow accents. It isn't hard to tell the nobility from the rest of us. Bastards! Spoiled, rich bastards," the Austrian ground out.

Hagen partook of his beverage. God! He hated beer. "It all sounds very cartoonish. Or have you ever heard of the English tale of Robin Hood?"

Kaltenbrunner shook his head. "Never heard of it."

"Robin Hood, according to legend, was a displaced English knight who returned from the crusades to find his home province in the grips of a tyrannical lord, taxing the peasants into starvation. He robbed from the rich and gave to the poor. Very benevolent. Supposedly no one was hurt who didn't deserve harm." Hagen explained the tale. "This all sounds very childish to me. Picking people up off the street, drugging them, and delivering them to border crossings? Stealing the treasury? Taking the weapons, but not hurting anyone? It's making your life pretty damn inconvenient, but no hurt. That is a very childish form of terrorism."

"I see your point," Kaltenbrunner admitted.

"Yet their intelligence on the party is not childish. I think you should take the threat this group represents very seriously. If they did turn violent you could easily get caught with your pants down." Hagen spun his glass in his hand. "Unpleasant unless you are finding the red haired minx alone," he added to soften his words.

Kaltenbrunner dropped his giant hand to the table with a percussive slap. "You think I haven't considered that, Doctor Kohl? You think that hasn't occurred to me?"

"What are your people doing about it?" Eugen returned evenly.

"We have naturally increased security in all areas. Moved our supply depots. Changed our meeting locations. Yet still they seem to know where we are and what we are doing." The Austrian screwed up his face. "It's so damn frustrating."

"Have you considered they must have a spy in the Austrian SS or the party?" Hagen stated the obvious.

"You don't understand how the party works here, Doctor Kohl. Austria is not a large country, and many of us have had long spells together in prison. We are the closest of comrades. I cannot imagine any of my Nazi Brothers turning traitors to this NAO. It is, quite frankly, inconceivable to me." Kaltenbrunner shook his head. "No. It can't be a member of the Austrian SS. You wouldn't understand what we went through after Dolfuss."

Hagen smiled grimly. "If there is one thing I've learned, it is that almost every man has his price, and if he doesn't have a price, then he has an agenda. Know a man's agenda and you can pander to it until you own him."

Kaltenbrunner narrowed his eyes. "Our agenda and mandate is to bring our glorious Fuhrer to Austria. We have no other. I can personally vouch for any man in my service that he is a dedicated, loyal National Socialist."

"In your service, perhaps. Did you think that this could be the work of the Austrian SA? I know there is no love lost between your two units." Hagen swigged his beer, swallowing it back before it could touch his tongue. It wasn't even good beer as beer went, but was light and thin. "They did betray you once over the Dolfuss affair and the '34 putsch. I can only imagine they would be willing to do it again."

"Those bastards. Yes. We did consider them, but no. We made very thorough inquiries and obviously I have spies in the SA here. They're just as mystified, and it's happened to them as well. If anything, they have been hit harder than us. In one night in Graz last year, twenty vehicles owned by SA members, or seventy-five percent of their available motor pool were sabotaged, and sabotaged severely. Each car with a note on the dash. I can't imagine they would have done that to themselves just to put us off the trail."

"Does seem a little excessive," Hagen agreed.

"Absolutely. That is why I didn't suggest it in my report to the Reichsführer." Kaltenbrunner finished off his beer and signalled to the waitress. "The SA here never had the power of the SA in Germany. Thank God. They had enough to screw us in '34, but since then have lost a great deal of ground, just as in Germany."

"As I understand, Von Schuschnigg denied knowledge of the NAO yesterday to the Fuhrer. Would you believe him?" Hagen asked quietly.

The waitress came over. Kaltenbrunner glanced over at Eugen and Hagen's drinks. "You aren't done yet. Too bad for you.

Another for me, my girl!" The girl left and Kaltenbrunner continued. "He might not. It's very possible he might not. We certainly haven't made a big deal of it to the police. How could we? We are a banned and persecuted organization under the law."

"The Graf von Reitersbach admitted knowledge of the group," Hagen countered.

"That fag!" Kaltenbrunner sneered, his face twisting up pugnaciously. "He and his kind need to be driven from this country! Just as you did in Germany." The man lit yet another cigarette. Hagen was amazed at the man's capacity for nicotine.

"Who is he?" Eugen asked, having missed the little display at the Berghof. Knowing Eugen's penchant for jealousy, Hagen had not elucidated on the man who claimed Galiena as his wife.

"The jester of the upper class. Lives in his big town house in Vienna with his 'private secretary', the Ritter von Glass. Our waitress is more of a man then that one. Completely useless," the Austrian paused, his small eyes opening wide. "But you know, if it is the nobility, he probably would have heard something. They say in Austria if you tell Reitersbach something, the entire country will know ten minutes later. The man can't keep his mouth shut."

"I wonder why Schuschnigg took him to a secret meeting with the Fuhrer?" Hagen murmured idly, seeing how well Kaltenbrunner's mind worked.

"If Schuschnigg didn't want to keep the nature of the meeting secret, von Reitersbach would be the perfect choice to have there. Von Reitersbach would ensure all of Austrian society knew what was said." Kaltenbrunner tapped his fingers on the table. "Come to think about it, it could seriously jeopardize our struggle if the country knew that the nature of the Fuhrer's demands on our government."

"Is Reitersbach a threat to us?" Hagen questioned, feeling his own worry at the possible implications and entanglements.

"Absolutely not. No. On the flip side, no one of any note takes him seriously and here in Austria the old nobility doesn't have any power. Legally they don't even have their titles," Kaltenbrunner explained, eyeing the waitress who was bringing his new beer. "Not since the end of Franz Josef and the empire. All that nonsense was stripped away." A large hand disappeared under the dirndl skirt and the girl gave Kaltenbrunner an exasperated stare.

"Then why do Reitersbach and his companion have use of theirs?" Eugen frowned.

"They aren't native Austrians. They are both Germans. Prussians I think. Or their lands straddled the old German Austrian border and they claim German citizenship. No. Not correct. Von Glass might be Sudeten, but that doesn't matter. They merely reside in Austria; but the government has not seen fit to deport them. I suppose they pay their taxes on time, and despite the rumours I have heard about their faggoty orgies, the police have never raided them." Kaltenbrunner's lips thinned to nothing. "They have plenty of time to come after us, but they leave the degenerates alone."

"Is the Graf wealthy?" Hagen queried. There was always a moment to gather information on a rival and Kaltenbrunner was a safe if biased source.

"Don't know. I am not interested in gossip from the upper classes, and that certainly isn't the sort I associate with, or would wish to. Completely useless, as I said. I know they have been harassed by the SA from time to time, but why should I care? Swishing around Vienna as if they own the place. It's sickening."

"Interesting. Perhaps we might be able to convince the Graf to assist us in exchange for temporary protection from the SA," Hagen mused. He wasn't going to share with Kaltenbrunner that he possibly had a connection to the two men.

Kaltenbrunner was aghast. "You would want to work with a couple of queers?"

Hagen narrowed his eyes. "I am not above using any means necessary to accomplish my mission. I have no compunction with using them now and sending them into a KZ later. I'm certainly not going to give them promises of protection from the government, for I know we will be the government soon, but I will offer to protect them from the Austrian SA if it serves my purpose to do so."

"They told me you were the iron man," Kaltenbrunner nodded, his face aglow with approval. "I respect that. Toughness is very important."

"Thank you, Doctor Kaltenbrunner."

The Austrian drummed his fingers on the table, and then sucked deeply on his cigarette. The burning ring crawled along the paper towards the man's lips and Hagen was positive he had never seen anyone smoke so fast. "So why are you here, Doctor Kohl? Why has Herr Himmler sent you to meet with me?"

"I am here to facilitate the eventual takeover by our people. I have been sent to investigate the serious obstacles, and this New Austrian Order appears to be one. Your report to Herr Himmler distressed him, but I believe he was anticipating that the people responsible would be the Austrian SA." Hagen answered truthfully. Himmler would love another reason to put Viktor Lutz on the mat in front of Hitler. Hagen wasn't adverse to the idea either.

"Yes. Herr Himmler is no friend to the SA. I am aware of the situation. I am sorry to disappoint in that respect," the Austrian agreed, appearing glum.

Hagen raised a brow studying the man. For someone so educated, Kaltenbrunner struck him as being both dull and stupid. There should be a law preventing those of limited scope from putting the honorific 'doctor' in front of their name if they didn't have the intelligence and creativity to back it up. "Not to worry, Doctor Kaltenbrunner. It might just be the Austrian SA in the end, you know. Or at least, that is the way the Fuhrer might read the report. Herr Himmler doesn't appreciate how the Austrian SA betrayed the Austrian SS in '34 and he has a very long memory. If it is convenient to negate the powers of the Austrian SA as German rule comes to Austria, then he hopes you will cooperate in the facilitation of such," Hagen replied blandly.

"He would purge them at the same time the Fuhrer establishes rule here in Austria?" Kaltenbrunner drew his giant head back in disbelief.

Hagen shrugged with exaggerated suggestion. "A large number of people will be arrested when Austria eventually comes under German rule. The SD in Berlin is making lists as I said and the Allgemeine SS will be coming to assist the Austrian SS in rounding up those in need of re-education. If members of the Austrian SA are accidentally rounded up at the same time, then it will be an unfortunate misunderstanding, and one to be sorted out at our leisure when the dust settles. If it takes a year or two, then it is truly unfortunate, but these things have been known to happen."

"I like your style, Doctor Kohl. You are a man after my own heart." Kaltenbrunner grinned, flashing his mouth full of yellowed and rotting teeth. "Come. I see you are barely drinking. Tell me more of these plans. You don't have to leave early, do you? I would like to introduce you to a few of my most trusted men who accompanied me here. It would hearten them to hear news of how things get done in Germany. As you can imagine, the struggle here is very tiresome." A fourth cigarette came out of the package.

Hagen looked at his watch. It was two thirty. Would his lungs survive this encounter? "I have a few hours but I need to leave by five thirty. I have an evening appointment with my fiancée and a couple of her acquaintance."

October 3, 1937
Dearest Poppet,

I'm not angry anymore. I just want you to come home. Haven't
you punished me enough? Don't you know how much I need you?
The forest mocks me. I have been such a fool.
Eternally yours,
Meinrad

Chapter 6
February 13, 1938

    Galiena was tipsy. The more she thought about it, she
might actually be downright drunk. Yet it didn't matter, for her
companions were as close as family and Freffie was decidedly
more drunk than she was. Wills was less so, but then Wills was
always the responsible one. Wilhelm Ritter von Glass stood six
feet tall, with wavy light brown hair and bluish green eyes. He was
quite broad through the shoulders, with a very athletic physique,
more powerful than Freffie's whip cord leanness. Wills was also a
little older than Freffie, thirty-one to Freffie's twenty-nine.
    The men had shown up at Göring's chalet at two thirty.
Lunch had followed and conversation was kept very light; the
champagne flowing like water. Freffie wouldn't press Galiena on
where she had been; content to wait until she felt the time was
right to tell her story. After lunch she showed them around
Göring's chalet and they had been duly impressed. About five they
went their separate ways to dress for dinner. Göring was dining
with the Fuhrer, so they had the chalet to themselves. Until Hagen
arrived, of course, sometime after nine. The men wore white tie
and she dressed to the hilt, as was proper for those who were raised
to be at court. She wore her Edwardian collar necklace over a
black gauze band to hide her burn and a boat necked dress to hide
the aubergine bruise on her collarbone. When would she be able to
get dressed and not worry if some new injury was exposed to the
public?

They met in the hall at six, and the men were so handsome in their tails it nearly took her breath away. Dinner consisted of further inanities. So now here they were, walking into the ballroom, the room illuminated only by the moonlight streaming in through the windows and the huge fire roaring in the hearth. They each carried snifters of cognac, and the decanter was dangling loosely from Freffie's fingertips.

He leaned up against the mantle. "Well, shall I call this meeting of the Anglo-Germo-Homo-Noblo Association to order?" the elegant Graf drawled.

"Absolutely. All present and accounted for, with the exception of dumb Dickey, the Marquess of more than I will certainly ever have!" Wills raised his glass to the ceiling in salute, then drained his glass. Galiena and Freffie followed suit.

"You know, this is certainly duller without Dickey and his kilt," Galiena giggled, happily lost in the memory. "And that terrible sporran of his. Moth eaten thing! You would think he'd have a better one."

The Graf refilled everyone's glass from the decanter before resting it on the mantle. "Indeed. Now, my sweet Gallie! You have some explaining to do, little wife! Stories before we dance? Or should we dance first and have stories after? What is this talk of marriage! Fiancés! Adolf Hitler! I am agog, my dear! I thought you loved me!" Freffie smirked as he leaned over with hooded eyes.

She threw herself into Freffie's arms. "Of course I love you! I love you most cruelly. But you will never love me the same way." She batted her eyelashes at him gamely. "Remember, Graf von Reitersbach, who abandoned whom first?

Wills bowed theatrically. "Madame, I apologize, but I am extremely grateful for your introducing me to your most charming Freffie all those years ago!"

"You stole him right out from under my very nose!" Galiena thrust an accusatory finger in the other man's direction.

"I let you marry him! You could have taken him back!"

"Oh don't give me that, Wills!" She moved to hug the other man. "Impudent wretch! Where was it? Saint Moritz? Or Zermatt?"

"November of '33. God! It's going to be five years, Wills! Can you believe it?" Freffie drained his cognac in one gulp. "I think I need another drink. Who would have thought it?" He filled his glass again, amber liquid sloshing onto the hardwood floor. "But you, my little chickadee, have changed the subject. Not well done of you, sweetheart! Why are you swanning around with Hermann Göring and not locked up in Riesa like a good little virgin! I would hate to think that my wife has been gadding about without me!"

Galiena walked over to the fireplace, a chill covering her that the roaring fireplace and alcohol couldn't dispel. She stared into the flames for a very long time. The last six months had been the hardest of her life and were it not for Hagen Kohl, Galiena doubted she would have made it as sanely as she had. Since the attack, Galiena had been at war with herself, fighting battles where there could be no winners, only losers. In the end, she conquered the tortured part of her psyche which threatened to destroy her, silencing that little voice gnawing at her soul, but not without great cost. In the end it had come down to a choice; death for her or death for her Grandfather. At the last moment she had chosen him and it was only the misfire of a pistol which prevented her from murdering the man in cold blood.

"Grandfather, he," Galiena paused, then like Freffie drained her glass. Dear God! It was so hard to express in words and not have the memories replay in the back of her mind. Talking about it was reliving it over and over again.

Freffie walked behind her and enfolded her shoulders in his arms. Galiena loved Freffie, and always would. The Graf von Reitersbach had been a part of her life since memory; she had called him Freffie because as a tot she couldn't say Freddie, and the name had stuck. He had been at her father's memorial holding her hand. Their English mothers dear friends; alone in Germany but for their spouses. Both families had intended Galiena and Freffie to wed, but Freffie was also not a man who liked women. Not in that way. "What is it, sweetheart? What happened?" Concern rolled in waves off his body.

Wills came over and wrapped his arms around both of them. "Did he hit you, Galiena?"

She nodded, and lifted her chin up to keep from crying, the ceiling melting into a watery haze. "Yes. God, yes!"

Freffie stilled completely, his body that of a statue around her. "What else, Gallie?"

It was still not a word she could say. "He hurt me, Freff." The words came out like that of a child; high-pitched and sing-song.

The Graf erupted in fury. "The devil you say! I'll kill him, Gallie! I'll call him out!"

"You can't. Hagen had him put into a camp somewhere," she breathed, not even recognising the sound of her own voice.

"When? When did this happen?" Freffie hissed at her ear.

Galiena turned to face him, her cheek resting against his chest. "Months ago. September. A lifetime ago. Don't concern yourself with it."

Wills kissed her forehead. "Why didn't you come to us, darling?"

Freffie refilled her glass from the decanter without dislodging her from his side. "We would have looked after you, sweetheart! You always will have a home with us! Or Dickey! By God! Does Dickey know? Dickey will tear Germany apart looking for the Pfalzgraf."

Galiena gulped back the cognac. It no longer burned a trail down her throat and her teeth were getting numb. "He knows I was in a car accident in September. I know how protective Dickey is! Anyway, the car accident. That was how I met Hagen; I hit his car when I was trying to get away. I understand he contacted Uncle Hermann once he found out who I was, for I had a letter from uncle Hermann in my handbag. To be honest I wasn't thinking very clearly, and I hadn't seen you in so long. I didn't know what to do." The tears she had been fighting seared down her cheeks. "Grandfather hurt me very badly. I just didn't know what to do." Those memories almost felt as if they belonged to another person.

"What happened, Gallie?" Freffie demanded again, his arms tightening around her waist.

Galiena dashed her tears away angrily, and pulled out of the men's embrace. "He raped me, Fref." The words were flat and vicious. "What do you think happened? Good God!" She stalked the length of the room to the huge windows; the snow covered terrace mocking her with the illusion of purity. The moon rebuked her in the sky. "But I should take comfort in the fact that I wasn't the only one, Freffie! He raped my sister too!" An ugly laugh rose in her chest. "You once said sodomy was an enlightening experience, but I can't say as I was enlightened any."

She heard his footsteps behind her before an iron hand on her upper arm spun her around. Freffie's eyes glowed like stars in the moonlight. "You let him bugger you?" he exclaimed.

Galiena's hand flew of its own accord, the crack of her palm against his cheek like a gunshot. "It wasn't as if I had a damn thing to say about it, you insensitive idiot!"

Her friend paled, realising the folly of his words. "Sweet Jesus! I'm sorry, Gallie! I'm drunk and this! I wasn't thinking! This is- This! It's just too much! A man just doesn't do that to a woman! Please forgive me!

"What is there to forgive, Freffie?" The anger and the sadness seemed to wilt, leaving Galiena an empty shell. "It wasn't like it was published in the Gotha. Meinrad Pfalzgraf von Steinberg tries to father new dynasty on granddaughter." Her skin crawled and she resisted the urge to claw at herself.

He wrapped her in his arms again. "Oh Sweetheart. I am so sorry. Tell me what I can do to make it better? Make you better?"

"Nothing, Freff. It's done. It's over. Just please, tell me that you don't think it's my fault," she whispered brokenly. From fury to despair. She desperately needed him to believe her.

"Lord no, you silly goose! Don't even suggest such a thing! By god! I would never think that!" Freffie whirled around her to press his forehead against her. "Never Gallie! I know it wasn't your fault!"

The gulped down brandy was making her even more unsteady the room taking on a motion of its own. She needed to escape these memories before she did herself harm. "You know, Freff! I feel like dancing! Do you want to dance? I have some fabulous records. I don't want to talk about Grandfather anymore."

"Do I want to dance? Do I want to dance?" Freffie laughed insanely, swaying from one foot to the other. "What do you think, Wills? We have the most beautiful woman in all of Germany right here and she wants to know if we would care to dance!"

"I'm up to taking a turn about the room!" Wills joined them, a strained joviality stretched across his face.

Galiena dried her eyes one more time and staggered over to the door out of the room. After picking up the phone in the hall and dialling the extension for the butler, Galiena ordered him to bring a record player and the box of records in her room down to the ballroom. He agreed and she wandered back to her comrades.

"So tell us about this Doctor Kohl, Gallie!" Wills pressed another drink into her hand, as he topped his up.

"He's quite perfect and very dashing in his uniform. You will meet him later. I told him to come tonight," Galiena said in a rush, clinging madly to the safe topic. Though in sober reality she wondered if Hitler's words that Hagen's appreciation of her was purely material were right.

"Uniform? Is he a soldier?" Freffie drew out the word. "I do like a man who cuts a fine dash in a uniform!"

"Paws off, Your Illustrious Highness! Hagen is mine and I don't ever intend to share. Well except for with Eugen. If you think Hagen's something, wait until you meet Eugen. He is a veritable giant!" She let her eyes go round and wide.

"So what service is he in?" Wills pressed.

"Schutzstaffel. He's a Standartenführer."

Freffie sighed, but seemed to be exchanging a look with Wills. "How frightfully boring."

Galiena poked Freffie in the arm. "Not boring at all. Don't be such a snob."

"And where is his Von, Sweetheart? I don't think I can let you marry someone who doesn't have a von! What say you, Wills! It's bad enough that I took up with a Breifadel, Gallie! What is this Doctor Kohl?"

"He's a commoner, Graf von Reitersbach!" Galiena curtsied and half fell over, Freffie catching her around the waist. "Oh! The floor keeps coming up to get me!"

"Dear Lord!" Wills exclaimed. "How ever will we all survive the shame? Gallie is chucking us for some dirt farmer!"

The door opened and a footman came in with the requested items. He set up the record player and left quietly. "He isn't a dirt farmer, Wills. He's a Standartenführer. It's like an oberst. There is a very large difference. And he's my choice!"

"You'll get kicked out of the Uradel if you marry him, you know, Gallie. Not that it means much these days." Freffie walked over to one of the three dozen chairs which lined the room. They had large velvet blue cushions with the Göring coat of arms on them. He picked one up and threw it at Galiena, hitting her in the rump. "Oh! That was fun." He walked down the room, and continued to throw the pillows at her.

"You could adopt him for me, Freffie! Now why didn't I think of that! He could be your son!" It had been on her mind for days and that would solve that little von issue. Not that Hagen wasn't perfect, but a von would make him more socially acceptable.

The Graf shook his head in warning. "He might not want me to adopt him, my dear! I am the most notorious fag in Europe! Well, after that Röhm fellow, I guess. But I'm damned unashamed of it, Gallie!"

"But you could adopt him, couldn't you? Then he could be your son. Or maybe your nephew. Nephew might be better, what do you think," she asked, putting the record *Sing, Sing, Sing* on the player.

"If you love him and you want me to adopt him, of course you know I will. It's the least I can do. It's not like that will make him a Uradel, though, Sweetheart. Nothing can ever change that! And no matter what, you can never take his name, for then you would really be in the soup! Now come over here and let's dance." Freffie ripped off his tailcoat and threw it across the floor.

Galiena allowed Freffie to lead even though the man was hugely unsteady on his feet. Galiena couldn't feel her teeth in her mouth, a sure sign that she was three sheets to the wind; what did it matter if her dance partner could barely move? Instead, she nestled against his shoulder, pleased to have him near. "Fref, I wanted to ask you, all that rot about the blood of the nobility and et cetera. Do you believe in it?" Galiena posed the question suddenly.

"Where did that come from?" The Graf fixed her with a bleary yet probing stare.

His neck and shoulders felt so strong, and he smelled divine. "It's come up recently, and I don't know what to believe anymore. Are we special? I know Dickey thinks so, as does Grandfather, but I've always fought against that particular elitism. Now someone else that I have a certain respect for, and not one of our class, has resurrected it and I'm quite lost."

Freffie dipped her slowly, her head's careful descent back allowing her to examine him. "We are superior in our own ways, Gallie, and I think that you are more superior than most. Well, you and Dickey to be sure. I don't know, really, about the rest of us, but you and Dickey are special. Is it because of his strange affliction and the fact that you are the way you are? Again, I don't know, but what I do know is that all my life I have been following behind the two of you, and it's always been like treading in the footsteps of the Gods."

Galiena stared at her friend in puzzlement, frozen in that moment, her body helpless before him. "I don't understand, Fref! What are you trying to say?"

"Dear heart, I'm not the great theosophist that Dickey has become, and nor am I a scientist, but you two are different, and I know that. It's never disturbed me; the knowledge that I am lesser. Perhaps I console myself with the thought that I'm your disciple, the one who will spread the word of who and what you are as you proceed to do it." Freffie pulled her body back up against his, an indescribable fervour in his expression. "But I've always worshipped you, Gallie. I hope you know that! You are my Freya." He ran a finger along her jawbone. "My valkyrie."

"I'm flattered, Fref, if a little confused. I ask you about eugenics and you bring up the Gods." Galiena felt a frisson of unease at the conversation.

"Men create gods after their own image, not only with regard to their form but with regard to their mode of life. I do believe Aristotle said that. Why would you not be my most sacred Goddess when you and Dickey represent absolutely everything I would ever and can never hope to achieve?" The Graf's face turned sad as he returned her gaze measure for measure. "Are you an Atlantean, Gallie? I don't know. Are you born to rule, should you rule, and is your bloodline of the most noble in existence? You don't need me to answer that one, sweetheart. You know the answer already. Of course you are above the rest of us, and I think that this friend of yours is quite right to suggest it, but not in the normal sense."

"In the name of Heaven, Frederick von Reitersbach, you make absolutely no sense at all!" Galiena exclaimed in frustration.

84

The man had the ill grace to laugh. "That's because I'm drunk, sweetheart, and you're quizzing me on the esoteric. I don't think that every poxy, louse-ridden aristocrat in Europe should claim superiority by blood, but I do think you are one of the very few who can, my most sacred angel. To use the eugenic term, your blood is true."

Galiena laid her head on Freffie's shoulder again. "Fine then. Keep answering me with your riddles, Herr Graf. What did I expect trying to get a straight answer out of you?"

"I do worship you, Gallie. Don't ever forget that. You are my most sacred valkyrie and I know you remember why." Freffie whispered before letting the subject drop. They danced for several songs, but in reality they were far too drunk and spent as much time falling over onto the floor as Swinging. Galiena traded between her partners, and when Wills wasn't dancing with her, he was grabbing the pillows from the chairs and building a great mound of them in front of the fire. They laughed and shrieked to the music and suddenly Galiena's hair fell out, cascading down her back in a crimson tangle. Freffie had been pulling the pins out on her, and she chased him around the room, trying to get them back. Finally Wills picked her up in his arms and carried her over to his great pile.

"Come, Cleopatra! Rest, and let us look after your every whim." He reverently lay her down.

"You silly thing!" Galiena breathed as he handed her yet another drink. There was a languorous quality to this intoxication and knowing she was safe with her two oldest friends encouraged her relaxation. "I don't think I should have this, Wills. I think I'm a little drunk."

Freffie chuckled wickedly. "Nonsense, Sweetheart. You certainly aren't drunk enough. I know I'm not drunk enough, therefore you can't be."

"You might make me sick, Freffie!" She said lifting herself up so he could sit beside her.

The Graf pulled her back against his chest, running his fingers through her hair, the feeling of his gentle fingers against her scalp restful. "There's a nobility to vomiting, or perhaps you're noble, ergo your vomit is. I don't know. I'm not so sharp myself at the moment." He kissed her forehead. "The thing is, a morning where you don't wake up absolutely hung over generally means you didn't have enough fun the night before."

Wills lifted up her feet and placed them in his lap. "I want to massage your feet. May I, Queen Cleopatra?"

Galiena wiggled her shoes at him. "Does this make you my palace slave, Wills?"

"Oh absolutely. I've been in thrall since the first moment I saw you." He carefully undid the buckles on her shoes, his deft fingers stroking her ankles.

"No. That was Freffie, old bean. You were in love with Freffie."

Freffie laughed. "Actually it was Dickey who caught his eye first. I know it. That Celtic charm. The red hair. The green eyes. Damn that Dickey."

"But it wasn't to be." Wills sighed theatrically as he pulled off her shoe. "My God! You know, Freff, women really do have nicer feet than men. Or at least her feet are much nicer than yours."

"I am insulted, Ritter von Glass! I should call you out for that!" Freffie retorted with mock indignation.

"No, Graf von Reitersbach. I forbid you to do so!" Galiena waved an arm in the air, before tracing his moustache. "This is very Clark Gable."

"I know. Do you like it?"

"It's quite the thing, Freff. I like it." Then she moaned with pleasure at the firm pressure of Wills' hands on her feet. "That is sinful, Wilhelm!"

"It would be even better if you let me take off your stockings." He wiggled his eyebrows at her then pressed his lips to the sole of her foot. "Come now, darling Freya! Let me pleasure you!"

Galiena blinked in surprise. "I should think not! How improper would that be?"

"I think we tossed propriety out the window a long time ago, Sweetheart. But it's okay! We are family. All Uradel are family. I know the peasant down at the end is just a Breifadel, but that can't be helped." Freffie grinned wickedly as he wrapped his arms around her chest. "You can count the silver when he leaves. Really, you should have had him come in the servants' hall entrance."

"I am so sorry my family wasn't ennobled until 1871. I know I am just a goat herder by comparison to your illustriousness." Wills patted her foot. "But I will forgive the pair of you for being half English." He kissed the top of her toe, before the digit disappeared into the cavern of his mouth.

The feeling of the warm wetness surrounding her toe was both alien and disturbing. Galiena tried to pull her foot back but Wills' grip on her leg was like iron. "Wills! What are you doing? Stop that!"

"Shush, Gallie!" Freffie answered soothingly. "Wills isn't hurting you, now is he?"

Her breath caught in her throat. "No. Not precisely, but this is indecent!"

The Ritter ran his tongue along the instep of her foot. "Ah, Gallie! Were it possible for me to make love to a woman, you would be at the very top of the list. Your feet are absolute perfection!" He devoured her digit again.

"Wills! Please!" Galiena begged, the foreign sensuality unnerving her terribly. Her friend was so far away from the sensitive parts of her person that she wasn't at the stage of panic, and yet! As he feasted on her foot, it felt as if he was somewhere far more intimate.

Freffie nosed her ear. "Wills has developed a terrible yearning for toes of late, and as you are our inspiration in all things, sweetheart, I'm altogether not surprised he felt compelled to taste yours."

"But Freff! He's sucking on my toe!" She whispered, taking another huge gulp from her cognac, before she drained the glass for good measure. The jolt from the alcohol and the tingle from the urgent suction on her foot seemed to arrive at the same and very surprising place.

"Yes, Goddess! He is!" The slurred words floated around her. "Freya has always been a notorious sensualist, but that bastard Pfalzgraf has made you lock that part of you away! I can tell, Darling."

"Freffie! What are you talking about?" Galiena lost all thought as Wills wove his tongue in between her smaller toes. Her silk stockings seemed absolutely no impediment to his actions.

"A year ago, this wouldn't have left you trembling like a leaf, Gallie. Your eyes wouldn't be rolling in fear like a frightened filly; you would be lying there, glowing with desire." The Graf stroked her hair again. "I can't believe how much you've changed. Come back, Freya!" More fluid sloshed into her glass.

"I am frightened." Galiena breathed as Freffie brought the glass up to her lips. "It hurt so much."

"Beyond leaving your stockings moist, Galiena," Wills moved his head to nip daintily on the outside edge of her foot. "Am I doing anything to harm you?"

She drew in a shuddering breath. "No. I suppose not."

"Then enjoy it, my glorious Freya!" Freffie picked up her hand in his own and pressed it to his smooth cheek. "Swoon and enjoy it!"

Galiena slid her face along his jaw to angle her eyes up to those of her companion. "What, Fref? Should I just lay back and think of the Reich?" There was a sarcastic quality to her actual words, but they were spoken breathlessly and on the edge of surrender.

Freffie grinned down at her with bleary eyes. "You are such a brat, sweetheart. But I love you anyway." He kissed her rather enthusiastically, making silly noises in the back of his throat until she giggled at the ridiculousness of it all. Maybe having one's toes sucked by one's closest friends wasn't such a bad thing after all!

The door into the darkened ballroom opened and a servant showed Hagen and Eugen into the room. They were both dressed in their uniforms; just shadows as they crossed the hardwood floor. Hagen did not look happy in Galiena's opinion, but that could just have been the poor light. She didn't know why he could be in a bad mood! The evening was still young!

Galiena lifted a languid hand. "Heil Hitler, Standartenführer Kohl! Heil Hitler, Hauptsturmführer Freisler."

How amazingly wide could Hagen open his eyes when he was of half a mind! Galiena noticed that they seemed to take up his entire face as he took in the tableau. "Heil Hitler." Why did his voice sound so very tight?"

October 10, 1937
Dearest Poppet,

It has been a month, and still you have not forgiven me. Was my transgression so terrible? Or are you merely ensuring I am suitably apologetic when you return. Enough with this game. Come home to me.
Eternally yours,
Meinrad

Chapter 7
February 13, 1938

There was a strange silence in the room as Eugen came up behind Hagen to stare at the group on the floor. Galiena couldn't understand why the quiet seemed to go on and on, seemingly indefinitely. There was a charge to the very air between the two groups of men, and she felt strangled by it. At the same time, she simply didn't know what else to say. Her Teufel had become so completely Teufel-ish; his eyes hard.

"Oh don't bring him up!" Freffie waved a hand, nearly hitting Galiena in the head as he did so. The sound of his words was like a glass shattering in the stillness, and she jumped in his arms. "I really think we should make this a demilitarized zone. For politics. You know what I mean."

Galiena rolled her eyes up to Freffie's. "Very wise, Freffie. Very wise." She scrunched her toes on Wills' face. "Come on now, Slave! Get up and get the officers a drink! Or do I have to do it myself?"

"Now that would be criminal, great Cleopatra. Wilhelm, your favoured palace eunuch will see to everything." The Ritter released the hold on her calf, lowering it carefully to the pillows before pulling her dress down to cover her ankles modestly. With a quick pat on her knee, the man climbed unsteadily to his feet.

"Eunuch? Perish the thought, my boy!" Freffie also moved out from under Galiena. He stood and bowed to Hagen. "I do believe I am in your place, Sirrah, as much as it pains me to leave such a magnificent creature." Her friend bent to kiss her arm noisily from wrist to elbow.

"Come join us, Hagen! It's like a puppy pile. You too, Eugen! Come down and entertain me." Galiena raised a hand to her face as a thought occurred to her. "Silly me, I haven't made any introductions."

"Quite all right, Galiena," Hagen spoke very quietly, his words falling like a hammer. "I am sure we can attend to it."

"I am Wilhelm, the palace slave." The man clicked his heels and bowed low before staggering at the effort.

"Oh just call him Wills. Everyone does. I'm Freffie, Lord High Pillow; and you can call me," he paused and then said his name as if in surprise. "Freffie. His Illustrious Highness Frederick Graf von Reitersbach is just such a mouthful not to be inflicted on anyone. Really reminds me far too much of my father, who was a violent, drunken, old reprobate with no social graces. It amazes me that my mother; poor sainted woman, ever took up with him." Freffie pressed glasses into Hagen and Eugen's hands while Wills came leaping over with another bottle of Hermann Göring's cognac.

Galiena tried to focus on Hagen who now appeared faintly bemused. "I see. I'm Hagen Kohl. Eugen Freisler behind me." Eugen said nothing, merely glowering about the room.

Galiena crawled up to her feet, swaying in turn with the rest of the world. Hagen's firm, steady hand grasped at her elbow and that was the only still thing in her universe. Galiena shut her eyes in hopes that would make everything return to stillness, but the whirling only became faster. When she opened her eyes up, she smiled at Hagen. "I am so pleased you have all decided to become friends, because you are the most important men in my life. Well, Uncle Hermann and Dickey are in that group too, but they aren't here," she said. "Did that make sense?"

"It did to me, but then I've had more to drink than you, sweetheart." Freffie placed another glass in her hand. "But let's toast to friendship anyway."

"Brilliant thought, Freff!" Galiena raised her glass. "As they say in England, here's mud in your eye." They clinked and drank, though she only had a sip; feeling that perhaps it was time to stop drinking. At least for a while. She looked at Eugen who seemed overly stiff behind Hagen and she launched herself at him. "Come Eugen! I want to dance. Do you swing?"

He was as immobile as a wall. Had he not caught her in his arms, she would have fallen. "No, Pfalzgräfin."

Galiena gave him a dirty look. "Do you waltz?"

"There's no music," He rumbled with noticeable irritation.

Freffie looked at the white haired giant. "Dashed set of pipes there, my man!"

Galiena ignored her friend. She had forgotten how Eugen sounded. "If we are going to be married, then you must dance with me," she wagged a finger under his nose.

"Wait a moment!" Wills pulled her off Eugen and pulled her against his chest protectively. "Wait a moment. You're marrying this one? I thought you said your fiancé's name was Hagen and he is Hagen."

"It's complicated. Eugen would have to explain it, because I don't really understand it myself. It's something to do with people following us," Galiena replied with a matter of fact tone. Wills could figure it out for himself.

Freffie furrowed his brow. "So then what you are saying is they are a matched set?"

Hagen's lips twitched. "Something like that."

"Well, well! Two for the effort of one." Freffie turned to Wills. "Whoever would have guessed? Rather novel, come to think about it. Makes me like the SS a little more, my boy!"

Galiena curtsied to Hagen. "Would you dance with me, Hagen?"

"As Eugen said, there is no music," Her Teufel stared down at her.

She went twirling off into the middle of the floor, her dress belling out around her thighs. "I'm surprised you can't hear it." Galiena continued with her pirouette. "Wills and Freffie can sing. They do it very well. You should hear them. Maybe not now though, they are a trifle squiffy."

"There's all these records over here, Gallie," Freffie called over, flinging a plastic disc at her.

Galiena and Hagen ducked the flying projectile. "No. No jazz," she returned in a stage whisper. "It's against the law." She tried to look ever so innocent for Hagen. "Of course we would never listen to degenerate Jazz in Uncle Hermann's house, Standartenführer Kohl."

The officer leaned down, his face very close to hers. "If you did, I would have to arrest you, Fraulein."

"Now that does sound exciting, Standartenführer Kohl, but you have to catch me first!" Galiena leapt away, but he caught her easily and pulled her back into his arms.

"You are drunk, Galiena! I don't think I have ever seen you this drunk!" He growled in her ear.

"Do you like it, Hagen?" she answered winsomely.

"No. I don't think so," he shook his head.

Even absolutely gooned as she was, Galiena could tell Hagen was displeased but she didn't care. "Pity!" She winked at him. "It doesn't happen very often, but I'm sure you will get used to it when it does."

Freffie and Wills had been rebuilding her mound of pillows by the fire while Eugen looked down in consternation. "Come back to us, sweet Cleopatra! We are desolate without you!" Freffie bowed floridly.

"Be desolate a moment longer, Freffie!" Galiena made a dismissive gesture with her hand. "You can worship me again in a minute."

"Yes, my queen!" Freffie fell backwards into the pile himself.

"Are you always so cruel to your admirers?" Hagen whispered in her ear.

"Occasionally, Standartenführer."

"Then I shall be forewarned." His brow almost disappeared into his hairline. "For I am your premier admirer."

Hitler's words flashed into her mind, as they had periodically through the last few days and she felt her eyes narrow, feeling the kernel of doubt which nagged at her constantly. No. Now was not the time. Galiena nodded at him, not trusting herself to speak and pulled out of his embrace. Arriving at an illusion of sobriety, she moved over to Freffie, and allowed him to assist her down. "Thank you, Freff," she whispered.

"Come now, Oh Julius Caesar! Your lady awaits." Wills bowed mockingly at Hagen.

The Standartenführer stalked over to the pillows, his boot heels sounding a sharp staccato all the way. Hagen's face seemed questioning as he searched hers, then he looked over at Wills. "It would not be appropriate."

"Oh stuff and nonsense, Standartenführer," Freffie exploded, crawling off the pile to slide onto the parquet floor. "Get down here, and show us how a brown shirt has fun." His eyes were very sly. "Or do you not know how?"

Hagen appeared unimpressed. "Didn't Galiena tell you how dreadfully dull I am?"

"You have comported yourself on the floor before, Hagen," Galiena reminded him quietly.

"Do you request that I join you, Madame?" His words felt cold and she wondered where he found the gall to sit in judgement of her.

"Of course I do, Hagen. If you are of a mind, that is," she retorted sharply, wanting him, but not wanting to play this dominance game.

Surprising Galiena, Hagen settled himself down, his legs straight out towards the fire; she sat up to lean back against his chest, as she often did in the car. He was very stiff and she could tell he was not comfortable with the situation. Responding to his willingness to give in, Galiena reached up an arm and stroked his cheek. Her officer relaxed somewhat. "You don't have to be the ever so perfect officer here, Hagen. This is my family," she breathed.

Eugen pulled over one of the chairs and sat with his legs crossed, his glass in his hand. Freffie and Wills sat down on either side of her feet. The Ritter moved to reclaim her foot, but the sharp slap of Eugen's sole against the floor seemed to forestall him. Freffie poked his lover in the arm. "Oh how it pains me to see my wife in the arms of another man!"

Hagen inhaled and Galiena could feel his body turn rigid. "Oh stop teasing Hagen, Freff! That's just cruel!" she paused. "Besides! I've always had to endure seeing you in the arms of another man for years."

"Touché, sweetheart," Freffie laughed.

"It was never legal anyhow," Galiena protested.

Eugen narrowed his eyes. "Then are you married or not?" His usual growl was even more feral tonight than was usual.

Wills grinned. "They aren't anymore but they were. It was probably the most half-baked scheme ever to come out of these two. I can't believe Dickey went along with it. He's usually the most sensible of the three of them."

Freffie looked hurt. "Come now! We wouldn't be living nearly so well if Galiena and I hadn't done it!" He glanced over to Hagen. "I needed to get married to secure an inheritance from great Aunt Wilhelmina. She had given up on it ever happening, was about to disinherit me and had sent me a letter informing yours truly of the situation. We were up at Dickey's hunting box in the Highlands of Scotland when I got it, and I just about had heart failure."

"It was quite amusing." Galiena smiled at the memory. "He was snorting about for an hour at least. Completely lost his composure."

"And Dickey was laughing his unmentionables off. Hard to believe it was four years ago!" Wills added in disbelief.

"So we are up at Kincaldie; one of Dickey's ancillary titles is Laird of Kincaldie and a Scottish laird has all sorts of strange abilities. So he suggests I find someone to hand fast to, because he can write up a licence of sorts to make it legal. Sweet Gallie immediately volunteered, so that, as they say, was that. Dickey called in the Kirk, some sort of a priest and we dressed up in kilts," Freffie shrugged as he said what to himself was the obvious.

Galiena cut him off, looking up at Hagen. "I did not wear a kilt. I wore a dress."

"I see." But her fiancé did not appear to understand.

"Anyway, we stood in the great hall at Kincaldie, in front of the Kirk, and jumped over a broom, tra la la! We were hand fasted." Freffie finished with an extravagant movement of his hand.

"But what does that mean?" Eugen asked, his brow furrowed.

"It's a trial marriage they used to have in Scotland. You are only married for a year and a day and if one doesn't go through with a formal ceremony after that time, the marriage is dissolved. No need for an annulment and it is formalized if the lass becomes pregnant, which was never an issue in this case. They don't do it anymore, but it is still legal in Scotland. It isn't legal here, or at least I don't think so. But it was good enough for the Baroness Wilhelmina." Freffie rested his hand on Galiena's knee before throwing a strange, almost challenging stare at Hagen. "Or almost good enough."

Hagen swivelled his head. "Almost good enough?"

Wills nodded. "We left Scotland and returned en masse to Vienna to confront Aunt Mina and she looks across the room at Freff and declares,"

Galiena and Freffie joined in, and the words were said in unison. "You, Frederick, have always been a buggerer and I highly doubt you have consummated the marriage with this sweet child!" The three burst into uproarious laughter at the memory.

"Which, of course, was absolutely the case. So we were escorted by the butler up to our room to attend to the deed!" Freffie added when he caught his breath.

Galiena stroked Hagen's cheek again. "There we were, panicking in the bedroom, both trying to figure out how to solve this problem when after about an hour, Wills bursts in through the window and comes to our rescue."

Wills leaned forward as he told his part of the tale. "Yes. The butler was standing guard outside the door, having locked them in like rabbits in a hutch. Dickey and I were searching for a way to salvage the situation, for we were damn sure Fref and Gallie couldn't possibly be inflagrante. So I climbed out the window of my room and clambered along the ledge into his. Thankfully I had some brandy first and didn't look down. I came in, slashed my forearm, spread the blood liberally on the sheet, and voila! One deflowered young lady and one happy old dragon."

Freffie shook his head. "Simply never would have occurred to me." His eyes darted around sheepishly. "Didn't know about that at the time."

Galiena half smiled. "Me neither."

Wills slapped Freffie on the back. "That's because you're absolutely useless, and she's innocent."

Hagen raised a brow. "And did the Baroness accept that as proof?"

Galiena giggled. "It was ghastly. She came in, inspected the bedding, looked at Freff and just said 'with practice he won't be such a brute.'"

"I thought we'd managed to fool her, but on her deathbed, about three months later; didn't know she was dying at the time, she took my hand and thanked me for going through with such an elaborate charade on her behalf. That it gave her no end of pleasure to pretend I had returned to the fold, as it were." Freffie added. "I really do miss Aunt Mina. I still have the portrait that was done of her as a young woman hanging over the fireplace in my study. They don't come like that anymore." Freffie drained his cognac and refilled it. He stood very unsteadily and raised his glass. "To Aunt Mina, wherever you are!" A gulp and the cognac was gone.

Wills also stood. "Grand dragon of Vienna!" He drank as well. "She and I always rubbed shoulders very well, but then she sponsored my mother as a girl." The two nobles sat down again.

"Didn't you feel like you were defrauding your aunt?" Hagen asked slowly.

"No. It was a game on both sides, I think. It's the way things are done. Or were done. I was born in the wrong time; I would have done better had I been spawned twenty five years sooner. I would have been an absolute corker in the aughts. Probably about 1905! Or the gay nineties in Paris."

Wills rolled his eyes. "Ah! Paris! Mais oui! I do love Paris. We haven't been in a while!"

"True. True." Freffie rounded on Galiena. "And whose fault is that? Hm? Who had to stay home and play dutiful nurse for the last two and a half years?" An accusatory finger thrust in her direction.

Galiena examined her hands. "I thought Grandfather was going to die, Freff. I wasn't going to leave him alone. He was so sick for so long." She started to tremble, her mouth going dry. If only she had known. Her eyes filled again. "It wasn't all bad, Freff! You have to believe me! Most of the time it was enjoyable. Especially when we were at Riesa! I was lonely for other people, but Grandfather was," she paused. "I don't know how to explain it." Galiena wrung her hands. "It was never my intention to become his-"

"Don't talk about it, Darling." Cutting her off, Hagen kissed the top of her head.

"It confuses me. I don't know how I feel about it. I hate him, and yet, he's my grandfather! There were good times," she answered brokenly, though not as desperately as had she been sober. Galiena was fast learning the amazing powers of alcohol and how it could make everything seem less terrible. "Does a night of madness erase twenty years of kindness?"

Wills rubbed her foot, ducking out of the way of Eugen's boot. "The man in black is correct, Gallie girl! You have all of us, or so it would seem. Don't think about the bad times. These are the thirties, after all! Eat, drink and be merry! Seize your happiness where you can!"

She smiled at him. "Wills, you are such a love!"

"Absolutely, sweet Gallie! Don't ever forget it!" Her friend winked at her.

They talked and drank more, but Galiena tapered off her intake. She didn't want to be sick, and she knew she was on the edge of it. The men discussed cars and Galiena mentioned the tragic loss of Hagen's without going into the details. She didn't want Freffie to know how close she had been to danger, and she absolutely didn't want Dickey to find out.

"Well, Gallie, my felicitations on your engagement," Wills said at last.

"Mine too, Kohl. You seem like a capital chap and you are welcome to visit us in Vienna whenever you should be in the neighbourhood. Yes. Capital." Freffie sounded very drunk.

"Thank you." Hagen's chest rumbled against her ear.

"You too, Freisler, even though you don't seem to say too much. Bit affected, that," Wills nodded slowly.

"So what did Dickey say about this engagement, Sweetheart?" Freffie slurred.

"Not much. He's reserving judgement. He said on the phone that he plans to come here in mid March to decide whether or not he will allow me to marry," Galiena told the Graf.

"What's this? I have your uncle's permission to marry you." Hagen replied, rolling a lock of her hair against his fingers.

"Oh no, Kohl. Göring isn't her family. After the Pfalzgraf, the man you need to talk to is Dickey and he is very protective."

Freffie patted Hagen's boot with his hand, almost stroking the polished surface. "Nice shine there," he remarked casually.

"Really?" Eugen returned flatly.

"Very protective. Isn't he your guardian, Gallie?" Wills questioned.

"Only financially in terms of my mother's trust. Dickey and Uncle Hermann. Why? Are you boys short of funds?" Galiena tried to focus on her friends. "You can have some of mine, darling. I have more than enough for a whole passel of useless aristos."

"Perpetually," Freffie chuckled. "No. In actuality, not at the moment. We've been behaving of late."

"After a fashion," Wills muttered under his breath. "But as for Dickey, he will be examining you with a fine toothed comb, Kohl. He always was the responsible one, in a highly irresponsible way."

Galiena winked at Eugen. "Dickey's the one who taught me how to smoke cigars."

"This is the responsible one?" Eugen questioned.

"I didn't know you smoked!" Hagen tilted her chin up to meet his indignant eyes.

"Rarely!" She shot him an arch look. "You don't know all my secrets, you realise." Then she added for good measure, "Thank God there are some things not in your precious files."

"I am beginning to understand that," Hagen replied evenly.

Freffie started lolling his head. "You know, Wills? I do think I'm done, love."

"God, Freffie! Do I need to take you outside and let you hang your head over the balcony?"

Freffie tried to crawl to his feet. "I think so. Damn my frail body!"

Eugen stood and effortlessly picked Freffie up by the back of his shirt; standing him on his feet. "There."

Freffie appeared to be swallowing hard. "Thanks. Bloody decent of you."

Galiena also stood. "The doors at the balcony open. I will send a footman out to escort you to your room when you are ready."

Wills sent her a grateful smile as he came to his feet. "Thanks, Gallie. Sweet dreams. He could be out there a while."

"I remember. Don't let him catch a cold. Breakfast is served English style, so come when you are ready," Galiena added.

"Righto, Gallie," Wills said in English, before continuing in German. "Pleasure to meet you gentlemen. Come, Freffie."

"Damn shame to end the party this way," Freffie muttered, as Wills supported him. "Night."

"Good night," Hagen and Eugen said at the same time.

Galiena watched as the two peers staggered to the end of the room and exited the door to the outside. She yawned and looked at Hagen. "Poor Freffie. He never knows when to stop. I don't know what would happen if he didn't have Wills to look after him."

"An interesting pair. I can't say as I approve of their lifestyle, however." Hagen moved to stand beside her.

"No," Eugen agreed.

Galiena held out a hand to Eugen who clasped her elbow as the floor moved abruptly beneath her. "It seems so second nature to me. Freffie was always different. I think we both knew it, even as children." She patted Eugen's hand as she steadied herself. "Thank you Eugen."

"My pleasure."

Hagen turned her to face him. "And I don't approve of some of your antics in the past. Why did you not tell me you were married, or hand fasted, or whatever you wish to call it?"

"It was years ago, Hagen, and it didn't mean anything. It wasn't legal," she explained again, wishing he could understand.

"You defrauded a woman to achieve an inheritance," Hagen pointed out to her.

"I didn't. Freffie did, or at least tried to. I told Freffie at the time he didn't need to worry, for if he needed money I would have given it to him. I still would. Or Dickey would. Either way, Freffie didn't need to worry at the time. But when Dickey suggested it, it seemed like such a lark," Galiena sighed feeling lost and yearning for those completely carefree days. "And at the time, I might have made it a more permanent arrangement. Being Freffie's wife in name only wouldn't be so terrible. But he never had the fortitude to stand up to my Grandfather and Grandfather is more than aware of Freff's peculiarities. In all honesty, it wouldn't be so different from how our marriage is going to be." Galiena shook out her dress. She never had a physical relationship with Freffie during their hand fasting because it simply wasn't an option; Hagen would have to understand that the same rules would apply to their union. It wasn't going to happen.

Hagen caught her chin in his hand. She wondered why his eyes seemed to be drilling into her. "What precisely do you mean, Galiena?"

Eugen turned and walked out of earshot. Galiena appreciated the man's discretion. "Hagen, I should think I wouldn't have to explain it to you?"

"Explain what?"

"I'm not a child, Hagen. I know what the Fuhrer said the other day was true. I know you don't love me. I have no illusions about that, no matter how much I would like to."

"I'd anticipated his words might make you upset. The Fuhrer was trying to shake you, Galiena. You must see that," Hagen told her firmly.

"But you don't love me, do you, Hagen?" He started to make an excuse and she cut him off. "No. Don't dissimulate. I deserve better than that. I don't ever want you to lie to me about your feelings, or tell me that you love me if you don't. Yes. I believe you care. I wouldn't have accepted your proposal if I didn't think that was the case."

"You told the Fuhrer that you love me," Hagen replied doggedly.

"And I think I do, Hagen. Yet loving you doesn't make me blind; and while I love you as a woman loves a man, I can never," she paused, looking for the proper words.

"Never what, Galiena?"

She took a step back, away from him. "Hagen, you, more than anyone else, should understand I cannot and will not allow a man to do to me what my Grandfather did."

"I wouldn't expect you to. For God's sake, Galiena! Over my dead body will it happen again!" he exclaimed hotly.

Galiena was so relieved and warmth spread into every part of her being "I knew you would understand, Hagen." She threw her arms around him. "You are such a wonderful man!"

"Darling! That you would think I would allow another man to touch you is ludicrous." Hagen kissed the top of her forehead.

Galiena was surprised that he was being so reasonable. She had been concerned this was going to be a major issue for him. "I was terrified of having children anyhow," She whispered against his throat.

He stilled. "What was that?" There was a dangerous tone in his voice.

"Well it means I don't have to worry about children either and quite frankly, I'm relieved. I had hoped you weren't desirous of having them." She gave him a quick squeeze, and then pulled away, turning to exit the room. "I'm so glad that is settled."

Hagen grabbed her hand. "Wait a minute, Galiena. I think we are having a slight misunderstanding here. How does my not allowing another man to touch you preclude us from having children?"

"I think that should be self explanatory." For such a smart man, he was being remarkably obtuse.

"I didn't including myself amongst the rest, Galiena," he answered her.

"I did."

"Galiena, I think we need to discuss this." Hagen looked a little angry. He obviously wasn't going to be reasonable after all.

"As far as I am concerned, Hagen, it is settled. Nothing will make me do that-" she paused. "That act again. I won't allow anyone to do that to me. I'm sorry! I've thought about it long and hard and I just couldn't submit to that again. I won't let it be done to me." Galiena pulled her hand out of his grasp and crossed her arms across her chest.

"Your Grandfather raped you, Galiena. I have absolutely no intention of ever doing so. I could never do that to you. The physical relationship between a man and a woman, a normal one, isn't like that." Hagen put his hands on her shoulders.

She shook her head. "No, Hagen. I'm resolved. I can't do that again." Galiena took an abrupt step back out of his grasp.

"You seemed to like it well enough when I've kissed you." Now he sounded furious.

"I did. That was fine. But kissing isn't," she kept fumbling for words. "Kissing isn't that!" Her heart felt like lead. Maybe this wouldn't work after all. Galiena could almost feel her heart breaking.

The Standartenführer inhaled and then exhaled very slowly. "We will discuss this again when you aren't intoxicated.

Galiena shook her head stubbornly. "Nothing is going to change!"

"I don't wish to argue about this now." The Teufel stood before her in all his blazing glory. The stark white ring around his compressed lips should have been a warning but it intimidated her not at all.

"Neither do I! I thought it was settled." She eyed him suspiciously. She knew she couldn't marry him if he didn't change his mind on this issue.

Hagen took her hand kissed it. "Good night, Galiena. Thank you for your hospitality." His words were icy with formality.

"Good night, Hagen." Galiena inclined her head mechanically, and then walked over to Eugen. "Thank you for coming, Eugen."

"My pleasure, Pfalzgrafin." Eugen's face was twisted with something she read to be concern.

"I shall, of course, see you both again soon." Sweeping passed Hagen and Eugen, Galiena left the room with the speed and intent of a battleship.

Chapter 8
February 14, 1938

Hagen was in a foul mood the entire morning. He knew that he had long surpassed irritability and was bordering on mean. He had growled at Eugen on the drive to the train and now his loyal compatriot was avoiding him; not even in the train car, but outside on the platform watching Bavaria go by. Hagen staked out two seats at the back of the saloon car and glared at anyone who came near. He'd even snapped at the steward when the man came to serve him refreshments. Hagen had no regrets. He didn't want anyone around him right now. The world could go to hell! He gritted his teeth and tried to concentrate on his file.

Hagen was going over his notes from his meeting with Kaltenbrunner, and working on a plan of action for the Austrian situation. He was preparing a fact-finding mission, for both himself and several of his people. Hagen could accent his German to sound more Austrian, and he was relatively certain that so could others on his staff. It wasn't such a hard thing. The Austrian accent and the Bavarian accent weren't so different. Von Ond had very little regional accent at all, the product of an upper class childhood.

Hagen had very special plans for von Ond, as soon as Himmler put through the man's promotion. Von Ond was going to infiltrate the New Austrian Order. He was the perfect choice to try; the right name, accent, and manner. He was young, aristocratic and Hagen was sure that if any member of his team could penetrate the organization, it would be von Ond. Hagen had a feeling that he personally couldn't do it, Eugen was out, Kappler was far too rough, Strohkeller and his men were primarily watchers; not suited to an active infiltration. No. Von Ond was the man for the task.

But he was going to have to move Strohkeller and his crew down into Austria; that was for certain. There were people who needed to be followed. Watched. Hagen pulled a map out of his briefcase. He would send them down over the border in threes, here and there, along the German-Austrian frontier. They could then make their way to Vienna and rendezvous with Hagen for further orders. Seven groups of three. That would be easy to manage. He would set Eugen up somewhere to collect the information at specific times, maybe even use some of his other analysts from the department to assist Eugen.

Hagen didn't want to use any Austrian SS in his operation. He wanted men he could trust completely. He also had serious concerns about the probability of a leak in the Austrian SS and he didn't want the information about his unit being on the street. The only person who would know about his presence would be Oberführer Kaltenbrunner. Hagen was quite sure the big man wasn't a traitor and he would impress upon Kaltenbrunner the need for secrecy. Although a man who drank and smoked far too much, the Austrian did not appear to be a fool. One thing was for certain, Kaltenbrunner was a Nazi down to his soul. He lived for the party and for Adolf Hitler.

Thinking on Kaltenbrunner's nicotine habit, and the stench in his suit, Hagen scowled. His clothing reeked, his camel hair overcoat would have to go to the cleaners for certain and his suit most likely as well. How could one man smoke that many cigarettes? In the three hours they had spent with Kaltenbrunner, the man had smoked at least twenty of the damn things. It was foul. Hagen had smoked during his time in the trenches; every man had as a way to conquer the boredom and fear. During the time of Hagen's injury at the front, his addiction had been broken and now he only smoked a sum total of five cigarettes per year. Only after a difficult interrogation or doing something of which he wasn't proud. Yes. Smoking was completely foul.

Hagen suddenly felt a hand on his shoulder. "What?" he snarled, turning his head.

Karl Wolff looked down at him with both eyebrows raised. "They told me the devil was at the back of the train, but I didn't believe them. Perhaps it's the case after all."

Hagen nodded, trying to adjust his mood. "Possible. I'm sorry. I thought you were Eugen or the steward."

"No. Eugen is outside on the platform and I think the steward has written you off." Wolff replied with a slightly lopsided grin. "What badger is in your trousers? I haven't seen you look this dyspeptic in a good long time."

Hagen moved his files into his briefcase so Wolff could have a seat. "Just busy."

"Really?" Wolff's tone spoke volumes.

"Is it so hard to believe?" Hagen indicated for Wolff to sit down.

"I know you, Hagen. You are one of the most even-tempered people of my acquaintance. For a man on the edge of promotion, in favour, engaged to the perfect woman and generally on top of the world, you don't look especially happy." Wolff lowered himself into the seat, being careful not to spill his glass of sparkling water as he did so. "And your present temper has even chased off Eugen, which is certainly saying something."

He certainly wasn't going to tell Wolff what was really bothering him. "Just have a great deal on my mind." An image of his Galiena's toes being sucked on by that man surfaced and Hagen nearly saw red. Those feet were his, goddammit, and if anyone was going to lick them, it would be him! And thinking of it, how dare she loll about in the arms of those two degenerates? Letting them both kiss her, and then have the unmitigated gall to tell her soon-to-be husband that there would be no sex in their marriage! It wasn't to be borne! Hagen winced inwardly at the pun. She was his, and he was going to make love to her as soon as they were married. Before if he could arrange it! Best to get these notions right out of her head before they had time to flourish.

"I heard through the proverbial grapevine that your fiancée has been married before," Wolff said quietly, breaking into Hagen's thoughts.

"After a fashion," Hagen replied curtly.

"Well?" The word was drawn out.

"Are you asking or is Himmler?" Hagen's tone did not show its usual deference. He wasn't in a mood to be prodded, even by Wolff. Why this interrogation? He had done nothing wrong. If anything, he had been a saint the last few days.

Wolff fixed Hagen with a flat stare. "I am, you stupid, suspicious bastard." It was the profanity which caught Hagen's attention. Very infrequently was Wolff foul mouthed.

Hagen tapped his fingers on the file he was holding in his hand. "It was some sort of prank in Scotland called hand fasting. It's a kind of Celtic trial marriage that lasts a year and a day, but it isn't legal anywhere, so she wasn't married," He explained curtly.

"And the previous groom was at the Berghof?"

"The Graf von Reitersbach. Yes. He was there. He is an old friend of Galiena's. Very close old friend." Hagen narrowed his eyes. Hagen would never consider Freffie as Galiena's previous spouse. That hand fasting had been a sham. What a foul waste of Galiena's generosity! Didn't Galiena say she would have just given the Graf the money had he requested it? Hagen felt his ire flare. Never would he allow her to randomly dispense her money or time to people who were undeserving! No one would use her with him around for he would protect her from anyone callous enough to try. Hadn't he taken care of Verina von Taschen? Her parasitic sister who was even now languishing in a sanatorium at the pleasure of the SS?

"And that has you jealous?" Wolff asked with a great deal of sympathy. "I know I would be a little dyspeptic under the circumstances."

Hagen barked out a short ugly laugh. "No. Not at all. The Graf von Reitersbach is about as interested in the female sex as Ernst Röhm was. Absolutely nothing to worry about there let me tell you." But it still didn't make him feel any better at the thought of her drunk almost into a stupor in Freffie's arms. Hagen couldn't touch her, but they could! That was it? Any homosexual in the offing could stroke her any which way, but he couldn't? No. It wasn't to be tolerated. She was his. He had no intentions of sharing. Ever.

Wolff rolled his eyes. "So then what is the problem, if not this von Reitersbach?"

Hagen shrugged, trying to make his visage less imposing. "There is no problem, quite frankly. I actually plan to reinitiate contact with von Reitersbach in Vienna in a few weeks. I was properly introduced to the man last night at Göring's chalet; he's a decadent, useless aristocrat, but may be useful to me. He's rather protective of Galiena, which raises him in my estimation, and seems to consider me as a family connection now." Obviously Frederick Graf von Reitersbach was one of those selfish individuals who cared for nothing but their own pleasure. Hagen had no time for that.

"Useful? How so?" Wolff asked.

"Supposedly the Graf von Reitersbach knows everyone of any note in Vienna. I plan to use him to discover the New Austrian

Order. Any entrée into the Austrian upper class would be of great value. I shall use myself as a beater and set the birds a flight so that my hunters can shoot them out of the sky." Hagen smiled grimly. It was a good plan. He could kill two birds with one stone. He would have to be very careful about separating Galiena from the Graf von Reitersbach. They were obviously much closer than Verina and Galiena, but nothing was impossible. She was his and his alone.

"You sound like you have a plan in the works." Wolff nodded, his open face considering. "What did you think of Kaltenbrunner?"

"Personally the man isn't to my taste. He smokes like a chimney and appears to be a drunk. I can't fault his loyalty, however; that kind of dedication is truly admirable. He's spent a great deal of time in Austrian concentration camps for his belief in the party. I can't say as I have spent a day in jail for the Fuhrer." Hagen admitted ruefully.

"Me neither, but then I'm not the old fighter you are, even. Certainly not like Freisler," Wolff agreed.

"So I think that puts Kaltenbrunner in a special class and he is a doctor at law," Hagen conceded.

"But you don't like him?" Wolff pressed urgently. Hagen could tell in the man's tone he also had concerns about Kaltenbrunner. Wolff's proverbial mission in life was to keep the Reichsführer's circle free of asses; if Hagen considered Kaltenbrunner an ass, it would probably be an impression they would share.

Hagen spread his hands expansively. "Karl! You know me! I don't take much stock in people who drink to excess. It doesn't impress. Neither does smoking. Kaltenbrunner has a surprising lack of refinement for his education. He isn't the sort of person I would relish seeing in a position with a great deal of authority. Supporting role, yes, but commanding? No."

"He has very big ambitions. As head of the Austrian SS, he has asked to be the security director of the new Austrian state when it is amalgamated into the Reich," Wolff told him.

"I think that would be a mistake," Hagen narrowed his eyes. "That's my feeling. Kaltenbrunner is weak. He has too many crutches."

"The smoking and the booze?"

"Exactly. And his organization isn't tight, though that might not be Kaltenbrunner's fault; could be part of the Austrian problem in general. In Germany we were always a political party, and were never universally banned. We were banned in Berlin, or in Prussia, or in Bavaria, and then only for a time, and not at the same time. In Austria they have been banned since 1934. Wholesale. I think that breeds a strange, almost fanatic kind of loyalty in the old fighters, and yet they are so desperate to fill the ranks, they haven't been as selective as we have. They have been hunted and persecuted by the government to such an extent that their members are very hard," Hagen answered thoughtfully.

"So you are saying that they are extremist?" Wolff crossed his arms over his chest.

Hagen pondered that one. "Fundamentalist is more the word I would choose. Kaltenbrunner introduced me to his cell in Salzburg, and it reminded me of the tales one hears of missionaries, fanatically devoted to the word of God, so much so that nothing else matters. The men I met yesterday were like that, only in this case, God is the Fuhrer."

Wolff chuckled. "Isn't that the way it's supposed to be?"

"The old Austrian fighters are pious to the point of perverting the message, Karl. It was disquieting. I don't think there is a limit to what those men would do if the Fuhrer told them to."

Wolff raised both brows. "Is there a limit to what you would do, Hagen?" he led dangerously.

"If the Fuhrer told me to put my service pistol up to my temple and pull the trigger, I wouldn't do it, Karl," Hagen said quietly, but directly. "There is a line somewhere. It isn't a question of loyalty, but of sanity. I have proven my loyalty."

"Yes. Of course you have though I understand your loyalty to the Fuhrer might have been strained recently." Wolff sipped his water.

"The Reichsführer has obviously been feeling chatty," Hagen growled, thinking back to the meeting at the Berghof.

Himmler had summoned him from the veranda in a terrible state. The Reichsführer-SS had been outwardly calm, but Hagen knew him well enough to spot the inner turmoil. 'The Fuhrer has requested your presence, Hagen. He's very displeased and I think we might have to change our plans. I didn't anticipate this. It's about your prospective union with the Pfalzgräfin. No. It's not good at all. I will do what I can to help you. You understand that, don't you?' Himmler's words had tumbled one after another in a string, a sure sign of the man's discomfort. Hagen had said nothing and braced inwardly for the worst. Yet Galiena had handled the situation well.

The feeling of Wolff's hot gaze snapped him back to the present. "You work for him and now you are working for me. You know Himmler doesn't like to take barometer readings of his men, that's my job. I am the chief of his personal staff, a staff that you are now on. Let me do my job, Hagen, and stop being so God damned suspicious all the time."

"I've worked for Heydrich far too long," Hagen grumbled, turning away.

"What are your feelings toward the Fuhrer?" Wolff asked.

Hagen blinked at Wolff in disbelief. "How am I supposed to answer that Karl? We are in the second car of the Reichsführer-SS' personal train which is hardly the most appropriate place for a discussion of this nature." He put his file down into his bag. "I've sworn an oath of loyalty to the Fuhrer, and I will carry out my duty as I have always done, with the strength and diligence fate has granted me."

"Your relationship with the Fuhrer is more personal than the average officer's, Hagen," Wolff said gently, glancing about. Their end of the train was empty. "It is relatively private here. You can talk to me."

"For Christ's sake, Karl! How the hell do you think I feel? I'm sure Himmler told you! I was summoned into the Fuhrer's parlour and found my fiancée on her knees before the man. It was disquieting, but I will bow to the Fuhrer's wisdom in the matter." Hagen looked at his hands. It was the only place he could. He focused on his Totenkopf honour ring. It meant so much to him. He ran his thumb over the Sigrunen on the underside. The SS was his entire life. Nothing else mattered. His loyalty to the SS was greater than anything in his life, and loyalty to the SS was loyalty to Hitler. The silence between them grew long. Hagen met Wolff's blue eyes. Deliberately he stated, "My loyalty to the Fuhrer is unchanged." He was saying it as much for himself as he was for Wolff. "It is as it always was." Try as he might, he couldn't push that terrible welt on Galiena's collarbone out of his mind. His Fuhrer had hurt his Galiena and Hagen's mind couldn't rationalize the two.

Wolff clapped him on the arm. "You're a good man, Hagen Kohl. Probably the truest I have ever met."

"There is nothing more important to me than the SS, Gruppenführer Wolff," Hagen reiterated formally. He would never let her get in between the SS and himself. He couldn't. That would destroy the order in his life. Everything had to remain in its place, welt or no. The SS was his soul.

"Both the Reichsführer and I were concerned after the events of the other day. He feels a certain responsibility for the incident between the Pfalzgräfin von Steinberg and the Fuhrer. He was unaware the Fuhrer had not been notified of the situation between the two of you," Wolff explained, as he stroked the beading sides of his water glass. "You know it's not his way to be indiscrete."

"It's of no moment, Karl," Hagen answered crisply. "It was of far more discomfort to her than it was to me." How his mind had frozen when he had seen that welt on her skin. The shape of a thumb, it had been. His imagination went wild trying to figure out how Hitler had treated her. Obviously the man had grabbed hold of her. Had she cried out? It was like maggot in his brain. He had failed her. Again.

"I'm sorry to hear that."

Hagen crossed his legs. "It's over. I'm sure Göring will have dealt with it by the time he returns to Berlin." She obviously had a handle on the situation as well. He had seen that spark again. The indication of her will. Hitler was a master manipulator but she seemed to hold her own against him. Damn Hitler for speaking of the veracity of Hagen's affections. Those words had done such damage, he could see that now. But she seemed to have calmed the Fuhrer down to the point of some reasonability, which would have taken cunning and skill. Perhaps she wasn't as helpless as he had initially surmised. What had she said? 'I did what I had to do, Hagen. I didn't have a large number of options.' Ominous words, echoing in his mind. What was she willing to do to get her way, and what options would she consider? He had to learn how she thought so that he could think ahead of her. Being forearmed was the only way to guarantee control.

Wolff nodded and then stood up. "Well then, I will leave you to it, Hagen." The man headed off between the seats of the train and Hagen was happy to see him go.

He crossed his arms over his chest and lifted the shade on his window. The countryside was beautiful in the winter. White with snow. It was cold, but inviting. The land screamed of hearth and home and leant him a modicum of calm. Peaceful villages lay off in the distance, glittering under ice. No wonder Eugen was outside watching it go by. Last night's storm had refreshed the old, dirty crust on the land. It was very lovely to look at. Untouched.

What was he going to do? His chest was as cold as the outdoors. There was absolutely no way he was going to have a platonic marriage with Galiena. It simply wouldn't happen. He wanted to have sex with her. The thought that she would deny him her body was infuriating, even if he could understand her position. It had never occurred to him that she would be this way! What did she think? He would live out the rest of his life just giving her a peck on the cheek outside her bedroom door and carrying on alone to his? The aristocracy might have separate bedrooms, but where he grew up they didn't.

No. She had to confront what happened in the first place. Perhaps it was time she went back to the scene of the crime as it were. Maybe he should take her back to Riesa and allow her to face her demons. The problem was he didn't have time for this. He hadn't had time after von Blomberg's wedding and he certainly didn't have time now. It was Monday today. Perhaps he could take next weekend and drive her down there. Leave on Friday, maybe even Thursday and come back the next day, in time to high off to Vienna. It would take a few days for his people to work their way down to Vienna anyway. Yes. Perhaps they could leave on Friday if she had no fixed engagements.

Vienna. The New Austrian Order. He had to find them. He had to get inside and remove them as a threat to the SS. They were no minor annoyance. To Hagen they seemed paramount. He had prepared a report for Himmler explaining the threat as he saw it. On his return to Berlin, he would set Kappler to interviewing all who had direct contact with the NAO; those who had been kidnapped and probe them for every little detail of the event. Those men had to know more. That, combined with von Ond infiltrating the group, would put them a great leap forward.

Hagen ran a finger along his lips as he thought, and an idea leapt to mind. Of course von Reitersbach would know Hagen was SS, but everyone else in Vienna didn't have to be aware of the fact. If both he and Eugen grew in some facial hair, it would disguise their true occupation some. SS men weren't allowed to wear beards. That, coupled with the fact Hagen certainly wasn't known in Vienna, should be an adequate enough disguise. He doubted the tales of the Schwarze Teufel had travelled that far. He felt his lips curl up. He might be able to eliminate his security detail for the time being! Now wouldn't that be a silver lining!

Hagen stood, and made his way towards the back door of the train. There was an observation platform between this car, the workers car, and Himmler's private car. He made sure his cap was well and truly secure and opened the door. Eugen stood there, his broad back leaning against the outside wall of the train. He had an unreadable expression on his face as he looked out at the scenery. His black greatcoat was done up and the man appeared very imposing. Hagen suddenly felt the cold; it was probably minus five or so and he didn't bring his overcoat with him. Oh well. He wouldn't freeze to death.

"How are the sights?" Hagen asked idly. He had snarled at Eugen several times in the last twelve hours and it would be his just desserts if his second in command was a little put out with him. He regretted taking his temper out on his friend. If there was one person he completely trusted, one person he would trust with his life, it was Eugen. The loyal man deserved better.

"Some days I miss Bavaria," the other man said simply.

"You have been away from it a long time," Hagen answered by way of apology. "I don't give you nearly enough time off."

"When you take time off, I take time off. You know the drill, Hagen," Eugen shrugged.

"I don't take time off."

The green eyes met his. "I know."

"You have a family. I don't," Hagen pointed out.

112

"Bah, Teufel. You know how it is. I show up and eat them out of house and home. They prefer it when I send a card with a few marks tucked inside. It's much easier on all involved," Eugen replied with a slight grin.

"What about time for yourself?" Hagen returned, as he always did. "You could go find yourself a woman?"

"And turn into you? Hardly! Besides, the one you found is going to keep both of us busy for a while." Eugen's grin turned into a smirk.

"Thanks."

"Don't mention it. So does the fact you are out here and turning blue mean you're over your irritation?" Eugen rumbled, eyes gleaming with amusement.

"One might say that, yes. Or at least it's under control," Hagen nodded.

"'Bout time, Hagen. I was considering throwing you from the train."

"It's been a tough week."

Eugen sobered momentarily. "Yes. After last night, are you sure you want to marry the girl?"

"How was last night different from any other, Eugen?" Hagen questioned, though he knew what the issue was.

"Come now, Hagen. I'm not blind. I know what I saw," Eugen said slowly.

"They aren't a threat to me, Eugen," Hagen stated crisply

A black gloved finger materialized between them. "But her behaviour was disrespectful to you."

"They were all very drunk, Eugen. It is my opinion those two men are like Galiena's brothers. Their ways are different from ours, I will admit, but they do seem protective of her. I respect that, Eugen. We only have two examples of her family, the Pfalzgraf and Frau von Taschen. In the balance those two fairies aren't so terrible."

"They seem very free with her, and she allows it," Eugen grumbled.

Hagen smiled grimly. "That will have to change, I agree. But her past is in the past, and I will endeavour to keep it there. I have no control over what she has done previous to our association. It isn't like I don't have a past myself." The wind threatened to rip the cap from his head.

"True. True. It made me angry. She shouldn't be so familiar with other men. I don't care who they are. She doesn't belong to them." Eugen shook his head. "The Pfalzgräfin is ours and I never was the sharing type."

"They could say the same of us, my friend. I think von Reitersbach could prove very useful to me. I want to go back to Austria next Sunday. Become better acquainted with my potential cousins in law."

"I figured as much," the large man nodded.

"I want you to stop shaving. Cover up that famous face with a beard. Make you look a little less like a soldier," Hagen told him.

Eugen gave Hagen an irritable look. "You aren't serious."

"Completely. I'm going to get us a Papal dispensation to be scruffy for the next week," Hagen grinned wickedly.

"I resemble Father Christmas with a beard. I look like an old man." Eugen said plaintively. Hagen had a sudden insight that Eugen had issues about his age.

"I can't imagine you looking like an old man, Eugen. But not to worry. I will be joining you in the ranks of the unshaven, and my facial hair leaves a great deal to be desired. You can wear civvies into the office. Welcome to the wonderful world of espionage." Hagen laughed with amusement.

"I'm abounding with joy, Hagen. Really I am. The things I do for you. "

"Yes. I know. I appreciate it. Also, I think it's time we took Galiena back to Riesa. I'm thinking Thursday night to drive down there if she is amenable."

"Do you think that is wise?"

Hagen nodded. "I do. I think Galiena needs to face her fears. If she doesn't face them now, I think they are only going to get worse."

"Makes sense. So you are going to send her over the top, as it were?" Eugen raised a brow.

"Over the fire step and right off into No Man's Land. Yes," Hagen agreed, liking and understanding the allusion.

"Best of luck to you."

114

Abruptly Eugen's face shuttered. "Hagen, about the Fuhrer? I've heard the rumours."

Hagen was fascinated by the snow blowing along the tracks. "I would rather not discuss this right now. I just reassured Wolff, Eugen," his voice dropped to a whisper. "That should be enough, even for you."

A huge paw clapped onto Hagen's arm. "The Fuhrer will do the right thing, Hagen. He always does."

His face bleak, Hagen met that of his best friend. "For once, I beg to differ. Please don't press this."

"You need to have faith in his wisdom," Eugen countered earnestly; his conviction honest and heartfelt. There was something in the large man's face which reminded Hagen of a simple, devout, country parson trying to explain the political and contradictory actions of the pope to his flock. Yes. This was Eugen; priest of the Schwarz Ordern. Kind, benevolent and reassuring.

"Eugen, you weren't there. Please don't explain to me what the Fuhrer said or did and don't ask me to tell you what I saw. Some things are not so simple," Hagen breathed carefully. This wasn't a wise conversation to be having on the back of Himmler's train.

Eugen's frown was black as a thundercloud. "What are you talking about?"

Hagen inhaled and slowly exhaled. "The next time you see Galiena; examine her left collarbone, for she bears a mark of our Fuhrer's favour."

"What do you mean?"

"I mean that you should look for yourself, Eugen. See what our Fuhrer did to our wife," Hagen used Eugen's terminology very deliberately.

There was disbelief and suspicion in his friend's face. "What am I supposed to find there? Explain yourself to me!" The large man demanded; a very rare occurrence for him.

Hagen smiled sadly at his closest comrade. "You will know when you see it, Eugen."

"Then I shall look, Teufel, and make my own decision when I see what there is to see," Eugen promised him.

"Thanks. I should go see if I can talk to Himmler. Get that papal dispensation." Hagen headed over to the other door.

"Glad to see the badger is out of your trousers," Eugen called after him.

Chapter 9
February 14, 1938

With Eugen's words trailing behind Hagen, he opened the door into Himmler's private car. Wolff was standing there talking to one of his underlings while Himmler's personal secretary, Fraulein Potthast, organized a stack of cards at her desk. The three of them looked at him with something close to surprise. Hagen supposed there were few interruptions expected today.

"Hello, Karl," Hagen said, as if he hadn't just spoken to the man.

"Didn't expect to see you again so soon," Wolff replied, obviously startled to see him.

"I need to talk to the Reichsführer," Hagen answered briskly.

"He's free at the moment, and I'm sure he would like to talk to you. One minute." Wolff disappeared down the companionway and ducked into a compartment. Hagen looked around Himmler's train car. It was all finished in dark cherry wood and was quite opulent. Hagen sat down on a bench built into the side of the train, and watched as the adjutant went about his work. Wolff eventually came back. "Yes. He will see you now."

"Thanks, Karl." Hagen stood up.

"Don't mention it. Glad to see you looking a little more human." Wolff sent him an arch look.

"Eugen was quite of the same opinion."

"I can only imagine." Wolff opened the door into what served as Himmler's sitting room.

Himmler was sitting in a large oxblood leather chair, his feet crossed on a matching ottoman. The small compartment was comfortable, even homey. There was a recent painting of Himmler's daughter on one wall, a rendering of Himmler's SS castle at Wewelsberg opposite. This was a private area of the train; Himmler's refuge. The man himself was reading a slim volume which he marked with a black ribbon bookmark and set on his lap. "Hagen. Do come in." He indicated the chair opposite him. Snow covered Germany seemed to melt by, the landscape slowly changing as the train moved along. Covered in white as it was, it was a languid transformation. Slow and gentle.

"Herr Reichsführer," Hagen saluted formally.

"I heard you were in high choler this morning, Hagen." Himmler always seemed to know how to position his head so that light reflecting off his pince-nez obscured his eyes. Hagen found the habit extremely annoying. He gestured to a nearby chair.

"Something I ate, no doubt," Hagen replied, settling himself down opposite Himmler.

Himmler cocked his head, and his eyes appeared. They were wrinkled slightly at the corners, evidence of Himmler's amusement. "No doubt, indeed. Don't worry about it, Hagen. We are all entitled to a bad mood occasionally."

"Thank you, Heinrich. It was not my intention to be disruptive," Hagen added ruefully, using Himmler's first name, encouraged as he was by his master's informality

"From my information, you weren't disruptive, just not amiable to interruption." The Reichsführer-SS smirked.

Hagen spread his hands. "I have a great deal on my mind of late. This weekend was rather full."

"Yes. Yes it was. The conference went quite as expected, however; I wonder how long it will take von Schuschnigg to renege on his promises to the Fuhrer?" Himmler pondered absently.

Hagen considered the question. "Not long, I think. He won't allow the Austrian Nazi Party freedom of movement. He will lose his country if he does."

"And he will lose his country if he doesn't. The Fuhrer has made that point very clear. Austria is our government's number one priority," Himmler stated matter of factly. "I understand you met with Oberführer Kaltenbrunner yesterday and were not impressed with what you saw?"

"The man seems able enough. He is a very devoted National Socialist," Hagen began carefully.

"Please, Hagen. Don't dissimulate with me. I didn't put you in the position you're in to have you start acting like all the rest. Tell me what I need to hear, not what I want to hear, unless I should tell you differently." The light was mirroring off the glasses again.

118

Encouragement if ever Hagen heard it. "The man drinks too much. For that reason alone I would consider him to be unreliable."

"Yes. I can understand that and I would also agree. He was the best man for the job at the time. After the Dolfuss affair, the Austrian SS was in a shameful state; any of the higher echelons were arrested and several of those executed by the Austrian government. Kaltenbrunner seemed a likely candidate to pick up the reins," Himmler explained, the skin on his face tightening defensively.

"That makes sense."

Himmler raised a brow. "I'm pleased you agree. After your meeting with him, what have you decided to do about this New Austrian Order? Do you think they are a wing of the Fatherland Front? Or are they separate?"

"As I am sure you know, the Fatherland Front is a mishmash of political agendas, fashioned because Dolfuss wanted to create a fascist state. One party, absolute power. Just like Italy or here in Germany. The difference is the Fatherland Front is composed of three main blocs. A nationalist bloc, a socialist bloc and a liberal bloc, and those blocs appear to be of equal power within the group. There is a complete lack of unity between them. Members of the Austrian Nazi party, Seyss-Inquart for a start, control the nationalist bloc. They are discrete about their involvement with the Nazi party after a fashion, and are elected under the banner of the Fatherland front. Same as with the socialist bloc, and members of the various communist parties. The Fatherland Front isn't much of a party as the diametrically opposite groups within it are tearing it apart. So in answer to your question, the NAO could very easily be a splinter organization of the Fatherland Front, but would it matter? By that definition, the Austrian Nazi party could be considered a splinter group of the Fatherland Front because the leader of the Austrian Nazi Party, Seyss-Inquart himself, is a cabinet minister under the banner of the Fatherland Front," Hagen clarified slowly.

"I simply don't understand how Dolfuss, or von Schuschnigg for that matter, thought they could keep a group like that under control. Obviously our own party has some pockets with varying agendas, those who are more socialist and those who are more conservative, Goebbels and Göring, being a perfect example of that, but in the end, they are all completely loyal to the Fuhrer," Himmler shook his head.

"And that is von Schuschnigg's primary problem with the Austrian Nazi Party. Those members, too, are completely loyal to the Fuhrer; ergo he has a very large segment of both his political party and his government who, not only are not loyal to him, are loyal to the head of a completely separate country. In most languages that translates into treason," Hagen shrugged mildly. "What would the Fuhrer's reaction be if he discovered that a section of the Nazi party owed its true allegiance to Neville Chamberlain and his Conservatives?" Hagen spread his hands as he made his point.

"Heads would roll. That is treason." Horror shone out of Himmler's eyes.

Hagen smiled. "Puts a whole new slant on von Schuschnigg's attitude, doesn't it?"

Himmler pursed his thin lips. "I see your point. Not that I have much pity for von Schuschnigg. He, or perhaps more truthfully Dolfuss, created that particular problem. Besides, union with Austria is the natural way of things. It hasn't happened thus far because the Weimar Republic was too afraid of the Treaty of Versailles and the possible repercussions. It has been amply demonstrated by the Fuhrer that the European nations aren't willing to support the treaty. Look what happened when we reoccupied the Rhineland? Nothing. Just as the Fuhrer said. Those men in Paris had no right to carve up Germany like a slab of sausage, paying no heed to what parts belonged to what! Germany and Austria belong together, as do the Sudetenland and the Polish Corridor."

"You know I am in complete agreement with you, Heinrich," Hagen stated quietly. How many times had they had this conversation?

Himmler sighed. "Yes. I know. So enough of European politics. What are your plans?"

"My top men and I will be going into Austria next Sunday. That allows us the time to prepare. Have you considered the matter of Scharführer von Ond? The young man I presented for promotion to Untersturmführer grade? He is a very capable man, and I think will be a credit to the officer corps," Hagen told his superior officer.

"Yes. Consider the man promoted. I shall attend to it tomorrow when I get back to the city. I assume you want to use him for this mission?" Himmler asked, his face alight with curiosity.

Hagen smoothed his hair with his hand. "I do. I hope we can use him to infiltrate the NAO. He's young, aristocratic, has the right name, originally Austrian, and I think has the tools to get the job done. He is also unknown, both in German and Austrian SS circles."

"Sound reasoning," Himmler nodded in approval. "Remind Wolffschen about the man's file and I will be sure to complete the matter."

"Thank you. I really believe this is for the benefit of the order. Von Ond is a very solid individual and was instrumental with several aspects of my previous mission," Hagen assured the other man.

"I trust your judgement." The Reichsführer gave Hagen a wry smile. "You are allowed to have bright stars. That's one of the rare perks of command. What are the rest of your intentions?"

"Von Ond will fly down as soon as I can brief him tomorrow. He can set himself up in a suite at some very upper class hotel in Vienna and act nationalistic and bored in the hotel bar. Make a name for himself bellowing Free Austria and the like to see if he gets contacted. I believe his family has connection with the Austrian upper class; he mentioned Rittmeisters in his background. Old Hussar family. See what he can stir up on his own. Maybe encourage him in the direction of the university," Hagen thought aloud.

"Why the university, Hagen?"

Hagen grinned. "What were you doing in university?"

Himmler nodded, his eyes sparkling. "I was a right terror. Duelling. Politically agitating. Hatching a new dream to save society every week. That sort of thing." He flashed his white teeth in a smile. "Forgive my momentary lapse of thought there. Of course you are correct. What better place to look than the university. Bored young aristocrats are probably worse about that sort of thing than the rest of us peasants."

"Not to worry, Heinrich. It just occurred to me as well. Besides, the actions of the NAO have a certain juvenile bent to them. Kidnapping people and dropping them at the border with a note around their neck? Stealing weapons and replacing them with hoes? It's like a bad motion picture, or pulp fiction novel. Doesn't that sound about the level of a university student?" Hagen rubbed his brow with his hand. He'd had a dull, nagging headache for days which no amount of aspirin would make disappear.

"It certainly does. It's not particularly well thought out, is it?" Himmler stroked the cover of the book on his knee.

Hagen raised a warding hand. "Maybe it is, and maybe it isn't. Kaltenbrunner labelled it a nuisance until meeting places started being firebombed. What would you have said to him if he complained that his men were being kidnapped and set free at the border?"

"I would have told him to get a better handle on his troops," Himmler agreed, obviously seeing where Hagen was going.

"Exactly. So all the while this group has exerted its perverse power over the Austrian Nazi party and its appendages, being a nuisance, consolidating its intelligence, that now it has all the information it needs to be a real threat. That demonstrates patience. Whoever is behind it, no matter how whimsical and you must admit there is a certain humour involved, must be a very cunning individual."

"I can't say as I see any humour in the situation, Hagen," Himmler replied tartly.

Hagen traced a curly-cue in the air with his finger as he tried to think like a whimsical anarchist. "But I would guess the perpetrator does. I would think he's laughing at us. Look at it from his perspective! In Austria the 'oh so tough' Nazis roam the night in packs because they are terrified of being picked up off the street, tied up in some strange pagan ritual, cursed and dropped off at the border?" He felt his lips curl up of their own volition as he said it.

"Put that way, I suppose I see your point," Himmler conceded, rolling his eyes.

"And if their intelligence is as good as I think it is, they are already about five steps ahead of Kaltenbrunner. This has been going on for a few years now? Just when did they infiltrate the SS?

Or the SA? Or the party for that matter? A man can gain a lot of trust in two years. Especially with the great state of flux in the Austrian Nazi party. The old core is probably not suspect, but anyone post Dolfuss' demise would be." Hagen rubbed a finger on the side of his nose as he thought. "If they do have insider information it could be very highly placed."

"You trouble me greatly, Hagen. I am glad I set you to this. Do you have an idea who could be behind it?"

Hagen shook his head. "No, I don't. Not yet. Society people, I would suspect. They have easy entrée almost anywhere. Kaltenbrunner thought military, but given my recent experiences with the military, I wouldn't agree. While the cunning and patience might point to it, military people tend to be very direct. Think about it, Heinrich. No one has been killed. Not one, even in the fire bombings. No Nazi and no civilian has been actually harmed. Would officers be that selective? They would see casualties as collateral damage, and their methods tend to be a little more direct."

"Really, it's more like terrorism of a sort? No one is hurt, but they are afraid. Each attack almost seems to say 'look how close to you I am.' They started with kidnapping low ranking members in outlaying districts and then worked closer and closer and closer, until they penetrated top secret weapons caches, and office treasuries," Himmler repeated himself slowly. "Look how close to you I am."

"I think you hit the nail on the head. The implied threat. Who knows what will happen to the next kidnapped man? Will he wake up from the drugs? Will he be murdered? Where will the next bombing be and will there be a full crowd in the targeted area?" Hagen blinked in disbelief. "All the while, no one has been hurt. Yet."

Himmler looked a little grey. "That's a very big yet, Hagen."

Hagen agreed. "It's a colossal yet." His palms dropped to his thighs with an audible slap. "Whoever is behind this is brilliant. Absolutely brilliant. They know exactly what they want to achieve, and I would hate to hazard a guess where they intend to go. It's obvious they don't want us in Austria, and they are willing to go very far to accomplish their goal."

"Then I leave it to you to stop them. Budget is not a concern. Wolffschen knows you are to be given a free hand. It gets you away from the SD budget bind. The Freundkrais Reichsführer-SS, my little corporate donation pool will be funding you," Himmler told him.

"The Circle of Friends of the Reichsführer-SS?" Hagen asked. "I had not heard of this."

"It's been around for a few years. A group of industrialists who donate money to me personally instead of actually joining the Schutzstaffel. They don't have the time to participate but they have the money, as it were. The directors of Krupp, I.G. Farben, Mercedes Benz and the like. I use the money for funding special projects. This certainly qualifies. My Ahenenerbe Society will suffer slightly, but they will still get their research trip to Tibet and Nepal." Himmler's eyes glittered as he spoke.

"Fascinating. As I said, I had never heard about it."

The Reichsführer scrunched up his shoulders. "We have monthly lunches. I might bring you to one once this project of yours is complete. I think they would be very interested to see where their money is going and you speak very well despite your reluctance. But enough of my Freundkrais, how do you plan to proceed from here?"

"With your permission, Eugen Freisler and I will be out of uniform for the next few days at the office. In an effort to be more discreet about our appearance, we are going to grow beards for our time in Austria. It isn't going to fool people who actually know us, but it will mask our identities from casual acquaintances." Hagen crossed one leg over the other.

"Yes. Best not to wear your uniform if you are going to do that. We will put it about you are going on holiday while your office is being set up, and that you are around to supervise but not actually on duty. I want the beards off when you come back to Germany, though. No beards allowed in the SS, as you know." Himmler rubbed a hand over his own chin, his fingers rasping against the blue-black stubble which seemed to appear seconds after he shaved and then grinned. "I know I would have a full beard if I stopped shaving for a week. What about you, Hagen?"

"I shall opt for a goatee, and hopefully it will grow enough to be of use. I haven't worn facial hair since 1918 when my mother shaved it off while I was wounded." Hagen smiled weakly.

Himmler chuckled, his eyes sparkling with amusement. "Oh the cruelty of mothers. How completely they show disapproval of the actions of their cubs."

"Indeed. So that is our plan. We will be very discrete. Only Kaltenbrunner will know exactly who we are. I will travel as Doctor Hagen Kohl, and I will be prevailing on the hospitality of my new acquaintance, the Graf von Reitersbach for accommodation. He and I are going to be family after a fashion." Hagen raised a brow.

"Hagen, do you really think it is wise to avail yourself of the hospitality of a notorious homosexual? People might talk. They might," Himmler paused and gave Hagen a very pointed look.

"Not every homosexual is an Ernst Röhm. I think my virtue will be quite safe." Hagen leaned back. "Besides, the entrée into Viennese society is too good to pass up. Von Reitersbach might know I am a member of the SS, but a properly worded note from my esteemed fiancée asking the good Graf to introduce me about and show me the ropes of the aristocracy will probably ensure the man's proper behaviour."

"Very cunning, Hagen. The Teufel at work again. I'm impressed. That should get you into places where our members tend to be barred," Himmler considered this. "And the Graf was the one at the conference who did mention the NAO. Do you think he might be a member?"

"I doubt it. The man would have been called a fop a hundred years ago. He's a dilettante. Never had to work for anything in his life. Committed a very elaborate fraud to ensure an inheritance; such was behind his so-called marriage to my Pfalzgräfin. He had to wed to convince a great aunt not to disinherit him," Hagen said with no little amount of disgust in his voice.

"That is deserving of contempt, isn't it? Why did she go along with it? She seems like an upright sort to me."

"Loyalty to her family. Seems to be how she considers von Reitersbach; for they are extremely close. I had the privilege of joining Galiena, the Graf and the Ritter von Glass for an aperitif last night. The Graf was quite desirous that I be admitted into the 'family circle' as it were. As I said previously, I intend to take him up on the invitation. While I have my doubts that von Reitersbach has entrée into the NAO, I wouldn't be surprised if he knew the identities of at least some of the members. Even Kaltenbrunner concurred. Von Reitersbach knows everyone in Vienna, and everyone knows him. I think he will be a very useful resource to exploit. I might be able to sniff out other people of interest while I am there." Hagen's lips curled up with pleasure. "I have no issue with using the man to the fullest extent I can. It gives him the passive opportunity to be of use to someone other than himself."

Himmler glowed with approval. "Oh absolutely. Brilliant, Hagen. Of course! Go ahead. Anything you need is at your disposal for the situation in Austria is critical. Those reports from Kaltenbrunner about this NAO have caused me a great deal of distress; I can't believe Kaltenbrunner didn't come to me sooner. Having them waiting on my arrival in Berchtesgarten was not a pleasure. I'll tell you that."

"I can imagine not. I also planned to spend Friday out of the office. It is my intention to take the Pfalzgräfin back to Schloss Riesa if she is amicable to the idea," Hagen told his superior.

Himmler's face took on a strange cast as he looked sharply at Hagen. "Was that your idea or hers?" he asked quickly.

"Mine. I haven't discussed it with her yet. Do you have an objection?" Hagen questioned, trying to read Himmler's sudden alertness.

"No. Not at all. I think it to be of some value. Do you think it is too soon for her, the situation with her Grandfather and all?" Himmler looked out the window, before returning his eyes to Hagen.

"I think she should face her past, Heinrich. No use hiding; one can never hide forever."

"Yes. There is truth in what you say. If you think she is ready, then by all means. Especially if you and Freisler are going to be out of uniform. I do hope your fiancée won't take it amiss?" Himmler lifted a sable brow.

Hagen frowned. "I hadn't thought of that. I shall inform her I am on holiday and trying to be more casual."

"Your scruffy chin and sudden desire to play the tourist in Austria? Galiena von Steinberg doesn't precisely strike me as a lackwit." Himmler gave him a sceptical look. "Will she believe that?"

Hagen shrugged. "Possibly. I don't know. It doesn't matter particularly to me if she does or not. It has become obvious that we both are guilty of keeping secrets." As he spoke the words, Hagen realised that bothered him. Galiena shouldn't have secrets from him. Certainly not secrets like her hand fasting to von Reitersbach.

"All the best to you on that score." Himmler tapped the book on his knee again and then looked at Hagen. "Oh, I must thank you. I followed your advice and had someone find this for me." He held up the spine of the book.

Hagen read the spine aloud. "The complete works of Andrew Marvell. An excellent choice."

"You said I might find the English metaphysical poets interesting, and indeed I do. My English is certainly nowhere near yours, or Heydrich's for that matter, and this is of great assistance in furthering it. I appreciate their vision of the world." Himmler tapped his lips thoughtfully. "Though I must admit they spend a great deal of their time either writing about God or their mistresses."

Hagen laughed wryly, understanding Himmler's statement very well. He'd asked almost the same question of a Don at Cambridge. "Like our generation, their generation went through a terrible war which ended in their ultimate defeat. I think it left a similar mark. Mysticism, sex or God," He sobered. "That's why I studied them in England. The quest for answers."

"What did you learn?" Himmler took off his pince-nez and cleaned with a handkerchief.

"That there aren't any answers." Hagen gazed out the window, abruptly feeling melancholy.

"Sounds a little bleak," Himmler replied. He opened the book and read from his marker. "*O, Who shall from this dungeon raise/A soul enslaved so many ways?*"

Hagen slid his gaze back to Himmler's. "*With bolts of bones, that fettered stands/In feet, and manacled in hands.* One of my favourites, Heinrich. *A Dialogue Between The Soul And Body.* I think I prefer the first stanza of the body, however. *O, who shall me deliver whole, from bonds of this tyrannic soul?* That piece always fascinated me. The duality of the human being. Body and soul. I did a paper on it."

"Really? Do you still have it?" Himmler asked, leaning forward with interest.

"It's probably around somewhere. At my Augsburg house, no doubt. All my old university work is there," Hagen cocked his head. "Collecting dust with everything else which predates the SS in my life."

"I would like to see it sometime. The duality of the human being. Yes. We are two creatures inside, aren't we? The man one is and the man one would like to be. I see it often in myself. The soul is indeed a tyrannical thing. It torments us, and yet gives us our strength." Himmler placed his pince-nez on the table beside him, then carefully stroked the bridge of his nose with his thumb and forefinger. "I have been reading eastern works on the soul. They intrigue me. We never learnt enough about other religions in school. I just finished reading the Koran a few weeks ago."

"And what did you discover?" Hagen asked, taking his turn to lean forward with interest.

"I discovered I had more questions and now I am reading Andrew Marvell." Himmler grinned.

"That is how young Hagen Kohl ended up with a doctorate in German Literature."

"Did young Hagen Kohl ever find the answers?"

Hagen shook his head, answering Himmler's expression. "No. In the end I decided that perhaps I would have been better served studying Philosophy and not Literature."

Himmler snorted derisively. There was a bitter mocking in his expression which seemed foreign on his normally bland face. Hagen always found it interesting when definitive emotions traversed the visage of his friend and master; it always caught him unaware. "Yes. One could devote a lifetime to looking for answers. What I think is important is that one has a great soul. With a great soul you can accomplish anything."

"I think most poets would agree with you on that one. But who has a great soul and who doesn't?" Hagen retorted.

"The Germans have the greatest soul," Himmler said slyly. "Of course."

128

"What of poor Mister Marvell there?"

"Come now, Hagen! The British Isles were conquered by the Angles, the Saxons and the Jutes. That makes all English people German."

"And the Celts?" Hagen asked, playing the Devil's advocate.

"They seem to have been remarkably clever in their own right. Probably Aryans as well. Some actually believe the Celts were the original offshoots of the Atlanteans. Atlantis, you know. That would make them higher on the Pyramid than us. But I trust you won't tell anyone else I said this."

Hagen allowed a smile to cross his lips again. "Your secret is safe with me."

The chief of all German police laughed at the irony. "I should hope so."

"Actually, the British romantics of the last century considered the Scots to be rather fey. Part of the neogothic awakening in the late Victorian era," Hagen added. "Quite unlike Marvell there who would have thought the Scots were a dour lot of barely civilised barbarians!"

Himmler looked at Hagen. "We should get you a drink or some other refreshment. I think this discussion might last a while longer." Himmler slapped his hands together. "It's been a while since I've had a good philosophical discussion, and it is several hours back to Berlin! I do hope you don't have anything too pressing waiting back in the work car?"

October 17, 1937
Dearest Poppet,

If I close my eyes, I can feel you here with me. Age has taught me patience. I know that you will come back. I can wait. Riesa is in your blood. So am I.
Eternally yours,
Meinrad

Chapter 10
February 18, 1938

Galiena sat behind the wheel of her newly delivered Horsch 853A cabriolet. It was very dark purple with brilliant chrome work and a black saloon. She had ordered it almost three months ago and it had been delivered just this week. Hers and hers alone; there was even a little bud vase fashioned in the dashboard, in which sat a stark white camellia from Göring's greenhouse at Carinhall. She stroked the wheel with her thumbs, pleased to have such a nice sedan, looking forward to when her new BMW roadster arrived, then glanced at her co-pilot out of the corner of her eye.

Her fiancé was not looking his usual elegant self. While his suit was definitely passable, this new attempt at a beard was a source of consternation for her. His insistence during his birthday lunch the other day that he was taking a vacation didn't sit right with her either, but then she didn't know Hagen well enough to accurately be able to pin him down on this subject. Suddenly out of nowhere, he was going on vacation? No. She didn't precisely believe him. And why, just because Hagen was growing a beard, was Eugen growing one as well? At least it somewhat resembled a beard now, and not just like he had forgotten to shave. Thankfully he had shaved some of his face, so it did look like a goatee. Galiena snickered inwardly. Who would have thought it would grow in so ferociously orange? It almost looked like some child had coloured his chin with a crayon.

Galiena had been floored when he had suggested they go to Riesa together. She had been wracking her brain trying to think of

130

a way to bring up the subject since her bargain with Himmler, and lo! He did it for her. In many ways the timing worked very well. She would meet tomorrow with Helmet Ritter von Kleist, no relation to the more famous von Kleists, her grandfather's chief business manager and Werner von Klopfer, her grandfather's private secretary, to become better acquainted with the problems facing the family business interests.

Galiena had to admit, she was terrified to go back to Riesa. Each passing mile only served to remind her how scared she was. It was probably why she had insisted on driving today; normally she would have let Hagen or Eugen drive. She needed to have the control, and Hagen seemed to understand for he had acquiesced to her cheeky assertion of the driver's seat with complete mildness. Eugen seemed far more irritated of the two. Interesting that. He was sitting in the back seat beside Idalie with his arms crossed over his chest, glaring out the window.

Galiena peeked into her side mirror. The ever present SS vehicle was behind them. Why did they follow Hagen everywhere? Now there was an interesting question. If he was on holiday, why did he still require a security detail? She supposed he needed it even when he wasn't on duty, but it still leant oppressiveness to the trip. She was used to servants; they were always in the background in her world, but this being actively followed all the time was something hard to get used to.

Galiena was torn. She wanted to go home and as she pondered the nature of the word, she realised Riesa would always be home for her. No matter where she travelled, or how long she had been away, the castle where she was born would always be there like a lode stone. Her family owned other castles, another even in Germany proper, but it didn't have the same feeling. The von Steinberg Zum Riesa family had lived at Riesa since 1156. That was great deal of history and was hard to deny despite the difficult associations the place had for her now. Why had her Grandfather done what he had done? She supposed she would never have the answer to that question.

They rounded a corner on the twisting pavement, and Galiena pulled the Horsch over to the side of the road. There it was; off in the distance. Magnificent on its hill, rising up to touch the sky. Schloss Riesa. Beige stone lifting out of the trees with steep slate grey roofing. Turreted towers made taller with points sharp as pencils. The turrets were all painted white, for a reason she had never known. Riesa. It called to her and as she looked out the window she discovered that Riesa owned her soul.

Hagen had been quiet beside her, but now he spoke up. "Is there a problem, darling?" Galiena ignored him, stepping out of the car to walk over to the edge of the road. The ancient edifice was like a pinnacle, jutting up from the rolling land. There was an illusion to the place. One minute there was nothing there, then a roll in the ground and it appeared like a like a lone tooth in the flatness. Her grandfather explained it was an effect of topography and the riverbed, but as a child it was magical to her. Hagen followed her, looking up. "Good God!" he breathed. "Is that it?"

Galiena turned and smiled at him. "A little place we like to call home."

Wide violet eyes stared down at her. "I had no idea!"

She laughed in disbelief. "With everything you seem to know about me, you never saw a picture of the old place?"

"I don't think I ever really looked. It's massive!" Hagen shook his head in wonderment.

"It's not so big. Only a hundred or so rooms. It's approximately twelve stories and built in a triangle around an inner courtyard, so what you see isn't as big as it looks. It's hollow on the inside," Galiena explained, her voice filled with love and pride at her family seat. "Not as ornate as some of our newer residences, but certainly the most beloved."

He put his arm around her waist, his face as close as her hat would allow. "You look a little pale, Galiena."

A tilt of her head and she could see his face again. "Perhaps a bit daunted. I know I shouldn't be afraid, but I am a little. No. Afraid isn't the right word. It's more like trepidation. The last time I drove this road, I vowed I would never come back."

Hagen squeezed her. "That was months ago. Not to worry. I won't let anyone hurt you."

Yes, Galiena thought wryly. Not like you let the Fuhrer hurt me. She turned back to the car, chiding herself for being unfair. "I know. Come. We have another half hour drive at least to get there, and we are expected."

They finished the journey and the light was fading as they drove through the gate and into the courtyard. As she pulled the car around the front, men came pouring from the castle. Her door was opened by Gebhardt, the major-domo; stark in his black uniform, his face pink with pleasure. As she stepped out of the car, she took his hand and squeezed it.

"It is good to see you, Gebhardt," she said to him.

"Welcome home, Your Serene Highness. Come. Let us get you inside. It's very cold. Very cold indeed. Now that you are back we would hate for you to catch a chill." Gebhardt bowed his head and escorted her until she came abreast of Hagen. His bustling was familiar and gladdening to her soul.

Galiena winked at her fiancé and beckoned him to take her arm. He did, and she noticed that his eyes seemed just a little wild. "It's not going to fall down on you!" She laughed as he looked up at the gothic spires above him.

"When was it built?" Hagen breathed.

"In this incarnation? The mid 1300's, but a great deal of it was damaged during the mid 1500's when my family was involved in a little contretemps with the Wittelsbach[8]," she told him as they passed into the massive entry hall.

The ornately vaulted room soared up thirty feet, with stained glass in the narrow casement windows. The floor was tiled in black and white squares of marble. She saw the place at the base of the gothic staircase where she had fallen when she had fled and tore her eyes away. No. She wouldn't think about that now.

The entire house staff of twenty had lined up to greet her, from the lowest kitchen maid to Gebhardt himself. She was touched by this show of respect and affection even though it was her due. She said a few words to Frau Silberberg, the housekeeper as well as Idalie's mother, and allowed the woman to smother her in a crushing embrace. Two big tears ran unashamedly down the woman's cheeks.

"So pleased you came back to us, Your Serene Highness!" the woman cried. "You are the mistress of Riesa! Our mistress!"

"I have a duty, Frau Silberberg," Galiena answered very softly. She was more than aware Frau Silverberg knew everything.

---

[8] The ruling family of Bavaria.

"The sins of the master shouldn't be visited on the house." The housekeeper was as much mother as Galiena had ever known.

She took a step back and addressed the assemblage. "Thank you all so much for your kind welcome. As you may or may not be aware, the Pfalzgraf, my Grandfather, has been detained at the pleasure of the German government. Efforts are being made to secure his release but at this time there has been no indication of how long he will be away." She paused, hoping that would be good enough. These people knew what her grandfather was; both prince and demon. She moved over and took Hagen's arm. "On a happier note, I would like to introduce you to my fiancé, Standartenführer Doctor Hagen Kohl of the Schutzstaffel. Please treat him as a member of the family, for soon he will become my family."

Galiena didn't fail to miss Frau Silberberg's eyes widen, darting to Hagen and back to her. Gebhardt's expression didn't change, but she could feel the man's demeanour change. Gebhardt stepped forward. "I am Gebhardt, Herr Standartenführer; butler and majordomo. If there is anything I can do to assist you, please do not hesitate to ask."

"Thank you, Gebhardt," Hagen replied quietly.

"Gebhardt, there are two men travelling with Doctor Kohl," Galiena turned to Hagen. "I assume one is your valet?"

Hagen shook his head, his face bemused. "Uh, no. They are my security personnel. They don't serve me personally."

She blinked and then turned to Gebhardt. "Ah. Well then, in that case, if you can assign one of the footmen to assist Doctor Kohl and another to assist Hauptsturmführer Freisler, it would be greatly appreciated. The other men can be quartered above the carriage house."

"Yes, Your Serene Highness," Gebhardt nodded with efficiency of movement.

"We have prepared the Peacock and Chinese suites for your guests, Your Serene Highness," Frau Silberberg interjected.

Galiena smiled. "Excellent." She touched Hagen's arm. "Kaiser Wilhelm preferred the Chinese suite."

"The Kaiser?" he repeated in disbelief.

She couldn't help but tease her fiancé. "Wilhelm the second. He enjoyed the hunting."

Frau Silberberg curtsied to Galiena. "We," she threw a concerned look to Gebhardt and he made a curt motion with his chin. The old woman continued. "We prepared your mother's suite for you, Your Serene Highness."

Galiena felt a coldness in the pit of her stomach. "Why?" Her mother's suite held nothing but bad memories, but for entirely different reasons than other rooms in the castle. Those haunted rooms tormented her even from childhood.

"The Pfalzgraf had instructions that your suite was not to be disturbed," the woman looked down.

Her face was going numb; she couldn't feel it at all. It was like a mask sitting on her bones. "I see," she said at last. "I see." She couldn't think. This felt like a terrible mistake, coming back to Riesa. The pressure on her chest made it hard to breathe.

Hagen leaned in; a firm hand on the small of her back. "If it isn't too bold of me to suggest, would you like me to accompany you up to your rooms, Galiena. Normally I would never propose such a thing, but perhaps it would be easier if you didn't face this alone."

Galiena felt such gratitude toward him. "Thank you, Hagen. Why don't I collect you when you have had a moment to refresh yourself?"

Her fiancé addressed Frau Silberberg. "If we inspected the Pfalzgräfin's suite now, would there be time to prepare it before she retires?"

The woman bobbed her head. "Of course." The tightness around her eyes suggested she was indignant he would need to ask such a question.

Hagen squeezed Galiena's hand. "Then why not now, sweet Galiena?" He raised his brows. "No time like the present."

"Yes," Galiena said weakly. "Of course." She took Hagen's hand and they climbed up the massive main staircase. "I hope you like stairs, Hagen. When I came out of the schoolroom, I picked the Aerie Suite for myself. It's in an older part of the family wing and hadn't been used since my great great aunt Eva died in 1877. It's also ten floors up, but the ceilings aren't so high here."

"Good exercise," he chuckled gamely.

"As they say in fairy tales, I live in yonder topmost tower. But on a sunny day it feels as if you can see all of Europe, and at night it's as if you can touch the stars."

Did her beloved just roll his eyes? "I can imagine."

Galiena showed him favourite rooms as they passed. The palatial Rococo library, which encompassed three stories, with its own internal staircases and galleries; the Hunter's Hall with its heavy leather furniture from England and taxidermies. They walked through the main portrait gallery and she introduced him to her ancestors as they passed up and up through the castle.

"This place would take weeks to explore," Hagen looked around. "Have you been in every room, Galiena?"

She laughed, even though trepidation filled her with every step closer to her suite. "I can honestly say that I have, but not in one day. Some of the rooms are not very interesting and are sealed up. The castle has been remodelled extensively as times; tastes and technology have changed, and old rooms often get abandoned. The last major remodel was in the aughts. Aught eight or nine. My mother was responsible for modernizing the main rooms; the Chinese suite and the Indian Suite came from my parents' honeymoon to those places. Chinoiserie was ever so much the fashion then, as it is now. They did a number of modernisations! Not to mention the wonders of electricity and running water! As the family shrinks and changes, there is an evolution to the place. The last ruling Pfalzgraf had twenty-five children from three wives. You can imagine they used far more of the castle than Grandfather and I did."

Hagen stopped short. "Did you say twenty-five?"

"Only thirteen lived to adulthood; six of the boys died fighting Napoleon at different stages of those wars, and four of the daughters never married," she dropped her voice to a hushed whisper. "And they all died here, old spinsters."

"Is there a ghost in your castle, my darling?" Hagen took her hand in his own, stalling her progress forward.

Galiena allowed herself to be pulled into his arms. Damn him! Why did he make her feel so safe when she suddenly didn't trust him the way she had before? Perhaps she should damn Hitler instead! "Several. Many people have met their end here. Sadly it's primarily the women who haunt the place. In the late 1600's, they bricked up one Pfalzgräfin in the South East tower because she went completely mad. They said she was cursed and a witch, so they fed her through a slot in the door." Galiena winked at him. "Are you afraid yet?"

"Perhaps. How long did she live like that?"

"She lived another eleven years, screaming like a banshee night and day. She still does it sometimes. You go up there in the summer time you can hear her shrieking."

He frowned, tightening his grip around her waist. "Let me guess. During a storm? I'm sure the wind howls up in the turrets."

Galiena rested her head against his shoulder. "It does, but the sound of the wind howling, and the sound of the tower Ghost are completely different."

"Fascinating." Oh how dubious were the uninitiated. If only he knew just how haunted the castle was. The place seethed with the dead.

Galiena pulled out of his embrace and charged up another flight of stairs. "Coming?" she puffed, feeling slightly out of breath. "Living up here seemed so romantic at eighteen."

His answering chuckle drifted up behind her. "Many things do at eighteen."

They came to a stairway, an old stone spiral staircase. On each step was a small potted plant. "Frau Silberberg kept my blossoms!" Galiena exclaimed, glancing at Hagen. "Blooming heather from Scotland in the winter. Tulips, of course, next season. The family did very well in tulips."

Was he sounding slightly out of breath now. "Tulips?"

"Tulip speculation in the 1640's, I think it was. Tulips were worth more than gold; far more. But if the ship with your bulbs didn't make it back from the Orient in time or God forbid, sank, then you were in very big trouble. The family was in a decidedly strained financial strait back then, and the reigning Pfalzgraf put everything he had left into tulips. The gamble played well. We were saved, the coffers replenished; so he did it one more time, and then quit; right before the bottom dropped out of the tulip market."

Hagen smirked. "High finance, Renaissance style, I see."

"Exactly."

They opened out into a hallway with several doors. Galiena went to the first, and laid her hand upon it, trying to find the courage within herself to push it open. Not all ghosts came from the dead. The heavy carved door was so old; and she felt her body tremble. Then Hagen's hands were on her shoulders. "I'm right here. He can't hurt you. He's far away."

"I know." Galiena slowly turned the knob then pushed the door open. She was hit by a blast of cold stale air. Her sitting room was dull under a layer of dust; exactly as she had left it. The servants hadn't been in here at all. It was eerie. The book on Catherine the Great she had been reading the day she fled was still sitting on the window bench. She moved into the center of the room, spinning around, her senses extended as if for danger. The room felt like a tomb; all the plants had dried to sticks. "It's like I died!" she breathed. "My father's suite was like this for years. Finally I convinced Grandfather to have it cleaned. Not cleaned out, I like to go in there and touch my father's things; just cleaned and dusted. I remember as a child, sneaking in there, and seeing the footprints in the dust. I used to think it was my father's ghost walking around," She stared at Hagen, in a strange state of shock.

"Maybe it isn't as bad as you thought?" Hagen replied, encouragement shining from his face.

"I hope so." Galiena moved into her study, down a little hall and stared upon the mess on her desk. Drawers she had torn open, looking for her money the night she fled. Searching for her letter from Uncle Hermann. Hysterical. Bleeding. Unable to see the things in her hands. She could feel it, in this room. The anguish. The terror. It enveloped her like a cloak and nearly drove her to her knees. Seeing it was reliving it.

"Him?" Hagen asked, casting his eyes about at the mess.

"No. Me."

Her fiancé took her hand. "Maybe he wasn't in here. I don't see any footprints in the dust."

"I know he was." Galiena retorted with absolute surety. "I can feel it."

"Did it happen in your suite?" His tone was gentle.

"No." Did she actually say the word or did her lips just form it?

Hagen brought her hand to his lips. "You could just be paranoid, Galiena. Maybe he wasn't in here."

"Oh, no, Hagen. He was in here." Galiena drew a long shuddering breath and met his eyes, even though she knew he would never understand. "He had everything of Verina's burned in the courtyard. Everything. Her suite was stripped bare. I wasn't here then, I heard about it from Frau Silberberg when I went looking for a memento of my sister," she paused, and whirled for a huge chest. Galiena threw open the lid, sighing in relief as she spied the old Hussar jacket inside. She pulled it out and buried her nose into the neck of the lining. It was there, ever so faint; the smell of her father. Every year it faded more and maybe she was imagining it even now. She slipped the uniform jacket, stiff with its piping, over her shoulders. It was like having him here. She picked the cuff up and pressed it to her lips.

Hagen raised a brow. "Whose is that?"

Galiena pulled the edges over her breast, enveloping herself in the garment. Her father had been a large man. "My father's. I stole it from his suite and took it with me to school when I was sent away. I am so glad it is still here." She flashed him a wan little smile. "It was sort of like my teddy bear."

His tone was dubious. "I see."

He didn't have to see. It wasn't his place to understand or comment. She moved further through the suite and into her dressing room. The inside of her cheek went between her molars as she strove to keep her composure. There on the floor lay the ruins of the dress she had been wearing; the dress she had wrapped around herself as she fled naked from his study. She could see the bloodstains on the dress and they chilled her. Then there was the bloody towel near it. And another. And another. Clothing torn from the hangers. She swayed on her feet. It was like reliving the nightmare. Things she had forgotten had returned to haunt her and there was no relief from it. The wardrobe doors all hung open.

"He had passed out," Galiena began, almost in a trance. "Exhaustion. The-" she paused. "The episode went on for almost a twenty-four hour period. I spent a great deal of it insensible. When I fought too much he would choke me into insensibility. But I do remember his perfect voice in my ear, telling me to wake up. I didn't want to. I pretended to sleep. Then he shook me until I couldn't pretend anymore. Then the last time he was inside of me, it was like he had an attack. He stiffened up and collapsed onto my

139

chest, a great dead weight. I thought Europa had killed him with her trident, from where she was on the ceiling. I clawed out from underneath and crept into the passages to come up here. I didn't want anyone to see what he had done. I didn't want them to know. I crawled under the tap in my bath and let the water flow over me. I was soaking wet and still bleeding when I changed. The blood wouldn't stop; I don't even know where it was coming from, Hagen. I don't even remember what I was wearing. I just grabbed things off the rack and threw them on."

Blazing violet eyes filled her vision. Fury. "Look at me." She did as he ordered, compelled by his gaze. "What he did to you was heinous! It was rape! It wasn't making love. It wasn't normal intimacy between a man and a woman. It was twisted and perverted. I want you to understand that."

"I know, Hagen." Galiena tried to look down, but he grabbed her chin in his hand and forced her to stay where she was.

"No, darling. You don't. Please don't throw that part of your life away because of him. I'm begging you, Galiena. Don't let him win." Eyes blurring and throat constricted into strangulation she tried to talk, but couldn't. He released her as he watched her struggle. He seemed to know this wasn't a battle he could participate in directly. "Please don't let him ruin the rest of your life."

"Thank you," she whispered and then turned from him to face the last door of her apartment. It was closed. That wasn't how she left it.

Galiena took a deep breath and opened the door. What she saw startled her. No dust. The room had been maintained. She walked into the large room, unlike the others, it had the full twenty-five foot high muralled ceiling of the turret. The bed sat in the center of the room, on a platform, as it always had; centred under the point of the roof, blue silk hangings coming from the ceiling to engulf the opulently made bed.

Close to the bed was a gown on a form. It was one of her great grandmother's court gowns from the 1860's with great hoop skirts; white with crystals and swansdown. Galiena had worn it before. She and her great grandmother were a similar size when corseted. It had been set up meticulously, and around the neck of the form was one of the most valuable diamond necklaces in the family collection. It most certainly shouldn't be up here like this. It should be down in the vault with the rest, and the last time she wore the dress it had been repacked very carefully in its cedar chest.

Galiena took another step into the room and moved closer to the bed. There was an indent on the end. Someone had been sitting there. Laying on the bed were envelopes; Twenty of them, each resting under a rose dried with age. The envelopes were all addressed to 'my Poppet.' She looked from the envelopes to the dress, and it suddenly made perfect sense.

She walked over to the bed and traced the indent. The envelopes were in even rows of five, and she picked up the one in the upper left hand corner. It should be the oldest. A bobby pin removed from her hair served an adequate letter opener and she slit the envelope open with it. A thick card, ivory with her grandfather's bold strokes across it, dated September 13, 1937. A Sunday. Six days after she fled. She sat down on the corner of the bed and read it.

September 12, 1937

Dearest Poppet,

I know that I have hurt
you, and because of this you
have left me. Nevertheless I am
here, waiting for you to return,
as I know you will. You belong
to me and I am desolate
without you. I miss you.

Meinrad

Again, her throat closed, cutting off her breath. Galiena clenched her teeth so hard her jaws ached. She picked up the next one along.

September 19, 1937

Dearest Poppet,

What have you done,
Poppet? What have you
allowed that foul Göring to do?
I am no longer your guardian.
What nonsense is this? What
did you tell him? He has no

141

right to interfere! I am most
seriously displeased. We will
discuss it when you return.

Meinrad

The third one disturbed her even more. She glanced at the
huge windows and pictured him standing there. Her eyes closed.
Her entire being felt like it was folding in upon itself. There
seemed to be nothing in there. No feeling at all. To find these
letters now! She knew she would read them all. She should burn
them for they confused her. Yet he had come up here and waited
for her to come home. In his sick and twisted way, he loved her. Or
did he? She had no control over her thoughts but as they whirled
frantically, her muscles froze stiff. She should hate him. Where
had it gone? Now it was just cold.

Hands on her face and she opened her eyes. Hagen was
there, cupping her cheeks between his hands. He looked worried;
lips thin, and eyes narrow. She was struck how he developed two
vertical wrinkles as he furrowed his brow. "Galiena?"

"Yes?"

"You're terribly pale, Darling. Are you faint?"

Galiena nodded. "Maybe a little." Her eyelids drooped
again.

"What can I do? Please! Let me do something." There was
a particular urgency in his voice.

His hands were so warm and they gave her strength. "You
have done a great deal already, Hagen." She pulled her scattered
wits together.

"Why the dress? Was that yours?" He cocked his head to
the side and pulled her head down to his shoulder, folding his arms
around her. "Lean on me, darling."

Galiena slipped off the bed and they leaned back against it,
looking at the magnificent gown. "When we were in residence,
Sunday was our special day. The day of rest. Grandfather never did
any business on Sunday. It was a day for pleasure. He wasn't
especially religious but I went to the church and sometimes he
accompanied me. Afterwards we would lunch then spend the
afternoon riding, or walking, or something of the like. When he
was ill, we would sit in the gardens and play cards, or do puzzles

and other calm things. In the winter we would go through the attics. It's fascinating up there, Hagen. It's like looking at history. Mostly it's clothing and personal effects, some hundreds of years old. Grandfather would teach me the history of the family, that sort of thing."

"Doesn't sound so bad," Hagen murmured.

"God, no! It wasn't! One day we were going through my great grandmother's ball gowns and I wanted to try one on. It was a lark. We called Idalie and Frau Silberberg, and while Grandfather waited in another room, they dressed me. Amusingly enough, it fit. Grandfather was entranced. He asked me to wear the gown to dinner and left so that I could be prepared. When I came down, he was wearing his Hussar dress uniform from when he was a young man. He surprised me by bringing up some of the special family jewellery from the safe. We had dinner and we danced in the ballroom. I felt so very special." She choked over the last word.

Hagen stroked her hair. "You don't have to tell me. Not if it's painful."

"It isn't painful, Hagen, it's confusing. After that, and it was over three years ago, it became part of the tradition. He would pick a dress and have it prepared for me to wear, having spent the time when I was in church to make his decision. Grandfather had my grandmother's dresses altered to fit me. She was a little rounder than I am, though her waist was much smaller due to the corset. He would direct Idalie to pictures of my great grandmother and grandmother, and insist she make me look like them. Grandfather would dress in his formal uniforms, and we would hold court in the Throne room. Then it became if he had a particularly bad day during the week, he would have a dress sent up and I would wear it to please him," Galiena took in a deep breath. "It wasn't until after I left here it occurred to me that he treated me almost like a doll. But you have to understand, the gowns were so beautiful." She pointed at the form. "That's a Worth Gown. Worth is considered the very first couturier. That is real swans down and the crystals come from Bohemia. My great grandmother wore it when she attended the Empress Eugenie."

"Galiena, darling, that isn't normal," Hagen's lips moved against her ear.

143

She rested her head against his chest. "I don't know what is normal, Hagen. I only know the life I have lived. It didn't seem so terribly odd for when I was with him, my grandfather insisted being around when the dressmakers came. If we were travelling, he would take me shopping and pick what he wanted me to wear. It wasn't until I started to live with Uncle Hermann that I actually picked my own wardrobe." Galiena smiled ironically. "I suppose it was my fault. When I came here after school, I was eighteen. I desperately wanted to please this aloof and very proper stranger I was living with. I asked him for advice on what I should order for our trip to Italy for I didn't want to embarrass him. I knew I was being presented to the King, as well as others. Grandfather was fascinated with my request and suddenly he wasn't nearly so proper. He insisted on sitting in and seeing all the sketches. He was exacting and the designers hated him. When we were in Paris last, I think the esteemed Monsieur Givenchy was on the edge of fits. If it hadn't been for the excessive amount of money grandfather spent, I think he would have been barred from the salon. If I bought anything when I was away on my own visiting Dickey, I had to be very discreet about it. Grandfather was very decided about what I should wear." She chuckled sadly at the memory.

"Darling, I will never tell you what to wear. Ever. You have my sworn promise on that," Hagen paused and then reiterated. "But it isn't normal. Don't ever think it is."

How could Hagen possibly understand? No. Galiena couldn't expect him to. "Listen to me rattling on. You must be tired."

The man with the investigator's eyes saw right though her. "No. Keep rattling. You mentioned to me once that there was an incident before the last one. What happened?"

Galiena dropped her chin to her chest. "I had a nightmare. I have them occasionally. My father's plane is falling from the sky and I am trying to save him and I can't. Or about my father's body in the coffin. Apparently I was screaming in my sleep and my grandfather heard. His suite is only a floor down. The sound travels quite well in the top floors of this place. I was crying. Inconsolable. He sat on my bed and held me for a very long time. Eventually I fell asleep. I woke up and he was kissing me. His hand was in my nightdress, along my neck and collarbone;

nowhere precisely nefarious. When I woke up, he apologized. Told me he had been asleep and didn't know what he was doing. It scared me at the time. I wrote uncle Hermann, trying to figure out just what happened, but I was vague. In the end I decided to believe grandfather's explanation. I wanted to believe it." She looked down. "For my own sanity I think I had to."

"Oh my sweet Galiena, what have they done to you?" he whispered, clasping her to him.

"I'm tired, Hagen. So tired. I feel like I'm a thousand years old." She could have fallen asleep right where she was.

"Lean on me, Darling. Let me be your rock. After today you don't have to think about it anymore." Hagen stroked her shoulders. "You can forget."

Galiena lifted her eyes to his own. "Have you ever forgotten about the war?" She retorted pointedly.

His eyes rolled up to the ceiling, not in frustration, but in memory. "No," he replied simply.

Galiena rose to her feet. "I thought not." She walked over to the dress. "This one was always one of my favourites." The fabric was soft under her fingers. "It's like he had me here in effigy."

Hagen moved to her side, also reaching out a finger to stroke to gown. "So it would seem. It's perverse."

"I liked it though; dressing in the gowns. Our special Sundays. I see it here and I want to put it on. Does that make any sense?"

"It means you don't hold the monster against the dress, I suppose. Perhaps the same way I don't hold the Great War against the English. I don't know." Hagen crossed his arms over his chest.

Her hands reached up and unclasped the glittering diamond necklace from the neck of the form. "This shouldn't be up here." She fastened it around her own neck. "I don't want to lose it." The weight of it pressed down on her shoulders.

Hagen traced a finger along the stones; the diamonds the size of his fingernails. "It's real, isn't it?" The amethyst eyes searched hers.

Galiena laughed. "Why do you think I put it on and not just in my pocket?"

"It will take me a very long time to get used to that."

145

"Hagen in Wonderland?" She watched him through her lashes.

"It isn't what I am used to."

Galiena walked over to the bed and picked up the envelopes. "I suppose I've always taken it for granted. Isn't that terrible? Look at me. Poor little Pfalzgräfin. How bloody useless my life has been." The bitterness welled up inside of her.

"Privation doesn't necessarily build character, darling." His eyes narrowed as she gathered the letters. "Why are you taking those? Leave them here. Let the servants destroy them!" he ordered.

Galiena shook her head. "No. They're mine. I will read them and then I will destroy them. Perhaps they will bring the hate back. The hate was far more comfortable to me than this blasted confusion. Please excuse my language."

Hagen chuckled suddenly. "Swear all you like, Galiena. I'm not going to be offended."

"How remarkably gracious of you, Doctor Kohl." Galiena cast her gaze about the room again. "I will talk to Montrose. He must have done the cleaning in here. I can't imagine my grandfather doing it and Montrose is the only one he trusts with his intimate affairs." She bundled the letters together and clutched them in her hand. "Come. Let's go."

Hagen followed her out of the suite. "Who is Montrose?"

"Grandfather's valet. Montrose has been with Grandfather for almost forty years. No. More than that. 1896, I think. He always refers to himself as Grandfather's souvenir from the Highlands of Scotland. His son served my father." She screwed up her brow as a thought struck her. "I really can't believe that you don't have a valet."

Hagen shrugged. "What use would I have for one, Galiena? I don't need one."

She rolled her eyes at him, trying to think of something normal to think about. "Every gentleman has a valet, Hagen! We are going to have to change that. We can't have you travelling without one! What would people say? It's scandalous."

"I'm a policeman, Galiena, not a prince," Hagen sounded resigned.

"Who attends your wardrobe? Your washing, and et cetera? The mark of a gentleman is in the quality of his valet! My goodness! You should hear Dickey go on about the necessity of a Gentleman's Gentleman. Freffie and Wills live together and they don't even share a valet. Each has his own. It's of vital importance, Hagen!" she answered emphatically.

"I don't need one, darling! I send my laundry out and I am quite capable of dressing myself!"

"So am I, Darling. I didn't have a personal maid in school but that doesn't mean I would ever go without one now! It would be like cutting off an arm!" Galiena reached the top of the stairs, and swivelled to fix him with a direct stare. "We will just have to find you one."

He looked very pained. "Is it that important to you?"

"Hagen, a man without a valet is like a car without tires. Sure it can roll along, but not very well! They're very useful. Even uncle Hermann has seen the light. He says he would be lost without Robert now!" She took his hand. "Please? Will you get one?"

"This means that much to you?"

"Hagen! People will look down on us if you don't have a Valet! They won't think you're a gentleman!" That sounded insulting and she knew it was very shallow. She raised his hand to her cheek. "I know you are. Please don't think I don't. But in this world, the world I grew up in, such things are terribly important. If you don't have a valet, people will think I've lost my money. They'll talk and the nobility are horrible gossips. So are our servants and they share with us everyone else's tragedies. They will always treat you as an outsider if you don't have the correct accoutrements and they can be very cruel." She searched his face. "I may not be able to give you my title, but I will be painted blue and pilloried before I let anyone treat you as anything less than my prince." She threw her arms around him. "Because you are."

He kissed her forehead. "I see I have a great deal to learn."

She inhaled, savouring the smell of him. "Do you still want to be my rock, Hagen?"

"Of course I do?"

"Even if being my rock meant you have to have a valet rock?"

"I don't think a rock needs a valet," he joked.

"Very funny, Standartenführer Kohl." She frowned. "You know, given your rank, I'm surprised you don't get one automatically! Goodness Gracious! What kind of organization is Herr Himmler running, anyway?"

Chapter 11
February 18, 1938

Hagen arrived at his suite to find Eugen waiting for him with a face like a thundercloud. The scowl was truly fearsome; it emerged from under the bristly white beard like the face of a demon. His eyes, narrowed to slits really, followed the servant who was unpacking Hagen's bag. When Hagen entered the room, they flickered up to him.

"Eugen," Hagen said simply, not in the best frame of mind either. The last hour and a half had been very difficult. Seeing the actual evidence of the attack on his fiancée had soured his mood. The stained towels had sent his blood pressure racing until his pulse had pounded in his skull like a drum. Then there were the damn letters. He tried to take them from her just now, but she evaded him. He hadn't even had the opportunity to glance at one, but he knew whatever they contained was pure poison. Her tale tightened his chest and it had taken every ounce of self-control not to lose his temper. He wanted to drive down to Buchenwald and kill the Pfalzgraf with his bare hands.

A living doll. That's what she was. There had to be something seriously wrong with a man who wanted to dress his granddaughter up like his mother. That rang every single one of Hagen's bells and he didn't know why she couldn't see it for herself. Was she blind? Didn't she know just how fundamentally wrong that was? The last person Hagen ever intended to associate Galiena with was his mother.

When she read those cards, all the light had gone out of her body.She turned pale, going completely grey and her lips bloodless. She was in so much pain and he couldn't help her. Perhaps he had made it worse. He didn't know. What he did know was that everything he had seen today had shaken him. Now he understood the root of her fear. Maybe he had forgotten in the last six months. Hagen had blocked out the bruised face and brutalized body he'd pulled out of the Horsch so long ago. He wanted to do something to take it all away. Fix it.

"What took you so long?" Eugen asked testily, focusing his ire on Hagen

Hagen glanced around at the suite, wishing he had a moment to himself. It was like being in a foreign land. The walls were bright red, and the furniture shiny black lacquer. It was unlike anything he had ever seen before, except in a museum; exactly as he pictured China to be. He walked past Eugen into the bedroom of the suite and was agog at the ornately carved canopy bed. Dragons chased clouds and chrysanthemums up the posters; the entire top of the canopy was the same. Intricately carved and painted dragons twined around the wood. Heavy red silk draperies hung from the canopy. He was in absolute awe.

Hagen returned to Eugen. "We went up to her suite. It's five stories above us in a different side of the triangle."

Eugen continued to glare at the servant, who bowed to Hagen and left the room. "This place is," the large man paused. "It's a castle," he continued somewhat lamely.

Hagen nodded. "We were aware of that," he answered gamely.

"It dwarfs the Carinhall," Eugen pointed out.

"It does, indeed."

"The Kaiser slept in this room. The crown prince slept in mine," Eugen whispered, his eyes wide and wild.

"Is that what has you upset?"

"I'm just a simple soldier. I don't belong here," his friend replied with a little shake of his head.

Hagen chuckled. "It's a new experience. Revel in it."

Eugen appeared to consider that. "Good point. Can't say as I liked having that man unpacking my clothing. I felt like he was assessing everything and finding it wanting. He isn't the bloody Pfalzgräfin. She doesn't seem to find fault with me." The large man's face twisted pugnaciously.

"I think Galiena likes you quite fine, Eugen. I wouldn't let the staff intimidate you," Hagen chuckled.

"I am not intimidated by the staff!" Eugen barked indignantly.

Hagen shot his friend a wry glance. "No. Of course not."

Eugen shot Hagen a black look. "Interesting sights on the way up here," he said by way of changing the subject.

"Oh?"

"That certainly looked like a synagogue in the village, didn't you think?"

"Yes. I noticed that," Hagen agreed, slowly thinking through his answer. "A very large number of the staff have all the eye marks of Judaism. Now we know the mystery of the little maid and her fear of the uniform. Frau Silberberg is her mother."

"So what are we going to do about that?" Eugen stepped closer to him.

"I'm not inclined to do anything about it," Hagen told his friend and subordinate. "Firstly, I am not in uniform. Secondly, this is Galiena's home. Thirdly, I don't really care about the Jews. Why should I cause my already distressed fiancée grief by upsetting her household?" Hagen thought of the affection in her tone as she talked about Riesa and the people here. "In actual fact, I want it buried. Tell the men they saw nothing."

"Yes, Hagen. Frankly, I agree with you, but then you know me. I don't care about the Jews either. But what about the law? The Nuremberg Laws?" Eugen furrowed his brow.

"If memory serves and it has been a while, a Jew cannot have a German maid of less than forty-five years working in their house. That's under the blood and honour law, but it might be the citizenship law. That isn't a problem here. Galiena, or rather the Pfalzgraf is a German and the employer. She can hire whomever she wants. It is of no concern to me." Hagen undid his jacket and slid it off his shoulders.

"You're the Standartenführer." The big man shrugged, and sat in a chair.

"Hell, Eugen. You know I don't go for Jew baiting. Between you, me and the wall, I've just never seen the point."

"There is the odd decent one." Eugen muttered under his breath.

"Exactly." Hagen looked down as he loosened his tie. It felt like it was strangling him. "I hate being out of uniform."

Eugen scratched his chin. "I hate this fur on my face. It itches."

"I'm sure you have the fortitude to bear it." Hagen chuckled again.

The servant re-entered the suite. He bowed. "Would the Standartenführer be requiring a bath?"

Hagen considered it. "Yes. Thank you." The man withdrew. "Problem number three," he murmured.

Eugen glanced up. "I don't know what to make of it, myself. Being waited on. I feel they are going to realise I'm not one of the gentry."

"Galiena insists I need a valet once we wed." Hagen rolled his eyes. "It's expected, she said."

Eugen snorted. "Foolishness."

"I agreed to look into it. She said it would make her look bad if I didn't."

The white head swivelled around as Eugen looked around the suite. "Will you live here, Hagen? We are only a few hours from Berlin."

Hagen blinked. "I don't know. I hadn't processed the future that far. What a strange thought. It's a trifle overwhelming."

"It's a very different world, Hagen." Eugen stood. "I feel like a stranger in a strange land."

"Galiena will guide us, I am sure."

Eugen's lips twisted. "Now there is a comforting thought. I'm off to prepare for dinner. I'm just across the hall, if you need me."

"Sieg Heil!" Hagen grinned.

"To hell with you, Herr Standartenführer." Eugen left the suite.

Hagen walked into the bathroom with its large tub. The servant was busy in the dressing room. The man looked up as Hagen passed. "What does the Standartenführer wish to wear for dinner?"

"I will wear the white double breasted dinner jacket, thank you," Hagen said before moving into the bathroom. He slowly divested himself of his clothing, contemplating the afternoon as he did so and sunk into the water. The temperature was absolutely perfect! How did the servant know? He could get used to this! Perhaps there was something to this valet idea after all.

Hagen half dozed in the tub, floating with his thoughts for three quarters of an hour. This was certainly not par for the course with him, but he had an hour and a half and nothing to do with it.

For security reasons he had not brought any work with him. One never knew who might be looking at his briefcase. Rising like Poseidon from the sea, Hagen left the tub and collected a bath sheet from the warmer, wrapping it around his lean hips. As he padded about, he occasionally felt the hairs on the back of his neck prick, almost as if he was being watched. He paced the suite, looking for signs of spying, but could find nothing. It was probably the castle servants moving about. His lips compressed to a thin line. Maybe it was a ghost. Hagen dressed carefully, and the footman reappeared as if from nowhere to help him. He wore his iron cross on his breast and his party pin in his lapel. When he was finished, he still had fifteen minutes, so he went across the hall to see how Eugen was faring. He knew if he was ready, Eugen was bound to be climbing the walls.

Hagen knocked on the other door and another footman answered, letting him in. Eugen's suite was like something out of the Arabian nights; all silks and jewel tones. Very exotic. Inside Eugen prowled like a caged beast. He wore his dress mess uniform, but his jacket was not yet on.

Hagen crossed his arms over his chest. "Well Hauptsturmführer, you look rather sharp," he complimented his friend.

Eugen spun on his heel. "This place makes me feel very edgy."

"How so?"

"I feel like there are eyes on me. Not right now. Earlier. I don't like it," the large man growled.

Hagen frowned. "I had the same feeling. Strange. I put it down to having people coming in and out of my room. You know me. I'm not one for strangers in my territory."

Eugen rolled his shoulders, stretching his back. "It disturbed my exercises."

Hagen snorted. "Watching you do those blasted one handed push ups would scare anyone."

"Keeps me from getting flabby. Use it or lose it, as they say." Eugen straightened his tie.

"Thought you would be dressed," Hagen said after a moment.

"Didn't want to get too hot. Suppose I should though." Eugen walked over and allowed the servant to help him into his jacket.

Hagen and Eugen discussed which Berlin area Standarte would win the upcoming SS football game and left the suite together after another ten minutes. A maid, her eyes modestly downcast led them through the halls. As they moved, Hagen suddenly registered the sound of two people arguing in English. He paused, following a secondary hallway to the source of the commotion. He held a hand up to Eugen to wait; his curiosity getting the better of him. He took another step down the new hallway and saw that it opened up into a round room, seemingly at the corner of the building. He moved closer. The voices were coming this way. Then he saw Galiena enter the circular room from the other side. She looked both beautiful and angry. Her violet gown clung to her torso and seemed to float around her legs. She spun on the person following her.

"Hear me, Montrose; I will do what I can, but I am not promising anything." Galiena spat viciously in a tone of voice he wasn't used to hearing. "That is the end of it."

A tiny man followed her. He was old, stooped and thin, with a balding pate of iron grey hair. Even from this distance Hagen could see the man's beady black eyes, and pointed nose. The old man held his little hands high in front of his chest like curled little paws, only completing the mouse-like visage. "But Madame! Please! He's sick! He needs me!" The voice was plaintive, almost desperate. From the sound of Montrose's voice, he was obviously of Scottish origin.

"I am aware now of the Pfalzgraf's deterioration over the fall, Montrose," she retorted. "But there is very little I can do about the situation."

"Maybe Herr Göring can help, Madame! Have you gone to Herr Göring?" The man stroked his fingers against each other.

"It was Herr Göring who sent him to prison, Montrose. I hardly think my uncle is going to get him out." Galiena sliced through the air with a hand

"What has he done to be sent away like this?" Misery emanated from the little man. Was it Hagen's imagination or had the man's eyes gone completely glassy?

154

Galiena's eyes flashed with fire. Her finger stabbed the air near the man like a dagger. "Don't pretend you don't know, Montrose. That's just bad comedy! He is a monster!"

The man called Montrose drew himself up. "He is the Pfalzgraf! He is a prince!"

"And divine right of Kings died out with Charles the Second." Galiena whirled to the window and looked out. Her face became very ugly as it twisted with bitterness. "No matter his rank he wasn't entitled to do what he did." There was a long silence, and she looked over her shoulder. "Did you enjoy it, Montrose? You watched, didn't you?"

The man dropped his hands to his side. "I did no such thing, Your Serene Highness. What do you take me for?" The words sounded weak to Hagen

Galiena turned and leaned against the window, her arms crossed against her breast. Her eyes were heavily lidded; they almost appeared closed. "Don't lie to me, Montrose. I didn't mean literally, though at this moment, I have my suspicions. You watched him destroy Verina. My sister, who lived as his wife for two years."

"The Frau von Taschen has been lying to Your Serene Highness." The man looked down.

"Has she, Montrose? I don't think so."

"She never understood."

"Then we share the same lack of understanding, for neither do I!" Galiena snapped back.

Montrose took a step forward, his paw shaking as it reached out for Galiena. "He didn't abandon you, Your Serene Highness. You abandoned him! You left him!" The fingers brushed the back of her hand, then pulled away swiftly after touching her. "He didn't mean to hurt you. He wanted to raise you above them all. You were always the special one. It broke his heart when you left. He became sick again. It's your fault."

"I've read the letters, Montrose. Forgive me if I'm not distressed."

"Then Her Serene Highness has become heartless and cruel." Montrose pointed a finger at her in return. "He raised you better than that."

"Go to Hell, you little bastard!" Galiena gasped, drawing back. Hagen could see the pain in her eyes, but the ferocity of her words surprised him. He wondered just what this Montrose knew and just what the man had done to Galiena. The little Scot was obviously more than a mere servant.

This time it was Montrose who turned on his heel. "His Royal Highness was right. They did poison you against him. Oh Madame! Where did our sunny natured little Poppet go?"

Galiena bent at the waist, until her eyes were even with the rat-like man's. Hagen had to strain to hear her feral hiss. "She died while her Grandfather sodomized her." She pushed her way off the wall. "Tell me, Montrose, did he do that to you, too?"

The tiny head dropped, the man's chin on his chest, then raised, an unholy light in the black eyes. "I love the Pfalzgraf, Madame, but he has never seen fit to honour me with his attentions. As it should be. I am a servant. I am not worthy."

"You make me lose my appetite, Montrose, and I have guests. It is only out of a sense of duty that I don't turn you out-of-doors this very evening. You have served my Grandfather loyally for nearly half a century and I find I cannot do that. You will always have a home here at Riesa, provided I do not see you." Galiena drew herself up to her full height. "But be warned, Montrose. I highly doubt the Pfalzgraf will ever return to Riesa. In fact, I intend to ensure he doesn't. Now get out of my sight!"

The man took a step back, bowed slowly and with reverence before leaving. Hagen looked at Galiena. Her pale face was transforming into an expressionless mask he had seen upon occasion in the past. That particularly blank expression which hid her emotions completely. She reached up and touched the necklace which was still around her neck. "I am going to have to put you away, aren't I. Damn. Maybe Hagen wants to see the dungeon." She half smiled and then laughed ironically. "And to get to the dungeon I have to go through the torture chamber."

Galiena started to move towards him, and Hagen ducked back to where Eugen was waiting. His friend raised a brow, but Hagen shook his head curtly and they followed the maid to complete their journey. The men were deposited in the Hunter's Hall and waited silently for Galiena to join them. Eugen examined the taxidermies with an interest born of boredom and Hagen stood with his back to the fire thinking on the scene he had just witnessed with his fiancée. She obviously hadn't followed them directly, for she arrived almost five minutes after they did. Her face was calm and Hagen was impressed by her ability to regain her composure. He would not have believed the tableau he had just witnessed between the woman and the valet was possible.

Galiena greeted Eugen graciously, and linked arms with him on one side with Hagen on the other. "I thought we would dine en famille in the Mural Salon. It's a little more intimate than the dining hall." Galiena smiled too brilliantly. "I don't think the three of us need a twenty five foot long table do we?"

"No. I don't think so." Eugen answered quietly.

Her body was very close to Hagen's own. He gazed down at her and wondered at her last comment earlier about the torture chamber. What an interesting turn of phrase. There was such tightness around her eyes. "Galiena," he began. "Is everything all right?"

"Yes, of course, Hagen. I'm fine," she responded without missing a beat.

He had his doubts, but he let them rest and allowed her to chatter about innocuous things. Galiena had slipped into a role, something he rarely saw. The same mask she wore around Hitler. Hagen wanted her to take it off and throw it away, for it unnerved him. He preferred Galiena without artifice. He liked to see her soul shining through. Her innocence. Her light. Right now that light was dull and hidden.

Gebhardt entered after twenty minutes and announced that dinner was served. Galiena rose and lead them into the Mural Salon. She explained how the room had been painted in 1717 after the school of Watteau. The pastoral scene ran up the walls and across the ceiling. The doors were mirrored on the inside, and the room was lit only by candles in white wall sconces. The effect was startling and beautiful. A black garbed footman stood behind every chair. The flatware was gold, the crystal glittered and the china unnervingly delicate.

Galiena sat at the end of the table and modestly put her napkin in her lap. "I hope you brought your appetite," she winked at Eugen.

"Always, Your Serene Highness." The huge man rumbled from his seat.

"Come now, Eugen. We are away from Berlin. It's just the three of us. I know you would be polite and respectful, but it's my house and my rules! Call me by my name." She batted her eyelashes at him.

"For tonight only, Galiena," Eugen answered with a sly wink.

Galiena laughed and seemed to relax for the first time in the evening. A glimmer of the light was back. That pleased Hagen; he and Eugen shared a look. They were on the same page. Eugen didn't like to see Galiena unhappy either. If Eugen had seen Galiena's quarters he would be dismantling things in his rage.

Dinner was ten courses and seemingly went on forever. Hagen found himself daunted by the delicacies which appeared at the table. The main course was an Osso Bucco so tender that the veal seemed to melt into his mouth. Hagen suspected that the chef at Riesa must be Italian, for there was a decidedly Mediterranean flavour to the meal. The cheese course nearly put him into ecstasy and the dessert was an elaborate confection of lemon and meringue.

The footmen served them quietly and efficiently; almost shadows on the edge of the room. Black-clad, white-gloved arms occasionally passed into view, bringing some new succulent food into range. Every different course brought a different glass of wine to accent it. He watched as Galiena ate very little, elaborately pushing the food around on her plate. It was artfully done, but didn't escape him. She also drank very little; sipping only a third of each glass.

Her colour came back for a while and then the distance returned. Her light faded again. She was still charming, but vacant. When the food was finished she gave them a different tour of the castle. Hagen noticed that her hand absently ran across the necklace at her throat. She was thinking about it; stroking it. Finally they came up a carved staircase, ending at an ornate door.

"And this is my grandfather's private study." Galiena pulled a key out of some mysterious location on her person. The iron rattled in the lock as her hands shook. In fact her entire body was vibrating. Then Hagen realised; this had to be the scene of the crime. She had to return the necklace to where it came from. This entire tour had been an attempt to steel herself into coming to this room.

The door swung open and he was assailed with the smell of cigars and leather. The room was opulent. The ceiling of this room was also heavily muralled; women indicative of the feminized nations of Europe. Britannia with a trident and a lion. Germania with her iron cross and eagle shield. Italia and Franconia painted as well in their turn. Heavy wood shelves held numerous books; several portraits were on the walls, including one of Galiena with bright eyes and a sensuous smile on her lips. A cold fireplace sat with huge leather chairs before it, and a great desk dominated one side of the room. Thick carpets covered the inlaid wood floor. This was the room of a prince.

Galiena walked into the room, as if in a trance. She moved to a place on the carpet almost in the center of the room; looking down at it almost contemplatively. Hagen followed her eyes. To his horror, the pattern on the carpet was different there. It was darker. Stained. Then she abruptly moved over to the bell pull and gave it several hard yanks. Within moments Gebhardt appeared.

The man bowed on entry into the room. "Yes, Your Serene Highness?"

Galiena pointed at the carpet. "I want this removed!" she ordered fiercely, pointing a sharp finger at the carpet.

"Yes, Madame." Even Hagen could hear the conflict in the man's voice.

"I want it burnt, Gebhardt. I want it burnt tonight. Douse it in petrol and set it on fire in the courtyard. Bring me the ashes in the morning," she said very quietly.

"The Pfalzgraf gave orders it wasn't to be disturbed," Gebhardt replied in obvious discomfort.

"I shall explain the situation to my grandfather when I see him next. Remove the carpet, now." The last word was spoken in a tone which brooked no refusal.

"Yes, Madame," the servant acquiesced.

Galiena inhaled deeply, her nostrils pinching as she did so. "In fact, send someone to me when it's burning. I might come down and watch."

"Yes, Madame." The man withdrew.

The troubled woman threw Hagen a sad smile. "Sometimes a girl just feels a need to redecorate."

Eugen walked over to her and put his massive paw on her shoulder. Hagen could tell that his friend had figured out the reason for the Pfalzgräfin's actions and Eugen's eyes burned hotly. Comfort registered on Galiena's face and she leaned her head against Eugen's shoulder. "I swear that I will kill anyone who hurts you, Galiena. From now on, I swear it!" Eugen whispered fervently.

"Thank you, my Ritter von Freisler." Galiena almost seemed to be mocking Eugen by her use of the knightly title, and yet her emphasis on the word made him realise she was not. When had Eugen become knight to Hagen's princess? Then, with a suspicious flickered glance at Hagen, Eugen snaked a finger along the cowled neck of Galiena's gown to reveal the greenish yellow thumbprint. "Eugen!" Galiena exclaimed in shock, pulling his hand away and readjusting her dress with a confused look on her face.

"I'm sorry," The huge man whispered as he returned his gaze to Hagen's. Green eyes collided with violet and for the first time in their twenty-one year relationship, Hagen saw bewilderment there. Eugen was clearly rattled to see proof of Hagen's assertion on the train. Not that Eugen wanted to catch Hagen in a lie, but his faith in the perfection of Adolf Hitler demanded it.

"You are forgiven, Herr Ritter," Galiena joked weakly; oblivious to the drama all around her, locked as she was in the drama within her. She patted Eugen's hand and stepped away, her eyes distant. She trailed a finger along the desk, and sat down behind it. She appeared to be feeling under it for something.

"What are you doing?" Hagen couldn't help his curiosity.

"Do you gentlemen want to see my dungeon?" she queried almost flippantly.

Eugen raised a brow. "You have a dungeon?" he repeated.

"Every castle has a dungeon, Eugen. You can't have one without the other. I don't like going down there alone, but that is where the vault is and one can only get there from this room. My Grandfather sealed off the dungeons from the rest of the cellars when the vault was upgraded; partially for safety, or so he said. There is an oubliette down there, and he didn't want to fill it in, yet he didn't want the curious getting trapped down there either." Galiena winked at him. "There's even an iron maiden. It's gruesome."

Eugen walked over to the desk. "What else is down there?" Did Hagen detect a certain professional curiosity?

Galiena laughed suddenly. "There are all sorts of things. We had a fully equipped dungeon and you never know when you might need a rack. Hate to get rid of equipment that's tried and true."

Hagen walked over and took her hand. "One never knows when one will have to put a man to the torment," he intoned with great ceremony.

"Exactly." Galiena chuckled again, and pulled a key out from under the desk. "I asked grandfather if he had ever put someone in the oubliette and he just smiled back. It was very strange. But the dungeon rooms are haunted. That I do know. Grandfather and I spent some time down there cataloguing things and you can hear screaming and chains rattling." She stood up. "I hope seeing it down there won't bother you gentlemen. I found my first experience down there a trifle disturbing."

"I believe we can handle it," Hagen answered with aplomb.

Galiena moved over to one of the bookshelves and moved a series of books aside, and reached her arm into a place behind the wall. Her arm disappeared for some time and then she brought it out again after a loud click. Then she moved over to another bookshelf. "Could one of you pull on this side?"

Eugen walked over and took hold where she indicated. The bookshelf swung away from the wall on a hinge, revealing a stone hallway with stairs leading down. They went into inky nothingness. "Clever." Eugen noted.

Galiena retrieved an electric torch from the top of the stairs. "There's no electricity down here. The upgrade on the vault was done in 1890, and Grandfather hasn't seen the need to let people down here since." The torch lit the stairway, and she moved back to let them enter. Then she pulled the bookshelf closed behind them using a large handle set into the back. Again there was a loud click.

Hagen felt shivers up his spine. He suddenly felt hemmed in and claustrophobic. It wasn't something he often felt within his soul, but then the only cells he ever entered he was the master of. The stairs, hewn out of the rock itself seemed to go down forever and the trio spiralled down on them for what felt like an eternity in the dark. "What is this?"

Galiena turned and grinned at him in the faint back light of the torch as she descended the stone steps. In the grim glow she looked almost demonic. "The passages, Herr Kohl. Only this one has been cut off from the rest." They came to an ancient heavy door, iron bound with great studs. They just didn't make them like this anymore. She inserted another key, and the door unlocked. The door opened to reveal another huge metal door set into the corridor with a combination dial and a wheel. "You might be the first strangers to come down here since the renovation in 1890. Grandfather would probably skin me alive if he knew I brought you." The Pfalzgräfin entered the combination and spun the wheel. The there was a clang inside the door and she stepped back to allow Eugen to pull the thick door open.

Hagen put a hand on her shoulder. "I appreciate the trust you are giving me, Galiena. It means a great deal." As the door opened he was hit by cold heaviness. Air escaping from the sealed area had the same feeling of the basement of Gestapo headquarters, only fainter. Misery. Despair. The smell of humanity was long gone, but the horror seemed to have sunk its way into the stones. The lantern cast its light down another corridor, this one lined with more doors like the one they had just passed through. At the end was another door. Hanging from the ceiling were more lanterns, like the one in her hand.

"When we are married I will show you where everything is down here so you can get things for me if I need them. I hate it in the dungeons." She lit the lanterns in the hall and it was suddenly less gloomy. "Grandfather locked me up in a cell once to make a point. I didn't panic, but it just increased my unease."

Eugen walked over and helped her with her task. Pushing the darkness away. "Why did he lock you down here?"

"He said when you are really scared having all the money in the world won't help you. I didn't understand what he meant and we had an argument about it. So he took the lantern and left. I was in the dark. All the doors were open and he was right. Not a single gold coin or necklace was able to help me conquer my fear of the dark or the cold." She turned on her heel contemplatively. "But that isn't quite true. We were sorting through some of the old regalia when he did it, so I put on a cloak and it made me feel braver and warmer. I sat down amongst the boxes and waited. I made up little fantasies in my head, it was much easier in the dark to do that, and I waited him out. I slept for a while as well."

"That's a way to make a point, Hagen commented, feeling another tremor of unease. The thought of being caged was abhorrent to him. "How long were you down here?"

"Overnight." Galiena seemed to sense his nervousness and stroked her hand across the lapel of his dinner jacket. "It felt like a year."

Eugen looked at her with something akin to horror. "In the pitch darkness?"

"It's not quite that dark. Three of the cells have long vents to the outside and there is some very faint light. The upshot is that I no longer fear the dark. I don't like it and certainly not down here, but I could do it again if I had to." The Pfalzgräfin walked over to one of the cells and fumbled with her key ring, going through the keys. She tried a few and found the right one. "Ah! The lengths we go to hide our plunder," She teased and entered the cell. "And you would not believe some of the plunder we have down here. There's even the odd religious artefact to be found, including five of St. Peter's kneecaps, particularly fascinating considering that most humans only have two, but to collect them was a particular fashion in the late middle ages."

Hagen and Eugen followed her into the dry, cold room. It was bigger than he was expecting; almost ten by ten feet. Shelves lined one wall, filled with square wood boxes, and on another were a multitude of smaller, flatter leather and velvet boxes. Two chairs and a table were in the middle of the room and a mirror was affixed to the wall. Galiena lit the lantern hanging from the ceiling and the room was illuminated. It all seemed very ordinary.

"I feel faintly disappointed," Hagen said ruefully.

Galiena's brow raised sharply. "What were you expecting? Great chests filled with gold coins? Ropes of pearls spilling over the edge? An unholy golden glow like in a comic book? Perhaps a skeleton clinging to the lip, it's grinning skull staring at its treasure in eternal longing?"

163

Eugen shrugged. "Now that you mention it. Yes!"

"Let me see if I can impress you, then. Have a seat." She grinned. "We're princes, not pirates!"

Hagen and Eugen sat in the wooden chairs and looked at her expectantly. Hagen could almost feel a child-like excitement growing in his chest for this was unlike anything he had ever done before. It wasn't everyday one got to view a royal vault. He thought it was silly how his nerves tingled at the thought, but he certainly wasn't going to walk out of the room.

Galiena looked at the boxes, each with its little label and brass handle. She pulled one down from the shelf. "This one will suit Eugen, I think. It's the first Steinberg Crown and it's from approximately 1050, but the dates are a little hazy. The Margraf Lothar von Steinberg commissioned it for his coronation as the old diadem was buried with his father as was tradition. The coronation was in January of 1051, but the calendars have changed several times since, so pinning down an exact date is a little difficult." She looked down at Eugen who was gazing up at her with rapt amazement. "Lothar was a little bit of an egotist, and ordered that his crown never be destroyed or buried, so that he could live on and it's supposed to be haunted by him. According to legend, When Lothar was dying, he marked the sign of the cross on the inside of the band with his blood and vowed that anyone who stole it would die a hideous death shortly after. Such has proven the case both times it was stolen." She opened the box and lifted out a crown built in eight arch shaped sections hinged together. The sections were all equal in size, and hammered almost smooth. White pearls outlined the edge of each section; cabochon spinels and sapphires the size of a man's fingertip in seemingly random patterns were inlaid in the centers. The effect was very primitive feeling. Savage.

Hagen examined the crown and felt something stir in his breast. He had never seen anything like this before, for it was Germany Galiena held in her hands so blithely. His country's history! His fiancée leaned forward and placed the crown on Eugen's brow. It perched on the big man's forehead, being from a time when men didn't come as big as Eugen. Hagen watched as his friend straightened and preened under the weight. She was right. It did suit Eugen.

"There!" She adjusted it with some satisfaction as her lips curled in pleasure.

"It's heavy." Eugen's ruined voice was especially ragged. Hagen wanted to say something witty, but nothing came to mind. Instead, he just stared at his friend.

Galiena returned to the boxes and pulled down another one. "This is my favourite. The family was quite powerful and very independent in the 1630's. We were autonomous from the Holy Roman Empire, or as much as anyone ever became, and Wilhelm von Steinberg Zum Riesa inherited. He decided he wanted a crown for his investiture, and he wanted one to rival the crown of Hungary. I should clarify; the crown of Rudolf II, who became emperor of Austria. Wilhelm, too, was a bit arrogant. This nearly bankrupted us and is the reason my family invested so heavily in tulips." She opened the case and removed a glittering fantasy. The crown's band of alternating grape sized pearls and thumbnail sized sapphires surrounded by diamonds was bordered in rows of finger tip sized pearls. From this rose twelve alternating fleur-de-lis and Maltese crosses; the fleur-de-lis were encrusted in large emeralds and diamonds, and the Maltese crosses in sapphires. From the points of the fleur-de-lis rose six spindly pearl studded arches which mushroomed outward, and curved back in to support an emerald sphere the size of a golf ball. Under the arches was a cap of soft blue velvet. It was an overwhelming and ostentatious display of wealth. Galiena pointed at the emerald. "That is the Riesan Eye. It came from India in 1468; it detaches and has a pendant it can be fitted to. Supposedly it came from the eye of a statue of Kali, the Indian goddess of destruction. Every Pfalzgräfin is supposed to wear it on her wedding night to bring the power of the Goddess into the children conceived. Make them conquerors and destroyers." She placed the crown on Hagen's head.

It was heavy. The pressure of it on his brow was unlike anything Hagen had ever felt before. It fit him very well and like Eugen he felt himself straightening. He felt kingly. It was like his uniform cap yet so much more. Even in this room far beneath the ground, the effect it had on him was instant. The feeling of the crown on his head also aroused him. Power. Underneath it, he had such a feeling of power. Hagen stared up at her, almost as if through another man's eyes, pleased when she smiled down at him.

"You look like an emperor," she whispered, running a finger down his cheek. God, he loved it when she touched him of her own volition.

"I feel like one." Hagen stood and met his reflection in the mirror. The man staring back at him was nearly unrecognizable. The image's eyes burned with unrestrained fire, the skin around them taught and hard. Is this the man he could have been, marrying a Pfalzgräfin, or the man he would become? Who was that stranger staring back from the glass?

"One moment." Galiena ducked out of the room, and he heard another door opening. A few minutes later she returned carrying a mound of folded purple fabric, encrusted with silver bullion embroidery of dragons grasping oak leaves. She draped the velvet over his shoulders, exposing an attached capelet of ermine. "The last coronation robes." They pooled around his feet in an embroidered pool of fabric.

"Well Eugen?" Hagen finally had a breath to address his friend.

"Don't know what to say," The man answered at last, his eyes wild.

Hagen grinned wickedly; a feral, predatory expression on the doppelganger in the mirror. "This is very dangerous. I want to grab my sword and send my troops out across Europe." He reached out, and pulled Galiena into him. She didn't resist. "Conquer countries and lay them at your feet, my empress."

"Crowns have a funny way of doing that." Galiena replied, her hands splayed across his chest. "It's been getting my family into trouble for a number of years now."

Eugen took his crown from his head and put it back in the box. "I don't want Lothar to think I'm stealing it." He smoothed his hair down with an automatic gesture.

"I want to kiss you." Hagen whispered against her forehead. Kiss her? He wanted to do a damn sight more! He wanted to push Galiena up against the wall and take his pleasure in her soft flesh. That which was his right by betrothal.

There was a terrible indecision in her eyes, then the tip of her tongue traced across those beautiful lips. "It is my duty to obey the man who wears the crown." She answered him.

The words made his blood run cold. Instantly he thought of her grandfather and it chilled him. He reached up; lifting the crown off his head and placing it on the table. "The only person you have a duty to obey is yourself, Galiena." He traced the line of her jaw with his index finger. "I never want you to obey me out of duty." Hagen realized as the words crossed his tongue just how much he meant them.

Galiena picked up the crown and placed it in the box, her eyes clouded. Silently she put both boxes back on the shelf and took the necklace she was wearing off and returned it to a leather case on another shelf. Then she lifted the State robes from his shoulders and disappeared around the corner. Hagen followed her into another cell, this one smelling of cedar and filled with larger trunks. She refolded the garment and put it away, all without saying a word. He wanted to know what was going on in that head of hers, but she wasn't volunteering anything.

Finally Galiena looked up at him. "Let me show you the dungeon." Her voice was thick and awkward.

"Galiena," Hagen began. "You never have to be afraid of me. I want you to know that. I will never hurt you. If I could make the past disappear, I would."

Her face was a mixture of longing and scepticism. "I am surrounded by the past, Hagen." The Pfalzgräfin's eyes dropped to the ground. "I belong to Riesa and have since the day I was born."

"You don't have to be chained to it," he responded, before backing up into the hallway; Eugen waiting silently behind him.

Galiena left the cell before moving down to the door at the end. It wasn't locked, for she pushed it open and there was another stairwell down. "Come." A hand gesture and they were descending further into the ground. The stairs opened up into what had once been a natural cave. The floors had been evened in the room and there was enough equipment to make any medieval torturer proud. Galiena hadn't been joking when she mentioned the Iron Maiden, or the Rack. What looked to be a forge sat in one corner, and rings were bolted into the stone walls. Everything was covered in a thick layer of dust; the feeling of horror even stronger in here. In the feeble light of the lantern the room was infinitely more sinister and Hagen immediately lit the lanterns spaced about.

Galiena pointed to a wood covered area of the floor with another ring bolted into the top. "That's the oubliette. When Grandfather brought me down here the first time he told me never to go near because if I fell down there, it's fifteen or so feet to the bottom, and they would never retrieve me alive. That's the point of an oubliette, I suppose. I will leave you both to explore at your pleasure. I would like to pick out a few pieces of jewellery to take back to Berlin and this place makes me terribly uneasy."

Hagen nodded, rather intrigued by his surroundings. "We will join you in a moment."

Galiena turned on her heel and left while Eugen walked further into the room. "Reminds me of headquarters."

Hagen smirked over his shoulder at his friend. "Heydrich doesn't have a rack, Eugen, though I'm sure he would like one!"

The large man padded over to a heavy shelf filled with boxes. He looked in one, and pulled something out. "Thumbscrews?"

Hagen assessed the object. "Could be. How vicious!"

"Seems a little cruel." Eugen radiated amusement. "But potentially very effective."

A glance at the ceiling revealed a block and tackle. "Wonder what that was for? Hanging people upside down?"

"Probably. Interesting." Eugen picked up a large ornately carved wooded block, hinged on one end, with one large hole and two small ones beside it. The carved scroll work on the device was worn down to smoothness, and the wood stained to a dark burgundy around the neck. "Looks like a violin," he commented slowly. "I think we have something like this at home. I think one of the boys called it a Shrews Fiddle."

Hagen pointed at a large platform, like a bed, with masses of nails pointing up for a mattress. "Ouch. One really forgets how savage the good old days were."

Eugen pursed his lips. "Yes," he said sagely. "It's certainly not like that today. All the better for it, I think. Though I must agree Heydrich would be like a child in a toy store down here. Or maybe Müller. He would really appreciate this place."

"Müller is a touch enthusiastic about getting results," Hagen muttered as he strode over to the oubliette. He lifted the hatch. It was a hole straight to hell. Blackness. He lifted the lantern but couldn't see the bottom. "Do you think anything is down there?"

Eugen wandered over. "I doubt it. Ten Reichsmarks says empty."

"It's a bet. Pass me that rope over there. I will tie it to the lantern and we can lower it down." Hagen held out his hand. "Not that I don't agree with you."

Eugen grinned. "This is silly, you know. Ghoulish." He passed over the rope.

"It is, isn't it?" Hagen attached the two items and with Eugen beside him slowly lowered the lantern into the pit. The rough hewn sides of the rock gleamed with dampness as the light went down.

"Jesus Christ!" Eugen swore abruptly.

"Wasn't expecting that," Hagen agreed, his gorge rising.

"I owe you ten Reichsmarks," The large man recovered, looking down into the gloom again.

The bottom of the pit was a mass of human bones. Skulls screamed up at him from the depths, their eye sockets empty and reproachful. It was much larger at the bottom than Hagen was expecting. Tatters of clothing covered some of the bones, and the garb at the top seemed to be overly familiar. "Eugen, does that look like field grey to you?" Hagen asked, his curiosity overcoming his horror.

"When you mention it, yes it does. Standard issue, 1917. Imperial to be sure. Cavalry from the looks of all that braid." Eugen scratched his head, almost glaring at the mummified body. "Looks like an officer. You don't think," he paused.

"Meinrad's been a busy boy." Hagen blinked slowly, trying to decide how one could have killed one of the Kaiser's officers and gotten away with it. Then again, given the slaughter in France, who would have missed one more name? "Or the vaunted Rudiger." He sighed, realizing he had an irrational jealousy of Galiena's devotion to her dead father.

"You want to look into it?" Eugen eyed the hole. "I really don't want to go down there in my dress uniform."

Hagen lifted the lantern. "Another visit perhaps. He's been down there twenty years at least. A few more months won't hurt. We don't have time for a mystery at the moment, and how do you

169

think Galiena will feel if we start brining up corpses from her basement." The bodies faded out of view, buried in the inky blackness. "It might knock her night off kilter."

Eugen agreed with a nod of his head. "She's had a pretty rough day as it stands. Once we're married we can come back and scoop our comrade down there out while she's napping."

Hagen retrieved the lantern with a quick hand. "I wonder if they are all from this century?"

Eugen shrugged, and then replaced the cover with a grisly chuckle. "How often does one clean out one's oubliette?"

"There could be eight hundred years worth of victims down there!" Hagen frowned. "They should be buried. No wonder this place is haunted."

"It's not especially pleasant; no," Eugen straightened his jacket. "But I don't know how much worse long dead bodies are than the fresh. The smell isn't as bad. Similar, but age certainly takes off the tang. I almost miss it."

"You know, after seeing that, I think it's worse than HQ. Much, much worse. At least we clean up after ourselves." Hagen started to walk towards the exit, turning out the lanterns as he went. "Cremation is a damn sight cleaner than that."

"I would agree. Leaving the prisoners down there seems a little on the grisly side." Eugen rubbed his head with the back of his hand. "I feel like someone just walked over my grave; you know! That itchy feeling betwixt the shoulder blades? It's not a nice feeling." The man's hands dropped from his head to his back. "I don't know if I like it down here."

They went up the stairs and shut the door behind them. Hagen wondered what was behind the doors Galiena hadn't opened, but it was an abiding curiosity which could wait to be satisfied. He could hear her humming from in the first cell they had entered and he felt better. Humming had to be a good sign. He entered the cell and her back was to him and he leaned against the doorjamb with an amused expression. She was placing boxes back on the shelf with all the studiousness of a woman rearranging her pantry, only this pantry wasn't filled with flour and sugar. He could see she had placed several of the smaller and a few medium sized boxes on the table. Her choices? She yawned delicately, and went back to her work.

"Galiena," Hagen said quietly, not wanting to startle her.

She whirled around. "See anything interesting?"

He almost chuckled at the irony. "There were a few surprises."

Galiena bobbed her head as if to avoid his eyes. "The existence of that room and the things in it isn't a part of my family history I am particularly proud of. I'm fully cognisant of the fact some of my ancestors, even those not yet dead, weren't the most gentle of individuals. Seeing the family dungeon just hammers it home."

"Not to worry, my darling. We all have skeletons in our closet." Now why in hell had he said that?

The Pfalzgräfin looked through her lashes at him. "I declare, Doctor Kohl, that you've seen most of mine." He heard Eugen snort behind him as she continued. "When do I get to see some of yours?"

Hagen winked at her. "My closet is rather free of skeletons. Why clutter up the house when you can bury the bodies in the back yard?" His tongue seemed to have a mind of its own.

"I never thought about that, but then I'm just a common, ignorant girl."

He shot her an amused glance. "Yes. Ever so common. I can't imagine a girl more common than you."

Galiena picked up a pile of boxes and handed them to him. "Absolutely. So tell me one skeleton. Just one."

Oh the agony of choice! "I occasionally have nightmares about the war. Speaking of skeletons in the closet," She looked so concerned and he continued. "Not very often, but sometimes. Two or three times a year."

Galiena brushed his hand with hers and then squeezed it. "Thank you for telling me."

"Don't share. Only Eugen knows."

She laughed and her velvet eyes twinkled at him. "Then you had best not tell anyone about my vault!"

Hagen held out his hand, and eventually she took it. They shook firmly. "Done then."

171

October 24, 1937
Dearest Poppet,

I keep pretending that you are away at school, but I must confess
that I did not miss you the same way when you were at school.
You were away so much and we were almost like strangers. You
were young, and I was busy. But the last few years, my dearest
Galiena, they meant so much to me. What I wouldn't pay to hear
your laugh echo throughout the halls again. Don't make me wait
too long to hear it again. I am an old man.
Eternally yours,
Meinrad

Chapter 12
February 19, 1938

Galiena escorted Hagen and Eugen back to their suite well
past one in the morning. They said their goodnights, and Galiena
gave Hagen a quick peck on the cheek before she left them. She
gave the men leave to explore the castle, but warned them of
getting lost in the passages, should they venture into them. Hagen
assured her they wouldn't get too lost and that in the event of
doing so, would shout.

Galiena walked down the hall and moved into the family
wing, up towards her sister's old suite. It had long been refurnished
into something luxurious but without meaning. She had decided
not to sleep in her own quarters. It just didn't feel right. It would
probably never feel right again. That was fine. She would renovate
a new place for herself, when Hagen chose a place to make his
own. She smiled. One hundred rooms. It shouldn't be too hard for
her to find a place with no connotation to it. Perhaps even on a
lower floor. Stairs no longer seemed as romantic to her.

Idalie was waiting for her in the suite and helped her out of
her evening gown. Her maid seemed very happy to see her family
again and chattered about it as she took the pins from Galiena's
hair. The auburn mass fell down below her shoulder blades and
gleamed as Idalie ran the brush through it. When they were
finished, Galiena slipped into one of her favourite night dresses. It

was like a renaissance gown with a cobalt blue silk satin empire bodice, snug under her breasts and falling in layers of pleated silk gauze to the ground. It was so full that if she twirled it flew straight out from her bust line in a filmy disk. Over top went a navy robe in the same style, and even fuller in fabric. The layers of translucent silk floated around her. Galiena put two combs in her hair, clasping the sides out of her face, before standing. She was keenly missing Emil, her lion. He was always a good companion when a girl had insomnia.

She felt a hand on her shoulder, and turned to see Idalie behind her. The dark haired woman held a sheathed dagger and a small roll of bandaging. "I thought you would be requiring this?"

Galiena smiled sadly. "You know me so well, Idalie. Thank you! I wasn't relishing returning to my suite to get those." She took the items into her hands.

White teeth flashed. "After six years if I didn't know your habits, I wouldn't be much good to you!"

"Yes, of course," she whispered slowly. "You may retire now. I won't need anything more tonight. If our guests get into any trouble, I will be in the family gallery, and after, the Pfalzgraf's study." Galiena instructed as she picked up a small kerosene lamp and left the suite.

The castle was quiet; the halls dim as she traversed them. Her lantern made it much easier to see. Her feet, clad in navy blue leather slippers, made no sound as they sank into the carpets lining the floor. She made the rounds of the floors, ghosting past the doors to Hagen's and Eugen's suites. Both seemed dark. It would have been very easy to check and see if they were occupied. The passages in the walls passed by both suites, complete with occasional spy holes, but Galiena certainly wasn't going to invade either man's privacy. Besides, she could always ask a member of the staff if she really felt the need to know. They would be watching, of that she had no doubt.

A part of her wanted to knock on Hagen's door and talk to him; spend more time with him. Galiena took a step closer to his door, her hand raised, and then she thought better of it. After all, she had someone she had to greet. With faint regret she stepped back and continued on her rounds, travelling in a cloud of billowing blue like a fairy.

Galiena entered the family portrait gallery and the room was awash in silvery moonlight. It bled the colours from the portraits, making them monochromatic and flat. She moved into another much smaller room, then into the Long Gallery. Dominating one end of the room was a life sized portrait of her Father. This was the room where his memorial had been held. His coffin had lain in state here for a day, draped in the old flag of Steinberg. She placed her lantern right where his coffin had rested and stood there, silently feeling the ghosts in the room.

How very vividly she remembered it, even though she had only been four. The huge black coffin on its plinth. Galiena only had one other memory of her father, on leave just two months before his death; home for Christmas. Rudiger von Steinberg holding her and kissing her forehead, calling her a little Valkyrie; the smell of his cologne on her cheeks from where she had snuggled up against him.

Then just a blink of life later and he was dead. Of course she remembered the memorial, she had sat on Uncle Manfred von Richthofen's knee, and he had looked down at her with those sad blue eyes. He had been on a tour of Germany at the time of her father's death, still recuperating from a serious head injury and been charged to attend the service. Galiena remembered that her silent tears had left a large wet mark on the handsome aviator's uniform as he had tried to explain to her that her father's death was one of great honour.

But even more memorable was the night before the service. Galiena moved to her father's portrait and stood underneath it, letting the memories pass over her. Coming awake to her mother shaking her hysterically; Verina standing just behind, watching. Her mother had dragged both girls downstairs to this room, the black coffin sitting alone, bathed in the light of standing candelabrums at each corner.

"We must bring him back, girls! We must bring him back! I can't live without him!" Jessamine von Steinberg Zum Riesa had cried piteously.

Verina, a vision of her mother at fourteen, had stroked the older woman's hand. "He's dead, Mother! We can't bring him back to life!"

"Yes we can, Vee! I'm a Kincaldie, and so are you! We have the power! If we want it badly enough, and pray hard enough, and bleed long enough, he will come back!" The distraught woman had pulled the flag from the coffin, and flung it to the ground; then she pushed the lid of the coffin to the side, exposing the body.

He had been grey-green, for it had been a week and a half since her father's death. As a measure of respect for his high station and the position of the Pfalzgraf, the body had been shipped home from the front by train. In retrospect, Galiena was thankful her father had died in February, and not June, considering the actions of her mother. She could still remember the faint but terrible smell which had emanated from the coffin. It scared her, and she quailed against Verina's legs. Time and hasty wartime embalming didn't make for a beautiful corpse.

Jessamine had stroked the peaceful face, for a very long time, and then kissed it. "Come back to me, Rudiger! Please!" A moment later, Jessamine pulled an officer's dagger, the dagger Galiena now held in her hand, from the folds of her dress. The woman snatched up Verina's hand and slashed her wrist before thrusting the bleeding hand onto the face of the dead man, all the while chanting in Gaelic. Verina had trembled and sobbed silently. Galiena hadn't. When her mother came at her with the dagger, she screamed blue murder. Scared, hurt, and bleeding, Galiena didn't want to touch the body. Jessamine had slapped her until she was nearly senseless and then placed her hand on the corpse, giving her to Verina to hold. Jessamine then slashed both of her own wrists and the blood spilled into the casket. "Come back, Rudiger, or let us join you! Don't leave me alone! Please Rudi!"

Galiena ran a finger along the ever so faint line along her wrist. It was nearly invisible now. She could still remember the feeling of that terribly cold skin. Clammy. Spongy even. Pools of scarlet blood across the lifeless face. Then the door behind them burst open and help was charging in. Gebhardt and two more of the footmen followed their furious master into the room. Meinrad had snatched Galiena out of Verina's arms, and clamped his huge hand around Galiena's wrist. The footmen dragged a hysterical Jessamine away from the casket and out of the room while Gebhardt attended to Verina. Meinrad saw Galiena's wounds were bandaged and soothed her, holding her in his strong arms until she slept, and she woke up snuggled to his chest on the sofa in his study hours later. He kept his promise to not leave her alone. Her grandfather became special to her in that night. A mountain; an oak tree to lean on in a time of terrible fear and uncertainty.

Galiena looked down at the knife in her hand and walked over to the portrait of her father. He was so handsome in his Liebens Hussar Uniform, worn with pride until he left that unit to fly. Six months after his death, their mother locked away in insanity, Verina had brought Galiena down here. Now Galiena was five, Verina said she was big enough to help keep father from going away completely. He was dead, but they could keep his spirit with them. Verina had produced her father's officer's dagger, and sliced her own finger, pressing it to the oils of the portrait. "Papa, come back and guide us." Then Verina had looked at Galiena. "Your turn, Poppet."

Galiena had agreed and choked back her tears as her sister nicked her finger. Pressing it into the painting, Verina helped Galiena repeat the words. "Always remember Father, Galiena," Verina had urged her. "You must give him your blood, or he will disappear forever and we will be alone! Mother started it and we must continue it. The dead need our blood, Poppet. I know you're just little and you don't know much, but mother would want you to know this. Don't worry. I will explain more when you're older!"

Galiena hefted the knife in her hand, and stared at the painting. She let the sheath of the dagger fall from numb fingers to hit the inlaid wood floor with a clatter. Nineteen years worth of bloody prints marred the portrait, but only in the places where the paint was dark enough to hide the marks. Galiena and Verina's blood. A moment of pain and she sliced a four centimetre cut on the edge of her palm, pressing it into the painted black jacket of her father's portrait.

"Papa, come to me and be my guide." Galiena intoned, looking into the eyes. Her throat threatened to close up with her grief. Then suddenly, just as it had the first time, she was suffused with a feeling of such warmth and tenderness. "Why did you leave us, Papa?" she asked, as she often did. "Why did you have to go and die for the Kaiser and leave us alone? We needed you more than Germany! Couldn't you realise that?" Her breath caught in her throat. "I need you so much! I am alone."

176

The blue eyes looked down at her; gentle and amused. "I don't know what to do, Papa. Please help me! Don't leave me to muddle through this on my own, because I'm not strong enough to do it! I have not the skills, nor the intuition." There wasn't an answer, but then there never was. She leaned her cheek against the rough portrait and closed her eyes. "Grandfather hurt me so badly, and I hate him for what he did. Yet I love him for all the years before it. Mother's memory terrifies me. After you died, she became crazed and terrifying. Then she followed you, as I think she wanted. I was sent away. Verina fled. Did you know he hurt Verina too?" Galiena's eyes closed as she communed with the portrait, her cheek pressed up against the sharp oils. "She was just seventeen, Father. Now she is desperately ill; I don't know if you knew that. Grandfather is in prison. The Ritter von Kleist says I am the only one left and insists I assume the reins of the estate but I think there is more to it. What if I make a mistake, Father? How many people rely on us for their livelihood? I don't know if I can do it and yet if I don't, Riesa might falter. Do I trust von Kleist? Why did you leave us? Why?" For a moment she felt a burning resentment. They had all left her to this fate; her father through war, her mother through grief and madness, even Verina's abandonment. She knew she was being irrational, but why hadn't Verina taken her away too? She knew intimately what the Pfalzgraf was. Why hadn't she saved Galiena?

Galiena glared up at the portrait. "This should have been your responsibility! I'm not ready! You were selfish, father! And now I'm lost!"

On the edges of her consciousness, Galiena knew she wasn't alone. Then she heard footsteps, quietly coming towards her. In her imagination she wanted to believe her father had finally come back from the dead to save her, but her rational mind knew he could not. None of the servants would dare disturb her in this room tonight. Galiena opened her eyes to see a man in maroon ghosting towards her. She blinked, pressing her back into the portrait as if she could hide behind the man painted upon it. Once, it might have been her grandfather coming across the floor. Ice cold terror washed over her even as she reminded herself it wasn't possible. Was she losing her mind? No. Out of the dark walked Hagen, in a brocade smoking jacket. He brightened as he approached the lantern, and became a shadow as he passed by it. Ominous; almost like a sign.

"You aren't lost, Galiena," he said slowly. "Come to me."

"Hagen." Her voice was tremulous, even in her own ears. "Can I help you with something?" The rough ridges of the oils caught the filmy silk of her gown and she was almost pinned to the portrait.

Hagen reached a hand out to her. "You aren't lost," he repeated. "I found you. You aren't alone." She raised a hand up, as if to push him away and he clutched at her wrist. "Good God, Galiena! You're bleeding!" He exclaimed.

"It's nothing. Just flesh. I'll be fine." How could one explain to one who would never understand?

He pulled his handkerchief out and pressed it into her hand. Mopping up the blood he gazed into her eyes. "What are you doing here in the dark, darling?"

Galiena glanced back at her father's portrait. "Asking for guidance." Perhaps even absolution.

"Your father?" Hagen queried softly.

She nodded. "Yes."

He stroked a finger down her cheek. "You live too much in the past, Galiena. It's your whole life. You need to look forward, or you will never move forward." He curled his hand around her wounded one. "Come. This room feels haunted, even to me."

Galiena allowed Hagen to draw her from the room, holding his hanky in her scored hand, and her father's dagger in the other. He picked up her lantern in his free hand as they passed it. When they reached the hallway, he gave her a questioning glance and she led him into the huge library, with its roaring fire. Hagen eyeballed the blaze. "I see you were anticipated."

Elegantly, Galiena gestured for him to sit down. "Idalie knows my habits. How did you find me?"

"I followed you." He winked at her slowly. "I heard footsteps outside my door and I was awake, so I investigated. It's my nature, I suppose. You lost me partway, but I managed to find you in the end," he shrugged. "I hope you don't mind."

"I could have been a footman, Hagen. You could have been on a wild goose chase."

Hagen sat down, and crossed his legs. "Possible, but very few of the footmen float through the halls like a Titian angel." He appeared to be appraising her.

Unsure of the situation and feeling a little daunted, Galiena changed the subject. "Can I offer you a drink?" she asked, moving to the sideboard. "Cognac?"

"Cognac would be fine."

"Always a perfect choice." Galiena placed the dagger on the tray and poured his drink, taking it to him immediately. He thanked her, and she went back to pour her own and retrieve the blade. She carried both back to the fireplace and sat down in the wing chair opposite him, toying with the knife openly. His eyes widened as he saw it and his lips thinned.

"Is that intended for me? Or did you have some other victim in mind?" Hagen asked wryly.

She opted for honesty. "No one in particular. I'm a little out of sorts this evening." Her gaze drifted in his direction.

"Why did you cut yourself?"

Galiena squeezed his hanky tighter against her palm. "Tradition or duty depending one whether one is feeling more English or German. I have a plethora of little scars from it over the years." A thought struck her; she had no idea of Hagen's spiritual beliefs, and how all of this would affect him. Moreover, what would he think when he met Dickey, or if he ever found out about the rites she, Dickey and Freffie had played at up in the Highlands of Scotland. Just as Jessamine had imparted her fey ideas to her children, Dickey's mother Leticia immersed the son no one thought would survive in the secrets. The occult was a game to the Edwardians, indulged in by many in the aristocracy, but for the Kincaldies it had been a centuries old tradition. "Every time I come back to Riesa I visit my father. Verina told me when I was very little it would keep him from leaving us forever."

Hagen sipped his cognac. "Is your father so bloodthirsty a ghost?"

"I don't know. Probably not." She placed the knife on the table beside her and picked up her beverage. Rolling it between her hands; swirling it around, over and over as she thought. "It's simply one of those things which must be done. I like to think he is watching over me."

179

"You never mention your mother. Why is that?"

Galiena was silent for a long moment. "My mother went mad when my father died. Round the bend with grief. Completely bonkers. It's a deep, dark family secret. She was never the same again. She tried to commit suicide the night before my father's funeral. In retrospect, she may have planned to kill Verina and me as well. Grandfather and Gebhardt managed to stop her and it caught him completely off guard. Not something that happened often to Meinrad von Steinberg, let me tell you! From the stories I've been told from both sides of the family, my mother was never strong. Dickey tells the most amusing stories of her antics; things I barely remember. Her nickname was the Faerie Queen. That should give you an idea. But after Father's death, she lost the plot. She would lay sedated in bed all day, with her two nurses watching over her. I remember the nurses so well. They were old dragons with enormous white aprons and high starched caps. I thought they were crowns. The nurses would chase me out of her room if they caught me nearby, which wasn't very often because I was terrified of her."

Hagen leaned forward. "Your childhood sounds very traumatic."

"That's the way of the aristocracy, Hagen. It builds character. My youth and Freffie's weren't much different. Boarding schools and summer holidays abroad. His father died shortly after the war." Another horror Galiena remembered. It was the first time she had seen a man die and the murderer had been her Grandfather. "Dickey's was little different either, and both his parents are still alive; yet he, too, was shipped off to schools. Eton and then Cambridge. But I shouldn't complain. I never wanted for anything. What about you, Hagen?" She cocked her head as she studied him.

His normally impassive face took on a faint glow; the hardness in his eyes softened and they drifted far away. "Quite the opposite. I was an only child and my parents were quite involved with my upbringing. My father was an outwardly stern disciplinarian, yet he was very tolerant of my hijinks when mother wasn't in the room. As I have told you, my father was a director of investment for the Fugger bank and we were quite well off. From when I could first read, my father insisted I read to him every night before I went to bed. I think that's where my love of literature comes from. I would read to him for an hour and then we would debate what I had covered. Because my father was in charge of foreign investment, he was very well educated and had travelled through Europe, giving him a unique perspective on the world." Hagen's eyes dropped. "He was a very gentle man, I believe. Very compassionate. He agreed with some of the ideas of Karl Marx even though he hated Bolshevism. Not so much about class, but that the lower classes shouldn't be treated as a lesser state. More in the American attitude that a man should be able to rise and fall on his own merit and that at some point we are all equal and the same. We had such arguments over the *Communist Manifesto*," his voice trailed off. "He was a much better man than I will ever be. He loved his king, but he loved man. He was a true humanist."

Galiena felt a burning envy for Hagen. To have known one's parents! "You were truly blessed, Hagen. I don't think you know how lucky you are."

Hagen looked around the great library, a slight smile about his lips. "My mother would not have believed this castle. She was a very simple woman; my father's second wife, and not of his class. His first wife was a distant member of the Fugger family who died with my other siblings in an influenza that passed through Augsburg in 1895. Father married my mother, who was the daughter of a wealthy farmer, in 1897. He hoped to have another family, but apparently I was so big my mother was unable to have children after me. She used to say her body was only able to give life to one child and I was the special one. Mother worked very hard not to embarrass my father and she was such a good, kind woman that everyone loved her. When they died in 1919 within a few days of each other, the funeral was quite large despite the raging epidemic. It astounded me, how many people they had touched in their lives and the genuine outpouring of grief at their passing affected me very much."

"They sound as if they were very special people," Galiena whispered, putting her glass down on the table.

Hagen uncrossed his legs and leaned forward. "Once she got over her shyness, I think my mother would have liked you very much. I see things in you which remind me very much of her." He almost sounded surprised as he said it. Hagen moved out his chair,

181

and onto his knees before her, taking her hand in his. "I meant what I said, Galiena. You aren't alone anymore." He pressed her palm to his lips, kissing it. "I will never hurt you. You don't ever need to be afraid of me."

"I'm not afraid of you, Hagen." And if she were a little wooden doll, her nose would be growing.

He chuckled, obviously seeing through her. "What a sweet little liar you are. If you weren't afraid of me, you wouldn't have carried that dagger in here the way you did. Do you really think that I could cause you harm?"

Galiena looked down into his pale violet eyes. He appeared so sincere. "Hagen, I-"

Hagen cut her off, rising up onto his knees and putting his hands on her shoulders. "You told the Fuhrer that you loved me. Has it changed, Galiena? Or did you lie to him in an effort to ensure our union?"

She felt trapped with him so close to her. "No." She could barely hear the word when she said it.

"No, it hasn't changed? No, you didn't lie to him? Or no, you don't love me?"

His words were very direct and cut her deeply. She didn't know how to answer. "No, I didn't lie to him," she replied.

Hagen cupped her face with his hands, tracing his thumbs across her lips, his eyes bright like a basilisk. "Then you must trust me, Galiena. If you love me, you must trust me. It's very simple, my darling."

"Hagen, please, it isn't that simple," Galiena cried. "You don't know," she began. "You- It didn't happen to you!"

"Come down here, Galiena. Come down to me," he commanded in that strange voice. His hands slipped down to her waist.

He was right. She was afraid. Terribly afraid. Her nerves were on fire. "I can't."

"Just this one step, Galiena. That's all I'm asking. Come down here to me. I'm not going to hurt you. You don't have to be afraid of me. We did this in Berlin, don't you remember? We lay together on the floor. Nothing has changed."

"Emil was there in Berlin and uncle Hermann was just down the hall. If I screamed, he would have heard. We are alone now," Galiena pointed out to him.

"You trusted me then. Trust me now. I am no different a man. If anything, I only care about you more. I would never cause you harm," Hagen replied evenly.

"You ask me to trust you, Hagen Kohl, but do you trust me?" She studied him intensely.

His brows drew together in a faint frown. "What do you mean by that? Of course I trust you."

Galiena shook her head from side to side, very deliberately. "Then why did you lie to me?"

The frown grew darker. "When did I lie to you?"

"When you told me you were going to Austria on holiday. I don't believe you, Hagen. I may be blind and terribly naïve, but if you think I'm stupid, then you are in for a shattering surprise." She raised a brow. "Don't forget, Doctor Kohl, I was at the Berghof last week. I heard the Fuhrer threaten the chancellor of Austria. Now suddenly you just happen to be taking a holiday, when according to your own self of a few months ago, you don't take holidays. And now you just happen to be going to Austria?" Her mouth snapped shut after the last word like a trap.

He ran a hand over his hair, smoothing it down; something she was beginning to notice as a 'thinking' habit. Had she hit the jackpot? "Oh Galiena! What am I going to do with you?" His voice echoed with consternation.

"If you were a humble clerk or a useless aristo like me then I wouldn't be suspicious of your trip. But you aren't. You told me you are an investigator. What are you going to investigate?" Silk gauze pleated almost magically between her fingers as she spoke.

"I can't tell you that."

"Ah-ha!" Galiena pounced. "So you did lie to me! I knew it!" She felt a slight thrill of pleasure at having caught him out.

"My mission to Austria is a Reich secret. I can't tell you about it. The less you know the better; as such I told you it was a holiday," he sighed. "It doesn't mean I don't trust you."

"You asked me to contact Freff for you. Arrange a meeting. Are you investigating him?" The balance of power between them shifted in her direction.

Hagen met her eyes. "No, but I think he might have knowledge of the people I am looking for."

"Then if you promise me you won't investigate him, maybe I can help you." Galiena tapped her finger on her chin. "As my fiancé, it only stands to reason that you would visit my closest family members; especially as Freff knows all of Viennese society. He could sponsor you for me. Teach you what you need to know to interact with the people of our class. I've already asked him about adopting you, so it's not going to look odd if you spend time with him."

"Adopting me?" The expression on his face was almost comical.

"It's a simple enough thing, Hagen. Freffie's the last of his line, his family is dead. There is no one who will make a fuss if you suddenly become a long lost member of the von Reitersbach clan." Galiena laced her fingers in her lap.

Hagen drew back his head. "What do you mean, adopt me, Galiena? Is my family not good enough for you? I am not ashamed of my ancestors!"

It was her turn to sigh. "Hagen, you could be a French ditch digger from the lowest slum in Calais, and I would still want to marry you. No. I don't care about your ancestors; but the other members of my class certainly will. It matters not a jot to me to make a morganatic marriage, but it might affect our children and as things stand now, they will inherit Riesa after me. Other Uradel will no longer consider me as one of them for marrying outside our class even Freff adopts you, but it's the gesture. It's what's expected."

He tapped a finger on his lips, his eyes distant and then they snapped back into focus. "It might affect our children, darling? Have you had a change of heart? Because all that nonsense about a stork being involved is simply that."

Galiena sent him a hard look. "I know where babies come from, you twit!" She used the English word unable to think up a good German equivalent. "As for having children, I don't know, Hagen. I don't want you to hurt me. I don't want to be hurt again. I would rather be dead than go through that again."

"Galiena, what can I do to reassure you?" Hagen asked; his voice rife with aggravation. "Why can't you trust in the fact that I

184

am not Meinrad von Steinberg? I'm not your grandfather. I am not going to hurt you! Hell! The thought is incomprehensible to me, with the sole exception being I am so frustrated that I want to shake you to make you see reason!" His eyes pleaded with her. "Please, Galiena! Give me the chance to prove to you that I will never abuse you!"

Emboldened by something in his voice she dropped to her knees in a cloud of fabric. She could feel the heat of the fire behind her, even as her blood felt like ice. "I trust you." She whispered at last.

Hagen smiled at her, his eyes gentle. "See now? That wasn't so hard, Galiena." He ran his fingers through her hair, pulling the combs out of it. "This is so beautiful. I've never seen it down before; you always wear it up." A lock in his fingers was raised to his lips and he kissed it reverently. "I adore your hair, Galiena."

"Thank you," she answered him shyly.

"The smell of it. The feel of it. Everything about it." His face grew more intense again. "I want you. I don't want to scare you, Darling, but I can't deny it."

She considered his words and traced a medallion in the carpet with her finger. "Hagen, I can't disallow a certain curiosity. Lord knows, before the attack, I was terribly curious. I did everything I could to encourage a certain member of," she paused. "Well, that doesn't matter now. The fact is, if there was a man that I would want to," Galiena found herself making useless gestures with her hands. Hagen's eyes danced as she futilely fumbled for a word. "You know what I mean!"

"I think I do, yes," he chuckled.

"It would be you, Hagen," Galiena whispered in the silence.

"Such a ringing endorsement, my bride to be." He enfolded her in his arms and pulled her close to him. "You never seemed quite so reticent before the New Year. What changed, Galiena?"

Galiena allowed his arms to hold her; in fact she melted against him. God! She loved his strength. The smell of his cologne. "Seeing him. Seeing my Grandfather. Hearing the words. It brought it back, Hagen. It wasn't six months ago. It was just yesterday. I'm not done with it. I tried to put it away, Hagen. Into my personal library, just as you said, but it wasn't ready to disappear. Coming back to Riesa, seeing it again, feeling it again, I think has helped, but I'm not done with it, and I'm not done with him." She ran a fingertip along his jaw line. "I beg you to be patient with me, Hagen. I just need time. Can you grant me that?"

"You have been very badly damaged, darling. Of course I can grant you time, provided you leave your ghosts behind when the time is up." He traced his lips along her earlobe and then made a sound between a sigh and a grunt. "Come now, Galiena. Let me escort you to your rooms, so that we can both get some sleep. I'm sure tomorrow will come very early." His lips traced the edge of her ear and it sent chills down her spine.

"I shall escort you back to your rooms, Hagen, but I'm afraid I will not be going back to mine. In the words of Robert Service, I have miles to go before I sleep," she replied ruefully.

"What do you have to do tonight?" His tone was stern. "No more ghosts, Galiena. Not tonight. No more."

She laughed against his neck. "Not ghosts! No. Not at all! I have to study before my meeting tomorrow. I have to rifle through the estate and company accountings and bring myself up to date on my Grandfather's affairs. I know where everything is; I handled things when he was quite ill two years ago, but I'm obviously not up to date anymore."

Hagen nodded. "I see. And you plan to do this in your Grandfather's study, yes?"

"Unfortunately, that is where all the material is." She squeezed his hand. "Not to worry, Hagen. I will be fine." Oh yes. Absolutely fine. So completely fine she tossed back her cognac abruptly.

Again, that grunt. "Let me keep you company. I might drift off, but I will sit in there with you."

Galiena felt a relief in her chest which was tangible. "How very authoritarian you sound, Standartenführer Kohl!"

His nose trailed through her hair and along her head. "Don't you forget it, Pfalzgräfin von Steinberg zum Riesa. It's against the law for you to disobey me. I'm an officer of the Gestapo, after all."

"I'm not afraid of you, Doctor Kohl. You don't scare me!" she replied cheekily.

His eyes gleamed wickedly. "It's about bloody time you admitted that! Now perhaps we can make some progress!"

October 31, 1937
Dearest Poppet,

It's all Hallows eve. This place is filled with ghosts and none of them kind. Your ghost haunts me most of all. I can smell you and it makes me lonely. You have humbled me, Poppet. I miss you so dreadfully. Please come home to me.
Eternally yours,
Meinrad

Chapter 13
February 19, 1938

As promised, he stayed with her the rest of the night. Galiena watched him sleeping in the leather chair by the fireplace as she read accounts at her grandfather's desk. She worked diligently until dawn peeked up over the horizon; but as light appeared in the sky, she found herself stealing glances at her fiancé. In sleep he seemed at peace, the cares slipped from his face, the lines of strain smoothing to invisibility. Galiena felt guilty with him sleeping in the big chair, his feet on the ottoman, when he could be in his comfortable bed upstairs, but she was happy for the company. A sigh and she went back to her paperwork. It was impossible. She wasn't ready for this responsibility and she didn't know if she trusted her grandfather's advisors. No. That wasn't right. She didn't trust herself. She would never trust herself. Meinrad spent a lifetime building this empire and she certainly wasn't equipped to summarily take over. One thing had cemented very firmly in her mind: she wasn't ready. Why did she have to be? Her grandfather wasn't dead, after all.

At seven on the nose, Gebhardt came in, his tray bringing coffee; the smell confirming the existence of God. But Galiena felt reticent about waking her fiancé, asleep as he was. She was a strange mixture of wide-awake and exhausted but she would have time to rest later when she returned to Berlin. Waking Hagen seemed the best option, for she was going to eat and then go riding before her appointments. If he wished, he could return to his suite and rise or sleep as he desired.

Galiena walked over to the sleeping man; so familiar, yet in so many ways completely a stranger. She gently kissed his cheek. "Hagen, darling, wake up."

His eyes flickered open, a confused alertness in their depths. Then they softened as they met her own. "Galiena," he whispered.

"Hi," she smiled at him.

"Hello." His lips curled up lazily. "I'm sure you can wake a man up slightly better than that," he paused. "Not that I have any complaints. It was a darn sight better than Eugen's usual method."

Her hand reached out of its own volition and squeezed his. "What did you have in mind, Herr Standartenführer? A bucket of cold water? Is that how they do it in the SS?"

"Not to me, they don't. Eugen usually pokes me in the shoulder until I open my eyes. You, on the other hand, could come up with something more creative, I'm sure." His eyes took on a hooded, snake-like look. "Kiss me, Galiena."

"I thought I did."

"Oh, not nearly well enough."

She decided to listen to the devil on her shoulder. "Are you always so demanding first thing in the morning?"

Hagen wrapped an arm around her waist and pulled her to him. "I intend to be considerably more demanding in the future. I don't usually have someone so charming to make demands of when I wake up."

"I think you entirely too used to getting your own way," she retorted, disentangling herself from his grasp.

"One could very easily tar you with the same brush, Your Serene Highness."

"Entirely true, I'm afraid. Guilty as charged." Galiena dove in and kissed him very fast on the lips, darting back before he could catch her with his hands. "But there you are. I will acquiesce in the interests of peace."

"I'm faintly disappointed by your cowardice, darling," Hagen narrowed his eyes at her, and then his face took on a dreamy fix. "Is that coffee I smell?"

Galiena laughed. Were men always so easily distracted by food and drink? "Of course. We aren't completely uncivilized here in the wilderness." She moved and poured him a cup, adding a generous dollop of whipped cream from the salver.

Hagen looked askance at the cream. "Isn't it a bit early in the morning for that?"

"It's the Herman Göring special, Hagen! Guaranteed to wake you up and cure whatever ails you. So he says, at any rate." She winked at him. "But before you drink that, you don't have to rise for the day if you aren't ready. I intend to go riding, but you are more than welcome to return to your suite and sleep. I didn't want you to wake up and find me gone."

"No. I will go riding with you," Hagen sipped his coffee and sighed. "Provided you have a gentle horse for me. I am no brilliant equestrian. I learned only a few years ago and have had little opportunity to practice."

"I'm just thrilled you know how!" Galiena poured herself a coffee and sat opposite him.

Hagen grinned ruefully. "Because I am a peasant?"

She gave him a very direct look. "No, because you grew up in the city. You aren't a peasant, Hagen." Would he ever get over this pathetic reverse snobbery? Or was it that he was intimidated by the differences in their station?

He seemed to drink his coffee with some haste. "I could get used to this whipped cream. It's very Viennese, is it not?"

"Absolutely. I have to say I prefer it that way." They spoke of banalities over another cup of coffee and then went their separate ways to change. Galiena stopped to tell Gebhardt which horses to have ready as she passed him. When Galiena arrived in her suite, Idalie had her riding clothing prepared, and Galiena was pleased to see that her breeches still fit. Nine months living with Herman Göring hadn't put that much extra weight on her; something of an accomplishment in itself!

Idalie helped her with her riding boots, blouse and cravat before holding the ornately frogged cream cashmere Hussar style greatcoat. Her long hair went into a matching snood and she dismissed her helmet. She hated to wear the darn thing; anyway she hadn't been thrown in years. Galiena put on a Russian style cream fur hat instead. Gold kid gloves completed the ensemble.

Galiena met Hagen in the entrance hall and he was completely turned out in black. He appeared to be wearing his uniform and yet it wasn't like she remembered. All the insignia were missing, making him look particularly crow-like. He wore a crisp white shirt with it and his black tie leapt out at her. The only thing which proclaimed him as SS was his hat. The Totenkopf grinned down at her from his brow with its usual sinister glimmer.

Hagen eyed her very intently, his gaze travelling from her boots to her hat and back down again. Then he inclined his head. "Your Serene Highness, might I say how very fetching you look for a woman who didn't sleep last night."

"Why thank you, Herr Standartenführer. Or should I say that? You seem to have lost all your plumage." She touched his sleeve where normally his red swastika armband would be. "You appear to have lost your political affiliations too, but I can't say as I am entirely displeased by that."

Hagen rolled his shoulders in a modest little shrug. "The men call it Teufel mufti. I occasionally dress down when I am training with the men at the Standarte. Some days it doesn't pay to broadcast who you are too loudly and it amuses me to stomp about dressed like a humble recruit. Keeps the men on their toes. I had one Untersturmführer give me a rather entertaining dressing down before he looked at the face and not just the uniform in front of him," Hagen paused, a mischievous gleam appearing in his eye as he told his story. "As for the swastika, I have an armband with me, but I didn't feel the need to stride about your lair looking the conquering Nazi."

"What would Herr Himmler say?"

He leaned down. "I don't really care at the moment." He kissed her cheek, his hand lingering at the small of her back. "Contrary to the propaganda, the wishes of the Reichsführer-SS and the Fuhrer aren't the only things on an SS officer's mind."

"That is contrary to the propaganda," Galiena winked at him. "Or at least contrary to what uncle Hermann says."

"Would you take it amiss if I told you that Hermann Göring doesn't know everything?" Hagen held out his arm to escort her.

"Now, Herr Kohl! That might just be treason."

He took a step into her space and looked down at her. His black chest filled her entire vision and she resisted the urge to take a step back. "Right now I can very honestly say that the wishes of

Heinrich Himmler and the Fuhrer are about the last things on my mind."

Galiena wrapped her arm about his and lead him out the doors. "Come! Let's go, Hagen." She led him down around the outside of the castle towards the stables. It wasn't especially cold, perhaps two or three degrees above zero and the snow had the looks of impending thaw. A few more days of this weather and it would be gone. The sun shone quite brightly and Galiena pulled her sunglasses from her pocket.

The horses were saddled and waiting for them. Galiena felt a surge of pure joy when she saw her massive Friesian stallion, Bastian and the quiet Oldenburg mare, Wanda. Bastian was an anomaly at over 17 ½ hands high and was pure black with a long wavy mane and tail. He had thick feathers on his legs and his hooves were almost completely covered by them. Wanda was much smaller, 15 ½ hands high and grey in colour, with gentle eyes and a straight mane.

As she approached, Bastian shook his mighty head and snorted at her, as if to say 'Where the hell have you been!' Galiena reached out and patted his nose. "Hello Bastian, my love. I've missed you."

Hagen gave the horse a truly askance glance. "You aren't going to ride that monster, are you?"

"Basty's a big baby. Don't worry, Hagen. He and I have been riding together since I was nineteen." Galiena pulled Bastian's head down by the bridle and rested her cheek beside his, as she produced a carrot from her pocket. "And the route to his heart is via his stomach." A finger directed Hagen towards his horse. "She's Wanda the Wanderer; very gentle and will walk or run as you direct. You don't have to worry about her having a fit of independence and taking off on her own." She looked into Bastian's eye. "Unlike some others I could name." Bastian whickered and his eyes gleamed with mischief. He lipped her cheek, then took her hat in his teeth and dropped it on the ground.

Hagen looked at the hat on the ground. "Having trouble with the troops, Your Serene Highness?"

"Bastian's never been one for women in hats. I don't know why. He's always taken a very childish delight in removing them for me." Galiena bent over and picked up the headwear, tucking it under her arm as she heaved her body into the saddle. That was the only problem with her horse. It was like trying to straddle a mountain.

"Well, Frau Wanda, I'm Herr Kohl." Hagen and the horse eyed each other with some suspicion. "I have never felt entirely comfortable trusting my life to a mode of transportation which thinks for itself. I find myself wondering what I would do was the situation reversed and the answer is never a pleasing one!"

Galiena grinned, the barest hint of a challenge on her face. "Come on now, Doctor Kohl! When was the last time someone put you to the harness?" She settled her hat back on her head.

"In my organization it happens quite frequently." Hagen muttered, almost under his breath as he mounted Wanda.

Bastian was eager to go and began to prance, proudly lifting his hooves to look like the medieval warhorse his ancestors were. Galiena led them off around the woods and into the trails which crisscrossed her lands. They rode in relative silence and Galiena assessed Hagen's skill level on his horse. He wasn't a novice, but she could tell that he wasn't truly comfortable either. Hopefully with time he would be more at ease. Wanda had been a good choice for him.

"Your horses are lovely," Hagen called to her.

"Thank you. They are from the family stud in Westphalia," she replied.

"The family stud?"

"My great uncle Maximillian's family. Grandfather's younger brother. They were almost nineteen years apart." Galiena supplied as she reigned closer to Hagen.

"Was?"

"He and his son, my cousin Edwin, died in the war."

Hagen drew up beside her. "I'm sorry," he said simply. "Where?"

"Uncle Maximillian was an Oberst under Von Mackensen and died at Tannenburg. Edwin at Caporetto. I don't personally remember either of them except as they were represented in Grandfather's stories." She shrugged. "Never let it be said the von Steinbergs shirked in their duty."

"Indeed, no," Hagen answered soberly

"So the stud returned to our family as there was no one else to inherit. Uncle Max' death was a terrible blow to Grandfather. He was the first one in the family to die in the conflict, and while the stud does still run, Grandfather never goes there. I've visited a few times; obviously when I picked Basty, but it suffers from neglect. It's sad to think a man's dream can die with him. Apparently Uncle Max was to bring the Friesian bloodline back to prominence. He saw them, oh, around the turn of the century on a trip through the Netherlands, and started working with them; breeding the Oldenburg line into the strain to strengthen it," Galiena explained.

"You sound as if you have an interest in breeding yourself?" Hagen questioned her as he appeared to relax into his riding.

"No. Not as such. Just a good listener and I enjoy horses. It's a very peaceful place and the house is beautiful, if in some disrepair now. Perhaps we should go there and take a look one day?" She dropped that into the conversation; sometimes a fishing expedition was a good thing.

"If you would like to later this spring?" He returned with a smile. "I have no knowledge of breeding or biology, but it sounds like a pleasant place for a holiday."

She was about to reply when something caught her interest. Someone was thrashing through the snow in the meadow ahead of them. Then the person dropped into the snow abruptly, obscured from view, before popping back up to keep running. "What is that?" Galiena asked, almost to her self.

Hagen shaded his eyes from the glare. "Looks like Eugen. He's drilling, I would suspect. He doesn't miss a day."

"Drilling?" A closer inspection revealed that Eugen was stripped to the waist, wearing just an undershirt inscribed with the double Sigrunen of the SS. His skin was pink with cold and his breath made puffs in the air; but what really arrested her was the fact that the man was built like an animal. His muscles rippled under his skin like Bastian's and were just as pronounced. She had seen mostly naked men before, but she had never seen one like Eugen, ever! Not even the labourers on the estate had muscles like that! She realised she was staring and dropped her gaze to her gloves, hoping the kiss of the cold on her cheeks would camouflage the blush that was crawling up from her neck.

"Eugen is a very sportive man." There was something in Hagen's tone, envy perhaps, which caught Galiena's ear. She looked into his face and found the expression unreadable. "He's a legend around the Hauptamt for his drilling. I doubt there is a man in better shape in all the SS."

"We all have our skills," Galiena paused. "Should we offer him a ride back home?"

Hagen shook his head. "No. He wouldn't want it and I am sure he would be embarrassed if he knew you saw him training. He has a very strict sense of propriety and this would probably be improper in his mind."

"How so?" She laughed. "Eugen's seen me in far less clothing."

Hagen's eyebrow disappeared under the brim of his hat. "Oh?" Volumes were spoken in that one word.

"At the Carinhall at Christmas. He walked in on me when I was swimming. That didn't seem to bother him," Galiena explained. She had been wearing a short silk chemise, which turned transparent in the water.

"But that was him seeing you. You seeing him would be entirely different. I can't define it for you, only he could. As I said, Eugen's sense of propriety defies me sometimes. He says it's because I am a bourgeois and he is a peasant. Different classes, different rules. The man can be down right prudish," the Standartenführer gave his head a mystified shake. "Eugen can be rather enigmatic at times."

"That is strange, I will admit." She reined Bastian around. "Then let us give him his privacy and go another direction."

They rode for almost an hour and a half before they returned to the castle with enough time to wash and change for brunch. Eugen joined them just as they were sitting down, garbed in a modest suit and Galiena couldn't help but picture him unclothed again. Hagen, who Galiena had also seen mostly unclothed in the spa at the Carinhall didn't look anything like his friend. Not that she was comparing, of course, for Hagen was certainly not a man in poor physical condition. Still, there was something rather thrilling about Eugen. She decided she wouldn't think about his person for doing so was making her blush.

Gebhardt entered the room and offered the gentlemen newspapers with their breakfast. Galiena asked him to put a call through to Freffie, with instructions that her friend was to be woken up as the call was extremely urgent. Ten minutes later Gebhardt returned and Galiena went into her grandfather's study to where the phone was.

"Freff, love! I need a huge favour!" She exclaimed in English out of habit.

The voice on the other end of the phone was displeased to say the least. "Gallie, you cad! Do you have any idea what time it is?"

"Almost ten, love!" She shot back.

"I only got to bed five hours ago! Wills says I should tan that adorable behind of yours for waking us up."

Galiena sat with her derriere on her grandfather's desk and slapped her hands against her thigh. "Sorry darling, but it couldn't wait. I have the most wonderful news for you."

"Unless it involves a massive annuity, then it's really too early for me to be interested."

She kneaded her thighs with her hands. "Don't be silly! No. Hagen wants to visit Austria and get to know you and I need you to show him everything he needs to know to survive in our world. You can do that for me, can't you? Please? Pretty please?" Galiena begged.

"Oh, Lord, Gallie! Do you know what you are asking me to do? He might be a little resistant!"

"No. He isn't. And who else to teach him how to be a Lord than you? On my soul! You have to do this for me. You said you would look after him if he came to visit so it's time to step up to the plate! You also said you would adopt him for me," she reminded him. "If you are going to do that, then you should really get to know each other first."

"You're a troll to remind me of obligations this early in the morning." There was a long sigh. "So when is he coming?"

"Sometime this week or next."

"Is this visit political, Gallie? Can he keep his goose stepping down to a dull roar? You know how I hate all that fuss.

Such a bother, all this political claptrap. Live and let live! That's what I have to say." Was the yawn on the other end of the phone real or purely for punctuation and drama?

"I promise he is on vacation, Freff. Just take him out and introduce him round. There's no one better for that than you." She toyed with her fingernails. "He's a good man, Freff. He really is. Trust me on this."

"Oh darling! You know I would do anything for you! All right. Wills is in agreement. Send him round and we will make a Graf out of your brown shirt. And if you want me to adopt him, have your lawyer draft up whatever paperwork is necessary, trot it down here and I will sign on the dotted line. In blood, if you would like. "

"You are a prince, Freff. Really you are!"

"No. I'm a Graf. Being a prince would be deadly dull. Look at you? Practically a princess and you don't get nearly drunk enough. It's a crime. A shame. Our class has been positively defanged since 1918. Even Wills agrees and that says something. Why would I want to be higher up the food chain? I would be bored, bored, bored!"

"I doubt that! Listen, Freff, let me send you a cheque to cover your expenses while you are entertaining my beloved. It's the least I can do." Galiena crossed and uncrossed her ankles primly.

"Don't be daft, Gallie!"

"No. I insist. I have pounds and Reichsmarks. What would be better for you?"

"Pounds, darling. Damn hard to spend Hitler's gold outside of Germany." There was another pause. "And last time I checked we were still an independent nation."

"And who doesn't want to be political? Must dash, Freff. The business managers are coming any moment to tell me that I am not equipped to look after the family firm, and I am going to agree with them."

"So who is going to mind the store if you aren't?"

Now there was a question to dodge. "Oh I will think of something, Freff! You know me. Ta! Ta!" She hung up the phone just as Gebhardt knocked.

"The Ritter von Kleist and Herr von Klopfer, your Serene Highness."

Galiena stood and greeted the two older men. "Gentlemen. Do have a seat. We have quite a task before us today. I need to know if it is possible for the business affairs of the family to be run from outside Germany. More specifically, could they be run if one was in Brazil. Secondly, if they can, I need to know what we can easily offer to the SS to secure my Grandfather's release. We also need to discern the exact nature of the charges under which my grandfather is being held I am absolutely positive that if he can be released, it will be conditional that he leave Germany, probably even Europe, never to return." After all, that was what she intended to propose to Herr Himmler when she saw him. The world was big enough for her and her Grandfather, but Germany wasn't. If she was going to buy him out of prison, she would set the terms, and his being close to her was absolutely forbidden. "Lastly, I need papers drawn up for Frederick Graf von Reitersbach to adopt Hagen Kohl of Berlin and formerly Augsburg."

Chapter 14
February 21, 1938

Hagen was travelling alone for the first occasion in years. When was the last time he went somewhere without Eugen right behind his shoulder? Had it really been since he came back from America? Eugen had been his constant shadow from the moment Hagen joined the SS and Hagen hadn't taken any holidays from that date. It was a very strange feeling. Almost as if he was wearing his drawers on the outside of his pants. Everything was fine, but something felt terribly wrong.

He chided himself. What was he thinking? He was a grown man! Thirty eight years old. He could go to Vienna without his uncle Eugen to wipe his ass for him like some six year old. He and Eugen weren't joined at the hip and it wasn't as if he had been away from the man for long. They had driven down from Berlin to Salzburg last night in an unmarked SS Mercedes. To keep up the fiction that Hagen was not in Austria on business to the Graf von Reitersbach, Hagen was taking the train from Salzburg to Vienna on his own, and his host was to collect him at the train station.

Hagen found an empty compartment in the 1st class section of the train, and settled himself down in comfort. The buttery leather upholstery was well stuffed and moulded itself to his frame. There was plenty of legroom and he thrust his legs out contentedly before him as he watched the station roll by. It was a feeling he could get very used to. He didn't see a life in steerage before him, and while the shock of Galiena's lifestyle had mostly worn off, there was great comfort in knowing poverty was never going to stare him in the face. He just hadn't contemplated the luxury. While he knew people lived like that, seeing it, and experiencing it for himself was an entirely different thing.

The door to the compartment opened and a dark hatted head poked its way in. Blue eyes, a thick dark beard, and two long curls framed the face. Hagen looked at the face in annoyance, and then sighed. A Jew. One of those orthodox ones. They had another name, but Hagen didn't know it. "Might I join you in this compartment, mein Herr?" The man's tone was high and nasal.

The kind of voice that gnawed at one's brain like nails on a chalkboard.

Hagen eyed the man and then shrugged, gesturing to the seat opposite himself. He wasn't at home, and quite frankly, he didn't care too much. The man didn't appear to have a passel of children, and would hopefully not be talkative. His new companion bustled opposite him, and with great flourish took off his greatcoat laying it across the seat. The process seemed to take an inordinate amount of time, but then the man settled, pulling out spectacles and a book. Stroking his luxuriant beard, the Jew read quietly to himself.

A quick scratch at the fur on his own chin made Hagen wonder if the other man thought Hagen to be Jewish as well. Beards certainly weren't the fashion in the Reich. He thrust out his chin and eyed the red gold stubble with some distaste. It was itchy. The urge to scratch was the very devil to resist. He hadn't worn facial hair since the war and now he remembered why. But it did serve its purpose. He certainly looked far more like an academic and far less like an SS officer. The only thing which would give him away to the initiated would be his Totenkopf ring, and they were still quite rare in the SS. Nonexistent in Austria at this time. It wasn't as if his host didn't know Hagen was in the organization and those people high enough in the Austrian SS who would recognize the ring should know who he was. He rubbed his thumb over the Sigrunen on the underside of the ring, somewhat absently as was his habit. It calmed him.

It seemed as if he had just closed his eyes when there was another discrete knock on the compartment door and a steward entered the compartment. "Excuse me, gentlemen, but can I interest you in anything from the dining car?"

Hagen and Eugen had eaten in Salzburg just before Hagen had boarded the train and as such, Hagen wasn't hungry. "No, thank you," He replied.

His companion also demurred and as the steward left the man began rustling through his pack. "I never eat on these trains. The cost is too much to be borne! Not when I have a nice mutton sandwich in my bag. Yes. The wife makes it for me in the morning." He pulled out the sandwich, made of thick, dark brown bread and attacked it with vigour.

Hagen attempted to keep from frowning. "Very lucky for you." He tried to be polite, returning to his window and musings. A childish part of him winced, however. Mutton. Yuck. The more he thought about it, the more he wanted to make a face. He was not fond of mutton. He had eaten enough tough stringy mutton when he studied in England to last a lifetime. Not that he was really all that picky about food. Back during the war he had ingested God only knew what and been thankful for it, but these days, he could afford to be choosy. In actual fact, the more he let his thoughts glide over his travelling companion's meal, the more he had a terrible craving for a ham and cheese sandwich. Followed by a side of bacon. What was it about knowing another's food restrictions that made another man crave it? The human mind was truly a strange thing.

Hagen opened his briefcase and removed a large envelope which Galiena had asked him to take to Fredrick von Reitersbach. He was burning to know what was inside. It was a large, heavy vellum envelope and she sealed the damn thing with an old wax seal. While with some effort he thought he could lift the seal; he had read of ways to do such things using a heated spatula but he decided not to do so. Hagen would respect her privacy, even though it was of terrible frustration to him. Hagen hated secrets. No. That wasn't it. He just hated her secrets and after she met with her advisors, she seemed to have a big one, because she kept slipping him sidelong glances which reeked of guilt. That worried him. It made him believe that she was up to something, and something that he obviously wouldn't approve of. Not good. Not good at all.

He raised the envelope to his nose. It smelled of her perfume. He was very fond of that scent and he let it drift on his nostrils for a moment, before he slid his hands up and down the envelope. It just felt like a letter. A thick one. She obviously had a great deal to say to the man. Gritting his teeth with irritation, Hagen put the envelope back into his case and pulled out a book. It was a compilation of the letters and writings of Madame Helene Blavatsky, a Russian mystic who founded Theosophy. The book had been sent to him by Himmler who wanted his opinion on the woman and her teachings. Thus far, Hagen thought she was a crank, but he was only a quarter of the way through. Blavatsky had been dead for forty years, and as far as Hagen was concerned her pseudo-Buddhist philosophy should have died with her. Himmler also wanted Hagen to read the Bhagavad-Gita; had raved about it, in fact. Hagen was idly curious. Himmler had given him a copy of that text as well. It certainly had to be better than this tripe from Blavatsky. Hagen wasn't a religious man, but he had his own spirituality. Like all high ranking members of the SS he had officially renounced his Christianity and in his case, had renounced it personally as well. Would he fill the gap with the teachings of a third century Hindu Brahman? No, probably not, but was it not the nature of man to struggle with the nature of God as he got older?

"That looks like a weighty tome, the way you keep hefting it," his companion remarked casually.

Hagen snorted. "One might say that."

"I just thought I did," the man said with a smile.

"Indeed." Why did the man keep talking to him? Hagen read the same page about three times and then flipped to the beginning of the book, reading the inscription. "My Friend! A little something for you to review, contemplate and absorb. Looking forward to our next discussion. H. Himmler." He would have preferred to review, contemplate and absorb his files, but he was not travelling with anything official or work related. That would be foolishness, given the circumstances. He wouldn't want one of his beloved files to get into the wrong hands. To do so would be tantamount to disaster.

In actual fact, Hagen was quite pleased with the inscription. When Himmler had sent him to work for Heydrich, Hagen had the very real feeling he had outlived his acquaintance with the Reichsführer. Now that he was back in Himmler's personal basket, he felt the glow of being close to the throne, as it were. To top it all off, unlike some, Heydrich included, Hagen genuinely liked and appreciated the Reichsführer. Being back in the inner circle made Hagen feel appreciated in return. His life was changing in leaps and bounds. A year ago if asked where he would be in a year's time, he would have replied, the same place I am now. More the fool he. Soon he would be married to Galiena, a wealthy and aristocratic woman. He was Heinrich Himmler's personal investigator. He had an understanding with Hermann Göring. Everything in his life was revitalizing at an incredible rate.

What was she up to? Hagen closed the book in his lap and glared out the window. What was going on in that mind of hers? Something. And he didn't like how she looked at Eugen. Was he jealous? He had ordered Eugen to spend more time with her. That was true. He had never had issue with Eugen's stature before. Eugen had always been bigger than Hagen, since the first day they met. What a day that was. Ypres, 1917. Yet Hagen had never felt insignificant to Eugen before, and that was how he felt, as he watched his fiancée ogle his comrade. No. She wasn't ogling Eugen. Hagen grinned in spite of himself. Not like she had ogled him back at Christmas in Hermann Göring's steam room. Now that had been a look and a half. That look gave him a great deal of hope for the future.

"It would appear Standartenführer Kohl is having a most pleasant thought."

"I am," Hagen replied. Then comprehension dawned. He never introduced himself to the Jew. He most certainly hadn't. And the man was sitting there, grinning at him like a complete idiot.

"Very kind of you to share your compartment with a member of the tribe," the Jew continued, his voice dropping. "I'm sure that the Standartenführer has broken at least one or two rules of the Reichsführer's by not throwing me out on my ear, but I understand that you are on holiday." The voice was so familiar and it terrified him.

Every muscle was on the alert and the adrenaline was pumping through his veins. "Who are you?" Hagen hissed.

"Now I am crushed, though I must admit you proved my point for me. Don't you remember we had a conversation a few years ago about how every man in Germany sees a Jew, but absolutely no man actually looks at him. It's a perfect disguise. Well, not always. I often get harassed by the SA, but then, so do you, don't you, Herr Standartenführer?" The man chuckled.

"Jesus Christ! Strohkeller!" Hagen blinked, as the identity of the voice penetrated the impossibility of the visage in front of him. "My God!"

Hauptscharführer Strohkeller, the chief of Hagen's group of watchers lifted his hat, and his curls incidentally, in greeting. Strohkeller was an acquaintance of Eugen's from the Great War, as were many who worked for Hagen, but other than that, the man was a mystery. There were a few things which Hagen knew about the man. First was that he had been a leader of a black hand gang during the war; a group of men who crept into No-Man's-Land, sunk themselves into the mud and gore, before springing up like wraiths to cut down unwary English patrols. It was a terribly dangerous task, few black handers seemed to survive the war, and most of them seemed to be a part of Strohkeller's crew. Tales of the brutalities perpetrated by the black handers on their victims were legendary in the trenches, and all of them were just the tiniest bit mad. Secondly, Hagen suspected that Strohkeller's sympathies did not lay with Adolf Hitler and the Nazi party; in fact, Hagen suspected that the watcher worked for him only as a means to an end. Something to keep him going for the world at large held very little interest for the man. Thirdly, there was much more to Strohkeller than met the eye, but the man revealed very little about himself. "Hauptsturmführer Freisler thought you might be lonely, and so he sent me to keep an eye on you. Really, Herr Standartenführer! You should be more observant! I could have shanked you in ribs and no one would be the wiser!"

It was like he had been tossed in a lake of ice cold water. Realisation mixed with uselessly late fear washed over him. "And I would have deserved it, too. Dear God! Do I feel like the village idiot."

"The Hauptsturmführer was concerned you wouldn't pay sufficient attention to your surroundings because you're used to having him do the watching for you. It's a simple enough mistake. I see it all the time. As soon as a man has bodyguards, he gets so busy enjoying the wonders in his brain and the stars in his eyes to actually look at the bastards all around him," Strohkeller paused. "With all due respect, of course!"

"You are quite right. You know, I pride myself on being observant." Hagen's mouth was completely dry.

"Germans don't look at Jews," the other man replied with a shrug. "As I said before, they see them, but they don't want to look at them. Brilliant propaganda. Can make my life a great deal easier." Then he smiled. "But they also never deign to dress like them either. I'm an aberration, but then that's why I'm so good at what I do!"

Hagen gave the man a pointed look. "I also don't consider myself to be a bigot."

"Obviously not, Herr Standartenführer! I thought I was going to have to stand in the passage like an organ grinder's monkey." The man gave Hagen a long look; leaving him with the feeling he had passed some sort of important test. "Not that I think there's any SA on this train, or at least if there are Austrian SA on it, they are keeping their hands to themselves. In Berlin I would have been hassled by now, if not spat on." Strohkeller plucked at his cuffs. "I hate the fucking SA. Pardon my language. I can watch just about anyone, but they make me want to vomit."

"No pardon necessary. They make me want to vomit as well," Hagen agreed wholeheartedly.

Strohkeller reached into his breast pocket and pulled out a thin flask and offered it to Hagen. "Vodka, that. From Ost Prussia. A little bird sends it to me."

Hagen opted for a sip for it would be impolite to refuse. "Zum Wohl[9]," he said in toast. The beverage was like lighter fluid and burned a trail right down his throat to his groin. It was practically melting through him! It was all he could do to keep his composure and not cough. He passed the mickey back to Strohkeller.

The faux Jew took the flask and raised it. "Mazel tov." He obviously was not so affected by the drink as Hagen.

"I didn't know you spoke Hebrew?" Hagen questioned, again observing the mystery which was Strohkeller.

"Don't really. Just a few words, here and there. Enough to convince someone who isn't a Jew that I am a Jew. I used to live around them." Strohkeller sneezed violently and rubbed his nose on his shirt cuff. "I owe them. It's served me well." There was something about that gesture; a minute hesitation which made Hagen decided it was forced. As if Strohkeller knew exactly what bad manners such an action was and forced himself to do it anyway. Then again, maybe it was all in Hagen's imagination. Goddamn it! The man was such an enigma.

"I can see that," Hagen agreed. "It's a brilliant disguise."

---

[9] Cheers

The spy winked at him. "So who are we watching in Vienna? Who do you want me to run down?" Strohkeller tucked into his sandwich again with vigour.

"I want you and your men to start with everyone close to Oberführer Ernst Kaltenbrunner. I think there is a leak somewhere up near the top of his group. Quite high up, I would guess. Someone who is telling the NAO exactly where and when to attack. I don't suspect Kaltenbrunner himself. He seems to be completely above board, but as for the rest? I know this goes against the grain, Strohkeller, but I wouldn't trust anyone you see in the black, because one of them is a traitor. We need to find out who the traitor is. I believe this person is even more dangerous than the head of the NAO, because if we don't find the traitor, he will just give his information to someone else when we are done with the NAO. Focus on people with access to the SS treasuries as two of those have been looted." Hagen looked out the window again; Austria was such a beautiful country. "And it's pretty damn hard for us to get the money back when the NAO gives it to orphanages, or, and worse, Veteran's widows groups."

"I see your point."

"I thought you would. It isn't that I don't feel pity for the people who are receiving the money. The Reichsführer-SS agrees with me on that point, which is why we haven't and won't take it back, but the Allgemeine SS isn't going to bankrupt itself to cover the lost funds of the Austrian SS if the Austrians can't plug their leak." Hagen slapped his thigh in frustration. "We must find the traitor. There is no option for failure."

"Of course. If he's out there, we will find him," Strohkeller said with complete confidence before his face took on a very sly cast. "I can find anything, include Hitler's missing testicle."

Hagen decided to ignore that. "I have no doubt as to your ability to sniff these bastards out, Strohkeller. You're the best. Hell! You just proved it yet again!" He tucked his book back into his briefcase.

"Thank you, Herr Standartenführer." The man elegantly buffed his nails on his trouser leg the languid motion betraying Strohkeller's earlier nose wipe on his on his sleeve. "It's nice to be appreciated!"

"Now I want you and your men to coordinate with Eugen in Vienna. I assume he briefed you on all of this?"

Strohkeller gave him a long, hard look as if to say 'don't be such an idiot.' "Pension Edelweiss. There's an original name if ever I heard it. On the Mozartgasse, close to the Neumanngasse. For all intents and purposes, it's going to be our safe house. That is what Freisler told me. Is that wise? Do we know that the place is safe?"

"The owner has no political affiliations whatsoever, and he's a very old friend." Hagen smiled faintly. "Doctor György Demeter would never betray me, so do mind the furniture when you are there. He isn't one of us, but he isn't fond of the Fatherland Front either. György's motto is live and let live. He doesn't have time for politics and never did." Hagen mused, almost to himself.

"Doesn't sound Austrian to me? Demeter?" Strohkeller questioned carefully. It wasn't said with suspicion, more like curiosity. Strohkeller existed by trying to find out as much as he could about people. It was how he stayed alive in his business.

"His family were Hungarians who settled in the capital. He was born there. His German is perfect, but he identifies himself as a Hungarian who lives in Austria. He doesn't care who runs Austria so long as Hungary stays independent. Interesting for a man who has never lived a year in his own nation, isn't it?"

"Sounds like the Baltic Germans." The watcher looked up, glancing out the windows. "It appears we are on the outskirts. I should move along. Don't want to be seen in the same compartment with you. I think I will head to the back of the train with the peasants."

Hagen held out his hand. "Good luck, Strohkeller. Don't get yourself killed."

Strohkeller raised a brow at Hagen's words. "That's never on the menu. Watch yourself, Herr Standartenführer. The SA can get you down here, just as easily as they can get you in Germany. Remember that." His ice cold hand slipped into Hagen's and they shook.

"Consider the warning heard," Hagen replied.

The other man nodded his head again, his curls springing along his cheekbones, and left the compartment. Hagen breathed a sigh of relief. He couldn't believe he had been so blind. Strohkeller was right. He was far too used to having Eugen watching his back all the time. This had been a very suitable wake up call. He wondered if Strohkeller would brief Eugen on Hagen's complete stupidity? If that happened, and it would serve him right if it did, Eugen would be intolerable. On the other hand, who was Eugen to send in one of the men to test him? His friend, that was who, he admitted to himself.

Hagen drifted over to his other friend, one who he felt a slight qualm at involving in all of this. György Demeter and Hagen Kohl met what seemed like centuries ago, but in fact only eleven years had passed. They met in England, when Hagen was at Cambridge, and György was at the University College of London. Two men, both scholars and former enemies of the country they were in, they had formed an association which lasted to this day. Demeter had been finishing his specialization in psychiatry, particularly war veterans' experiences and shell shock. He had published a note in one of the many Cambridge student newspapers looking for veterans who were willing to discuss their experiences. On a whim, Hagen had contacted the man, and their discussions had quickly turned from the war to culture and literature. They had a mutual understanding of how difficult it was to be one of the enemy at the university.

György was probably the smartest man of Hagen's acquaintance. He spoke Magyar, German, Czech, English and Italian fluently. Not only that, he could communicate adequately in French and Spanish. The same age as Hagen, he had missed the war but had lived through the subsequent revolution in Austria at the war's end. He had never truly explained to Hagen his interest in war psychiatry, only to say simply that his father, a Vezérörnagy[10] in the Austro-Hungarian army, had been terribly afflicted by his experiences in the war. That was a good enough answer for Hagen. He knew what the war was like.

They had maintained their friendship over the years. György was often in Germany to speak at conferences and universities, being quite eminent in his field these days. They wrote each other letters every few months. It was a comfortable, intellectual friendship. When they saw each other, they spoke long

---

[10] Generalmajor

into the night and copious bottles of wine were consumed. Hagen had never been to Vienna stay at the Pension which György inherited from his mother. He felt a little guilty about it, but life had been too busy.

Now he was involving his friend in work, and that was perhaps not the kindest thing Hagen had ever done. When he telephoned György to see if there were rooms available, the man had been most amiable. György Demeter knew that Eugen was going to stay at the pension, and that Hagen needed two other rooms for business reasons. It hadn't been a problem in the slightest. Hagen had to insist that the rooms be paid for, as his friend didn't even want to charge him. Proof doctors weren't good businessmen! György also knew that Hagen was going to be in the city, but that he, himself, would be unable to stay at the Pension Edelweiss. That also hadn't been a problem. György wasn't the sort to get hurt feelings over such things.

György was an interesting fellow in that he really wasn't aware of politics. He was interested in his research. György was fully aware of the source of Hagen's employment, and a vague idea that Hagen was a policeman of sorts and beyond that didn't want to know. No. That wasn't quite accurate. Doctor Demeter had been very interested the interrogation techniques Hagen used, and had given him many ideas on how to hypothetically conduct an interrogation. Sometimes György could explore an idea in directions which even left Hagen a little cold. Yet for his friend, it was completely theoretical. While György specialized in putting the mind back together, the act of breaking it was naturally of interest. Maybe it was the cold humour of medicine, of knowing too much about how the human being operates which chilled Hagen. Sometimes György would get a look in his eye which made Hagen feel just the tiniest bit like a lab rat.

Now Hagen was sending him Eugen! Now there would be an interesting living arrangement. Of course the two had met, but Eugen was completely silent around György. The giant viewed the psychiatrist with a suspicion which bordered on fear. That, too, was probably understandable. The doctor was quite fascinated by Hagen's war stories of Eugen. Eugen's comparative morality was also of great interest to György. Hagen was almost disappointed to be missing the show. The small Hungarian stalking the huge

Bavarian through the pension, trying to lure Eugen into speaking. It was almost too much to contemplate.

Hagen surveyed the city outside. They were pulling into the station and he carefully repacked his briefcase. He didn't want to leave anything behind. No scraps of paper to fall into the wrong hands, not that he had such things, but the paranoia was settling in. There was something about a new operation which set the blood astir. He took a deep breath, putting his persona in place. A slightly different Hagen Kohl. A Hagen Kohl who was coming to Vienna to be educated in the nobility. A Hagen Kohl who was also coming to root out the New Austrian Order. Two different men, inhabiting the same body. That was a new experience. He had never played the beater in the hunt before. No. Usually he was the man with the rifle, to bring down the prey. He didn't know if he liked this feeling. He felt naked and exposed. Inwardly Hagen shook himself. He had a job to do, and he wasn't going to shirk now. His task was by far the easiest of all. If he survived the visit with Freffie von Reitersbach; he had to clarify that point in all fairness to himself.

Chapter 15
February 21, 1938

Hagen smoothed his navy double breasted jacket and closed his black overcoat as he stepped onto the station platform. Vienna was chilly and overcast, the sky depressing in shades of slate. Ominous weather, to be sure. He adjusted his hat and surveyed the Westbahnhof Station, looking for his host. Surprisingly enough, Fredrick von Reitersbach and Wilhelm von Glass were lounging indolently against a light stand not ten feet away; looking every inch the bored aristocrats they were. They were turned out exquisitely in charcoal grey; their suits almost identical, but with different shirt and tie colours from each other. Von Reitersbach was tapping the silver dragonhead of his cane against a tailored shoulder in tune to a tempo heard only in his mind.

Hagen picked up his briefcase and approached the pair. Von Glass saw him first and nodded slowly, stroking a grey leather clad finger on von Reitersbach's sleeve. It was an intimate gesture and Hagen's skin crawled as he watched it. The Graf's grey fedora lifted and the blue eyes searched his before the man bounced his body away from the black iron pole and approached Hagen.

"My dear Doctor Kohl! Roaringly splendid to see you, old chap!" The words were spoken in English. It appeared to Hagen that von Reitersbach preferred the English language to German. He tossed the cane from one hand to the other, grasping it in the middle of the shaft.

"Your Illustrious Highness," Hagen replied politely, using the German words for their titles. The English translations for those words escaped him. "Ritter von Glass."

"Ye gads! I am neither illustrious nor high! Call me Freffie. You are practically family, Kohl and no one in Vienna calls me Frederick. Well, there might be the odd one, but they're all over the age of eighty and you are a damn sight under that age," Freffie replied in a bored tone. "Besides, old chap, the last Graf von Reitersbach was a terrible man who was, thankfully, sent to the heavens by an irate old warhorse. I certainly don't want to be associated with him."

"As you wish," Hagen acquiesced, feeling chilled at the complete disregard shown by Von Reitersbach for his sire.

Von Glass appeared to sense his feelings. He clapped Hagen on the arm. "One gets used to it, Kohl. Do call me Wills. I am in complete agreement with Freff. You are practically family."

"Hagen, gentlemen, please!" He wasn't going to stand on ceremony if they weren't.

"Capital, Hagen. Capital," Freffie laughed gamely. "Now, Gallie tells me you don't have a man, so I suppose we shall have to acquire your baggage and head off to the town house. We have a busy few weeks ahead of us. Things to do. Places to go! People to see. I'm under strict orders, don't you know!"

"So I am given to understand," Hagen replied.

"Gallie is a stern taskmistress." Wills gestured away from the platform. "But she is our Goddess and we worship her."

Hagen glanced over at the man's rather aristocratic profile. "That is an interesting way of describing her." He commented as they move off down the stairs.

"Isn't she yours?" The blue eyes were like ice.

Freffie gestured with his cane. "I think the baggage comes out down there. Wills, be a good boy and go take a look. This is rather new for me. Shoo, love!"

"Yes, my master. Whatever you say!" The older man tipped his hat and moved away.

There was something about the man's apparent submissiveness to von Reitersbach which Hagen feel more than slightly awkward. "I can attend to my own luggage."

"Nonsense. You are our guest. And don't mind him. He's in a bit of a mood at the moment." Freffie lead them off. "I think he's a little put out by Miss Gallie getting married to a complete stranger. He will get over it with time."

The words complete stranger felt like a substitution the way Freffie spoke them. "My apologies if this visit isn't at the most opportune time," Hagen returned evenly at he watched the Graf.

"Tosh, man! Wills can get over his snit. He thinks you are going to marry my girl, take her money and break her heart. It's making him terribly cross." The cane returned to its journey from hand to hand.

The subject was coming up far sooner than Hagen had expected. "Is that what you think?"

Freffie shot him a remarkably shrewd look. "What I think is hardly important, my man. What is important is what Gallie thinks." Then that flippant grin spread across his face. "And it would be hard for even me to render Gallie penniless."

"That is hardly an answer, Herr Graf." Hagen used the man's title to make a point.

"Then to use the vernacular, Hagen, the jury is still out. You would be a damned fool not to marry her for her money. Hell! You would be a complete idiot if the thought never crossed your mind, and you do not have the marks of idiocy. No. Not at all," Freffie appeared to be considering his words very carefully. "I dislike your politics, Hagen, and I know your politics dislike me. Makes things rather difficult, but Gallie professes to have an attachment to you, and if I were to get in the way of that, it would drive you ever closer into her affections, and me out. My somewhat unique situation allows me to watch this running around of men and women with a slightly different perspective from the rest of you. So what am I to do?"

"I think you are going to examine the crude bourgeois barbarian and if he doesn't live up to your standards, you will very carefully and subtly undermine him until your Gallie changes her mind," Hagen supplied easily, for it was exactly what he would do.

The silver head of the cane slashed out as Freffie bowed rather extravagantly. "Ah my dear Doctor Kohl! You malign me. Of course you are right, but I feel slighted to hear it so bluntly spoken."

"My most insincere apologies," Hagen inclined his head.

"You might just be better at this than I thought." Freffie straightened as Wills appeared with a porter. "In all frankness, it's a tangle for me, Hagen and I won't lie to you. On the other hand, I really don't need to deal with it. If you pass muster, as the soldier boys say, then I will prepare you for the acid test. You might be able to woo Hermann Göring. The man is a German and a Nazi, as are you. I'm sure it's a bond of some sort. The person I am referring to is Dickey. Jackboots, swastika, swagger stick and all, he will grind you up and feed you to his hounds if he decides you are using Galiena." Freffie leaned in with slightly narrowed eyes and made an elaborate and useless gesture with his fingers. "He's entirely Scottish, you know and despite all that stiff upper lipped civilization, they are really quite insane. Make your average German look quite civilized. Have you seen what they eat? Haggis! Heard their music? Dickey plays the bagpipes? They go into battle in skirts. Right bunch of loonies. What is it Noel Coward says? Mad dogs and Englishmen? The Scots are rather worse."

"I do believe that is the song, yes."

"That was written with Dickey in mind. And unlike me, he doesn't have an artistic sensibility. Not a shred. Not a drop. That's the Scottish blood. Savages. Brutes." Freffie grinned. "Damn! I miss Scotland. The thighs on those Highlanders. Bless me!"

Hagen was lost by Freffie's tirade. "I've never been there." During his sojourn in England he had stayed in the south. Small towns had big memories of an entire generation of their sons dead in Flanders and in rural England, a German was still the enemy.

"Well after the wedding we shall all have to go! Perhaps on the honeymoon." Freffie glided over towards Wills and the porter. "Well, Wills, what have we here? The luggage man? I see no luggage. Where is it?"

Hagen handed over his luggage tickets to the porter who promptly disappeared. "Must be collected."

"Ye gads! How completely tiresome. Yes. We really must get you a man. Do you always have to go through this when you travel?"

Hagen blinked, astounded by the man's ignorance. "No. When I travel it's usually work related and I have someone who attends to these details!"

"Oh! So you do have a kind of man? A batman or an adjutant or some such thing," Wills asked, a snide undertone to his words.

"My men do look after the movement of my cases, yes. Do I have a body servant? No. Galiena was quite disturbed to find out I didn't have one," Hagen corrected him.

Freffie nodded. "Dear me, yes you do need one. Very important." He pursed his lips. "You should have brought one of your men with you. That would have been just fine with us."

214

Hagen met Wills' eyes and said very directly, "No. I decided that I should leave work behind and travel light. It's quite refreshing to not have someone watching me all the time." He couldn't resist saying it, for Strohkeller the Jew casually strolled past them, almost close enough to brush Wills' overcoat.

"Yes. Yes, I can imagine. Well you can relax now. No Nazis at our place. They tend to avoid Wills and me," Freffie replied with exaggerated innocence. "Can't for the life of me think why!"

Wills rolled his eyes at Freffie. "There's the porter. Shall we adjourn to the motor? Cleves is waiting outside and I'm quite sure the man with the luggage can follow us."

Hagen followed as the two men led him through the crowds and out of the Westbahnhof. Freffie stopped talking, and breezed his way along like a tidal wave. There were people in the station who called to him, and he acknowledged them with a regal inclination of his wide brimmed hat, but didn't stop. There was an élan about the man, a flair that Hagen noticed and was reminded of a General reviewing his troops. He was completely at ease with his power and influence. It was something that one or two of Hagen's superiors could learn.

As they exited the Westbahnhof, a stern looking, elderly matron stormed up to them, the black ostrich plumes in her hat shaking furiously. "Frederick! I should turn you over my knee and spank you! You quite ruined my soiree!" She spoke in German.

Wills leaned into Hagen. "One of the very few who call him that. Prepare yourself, Kohl. You will be on stage in a matter of moments," he whispered conspiratorially.

"Tante Stanzi!" Freffie clicked his heels and leaned in to kiss the old woman on both cheeks, but an imperious hand stopped him.

"No, Frederick. You may not kiss me. Wilhelm may, for I am sure that he is entirely innocent of your crimes!" The woman presented her cheek to Wills. "Greet me, Wilhelm."

"Of course, Madame!" Wills kissed each cheek and then stepped back. "I am always innocent, Madame! He's the rogue."

"What on earth did I do, Tante Stanzi? You've wounded me, and astounded me, all in one blow. Can't think of how many times that's happened!" Freffie looked quite hurt.

"You assured me that you would drift by my musical evening Tuesday last and you did not show. I was quite counting on you to come lighten the evening, and it turned out a complete disaster in your absence. I should have you horsewhipped through the streets. Why were you not there, Frederick?" The old woman pointed a black leather gloved finger right under Freffie's nose.

"Tante Stanzi, I really must apologise. Did I not send round a card? Something else interfered at the very last moment and I was completely unable to attend. I'm sure I sent around a card! Flowers, too!" Freffie rounded on Wills. "Didn't we send flowers?"

"Camellias from the hothouse, or so I recall," Wills supplied helpfully, addressing the Gräfin.

"Hothouse blossoms and a note after the fact do not salvage my musical evening." The old woman returned with burning eyes and then she softened. "It turned so positively dull, Frederick. The same old songs. The same old conversations."

"I can hardly believe that, Madame!" Wills interjected.

"Really, Tante Stanzi! I do apologize. I prostrate myself before you. It was beastly of me not to attend, especially with so little notice. I shall endeavour not to do it again," Freffie answered, trying to reassure the Gräfin.

There was a loud harrumph, and Hagen felt the grey eyes turning on him. "And who is this, Frederick? Have you so completely lost your manners that you don't introduce me to your associates?"

"Might I present Doctor Hagen Kohl to you, Tante Stanzi? Hagen, this is the Gräfin von Manderscheid." Freffie laid a finger alongside his nose. "He is the fiancé of our little Galiena."

Hagen clicked his heels and bowed very formally. "Madame Gräfin."

"Oh!" The Gräfin replied and then slapped Freffie in the arm. "Do you mean to tell me Meinrad von Steinberg is actually letting that sweet child out of his grasp? I almost refuse to believe it, Frederick."

Wills adjusted his gloves. "It is the truth, Madame." Disapproval reeked from the man with every gesture.

"Wonders will never cease." The woman studied Hagen. "And who is your family, Doctor von Kohl?"

Hagen was about to correct her, when Freffie interjected. "Distantly one of mine, Tante Stanzi. Very distant. Cadet branch. Bit of a surprise that. It would appear great great Uncle Hugo had a life we knew nothing about. Hagen doesn't use his von yet, but I plan to make him a true blue von Reitersbach soon After all, I'm the last of the line, and we would hate for it to become extinct on my death."

"Your great great uncle Hugo was a notorious buggerer, Frederick. Even I know that. I remember him. That's how we know you come by it honestly." The Gräfin poked Freffie in the shoulder. "Why we don't think you are completely unnatural!"

Freffie smiled lazily. "Not so, Tante Stanzi. I've seen the papers m'self. It was after being denied his true love that old Hugo turned to a life of Greek delights. No woman could ever match her."

"Interesting. I would refine your tale, Frederick. That's not going to wash. No. Perhaps I will refine it for you. Much better." The Gräfin smiled at Hagen. "Not to worry, Herr Doctor. Your secret is safe with me. You are a smart man, marrying the chit. Unlike this foolish boy, that is a family of substance."

"Thank you." Hagen bowed again.

"Do remember me to the Pfalzgraf when you see him." The old woman almost seemed to flutter.

"Of course, Madame." Hagen responded trying externally not to let the irony taint his words. He didn't intend to see Meinrad von Steinberg for a very, very long time. If he went there sooner he would probably kill the old bastard, so deep and complete was his rage at the man.

Again he felt inspected and he met the old woman's gaze quite directly for a second time. "Who are you, Doctor Kohl, that you have managed to inveigle yourself into one of the oldest, most wealthy families left in Germany? You are a stranger to me; couple that with a man who must concoct a tale of family to be accepted by my class, and you are quite correct to concoct that tale, leaves me most curious as to how you became affianced to our dear young Pfalzgräfin. Meinrad von Steinberg would never accept you," the old woman hissed. "Never. You betray yourself with every gesture. You are not one of us."

217

Hagen was taken aback to be spoken to quite so directly, and Freffie had paled noticeably. He sized up the woman carefully. This woman was not the sort one lied to and a thought came to mind. Months ago, Hermann Göring had shared with Hagen that his Austrian godfather, the Ritter von Epenstein had taken an interest in the von Steinberg family. Perhaps that glimmer was a way out of this situation. "I am continuing in the interests of the Ritter von Epenstein," Hagen said finally before smiling. "That and she absolutely entrances me."

The ancient Gräfin studied him. "Does she, indeed?"

Wills' eyes also focused on him. "Interesting turn of phrase that, Hagen."

Freffie smiled brilliantly at the woman. "Isn't he a love, Tante Stanzi?"

"Not your kind, Frederick." There was a long pause. "Send him around my place next week. I will do what I can to help you both. Great great uncle Hugo indeed! Frankly Frederick, I simply don't understand you and your antics. Why can't you settle down and act like the peer you are?"

"My dear Tante Stanzi, there are so few options available for a man of my skills. I'm no inventor, so I cannot be a von Zeppelin. I'm no great warrior, so I can't be a von Hindenburg. I'm nothing really! No talents. No abilities, ergo I must be content with myself and continue to be as I am." Frederick bowed again. "And I am quite content, Tante Stanzi. I assure you. I have no ambitions towards any further greatness."

"You are simply impossible Frederick. I cannot understand why a solid young gentleman like Wilhelm tolerates you," the old woman harrumphed.

Wills chuckled. "I do believe it's because his tailor is quite gifted."

The Gräfin von Manderscheid swatted Wills in the arm with an elegant hand. "Rogue! Don't be impertinent with me!"

A station employee with far more braid on his uniform than the porter came up to the Gräfin and snapped his heels together. "Madame Gräfin."

"What is it, young man?"

218

"The train is scheduled to depart immediately, Madame. If you will accompany me, I will ensure that you do not miss your train," the man stated.

"If I must."

"Good bye, then, Tante Stanzi. When will you be back in our beloved Austria?" Freffie asked as he took his aunt's hand again.

"Next week. I am going to Salzburg to visit the Baroness von Braun. She is quite terribly afflicted at the moment. A feminine complaint, you know."

"Then we wish you good journey. I shall ensure we ring you Wednesday next, Madame," Wills inclined his head.

The old woman nodded once and then followed the station master down the platform. Freffie watched her with a strange look in his eye, and then returned his gaze to Hagen. "It would appear you've made a favourable start, Hagen. Tante Stanzi does not give her approval to strangers easily and yet you seemed to have charmed her. With her help we can make your lineage as old as mine and twice as respectable. I wonder why she's being so engaging?"

Hagen shrugged. "I wouldn't have the foggiest, having just met the woman."

"It's not for either of you," Wills replied very quietly. "It's for Meinrad von Steinberg. She's been in love with him for years. Supposedly they had an affair in the mid nineties. Mother told me it was rather torrid."

"Gad, Wills! You are a positive font of information." Freffie gave his friend a brilliant smile.

Wills looked down and shrugged. "I made it a point to learn everything I could about the von Steinbergs a few years ago."

Hagen studied the man. "And why would you do that?" He tried to sound casual and control the muscles which tightened around his eyes.

"I like to know about the people I care about," Wills answered blandly.

"Makes sense to me." Freffie grinned before reaching into the breast pocket of his overcoat and pulling out a flask. He popped open the lid and took a deep swig. "Damn. This is moving about of luggage is thirsty work. Now where shall we go play tonight?" He moved off towards a pale cream 1929 Isotto Franschini Tipo 8 Castanga limousine.

"Our guest might not want to play, Fref. Hagen could be rather tired," Wills reminded him.

The chauffeur, who had been loading Hagen's bag leapt forward to open the doors for his master. Freffie swept past the man and practically vaulted into the car. "Nonsense, Wills. He's here to learn the way it is, and learn he shall. Lesson number one is that we never rest, with the exception of between the hours of six AM and noon."

This time it was Wills' turn to smile apologetically at Hagen. "He's impossible to reason with when he is like this." Wills gestured for Hagen to enter the car. "Après vous."

Hagen stepped into the beautifully maintained car and sat down. "I rested on the train, so I'm sure that I can keep up with you gentlemen."

Wills joined them. "Is that a challenge then, Hagen?" He grinned wolfishly; a cold predatory smile which certainly didn't reach his eyes.

"No. Not a challenge in the slightest." Hagen shook his head and reached into his own breast pocket, to remove the letter from Galiena. "Before I forget, your orders, Herr Graf."

"What's this?"

"From Galiena. She pressed it into my hand just before we left each other in Berlin. I was instructed to deliver it the moment I saw you."

"My thanks." Freffie tore open the envelope and pulled out the letter. As he unfolded it, a bank draft fell into the man's lap. He snatched it up to examine and blinked before tucking it into his pocket. His eyes scanned the letter and he laughed openly before becoming serious once again. Hagen was burning to know the amount of the draft. Why was Galiena giving this man money?

"What does our Goddess have to say?" Wills was curious. "What is so funny?"

"Our sweet girl is conniving, Wills. Naughty little thing. We are under strictest orders to show Hagen here the ropes." Freffie glanced at Hagen. "But I have to say, I find this somewhat disquieting. And I quote, 'I've placed an iron in the fire, Love, and I swear removing it may sear my hands away. As Dickey says, there always comes a time to cut cards with the devil. They say that those who have to make choices between their duty and their desires are the loneliest in the world. I have joined their number. It weighs heavily on my heart, but I think in this case, duty is the only choice. Why is it that to do my duty is a betrayal of my self? You more than anyone else should understand this place to which I have come.'"

"What the Hell does that mean?" Wills narrowed his eyes at the letter. "Hagen? What is she talking about?"

Hagen was just as mystified. "I don't know. We were at Riesa on the weekend, and she faced a few of her ghosts, or so I thought."

Freffie tapped the letter on his knee contemplatively. "Duty means family. Lesson one. In our world, duty always equates to the ancestors."

Realisation dawned on Hagen. This had to be about the nature of their future relationship. Sex. Obviously she was coming around. A betrayal of self indeed! Galiena had such moments of sense so why did she occasionally engage in these feminine dramatics? He had been very clear that he wouldn't hurt her. Why did she have to doubt him? The subject should have been closed. He felt a slight twinge. Did she really look at sex as a duty? Christ! The last thing he wanted was her laying back and doing her duty for the Fatherland when he finally took her to bed! He grunted and rubbed the bridge of his nose between his thumb and forefinger. The beginnings of a headache were starting behind his eye.

"You look as thought you know what she's talking about?"

"Yes. Yes I do. It's nothing to worry about. Something I will discuss with Meinrad von Steinberg when I see him next," Hagen supplied, trying not to grind his teeth.

Freffie nodded. "Now there's a conversation I would love to hear. Mind if I join you? I might be able to add a few things you forgot."

"I have a point or two I would bring up as well," Wills growled. "The one on the end of my sabre, for a start."

Hagen felt one side of his lips slide up into a smile. "Do I detect common ground?"

The wolf-like smile returned. "I don't like it when the people I consider my own get hurt."

"In that we are in complete agreement." It was a small start, but a start to be sure.

November 7, 1937
Dearest Poppet

Friends have told me of you. They tell me you are about in society, and every inch a Pfalzgräfin. Why do you let that upstart Göring parade you around like some sort of trophy? Don't you understand he's just using you to advance himself? You should be on my arm, not his. I am terribly put out. Why do you cast your pearls before swine? They don't love you. I do.
Eternally yours,
Meinrad

Chapter 16
February 21, 1938

Galiena held Emil's leash firmly as they walked the grounds of the Carinhall. Emil was a powerful entity and one who was less than impressed with the snow. It had taken a great deal of coaxing to convince the lion that he did want to go for a stroll. His tawny eyes surveyed the whiteness with something akin to distaste, but he was obedient to his mistress. Galiena reached down and patted the lion's head. Emil kept pace with her, his shoulder at her hip. A loud chuff told her that such attentions were more than welcome. Galiena felt very tangible guilt. She had been away from Emil for far too long, and made a vow that in future he would travel with her.

"It amazes me that Emil will walk in this, your Serene Highness. I don't think I've ever seen a cub quite so eager to please." The dusky voice came from her shoulder. "Lions generally don't appreciate snow."

Galiena threw a glance at her companion. Swanhilde Stammler was the granddaughter of Herr Stammler, Hermann Göring's lion trainer, and now a member of Galiena's personal staff as Emil's keeper. If Galiena was ever going to be intimidated by the appearance of another woman, it would be by Swanhilde. The woman was just over six feet tall, her white blonde hair braided into a coronet on top of her head, and the clearest blue eyes

Galiena had ever seen. She was also strong as an ox, having flipped Emil onto his back as a punishment just the other day. Yet despite her amazing strength, Swanhilde Stammler was also lithe and graceful and beside her Galiena felt like a dumpy mountain pony. Swanhilde was almost thirty and had never been married, despite her spectacular appearance. Galiena wondered why. Emil, who was less fond of men, seemed to obey her and in the end that was why Galiena hired her. But just once, could Galiena see her with a blemish? A little one?

"I do believe he missed me when I was at Riesa," Galiena replied, halting in her steps.

"I would agree," the other woman nodded.

Galiena crouched down and placed her forehead on Emil's, scratching behind his ears. "He could show it a little better than he did last night. He was a positive terror in bed. Wiggling around and stealing all the covers before sprawling dead center in the middle and pushing me out." Her tone was firm but Emil did not appear too chastened.

"I can't say as I entirely agree with you sharing your bed with the cat, Your Serene Highness," Swanhilde muttered with a quick shake of her head.

"Emil won't hurt me," Galiena said with complete resolution. Underneath her, Emil's head vibrated has he gave a half purr.

"I agree. I doubt he would hurt you, particularly after he is gelded next month, but anyone else that enters your chamber may not be so lucky."

Galiena chuckled wryly. "Emil seems comfortable enough around Idalie, and she with him. Emil likes women. Really, he's a bit of a hound."

"Emil considers you as his territory, Your Serene Highness. Males can be very possessive." Swanhilde appeared to stifle a bit of a chuckle herself.

"Tell me something I am not aware of, my dear lion tamer."

"What I am trying to say, Your Serene Highness, is that Emil might take it amiss when there is another male in your bed; a place he considers his." The pale skin pinked slightly.

"I assume you are referring to my esteemed fiancé?" The woman nodded and Galiena sighed. "Hagen and Emil seem to tolerate each other, but you may have a point. Perhaps we could train him to sleep in on a chaise or a nest of pillows."

Swanhilde crossed her arms over her chest. "Perhaps it is time to consider training Emil to sleep in another room."

"And have him try and claw through another door to get to me? No. The racket last time woke the house and I won't put aunt Emmy through the cacophony." Galiena rose to her full height and Emil playfully butted her hip with his head. "Besides, Meike sleeps with uncle Hermann and aunt Emmy."

"Not to be indelicate, Your Serene Highness, but der Dicke[11] is a much larger person than yourself and very strong," Swanhilde used the popular affectionate term for Göring. "He can control Meike. You won't have that ability with Emil."

"Yes. He is growing very large." Galiena conceded and started walking again. "I will consider what you say, Swanhilde," Her voice dropped as she spoke. She didn't want to lose Emil's presence at night as he made her feel safe. No one could sneak up on her with Emil around, and that was the way Galiena liked it.

Her companion seemed to sense her unease. "It is lucky that Emil is small for his age. I don't think he will be a large cat, and he isn't aggressively dominant, as Meike tends to keep him docile. What a difference three months makes in the cat world. Once Emil is gelded he won't be such a worry. Perhaps I am being paranoid."

"Not very big? You told me Emil was over one hundred and fifty pounds!"

"Which is big, but look how much bigger Meike is. Almost two hundred and fifty. I would expect that Emil will be about four hundred when he matures. Meike will grow to be approximately five hundred. Far less manageable as a pet," Swanhilde supplied and patted Emil's flank.

Emil sat down on his haunches and gazed up at Galiena, adoration in his eyes. "Poor Emil! Small for a lion, but certainly big enough for me!" Galiena smiled and then giggled. "And far, far too big for Hagen's piece of mind."

---

[11] der Dicke - the fat one

Swanhilde walked behind Galiena and tapped Galiena's shoulder with both hands. "This is what we have been working on. Up Emil. Come on. Up!"

One tawny ear went back and there was some lashing of tail before Emil raised himself onto his haunches and placed his front paws on Galiena's shoulders. He chuffed happily and she was wilting in a cloud of hot lion breath. His very cold nose rubbed her face and she giggled again, stroking his long muscular front paws. "Why Emil! Shall we dance?"

"I think the waltz might be a little beyond him at this juncture," Swanhilde answered wryly. "But he's very smart. He would be a fabulous circus lion." Herr Stammler, in his youth a famous lion tamer, had been teaching his granddaughter the many tricks of the trade. She, in turn was teaching Emil.

Galiena took a slow step back and Emil leaned forward. Then the lion rose up higher on his back feet and shuffled forward. As he tried to keep his balance, his claws slowly unsheathed themselves into her heavy Melton coat, and she froze. He relaxed, and the claws disappeared. "Well those are certainly sharp enough," Galiena grunted.

"That might not be such a good idea, Your Serene Highness," the woman said behind her. "Did he pink you?"

"No. I don't think so. Just getting his balance," Galiena reassured her companion, hoping it to be the truth.

Swanhilde carefully lifted up Emil's paws. "Down, Emil!" she ordered and Emil dropped back to his sitting position looking very proud of himself.

"Shall we return to the house, Emil?" Galiena turned back on the path and the three of them walked along the path again. As they passed the administration buildings, Galiena could feel the eyes of the workers inside watching her, or more likely, Emil. The Luftwaffe administration buildings were quite large, with room for a few hundred when Uncle Hermann was in residence. As he was presently in Berlin preparing for the Werner von Fritsch's hearing, there were only fifty or so in the large building. They had quarters on a different part of the compound, and it was known to be a show of favour in the Luftwaffe to be assigned at Carinhall. Galiena rarely mixed with the Luftwaffe staff here. Not because of

226

any snobbery on her part, but because proprieties had to be respected.

As they entered the house, Galiena could see a large Mercedes staff car coming up the drive from the airfield. She shrugged. It wasn't uncle Hermann's car and she wasn't particularly interested. Instead, Galiena turned to Swanhilde. "I think I'll keep Emil with me for now. I'll call if I need you. Once he sees a fireplace he will be out like a light for hours."

"Very good, your Serene Highness." The woman bobbed her head and left.

Galiena unhooked Emil's leash and handed it to the butler before drifting off in the direction of the library. A glance at the clock showed it was four in the afternoon and she knew that Emmy Göring would be resting in her chambers. Emmy's pregnancy had aggravated her sciatica and the woman spent much of the day in bed. Galiena generally spent the early afternoon with her aunt and left when Emmy wanted to sleep.

Emil butted her hand and she moved off the library, the lion's favourite room. The lion seemed to favour the roaring fireplace. Galiena poured herself a large glass of port, tossed a few pillows off the chairs and then lay down on the carpet near the blaze. She arranged the pillows under her head, watching as Emil circled and eventually settled down beside her, his massive skull and paw resting on her stomach. He exhaled a purr and the end of his tail twitched, running along her neck and up to her head where it rested against his tummy, seemingly with a mind of its own. She drank the port, closing her eyes, warm and content. When her glass was finished, Galiena used tried to use the force of her will to bring the decanter closer. Deciding after about half a second that the only way she was going to have any success getting her glass refilled; she would have to do it herself. After debating rest versus alcohol, rest won and she sighed, closing her eyes.

Galiena supposed that she slept, for the next thing she knew, the butler was announcing General Ernst Udet. Galiena could feel Emil tense and she drifted a hand to his head. "Hush, darling."

"Where is my Leutnant Girl? I have a surprise for her?" Ernst Udet strode into the room and straight to the sideboard, pouring himself a scotch. Behind him came another man, a younger man in a Luftwaffe uniform walking heavily on a cane. The young man stared at Emil in horror and stayed near the door.

"I'm down here, my very dear General Udet." Galiena tried to push Emil's head from her stomach but the lion was having none of it. He was watching the intruders with avid interest, his claws unsheathing themselves.

"Dear Lord, woman! You've got that damned cat with you!" Udet exclaimed in surprise.

"Yes, so it would seem! Do sit down, my professor! I wasn't expecting company." Galiena managed to wiggle her way out from under Emil and rose to her feet. She allowed Udet to kiss her on the cheek before facing the other man.

"As I said, I brought you a present. I can't maintain our schedule of training and if you are going to get your wings next month you need to be diligent. As such, I have knocked skulls with our Lord and Master, and voila! I have another ace to train you." Udet threw back his scotch and poured another one for himself, then filled an additional tumbler.

Galiena smiled warmly at the war hero. "And are you going to introduce me to this paragon, General Udet? Or are you merely going to extol his virtues?" She looked at the other pilot and her heart caught in her throat. The stranger was simply the most beautiful man she had ever seen. His wavy, dark blond hair was combed straight back from his high forehead and his eyes were a rich cornflower blue. He had a pencil thin moustache on top of generous lips, high cheekbones and more jaw than any man deserved to have. He appeared to be very close to her age. While perhaps only an inch or two taller than Galiena, he had an air of confidence, enhanced by his immaculate Hauptman's uniform.

"Yes, of course. Your Serene Highness, might I present Hauptman Klaus Ritter von Schilling. Recently wounded hero of the contretemps in Spain, this is one of my favourite Condors. Klaus, this is the Pfalzgräfin von Steinberg, soon to be Hanna Reitsch's equal, if I have my way!" Udet's eyes sparkled at her. "Klaus was my other star pupil. Only eight kills to his name, certainly nothing on my sixty-two, but given he's a Stuka man, quite impressive."

The man limped forward and carefully clicked his heels together. Galiena could tell the motion caused the man pain from the tightening in his jaw. "Your Serene Highness." His voice was very deep and had an upper class accent.

Galiena held her hand out to him, and was rendered faint as the pilot gallantly kissed it. "Ritter von Schilling." Did she sound breathless to the men? Her mouth was suddenly like dust as she gestured to the chairs. "Do be at your ease gentlemen and don't mind Emil. He's feeling his oats this week. I went away and now he is rather possessive."

Udet handed the other scotch to von Schilling and raised a brow to Galiena. "I feel somewhat that way about you myself, Pfalzgräfin. What can I get you from the sideboard? It's absolutely intolerable that you aren't drinking with us; I don't care what that Schlotz-Klink woman[12] says."

"I was drinking port, my Master," Galiena smiled again. "It's perfectly acceptable for a woman to have a wee port in the afternoon, or so my English Grandmother always said."

"Smart woman, even if she was one of the enemy," Udet muttered and poured Galiena a fresh glass. He brought it to where she was standing and lead her to the settee, sitting himself beside her. Von Schilling took a chair close by, awkwardly stretching his wounded leg out in front of him. Emil's black-lined eyes glowered at Udet and he rose to his feet to sit on his haunches.

"Enemy indeed!" Galiena rolled her eyes, before directing them towards von Schilling again. "Do tell me about yourself, Herr Ritter. If you do not speak then dear General Udet will take it upon himself to insult my ancestors again." She stopped for a moment. "You seem vaguely familiar to me for some reason."

"I had the pleasure of making your acquaintance seven years ago in Potsdam at President Hindenburg's birthday. You were with your esteemed grandfather."

"Yes. That's correct. I remember now. We had just returned from Italy. I was recently out of school." Galiena mused, drifting back. How could she possibly have forgotten? "How has the time passed for you since? You have become a pilot, I see?"

---

[12] Reich Women's Leader Gertrude Schlotz-Klink was in charge of the female arm of the Nazi Party and believed in very traditional roles for women.

Udet grinned blearily. "Klaus here is a Guernica man. He could tell you stories, I warrant. Stories almost as interesting as mine."

"If you gave him the opportunity, he might!" Galiena replied tartly.

A quick shadow passed behind von Schilling's eyes. "The strife in Spain is most unfortunate. While it has been my honour to aid the nationalist forces, war is not pretty, Madame."

Galiena found herself nodding, quite entranced by the man's voice. "How long were you there, Herr Ritter?"

"December of '36, your Serene Highness. I was of the second wave to go over under General von Richthofen. I served until January second of this year when I was shot down by flak." The man rubbed his thigh with his hand.

"You served under Wolfram von Richthofen? I have met him on several occasions." Galiena told the man. Wolfram von Richthofen was the cousin of her 'uncle' Manfred von Richthofen.

Udet chuckled to himself and contemplated his glass. "Ah, yes. The lesser von Richthofen."

"Now, my Master, I'm afraid I must protest! Just because General von Richthofen didn't have either of his cousins' number of kills during the war doesn't make him lesser. I would say his long term experience easily makes him the equal of the other two!" Galiena exclaimed.

"Manfred was my inspiration, Lothar was my friend, and Wolfram attempts to be my rival. Forgive me if I don't agree with you, Leutnant Girl," the general muttered to himself, his voice becoming lost in the bottom of his glass.

"General von Richthofen is a skilled tactician, Madame. His choice of targets and methods of engagement are second to none. We have suffered no defeats, I must admit, but he has not General Udet's skill in a plane. He is not the plane, more accurately; he sees the entire formation in his mind and on the map. He is an excellent commander." Von Schilling's lips curled up into a boyish smile.

Galiena discovered a burning curiosity about this divinely handsome man. "How were you injured, Herr Ritter? Were you shot down? Was it the first time?"

"Not the first time for crashing, but the first time I didn't manage to find a soft place to land." The expression on von Schilling's face turned vaguely self-conscious.

"Don't be ashamed, lad. Any crash you walk away from is one to be proud of," Udet snorted. "My dear Pfalzgräfin, why don't we tuck into some of the Lord and Master's champagne? Make this more merry?" The General rolled his empty glass between his empty hands. "Flying up here has given me a powerful thirst."

Galiena laughed and moved to the bell pull, giving it a good yank. "General Udet, breathing gives you a powerful thirst!" She eyed him with amusement. "You never change! Powerful thirst indeed!"

"I haven't in all the years I've been on this planet." Udet chuckled. "And after a bottle or two, why don't we go to heaven and watch the sunset? The three of us."

"A possibility, my dear General!" Galiena turned to the butler and asked for a bottle of champagne and three glasses. "May I ask, Herr Ritter, how you were wounded?"

"I broke my right leg in four places, my left arm in two, and four ribs. I also had an abdominal tear from a bullet which penetrated my cockpit. It was fortunate I landed close to our base, or I might have perished." Again the faint shadow before a warm grin. "But they didn't get me and when I am better I intend to go back. If my friend Werner Mölders doesn't get the job completed in my absence, that is. They sent him to replace me and now I am here, recuperating until I can return."

"After everything you've been through, you would go back?" Galiena couldn't keep the surprise out of her voice.

"Of course. I'm a pilot! If my Fuhrer summons me back to Spain I will go most willingly." An honest and fervent declaration if ever Galiena had heard one.

Udet rolled his eyes. "He's as bad as we were. Ah well! Once it's in the blood, it's in the blood. The danger. It's just so damn fun! Pardon my language, Pfalzgräfin!"

"I would forgive you nearly anything, General Udet!" Galiena touched the man's forearm with a quick fingertip; knowing it would please him.

Udet jumped up to open the champagne which the butler brought into the room. "And would you forgive me for stealing a kiss from those soft lips?"

Galiena leaned over and batted her eyelashes at the older man. "I might forgive you, General, but Hagen would definitely object. Poor Eugen would probably have apoplexy."

Udet's grunt was insultingly dismissive. "Where is your flock of crows, Leutnant girl? Please tell me you've sent them away, never to return? They're always swirling around you like an angry cloud."

Galiena looked down, feeling an emotion that she found hard to put a name to. "Don't call Hagen a crow, General Udet. It shows a want of feeling." She looked over at von Schilling. "My fiancé is a member of the SS."

A silky blonde brow rose. "How terribly unfortunate for you."

Udet passed out the flutes and as he did so, he winked at von Schilling. "That's the way of it, Lad. Damned unfortunate. A toast." He raised his glass. "Confusion to Himmler's Black Order."

Von Schilling eyed Galiena. "I will only drink to that if the Pfalzgräfin von Steinberg does."

Galiena felt gratitude grow in her head for the handsome flier. "General Udet! You, more than anyone, should know I couldn't drink to such a toast! It would be contrary to my own interests."

"Fine then. To the health of the Fuhrer. Better yet, to a fast plane, clear skies, and a full tank of petrol!" Udet countered, his teeth flashing. "Let's agree to something before my champagne goes flat."

"Either will suffice for me," Galiena giggled. Von Schilling raised his glass, and they all drank.

"So where is the esteemed SS officer, my girl?" Udet fixed her with an interested glare.

"He is on holiday," Galiena replied simply.

"And he isn't here with you?" von Schilling asked quietly, his tone curiously even.

"No. He's in Austria." To say it made her throat constrict. Why did Hagen have to go away right when she was feeling these doubts? She needed him right now.

"I would say that is an adequate distance away. Just about right, really," Udet grumbled. "Will save von Schilling here from that glaring adjutant of his. The one who can't speak. Or is that one about?"

"Eugen is with Hagen, General Udet; and he does speak. You aren't being fair." Galiena felt the need to defend Eugen. "Don't mind his glaring, he doesn't like planes. I hear he gets terribly airsick."

Both men exchanged a condescending glance and grinned almost in unison. Galiena noticed that von Schilling's teeth were nearly perfect. "How unfortunate," von Schilling repeated with a lazy drawl.

"Well you don't need them to keep you company, my dear! You have us," Udet shrugged before grinning at her again.

"My dear Professor, when did you become so vitriolic about my choice of friends?" Galiena examined Udet under her lashes.

"Since your friends included such terrors as Himmler. I saw you with him at lunch a few weeks back. Don't think I was too drunk to notice, Pfalzgräfin! That man is dangerous and not dangerous in the way that I am dangerous, for I am the good kind of dangerous. Himmler is like the flu. You never think it's very serious, until it's got you by the neck and your gut is griping. Then you sit up and take notice, but by the time you does so, it's usually too late, and you're six feet under." Udet thrust a finger at her. "You should know better, my girl!"

"General Udet, my relationship with the Reichsführer-SS is primarily political in nature. He is my fiancé's superior officer." How easily the lie rolled off her tongue but Udet would simply never understand about her association with Himmler.

"Which is why a smart girl would leave the crows alone."

Galiena drained her glass in some frustration. "General, you are being ridiculous and paranoid! Himmler wants nothing but for me to marry Hagen. You are beginning to sound like Uncle Hermann. I thought he was coming around, but in the last two weeks he's been winding up about it again!"

"On that score we are in complete agreement. Perhaps an obedient girl would listen to her elders." The bleary blue eyes of the famous pilot locked on her own with a penetrating acuity.

"Why is it of so much concern to you?"

Udet fixed her with a smouldering stare. "Perhaps it is because I care, dear girl! You are Rudiger von Steinberg's daughter. I have a duty. One that circumstances make me less able to handle personally."

Galiena gave a little moue, trying to lighten the mood. She didn't want to argue with Udet about her fiancé, not when she was feeling so conflicted about Hagen. "And why must you abandon me, General?"

"In particular, since the Lord and Master wants me to spend just a tad more time in the office, I must give you Klaus over there. I've secured him a bunk up here at the Carinhall, and another in town so that he is completely at your disposal in the coming months until the doctors give him his wings back. Damn unfortunate that." Udet swallowed his champagne back.

"They took your wings away?" Galiena exclaimed, facing the younger man.

"Until I can run on my leg, yes. It shouldn't be too long. Six weeks and three days ago I was shot down. They said I might never walk again. A fortnight ago they took me out of traction, and now look at me. Another two months of therapy, and I will be dancing the Charleston, good as new," von Schilling shrugged. "But I don't need my legs to teach you; what you need is between my ears."

"I have no doubts as to your ability to teach me how to be a pilot, Herr Ritter." Galiena looked down at her hands, which were becoming damp. She patted Emil, scratching his alert neck, and could feel the muscles bunching in his shoulders. The cat wasn't ready to spring, but he was certainly not going to relax around this stranger.

Ernst Udet stretched his feet out in front of him, resting his arms on the back of the settee. "Von Schilling will get the job done. It's hours you need, my little Leutnant Girl, and practice. You could ace that exam now, but you haven't the hours. I've told von Schilling to treat you like any recruit when you are in his care and I expect you to do as your bid, or you will answer to me"

"Now General Udet! Is that a threat or a promise?" She couldn't help herself and the fluttering of her lashes was probably a tad over the top.

234

"It's a promise, my girl."

"As such, I think we need to make you think like a recruit. No more of these leisurely ten a.m. to one p.m. lessons, your Serene Highness. A good pilot has more toughness. I think your schedule needs to be shaken up a tad," von Schilling winked at her, but his expression was impassive.

"And just what is that supposed to mean?" Galiena froze in her flirtation with Udet.

"I expect you to be on the airfield at six a.m., bright eyed and bushy tailed. We will fly or do theory from six until one every day." The young man's eyes sparkled. "Sunrise is the best time to be in the air."

Galiena sucked back a stuttering breath. "You can't be serious, Herr Ritter!"

"Absolutely I am serious, recruit von Steinberg. Tomorrow we begin. Consider this your last day of freedom." Von Schilling's eyes gleamed with an almost cruel light.

"Civilized people aren't up at that time of the day! Heavens above! I would have to be up at five a.m. at least!" Galiena rounded on Udet. "You don't fly at six a.m.!"

"I'm not an apprentice pilot, my dear girl! You are. I did my fair share of daybreak flights in my younger years." Udet reached for the champagne bottle and refilled their glasses. "Come now! The night before boot camp is traditionally a celebration of the hell which is to come! Drink, Leutnant girl, for tomorrow your life will change."

"Just one moment, gentlemen! Don't I even have a say in this plan you have for me?" Galiena protested with very real feeling. "I do have business that I must attend to during the day! I'm no more a free agent than the next person."

Udet reached over to pat her on the cheek; Emil following the hand with his snout as it passed over him. "You're just going to have to do it in the afternoon like the rest of us human beings, my dear! Do you want to be a brilliant pilot, or don't you?"

"That's hardly fair, General Udet! You know I do!"

The General shrugged. "Then what is the issue?"

"The bored officers of the German Luftwaffe can't summarily commandeer my life without so much as a by your

235

leave! I do have duties I must attend to!" Galiena retorted again, hoping the men would see reason.

Udet cupped her chin in his hand. "Come on now, Pfalzgräfin! It's your passion. I know that it is and I understand how passion works. You should feed it, my girl, not suppress it." His lips turned up, and the words rolled off his tongue like honey. "I'm giving you what you need."

Her mouth was completely dry. Galiena hated it when Udet turned up the wattage on his very considerable charm. It made him ever so much harder to resist. "Has Uncle Hermann approved of this?" Why did she suddenly feel naked?

"So much so, he sent us up with a little present for you since you've been such a good girl!" Udet released her, and looked back at von Schilling. "I think it's a good present, at any rate. What do you think?" His voice had returned to its normal pitch.

"I think Feldmarschall Göring has excellent taste, General Udet." Von Schilling caught her eyes. "I even like the colour."

Galiena had a dawning suspicion. "What did you bring me, General Udet?" She caught her bottom lip between her teeth in excitement as she wrapped her arms around Emil's neck and rested her cheek on his great head. The lion chuffed happily.

"Well now, down at the airfield there might just be a brand new BF 108B Taifun in the von Steinberg family livery. At least your father's wartime livery of purple with a black stripe running down the fuselage," Udet shrugged idly. "It's the new four seater so that when you decide to go for a spin, you can take a few friends." He stared down at Emil in consternation. "But I wouldn't advise taking the cat. He might not like it, and I know I certainly wouldn't like it."

"A Taifun?" Galiena breathed in disbelief.

"A Taifun," von Schilling repeated. "Heil Messerschmitt! The man's a genius."

"And when you have your private licence, plus one hundred hours in the plane, the Lord and Master says you can fly it on your own." Udet refilled her glass and his own again. "What do you say to that, my girl?"

Galiena turned to von Schilling with abject devotion. "I will be your most devoted pupil, Herr Ritter! What time did you say you wanted to start in the morning?"

236

Chapter 17
February 23, 1938

The explosion rocked the elegant house on the Wollzeile, rattling the windows and the pictures on the walls. There were cries from the women, and more than one man dove to cover his escort. The chandeliers swung dangerously overhead and puffs of plaster came from the ceiling, dusting the shoulders of tuxedo jackets like fresh snowfall. Then came the strange sound of silence as all the people in the room looked from one to another in stunned confusion before the wail of sirens punctuated in the distance.

"What a terrible bother!" Freffie broke the silence in the room, looking askance at his martini. "There's dust in my drink."

"Bloody anarchists," an older gentleman, General Robert Freiherr von Zedanski, piped up from an overstuffed chair, his medals glinting on his chest.

"Your Excellency! Really!" a younger woman said from the settee.

Hagen moved to the window and saw a sooty glow a street over. There was a terrible pit yawning in his stomach, and the policeman in him wanted to charge over to investigate. He knew beyond the shadow of a doubt the target had to have been his party. Yesterday's demonstration by the Austrian SA had stopped traffic on the Kartnestrasse for hours. Several civilians had been hurt, or so the papers said this morning. Couldn't Seyss-Inquart keep his thugs under control? They couldn't risk bad opinion, especially at this delicate juncture.

"I hardly believe it's anarchists," Wills drawled, entering the room. "Freff? You sound, my man?"

"Fine. Hale and hearty. Takes more than a far off blast to ruffle me."

A middle aged gentleman with a pointed goatee joined Hagen at the window. Hagen knew the man to be the host of this soiree, August von Hellenberg, the Prinz of Zerbst, a now defunct principality. "What do you think, Freff? Nazis or Sozis?"

"For Christ's sake, August! Does it matter? You know I don't pay any attention to that sort of thing. Let the rats play their games, so long as the champagne holds out!" Freffie shook his head in disgust.

The Freiherrin von Zedanski, a woman past sixty with a bored expression and overdone coiffure drifted over and Hagen made room for her. "It's so terribly vulgar. I just hope they haven't hurt anyone important this time." She glanced up at Hagen. "Those Nazis completely interrupted my marketing. Why do they think gadding about shouting in the street is necessary?"

"Because they're workers, my dear," von Zedanski said to his wife from his chair.

"But that is the point, husband! If they are workers, then why aren't they working? I've never understood why the workers are always agitating? And how is it that there are National Socialists, and plain socialists? What is the difference? Why don't they return to their factories and do as they're told?" The woman huffed.

The Prinz smiled down at the woman. "Ah, my dear Freiherrin! As always you show yourself as one of the people!"

"Well if you are so knowledgeable, Your Highness, why don't you explain why it's always the workers? You never see our class as anarchists! We don't go around blowing buildings up." There was a sharp crack as the Freiherrin snapped her fan shut.

"Madame, when our class feels the need for a little anarchy, wars get started. I do believe we were responsible for a great deal of destruction over in Flanders a few years back. We can't be anarchists when we set policy." Freffie sauntered over to stand behind the Freiherrin. "Cheery looking blaze, isn't it?"

Hagen watched as the sky lit up and the sirens grew closer. Hopefully it was only one building and the flames weren't jumping to others. The old quarter of Vienna was densely populated; the buildings were very close together. A serious blaze could be a major problem. "I don't see much cheery about buildings burning," Hagen murmured unconsciously. He had seen death by fire before.

Von Zedanski chuckled, unaffected by the situation. "Our class being anarchists indeed! The lad has the right of it, wife!"

"You still didn't tell me the difference between a Nazi and a Sozi! Shouldn't they be allies since they are both socialists?" The woman bleated gratingly.

"Madame Freiherrin, Sozis are communists. They are supported by the Comintern in the Soviet Union and believe the workers should control Europe regardless of national boundaries. They argue that the international bourgeoisie has kept them enslaved and will stop at nothing to eliminate their enemies. They wish to achieve dictatorship of the proletariat, and as such they do not believe in an aristocracy, nor do they believe in social norms such as family and property. The Russian Revolution should be case and point," Hagen said quietly, explaining the differences as he understood them. "National Socialists believe in the strength of the nation and its people. Together the nation can solve its own economic problems through use of its own resources and labour. Groups, such as the Comintern, destroy the fabric of the nation with their divisiveness and will bleed the strength of the people with it."

The Freiherrin's mouth dropped but she closed it quickly. "You seem well informed, Doctor Kohl. Just how is that you have this knowledge?"

Hagen raised a brow at the woman, unable to contain his dislike. "I read, Madame. I've read the *Communist Manifesto*, the *Fascist Manifesto, Mein Kampf*, Marx, Engles, Trotsky, Smith, and far more. My father believed that to understand the human condition from different perspectives brought the soul closer to God."

"A wise man, your father," The Prinz nodded his head approvingly, offering Hagen a cigar.

Hagen took the item with a reciprocal nod of his head. "Quite the wisest I have ever met. I think he had secretly socialistic leanings despite his innately capitalist nature." He held out the cigar as the Prinz clipped the end.

"I simply can't believe Hitler is actually an Austrian. What a common little man," The woman harrumphed, her face flushing like an apple. "Have you met him, Doctor Kohl? You being a German and all?"

Hagen considered his answer carefully and then relaxed. Many Germans had met Hitler, particularly those of a certain class. He wouldn't give himself away by answering to the affirmative. "Yes, Madame. I have met the Fuhrer on several occasions."

"And what is he like in person?" Von Zedanski asked, lifting his head, his interest obviously piqued.

"He has a very strong personality. He dominates a room simply by entering it." Hagen himself was torn. His relationship with the Fuhrer was in such a tangle at the moment. He worshiped the man and yet now there was a kernel of another, stronger, more negative emotion; something more than doubt. It surprised him with its intensity. How much had Galiena's interaction with Hitler affected him?

"The man is a peasant and a dreadful bore," Freffie interjected firmly.

"That's right, Freff! You were up there, weren't you? With von Schuschnigg and the rest?" The Prinz stabbed the air with his cigar. "What did you think of the great German Fuhrer?"

"August! You know I never involve myself in politics! Besides, I just told you! The man is a peasant, and you really can't take that kind anywhere." Freffie downed his alcohol. "You know that I am the great proponent of the bourgeoisie! Once a long time ago, we were all bourgeoisie, really, except for Gallie's family. They have been noble as far back as anyone can go, but as I was saying, the middle classes have a certain unused charm. Or perhaps they just aren't as inbred as the rest of us; we're so inbred we've gone stupid. Now the peasants are over bred. They spend so much time breeding; they don't have any good strains left. Oh yes. Every so often you get a clever one, but all in all, they are just the worker ants. Toil, toil, toil! That's what they should be doing!"

"How positively enlightened, Freffie!" Wills laughed, dusting the arm of a wing chair before perching on the edge.

"Come now, Wills! You didn't meet him. Hitler is a peasant, and most of those who serve him are." Was that a direct challenge?

Hagen cocked his head to the side. "Hermann Göring could hardly be described as a peasant!" He interjected.

"Doctor Kohl is quite right there! Göring is the godson of the Ritter von Epenstein, as noble a man as I have ever met. Physician, you know. Very clever man!" The Prinz spoke up. "For a member of the newer nobility." He laughed suddenly. "Nice enough chap for a Breifedal."

"Yes. I will admit that Hermann Göring is a bit of an aberration. Don't quite know what he is doing with that group. He made a good showing of himself at the Obersalzberg," Freffie admitted modestly.

"So Freff, you would agree that Hitler is a common little thing? And these Nazis with them?"

"They're bullies, August. Nothing more, nothing less. Or the vast majority of them are. I think there could be the odd good egg here and there, Göring for example, but the rest? I pooh-pooh them." Freffie's eyes gleamed at Hagen. "But as we have established, they're workers and I despise workers."

"I completely agree with you, your Illustrious Highness," The Freiherrin concluded. "And I don't like them agitating in Austria. It's so terribly disruptive."

"Sometimes a little revolution is not entirely a bad thing, Madame." Hagen sipped his drink.

"Nonsense! Look what happened here after the war! We were stripped of our titles! What kind of vulgarity is that?" The woman was beginning to sound shrill to Hagen's ears and he just wanted her to be quiet.

"I do believe that was an extremity which was not correct," He answered to please her.

"Then of course you believe a monarchy is the most intelligent form of government?" The Freiherrin words were spoken as a statement and not as a question.

"No. Not as such, Madame. Why would I believe that?" Hagen returned, catching the woman's eye.

Von Zedanski sipped his drink. "Because ruling should be left to those who have it in their blood. They are conditioned from birth to rule. They have a closer tie to the blood of the nation."

"Now that I might agree with, Herr General, but what happens when the ruler is an imbecile? Even the noblest families occasionally have a bad seed," Hagen pointed out, addressing the woman's husband.

"Ridiculous. Noble blood is untainted."

"Not true. I must stick in my proverbial oar. George the third in England. He went mad as a hatter." Freffie raised his glass to Hagen.

241

"But you must admit it is rare! Look at the great ruling families! The Hohenzollern here in Germany? The Romanovs in Russia? The Saxe-Coburg-Gotha in England?" The woman protested.

Wills sighed. "The latter are now the Windsors. They changed it during the war to be less German."

"Yes, Freiherrin von Zedanski. I'm surprised at you!" Freffie winked at Wills. "The merry wives of Saxe-Coburg-Gotha!" He chortled out Kaiser Wilhelm's famous wartime joke.

"That is irrelevant, Herr Graf! The point is that the families with leadership in the blood should control the countries, not trumped up little peasants with delusions of grandeur." Again the fan snapped with displeasure.

"Well thank the Lord in Heaven that I have nothing to rule. I would be a terrible Prinz if I actually had to engage in that profession." August von Hellenberg lit his cigar with several puffs of his cheeks. "I don't have the constitution for it."

The fan hit Hagen in the shoulder. "I am terribly surprised at you, Doctor Kohl, that you would have such an attitude, given you are marrying the Prinzess von Steinberg."

"Madame, I realise that you are merely a Freiherrin, but even you should know the von Steinbergs consider that title an insult when used to describe them." Freffie's voice was low and rather dangerous. "I won't have my Gallie insulted in my presence."

Hagen resisted the urge to furrow his brow at Freffie. He had no idea what the man was going on about but it had to be noteworthy given the reaction. The Freiherrin spluttered and the Prinz hid a grin by puffing on his cigar. The woman drew her head back like an affronted bird. "The Kaiser always referred to the Pfalzgraf von Steinberg as the Prinz von Steinberg. I am merely following court custom, Your Illustrious Highness."

Freffie heaved a theatrical sigh. "My dear lady, in the aftermath of the Congress of Vienna, the Hohenzollern's appropriated the lands of Steinberg and Riesa as punishment for that particular Pfalzgraf's cooperation with Napoleon. As a sop to one of the more ancient families in Germany, Frederick Wilhelm the third titled the Steinbergs as Prinz, but the title Pfalzgraf von

Riesa originally came from Charlemagne; as such, that is the one they use."

"Kaiser Wilhelm always called the present Pfalzgraf Prinz von Steinberg," Freiherrin von Zedanski repeated doggedly.

"And the Pfalzgraf once suggested to the Kaiser if he held onto his horse's stirrup and clucked, that our liege's infamous withered arm[13] would grow to a normal length when the horse moved. Doesn't mean you could say the same, Madame." Freffie retorted, his eyes strangely flat.

A swirl of silk and the woman stalked off. The Prinz started to chuckle, ash from his cigar falling to the floor to mix with the dust of the plaster. "Ah Freff! You are pure gold, you do know that."

"My apologies for my wife's self-important tongue." Von Zedanski smiled weakly. "I'm sure she didn't mean to offend."

"She should be thankful Tante Stanzi wasn't here." Freffie stood up and walked over to the window. "Tante Stanzi is very protective of the Pfalzgraf's dignity."

"So she should be, given she was his mistress for a good ten years." The Prinz replied with a slow wink.

"Tante Stanzi? You must be joking, August. Not that I want to picture Tante Stanzi intimate at all. That's a positive mind destroyer," Freffie said with a shudder which consumed his entire being.

"Now that you mention it, your Highness, I can picture it. The Gräfin seems to glow when the subject of Meinrad von Steinberg comes up," Wills spoke quietly.

Hagen, too, puffed on his cigar, tasting the smoke in his mouth before blowing it out. The back of his throat tingled from the tobacco. "Is that the truth about the title?"

Freffie nodded and looked out of the window. "Tis indeed, my son. There is only one man on this planet who calls Gallie 'Prinzess' and that is Dickey. Within the family itself, they are very careful never to use the title. If you hadn't noticed, Galiena refers to her Grandfather as the Pfalzgraf, often to his face."

---

[13] Trauma at birth caused Wilhelm II's left arm to be significantly shorter than his right. It was a source of embarrassment to the Kaiser and never mentioned at court.

"He calls her Poppet," Hagen said, almost to himself, his mouth turning sour as the words rolled over his tongue.

"They all did, but in public he will refer to her as the Pfalzgräfin. Meinrad has always been sensitive about that point. Perhaps because he was such a chum of poor old Kaiser Bill."

"How is the Pfalzgraf anyway, Freff? He hasn't been up to Vienna in a hound's age. Eight months at least. I last heard he had taken poorly in the fall, but gossip says he recovered," the Prinz asked, inquiry etched across his dissipated face.

"Haven't the foggiest, old boy. Last I heard from Gallie, he was off taking the cure somewhere in Germany, but I couldn't tell you where." Freffie replied with deft evasion.

"Damn and blast! He always finds the best places."

"I'm sure he's enjoying his stay." Hagen couldn't help but answer as he returned his gaze to the conflagration. "Does it look to you like the fire is spreading?"

"Possibly." Freffie shrugged and deliberately turned his back to the window. There was such dismissiveness in the gesture that it disgusted Hagen.

"I highly doubt it. I'm sure the fire brigade will attend to it," Wills replied, accepting another drink from a passing footman.

"I was having the same curiosity myself," the Prinz said to Hagen.

"Want to go for a stroll and take a look? Perhaps they could use a hand?" Hagen suggested.

August von Hellenberg looked on him with astonishment. "You mean walk to the site of the blast?"

"Why not? You just said you were curious," Hagen tossed out, almost mocking the Prinz.

The man's brow furrowed for a moment and then smoothed. "How terribly novel! It might just be fun. I haven't seen anything like that since the war."

Freffie looked more than faintly pained. "Lord, August, it's bad enough I'm wearing your plaster on my favourite jacket! Do we really have to go tromping about a disaster like a cluster of penguins?"

The Prinz glanced at Hagen and back to Freffie. "Yes! Why not? It's not often that something of such a nature happens on one's very doorstep. Lord knows, I couldn't have planned better entertainment for my guests."

"You know, Freff, don't be such an old stick." Wills shrugged. "A modicum of adventure might not go amiss. You're always going on about how nothing exciting ever happens in Vienna anymore."

"I really can't believe you are seriously considering this. Carnage shouldn't be a spectators sport. Aren't we somewhere beyond the gawkers at the Roman coliseum?" Freffie said plaintively.

"You can always stay here with the rest of the guests," the Prinz replied blandly. "Quite frankly, I'm intrigued," he returned his eyes to Hagen. "You might just be a breath of fresh air in this otherwise stale society, Doctor Kohl."

Hagen inclined his head. "Why thank you, your Highness."

"Not at all, Kohl. Not at all. Shall we get our coats?"

Chapter 18
February 23, 1938

There was a smell of burning on the wind as Hagen stepped out of the house and into the street. Hagen, and the group of nearly twenty who felt the need to go a-gawking' as Freffie put it, had taken an overly long time to arrange their hats and cloaks before finally exiting the building. Hagen wished he could trade his top hat, tails and evening cloak for his uniform; his sudden bosom companion, August Prinz von Hellenberg for his loyal Eugen; and his status as future aristocrat and tourist for the rank and title he held back in Germany. At least he was moving to investigate, if only in the capacity as a gawker. Sadly he had to take this sideshow of the bored and wealthy with him, but some things simply couldn't be helped. One had to adapt to the situations at hand.

Hagen headed left down the Wollezeile, leading the group with the Prinz at his side. They moved no faster than a brisk walk, for three ladies had decided to attend the excursion, and could not move so deftly in their heels. A fire brigade truck screamed by them, red lights strobing, painting their faces scarlet. The roaring sound of fire came from the edge of the block opposite them, increasing in volume with every step. Hagen felt the thrill of adrenaline pumping through his veins. So much better than alcohol, this rush from his own body; yet underneath it all, he felt sick. The bomb had to be targeted at his own people, and the potential loss of life, property and equipment could be catastrophic. No matter what he saw, there was very little he would be able to do. Maybe he was just torturing himself with this little expedition. No. He had to be useful. Two days of dinners and parties with Freffie and Wills had left him feeling like the lowliest sort of wastrel in the world. Not a feeling he enjoyed.

"You know, Doctor Kohl, this is the most alive I've felt since Caporetto." August von Hellenberg's eyes gleamed like coals in the darkness.

"Infantry, artillery or cavalry?" Hagen asked, not feeling the curiosity the question implied.

"Hauptman, infantry. You?" the man returned crisply with practice.

"Offizier-Stellvertreter; infantry as well," Hagen paused, looking down an alley and followed that route. The Prinz looked slightly dubious and trailed along.

"Whereabouts?"

"Primarily Ypres. That general neck of the woods." Hagen tried to hear beyond the sirens. His tail of partygoers seemed apprehensive of the alley behind him, milling at the entrance. Hagen wished he was carrying his side arm. What had he been thinking? Taking a walk over to a bombing without proper backup. He deserved to get his head smacked for this. On the other hand, it was Vienna, and Vienna was a civilized place.

"Oh! Ypres. Bad luck that. Caporetto was no picnic, but nothing on the Western Front. Thankfully by that point, the Italians weren't interested in fighting too hard," the Prinz chuckled into his beard.

"If it hadn't been for the English, we would have had it much easier," Hagen agreed. "They simply couldn't leave well enough alone. On the other hand, we might still be camped in the mud in Belgium were it up to the French."

A sharp bark of laughter beside him. "The French have a very decided notion of how a war should be fought; whatever way is easiest for them. Unfortunately the Italian is a lion, though thankfully only in short doses. They fought well, until they were far more irritated with their own officer corps than with us, and it all fell apart for them at that point."

"Like the Frenchman, the Italian is a different sort of creature. I think it's the warm weather." Hagen could see activity at the mouth of the alley and wondered what they would find.

"Absolutely, yes. It's always been a problem for us Austrians. At least you Germans have us as a buffer," the Prinz said wryly. "Though I do believe there are those who would change that in your country."

"And how would that make you feel, Your Highness?" Hagen asked cautiously, wanting to feel the man out.

"Now Doctor Kohl, when you are in a position like mine; a Prince without a Principality, living in a country that isn't yours by birth but by an arbitrary division after a lost war, you wouldn't consent to answer questions like that. Perhaps it would be better served if I asked you instead; you being a German and a stranger to boot. I am not allowed to have an opinion about the state of my adopted land, but you on the other hand can have any opinion you would like," von Hellenberg spoke slyly, tapping the side of his nose with an elegant finger.

Hagen turned to examine the man, noting they had outstripped their companions by almost twenty five feet. "Ah, but as von Reitersbach constantly reminds me, I am a stranger in a strange land and my behaviour will have a lasting impression on how I am perceived by your class. I am under orders to not embarrass my future queen."

"Oh dear Lord, Doctor Kohl! You even sound like Freff when you say that. Let me tell you one thing about our class. We are a dying breed. Most of us are dead already and just cling to the past. We have no skills and have no use, more importantly; few of us have any money in this brave new postwar world. We are reduced to being relics, only we are relics that live and breathe and are generally far too scared to acknowledge the fact we have long outstripped our usefulness. I think your opinion matters a great deal indeed; far more than that of any of us."

Hagen studied the man before him carefully. The man was close to fifty, had a dissipated air, but more than that, there was a sadness about him as he made his speech. He couldn't help but wonder what it cost von Hellenberg inside to make the admission he did. A man should never admit to a stranger, let alone himself, that he's useless. "Thank you, Your Highness. My opinion? My opinion is both our countries were harshly punished for a war that Nicholas the Second wanted. I think we should stand united against the Treaties of Paris and reclaim what we lost."

"A Nationalist, then," the Prinz nodded slowly. "Just like the rest of us."

"I love my Fatherland, your Highness. No truer words were spoken than Deutschland, Deutschland Über Alles," Hagen replied with barefaced honestly.

"An interesting answer, Herr Doctor. History says those words came about as a rallying cry for the German states to put aside their differences and unite to make one centralized country.

Today people say those words mean Germany over Europe?" Von Hellenberg crossed his arms over his chest.

This man was depressingly intelligent. "I merely want to see Germany as a strong, proud nation once more. I never want to see her suffer as she did after the war. It must never happen again."

The Prinz nodded as the rest of the group trailed to where they stood. "To answer you, Doctor Kohl, I feel precisely the same way."

The lure of the carnage was more than Hagen could bear. "Stay or leave, I am going to take a look around," Hagen told the other man.

"I think I will mind the children, Papa," von Hellenberg replied dryly. "But don't worry; I won't go back without you!"

Not particularly caring either way, Hagen poked his head out of the alley and looked down the road. Two large buildings were burning; glowing embers showering up into the sky and men running in and out of the most damaged one with all manner of boxes. He saw more than one swastika flag come out as well, as well as several insignias of the SA. Countless people lay on the ground, obviously wounded, and others were tending them. Men milled about everywhere, some with confused, shocked expressions on their faces. The police were trying to cordon off the area, but the men moving the boxes interfered.

Hagen stepped into the maelstrom of people, not mindful of the chaos, alert and listening for answers. This had to be a Nazi command center of some kind or another and Hagen knew its destruction would be a great loss for the party. The extent of the damage was terrible. The building's upper floors were an inferno. It had to have been a decently sized bomb, though Hagen had very little knowledge of such things.

There was a pocket of calm ahead of him, a place where there were no people, and he pressed his way into it, trying to absorb the destruction around him. The air reeked of charred wood, burnt hair and a miasma of other smells he couldn't define. The roar of the fire was almost drowned out by the scream of sirens arriving, the cries of the wounded and the sobbing of the terrified. It was almost like being back in battle. Hagen turned in a circle and something caught his eye; a huge silk banner, hanging from the building on the opposite. 'Nazis to Hell.' It read. The words seared

249

into his brain and if he had doubts before, they were gone now. This had to be the work of the NAO, for they were simply too fond of leaving calling cards. The sheer arrogance of them! How dare they?

There was a shift in the people around him, and as the police and fire brigades arrived in droves around the buildings, many of the bystanders melted away. Hagen cast his eyes and saw a group of men, one of whom was Ernst Kaltenbrunner. The Austrian-SS leader and another man were arguing loudly. Several others were trying to get the boxes of Nazi paraphernalia into cars and trucks. Of course. The Nazis were banned. The police would be obliged to confiscate any party propaganda they found. It was a perfect situation for the NAO. The police would clean up the mess, and harass the victims of the attack in the process. God damn them.

Hagen moved to intercept a man whose arms were full of papers. "Excuse me! What happened here?"

The man looked at him, his eyes wide with panic. "Hellfire! The room exploded in flames! It was Hell!"

"Get a hold of yourself, man!" Hagen used his officer's voice to cut through the man's panic. "What happened?"

"We were to have a meeting. Some were in and some hadn't arrived! It's terrible, mein Herr! Terrible!" The man clutched his papers to his breast and swastikas leapt out at Hagen from the pages.

"Was anyone killed?" Hagen demanded calmly.

"No! I don't know! I don't think so!" The man looked back at the burning building. "I don't know! I don't know!" The voice was on the edge of hysteria.

"Carry on then." Hagen moved away, trying to edge closer; feeling the heat from the blaze on his face even though he was at least twenty feet away. He turned around again, his cape swirling and searched for any clues as to the perpetrators, as well as trying to commit the scene to memory. This was something he could never forget. There was yelling from the inferno; then a man burst forth, his clothing alight. His appearance was that of like a shooting star, coming towards the line of police and firemen. The police tackled the man, pushing him to the ground and pouring water on him, the poor wretch's screams blistering to the ears.

Fire hoses were run out and the men of the fire brigade let fly on the fire. The wind blew the spray back in Hagen's direction and dewed his face with moisture, mixing with the faint sheen of his own sweat. The streams of water seemed to make little difference on the conflagration, and there was a loud crash as a floor inside one of the buildings collapsed. More sparks floated into the air like faeries against the blackness of the night. How much accelerant had been used to make the fires spread this fast?

A man on the ground screamed out in agony and Hagen bent down to see if he could render assistance. The skin on the man's forehead was blistering to a liquid mass, and black claws reached to clutch at Hagen's clothing. The damned creature, if he survived, would never be the same again. An acrid smell emanated from the body, a mixture of smoke and urine, souring the back of Hagen's throat. "Help me!" the man hissed though frothing lips.

"Don't speak, man!" Hagen took off his cape and covered the torso of the victim. "I'm sure a medic will be here soon." He had seen men injured like this during the war. Burns of such an extensive nature were hard to heal. He would do his best to make the man comfortable, but he doubted his ability to do much more than that.

"What the fuck are you doing here, Doctor Kohl?" Someone bent down beside Hagen.

Hagen whirled his head up. Strohkeller the Jew was on the other side of the body. "I was in the neighbourhood and thought I would see what I could do. Why are you here?"

"Followed your pretty boy. Our little Austrian," the man hissed through clenched teeth. "Get out of here. We have it covered."

"Was he involved?"

Strohkeller nodded in sharp affirmative. "Would have been a slaughter if he hadn't tipped us off right before. No fatalities yet, but it's bad." Strohkeller reached into his thick black overcoat and pulled out a mickey, holding it to the man's lips. "Drink this, friend. It will take some of the pain away. Slowly now." The agent let a few drops of the vodka hit the man's lips.

Hagen pulled out his silk pouf and reached for the vodka. He soaked the edge and tried to daub the worst of the dirt from the victim's forehead. "What do we know?"

251

"New orders came down from the Grandmaster today. Crack the lice. It's only going to get worse from here, I think. But we do know that these offices were supposed to be empty tonight. This meeting of the faithful was scheduled at the last minute. We don't think the NAO meant to have this loss of life." Strohkeller's eyes focussed on the injured man. "These idiots! We tell them to get out and they start packing. Get out means get out! I despise the grotesque stupidity of fanatics. They get what they deserve."

Hagen ignored that outburst. "Have you seen Freisler?"

"Yes. We made contact yesterday."

Hagen poured more vodka on the wounds to clean them, and the man screamed out piteously. "Can you tell him to meet me in St. Stefan's at ten a.m. in two days?"

"Will do. Don't you think that's a bit risky?" Strohkeller's smooth face lined with displeasure.

"No. My hosts don't arise before the strike of noon. I can get in and out with no one the wiser, I think. Besides! Going to a church is a good cultural thing. My host should approve," Hagen commented, sparing a thought for Galiena's friend in the alley.

"You fucking filthy Jew!" A hand reached down suddenly and picked up Strohkeller, throwing him away onto the pavement. Hagen knew that voice. Kaltenbrunner. "Get away from him, you bastard!"

"Apologies, mein Herr. Many apologies." Strohkeller tried to crab away and received a kick in the ribs which sent him flying.

"You, too!" Hagen twisted around to see the end of a billy club flying towards his head. He raised up his forearm to ward off the blow, and took the brunt on his left forearm. The impact stunned him, the pain greater than anything he had felt in many, many years. He knew his arm wasn't broken, but the bruise was going to be with him for weeks.

Hagen attempted to get to his feet and another man was on him, throwing him into a parked car. "What gives you the right to touch him, Jew!"

His shoulder impacted into the hood and exploded into agony. "Jesus Christ!" He swore loudly. "I'm not a Jew!" He ground out, lifting his bare head. His top hat had gone flying when he hit the car; rolling away from him and as he followed its trail and saw he was surrounded by the group of men who had been arguing with Kaltenbrunner. Obviously they had united against a common enemy. "Open your eyes, idiot! You ever see a Jew in tails?" An inane thing to say perhaps, but it was the first thing to spring to his mind.

The man with the billy club advanced on him. "Then you're a fucking aristo and this is going to be nothing but pleasure." The man was covered in soot from his head to his toes, and from the blackened face the whites of the eyes glowed.

"You're about to make a huge mistake." Hagen dropped into a crouch. The crowd was forming a half circle around them, blocking Hagen against the vehicle. There was no way to go but through the crowd.

"Finish him off, Brigadeführer Rodlauer!" One of the other men jeered. "Make him dance!"

His adversary had at least forty pounds on Hagen, a weapon and a cheering section. Hagen had nothing. His cheering section had probably run back to the party. He felt at a distinct disadvantage. The only person here who knew he was a Nazi was Kaltenbrunner, who was busily screaming epithets at Strohkeller. Retreat seemed to be the best option at this moment. "I'm sorry I tried to help your comrade. Let me go, and let's call it a night."

"He's a fucking coward, too! Fucking aristos! Think your so high and mighty 'til the chips are down!" The billy club swung down in a sharp arc, but Hagen dashed sideways and the club impacted into the fender of the vehicle, denting it deeply.

Hagen saw an opening and drove his fist into the man's ribs, connecting solidly. He grabbed around the barrel of the man's chest with the other, holding him close and punched again. He felt a rib give way with satisfaction. "Back off. I don't want to play with you," Hagen ground out.

"Fuck you!" The man wiggled from side to side, trying to bring his club to bear on Hagen's back and shoulders.

Hagen clawed at his adversary's face and shoved up with all his might with the palm of his hand, trying to break the nose. He drove his toe into the man's shin and the man toppled, completely overbalanced. The Brigadeführer went down in a sprawl. "I'll be leaving now."

"You fucking bastard!" The giant Kaltenbrunner stepped over the fallen man to fill the breach.

This was certainly not working out as he had planned. Kaltenbrunner seemed much bigger at this proximity and situation. "It's over. Let me go," Hagen returned evenly, trying to meet the other SS man's eye.

"Not bloody likely." The huge hands were on his shoulders, driving him back against the car.

Hagen thrust his face into Kaltenbrunner's. "Himmler would be damn pissed if you took my face off!" Hagen hissed quietly. "Open your eyes, man!"

He was slammed backward into the side of the car again, suddenly seeing stars. "You aren't worthy to mention his," the words were spoken automatically, and then trailed off. "Kohl!" Kaltenbrunner exclaimed.

"You know this aristo, Oberführer Kaltenbrunner?" One of the others called.

"Yes," Kaltenbrunner said over his shoulder and turned back to Hagen. "Kohl! What are you doing here?"

"I sent you a note I was in town," Hagen replied with a diffidence he didn't feel. "Could you let me up now?"

The hands dropped him abruptly. "Hell, Kohl! I'm sorry."

"Perhaps you should kennel your dogs before they beat up any more bystanders," Hagen growled.

"Not mine. They're SA, but I will apologize. Tempers are a little frayed tonight." Kaltenbrunner held out his hand but Hagen refused to shake it. The untaken limb soon dropped uselessly.

"I won't tell Himmler you tried to concuss me," Hagen reached over and picked up his hat. There was dirt on the brim and he wiped it off with his forearm before he replaced it on his brow.

The towering SS man parroted his earlier comment stupidly. "Didn't know it was you, Kohl. But what are you doing here?"

Hagen allowed his gaze to travel up to Kaltenbrunner's eyes. "What the hell do you think I'm doing here, Kaltenbrunner?" He looked past the officer to the burning fire. "I'm sightseeing. Vienna is ever so lovely this time of year."

"Yes. Yes of course." The man bobbed his head almost subserviently.

"Who's he?" Hagen asked, gesturing to his earlier opponent on the ground who was writhing as he clutched at his ribs.

"SA Brigadeführer Adolf Rodlauer." Kaltenbrunner's voice was a bare whisper above the din.

"Thank you, Oberführer. If you don't mind, I should get back to my host. I wanted to appraise the situation, and it would appear I have the essence of it." Hagen narrowed his eyes at the Austrian-SS chief. "I'm sure the Reichsführer will be heartened to see the depth of the cooperation between the Austrian-SS and the Austrian-SA. I doubt he expected it would be so cordial that you would fight each other's battles." He found himself unable to resist that final dig.

"Of course." Kaltenbrunner's expression turned sickly. "Thank you for your assistance."

Hagen looked over his shoulder at Kaltenbrunner and felt his eyebrow go up of its own volition. "It was my pleasure to be your punching bag," he said with a great deal of irony.

"Yes. I am sorry for that."

Hagen walked over to the man he had felled. The SA man was trying to rise to his feet and Hagen very calmly stepped on the man's hand. He ground his heels into the fingers, and crouched down. "I would advise you, Brigadeführer Rodlauer, to use a little more discretion before you start assaulting those trying to help you. You might offend the wrong person." He lifted his foot and stepped over the man's head, walking calmly toward the alley. He was pleasantly surprised to see the Prinz was waiting for him. It would appear amongst the popinjays there was one who wasn't a complete coward.

November 14, 1937
Dearest Poppet,

A quick note tonight. I am not myself. The old complaint is acting up and Montrose is quite concerned. Why aren't you here? I need you. Don't you know how much I need you?
Eternally yours,
Meinrad

Chapter 19
February 24, 1938

The Taifun banked to the left with sickening speed, completely rolling over on its axis before going into a dive. Galiena gasped in fear and then blinked before reaching to grab the stick.

"Do I have your attention, Recruit?" The plane evened out slowly. "The next time you pull us out of the dive," Von Schilling reproved Galiena frostily.

"Apologies, Herr Hauptman!" She stammered in embarrassment.

"Not good enough, Recruit! You will pay attention!" The man yelled the last word. "You are my observer. What do you see?"

Galiena looked out the windows, her eyes so tired the lids weighed a thousand pounds. They had spent almost twelve hours in lessons yesterday, and had just surpassed the nine hour mark today. Six in the morning yesterday had turned into four thirty this morning. Galiena had made the critical error of concurring with Udet when he told von Schilling to treat her as any other recruit. She thought that meant in training; what it had turned into was something vastly different. Von Schilling had convinced Uncle Hermann's butler to have Galiena awakened and dressed at a time when civilized people were going to bed. When Idalie had shaken her awake at ten to four, Galiena had been unable to believe her ears. Then the bloody man had the temerity to yell at her for not being ready in less than thirty minutes! Whenever she made the first note of complaint, those dark blue eyes just narrowed, and he would ask if she did or did not have what it took. Those words forestalled any comments from her.

It wasn't that Galiena didn't love the Taifun. She did and couldn't wait for her first solo flight. She was even quite entranced with von Schilling, when he wasn't driving her to do better. But it had only been two days and he had reduced her to silent, frustrated tears three times. Not that she let him see her cry. Quite thankfully she wore goggles when flying which made hiding her shame easier. Away from the plane, he was completely charming, but in the plane her teacher became completely tyrannical.

"No offence to the esteemed General Udet, but your training has holes I could fly a bomber through. You know more about aerial tricks and hot dogging then you should for your hours, but your basics are lacking. The general only showed you what was interesting, not what is required. You already have fifty-nine flight hours, and twenty of them easily have been wasted. Your theory is a complete shambles!" Von Schilling told her over lunch in the hanger yesterday. "We must work longer and harder if you are to pass your flight test, because I won't let you take it unless you can ace it."

So now Galiena ate the plane, slept the plane, and dreamt the plane. Three almost hellish days and she was exhausted. Is this what soldiers went through? Getting up in the middle of the night and being yelled at all the time? They had flown until the sun set around six and then Galiena returned to the Carinhall to read the daily reports from the Ritter von Kleist on the family business. She hadn't gone to bed until midnight after making the necessary phone calls, but she couldn't let him break her. Galiena wouldn't give him the satisfaction. The Ritter von Schilling would not win. It wasn't going to happen!

Galiena scanned the clouds, returning to the present with a snap. "I see," she began.

"Now, Recruit!"

Then her eyes focussed on a dark speck ahead of them. "Port Quarter. Eleven o'clock. Approaching." She spat out the correct military terminology in time to hopefully escape another dressing down about civilian puddle jumpers.

"Very good. Looks like a multi engine transport. That is the enemy," von Schilling replied crisply. "Moving to intercept. Looks like Juan Negrin's plane to me! I see three escort planes with it."

Galiena knew Juan Negrin was the prime minister of socialist Spain and that wasn't the man's plane. She also didn't see any escort. What was he talking about? "Excuse me?"

Von Schilling let his gaze roam over her. "Open your eyes, Recruit! Before we intercept! This is going to be a hot one!"

Had he lost his mind? "I see one plane, Herr Hauptman, the transport. I see no escort planes!"

Von Schilling turned his head and winked at her. "I see three escort planes. Don't you?"

There was something in the way he said it; loud over the propeller, which clued her in. Galiena didn't know what his game was, but the merriment in his eyes suggested it was going to be fun. "I do believe you're right!" She replied gamely. "Dear Lord, Herr Hauptman! There are three more behind!"

"Six! Christ on the cross!" The man swore theatrically. "I wasn't expecting that! Where are our wingmen?"

Galiena swivelled her head. "Udet's on our aft port quarter, coming up fast."

"Good. Mölders is covering starboard. Three against seven's much better odds." Von Schilling threw back his head and laughed loudly and evilly; the burst of laughter was short and chilled Galiena's soul. He glanced over at her. "Now it's your turn!"

"What?"

"I always laugh before I go into combat, Recruit. Stops your guts from turning to water. Makes you know you can win! Now get on with it!"

Galiena forced out a giggle. "Good enough?"

"Not hardly! You laugh like a girl! Come on now! Laugh to strike fear in the hearts of your enemies!" She tried again, and he chuckled. "Good enough. Come now! Let's charge Negrin! Moving to intercept!" The plane banked left sharply, lifting up to surpass the attitude of the oncoming plane. "Let's see the whites of their eyes!" Galiena's stomach lurched dangerously, and she clung to his next words like a lifeline. "Always get above them. They can't see you when you come out of the sun. You can see them, but they are blinded by the brightness."

The new, sophisticated radio crackled to life. "Oncoming plane! Identify yourself. Over."

The plane was approaching very fast. They were perhaps forty kilometres apart, a distance easily met when both parties were travelling at 200 km/h. "That's a Junkers 52, Recruit! Never forget it!"

Galiena felt her blood singing; this was probably the scariest but most exciting thing she had ever done. She remembered back to the flash cards von Schilling had shown her over lunch. "Crew of two. Passenger plane. Max passengers seventeen," She repeated.

"Correct. Unless it's fitted for cargo," von Schilling swivelled his head. "Udet and Mölders are peeling away that escort rather smartly. Now it is our turn at the enemy! Come on now!"

"Unidentified aircraft! This is controlled airspace! You will identify and alter course. Over."

"They're being cagey. They want us to identify, but aren't identifying themselves. A cunning ploy. It must be Negrin's plane!" The other plane was growing larger through the windscreen and was much, much bigger than theirs. Von Schilling seemed completely unfazed.

Galiena could see the disturbance of the three props coming straight at them. "Junkers dead ahead and closing."

"Let's get behind them and blow them straight to hell! Grab the stick and pull up!"

Galiena did as she was told and reefed back on the stick. She was sure she could see the pilots in the plane charging them, and was more than a little afraid they were going to collide. She trusted von Schilling knew what he was doing, but she also didn't want to die! It felt like an eternity before the plane lifted its nose, and then suddenly they were shooting upwards into a Cuban eight. The Junkers passed below them, seeming hideously close, but Galiena knew it wasn't as close as it appeared. She was sure she spied her Uncle's pennant on the tail livery as they lifted.

At the apex of the circle von Schilling righted the plane and dove down to chase the tail of the Junkers, pushing the throttles forward. "Let's see what this baby can do, shall we?"

259

"We've never put it to the boards before!" Galiena felt a thrill of adrenaline coursing through her.

"Damn shame that!"

The radio reverberated to life again. "Unidentified plane! What the hell are you playing at? Over. "

Von Schilling picked up the microphone. "Sonderflug Hermann, this is the Wing of Riesa. Ask Der Dicke if he wants to play! Over." He placed the mike back and grinned at her.

"Do you think they will?" Galiena asked him in complete disbelief.

"Let's really get their attention!" Again the loud, evil laugh.

They were closing on the Junkers fast and von Schilling veered sharply to starboard, coming almost abreast of the other plane. He measured their progress carefully, gently pulling back the throttles some. Galiena could see the other pilots in the Junkers, staring at them and pointing for the other plane was only thirty or so feet away. Back in the fuselage, she could see someone waving at her plane.

"Wing of Riesa, you will withdraw! You do no have authorization to fly so close! You are contravening several regulations! Over."

"Regulations? Bah! This is war!" Von Schilling pushed the throttles forward and grinned. "Hold onto your lunch, girl!"

The plane dove slightly to increase speed, then pulled up and over, barrel rolling over the Junkers. Von Schilling timed it so carefully that they maintained pace with the Junkers, passing over the top of the fuselage without losing any ground. The Junkers maintained its attitude perfectly, its pilot very well trained. They continued the roll on their longitudinal axis, dropping down beside the wing of the other craft, and carrying over to return upright underneath. To complete the manoeuvre, von Schilling pulled the throttle back to slow down and pull into their original position.

Galiena didn't have a second to be terrified during the manoeuvre, but as they evened out, she felt it. Her face went completely numb and she felt her hands twitching on their own. "Are you crazy?" she breathed.

"Come on, recruit! Where're your balls?" The man laughed again. "Just for that, we'll do it again!" Von Schilling repeated the roll, this time faster. The little Taifun was perfectly responsive in the man's hands, reacting enthusiastically to his direction. The engines purred happily as he adjusted the throttle, and the other plane was very careful to maintain its course.

As they came abreast of the Junkers for a second time, it dove abruptly. "This is Sonderflug Hermann. Feldmarschall Göring says we can play for ten minutes, but if the Minister for Propaganda tosses his lunch then the pilots of the Wing of Riesa will be ordered to clean his plane with a toothbrush. Over."

Galiena giggled and reached for the mike. She glanced at von Schilling, and waited for him to nod at her before she spoke. "This is Wing of Riesa! Do inform the Minister for Propaganda that if he disgraces himself I shall apologize to him personally! We agree to the Feldmarschall's terms!" She replaced the mike.

Von Schilling glanced at her again. "You know what that means, don't you?"

Galiena eyeballed him flirtatiously. "What, my master?"

"A Hauptman in the German Luftwaffe never cleans up vomit, so if Herr Doctor Goebbels does toss his lunch, you're the one cleaning it."

"Uncle Hermann wouldn't actually make me clean up his plane. He's just threatening," Galiena replied with more confidence than she felt.

"You will do as you are instructed, recruit." Von Schilling retorted firmly. "No making that pretty little maid of yours do it." The man removed his injured arm from the stick. "Take control, recruit, and don't let them shake you," The last word was hissed through clenched teeth.

"Are you ok?" Galiena asked as she banked left and dove to follow the Junkers.

Von Schilling rubbed the broken arm with his good one. "Just a twinge. There's aspirin waiting for me down on the ground."

The Junkers banked right abruptly and then pulled up, decelerating. Galiena wasn't fast enough in pulling the throttles back and she overshot the larger plane. "Damn!"

"Now you sound like a pilot," von Schilling muttered.

"Thanks, ever so!" She grunted, thinking about the best way to find her target. Perhaps the direct chase wasn't the best idea, Galiena considered, throwing the stick up and to the left to circle around and chase the Junkers.

The little plane responded with enthusiasm and she completed the turn tightly. The Junkers had also completed the wheel around, and it was Galiena's very great surprise to see it coming directly at them at a mind-numbing velocity. The two planes were literally hurtling towards each other. She nudged the stick down quickly, for the Junkers was on slightly higher axis than the Messerschmidt, and passed underneath the airliner, shuddering in the bigger plane's wash.

"Instinctively very good, Recruit, but executed poorly." Von Schilling put his fingers back on the stick. "For now you're flying away again and you don't know your Cuban 8." Von Schilling executed the move, and once more they were spinning through the air.

"Wing of Riesa, this is Sonderflug Hermann. Please break off pursuit. You've had your ten minutes and Herr Doctor Goebbels is aching for Terra Firma. Over."

Von Schilling picked up the mike. "Sonderflug Hermann, this is Wing of Riesa. Pity you have to obey the cargo. We will discontinue pursuit and meet you on the ground. Over."

"Wing of Riesa. Easy for you to say when you're in the BF108. Try doing a Cuban in this kite! Over and out." The voice was highly amused.

Galiena watched as the Junkers banked to port, changing course to close on the Carinhall airfield. The turn was flawless and she wondered what it was like to fly such a large craft. Would it feel the same as the tiny Taifun? Would it require different skills to land such a great beast?

"I suppose the recruit would like to have the rest of the evening off to interact with her commanding officer?" Von Schilling grinned, his white teeth flashing at her.

"Is that allowed?" Galiena pondered von Schilling's phrasing. Was he referring to Göring or himself?

"Perhaps. We need to refuel anyway." The Taifun's course altered to follow that of Sonderflug Hermann. "And I think some food might be in order as well," Von Schilling added, rubbing his growling stomach.

Galiena tried to stifle a yawn as the plane descended, the singing in her blood of earlier having been depleted. Now she was just exhausted; she would be lucky if she didn't fall dead asleep in her plate. Her eyes watered behind her goggles and she tried to blink the moisture. "The recruit wouldn't object to food."

Her instructor looked over at her with a shadow of a grin. "You did very well just now."

"Thank you, Herr Hauptman." Galiena felt the corners of her mouth turn up for his praise meant more to her than she could say. Perhaps it was because it was praise she knew she had earned, whereas so many others liked to pat her on the head simply because of her position as a way to curry favour. Galiena didn't think von Schilling to be that sort.

Von Schilling landed the plane smoothly, perhaps a little closely on the heels of the Junkers for the other plane's comfort, but that was hardly her concern. That was between von Schilling and her uncle's pilot! The Taifun taxied into the little hanger which housed the plane, and had practically become Galiena's home away from home. She and von Schilling had spent so much time at the little table with its hard chairs studying, eating and discussing techniques when they hadn't been flying in the last three days.

A Luftwaffe mechanic leapt onto the wing of the Taifun, scrambling up to unlatch the cockpit cover and help her out of the plane. The blast of fresh air was more than welcome after three hours in the cockpit. It helped to clear Galiena's head as she and von Schilling went through their post flight checklist. She pulled off the tight leather flight cap on her head and handed it to the mechanic as von Schilling finished off.

"You look tired, recruit." Von Schilling whispered in her ear. "Has the pace been too much for you?" The words were like absolution from God's lips.

Galiena whirled to search his face, his eyes were half closed. What did he want from her? An admission? "No. It's just taking some getting used to."

"Then if you aren't entertaining your uncle and his guest this evening, might I invite you for a spell of contraband this evening?" Von Schilling leaned in, his lips almost touching her ear. "A friend of mine is up from Berlin this week. A fellow downed condor who has smuggled in some jazz records. Some of the boys and girls in the Admin building are planning a sock hop in the basement."

Galiena was taken rather aback. "I," she stammered. "I don't know."

"Come now! You aren't one of those boring BDM girls! All Sieg Heil! Lets be all withered up and dull for the fatherland, now are you?" Von Schilling chuckled, his voice containing all the seductive power of the devil. "I know you aren't, Leutnant girl of General Udet. No BDM woman would be in a plane with Germany's most notorious rake learning how to fly."

"Are you making some kind of slander against my reputation, Hauptman Ritter von Schilling?" Galiena retorted coldly, her eyes narrowing dangerously. "I can assure you that I am not a fast woman. If that is what you thought, then you are sorely mistaken."

She rose to her feet in the open cockpit, but he caught her arm. "Stay your feathers, lass. I meant nothing of the kind and certainly no insult. I merely thought you might enjoy that sort of engagement."

The lure of a dance was almost too much to resist. "I don't know." Galiena told him, the word engagement echoing in her mind like a gun. "My fiancé would not approve."

"I assure you, as an officer of the German Luftwaffe and a Ritter of the second Reich, nothing will happen this evening which would cause your absent fiancé distress." Was there extra emphasis on the word absent? "Besides, General Udet would have my tripe for his lunch if I did anything to compromise your honour, Your Serene Highness." Von Schilling smiled completely disarmingly. "Does that settle your mind?"

"Can I bring a chaperone?" Galiena asked quietly, thinking of Swanhilde Stammler.

"Provided it isn't Herr Doctor Goebbels, I can't see why not!"

Galiena blinked and stared into the pilot's blue eyes. "You bad man! I can't believe you would have a jazz party on the very night that the man who banned jazz is in residence!"

Von Schilling shrugged innocently. "Didn't know it when we planned the party and my friend goes back to the capital tomorrow. Seems a shame to cancel, wouldn't you say?" The last word was tossed out like a lure.

Galiena swivelled her head around the plane, using the movement to cover her indecision. "All right, I would love to attend. Guilty as implicated. I love jazz." She winked at him. "Pray don't report me to the Gestapo!"

"Never!" His smile broadened. "Then I will collect you at 21:00, from the spa door. You and your iron fisted chaperone."

Galiena nodded and lifted herself out of the plane to stand on the wing. The afternoon sun was shining with a fervour not usually seen in February and it had to be at least eight or nine degrees Celsius. Certainly warmer than the cold cockpit. She unzipped the jacket of her new two piece navy leather flight suit, exposing the thin cream cashmere sweater she was wearing underneath. It felt plastered to her skin with a layer of cold sweat. Her legs felt similarly stuck in the tight leather britches, and she would have sold her soul to rip her boots off right here on the tarmac. Galiena settled with unwinding the coronet of braids from the crown of her head and unthreading the plaits as von Schilling carefully deplaned.

"Where's my favourite aviatrix?" came a faintly slurred voice from across the tarmac. "I know she's about somewhere!"

Galiena walked around the Taifun to intercept her uncle, completely resplendent in full military uniform. His cheeks were very rosy; artificially rouged at closer inspection and his eyes were bright and glassy. Galiena ran to him. "Uncle Hermann!" She darted in for a quick hug to examine him a little closer. "Are you quite all right, Uncle Hermann? We didn't scare you with our antics, did we?" Those strange eyes claimed her own, yet they were like a shield; separating her from his soul.

"No, Liebschen. Not at all." Her uncle grinned. "Not at all."

This was not the first time of late that her uncle had been like this. Since his terrible toothaches of last fall, he had been taking painkillers by the handful, seemingly long after the toothaches had ended. It caused Galiena a frisson of concern, and yet it wasn't her place to inquire too strongly. Hermann Göring had to know what he was doing; it was his health after all. "Then I am doubly glad to see you!" She hugged him again, clasping him close. "I love the Taifun, Uncle Hermann! I could kiss you to death every time I see it!"

The great man chortled. "Emmy might have something to say about that, my dear girl! She seems to like me very much alive!" His hand rubbed her back absently. "But I'm so glad it pleases you. Willey Messerschmidt assured me it was quite the right plane for an eager young pilot." The turquoise eyes blinked owlishly. "And I could hardly give you a 109, now could I? As much as you know I would like to."

"A single passenger plane wouldn't allow for me to have my esteemed teacher with me." Galiena moved her hand, gesturing to von Schilling, who had come to attention at her side.

"Heil Hitler!" The young man saluted.

Göring threw his hand up haphazardly. "Heil. Yes. Von Schilling, how's my girl doing?"

"Very well, Herr Feldmarschall. She has an instinct for the plane," von Schilling replied crisply.

"Excellent. What we like to hear." Göring paused and examined the Hauptman through bleary eyes. "And how are the wounds healing up? I see you've been flying, so the arm can't be too bad!"

"Twinge now and then, Herr Feldmarschall. I shall be right as rain soon enough."

"Capital. We need our best men hale and hearty." Göring clapped von Schilling on his shoulder.

"Thank you for indulging our antics, uncle Hermann," Galiena smiled winsomely.

"Ach! T'was nothing, Liebschen, or at least nothing to me. There were others on my plane who were perhaps not so enthused to be on a non-standard flight plan," Göring chuckled wickedly.

"I heard that, Göring!" A tiny man, pasty beneath his black hair limped around the tail of the Taifun. "No making fun of me. I'm a talker, not a flyer." The sonorous voice of Paul Joseph Goebbels, Reich minister for Propaganda reached Galiena's ears. Goebbels looked like a cat whose fur had been rubbed the wrong way.

Galiena executed a quick curtsy. "Tis entirely my fault, Herr Doctor," She smiled warmly at the little man who was a strange friend of hers. "Do forgive me."

"My dear Pfalzgräfin von Steinberg, I could forgive you almost anything." The infamous smile broke across the homely face. Goebbels limped forward to kiss Galiena's hand, lingering a moment longer than was correct. "Especially when you dress like that," He added. "How are you?"

"Worn down to the nub, Herr Doctor. The esteemed officers of the German Luftwaffe have decided to treat me like any raw recruit and the pace is exhausting." Galiena looked down at Goebbels through her eyelashes. He always flirted outrageously with her and yet she felt safe with the man. She instinctively knew he wouldn't go farther with anything than she willed. On the other hand, with the slightest instance of real encouragement, she knew he would try and seduce her in a heartbeat. Goebbels, like Udet, was a hedonist of the highest order.

"Now my dear! Look at you!" Goebbels' grin turned positively lascivious. "Indeed! Look at you. Not your usual attire."

Galiena rolled her eyes and as she did so, she noticed von Schilling bristling at Goebbels' ogling. "Herr Doctor! Really!" She shook her head, as she pulled her hand out of the man's grasp.

"But my dear! What would the Fuhrer say if he saw you now?" Goebbels face was a picture of innocence.

Göring grunted sourly. "I don't think that needs to be addressed."

The one side of the propaganda minister's grin re-emerged; that patented derisive look of his. "And more importantly, dear Pfalzgräfin von Steinberg! What would Herr Himmler say?" The low voice dropped down even lower. "Or your Standartenführer Kohl?"

"Hagen thinks my flight suit is distracting and as for Herr Himmler," She frowned at both her uncle and the Doctor. "I don't give a fig about what the Reichsführer thinks!"

Goebbels laughed after a moment; a gleeful explosion of sound. "Very few would have the nerve to say that, Pfalzgräfin von Steinberg!" He took Galiena's hand in his. "But it is one of the reasons I am so fond of you."

"Well it's certainly a start." Göring harrumped. "Maybe now she'll leave the crows alone." He offered an arm to Galiena. "Can we escort you back to the house?"

"I think so." Galiena glanced at von Schilling. "Am I free for a while?"

"Until 21:00," Von Schilling winked broadly behind her Uncle's back.

Goebbels squeezed Galiena's hand. "And who is this young officer?"

Galiena blushed with embarrassment. "My apologies. Doctor Goebbels, may I introduce you to my flight instructor, Hauptman Ritter von Schilling, lately of the Condor Legion?"

"Herr Hauptman," Goebbels nodded and his eyes gleamed slyly at Göring. "Not a crow?" His eyebrow lifted faintly.

Now it was Göring's moment to be a picture of innocence. "How could her flight instructor be a member of the SS? The only decent one I know is Hans Bauer[14] and he's a little busy at the moment."

"I really dislike that term! Both of you!" Galiena frowned theatrically. "And I will be very put out with you both if you continue to use it."

"Yes, Madame," Goebbels nodded with mock contriteness. Göring just grunted as his limousine approached.

"Incorrigible men! I wonder why I choose to spend my time with such reprobates."

Goebbels brought a pale hand to his brow. "Because we amuse and you were ever so bored before we came to entertain."

"Something along those lines, to be sure!" Galiena couldn't help but grin.

"And speaking of amusement, Pfalzgräfin, I have come with the most amazing proposition for you to consider." Goebbels' eyes sparkled merrily. "I don't know if you were looking for one, but I have found you the perfect house. Come down to Berlin on the 26th and I will have the time to show it to you!"

Galiena blinked. "A house? I wasn't precisely in the market for one. A house in Berlin?"

"We would practically be in each other's pockets. A place on Schwanenwerder is coming for sale, and I think it would be quite darling. You can't live with old Göring forever!" Goebbels shrugged elegantly. "Would you like to see it?"

---

[14] Hitler's personal pilot.

"Schwanenwerder, you say? A home of my own?" The thought was very appealing. The von Steinberg family had a villa in Potsdam, but that place was old and quite outdated. It also wasn't hers. It belonged to her Grandfather. A place of her own in Berlin! It was a magical thought, the more she contemplated it. Some might call it a waste of funds, but they were her funds. If Uncle Hermann would allow the purchase.

"It's an older property for the island, bit of a fixer upper, I would say, but I think it's an absolute gem. Huge grounds. With the right touch, I think you could ramble around there quite nicely and the beach is perhaps even better than mine." Goebbels made a little moue. "Not that I would ever admit it to another soul."

Galiena cocked her head at her uncle. "What do you think, Uncle Hermann? Should I go take a look?"

The glassy eyes crinkled as the Feldmarschall smiled. "Whatever you would like to do, Galiena, I will support. Emmy and I love to have you near, but it might not be ideal for you! If you would like a home of your own, I certainly won't stand in your way," The big shoulders rolled. "And Wannsee property is a very good investment."

"Then it is settled. How about the 26th at noon? We can have lunch first at my place, and then drift over and look at this villa," Goebbels smiled brilliantly again. "Smashing plan!"

Chapter 20
February 26, 1938

The woman who sat in the foyer of von Reitersbach's house was an expression of misery. Perhaps it was her tired, worn features, or the dejected slump of her back. Her simple charcoal suit hung from her shoulders, and while it appeared to be of an expensive cut, it looked old and worn. The feather in her small hat drooped limply along the brim, drawing the eye to the greyish cheeks. She wore no makeup, and Hagen figured she had to be younger than her lined and worn face suggested. Her gloved hands clutched a black leather folio to her knees in a tight grip; obviously the contents were important.

As Hagen descended the stairs he studied her. There was something about her features that was familiar. He knew he had never seen her before and yet- the cheekbones, or the lips, or the mouse brown hair streaked with white coiled at the back of her head rang bells in his mind. Who was she? Why was she here at quarter after nine in the morning?

"Wilhelm! At last!" The woman looked up at his footfalls on the stairs, her words coming before she realised that the man before her was not the one she thought. The eyes met his then dropped to the floor. "Apologies, mein Herr. I thought you were the Ritter von Glass."

"Nothing to apologize for. I am Doctor Hagen Kohl. I'm a guest of the Graf von Reitersbach. Can I assist you, Madame?" She seemed so familiar!

The woman shook her head dejectedly. "No, Herr Doctor. I don't think so." She wrung her hands for a moment and then glanced back up at him. "I'm sorry. I am Frau Drexler. I am Wilhelm's sister." The last words were a bare whisper.

At closer inspection the woman was probably not yet forty, yet she looked to be in her sixties. Her pallor was dreadful and the hurt in her eyes tore at him. "I am pleased to meet you, Frau Drexler." He clicked his heels and bowed his head. "Is there naught I can do to help you?"

She sighed. "No. I should have expected this would happen. Wilhelm never keeps his appointments with me. It's just every time I hope he will, and I sit here and I wait, and I curse myself for being a fool," her voice was thick and the end of her nose turned pink.

Hagen offered the woman a hanky. "Would you like me to send his valet to rouse him?"

"Thank you." Frau Drexler took the hanky and daubed at her eyes. "But he will not come. He seeks to remind me of my place. Of my sin." The last words were spoken with so much derision and regret, before she looked up at him, smiling sadly. "I'm sorry. I shouldn't be rattling on like this."

Hagen had a few moments before he had to leave to meet Eugen. He sat down on the settee beside Frau Drexler. "No. Continue," he said gently.

"You know Wilhelm, I'm sure. He's an idealist; always has been. He doesn't forgive those who fall in his eyes, and that was my mistake. I married the wrong man. Disgraced the family. Married beneath me. Betrayed my class once, then betrayed it again, or so he says." Frau Drexler glanced down. "But it's my own fault I suppose. I come here like a dog begging for scraps at his table and what do I expect?"

"His behaviour towards you is reprehensible," Hagen replied quietly. "No sin could possibly warrant this."

"I shouldn't even be talking to you. I'm sorry." She rose to go, clutching the folio to her breast.

"Are you in trouble, Frau Drexler?" Hagen asked with concern.

The woman hefted the case in her hand. "I need this to go to Wilhelm and I'm afraid to leave it." Her eyes scanned the room.

"I can ensure it gets to him, Madame. On my honour, I will." Hagen stood up.

Her gaze returned to his. "I don't know," Frau Drexler whispered again. "I have to leave. I have to get to my office." She looked at her watch. "I suppose I can wait a few moments more."

Hagen reached out to touch the woman on her arm, trying to calm her as the frenzied hand wringing began again. "As you wish, Madame."

She considered his hand a moment before studying him. "And are you one of Wilhelm's special friends? Is that where I have heard your name before?" She slid her fingers along the edge of the folio almost contemplatively.

Hagen examined her. Did she think he was a homosexual? That was a tad blatant. "Madame, my connection to your brother is through a mutual acquaintance of the Graf von Reitersbach, but our association is very new. I would not go so far as to call us friends, special or otherwise."

"Then why do you stay here?"

"Because the Graf von Reitersbach is in the process of adopting me. It was thought politic we get to know each other," Hagen replied with simplicity.

"Doctor Kohl?" she said almost as if to herself. "Are you the German who is to marry the Pfalzgräfin von Steinberg?" Frau Drexler stuttered before she said the word German, as if she had been about to use another.

"It is my honour to be that man, yes," Hagen nodded.

"If you will forgive my forwardness, Doctor Kohl, you have very kind eyes," The woman spoke almost as if to herself. "The Pfalzgräfin must be a blessed woman."

Hagen cocked his head. "Thank you. The Ritter von Glass doesn't appear to agree with you on that score." He noticed her stockings were down at the ankles. Old, probably. "Will Galiena's sin be as great in the Ritter's eyes?" As the words left his mouth he worried at their cruelty.

"Wilhelm is fond of Galiena and I highly doubt it. She isn't pregnant and running away with the under coachman." Frau Drexler shook her head and took a deep breath. "No. Her sin will be nowhere near as great."

"Why do you see him, then? Does your husband have nothing to say about your brother?" Hagen questioned.

"My husband died in 1934," Frau Drexler answered primly.

"I'm sorry." Hagen bowed his head.

"Don't be. My husband made his share of mistakes as well, as he paid the price for them." It was an interesting turn of phrase. "It wasn't an ideal marriage, Doctor Kohl. I stopped mourning my husband about ten minutes after I buried him."

Again, Hagen didn't know how to respond, so instead he chose to retreat. "Then if I cannot be of any service to you, Frau

Drexler, I will bid you adieu." He raised his hat from his head in parting.

"Thank you again for your kind offer, Herr Doctor. It was most considerate."

Hagen did up his own overcoat, the black cashmere smooth under his hands. "Perhaps we will meet again?"

Her eyes narrowed ever so perceptively. "In the circles you travel in, it would seem unlikely." She inhaled, her nostrils pinching as she did so. "Why are you staying here, Doctor Kohl? Why?"

"I believe I already told you the reason," Hagen answered, his tone slightly harsher.

"You do realise this household is accursed for your kind." Frau Drexler tried to convey something to him with her eyes, but he simply didn't understand where she was going.

"Accursed? Because of the relationship between your brother and the Graf?" Hagen threw out the most obvious reason.

"What they do is against the laws of God and man, it's true," the woman sighed. "No matter. Be careful here, Doctor Kohl. You are a kind man. I don't think that you deserve what is coming."

"What is coming, Frau Drexler?"

"I don't know." There was a world of agony in those three words; agony as if she knew something more. Hagen looked into her eyes to see madness. This poor woman was obviously hanging onto her sanity by a slim margin; a result of her brother's callousness, no doubt. Then the agony was gone and the eyes shuttered. "But I shouldn't detain you any further."

"Good bye." Hagen knew a dismissal when he heard one. He put his hat back on his head, and moved towards the door. Another quick look at his watch told him that he had no extra time to meet Eugen. A last backwards glance before he went out the house proved she was still watching him. Her eyes almost burned through his jacket. Strange.

The air was warmer than he was expecting; winter was lessening its grip on the city. Four degrees at least today; perhaps closer to five or six. Pleasant weather. The world bustled outside the grounds of the villa on the Schubertring, and it took very little time for Hagen to find a taxi. He gave the order for St. Stephan's

Cathedral, and settled himself back as the old center of Vienna melted by. There was a feeling to Vienna that was so unlike any other place he had been. Berlin would always hold his soul but Vienna captivated him. The culture of the place, perhaps. So much art, so much literature, so much science had come from this city. From the time of Roman Vindibona, it was a very multicultural place. The former capital of a far flung and diverse empire. The more time he spent here, the more he understood how his friend György could love it so much. The less he wanted to see the place torn apart by NAO bombs.

The taxi stopped in the plaza outside the Steffl, as the locals called the Cathedral, and he paid the driver and left the car. St. Stephan's rose above him, the great gothic cathedral majestic in the morning sunshine. The white octagonal towers rose above him, as if to touch the blue sky and Hagen wondered how medieval engineers built such a wonder. Perhaps the hand of God was in man; that he could create such beauty. How many had slaved to craft this building, with its gables, buttresses, stained glass and intricately tiled roof? How many had died whilst creating it, their epitaph in each and every chisel stroke? Hagen wasn't normally so affected by buildings, and yet this one called to him. While his Lutheran past cried out against the excesses of Catholicism, he could feel a stirring in his chest at this mighty temple to God.

Hagen passed through the huge doors into the nave which rose above him like a vast cavern. The piers rose up with majestic regularity, supporting the vaults and arches that formed the roof. The sunlight streamed through the stained glass, painting the floor in brilliant shades of blues, reds and greens. Directly ahead down the red and white tiled floor lay the apse and the high altar; dwarfing him. The cathedral reminded him of his insignificance. It had been built long before his time and would remain here in this location long after he was gone. He was but a speck in the Cathedral's existence.

Hagen shook his head to focus on the pews. It was time to work, not play the tourist. It was a Saturday and the cathedral was quiet. Scattered about the pews were worshipers in various positions of prayer. Hagen scanned ahead, looking for his friend. Up near the front, a bent white head and giant shoulders in a camel hair coat had to be Eugen. As he approached, Hagen could see that

Eugen was down on the kneeler; head low, lips moving silently, and fingers rubbing the beads of a rosary. Hagen was completely taken aback. In their entire association, Hagen had never seen Eugen pray. He'd never heard Eugen even acknowledge God, except to take the Lord's name in vain.

Hagen slipped into the pew beside Eugen and waited patiently for the man to finish. Hagen took in the man's shoes, hardly worn on the undersides. Eugen rarely wore mufti in Germany; living instead in his uniforms. Yet here he was; the press in his trousers was like a knife blade and his socks a frisky argyle. That too, surprised Hagen. He'd never especially noticed Eugen's socks before, but would have put him as a basic black or brown man. Hanging from Eugen's neck was the emerald green scarf Galiena had given him for Christmas. The beaded fringe sparkled in the light with every movement of the huge man's arm. Hagen knew the scarf had special meaning for Eugen.

Eugen took his time, obviously not intimidated by Hagen's presence. He dropped the beads from his fingers and pressed his forehead against his clasped hands. A moment more and he raised his head, staring forward before crossing himself deftly, before joining Hagen on the bench. The men were silent, each breathing slowly, lost in thought.

"Glad to see you, Hagen." Eugen spoke at last. "Strohkeller told me you took a bit of a pounding the other night. What the hell," Eugen paused and crossed himself suddenly. "What were you thinking?"

Hagen swallowed a grin at Eugen's sudden showing of piety. "A bomb went off a block and a half from where I was and I had to take a look for myself?"

"Not good enough, you idiot!" One of those big fingers appeared right under his nose. "I hate it when you're stupid, Hagen! Your presence here isn't a complete secret! Don't you think if the SA found out you were down here alone and unprotected they would make an attempt on your life?" The man growled with abject ferocity.

"And how many times do I have to tell you, Eugen, that I won't let the SA dictate my movements to me," Hagen retorted smoothly.

With a lightning hand, Eugen grabbed the exact place on Hagen's arm where the Billy club impacted. Hard. Hagen tried to hide his reaction, but a quick in draw of breath told Eugen everything he needed to know. "Bloody fool you are! Great bloody fool."

"Strohkeller has a big mouth," Hagen grunted with irritation.

"Because he's more afraid of me then he is of you." Eugen sat back with some satisfaction. "Which is the way it should be."

"You're a bully, Eugen. Pure and simple," Hagen grinned, almost by way of apology.

"Absolutely."

"So what do you have to report?" Hagen leaned back.

"Von Ond is in, or so it would seem. He's based out of a hotel very close to where you are. Living quite the high life with a group of young blades. University men. There seems to be a large amount of frivolity and alcohol in everything these boys do; yet every so often they completely disappear and the bad things start to happen," Eugen began.

"Aren't they being followed?" Hagen felt his brows draw together.

"Of course they are, Hagen. This is hardly amateur hour! How do you think we got a five-minute heads up on the bombing? He has a rotating tail comprised of four of Strohkeller's best men at all times. When they can't be right in von Ond's back pocket, they cover all the entrances and exits to the buildings he's in. So far it's worked quite well. The problem is, we don't know which of this group of young agitators the contact is," Eugen paused. "Nor do we know how the information to move is being passed along, and von Ond hasn't been left alone long enough to tell us."

"How did he let you know about the bomb?" Hagen asked, unable to contain his curiosity. He knew von Ond to be resourceful which is why he chose the young man for such a sensitive operation.

"Somehow he managed to write the location and the time on a slip of paper and dropped it when he crouched to tie up his shoe. I think he was hoping we would have a man close enough to spot the drop, which was the case. Thankfully Strohkeller's men are damn good. I had the note in my hand less than fifteen minutes later, and I contacted Kaltenbrunner. The damned Austrian-SS were slow on the uptake, but they managed to get the building mostly cleared out before the bomb went off." Eugen studied the rosary still wrapped about his wrist, the cross swinging slowly on its beaded chain. "Nine still died, however."

"Damn!" Hagen muttered, thinking. "We need to get someone closer to von Ond. We need faster information. More reliable. What if we missed him dropping that note? It would have been far worse."

Eugen shook his head. "He is never alone. One of the cadre is with him at all times. They're a pretty debauched group. In the course of doing his duty for the Fuhrer, I think von Ond has screwed half the whores in Vienna. Drunk enough brandy to float the Graf Spree!"

Hagen considered this. "Where do the girls come from? All over? Or a single brothel?"

"Generally a single brothel. The pension Schöneberg."

"Do you think we can get to one of the girls? Convince her to work for us?" Hagen spoke his thought aloud. "Maybe one has a dirty little secret we can exploit; or perhaps a party member in the family. An angle we can work?" He had used this tactic many times before, to great success.

Eugen shook his head. "We can try obviously, but this isn't Germany, we don't have the same resources. That's hard information to get when we don't have the entire department here to back us up. Frankly, Hagen, this is like shitting out a window on a train. Messy, stupid, and the chances of getting hurt are pretty damn high."

Hagen chuckled, almost against his will. The noise sounded out in the echoing cavern of the church. "That's quite the analogy, there, Eugen. Shitting out the window of a train. Can't say as I've ever done that."

Eugen sent him a pointed look. "It's an expression. My point is that our resources are at a minimum right now," the large man paused. "On the other hand, we can use Heydrich's men to do that filtering for us. I know where the SD offices are here in Vienna. I've passed by them a time or two since we have been here. It's full of Heydrich's spies; three of them, I think. Perhaps they could be of some use to us."

"No. I don't want to use Heydrich if I can help it. I can't imagine that he's a member of my club of admirers. Somehow I think any 'help' he gave us would be tainted. What about our men? Don't we have enough here? Most of the department should be over the border right now," Hagen retorted.

"For sure. They are and set up to boot. Dr. Demeter is astounded at the activity in his house. No. The problem is that in Germany we have to Herr Heydrich's most excellent and thorough files. Here in Austria, we can't send one of the troglodytes down to the file room to get everything we know on an individual and it's making our job a damn sight harder. If we could access the Austrian SS files, it might make a difference," Eugen said the last few words almost like a question.

"No. Not possible. Then the leak would find out about us and I don't want that to happen. It's bad enough Kaltenbrunner knows. I don't trust his people; not with the lives of mine. No. We do this the hard and old fashioned way. Feel for a crack," Hagen pursed his lips. "So tell me what we do know. Start with this cadre. Who are they? What are they? Give me the details, my friend."

Eugen opened a folio in his hand; a black folio, strangely reminiscent of Frau Drexler's. He pulled out a picture of a young man, faintly grainy, obviously taken at a distance. "Anton von Harpe, twenty-six, family held a barony in northern Austria. Absolutely bankrupt. Attends university here in Vienna. Working on his doctorate in history, his specialty being the pan-Germanic movement here in Austria at the turn of the century."

Hagen nodded, drifting back to his own university years. He wrote a dissertation on that very subject for his masters degree. "I might know a thing or two about that. I studied the literature of that period. Is he a particularly sportive man?"

"Not especially. Certainly not by our standards. I can't picture this boy being a terrorist."

"You never can tell. Who's next?" Hagen eyeballed the next dossier.

"Rittmeister Karl von Edelsheim. Son of the General Alois Ritter von Edelsheim. Father died at 12th Isonzo. Von Edelsheim is a member of the auxiliary cavalry, most likely riding on his father's coattails. However, he is an expert rider and being considered for the Spanish riding school; yet his military training and performance is not what one would call stellar. His interest in the military does not seem to go much farther than his uniform. Twenty-nine years old, he appears to be the head of the group."

"A more interesting prospect. The age is also better. Old military family; would certainly have better connections, I think. The right connections. Put men on him. I think it might prove interesting," Hagen instructed, alight in his soul at being on the trail at last. After these weeks of playing at being an aristocrat, this sense of purpose renewed him.

"Absolutely. Then we have Wolfgang von Lüttwitz. Twenty-one years of age; this is the man who befriended von Ond in the first place. Father also dead in the postwar revolution here in Vienna. 1918. Nephew of Feldmarschall Hermann von Lüttwitz, one of the heroes of Gorlice and Tarnow. Artillery man. But young Wolfgang has spurned the forces, despite rumours of encouragement from the Uncle. The boy is the youngest of six sons, three of whom went military. Young von Lüttwitz is at the university, training to be some kind of chemist; we haven't discovered what kind yet. Again, family is impoverished and lives on the sufferance of the Feldmarschall's good will. Wolfgang would be an unlikely military candidate. He's not at all sportive, and almost as round as he is tall, which isn't very. I can see why he wouldn't join in the family business," Eugen supplied carefully.

"Again the military connection. Interesting. What do we know about the Feldmarschall?" Hagen asked, distracted by a nagging feeling in his gut.

"Not much at the moment. Was a General during the war; ranked to Feldmarschall right before Franz Josef abdicated, primarily as a reward for acts above and beyond. Retired from active service in 1930 at the age of seventy-one. Health is still excellent and is very highly respected in military circles. I'm told he's a very good friend of our Feldmarschall von Mackensen." There was a note of awe in Eugen's voice. Hagen knew that von Mackensen was a particular hero of Eugen's during the war.

"Put men on the Feldmarschall as well. Could prove worthwhile, I think. Who else would have the sorts of skills to start something like the NAO? My gut really likes this one. Also the brothers; keeping it all in the family. That wouldn't surprise me." Hagen narrowed his eyes as he studied the red leather cover of the

279

prayer book in the pew ahead of him. "Yes. Pursue it if we have the men to spare."

"Most of the department is down now, so a man for tailing isn't a problem. It's the information gathering that is proving slow. But we'll get on it, Hagen. Even if I have to drive them myself," Eugen grinned nastily.

"I'm sure that's not going to be necessary, Eugen. The men know their jobs."

The look from his friend was positively impudent. "Yes, Mommy!"

"Can it, Freisler! Or I will put you down for insubordination." Hagen's brow rose of its own accord.

Eugen snorted, undaunted as usual. "Lastly we have Albrecht von Gazen, dilettante extraordinaire. Twenty-four years old, wealthy and of seemingly no occupation. Very much like your Graf von Reitersbach. Were it not for the revolution, would be the Graf von Gazen, and still addressed as such by many Austrians to this day. Very well connected in the country, his Grandmother is the sister of the Gräfin von Manderscheid, one of the pillars of Vienna society."

Hagen's head went up like a hound. "Constanze von Manderscheid?"

Eugen consulted his notes. "That would be the one, yes. Why?"

"We have become acquainted. According to gossip, the Gräfin was the mistress of the Pfalzgraf von Steinberg," Hagen supplied easily, rounding out the picture for his number two.

Eugen's lips twisted wryly. "What an inbred group of people."

"You don't know the half of it. She's also von Reitersbach's 'Tante Stanzi' and my ally. Perhaps I can work on the von Gazen angle personally. I believe we have an appointment with her sometime this week." Hagen looked at the notes in Eugen's hand with envy. He wanted to be at György's, in the thick of it, with his men! Yet he knew if he went there, it could compromise the mission.

Eugen wrote a few things down in his notebook. As always, Hagen was amazed by the man's neat printing. Eugen rarely wrote cursively, and his handwriting betrayed his lack of education, but his printing was perfect. Hagen felt a sense of pride at that. He had taught Eugen how to read and write himself, so many years ago. "Anything you can discover on the inside would be a great help."

Hagen considered. "I also want you to run down August von Hellenberg, former Prinz of Zerbst and my host of the other night. I have a feeling about him, too. Infantry Hauptman at Caporetto, among other things. Is a singular exponent of the worthless lifestyle, and yet when he was creeping down alleys with me the other night he could still handle himself like a professional."

"Caporetto, hm? Where von Edelsheim's father was a General. Caporetto was," Eugen paused, stirring his brain, lining up the names of battles with the dates.

"Caporetto was the twelfth battle of Isonzo. When Alois von Edelsheim died. Do you think it might be a coincidence?" Hagen did the math faster than Eugen, but came to the same conclusion.

"Don't believe in them." Eugen scribbled away furiously. "But they might not have known each other. Cavalry general and an infantry Hauptman? There were a fair number of men at Caporetto, weren't there?"

"Yes. On both sides, but György once told me that one of the problems in the empire was always that the different racial groups didn't mix. German Austrians with German Austrians, Magyars with Magyars, and so on. Same age, same circles. It stands to reason that they must have been aware of each other," Hagen frowned; his face feeling like a mask on his bone structure. "And the nobility have no love for our party."

"You want him followed as well?"

"Yes. We are going to have to prioritize, however." Hagen gave Eugen a very direct stare, waiting to speak until his friend met his eye. "Pull the men you have on me off."

"I don't have the foggiest notion what you are talking about," Eugen muttered, tearing his gaze away.

"Yes you do," Hagen contradicted swiftly. "I am not important. The mission is. Keep the men you have on von Ond on him. That is number one for the boy saved lives the other night. It wouldn't do to put him out in the weeds. Next I want von Lüttwitz, von Edelsheim and von Hellenberg; put good tails on them.

Afterwards the rest of the boys. I met von Gazen the other night and I don't think he would be a person of interest. Perhaps a man on him, but I would put him in a class with my hosts. Young, vain and useless."

"Well given that he has no military connection or training, my gut says he must be of less importance to our investigation. While I would bet this month's pay that if he's involved, he must be a minor player." Eugen agreed. The large man shook his hand to emphasise his words, and the rosary glinted in the light.

Hagen brushed it with his finger. "This is not your standard uniform, Eugen," He said very quietly. In fact it was an article which could get him reprimanded or even expelled from the SS if Himmler found out.

A bright flush rose on Eugen's neck. "Camouflage," he grunted. "This is a cathedral, after all."

"Ah."

The silence dragged on for a few moments, and then Eugen turned to face him. "We aren't in Germany, Hagen. Things are different here. The rules don't have to apply." Again the silence. "I scouted out the location yesterday and for some reason I ended up in the confessional." There was a strange glow in Eugen's brilliant eyes; almost like pain.

"I didn't know you worshiped, Eugen?"

Instantly the shoulders straightened. "I don't. I haven't in years. I broke with God in '16; during the war." Eugen's brow twisted in agony. "I renounced the church, well and truly, Hagen. When I came in here yesterday, something compelled me. I don't know. I'm an old Catholic boy, like most of Bavaria, I suppose." There was another silence and Hagen was content to wait Eugen out. "I haven't been in a church since the beginning of the war but when I came in here, it all came back."

Hagen felt his chin dip in unconscious agreement. "Eugen, do what you have to do, just don't let anyone in the organization see you. I don't think I could save you from Himmler if he was informed that you were practicing Christianity."

Eugen bobbed his head curtly. "Of course, Hagen. I would never do this in Germany. Never. And when Austria is ours, when the rules apply here, I won't do it then. I promise you."

"Eugen, I'm not going to be your conscience. Do what you have to. I'm your friend before I'm your superior officer."

Eugen inhaled slowly after a long silence. "How many people have you killed since the war, Hagen?"

Hagen blinked at the question. "I don't know. Let me think. Five or six. Lichtermann. The von Schleisers. A few others during Long Knives. I've pretty much blocked it out."

"Eighty-seven, Hagen. I remember every single one of them." The big man frowned. "That's what I confessed to."

"Eighty-seven? When have you had the time?" Hagen was aghast.

"Bah, Teufel." This was the old Eugen back. "Most were well before you joined the party. Back in the twenties. I killed quite a few Communists in the riots. They always tossed me in the vanguard because they knew I would thin out the ranks of the enemy. Number's smaller after you joined. Only thirty-one since then. That's not so bad, is it?"

Hagen didn't know what to say. "I suppose not, when you average it over the years." Was that the best he could come up with? "But it doesn't count when you're following orders. Have you killed anyone when you haven't been ordered to do it? Have you killed a man in anger, or on your own?"

"Certainly not!" Eugen was completely affronted. "I'm not a murderer!"

"Then there you are. You aren't a murderer. You're a soldier. Soldiers shouldn't contemplate these things. How many did you kill during the war?" Hagen questioned his friend.

"You think I know that? I lost count after '14." The shoulders of the camel hair coat rolled in an irreverent shrug.

Hagen raised a brow. "Think of it this way, Eugen. For us, did the war ever end? We're still fighting it."

"That's for damn sure." Eugen unwrapped the rosary and put it in his pocket. "You're correct. You've put me to rights. Don't know what I was thinking."

"This place affected me too, Eugen. I haven't been in a church since my parents' funeral."

Eugen rolled his eyes. "Don't go dwelling on that, Teufel. Don't need you getting all moody. We don't have time for it. So much to do."

"Yes. That we have." Hagen changed the subject. "How is it working with György?" He asked slyly.

Eugen sent Hagen a black look. "That man chatters incessantly. Questions, questions, questions. I swear before God, if he tries to get me to talk one more time, I might just put my fist through his teeth."

Hagen chuckled loudly, again unable to contain himself. God! He had missed having Eugen around. "He's just curious about you. You're unlike most of the people he comes in contact with. Ignore him if he gets too tiresome. Remember, he primarily deals with the insane. You certainly aren't that."

Eugen grunted again, in agreement. "He wants to meet you in the next few days. Perhaps you could use it as an opportunity to pass on some information? Monday morning for breakfast, I believe he suggested."

"My hosts tend to lie abed late into the morning, so Monday morning would be fine." Hagen nodded, contemplating seeing his friend. "Very fine indeed."

November 21, 1937
Dearest Poppet,

The surgeon is coming up tomorrow from Vienna. The doctor is very alarmed. They might have to operate again. I am scared, Poppet. I might die, and never see your beautiful face again. Why did you leave me, Poppet? I just don't understand why!
Eternally yours,
Meinrad

Chapter 21
February 27, 1938

Galiena stood on the wide stone balcony, staring out across the Wannsee as the wind whipped the placid lake into whitecaps. The sky was grey and rain was going to fall at anytime, but it didn't matter to her. The vista before her was beautiful, as was this house. It would be hers; that she had decided. The grounds were extensive; more than enough room for an enclosure for Emil, and the lake entranced her.

The house itself needed some work. It was sixty years old and had been modernized very little in the intervening years. Galiena found that a positive for she could make this her house from the inside out. A haven for her and her alone, with no history and no memories.

As she thought of memories, her mind's eye drifted back to the other night when new memories, memories which left her feeling guilty, had been made. The quest for a chaperone had yielded Swanhilde Stammler, and together they met von Schilling and his friend Hauptman Theodor Freiherr von Obstfelder at the door. Swanhilde seemed generally pleased by the invitation; little excitement of any kind happened up at the Carinhall for a younger woman and an opportunity for fun was always relished. Galiena had appropriated a bottle of good brandy from her uncle's cabinet as an offering for the engagement and was very glad she had.

Von Schilling and von Obstfelder, dashing in their uniforms, had taken them into one of the main admin buildings and led them into the basement to a large room. They could hear the music from several feet away. Some of the communications men had rigged the record player up through a PA system and into some large speakers. The sound wasn't as good as in a proper Cabaret, but it certainly did the trick! Duke Ellington and Count Basie fairly shook the room the volume was so high.

There were perhaps twenty-five people in attendance, mostly men, but a few female secretaries as well. Red gels had been placed over the lights, creating a sea of scarlet; candles flickering on several surfaces coupled with the haze of cigarette and cigar smoke created an atmosphere which was quite primitive. People were dancing wildly in the center of the room, arms and legs flailing, swinging with abandon. Galiena was taken back to dark jazz clubs she had been to in England and felt suddenly at peace. She had missed this. There was something about an underground club which stirred the soul and got the pulse racing. That it was all happening right under the nose of Joseph Goebbels just added to the manic flair of the event.

While von Obstfelder devoted his time to Swanhilde, von Schilling was excessively attentive to Galiena. This wasn't the same ogre who was her flight instructor; this was a very charming, very handsome, very cocky pilot who knew the devastating effect of his smile and exploited it for his benefit. Von Schilling even managed one dance with her before his injured leg got the better of him. He hadn't cried uncle on the dance floor, but she could see in the lines of strain around his mouth that he was in pain, so she took pity on him. They sat in a corner of the room, drinking brandy, chatting about their upbringings and how similar in some ways they were.

Von Schilling came from an old military family. His father had been an Oberst in the Great War, and his Grandfather had been a General der Infanterie, both stationed on the Eastern Front. That von Schilling had chosen the Luftwaffe and not the Heer had been of great upset to the family, but felt he had to forge a different path. Also, there was an older brother who had done his duty and joined the Heer. They laughed about the old Junkers, and how they seemed unable to accustom themselves to the new order sweeping the world. How old von Hindenburg had feared Hitler and the Nazis. It was so nice to talk to someone who understood about the traditions which ruled their class, and how it was so hard to fight against the old ways and ideas. The pilot had made the yearly circuit of the aristocracy: Vienna in the winter, Berlin in the spring, Heiligendamm or some other Baltic resort in the Summer and then back to the family estate in the fall, just as she had, knowing so many of the same people.

Von Schilling was comforting and didn't expect anything of her. He asked after her Grandfather and as usual she deferred the question. It was also a relief to know he was completely unaware of the situation between the Pfalzgraf and herself. It added to her armour. His ignorance was a balm. There wasn't sympathy or pity or guilt in his eyes. He didn't know of her stain. Galiena didn't realize just how oppressive it was to have so many of the men in the periphery of her life knowing about the past.

The more they drank, the more the Hauptman opened up. She asked him about Spain, and he became very candid. "We have become an instrument of terror against the communists," von Schilling said quietly. "They are helpless against our airpower. War has changed for we have forever eliminated the siege. We level entire cities from the air, and when we pass, there is simply nothing left. At Guernica it was slaughter. The glorious propaganda of victory has nothing on the reality of seeing a city turned to a smoking ruin." His eyes had clouded. "I am proud of my unit, my men, the Luftwaffe and the Fatherland, but I am not proud of what we did to that city." Then he described it for her, as he had seen it from the cockpit of his plane, flying over that blazing inferno, people on the ground running like so many ants in the darkness. His words were so vivid; she could almost smell the smoke in the air.

Von Schilling had gestured to the dancers, their movements becoming more frenzied as the alcohol flowed like water. "Many of these men are Condors being rewarded with work here at the Carinhall. They've experienced the knowledge that today might be your last, so make every moment count. That's why we're down here listening to the music we discovered over there. Perhaps it's why we snuck into the country and are listening to it right under Göring's nose. Nothing matters when you could die tomorrow. What is a punishment or a reprimand for an exquisite moment when the next time you go up in your plane it could be over?" Then that perfect grin again. "Not that Göring would care. He remembers what war is. How we live in Spain? Like kings, Pfalzgräfin! Nothing is too good for Göring's Condors. He understands very well."

Then a breathless von Obstfelder and Swanhilde had joined them. In this case it was Swanhilde who drank the beer and von Obstfelder who partook of the brandy. The men leaned in and told exciting stories of Spanish night raids, where almost every line started with 'not a word of a lie, there I was when…" So many of their tales were funny, and Galiena laughed until tears came from her eyes.

The party began to wind down around four a.m., and Galiena had cheekily poked von Schilling in the knee. "So since I've now been up for twenty four hours, I suppose the flying lesson is cancelled? I can't imagine you are going to take me up now?"

Quite the wrong thing to say, for suddenly von Obstfelder lifted his sable head. "We have access to a plane? Let's go watch the sunrise over the Baltic! Show these lovely ladies how a night should end!"

That was that! A couple of blankets, a satchel with several bottles of beer, another bottle of brandy; some pastries and oranges looted from the Carinhall kitchens, and the party set out in a pilfered car for the airfield. The duty officer was used to the early arrival of Galiena and von Schilling, but he looked a little askance at the drunken group of four trying to cram themselves into the Wing of Riesa. The man said nothing, however; for he was merely an Oberleutnant, and what was he going to say to two Hauptmans and Hermann Göring's niece?

The satchel was stashed in the small cargo space and eventually everyone was tucked in and ready to go. A mechanic cranked the engine on the plane and von Schilling lifted them into the heavens. Galiena could tell it wasn't his best lift off. What did it matter? This was an adventure.

The night was clear and she could almost touch the stars from the cockpit. Below them Germany was sleeping and there were very few lights to guide them north. Von Schilling flew them in the right direction, for soon land gave way to the inky blackness of the Baltic. They flew for almost an hour and had covered some distance as von Schilling flew with the throttles all the way forward. Civil twilight arrived and the black landscape was painted in shades of grey.

Galiena assumed that they would just circle until the sun rose, but the men had other ideas. "Put her down, Klaus! Let's picnic on the sand!" Von Obstfelder slurred. "It's false dawn anyhow. There's enough light to see by!"

She had felt a moment of real fear then. "Put her down where, Freiherr von Obstfelder? There's no airfield!"

Von Schilling just laughed. "You think I need an airstrip to land on? Au contraire, Recruit! I may not be Ernst Udet, swanning down on top of a glacier, but I can still land this kite on a pfennig."

It was the most harrowing experience of her life! Von Schilling had put the plane down on the middle of a road, more of a track, which had a small straight stretch near the sea. As the plane hurtled across the bumpy gravel, Galiena was sure they were going to lose control and crash. No. The Taifun handled well and soon they were stopped right in the middle of the road. Von Schilling popped the cockpit and the sea air surrounded them, clearing the heads of the quartet. He scrambled out onto the wing and helped the ladies down with von Obstfelder securing the provisions. Galiena could tell that von Schilling was nowhere near as drunk as the rest of them.

Off the road and through the brush to the sand where the exceptionally pale Swanhilde took the brandy bottle with a shaking hand and drank a very generous portion before collapsing on the blanket laid out by von Obstfelder. When the ladies were comfortable, the men searched out some driftwood which burst into a cheery flame once von Schilling poured out most of his lighter's fluid onto the pile. They drank and ate as the twilight increased and the grey world became brilliant with colour.

Galiena licked her lips and leaned against von Schilling's shoulder. "You have been teaching me the Airlaw, my master, and I'm sure we just contravened several of the aforementioned articles."

The pilot dropped his chin, his lips resting against her forehead and she could feel his wide grin. "Oh hang the Airlaw. Some rules were made to be broken."

"That isn't what you said the other morning. As I remember, you said 'these are the laws and are more iron clad than

Bismarck's corset.'" Galiena lifted her head to meet his cornflower blue eyes. "I remember it well because a gentleman should never mention any form of undergarmentry in the presence of a lady!"

"While that is correct on all counts and absolutely applies to you as a cadet, when you are a Hauptman in the glorious German Luftwaffe, you will learn when and when not to take liberties with the law," von Schilling's voice lowered silkily as he stared at her.

Galiena knew she was skating on very thin ice. She could sense a change in her escort, a change which generally frightened her, but for once she felt immune from attack. "And are you taking foolish risks, Herr Hauptman?" For she felt that she most definitely was.

Von Schilling picked up her gloved hand, holding it between his own. "This moment would be worth the strongest reprimand." He kissed her fingertip. "Besides I'm a hero, so they would hardly strip me of my licence. If I really annoyed someone, they might demote me, which wouldn't be so bad. A mere Leutnant has far less paperwork to do!"

Galiena curled her fingers around his. "A desire for less responsibility? That's hardly the Prussian way, Ritter von Schilling."

The white teeth flashed at her impudently. "Oh hang the Prussians too!" There was a moment of silence and then von Schilling came closer. "I think I'm going to take another risk and kiss a Pfalzgräfin."

Her fingers went to his lips, pushing him back. "You forget, Herr Hauptman, that I have a fiancé."

His eyes positively smouldered. "Oh hang your fiancé."

Then Galiena shook her head. "No, Herr Ritter. I wouldn't hurt Hagen that way, so please don't opportune me further."

"As you wish it, my lady. Friends then, but don't think I won't try again another day." Von Schilling handed her the brandy bottle and grabbed another beer for himself.

"My answer will remain the same," Galiena tried to say with conviction.

Blue eyes met brown with a challenge. "Will it?" The words hung in the air like a red flag before von Schilling awkwardly climbed to his feet. "Come, von Obstfelder! A song!

Let's show these lovely ladies how a duo of Luftwaffe men strangle a tune!" The men sang the sun out of the sky; starting with the Luftwaffe Lied, then into popular favourites like *Wenn die Soldaten* and *Jawohl Mein Herr'n*. Von Schilling had undone his jacket, and von Obstfelder's tie was around his head like a bandanna. Even though she had transcended exhaustion, she managed to keep her eyes open. When the sun was up they walked along the surf, and the men flipped over rocks to pick up the crabs underneath. Von Obstfelder pulled off his high boots and stockings to caper about in the icy waves, looking the complete fool in his riding britches, overcoat and bare feet. They were all so drunk on life and alcohol that everything was amusing.

Though as it always does, reality came crashing in as an elderly man came down to the beach looking for the idiot who had the temerity to block the road on market day with an aircraft. How had eight a.m. come so quickly? The old gentleman was not so impressed with the officers of the mighty Luftwaffe, and both of the young men were given a severe dressing down for profaning their uniforms as they had. Sheepishly they had packed up their breakfast and returned to the plane only to find it being examined in some detail by two members of the Ordnungspolizei.

It was the sight of those two policemen which started the gnawing of guilt. All members of the police were members of the SS, and the SS reminded her of Hagen, who would certainly not have approved of this evening's antics. Von Schilling was very quick to smooth over the incident and promptly paid the fine insisted on by the policemen, promising never to land his plane in the precincts of the town of Straminke again. The names of the ladies were never once mentioned to the authorities, for which Galiena breathed a sigh of relief. She was in the clear, as far as her fiancé finding out about the evening. They boarded the plane and as they flew off, Galiena spotted the old man waving to them, a small smile on his face. Perhaps it wasn't as bad as she thought?

They flew out over the sea, passing far too close to a Kriegsmarine vessel offshore. The sailors waved at them enthusiastically as they buzzed over the deck before returning inland. The world felt perfect. She fell asleep in the plane on the way home to the Carinhall, lulled by the familiar sound of the engine, and woke to von Schilling smiling at her as he opened the cockpit. Round trip had been almost 350 km, but it had seemed like nothing at all in the fast little plane. The two Hauptmans had escorted the ladies back to the great house, and Galiena dragged her weary body up the stairs to her room. She fell into bed beside a somewhat irritated Emil. The last thing she remembered was the lion's nose wuffling through her hair, smelling the salt and the sea.

A hand arrived at the small of her back, startling Galiena from the depths of her memories. "My dear Pfalzgräfin, you are obviously somewhere very far from here, where raindrops don't threaten to ruin that fine chapeau of yours." Goebbels' touch almost burned her through the suit and coat she was wearing.

Galiena felt the drops then, before eyes registered the water in the air. "Far away? No. Just enjoying the view of the lake." She allowed herself to be directed into the magnificent Belle Epoch era salon on the second floor of the house. Many would say it was overdone, but it suited her mood. It reminded her of the opulence of her past, with the muralled ceiling and gold leaf.

"I am on the other side of the island and my view is not as perfect as yours. As it is, I rise every morning to see the sunlight on the water and feel as if I am master of the universe," Goebbels smiled blandly.

Galiena touched his gloved hand with her own, the leathers sticking against each other. "And are you not, Herr Doctor? You are master of what Germany thinks. Is that not the universe?"

He chuckled and brought her hand to his mouth, brushing her knuckles. "From your lips to God's ears. I would, you know. Control what everyone thinks. Unfortunately it's far harder a thing done than said, my dear; but then I think you would know about that dilemma, now wouldn't you?" Goebbels blue eyes searched hers. "I sense a change in you. One I don't know if I approve of."

Galiena forced a laugh. "And what could you possibly mean by that, Herr Goebbels? I am as I ever was."

Goebbels shook his head. "No." He was silent and led her by the hand over to the chaise, pulling her down beside him as he sat. "You have changed."

"We all change, Herr Doctor. It is inevitable. That is the nature of growing up." It was a guarded answer, but she was learning the value of walls.

"I am your friend, Pfalzgräfin von Steinberg. Far more than any of the other jackanapes about you. Tell me! What's happened? For I see it quite plainly and I don't like it." Goebbels reached out as if to touch her and then drew his hand back. "You have nothing to fear from me."

Galiena watched him from the corner of her eyes, not actually turning to face him. "Come now, Herr Goebbels. How can I not fear you? How can I not fear anyone? You told me once to open my eyes that I should not be taken aback by the grime. Now I have opened them and you chastise me for altering in response to what I see?"

Goebbels considered her for a long moment, assessing, as was his habit. His eyes scanned right through to her soul. "Why are you getting married, Pfalzgräfin? You go into seclusion here in Berlin, and then the next thing I hear from old Göring is you are affianced to that SS officer. A few days later you go to Berchtesgarten; the SS officer is gone and I come to the Carinhall where a handsome Hauptman from the Luftwaffe is escorting you about. The following morning I see you crawling up the stairs to your chamber, in that famous trudge of a woman who has been out far too long. I am not blind, Pfalzgräfin von Steinberg. I have a passing acquaintance with the ways of the world."

"Hagen isn't gone. He is away on holidays," she replied simply.

"Why are you marrying him? I realize it's a rude question, my dear, but I would like to know," The tiny man laughed self depreciatingly. "I've always had an inquiring mind."

"Because he asked me, Herr Goebbels, and it seemed like a positively brilliant idea at the time," Galiena replied, trying to put a smile on her face.

Goebbels shrugged elegantly. "But my question remains why? You hardly need to."

"I fail to understand what you find so elusive?" Why was he pressing her like this?

"Pfalzgräfin von Steinberg, you are in a very unique position to do what you want. The regular rules don't apply to you. It's not like you need to get married for respectability or advancement; you're already at the top of the pile. You have enough money you can do what you want. So why marry the first man who asks you?" Goebbels clasped his hands in his lap. "It's not that you should fear for other offers."

"There are other reasons a woman gets married, Herr Goebbels. Security," Galiena supplied, trying not to appear like she was grasping at straws.

A short bark of laughter. "Now there's a reason." The amount of irony in his tone! "You should marry someone you love, girl, not the first man who asks." His voice became almost wistful. "Don't make the same mistakes others of us have made."

"Now Doctor Goebbels, what could you possibly mean by that?" Galiena couldn't help but let a hint of derision into her tone. This was, after all, her sister's former lover, and a notorious hound to boot. "You would be the last man I would expect to give me a lecture on the importance of love in a relationship."

The little man's face twisted bitterly. "I might have more to say on the subject than you think, Pfalzgräfin von Steinberg. You don't know the secrets I keep in my pocket. But then let me be cold blooded for a moment. You, who are an engaged woman, why were you out all night with that flier? I think before the wedding is a bit soon to be taking a lover, or is that the fashion these days?"

Galiena recoiled as if she had been slapped. It was as if he had been reading her mind. She had heard that Goebbels could use his tongue like a blade and now she felt its kiss. "How dare you!"

"Why shouldn't I dare? Are you not used to being spoken to in such a fashion, Your Serene Highness?" His eyes glittered mockingly.

"Damn you!" She hissed, surprised at her use of the word. It slipped out before she could stop it.

Goebbels clapped his hands with pleasure. "Well! Well! Well! The kitten does have claws. Now this is a woman! Not that ever so perfect Pfalzgräfin von Steinberg, with her big, wounded eyes, ever so happy to please everyone, while everyone uses her to their advantage! Good God, girl! It's about time you showed some emotions!"

"You arrogant peasant!" Galiena snarled through clenched teeth.

The smile she received was huge, every tooth gleaming at her. "Absolutely, Pfalzgräfin. I absolutely am. Come now. Tell me what you want! I'm your friend and I would ask."

Galiena stood up abruptly and moved to the window, collecting herself carefully. She had let too much of her mask slip. "Are you, Herr Reichminister? You are very free with that word. So many in the Reich are free with that word. You are my friend. Herr Himmler is my friend. Herr Hitler is my," she almost choked on the word. "Friend."

"Ah. Yes. Now I see. So that is where this all stems from. The Fuhrer," Goebbels nodded sagely. "It is a difficult situation. I understand that."

She rounded on him. "Do you, Herr Doctor? Do you really? I look at this magnificent German Reich with all its similarities to Rome, and two things leap very strongly to mind. Firstly, Fuhrer's Princip. His word is above all written law. How positively ancient. Secondly, render unto Caesar what is Caesar's. So where does that leave me? I can imagine that your price is a great deal more than thirty pieces of silver but I'm sure you have one. Don't call yourself my friend. You, like all the rest, would sell me to Hitler if you thought it would get you just a little more power!"

"Well at least you finally see it for what it is," Goebbels drawled. "I'm sad to see it happen, but it's a start."

Galiena looked at the walnut floor with its intricate border of inlays. The pattern consumed her. "You ask me what I want? I want peace, Herr Doctor. I don't want to be afraid." He had knocked the air from her, speaking so frankly; making her acknowledge what was in her heart. She moved back to the window where the storm was whipping up into a frenzy. Her finger trailed along the sill. "I want this house."

His footsteps sounded behind her, and then he was at her elbow. He had obviously decided to take pity on her. "I will arrange it. I'm rather surprised that your family doesn't have a house in Berlin already." His gloved hands rested on the sill beside hers.

"We do," Galiena paused. "In Potsdam, actually. Near Sans Souci[15], naturally."

"Why would you buy this place when you could live there?"

---

[15] The Imperial German palace outside Berlin.

Galiena shook her head. "No. Too many ghosts there for me. I want a place of my own." She plastered a fake smile on her face. "Isn't that the prerogative of children? To leave the nest?"

Goebbels' hand covered hers again. "You are so terribly afraid of him, Pfalzgräfin. Just like Verina. Every time she heard he was coming to Berlin she would phone and beg me to use my contacts to have him detained. What did your Grandfather do to you both? He's the reason you've been hiding under Göring's protection, is he not?"

Galiena clenched her jaws until her teeth hurt and her face started shaking. Her eyes closed, and her hand, under his gripped the windowsill. All she could manage to answer him was a curt nod.

The minister placed his delicate, fine boned hand on her cheek. "Relax, Pfalzgräfin. You have nothing to fear from me. Where is he now?"

"Hagen had him taken away. He's in a camp." It was like the air was being sucked from her lungs.

The hand dropped to her shoulder. "Ah. So then he knows?"

"Yes. Hagen knows. I owe him a great deal because of it." She thought she loved him because of it, but now wondered if she had confused love with gratitude. Galiena didn't know the answer.

"So they all know. The SS. Or at least the higher members?" Goebbels had moved quite close, almost whispering. Like the Serpent in the Garden of Eden.

Galiena nodded again. "Oh yes. They all know. Herr Himmler has confronted me with it. Someone said to me what one knows, they all know. Yes, Herr Doctor. They're aware of the situation." She supposed she didn't need to reiterate the statement so many times, but it just happened.

"What a terrible thing to have as such common knowledge. What a boor Himmler is to confront you with it. I would have expected better, even from him." Goebbels had moved so that both hands were on her shoulders. He was completely behind her.

"No. It wasn't like that. He was very respectful. I have no issue with the Reichsführer." Galiena answered evenly. She didn't want Goebbels to know of her interactions with Himmler.

Goebbels was too clever by a half and might put two and two together.

"You worry about me selling you for thirty pieces of silver and yet you meet with him? He wouldn't require the silver. He would give you to the Fuhrer merely at the request," Goebbels snorted derisively.

"The Reichsführer and I have an understanding. He owes me a favour, and I think it weighs on him whenever he sees me." A flash and she was in Himmler's arms as the glass of the car window shattered above them. His lips on her ear as he told her not to be afraid. The faint smell of cigars in his uniform. It was a moment etched into her brain.

"Don't underestimate the Reichsführer, Pfalzgräfin. He has a serpentine kind of cleverness. One never counts on it until it's far too late," Goebbels warned her.

"I think, Herr Goebbels, that the Reichsführer is in the process of underestimating me, and I know I will only get the opportunity once," Galiena spoke quietly. "He's rather focused on what's pumping through my veins, instead of contemplating what's pumping between my ears."

Goebbels let out a short bark of laughter. "You are acquainted with the Reichsführer, aren't you, my dear!" Then he sobered. "Be careful, whatever you are playing at. He isn't the sort of enemy you want to have." The Reichminister swung around her to rest his back against the sill. "Be on your guard, whatever you are up to."

"I would entirely agree. I sense that he can be quite ruthless." She touched Goebbels on the shoulder. "Just as I sense that you can be quite ruthless. My uncle as well. I think as a group you're a terrible ensemble of predators."

This time the grin was slow and feral. He made a tsk-ing noise and looked at her through hooded lids. "Now my dear Pfalzgräfin, I'm not the one with a- how do the English put it? A murder of crows at my disposal? What would make you lump me in with Heinrich Himmler?"

"I lumped you in with Hermann Göring as well. Is that not enough for you?"

"It's a step in the right direction, to be sure, but I tend to look at myself as a cut above in the predator department.

Himmler's too much the pedant, and Göring's too wrapped up in being the great renaissance lord. I'm not blinded by either folly." The propaganda minister looked so expectant. He wanted to play with her.

"Ah, but you rely too much on the power of your tongue, Herr Doctor. What are you without it?" She lightly covered his lips with her finger. His skin was warm through her thin gloves. "There. I've muzzled you."

The eyes narrowed, assessing her, and then he'd taken her finger in between his teeth. It was a very intimate thing to do, but she resisted the urge to tear her hand back. Why hadn't she expected him to do this? She'd meant to make him draw his head back. Instead he just fixed her with a basilisk's gaze while he exerted just enough pressure to let her know he had her. The he slowly reached up and took her wrist in a gentle but firm grip, his thumb penetrating the opening of her glove, tracing a circle around and around on her pulse point. The teeth removed themselves from her finger and he kissed the tip before pulling her hand away. Her blood was pounding in her skull but she didn't move, nor show anything externally.

Goebbels shifted his weight, so that he was no longer leaning on the window; he was in front of her. Close. Nostrils flaring as he inhaled deeply, and eyes glittering with his will. His other hand came up to her face, his thumb in the softness under her chin and the hand completely covering her mouth. It was an awkward position for him, but the pressure of his thumb on the inside of her jawbone made it difficult for to just jerk her head back.

His glove smelled of leather, cologne, and cigarettes. It was tight to his hand, and Galiena could feel the warmth of his palm against her face. She was consumed with claustrophobia, and yet vowed she wouldn't give an inch. She had height on him, giving her a slight advantage, for all she had to do was conquer her fear, while he had to hold up his inverted arm. She was bigger than him, after all. Much bigger. Unlike almost every other man in her life, he was slight and short; there were no bunching muscles under his suits. Goebbels had bones like a bird. For absolute certainty she knew that he couldn't force himself on her. It calmed the panic of having his hands in her space. She wasn't afraid of him. Not at all.

She had been taught the hard way to fear the power of the male animal, but this one couldn't hurt her unless she allowed it to happen. It was a startling realisation. What an amazing thing power was!

Time ticked past as they stared at each other, unblinkingly. He was trying to use what he knew of her to force her to bend, and she just waiting him out. Each trying to make their point and save face. Then she felt it. The faint tremble in his thumb. She was like iron. It was an impossible stalemate. He'd gambled and lost. The hand came down from her face.

"You are not Verina," Goebbels said at last. "That would have reduced her."

"I am not Verina," Galiena answered with absolute surety.

Goebbels nodded. "Verina had no strength of will. Care for her as I do, it was always apparent. She never faced anything head on and never confronted her fears. They always dominated her. That is a terrible failing." Galiena said nothing and he continued after a moment. "I think it might be easy to underestimate you. You might just get the upper hand over Himmler if you play your cards right." Still she was silent. "This is a side of you that I think you hide very well. If some, the Fuhrer for a start, were to see it, I don't think they would like it very much. Strong women are very intimidating."

"Do you find them so?" Galiena ventured finally.

Goebbels let his breath out in an embarrassed half smile. "I like control, Pfalzgräfin von Steinberg. What do you think?"

Galiena felt her eyes grow hard, her body assuming the persona of the Pfalzgräfin von Steinberg. "You might find what I think to be a little uncomplimentary."

"Oh, Touché, Madame! Touché indeed!" Goebbels backed away to a more respectful distance. "This is why I would rather be your friend and not your enemy. I'm not the only one who uses their tongue like a razor."

Galiena curtsied gracefully. "Thank you, Herr Reichminister. I will take that as a compliment."

"So then tell me, dear Pfalzgräfin, what does your fiancé think of this hidden side? Has he seen it?" Goebbels asked.

"I don't know. One might say I took a right turn at Yesterday and decided to follow a different path than the one I had been on. When I arrive at Today, I'll give you an answer," Galiena shrugged. "The poets talk about the road not taken, and I think I'm on it."

"You sound very uncertain."

She decided to go out on a limb and confide in him. Goebbels was many things; a devoted student of human nature being one of them. "I do have some confusion about my engagement. I must admit that the company of the Ritter von Schilling pleasantly surprised me. It was unexpected."

"He is much younger than your Standartenführer Kohl. That is true," Goebbels dropped his chin, his eyes distant as he considered the situation. "And from what I saw, had that devil may care attitude common to pilots. That might be more attractive to a woman of your years than an officer old enough to be your father."

"Not quite that old, Herr Goebbels. Hagen is only thirteen years my senior, and I doubt he was that precocious as a lad." Perhaps that was part of the problem. Hagen was so very serious, so very secretive. There was no happy medium.

"But he was your saviour, was he not? And you let yourself fall in love with him because you wanted his protection?" Goebbels spoke quietly, and reached out to rub her arm. "And now you wonder what he wants in return. What a terrible pickle for you, Pfalzgräfin von Steinberg. Now you see a different man, you spend much time with him, and he's charming, gallant, and here. You have a conflict. Yet you must ask yourself, what does the young man want? Or had you not thought of that?"

"Could he not just want me?" Galiena asked wistfully, before she shook her head. "No. I am not that innocent. They probably both want the same thing, really. A Feldmarschall's baton. Come now! Von Schilling is a young flier who is being attentive to the boss' niece. He sees advancement, fortune and position. Just as Hagen does," she paused and turned on her heel. "Hitler made that very clear."

Goebbels frowned suddenly. "The Fuhrer did? When did he do this?"

"At Berchtesgarten when he found out about my engagement. He wasn't pleased. Called Hagen in and derided him something fierce. It was hard but good to hear. It took the rose coloured glasses from my face. Allowed me to assess things a little more clearly." Galiena's mouth turned dry at the memory.

"May I tell you a little story?" Goebbels spoke slowly, obviously choosing his words with care. "One I would prefer not to travel beyond these walls."

"Of course."

Goebbels led Galiena back to the chaise and they sat together. "My dear, you know of my relationship with your sister, and you know of my relationship with my wife. It does not exist much, these days. We are strangers who live in the same house. I have my peccadilloes, and she has hers. With one of my right hands at the moment, which is a source of some consternation. I thought I was content. There are always plenty of women eager for an adventure, especially when a man is powerful and famous, as I am. In that, you and I are alike. Whereas I have power, you have money, and we both have prestige in our circles, you doubly so for while we Nazis flock around you like pigeons, you also have a dominant position in the aristocracy."

"I'm not sure I completely understand," Galiena said, wondering where her companion was going.

"Because I digressed. I thought I was content, and then I met a woman who has completely changed my life. I love her. I would do anything for her. I would give up everything to be with her, and it is my intention to petition the Fuhrer for a divorce from Magda so that I can marry this woman. The point I am trying to make is that you don't need to marry Standartenführer Kohl for protection. You should marry him because you love him, and for no other reason. When I married Magda, I was quite entranced with her. She was a wealthy divorcee with an unquestionable place in society. She had a quick mind, and I must admit, she had another serious suitor which made her ever more the challenge." Goebbels touched his hand to his breast. "Yet in my heart I didn't love her, and very soon we both tired of each other. Now that I know what love is, now that I have felt it, I would ache to see you settle for anything less. You have so many choices before you. I know the Fuhrer has his strange fixation with you, but if he was to see this new side of you, this strong side of you, he would shy away, I guarantee it. He has always said that intelligence in a woman is wasted. He, more than anyone, can't accept that kind of challenge."

"I appreciate your candour, Doctor Goebbels," Galiena spoke quietly.

"It's more than candour, my dear Pfalzgräfin. It's power. No one, as yet, knows the depth of my relationship with this woman, and if it came out too soon, I could be in the soup. Not that it would matter, for she's worth the soup, but still I would choose my time. Do you love your Standartenführer? Would you give everything away to be with him? The money, the cars, the lion?" There was a long breath. "The plane and the handsome young flight instructor?"

"I don't know. I thought I did, but now I don't know. I keep hearing the Fuhrer's words in my head." Her whisper was tortured and broken.

Goebbels looked at her sadly. "Which was his intent. The Fuhrer isn't above controlling people for his own amusement. You need to decide what you want."

"What I want has nothing to do with it, my dear Doctor. It's a very sad fact in my life that I'm a rich woman of important family. I don't expect any of the suitors at my door to see anymore than that when they look at me." She didn't say it to elicit pity, merely as a statement of fact.

The little man cocked his head to the side, almost like a bird. "I adore it when you are cynical."

Galiena laughed and brushed her shoulder against his. "You are a beast."

"I am. I admit it, but then I've never made any sort of secret of the situation."

She was quiet a moment. "You know, I always expected to have an arranged marriage; or at least the choice of a selection from the Pfalzgraf. He would vet two or three and I could pick the winner. All the atrocious wheeling and dealing would happen away from my eyes. It always seemed like a dreadful shame at the time, but now that I'm faced with it for myself, I think I would prefer it."

"I think you are even more cold-blooded about romance than I am!" Goebbels exclaimed with a laugh.

Galiena winked at him. "That isn't romance, Herr Doctor! In my world, once you produce an heir, a private life is allowed and occasionally encouraged." Even the words chilled her. It made the loneliness tangible. "It's not as if I can disappear to a place where no one knows how much money my family has. My suitors see a commodity. They are plenty charming now. Once they've snared me? I'm sure it will change."

"Don't the Americans have a golden rule? He who has the gold, makes the rules?" Goebbels suggested with a leer. "Defy conventions and keep your husband on a very short leash."

"Now that's hardly the National Socialist way, Herr Doctor!" Galiena giggled wickedly. "I know what your own ministry says about the role of a wife, and I'm sure that isn't it."

The little man rolled his eyes dramatically. "That's for the peasants, my dear! I would never apply those rules to you! You are far too much fun for that folderol!"

"You hold your wife to it! How many children do you have?"

"Four and one due in April." His face took on that look of a male well pleased with his prowess.

"Yes. Folderol. I see." She gazed at him sceptically. "I can absolutely see how much you consider it folderol."

"You aren't Magda, my dear and you aren't married to me!" Goebbels retorted with a grin. "Did I say I don't have occasional moments of hypocrisy?"

"My perception of you is wholly shattered, Herr Doctor!"

"Somehow I think not," Goebbels widened his smile to its full wattage. "My thought is that you buy the husband you think will be the most innocuous, but with whom the duty of procreation won't be a total chore. When Riesa is secured, then be a scandalous bon vivant."

Her eyes narrowed as she processed that. "Oh! I see. Like Verina?"

"No, darling Pfalzgräfin. Not at all like Verina. She's not got your panache. I think you know what you want; deep in your soul. I think you want to rule all of us. In your own special way, of course."

His words gave her something to ponder, but now was not the time to do it. Galiena pushed it all aside, done with this conversation for now. She leaned in conspiratorially. "What I want is to buy this house. It I know I love."

"And it can be yours for the princely sum of two hundred and eighty seven thousand Reichsmarks," Goebbels grinned gamely. "Do you have access to that?"

Galiena smiled at him brilliantly. "My guardian, Hermann Göring, I believe you are acquainted; has already agreed to release the funds from my trust, so, as a matter of fact, I do!"

Chapter 22
February 28, 1938

Hagen walked into the small restaurant on the Canovagasse, just a few blocks away from the von Reitersbach residence. It was a dark day, as the weather had turned stormy. As protection from the weather, he carried a large black umbrella, feeling very much the Englishman. Underneath the black great coat, his suit was very dark, almost black, and his matching vest gleamed against his white shirt. His tie was almost blood red and was a striking foil to the sombre colours with his matching pouf. The suit was new; having been delivered to von Reitersbach's yesterday, part of his new aristocratic wardrobe. His goatee was quite full now, and he began to feel the part he was playing.

The waitress came over and took his coat, hat and umbrella before escorting him through the nearly empty restaurant to György. Hagen smiled with genuine pleasure when he saw his friend, who rose and pumped his hand warmly. György was unchanged, with the exception of a few streaks of silver in the coal black hair which curled about his head like a demonic halo. The well trimmed beard still came to a point beneath his chin, accentuating perfect white teeth and the hazel eyes sparkled with amusement and intelligence. György was resplendent in a shade which was slightly too bright to be navy; almost royal blue in colour. His double breasted suit was immaculate almost to the point of fussiness, the cut very exacting. The shirt he wore was also starkly white, and his accessories were bottle green. Even in London, so many years ago, György had been ever the dandy, and nothing had changed with time.

György Demeter was shorter than Hagen, just under six feet, but like Hagen had always been thin. The last two years had put more flesh on his body, but hadn't changed him terribly; if anything, it made the man more powerful a figure. He looked like a man of authority. Perhaps his position had aided the transformation. The flash young man and the eminent psychiatrist had melded into this creature before him. Someone who knew the answers, and might just share them if you stroked his ego until he deemed you worthy.

"Well, well, well! Doctor Kohl visits Vienna at last. The one-sidedness of our friendship was beginning to wear on me." György's German was completely without accent, as were the rest of the languages he spoke. He considered it a point of honour. His voice was deep and calm. It slipped from his lips with ease and filled the air, reminding Hagen of the way Goebbels spoke.

"György Demeter, leech extraordinaire. How are you?" Hagen asked warmly.

György pulled Hagen into a rough embrace and kissed both cheeks in his ebullient Hungarian fashion before they both sat back down. "All the better for seeing my old friend. Oldest friend, even. To my eternal shock and surprise, you are even out of that rather sinister uniform, unlike last time! How long has it been?"

"Thirty-six, I believe. In the fall. You were up for something or other in November. At the Kaiser Wilhelm Institute," Hagen supplied, trying to remember himself.

"Right. Of course. So a year and a half. How time does get along when a man is busy, as I hear you have been. Promotions. Honours. Titles to come, and now I hear a wife? Dear God! Is this my monolithic black clad friend falling to the enchantments of a mere female?" György leaned forward, a glint in his eye. "Come now, Hagen. Men like us don't get married. We plough the lasses when we have an itch, we might even set them up in a little house on the outskirts of town, but we don't marry them."

"Galiena's not the sort of woman one sets up on the outskirts of town. If anything, with some of the inequalities in our stations, I would more likely become the one in the little house," Hagen shrugged. "Besides, maybe it's time I settled down and enjoyed the adoration of just one woman. I'm told there are benefits."

György sipped his water. "Well then, tell me, is she young or old? Nubile or withered? I'm assuming you've plucked her, or you wouldn't have succumbed to the inanity of all this marriage nonsense."

"Younger. Twenty-four. Unplucked by me. In actual fact, György, I think she might prove very interesting to you." Hagen chose his words very carefully. "She's somewhat damaged. Shell-shocked almost." He saw his friend's eyebrows rise. "Not in that thousand yard stare sort of way, nor is she catatonic, but she went

306

through a battle all of her own, and the same sort of situation causes her to completely fall apart."

"There's a word for that, Hagen. It's called hysteria. Once upon a time surgeons removed the uterus to stem it, hence the term hysterectomy. My profession and other charlatans make a great deal of money off of women like that and have since time immemorial. Then there was the feminine massage to cure hysteria, which they still do in some areas. Genital stimulation to temper the female whose husband can't get his mast up to do the job. Dissatisfied women are a godsend for quacks! Look at Mesmer. Or Rasputin. Hell! That old scoundrel Freud has them lined up around the block, convinced that they all want a cock and dream of riding their fathers." György licked his teeth, a lascivious gleam in his eye. "Tell me, Hagen, does she want to mount her father?"

"She was raped by her Grandfather, György," Hagen replied simply. "So, no. I rather doubt it."

György leaned back in his chair, the gleam gone, but the amusement still there. "Well there you go. I've always considered Freud to be completely overrated at the best of times," He sighed and stroked his beard. "Raped? Really raped? Not just something she imagined or fantasized about? People can do that, you know. They believe these things to be true because they think about them so much."

"Oh yes. Confirmed by the horse himself. Considers Galiena to be his wife. Some of that strange Victorian nonsense about fathering a race of super beings with ancient bloodlines who will take over Europe. Quite insane." Hagen was silent as the waitress brought them coffees smothered in whipped cream. It reminded him of Galiena, weeks ago at Riesa. It occurred to him just how much he missed her. Hagen felt he should phone and make sure she was keeping out of trouble. "The man is completely unrepentant. In fact, given the slightest opportunity, I know he would do it again."

"She's one of your cases, isn't she?" Hagen was silent, and György shook his head with a faint chuckle. "You're eternally picking up strays. Me, for instance. That intriguing giant you have staying at my place for another. Your whole damn Nazi party for a third. Now this poor woman. One could spend a year psychoanalyzing you just for the pure enjoyment of it. Why, Hagen? Why do you do it?"

Hagen shrugged. "All my strays have served me very well, György. Why should she be any different?"

"You tell me, Hagen! But you have whetted my interest. I don't generally like to work with women, but one can always make an exception for a friend. I will even keep my hands off her nether parts out of friendship, even if I think there could be some medical necessity! Still, enough about her. What are you doing in Austria, old boy? I know you're up to something and it's not a holiday. I've been at you to visit for years, and finally you do; only it's when Hitler is on our border, slathering after us like a pervert after a virgin. Tell me, Standartenführer Kohl of the SS, who are you here to kill?" The gleam was back and György moved forward, elbows on the table waiting for Hagen's answer.

"Now who's the pervert and who is the virgin?"

"I'm a psychiatrist. I'm eminently the pervert. I sift through people's minds and try to make them whole again. It's like pawing through trash or dirty laundry for someone's secrets. But don't distract me with me, or I will get derailed. Come now, I would very much like to know." György tapped his finger on his lips.

"I'm here as a guest of the Graf von Reitersbach, György. I'm learning how to be a Pfalzgräfin's consort. It's really nothing more involved than that," Hagen grinned. "Am I in uniform? No. Am I surrounded by a restless group of hell bent Germans? No. I'm simply a man on a vacation."

"Which is why you and your infamous right hand man are staying in separate dwellings, sneaking around to meet each other. Why men I don't know keep showing up at my pension to meet with said right hand. Why there is another room with two other gentlemen in it who do nothing but sort pieces of paper, and fairly quiver when the giant passes by. Why I couldn't call on you at your lodgings, when I am acquainted with von Reitersbach on a social level." The psychiatrist rolled his eyes. "No. Not up to anything at all. Absolutely innocent as a new born babe is my old friend Doctor Kohl. Yes. It's as plain as the nose on your face."

Hagen's grin widened as he rolled his shoulders innocently. "Maybe you're just jumping to conclusions. Maybe you've been about the delusional so long that you're seeing conspiracies which aren't actually there?"

"Yes. Absolutely that's it. More to the point, I was really born yesterday. I came springing from my mother's loins like Athena from Zeus' brain, fully formed and brilliant. Come now, Hagen. You've never treated me like an imbecile before."

Hagen looked directly into his friend's eyes. "Do the words secret or classified mean anything to you?"

György nodded his head. "As a matter of fact, they do." The Hungarian was silent as he sipped his coffee. "Are you still having those nightmares periodically? The ones about the war? Where you fall into the pit of dead men?"

The complete change of track jolted Hagen. He wasn't expecting it. "Yes. Not in a while. The last one was in September. The night after I met Galiena, actually. Why?"

"Now that is interesting in itself. We will come back to it. So we have just consulted over medical issues. Doctor-patient confidentiality you know. You can tell me all your secrets, Herr Kohl, and I won't tell a soul." György's teeth flashed in his beard. "Gotcha."

"Those sorts of things don't mean a whole lot where I come from, Doctor Demeter," Hagen frowned. "Let me put it to you this way. That bombing last week? Near the Wollezeile? I'm looking for the people who are doing that."

"You mean the New Austrian Order?" György chuckled. "I know rather a fair amount about them."

Hagen's eyes narrowed. "What do you mean?"

"You know what I just said about doctor-patient confidentiality?"

"Yes?"

"I have a number of patients in the military, or who were in the military. They talk. Yes. I know about the individuals. I don't really know who they are, and if I did, I couldn't exactly tell you, but I do know about the organization." The dark head bowed over the menu and then looked up again. "But I can't help you over much, because I don't know who the leaders are."

Hagen felt a griping in his gut, and tried to keep his face expressionless. "You aren't involved are you?"

"Heavens no! You know me. Until Hungary takes its proper place as overlord of Europe, I couldn't give a fig for what the rest of you do in your spare time. Well, no. I would very much prefer that the Turks didn't make another stab at European domination, and I'm still a little irritated at their former aggressiveness against my people, but other than that, I don't care especially. One regime is very much the same as another when you are a stranger in your own country." György turned his head as he watched the waitress approach. "Might I recommend the apricot palacsintas? It's a taste right from home."

Hagen addressed the waitress, whose auburn hair reminded him greatly of Galiena's. "I will have the palacsintas."

"Excellent choice. I will have the same," György replied, before the waitress took the menus and left.

"So what do you know, György?" Hagen asked. "What can you tell me?"

"That it's very serious to the people involved, and that some of the people involved are not to be taken lightly."

"I think the bombing indicated as much." Hagen responded, tapping a finger on the tablecloth.

"Yes. What can I tell you? The group formed as a response to the Dolfuss affair. Now most of the aristocracy are Legitimists, or monarchists. The want to bring back young Archduke Otto from wherever it is he's mouldering in the Netherlands. They had no real love for Dolfuss, but he brought about a modicum of stability. The violence stopped. Then the Nazis here murdered Dolfuss, and that stability was rocked. But after those lads of yours killed the chancellor, the NAO decided to make confusion to the Nazis their first priority. They hate you like poison, my friend." György smiled sadly at Hagen.

"I rather supposed as much, György. They've hardly shown themselves to be encouraging of our presence," Hagen returned wryly. "Tell me more."

"The leaders of the NAO were incensed that Hitler thought he could pull a coup in Austria by arranging the murder of the Chancellor. Gentlemen don't do such things, you know. Von Schuschnigg managed to keep order; but for the NAO, it backburnered their plans for the Archduke and left them free for their mayhem. Play pranks against the Nazis and the like. At that juncture it was almost more of a game, but last year when Germany began stirring in our direction again the leaders of the organization decided to ramp up their efforts. They realised they had a connection to someone very high up in the Austrian Nazi party and, as I understand, are blackmailing this individual for information." György stemmed his monologue for a moment. "I don't know who the individual is. Just that they have access to everything in some form or another, and are trusted implicitly by the people in control."

"Do you know how many members there are?" Hagen pressed, his nerves on fire. If only he had known this sooner.

"My guess would be in the range of forty or so, but many of them aren't active in the events of late. They just contribute in some form or another. Money, resources, that sort of thing."

"We have an idea of some of the members. Young men," Hagen returned, trying to jog György's memory without giving anything away.

György nodded, a slow and deliberate motion. "That would sound about right, but my patient isn't young. Not in the slightest. I can't tell you much more than that."

The gears in Hagen's mind were moving, albeit torpidly. "You primarily work with war neurosis, György. We had suspected there were Great War veterans involved in the organization. Maybe in the leadership?"

György leaned forward. "These men, Hagen, they aren't regular soldiers. They're officers and some of them are quite unstable. These are men who are fanatical to their class and station and don't take kindly to a worker's party having control. Couple that with the knowledge of what they went through during the war; their experiences, the things they did. The things they ordered. Human life has very little value to them in terms of those they consider to be unworthy or beneath them."

"I understand the mentality, György. I was in the war. I remember," Hagen spoke firmly.

The other man shook his head curtly. "No, Hagen. You don't and you can't. I know your uniform affords you a measure of power in Germany. You have learned what it means to have authority over other human beings. These people didn't learn it. They were born with it. All that nonsense of Divine Right of

Kings? They believe it, because on their estates, they still have it. My patient became my patient because he cut the hand off a maid who spilled a tray of china in the parlour. Started raving she was an Italian spy and grabbed her, the sabre, and chop! It was hushed up, of course, but the individual's wife and son convinced him that maybe he should take a little holiday at a sanatorium and called me in."

"That makes no sense!" Hagen exclaimed.

"Not to you or me, but it made perfect sense to him. He even considers it as no great loss. He has another maid and the new one is very careful," György shrugged. "In his mind it was completely justifiable. The maid was a peasant and had no value."

Hagen tapped his head. "Why weren't the authorities called in? The aristocratic system no longer exists here in Austria."

György let out a short bark of laughter. "Right. Yes. The abdication of one emperor and the establishment of what many of these people consider an illegal republic wiped the slate clean of a thousand years of tradition. You can't get rid of an aristocratic system unless you get rid of the aristocrats. Hell. I am the son of a Generalmajor and my father's old men still genuflect when they see me as a sign of respect."

"I see." Hagen considered this information very carefully. "It is a different world, isn't it?"

"Very different. An outsider has to prove himself worthy to be admitted into the club. People who marry outside of it are usually cast out. It's rather like a religion. Either you demand admittance, and work for it, or both of you must leave," György smiled faintly. "Didn't you say you were marrying into it?"

"Yes. I am here for von Reitersbach to adopt me," Hagen admitted ruefully.

György blinked, drawing his head back. "The Graf von Reitersbach is actually adopting you? I had no idea I was dining with such distinguished company."

"Galiena says I need a von." He couldn't keep the sheepishness out of his tone, no matter how he tried. György's words had made Galiena's position make a touch more sense. "I don't intend to call myself Kohl von Reitersbach, however. Plain Hagen Kohl is good enough for me."

312

"You do realize you will be Hagen Graf von Reitersbach when he adopts you, or certainly when he dies." The psychiatrist crossed his hands over his chest. "Are we now playing at 'if we can't beat them, join them'?"

Hagen's brain went blank for a moment. "What?"

"If he adopts you, and he has no other heirs, you will become Graf on his death. Heir to one of the older titles around. He's a Uradel, if memory serves." György furrowed his brow. "How did you manage to get him to adopt you? You mentioned your fiancée. Who is she that she has so much influence over the Graf von Reitersbach?"

"The lass who has consented to become my bride is Her Serene Highness, Galiena Pfalzgräfin von Steinberg Zum Riesa." Hagen felt a moment of pride as he said it.

György was silent again as he slowly assessed Hagen. "Maybe I was wrong about the strays part. Hell, Hagen! Why did you sell yourself so cheaply? Why didn't you hold out for a Hohenzollern? Or a Hapsburg?

"Am I given to understand that you recognise the name?"

"Me? Vaguely. My mother, however; would be in fits if she knew. She follows the nobility and all their adventures. The Pfalzgraf was here, what was it? Last year, with his granddaughter. It was a big deal in society." György uncrossed his arms. "As I said, I'm the son of a Generalmajor. A titleless Generalmajor. That is a stratum of society beyond me, though I know Freffie von Reitersbach because he and I frequent some of the same amusements."

"Society has never been of interest to me," Hagen replied. "I find Galiena's rules occasionally surprising. She's insisting I find a valet." He felt like an idiot just saying it.

"Of course she would. You must understand that theirs is a very different world. It's like the NAO, Hagen. Or my patient. They have entirely different rules for how they go about life. No offence intended, but von Reitersbach would never adopt someone like you if he wasn't asked to by someone of her status. He would almost take it as a royal command."

They both fell silent as the waitress brought their breakfast. The crepe-like meal with its apricot filling made Hagen salivate. "You've given me something to think about," He said at last.

György tucked in to his breakfast. "I would like to help you where I can with this NAO. As I mentioned, they are dangerous, and becoming ever more so. They have a number of military and former military in their ranks, but from what I understand their leader isn't. I don't know much more than that."

"We know they have a grandmaster. Or they call their leader the Grandmaster." Hagen ventured.

"You know how you once told me that your organization was built on a religious foundation?" György asked.

"Well quasi-religious. Supposedly a la the Jesuits. The religious aspects crop up from time to time, but I wouldn't call it so." Hagen had taken oaths that he wouldn't discuss such things with the uninitiated; as such, he kept his answer vague.

"I would say as certain members of the NAO lose their grip on reality, their group is becoming more and more 'holy' in their mind. I think the Grandmaster aspect started out as a lark, but it's growing in importance to them. That's my supposition, not a fact; but I do know that their leader isn't one of the old military men. I know because my patient finds it novel to be taking orders from a puppy," György smiled. "But don't let that confuse you. My patient calls me a puppy too."

"So puppy could be anywhere between twenty and fifty-five?" Hagen raised a brow.

"I think that would be a very accurate age spread." The psychiatrist made an open gesture with his hand.

"Just lovely." Hagen bit into his breakfast and let the taste of apricots take him off to another place. Somewhere exotic and foreign. "You could just tell me who this person is, György. It would make my life so much easier."

"And break my oath? The relationship between a doctor and his patient is sacred, Hagen." The smaller man replied with a particularly amused tone. Just how strongly did György take his oath? Could Hagen break him from it?

"I'm an officer of the law, György," Hagen retorted quickly.

"Not in this country."

Hagen let his lips slide into a lazy smile. "Give it a few weeks."

"Besides, I didn't think the SS was a police force for normal people. Just your party," György challenged him.

"Let me introduce you to the other me. Hagen Kohl, Oberst de Geheime Staatzpolizei," Hagen inclined his head. "At your service."

"That's new, isn't it? I seem to remember you saying very clearly that you weren't a member of the Gestapo," The words were almost an accusation.

Hagen let out a long mock sigh. "It became politically expedient during my last case for me to be so, and there it is. I've found it to be very useful," Hagen narrowed his eyes. "If this was Germany you would tell me."

"Why Hagen Kohl, is that a threat?" György sat back in his chair, appraising him.

Hagen shook his head. "No. Not at all. You're my friend, first and foremost. Even if this were Germany, I wouldn't force you to go against your morals."

"But you could. In your organization, with your rank, you could?" There was a whole new light in György's eyes; something Hagen had never seen before.

"Doctor Demeter, in Germany I can do almost anything I want to, especially of late. I answer only to two men, Heinrich Himmler and the Fuhrer. Everyone else can take it up with those two if they don't like what I'm doing." Hagen didn't mean to brag, and in essence he wasn't. He did have that kind of power.

"But what about checks and balances? What if you were to abuse your power?" György asked quietly.

Hagen lifted another bite to his mouth, chewing slowly and deliberately. The palacsintas were truly delicious. "There aren't any, György. People don't get to where I am without proving themselves first. People can jump the ranks on a recommendation, of course, but once you get to the upper echelons, especially in the SS, the only person you answer to is your direct superior and those of similar rank." He sipped his coffee. "We can't even be tried in civilian courts."

"So you're completely outside the law," György looked fascinated.

"Doctor Demeter, in Germany, I am the law."

November 28, 1937
Dearest Poppet,

To Nuremberg tomorrow for surgery. There is another tumour to be removed. It is in my abdomen and quite large. If I should pass on, then all of this will be yours. God! How I love you, my dearest Galiena. Even though you are away, and Göring has poisoned you against me, I want you to know how much you have always meant to me. If I should survive this, I will make everything right. When you come back, I will make it right. I love you. I worship you. I shall hold your handkerchief during the operation to comfort me. With some little part of you there success is guaranteed. Why did you leave me to face this alone? I need you, Galiena. I need you so very much. I don't want to die alone.
Eternally yours,
Meinrad

Chapter 23
March 1, 1938

Galiena awoke, a heaviness on her chest making it hard to breathe. She was on her back, completely pinned to the bed by Emil who lay very contentedly on top of her. His muzzle was nestled in between her breasts, and his amber eyes glowed at her in the gloom. One paw cupped her shoulder and the other was on the pillow beside her head. She wasn't entirely sure where his hips were, for the weight of him was causing pins and needles in one leg. Carefully she wiggled to get the offended part out from underneath him, and he slid from her hip rather indelicately. He made a very discontented sigh and stood up, turning around to lay down beside her, with his head on her shoulder. She wrapped her arms around him and buried her nose into the stiff fur of his neck. He smelled the way he always did in the morning, that strange combination of big cat and her perfume. For her it was heaven. It was safety. With Emil in her bed, no man would ever hurt her. He rolled onto his side, so his entire spine ran along her torso and arched his head so that his nose rested against her cheek. Carefully she scratched under his chin and along his chest, drifting.

She'd been given this morning off from her flying lessons, for Herr von Klopfer and the Ritter von Kleist were coming up this morning to discuss business and more than business. The word had come from Gruppenführer Wolff yesterday in the form of a lovely floral arrangement with an elegant card informing her that the trip to Buchenwald was scheduled for Friday the fourth. She was to be at the camp at two in the afternoon. There was so much to prepare between now and then. So much to do.

Galiena sighed as she rested her head against Emil. Right now he was so much the giant kitten, but soon he would be a four hundred pound predator. He had such a sweet disposition, but still Galiena wondered about the future. He was a lion. Would he always be such a gentle animal? Or would he turn wild when he was bigger? Right now she knew beyond a shadow of a doubt that she could give him all of her love and that he loved her in return. Not because she had a large fortune, or was Hermann Göring's niece or had an impressive title. Everyone around her seemed to want something, but Emil just wanted her attention. Would he turn on her? Would those teeth and claws rend her flesh from her body?

Galiena stroked the cat, and he chuffed sleepily. No. She couldn't live her life waiting for him to betray her; she owed it to him and she owed it to herself. Uncle Hermann had been quite explicit in his instructions regarding Emil: never let him know when you're afraid of him. The cat will be able to sense it, and he will know that he's the one in control. A definite mistake.

Perhaps she could apply that to her life at this juncture. Galiena wouldn't let her Grandfather know she was afraid, and she wouldn't let Himmler know she was afraid. Galiena had to have some courage. She was in bed with a lion after all. How many could do so? She tried to picture Hagen nestling up to Emil, and failed. They tolerated each other, but there was a definite wariness on either side.

Emil lifted his head as Idalie drifted into the room. He knew her, and tolerated her as well. He dropped his head to the pillow and returned to his feline torpor with a small snort. Idalie was carrying hot chocolate for Galiena and she placed it on the bedside table and dropped into a low curtsey. "Good morning, Your Serene Highness." Before the advent of Emil in Galiena's life, Idalie would wake Galiena by kissing the hem of her nightdress and addressing her. Emil was very hard on night clothing, trying to climb inside to press himself against her skin, so Galiena slept naked instead and the tradition had been discarded.

"Good morning, Idalie. If you're here, it must be eight," Galiena said with some resignation. "And I must get up."

"If you wish to attend your meetings this morning, yes," Idalie curtsied again.

"You say that as if I have a choice," Galiena retorted as she raised herself up on her arm.

"You are the Pfalzgräfin. They wait on your sufferance, Madame," Idalie replied tartly as she moved to hold up a robe for Galiena to slip into.

"Have you met the Ritter von Kleist? Or more, von Klopfer? They wait on the Pfalzgraf's sufferance and in their minds, I haven't earned the right to treat them as he does." Galiena disentangled herself from Emil and slipped out of the bed, bending to kiss him on his great wedge shaped head. Emil stretched and promptly took over the entire bed for himself, rolling onto his back with his paws in the air.

"It's not your duty to please them, your Serene Highness. You shouldn't let them intimidate you." Idalie had a very strict sense of the status quo and the position of her mistress. She was also very protective of Galiena.

"Why? You bully me all the time!" Galiena chuckled as she allowed Idalie to put the robe on her.

"I'm your body servant. Your body is my priority, and as such it is my duty to ensure that your body is where your mouth says it should be, in the state it should be in. That gives me particular latitude with your person. They manage your affairs, and your family's affairs. They do so at your convenience, and you should never forget that." Idalie took Galiena by the hand and lead her to the dressing table where she sat Galiena down and pressed the cup of chocolate into her hand. "So if that makes me a bully, so be it. I would be the first person you would think to have shot if you were late."

"I would never have you shot! Flogged perhaps, but never shot!" Galiena winked at her maid. "Maybe we should trade. I'll clean up after me, while you deal with the Grim Reaper and his portly henchman." She laughed and sipped the chocolate.

Idalie picked up her Marcel irons and went to work on Galiena's hair, carefully curling it. "You need to be firm with them. Make them do what you want them to do." Deftly the maid rolled the hot tong to Galiena's scalp. "Not give into their demands that you have the Pfalzgraf released," she said at last.

Galiena looked down as best she could. "That I have to do, Idalie. I know you don't understand, but I can't run Riesa on my own. I don't have the experience. It's not just the estates. It's the factories, and the corporations. It's my duty to ensure it grows."

"He doesn't deserve to be out of prison, Madame," The maid growled ferally, causing Emil to lift his head from the bed to watch with narrowed amber eyes.

"No. He doesn't," Galiena agreed, blowing a kiss to the lion through the mirror. Emil blinked at her lazily, and then rested his chin on his paws.

"It's not fair to you. How they can expect you to have the Pfalzgraf released after what he did!" The maid exclaimed, and then dropped into a slight curtsey. "I'm sorry, Your Serene Highness. I spoke out of turn."

Galiena made a dismissive gesture with her hand. "They don't know, Idalie, and I am not going to tell them. As far as they are concerned, he's being detained at the pleasure of the Gestapo under no formal charges. Why would they not expect that I would do everything in my power and use all my connections to get him released? It would be a reasonable expectation were the situation different."

"Your Serene Highness is right, of course," Idalie said in a vaguely sincere tone.

"No. I'm not right. For Galiena von Steinberg, I am probably making a huge mistake, but for the Steinberg Gessellschaft, I'm making the only decision I possibly can." Galiena met Idalie's eyes in the mirror. "He will be going away, Idalie. Far away. As far as I can send him. It's part of the bargain." She was silent for a moment. "It's my duty, Idalie. I have to do my duty."

"May I speak plainly, Madame?"

Galiena knew she would hear Idalie's opinion one way or another. "You may always speak plainly, Idalie. You know that." In all honestly, she had always valued her maid's thoughts. Idalie's perspective on everything was fascinating and in the end, she was probably the person closest to Galiena in the entire world. Idalie knew all Galiena's secrets, and protected them.

"You are not in service to Riesa. You don't owe it anything, certainly not at the expense of your safety and sanity. I've watched you for years, Madame, being his doll. His pet. Doing everything he wanted." The black eyes hardened to obsidian. "It. Was. Sick." Each word was bitten off. "You owe him nothing. You owe Riesa nothing."

"I am the custodian of the line, Idalie. I have to protect it, as it was protected for me," Galiena protested with the words she had heard all her life.

"Let von Klopfer and von Kleist look after it. Give them the power. Sign what they want you to sign. Leave the Pfalzgraf where he is! In prison! What he did was a crime, both in the Torah and the Bible!" Idalie exclaimed, her sense of propriety lost in her fury.

"Rapists go free all the time, Idalie." Galiena looked down, unable to meet the older woman's eyes. Dear God! This whole affair left her feeling so broken inside; fractured, like a mirror.

"And your officer? Hm? Herr Doctor Kohl? What would he say of this? You plan to marry him, but you aren't telling him of this, are you? No. I know you are brokering with the Reichsführer! Feldmarschall Göring would be in fits if he knew!" Idalie gestured at Galiena in the mirror with the tong. "You are betraying everyone you profess to love with this, but most of all, you're betraying yourself, and that's just pitiful." The words came fast and furious; each a dart in Galiena's hide

"Damn you, Idalie! I don't have a choice! I'm the only one left! It all falls to me! I have to do the right thing!" Her voice shook as she tried to keep from crying.

"It doesn't have to be all you, Madame. There is another. Train him to bear the weight. Don't do this. Don't let that monster free!"

Galiena searched her brain. There was no one left. Not as she understood. No one who would be acceptable to the Pfalzgraf. "Who?"

"Your uncle," Idalie whispered. "And your nephew." The hiss of Galiena's hair sliding from the tong was deafening in the silence.

Galiena whirled to face her maid. "Who are you talking about?

"Your sister's eldest son. I believe his name is Rudi. He is not the son of the Ritter von Taschen, but of your Grandfather. My mother told me years ago that when Verina fled to Göring, she was pregnant with the Pfalzgraf's child. That is the one who bears the responsibility," Idalie spoke clearly and quietly, but each word was a detonation in Galiena's skull.

"But he's a boy, Idalie. He would be how old? Fifteen? Sixteen? Raised the son of a Heer officer? As if, for one breath, he would be capable of assuming the reins, even if it would be legal and it's not. No. I must do as my conscience dictates." But the worm was turning in her brain. She had to discover if this was the truth, and that meant a visit to Verina, something she dreaded. Maybe von Schilling would take her; or at least go with her as far as the door. She wouldn't allow him to see Verina. See her shame.

Idalie bowed her head as she finished Galiena's hair, obviously knowing that the discussion was definitely closed. "Yes, Your Serene Highness."

Galiena was still as Idalie worked her magic and then applied her own cosmetics before changing into her suit for the day. It was navy, and she wore Hagen's pearls to accessorize with it. As she placed them around her neck she felt such a sense of loss. She missed him, more than she wanted to admit to herself. She hated what she was doing, going behind his back, but he would never understand. Why couldn't any of them understand? Riesa wasn't hers; if anything, she belonged to Riesa!

When she was dressed, she roused the lazy Emil and he followed her down to breakfast, where she fed him sausages from her plate. In fact, he ate far more than she did, and eventually she placed her plate down on the floor for him. Her stomach was in knots as she read through the thick folder of information von Kleist had sent up for her. One came by courier to the Carinhall every few days, full of paperwork, figures and expectations. Some she understood, some eluded her. At least when she had been in control when her Grandfather was sick, she could ask him questions in lucid moments, but this? This! A strike at a woollens mill in England, and she had to make a decision on what to do! Her immediate thought was to give the workers what they wanted. Wasn't that the humane thing? Workers should be respected. They had to survive, just as she did! Yet beside was a evaluation of what giving into the workers would cost, and how it would eat into profits, profits which were being invested in purchasing farms to raise more sheep on. If it was simply a case of looking after the workers, she would have been less concerned and agreed to the demands, but seemingly all the money was promised to something else. It wasn't just going into some nebulous pot attached to her cheque book. How did her Grandfather do this every day? Make decisions which affected so many lives?

There was a discrete knock on the door and one of the footmen came in, startling her back to the real world. "Herr von Klopfer and the Ritter von Kleist have arrived, your Serene Highness." How long had she been staring into space?

"Yes. Show them into the solarium." There was plenty of room for Emil to play in there, even though he tended to wreak havoc on the plant pots. "Wait," Galiena paused while the man turned back to her. "Can you please have Emil's ball sent to the Solarium? Fraulein Stammler will know where it is." There was absolutely no way in hell she was going off to this meeting all alone. Emil might not be the most supportive creature in the world for this sort of thing, but the effect on her moral would be enough.

Galiena stood and Emil lifted his face, licking his chops as he looked at her. "Come on, kitten," She said to him, taking his leash and heading towards the door. He looked at the plate with an irritated regret, his ears at half mast, but he followed her. Swanhilde always fed him his big meal at midday and he wasn't truly hungry. Galiena sometimes helped with Emil's lunch, but the sight was almost too much. Watching her baby rip apart the chunks of horse, cow or whatever was on the menu could be rather gruesome, for his muzzle would turn completely scarlet with flesh and blood. Faced with a carcass, Emil was not a delicate eater; if anything, he became a ravener. She supposed it was in his nature, but seeing him covered with gore was not a vision she enjoyed. Especially not at lunch time.

They moved quickly through the halls, reaching the solarium well before the two men. Galiena sat on an oversized wicker garden chair, with enough room for Emil to sit beside her. He did so, his body curling around hers, his giant front paws and head on her lap. Soon he would want to play, but for now he seemed content just to be near her. Galiena felt a pang. While she played the pilot with von Schilling, Emil was being neglected. She had to make more time for him. Why were there only twenty four hours in the day?

The footman rolled a heavy rubber ball into the room as he showed the guests in. Helmut Ritter von Kleist was a tall man, six foot four at least, and thin as a rail. He was so thin as to be emaciated looking and his hawk like cheekbones seemed to carve their way across his face, accentuating his sharp nose. He was completely bald and his sunken eyes were so pale a blue as to resemble the milky film of cataracts. If he'd ever had lips, it had been a long time ago, for now his mouth was just a slash before his prominent jaw bones.

Almost completely opposite was Werner von Klopfer, who at just under six feet was corpulent, bordering on the obscenely obese. He was one of the few men who made Hermann Göring look slender. He had a shock of greying, curly blond hair which was so thick and riotous it defied all oils trying to tame it. Instead it became a glistening brillo pad on the top of his head. As with so many large men, he was almost unwrinkled, his large moon face jolly looking with its scarlet cheeks and nose. His eyes were a golden brown, and they always seemed to sparkle.

In temperament, the two men were almost the opposite of their physical stereotypes. Von Kleist, for his fearsome appearance, had always been kind to Galiena. While his almost colourless eyes unnerved her, there was something very genuine about him. He took the time to explain things to her and was always very patient. His manner was gentle and understanding, not at all condescending; of the two of them, he was the one she trusted.

Von Klopfer was dry, his cynical comments about her youth always wearing. There seemed to be a smirk behind his eyes, like he was waiting for her to fall and would laugh when she hit the bottom. Perhaps it was because she saw so much of von Klopfer as he was her Grandfather's private secretary and had been since about the time she was born. There was something in his demeanour, something which made her very uncomfortable. Something which made her wonder of late just exactly what he knew about the Pfalzgraf's intentions towards her.

The men bowed as they entered the room, before their eyes centred on Emil with alarm. It was a reaction she truly enjoyed. There was nothing like putting the ones who never seemed to be unnerved on their guard. "Your Serene Highness," von Klopfer spluttered.

"Herr Ritter, Herr von Klopfer. Welcome to the Carinhall. Do take a seat," Galiena responded to their salutation. "Please forgive me if I don't rise."

"Not at all, Madame," Von Kleist's tone was urbane as usual. The Grim Reaper was never flustered. "You are obviously occupied at the moment."

"Indeed," was all von Klopfer uttered.

"Your-" von Kleist paused. "Pet has eaten, has he not? I would hate to become the cat's breakfast."

Galiena rubbed a hand on the lion's head. "Emil is quite content." Only Emil didn't appear to be very content. His ears were almost all the way down, and the tip of his tail was lashing.

"Excellent." Von Kleist moved to another of the large chairs, opening his briefcase as he did so. "We have both been very busy since we met at Riesa ten days ago. First off, the Pfalzgraf is being held at KZ Buchenwald, as you suggested to us, and is there at the pleasure of the Prime Minister of Prussia, but not under any formal charge."

"I was aware of this," Galiena spoke shortly.

Von Klopfer fixed her with narrowed eyes. "Interesting, that you are in the Prime Minister of Prussia's household and you wasted our time searching for the Pfalzgraf."

Galiena returned the stare, measure for measure. It was amazing how having a lion in your lap increased your strength of will. "I wanted confirmation of the circumstances of my Grandfather's imprisonment, Herr von Klopfer. Is this an issue for you? As you work for the Pfalzgraf, in his absence you work for me, and I don't consider any of my directions to be a waste of time."

"That time could have been spent not using our government contacts for frivolous purposes," Von Klopfer retorted coldly.

"Let me put it to you this way, Herr von Klopfer. If I was to use my personal connections to secure the release of the Pfalzgraf, avenues which my guardian, the Prime Minister of Prussia might not approve of, do you think I would honestly alert him to the possibility of my doing so by asking him for the details of my Grandfather's incarceration?" Galiena raised a brow, taking a page from Hagen's book.

The man squirmed minutely. "No. Put that way, I see your point."

"What an amazing thing," von Kleist winked at her. Perhaps these two weren't as simpatico as she originally thought.

"Furthermore Herr von Klopfer, the direction I intend to use is down a road where a questor shouldn't venture without having every I dotted and T crossed." Galiena pressed on, enjoying making the loathsome von Klopfer back down.

"Which avenue do you intend to use, Your Serene Highness?" Von Klopfer licked his lips. "I doubt you're going to go to the Fuhrer?" He chuckled condescendingly. "To up the Prime Minister of Prussia, one would almost have to go the Fuhrer."

"In actual fact, I am owed a favour by the Reichsführer SS, and will be meeting with the Pfalzgraf and Herr Himmler on the fourth." Both men looked rather surprised at this. "But to secure his release, I need to offer the Reichsführer something which will astound him. Grandfather has always reiterated that to win in business, one has to offer the adversary something too good to refuse on a time limit which doesn't give him enough time to consider the ramifications of his actions. With that in mind, we need to figure out what, on a 'this day only' basis will tempt the Reichsführer into going behind Hermann Göring and releasing the Pfalzgraf, which is, I believe, the task I set to you ten days ago."

"The key to the SS is their greed." Von Kleist ran his gnarled hands over his briefcase. "It is well known that they have a capital problem, less so these days, but certainly a need for liquid cash flow separate to that distributed by the party. The Pfalzgraf was approached by friends on the boards of Daimler-Benz and I.G. Farben to join the Reichsführer's Freundkrais, but he refused. The

Freundkrais are businessmen who donate to the Reichsführer personally in exchange for, shall we say, special considerations."

Galiena frowned as she considered that information. "What is my status in the Company, Herr Ritter?"

"You are a director," von Klopfer supplied flatly.

"And how many other directors are there?" Galiena asked.

"None. Only you and your grandfather. He has a seventy-five percent share and you have a twenty-five percent share. The company is privately held between the two of you. There is no board," von Kleist told her. "This was set up years ago when you turned nineteen. If you will remember all the paperwork we had you sign then?"

"Voting or non-voting shares?"

"Voting, but it doesn't exactly matter. You can't outvote the Pfalzgraf," von Kleist answered, before making a little gesture with his hand. "At least not usually."

Galiena patted Emil, whose ears had relaxed somewhat. She controlled twenty-five percent of the company? She had no idea! More importantly, she understood the last part of the statement. While her grandfather was in prison, she could outvote him, for he couldn't vote. That was why it was so urgent to these men she get paperwork from her grandfather to take control of his shares; so she could legally have the necessary power to run the company. Her head was spinning and greed reared its ugly head. If she left her grandfather where he was, it was all hers. No. She couldn't do that. As secretly tempted as she was when hearing it put that way, she couldn't do it. "I'm not ready to try and outvote him," she said finally.

"Thank heaven for small mercies," von Klopfer muttered.

"Herr von Klopfer, such comments are neither welcome nor desired. If you cannot add anything of value to this discussion then you are dismissed." They were words she'd heard her grandfather use a thousand times, but had never dared use herself. She tried to mimic his tones and inflections as she said them and was rewarded as von Klopfer almost seemed the flinch.

"Yes, Your Serene Highness."

"Thank you. So with my twenty-five percent, can we join this Freundkrais in my name, not my grandfather's?" Galiena reiterated.

"I don't know if there are any female members, Madame," von Kleist commented appearing deeply contemplative. "I don't know if a female could be a member. The ruling government is notoriously backward in terms of the position of women in business, and the SS is their strongest arm."

Galiena cocked her head and smiled at him. "Well then call someone who might know. Alfried Krupp von Hollensbach would be a good place to start."

Von Kleist gazed at her with a measure of respect. "One of his people might just owe me a favour."

"Excellent. If I can become a member and the Reichsführer might be willing to make an exception as he does seem to be very well disposed towards me at the moment, find out what the general donation is, and then double it. Maybe even triple it," Galiena considered for a moment, going over her secret assets in her mind. "No. Double it. Chances are I can do it in gold, and give it to him on the spot."

Von Klopfer gave her an arch look. "And where, pray tell Madame, are you going to get your hands on that much gold? Are you going to ask the Prime Minister of Prussia for a loan?" He scoffed.

Obviously her grandfather had never informed his two closest advisors of the secrets of the Riesa dungeons. One of the cells contained a carefully tiered stack of gold bars. Probably two hundred or more. Grandfather called it the rainy day fund, and usually added one bar per month while she lived with him. He loved his bars of gold, spending an evening by the fire polishing the new one before laying it in the stack with its fellows. Grandfather was very quick to maintain that there were only two places you could always keep your money safe: land and gold. Banks, stocks and investments were all well and fine, but they had a value which was ephemeral and left you nothing in your hand at the end of the day. Nothing to prove the money was there, other than a slip of paper, with an arbitrary value assigned by a government.

"Leave finding the gold to me." She winked at her grandfather's secretary, solely to irritate the man. "As you see, Herr von Klopfer, I do assign myself difficult tasks."

"Quite. Your Serene Highness, I don't think you've any idea of the amount you're contemplating," von Klopfer's drawl hit a level of condescension which grated on Galiena.

"Then enlighten me," she retorted, stroking Emil's head.

Helmut von Kleist crossed one leg over the other. "It is rumoured Fritz Thiessen's donations to the Nazi Party have been in excess of one million Reichsmarks. I know Your Serene Highness can access that sort of collateral through the estate accounts, but in gold? That quickly? You said you would need this by Friday."

"A gold bar, about six inches by two inches by three inches; I believe about 400 troy ounces, what value would that have?" Galiena asked idly, knowing the answer to a rough surety.

"I would suppose it to be about fifty thousand marks, give or take a few thousand," von Klopfer commented.

"Then I would need twenty by your reckoning?" Galiena opened her file, resting it on Emil's head. The lion snorted as she wrote that down. "Consider it taken care of."

"Obviously Her Serene Highness has access to assets we know nothing about," von Klopfer exhaled nastily.

"You think the von Steinberg family rates you worthy of all its secrets, Herr von Klopfer? You do have an exaggerated notion of your own importance." Galiena decided to bait him verbally in an effort to keep from slapping him. "Besides, gentlemen, something tells me this is the sort of transaction which would be better served being off the books and not on. It's also my supposition Herr Himmler would prefer as well." But she wasn't precisely sure what her 'brother' Heinrich would do when faced with her proposal. Could he be bought? Or would she have to use another currency? Currency of a more personal nature? Oh, not sexual currency, but access by his specialists to her person and her history. Was she willing to pay that much? How many of her secrets was she willing to share to buy her grandfather's way out of prison? How much of herself would she have to give away to save the man who almost destroyed her?

Von Kleist nodded. "I think that would be a wise assumption, Madame," There appeared to be a faint respect in his eye. "You have matured, if I may say so, Your Serene Highness."

Galiena smiled at him. "You may, Herr Ritter, and thank you." She looked at her notes. "Now were you able to look into transportation out of Germany for the fourth or fifth with a destination of Brazil?"

"The Graf Zeppelin is scheduled to leave for Rio de Janeiro on the morning of the fourth, but Your Serene Highness' meeting is not until later in the day, so unfortunately that option is negated. Otherwise we are looking a sailing out of Hamburg later on in the month, or sailings from Cherbourg or Southampton, also at times to be determined, but not immediate," von Klopfer answered.

"Not good enough. Not good enough at all. I like the Graf Zeppelin. I have good memories of it. Next question, how much will it cost to delay the flight of the airship to put my Grandfather on it?" Galiena grabbed the tip of Emil's tail, which he was lashing into her arm. She kissed the tip and then let it go, removing her file from his head for good measure. He was being such a good baby and she didn't want to abuse him.

Von Kleist drew his own head back. "Delay it? You want to delay the airship for a day?"

Galiena addressed von Klopfer. "Come now. You know it's not impossible. Certainly not for the Pfalzgraf von Steinberg. We did it before when we took the Graf in '35 and were late getting over from Paris. They delayed the flight for two days. You arranged it, as I remember."

"I did. It's true, but the cost was-"

Galiena cut von Klopfer off. "When I am planning to spend one million marks to get my grandfather out of Buchenwald, don't presume to lecture me about costs, mein Herr! I don't have time for it. You will find out how much it will cost and I will pay it. Or The Steinberg Gessellschaft will. It matters not to me. What matters is that it happens."

The man dropped his gaze. "Yes, your Serene Highness."

"Thank you, Herr von Klopfer," Galiena considered the man. She was hit by the fleeting thought that she could be rid of this particular trial. Every cloud did indeed have a silver lining. "Of course, as my grandfather's secretary, I would expect that you would follow him into exile should you wish to maintain your present position. We will, of course, provide you with adequate compensation for such a relocation, both for you and your family should they wish it."

It was obvious von Klopfer hadn't processed this very far. "Me? To Brazil? You want me to go to Brazil," he spluttered uselessly.

"Well obviously you can't remain here in Germany and retain your position as grandfather's personal secretary, can you? He will need you, at least until you can train a replacement. Of course I expect you to go with him. He will more than expect your services; especially with the difficulties he will endure controlling our empire from South America," Galiena answered calmly, enjoying the man's discomfort. "Of course, I think a bonus in the form of two of the aforementioned highly portable gold bars would adequately serve for your troubles?" Galiena looked to her target. She knew he was an avaricious man and that the lure of gold would captivate him.

"More than adequately. It's very generous. Gold isn't tied to anyone's currency. Marks are very hard to spend outside of the Reich," von Kleist intoned.

Von Klopfer shook his big head, sweat breaking out on his brow. "In four days? You want me ready to go in four days? I can't do that! I have appointments."

"Cancel them," Galiena tilted her head. "Or resign."

"What about him?" Von Klopfer pointed at his counterpart.

"The Ritter von Kleist is the director of Operations for the Gessellschaft. The German division, which I plan to retain for myself, will need him; as will I, to better learn the business for when I need to manage the entire organisation. My necessity is greater than my Grandfather's. Besides, when the Pfalzgraf and I travelled in the past, you always accompanied us, Herr von Klopfer, while the Ritter watched the shop at home. I wish to maintain the status quo." Galiena rubbed the bridge of her nose between her thumb and forefinger. "It's your choice, as I said."

"You give me no choice. I will follow the Pfalzgraf into exile."

It was a small, hollow victory, but it gave Galiena a great measure of confidence. "Excellent. You are very efficient, Herr von Klopfer. I will expect you to continue your liaison with the Ritter von Kleist to ensure that communication between the Pfalzgraf and myself happens seamlessly. This is a new era and communication is very fast. Telegrams and overseas phone calls

330

mean the distances between Europe and South America can be reduced to negligible. As I understand, the turnaround time with the wireless is a matter of days, not weeks, and with the rumours of transatlantic aeroplane companies, it will be even shorter still. The war chest is such that the cost, which could be prohibitive for some, will not affect us too terribly. If anything, this division may serve to be a benefit. Certainly it will be better then the present static for which I am primarily responsible."

"It is admirable that the Pfalzgräfin has come to understand her limitations," von Kleist said quietly. "That did not come out as intended. What I meant is that a more immature person might have tried to take control of something they weren't ready for. I am proud that you have embarked on your present course."

Galiena took pity on the man. "I thank you for your compliment, Herr Ritter, and I understand how it was intended. I want to learn from you, Herr Ritter. You have years of experience and knowledge where I have none. I want to be a responsible custodian for what my grandfather has built. It would be vanity and folly to think I was ready at this juncture."

The man bowed his head. "It will be my pleasure to educate you."

Galiena switched gears. "Next. The paperwork regarding the Graf von Reitersbach's adoption of Doctor Kohl. Was it sent to Vienna?"

"Yes. It should have arrived on Friday last. I sent one of our attorneys down with it personally," von Kleist responded.

"Perfect. Next I want a legal document limiting the power any husband of mine would have over the estate and Gessellschaft. I'm not so clear about what is standard under German law in the case of marriage, but I don't want my husband to take control over my shares. Don't make it so blatant as to be insulting to Doctor Kohl. He's an intelligent man, but on the other hand, if he's marrying me simply to take everything I have and then cast me aside, I would like to re-educate him on the nature of the situation," Galiena dictated firmly, glancing at her notes again.

"It's about time that occurred to Your Serene Highness," von Klopfer replied snidely.

"Thank you for the vote of confidence, Herr von Klopfer." The corpulent man would make a fitting midday meal for Emil. If only he knew how close he was to being someone's dinner. Then again, the sheer gall of the man might make her beloved lion sick.

Von Kleist interjected. "I will set our attorneys to it when I return to the city. It shouldn't be too difficult. Your grandfather had interim documents drawn up in the twenties before the-" he paused, obviously choosing his words. "Runaway marriage of your sister. He knew that one day you both would marry and such things might be required to differing extents. When your sister and her line were disinherited, the point became moot, of course."

"Then have them redrawn in the name of Hagen Kohl Graf von Reitersbach," Galiena instructed. "And please have them ready by Friday in some form or another."

"That person doesn't exist unless the present Graf adopts Doctor Kohl, Madame." Von Kleist reminded her gently.

"I know, but I would have something to show my grandfather when I see him." Emil lifted his head, his wet nose touching Galiena under the chin, his painfully rough tongue running along the column of her throat. She kissed him on the nose and gently moved his head down.

"There is wisdom in that." Von Kleist frowned as he stared at the lion. "Speaking of which, Your Serene Highness, should you be allowing your pet such unrestricted access to your person? That is a lion, is it not?"

Galiena laughed. "Emil sleeps with me, Herr Ritter. I trust him implicitly," More than she trusted the Pfalzgraf and his cronies.

"As you wish," the cadaverous man acquiesced with typical Prussian reserve.

Galiena inclined her head in his direction before continuing. "Of course arrangements must be made for appropriate household to go with my grandfather, and I am assuming there will be space for such on the Zeppelin. Money is not an object. I have contacted Montrose, the Pfalzgraf's valet, and he is preparing my grandfather's things for transport. It is my intention that you will all wait at a hotel in Weimar while I go to the camp and secure my grandfather's release, and when I have done so, I will call you there to take him to Friederichshaven."

"You've obviously considered this very carefully, Your Serene Highness," von Klopfer said at last.

"I've had a great deal of time to ponder the problem. If the Reichsführer acquiesces to my request, I want the Pfalzgraf out of Germany before he can change his mind, or gets even greedier. Speed is of the essence. I was listening when Hagen was discussing his superior officer. Himmler can make decisions based on emotions in one minute, and change his mind when more rational heads prevail in another. We cannot allow him that opportunity." She sighed as Emil dropped from her to inspect his ball. The lion could be an overly warm blanket and she was relieved to have the weight gone.

"I had not heard that the Reichsführer was of a mercurial nature," von Kleist seemed unruffled, but he did mark Emil with his gaze.

Von Klopfer's eyes bulged as he watched the lion playing. The well mauled rubber ball rolled across the floor almost to his feet. "Madame!" He squeaked.

The noise seemed to annoy Emil, and he crouched low, watching the fat man. "No fear, Herr von Klopfer," Galiena whispered. "Just be still. Emil will be curious a moment, and then will go back to his game." True to her words, Emil relaxed and then snaked out a paw and pushed his ball in another direction.

"There was one last item," Galiena added, going over her earlier conversation with Idalie in her mind. "Something I want investigated, and the timing is less sensitive on this one. I would like the location of my nephews, the sons of my sister Verina and the Ritter von Taschen. I feel I should become acquainted with the boys and I haven't the foggiest notion of where they are. Verina told me their father has an estate in Aachen, or somewhere nearby in Westphalia. That should give you a place to start."

Von Kleist wrote that down. "I can put some men to it, for it shouldn't be too hard to find. The Ritter von Taschen is a Generalmajor in the Heer. The Pfalzgraf maintained a small file on him. We have access to them."

Galiena looked up for she had no idea. "Files? Where?"

"Some are at Riesa. Others are in Berlin at the Gessellschaft offices," von Klopfer replied, somewhat more calmly. Emil had disappeared behind Galiena into the forest of potted trees.

"May I have access to them?" Galiena asked intently. Knowledge was power, and with her grandfather's knowledge she would gain a surprising amount of power. The Pfalzgraf always seemed to know everything about everybody.

"You would have to negotiate that with the Pfalzgraf. They are his files, in his office. He has the key to the cabinets," The large man narrowed his eyes at her.

"So do you," she reminded the corpulent man belligerently.

"But I do not work for you, nor do I keep the files for you." Again the belligerent tone.

She wasn't going to get into a power struggle with him, as von Klopfer would soon learn the mistake of his arrogance. Her grandfather wouldn't appreciate von Klopfer's lack of co-operation with her when he was told. The Pfalzgraf had a very finely tuned sense of rank and order. Whatever von Klopfer's position or social status, to the Pfalzgraf he was a servant, and a servant who didn't serve was useless. Von Klopfer didn't seem to understand his position.

Instead Galiena turned to von Kleist. "I know that my grandfather has disinherited Verina and her line. If I wanted to re-inherit them, or even adopt them as my own heirs, would that be possible? If I felt one was deserving?"

"I will have to read the will, and the law. I couldn't tell you off the top of my head but I'll find out," von Kleist said. "With Herr von Klopfer leaving, we will also have to find you a personal secretary. Someone to look after these things for you."

Galiena dropped her head. "There seems to be a dearth of new people on their way into my life. In this I shall defer to you, Herr Ritter. Put together a list of ten or so suitable candidates, and we can interview them together." The corners of her mouth turned up wanly. "But not this week! I have far too much to do!"

Chapter 24
March 2, 1938

Hagen and Freffie lounged in leather wing chairs on either side of a huge fireplace, each reading the paper and drinking a very fine armagnac. They were at Freffie's club, 'recovering'- to use Freffie's word- from an arduous journey to the tailor. The man seemed to spend an inordinate amount of time at the tailor and spent a truly grotesque amount of money on clothing. Almost every second day they were there for fittings, or to pick something up; sometimes simply to examine fabrics, ties or poufs. Hagen very rarely emerged unscathed from these visits, and realised that he would have to return to Germany soon or be bankrupt. On the other hand, Hagen himself was a bit of a clothes horse, and there was nothing quite like a good tailor. The man also did uniforms, which was something to consider when Hagen could order such things.

Freffie's club was also quite to Hagen's liking, and the Graf had signed him up for membership. Apparently his application needed to be vetted by the membership committee, which, according to his host was merely a formality. The soon-to-be son of the Graf von Reitersbach would be welcome anywhere. It was a large club, quite full this afternoon, with men ranging in age from early twenties to early nineties. The young men here were sombre in their demeanour. When their tables became too boisterous, a club steward would walk over with a gentle reminder of their location and the volume would cease.

The club had existed for well over one hundred years; Freffie's great-grandfather being one of the founding members. Perhaps that was why this prime place by the fire was always here for him. Even the older gentlemen left it when the Graf arrived, a deference which surprised Hagen. He thought of György's words on rank and tradition, but even then such things didn't process well with him. Freffie's ancestors were the ones who were accomplished. Freffie himself was fairly useless, if harmless, in his own extravagant way.

Wills, on the other hand, was an enigma. He was a much harder man than Hagen would have figured, with eyes that followed Hagen wherever he went. It wasn't lust in those looks; more banked rage. Last night Hagen had tried to raise the topic of Galiena, but the Ritter merely shrugged off the questions and left the room to make a phone call. His hostility, though glacially polite, was a tad unnerving.

Hagen dropped his paper to look at Freffie, who was reading a day old London Times. Freffie always read three papers at the club: The Times, the Wiener Zeitung, and surprisingly enough, the Volkisch Beobachter. When asked why he read the national Nazi newspaper, which was illegal to posses in Austria, though readily available to those with influence, Freffie merely shrugged. The Graf was also following the von Fritsch trial. That stopped Hagen in his tracks. He knew enough about von Fritsch to last a lifetime. Curiously enough, when Freffie was reading the Zeitung, no one ever disturbed him. Not even the club stewards, who usually materialized the moment Freffie's empty glass hit the coaster, came near when the Zeitung was raised. The instant the Zeitung was dropped, they were at his elbow with a fresh brandy, but not while the paper was in the air. It was reminiscent of Heydrich fencing in the gym at headquarters. People never disturbed the Blond Beast when he was drilling; he disturbed them when he required a partner. It was one of those unspoken rules. Hagen wondered if he possessed habits like that himself. Most likely, but he was unaware of them.

Freffie sighed and shook the Times before laying it down on the table beside him. "Ah London. I miss it. I've been playing the Jewel of Vienna for far too long. It's about time I spread my sunshine elsewhere."

"Are you so bored here?" Hagen asked quietly, folding up his own paper.

Freffie frowned, and raised a hand, a call to the steward. "Not bored precisely, but I must confess ennui is creeping up on me. Perhaps it's an over-familiarity. There's been little travel of late, just work, work, work," Freffie winked as he said the last word, then turned to the steward. "Champagne de Venoge for the Doctor and myself. It's time to do some work and work requires champagne."

The man nodded, moving away. Hagen glanced quizzically at Freffie, who reached down and picked up his briefcase. "Work?" Hagen repeated in disbelief.

"It's ghastly, I know." The case opened and out came a large folder. "Gallie sent up some papers on the weekend. The Grim Reaper had the temerity to phone and remind me about them last night."

"The Grim Reaper?" Hagen was beginning to feel like a parrot and wondered why he couldn't think of a more intelligent rejoinder for the Graf.

"The Ritter von Kleist; the von Steinberg Gesselschaft's man of affairs. Looks dreadfully cadaverous." Freffie hefted the folio, untying the black ribbon securing it. "Still, it was a bit of a shock to have him on the other end of the phone. He extended himself for her, which means she must have impressed him, for the Pfalzgraf's creatures have been a handful for her in the past."

"Have they?" Hagen said flatly. That would change when Hagen was married to her. They would treat her with the proper amount of respect, or they could be replaced.

"Maybe there has been a change. Anyway, these are the adoption papers to make you my son." Freffie's eyes gleamed sardonically. "Funny that, given you have nine years on me."

Hagen studied the younger man. "Why are you doing this?" He opted for a moment of honesty. "I can't imagine you would elevate just anyone to your family"

The Graf's eyes clouded, staring absently into the fire for a long while before returning to Hagen. "Because I love her and she asked. She's never asked anything of me before and she has given more than I can possibly repay."

"I understand."

Freffie's eyes narrowed. "No, Hagen, I don't think you do. You don't know Gallie well enough yet. That woman you see on the outside is a shade of what is really there. The single biggest failure in my life is that I let her go when I was too stupid to realise what I had. On the other hand, it wouldn't surprise me to see the von Steinberg line has bred true. I warrant she could chew us both up and still have room for tea." The Graf's eyes dropped to his folder again. "This adoption is a drop in the bucket to what I owe her."

"I plan to protect Galiena with all the resources at my disposal," Hagen paused, strangely desirous to reassure his companion. As he said the words it was like saying a pledge anew. "I'm not a man without influence in my own country."

Freffie waved a dismissive hand. "You're a Nazi, Hagen. I know what you are. I know what your people are. I'm not fooled by all the propaganda," he smiled bitterly. "But as they say, your country has places for people like me, does it not? But it doesn't matter, for I plan to leave before it becomes an issue."

Hagen made an impulsive and probably foolish decision. "Freffie, you have my word that when Germany comes, I will protect you as well."

"Why would you do that, Hagen? Isn't that against your vows?"

"For Galiena," Hagen replied without hesitation. "Because you are her family." The word almost stuck in his throat as he considered what he'd done to her sister, Verina.

"Maybe there's hope for you yet." Freffie leaned forward and offered his hand to Hagen.

They shook quickly. "Perhaps. I'm more than a uniform, Graf von Reitersbach," Hagen answered. "Far more."

"I'm beginning to understand what Gallie sees in you. It's these moments of being toweringly noble, I think. Only being from the towering nobility, I've oft noted the towers are crumbling at the base and there's inevitably some sort of very dangerous nastiness underneath it all," the young man said dryly.

Hagen merely smiled. "We all have skeletons in our closet, Freffie. Don't ask to examine mine."

The effeminate dandy returned. "Oh Lord love you, no! I don't care to be appraised in the slightest, my son." He shuffled through the papers until he found one marked with an elaborate trefoil clip, and pulled out an ornate fountain pen from his pocket. With a deft flourish he signed his name on the paper before handing both the folder and the pen over to Hagen. "Now sign your life away, my boy, and it's all finished."

Hagen scanned the papers as the steward brought the champagne. It seemed very standard to him. He was being adopted as the son of the Graf von Reitersbach. True to what György said, he would become Hagen Kohl Graf von Reitersbach if he signed. It was almost unnerving. He met Freffie's eyes again. "Why? Why would you invite me to join your family? It goes back hundreds of years. You're Uradel. I know this. And I know how Wills feels about us common people."

Freffie rolled his eyes with overdone exaggeration. "Wills' 'Ritter' is so new it squeaks if he turns around too fast. Perhaps when one is born at the top of the food chain, one realises that it's all a case of semantics. My father was a monster, quite in line with the Pfalzgraf, believe me." Again the far away look on the elegant face. "No amount of nobility did either of them any good in the humanity department. Wills is terribly concerned with station, rank, and all that rot. I'm more interested in nobility of spirit. Yet at the same time, I have this notion of duty. My name is eight hundred and some odd years old. I won't have children, so when I die, it dies with me. If I adopt you, my family name lives on with yours. If you are a quarter of the man she professes you are, then there will be far more nobility going into the line then there was to begin with." He laughed self depreciatingly. "Besides. The royal line of Sweden needed a shot in the arm, and they adopted a commoner, a Frenchman to boot! I'm not so far above the kings of Sweden that I can't adopt a fellow German to take my title. It doesn't come with anything, particularly. A crumbling, neglected pile in Saxon-Anhalt on my death which is rather heavily mortgaged and the house here in Vienna which is less so. Or was. With those papers signed by me, the Steinberg Gessellschaft has released the mortgages, whether you sign or not."

Hagen dropped the papers into his lap feeling hugely disappointed with the Graf. "So then it was about money."

Freffie shook his head. "The Pfalzgraf held the mortgage. It wasn't precisely an issue. He paid me to release Gallie from my company by buying up my debt. The loss of my marker was an agreement I made with von Kleist last night, though I would have signed the papers for Gallie whether the Reaper made the offer or not." The Graf looked troubled. "Gallie doesn't know about that, by the way. That the Pfalzgraf bought me off. At the time I was desperate, but I've always been heartily ashamed. He didn't want her to be polluted by my lifestyle. Perhaps on some level I agreed. I couldn't contact her. Those were the terms of the agreement. She could contact me if she felt like it, but he kept her very busy. Very focussed on him."

"I see."

Freffie balled his fists in his lap. "By God, I feel rather responsible for what happened. So much for my great love. Meinrad von Steinberg is probably right about me. As much as I try, I'm not made of what one would call the 'sterner stuff'." Then Freffie's faced firmed in resolution. "But I'm working on it now. I'll make her proud of me one day. Even if it kills me."

"We all have our skeletons," Hagen repeated, searching for a sliver of understanding in his soul and finding none.

"I'm a different man now. I grew up, if you would care to believe it." The words were spoken without a trace of irony. "These days I do believe in something more than my own pleasure."

Hagen had trouble believing the man's declaration, but he wasn't going to spoil Freffie's illusions of himself. It explained the comments about towers rotting from underneath. No. Galiena didn't need to know. She would be devastated if she knew; yet maybe she did on some level. Galiena fled to Göring after the Pfalzgraf attacked her, not to Freffie. Galiena was a smart girl. She have know Freffie was weak.

A moment more then Hagen put the pen to paper and signed, and when he was done, he was almost surprised to still feel the same man. Nothing had changed, yet legally he was now a Graf. While he had no intention of actually using the name, he was now Hagen Luitpold Kohl Graf von Reitersbach. A Graf. Him. With the stroke of a pen. What a strange world this was. It didn't mean anything and yet on some level it did. He was a Graf!

Freffie rose to his feet, pressing an overflowing glass of Champagne into Hagen's hand. "Gentlemen, I would like to propose a toast." All the men in the room stood, charging their glasses. "I would like to present His Illustrious Highness, Hagen Graf von Reitersbach. Perhaps a little long in the tooth, but my son nonetheless."

"To the Graf!" The men cheered, drinking up. "Three cheers to His Illustrious Highness."

Hagen also stood. "To Freffie who adopted me." He raised his glass and poured the champagne down his throat.

The men crowded near, shaking hands and slapping backs. All in all, it was far more festive then Hagen was expecting. He was introduced to almost every man in the place, including Feldmarschall Hermann von Lüttwitz, the uncle of one of the boys on Eugen's list. Hagen talked to the man for a brief time, and wondered if this could be the patient György described. Von Lüttwitz didn't strike Hagen as the type of man who was suffering from War Neurosis. The other Feldmarschall in the club, Joachim von Lohausen, a stern looking man in his late sixties, looked very much the type with his hard eyes and expressionless face.

Hagen was talking with the two Feldmarschalls, who seemed to know each other very well, when suddenly Freffie drawled, "And if it isn't young Snotty! Afternoon, Wolfgang!"

"G-G-G-G-ood D-D-ay, Graf F-F-F-Freffie." The young man, the exact image of the picture Hagen had seen in Eugen's hands, had a terrible stutter. His face twisted up as he tried to force the words out.

"Only have three F's in my name, Wolfgang, but I appreciate the elevation." Freffie handed his glass to the boy. "Finish that off, boy, for it will cure what ails you."

"Thank-you, G-G-G-Graf Freffie." The boy drained the glass in one gulp.

Freffie turned to Hagen and winked. "What can I say? I make the lad terribly nervous. Must be my own towering nobility." Freffie looked behind Wolfgang. "And you have your new little friend with you. Hello there, friend of Snotty!"

Hagen looked up, straight into the eyes of Hans von Ond. He knew this moment would come, and hoped that von Ond had the possession to handle it well. "Your Illustrious Highness," von Ond addressed Freffie with a bow of his head.

Freffie took Hagen's arm. "Young Snotty here is Wolfgang von Lüttwitz, the Feldmarschall's nephers. His father was known to all and sundry as Snotty, due to some sort of permanent nasal congestion. I'm not entirely sure what that was about. Bit before my time, don't y'know. But all of his sons are eternally known by the same name, and young Snotty is the youngest of the Snotty progeny," Freffie looked back at Wolfgang. "I don't know, young Snotty. Perhaps I should call you youngest Snotty, but as I never see your sibs, I think young Snotty would do it."

"Wh-Wh-Wh-Whatever you s-s-s-say, Herr Graf," The boy choked out with a shy grin, obviously glowing from the attention.

His uncle rolled his eyes at the stutter and took von Lohausen's arm. "Not a voice for the parade ground, that. Come! Let's go find more cognac." The two men drifted away.

"So, young Snotty, this is my son, the other Graf von Reitersbach, Hagen. Mind your manners around him. He's far more than he appears to be." Freffie winked at Hagen.

"Pleased to m-m-meet you, H-H-H-Herr Graf." The boy clicked his heels and bowed his head.

Hagen returned the gesture. "My pleasure, Herr von Lüttwitz."

"And this one here is new," Freffie continued in his light-hearted manner. "Herr Hans von Ond, fresh from the Reich," He leaned in conspiratorially to Hagen. "Left with a passel of Nazis on his tail, or so I hear. Dogging his steps right up to the border."

Von Ond grinned. "Nothing so exciting, Your Illustrious Highness, but I did get an escort to the train. They seemed very happy to see the back of me and I was more than pleased to have left their company."

"Discretion, young V-O," Freffie chuckled wickedly. "One never knows where one of those sneaky reprobates might be lurking."

"If I saw one in front of me, Herr Graf, I would spit on his shoes and then call the bugger out," von Ond replied with some heat.

"You might want to back up," Freffie cheekily whispered to Hagen.

"Ah, the choler of youth," Hagen imitated Freffie's bored tones and elaborate hand gestures.

Freffie's eyes widened and he clapped Hagen on the back. "You are my son, after all. A father couldn't be prouder."

"Thanks," Hagen paused, rolling the word around on his tongue. "Daddy."

'Daddy' rolled his eyes. "Now let's not go too overboard with that, Hagen. People might think I'm older than I am and thirty is staring me rather pointedly in the face."

Hagen extended his hand to von Ond. "Herr von Ond, it is my pleasure to meet you."

Von Ond shook with Hagen. "The pleasure is indeed, all mine, Your Illustrious Highness. My congratulations on your elevation."

Hagen inclined his head. "Thank you, Herr von Ond."

Von Lüttwitz turned back to Freffie. "Are you attending v-v-v-v-von G-G-G-Gazen's rout on F-F-F-Friday night, Graf F-Freffie?"

"Do you think I would miss one of his ever so naughty parties? Of course not. Might take the boy here if he's up to it." Freffie turned to Hagen, slapping him sharply between the shoulder blades. "Do you think you can handle an evening of completely unbridled debauchery?"

Hagen appraised Freffie, trying to address what an evening of unbridled debauchery might mean for the man. "I'm sure I won't be too shocked."

"Von Gazen says he hired those g-g-g-g-girls that the Prinz of Zerbst had at his party last month." The young man's eyes grew as round as saucers. "The F-F-F-F-French d-d-d-d-dancing g-g-g-g-girls."

"They were entertaining," Freff nodded and then punched the boy in the arm. "Didn't you pluck one of them, boy? I'm sure I heard you did." Freffie tapped his lips. "On the buffet table at the end of the evening?"

The young man blushed and examined his shoes. "Th-Th-Th-There were t-t-t-two, Herr Graf."

Freffie burst out laughing. "Good show, young Snotty! That's what we like to hear!"

Hagen was beginning to have a clearer picture of the unbridled debauchery. He'd been to some debauches when he'd been at university; who hadn't? But nothing where a great deal of money had been invested. He wasn't particularly interested in going to such a thing, but as they said, there's always time to cut cards with the devil.

"Thank you H-H-Herr Graf."

Freffie patted Hagen's arm again. "Well we should be off. Must get home and change for the evening's rounds. Tante Stanzi is back and having another musical evening, and if we don't go, my life won't be worth a pfennig."

They moved off from the boys, who bowed, and made their way out of the club. It was late afternoon and the street was awash in a sea of red swastika banners. The Austrian SA was marching, in defiance of the police. The Nazis were wearing mufti, but despite their appearance their affiliation was obvious. The police seemed disinterested, those who weren't cheering the Nazis on. Times were changing in Vienna. The air was becoming ever more charged with the inevitable, and the common man seemed to crave Hitler's arrival. The parade made Hagen homesick and he yearned for his uniform. He missed how it made him feel. Being a bought Graf was all very well and fine, but the title which warmed his soul was SS Mann. He missed his office, his Standarte, his men, and his Galiena.

"Let's walk home," Freffie suggested; his brows drawing together over his nose in a frown. "It's only a few blocks, and we'll never make it in the car through this. When it comes to Tante Stanzi, fashionably lacking in punctuality is not the best choice. Ergo let us be unfashionably seen strolling through this rabble. The car can come later, when the streets thin out."

Hagen gestured forward. "As you say," he replied, assessing the situation. It also struck him how Freffie considered strolling fashionable when one had no plan but to be seen; yet walking to a destination was the height of déclassé.

"You smile. I suppose you approve of this chaos," Freffie answered somewhat bitterly.

Hagen considered his words carefully. "Of this? No. I don't approve of the Austrian SA. I don't approve of the German SA either. But the party? Of course I do. The Fuhrer has been very good for Germany."

"If a man conforms and is one of the many, for sure. I agree. Unemployment is down. Morale is up. All very important. Yet what about those considered enemies of the state? Your government is no friend to the Aristocracy! Or the Jews. Let alone humble little fags like myself." The word was so ugly coming from Freffie's lips.

Hagen didn't want to have this fight with his host. "No government is perfect," He said at last. "Even the English sent Oscar Wilde to hard labour. We Germans aren't the only people who disapprove of your lifestyle."

"Ah, yes! Poor Oscar. How I would like to be as splendid as he was," Freffie glanced at him out of the corner of his eye. "But you talk of disapproval and the laws your country upholds. It's small comfort to those who aren't members of the club." He hefted his walking stick. "Remember that, when you sit in the confines of your Germany, secure in the knowledge that you aren't one of the persecuted. Like von Ond, I had to leave and very quickly, because of what I am. Because I choose to be unashamed of it." The silver handle of the cane came up and lightly tapped Hagen in the arm. "Besides, cher Oscar was sent down over thirty years ago in a far less civilised era. Have we progressed naught in that time?"

Hagen had no reply, so he stayed silent and merely strolled beside Freffie, watching as the parade slowly began to break up. So far it wasn't a violent situation, but the possibility was there, as riots had broken out in the last few days. Riots which which had left several hurt. The riots angered Hagen. It wasn't the way the Nazis here should behave! Didn't they know Hitler's supremacy over von Schuschnigg was inevitable? It was simply a matter of time until the Anchluß happened.

"Well, well, well! What have we here? If it isn't the fairy von Reitersbach!" A voice familiar to Hagen growled. Hagen turned to see the somewhat battered face of Brigadeführer Adolf Rodlauer coming across the road, a few of his flunkies trailing after him. Rodlauer wasn't looking too good, which pleased Hagen, who still bore the purple bruise from the man's truncheon. Freffie ignored the man, and continued in his walk, staring through the group of SA. "You will stop when I speak to you!" The paw grabbed Freffie's shoulder.

Freffie pursed his lips. "I'm sorry. I didn't hear you," he drawled.

"Arrogant faggot! Your time will come! Then we'll show you the way of it."

Freffie looked tremendously bored as he looked up at the big man. "Which part, mein Herr? The marching I saw. The shouting, I'm hearing. Really, I think I've had enough education for one day."

Rodlauer raised his fist. "I could show you the way of it now, Faggot. I doubt the police are going to stop me. They might even cheer. They know who's going to be in charge around here."

Hagen decided to intercede. His distaste for Rodlauer was growing by leaps and bounds. "I think you've said your peace, Brigadeführer. Now take your men and move along," he said in his Schwarze Teufel voice.

"Oh, another one. Who the hell invited you to get involved?" Rodlauer growled; his working class dialect almost fouling Hagen's ears.

"Herr Brigadeführer, isn't he the one from the other night?" One of the men said quietly.

"Hagen, don't interfere," Freffie wearily told him, raising a hand.

Hagen exchanged a look with Freffie and shook his head. "This is my department, after all." He moved closer to Rodlauer; well within range of the man's fists. He drew himself up to his full height which was an inch taller than Rodlauer and glared down into the small piggy eyes. "You're a bully, Rodlauer, and you're terribly stupid. I will forget about this incident, provided you leave right this very moment." He looked at each man in turn. "Then I will work very hard at forgetting each and every one of you."

"Who the fuck are you?" Rodlauer obviously hadn't recognized him.

"I'm going to tell you a story, Rodlauer, though it's probably far above you," Hagen began. "In every town, during the time of the inquisition, there was a fearless traveller who worked for the holy fathers. No one knew who he was until it was far too late for them to do anything about it." Hagen smiled slowly and deliberately, taking a page from Eugen's rather thick book. "I might just be that traveller." He raised two fingers and pointed them at the SA Mann.

Rodlauer shook his head. "What the hell does that mean?"

"Herr Brigadeführer! He's the one! The one from the other night! From the bombing! Kaltenbrunner's comrade!"

Hagen took his two fingers and jabbed them hard into Rodlauer's chest, right where he had broken the man's ribs in their scuffle. Rodlauer gasped and went pale. "It means that I'm the one who doesn't want to play with you anymore. Need I break more of your ribs before you learn I'm not here for your pleasure?"

"He's the one Kaltenbrunner's so afraid of!"

Rodlauer took a step back, holding his chest. "I won't forget about this," He hissed through clenched teeth. Obviously Hagen had done a very good job of breaking that rib. And broken ribs were so terribly painful. Slow healing too.

"You should pray, Rodlauer that I forget about this, and forget about you." Again he looked at every man in the group. "But be notified that the Graf von Reitersbach is under my personal protection. Were something to happen to him, I would know precisely who was responsible."

"Why are you protecting that faggot?" the Brigadeführer asked.

"That's really none of your business." Hagen inhaled slowly. "As a comrade of Kaltenbrunner's, I might be on the Reichsführer's business, and you should be well aware of the Reichsführer's actions the last time the SA involved themselves in his business?" It was a blatant allusion to Long Knives, one no SA man would miss.

True enough, Rodlauer stiffened. "I won't forget this either." He turned on his heel and strode off. One of the lackeys, the one who spoke up, looked at Hagen and clicked his heels in salute before leaving. Hagen crossed his arms over his chest in satisfaction as he watched them go. He detested bullies. Nothing made him happier than making them run, tails between their legs.

"Very well done. I've had problems with that one in the past. Bit of my gadfly. Constantly trying to bite me." Freffie muttered under his breath.

"Rodlauer is an embarrassment to his armband." Hagen brushed off his sleeves and dropped his arms.

Freffie gave him an arch look. "So why is this Kaltenbrunner so afraid of you? Who are you, Hagen Kohl?"

Hagen smiled. "In Germany, I'm the SA's bane. They aren't fond of me because I've sent many to prison for crimes they thought they could get away with. Abuse of power and the like. It's given me a very unique position with the Reichsführer."

"Fascinating. Galiena said you were a policeman of sorts," Freffie appeared rather confused.

Hagen decided to tell Freffie the truth, as it was a year ago, as they restarted their walk. "I police the apparatuses of the party for criminal wrong doing and punish them accordingly. One could say I'm the inquisition for the inquisitors."

"But you aren't in Germany, so is not what you just did an abuse of power?"

Hagen shrugged innocently. "I carry my authority with me. I have Himmler's ear whenever I need it."

The Graf stopped in his track. "I thought you were on vacation?"

"I am," He held out his hand to Freffie with genuine intention. "Doesn't mean I can't use that authority to protect my friends from pugnacious swine like Rodlauer."

Freffie was still, and then shook Hagen's hand. "You have my thanks. Maybe Gallie is right. You do seem a decent sort of a chap."

"Thank you," Hagen replied neutrally, feeling that something in his relationship with the Graf had changed.

"Still doesn't mean I agree with your party, your politics, or your country trying to absorb mine," Freffie added in his usual tones.

Hagen felt the corner of his mouth turn up. "Aren't fathers and sons supposed to disagree on such things?"

Freffie's lips twitched and then he laughed aloud. "Something like that. Oh how fast the children grow up! I have you just a few hours, and already you're defying me."

"Just making up for lost time, Daddy!"

December 5, 1937
Poppet,
Still alive. Miss you. Love you!
Meinrad

Chapter 25
March 3, 1938

The hardest part was the timing; the second hardest part was the secrecy. Galiena had thrown all her balls into the air. Hopefully they would land where she wished. Instructions were left for everyone. Idalie was to pack clothing for three days into the Horsch, which Swanhilde and Emil would drive down to Berlin to meet her at Göring's palace before their final journey to Riesa tonight. She had given the plane to von Schilling for the weekend, so long as it was at Carinhall by Sunday night, that was all which mattered to her. He was talking of taking it to see his parents in Kiel. At Riesa, Montrose was packing the Rolls Royce limousine for both himself and his master, to be ready to follow Galiena to Weimar where they would meet Von Kleist and von Klopfer at the Hotel Elefant. The men would wait there for her phone call of success or failure, while she and Emil drove on to Buchenwald with the twenty gold bars in the trunk to, as the poets say, death or glory. Galiena knew it might be foolish to take Emil with her, but she wanted the modicum of protection. She was going to have a million marks worth of gold bullion in her car and she figured that Emil would better serve her than a pistol.

But today wasn't for rest. She had been up at five to meet von Schilling for six, and they had flown until just this moment, three in the afternoon, when they landed at the Berlin Templehof airport. Von Schilling had agreed to come with her to the hospital where her sister was being treated. Galiena had to know the truth about her nephew Rudiger. Von Schilling didn't know much, but had reacted very compassionately to Galiena's awkward and hesitant query for assistance. She didn't want to go to that terrible place alone. Her anxiety had caused the worst landing of her flying career; she'd dropped the plane with a dreadful jolt which rattled the entire length of her spine.

But again, von Schilling had been kind. Her frustration, fear and stress had manifested itself in her eyes filling with tears, but his gloved hand just covered hers, as he said "The worst landing of my life was when I landed to rearm after Guernica. I didn't want to go back, because I knew my bombs on the second run would land on the innocent. I think I wanted to crash, but I pulled myself together and performed my duty."

Von Schilling understood duty and he understood fear. She knew when she looked in his eyes. In that moment he became her friend; Lord knew, they spent so much time together. How could he be anything else? The pilot rubbed her shoulder as she got out of the plane; nothing sexual, more a gesture of comradeship. He'd handed her the garment bag she'd tossed in the back seats of the plane earlier. Here she was, in a change room for pilots, dressing, putting on makeup, doing hair, and attaching hat as to look like a Pfalzgräfin at the hospital. Her hands were almost shaking. She had only been to that place once before, but once was enough, in her opinion.

Galiena took a very deep breath, smoothed her green gloved hands over her skirt, collecting herself as she crumpled her flight suit into a ball in the bag. Another breath and she held her hand out flat in the air in front of her face. To her shame, she was shaking. Galiena left the bathroom, and continued to where she saw her escort. He had repaired to his daily uniform, looking the very debonair officer.

When von Schilling saw her, he snapped to attention and bowed low. "Madame, I salute you!" He grinned boyishly. The pilot was far too handsome for her peace of mind. If only he had some sort of flaw; a hunchback or a disfiguring boil. It would make things so much easier for her. Even his limp added to his charm.

"Thank you, Herr Ritter. You look very flash too," Galiena allowed her lips to curl up, albeit wanly.

He winked at her and took her by the arm, escorting her to the limousine Göring had sent. She gave the man the address of the hospital in Potsdam and they were away with typical efficiency. Von Schilling took her hand in his again, idly stroking her fingers with his thumb. "This is the first time I've been in Hermann Göring's car," he said with a wicked smile.

Galiena laughed at him. "It's like any other car."

"I've never been kissed in a Mercedes limousine," the pilot winked at her.

She was shocked, but it alleviated her tension. "Learn to live with the disappointment." The laugh escaped of its own accord.

He raised his hand to his brow. "You, Madame, are cruel."

"You, Herr Ritter, are still fragile and easily re-injured," Galiena reproved him mockingly.

Von Schilling's hand went to his breast. "What are you saying?"

"It's complex, mein Herr, but I think the answer is no."

He chuckled easily and kissed her knuckles. "Can't blame a flyboy for trying."

"When you are this charming, I find you very hard to resist at all," Galiena winked, enjoying the man's flirtation.

Von Schilling seemed to slide closer in the car. "From your lips to God's ears, Pfalzgräfin," He kissed her hand again.

Galiena was silent for a long time, as Berlin melted into Wannsee, and then to Potsdam. Thinking about what she had to do. "I don't think that God is listening to me today. Perhaps I am among the damned," she said very quietly. Dear God! She didn't want to see Verina. In her heart, she knew Idalie's words had to be the truth. What good would confirmation do her? It would just scrape the wounds raw. Her soul felt like a sailor at the gratings; flayed open and bleeding.

Her eyes traveled up the stone villa, to its swastika flag at the tallest spire. Once that was the flag of the second Reich, not the third. If this were the second Reich, things would be so different. Her title would convey instant obedience, not mere indulgence. Galiena looked at von Schilling beside her. They both tried to straddle both worlds, like a rider on two horses in the midst of a steeplechase. A foot in the past and a foot in the present. No. With her will, she could rule now and she didn't need to be afraid. Goebbels told her she had the tools to rule in this era. Her will was strong enough. Finally she spoke again. "Damned, Herr Ritter, but not without my weapons. Even the damned can fight back. Perhaps they fight harder, because they have nothing to lose."

"Ominous words," von Schilling answered with all amusement gone from his features.

Galiena touched his cheek, "Herr Ritter, I'm behind the eight ball this weekend."

He stared at her for a very long time, appraising. "Can't you convince the players into stepping away from the table?"

Again a frisson of uneasiness claimed her. "And do you think I'm a God, Herr Ritter? That I can control the SS?"

Von Schilling kissed her hand one last time. "Then leave the bloody crows alone, my dear!"

Galiena rolled her eyes as she got out of the car and walked up the pavement to the door of the hospital. Her gorge rose, the acid in her throat as she pushed through into the thick air. Cleanser, filth and something else assailed her. It was just like last time. She wanted to be out of here, free, and in the cleanliness. Instead she forced herself to the nurse at the desk. "I'm the Pfalzgräfin von Steinberg Zum Riesa. I believe Doctor Weber is expecting me."

The nurse looked at her notes. "Yes. If Your Highness would please sit and wait for one moment, the Doctor will be here momentarily."

Galiena resisted the urge to say, 'I'm Serene. A Serene Highness.' Now was not the time to quibble. It wasn't the second Reich after all.

Doctor Hamlin Weber wasted no time coming to the front. Perhaps he was as unnerved by her visit as she was by visiting. "Your Serene Highness! You gave us very little warning of your visit," he said as he bustled toward her.

All Galiena could see was this man with his thick fingers pressing a needle into her sister's veins on her last visit. The look in his eyes. His pleasure. No. She wouldn't think about that. It would defeat her and she needed to have all her wits about her now. "My apologies, Doctor Weber, but it was a matter of extreme urgency. Family matters and immediate legalities. I'm sure you understand," she told him.

Weber nodded slowly. "That I can understand, but I was under the impression you wouldn't be back."

Galiena forced an idle laugh. "And just who gave you that impression?" She decided to throw out a guess. "Herr Himmler?"

Her casual use of the name obviously caught him off guard. "No. Standartenführer Kohl."

Galiena tried to keep that casual sound. "And why would my fiancé stop me from seeing my sister, Herr Doctor? You must be completely mistaken."

It was a slip, and one easily caught. One which confirmed that it indeed was Hagen. "No- I- Perhaps I am, Your Serene Highness. Yes. That must be it."

She smoothed her gloves and returned her gaze to those ice blue eyes. "Well I do appreciate you taking the time to allow me to see Verina. It's of the utmost urgency, Herr Doctor."

"So you said, Madame." The doctor gestured down the long hallway. "If you will come with me, Frau von Taschen is on the terrace in the sun. She is having a very lucid afternoon."

Galiena hazarded a desire to know what that meant, but chose not to ask. It would probably make her upset to know. She glanced about the halls as they travelled through the building, and noticed the large portrait of Himmler on the wall, only slightly smaller than the one of Hitler in the lobby. He was staring off into the distance with an almost questioning expression on his face. It made him look so very young, younger than his thirty-seven years. She wondered if she could best this man in their duel tomorrow. Uncle Hermann thought so little of him, and Hagen so much. One of them had to be wrong, and in this case, Galiena suspected her Uncle's prejudices were getting in the way of his better judgement. There was something to the man which didn't show in his portrait. Something she felt as she shivered in his arms while the bullets flew during the ambush. Something she couldn't precisely put into words. Maybe it was drive. The intensity of the man's will just didn't come across in his pictures. Then Galiena frowned. The fact that his tie appeared to be crooked didn't help either.

Weber had stopped and turned to wait for her, his gaze bored. Galiena hastened to catch up to him. "The Reichsführer is commanding as always, but why his portrait?"

"This sanatorium is funded by the SS, Madame. Didn't you know that? You saw my ring last time you were here!" Galiena did not allow the condescension in the man's voice to affect her, but followed his hands as he gestured at the photograph.

His ring. The same as Hagen's. The Totenkopf honour ring, or so Hagen had called it. The worm began its turning in her brain. This was an SS installation. Standartenführer Kohl told Doctor Weber that Galiena wouldn't be back to see Verina. Her heart chilled in her breast. Why. What did Hagen know that she didn't? Why would Hagen have even spoken to Doctor Weber? There was more to this than she knew. Far more. She would have to find out.

"Of course. How silly of me." Galiena flashed the man a blank smile, knowing full well the effect it would have.

"Yes." She could almost see him stifling the urge to roll his eyes. "Shall we go? I am very busy."

Galiena nodded and followed the man out a large door and onto the terrace. The sunshine, warm for March, covered the stones, and interspersed about were lounges. He led her to a tiny figure wearing a large sun hat and inclined his head. "Frau von Taschen? I have a visitor for you."

Galiena looked down at the poor wasted figure under the blanket on the chaise. Verina was thinner than before, if possible. Her pasty skin stretched taut on her bones; the skin under her eyes like terrible bruises. The veins at her temples shone indigo, giving her an almost alien appearance. Those eyes; brilliant but glassy. Her lips were dry, almost to the point of cracking, and her cheekbones sharp and prominent. Galiena's heart ached for her. Whatever her sins, Verina didn't deserve this terrible affliction.

"Vee? It's Gallie," she said gently, sitting down on the lounge beside her sister.

The voice was not so slurred as the last time she saw Verina. "Galiena? Is that you? Am I dreaming this?"

Galiena reached out and stroked the bony claw, thankful of her gloves. "Yes, Vee. It's me. How are you?"

The whites of Verina's eyes were almost beige in colour. "Fine, Galiena. I'm fine."

"That's good to hear," Galiena said slowly. "I'm sorry I've been away so long. It's been very busy of late."

"The days stretch from one into the other at this place, Galiena. I hadn't especially noticed. I don't notice much these days." The slur was gone, but the words were slow. Spoken as if through the fog of sleep.

354

"Vee, I'm going to get married," Galiena spoke quietly, talking of inanities until Weber drifted away. It didn't take very long, and the man moved off to check on other patients. Verina seemed disinterested in her tales of flying and wedding ideas. Finally Galiena decided that Weber was far enough away to talk about the reason she had come. "None of this is why I am here."

"Oh? I'm pleased that you're a pilot, sister. Father would have liked that," Verina answered blankly.

"Vee, I need to know the truth. Your son, Rudi. Who is his father?" Galiena took the claw in her hands again. "I need to know. It's terribly important."

"His name is von Taschen. Why would you suspect anything otherwise?" The hazel eyes turned hard like agates. What would make you think anything else?"

"Because I know what the Pfalzgraf did to you. You told me. He made you his wife," Galiena choked on the words as she spoke them. "And sometimes wives bear their husband's children."

"What would you know of that, girl? What would know about being his wife? Were you his wife?"

Her throat closed up and her eyes burned. It was almost like she was being strangled. "Only that one time, Vee."

The gnarled claw clutched at her hand like a vice, crushing the knuckles together. The heroin certainly hadn't drained Verina of her strength. "How did you get away?"

"I fled, Vee. After that first time. I wanted to die. I pushed him off me, and I ran. Through the halls, and down to my car. I ran as far as I could." Flashbacks almost blocked her vision. Glittering violet eyes. Hagen's eyes. Tearing the flesh on his cheek as he pulled her from the car wreck. Shame that he would know. Shame of what had been done to her. Craving the courage to kill herself and finding herself too much the coward. Living because Hagen shamed her into it. Suddenly she ached for him. For Hagen. The distance between them cut into her chest far better than any knife or sword ever could. Somehow he made her safe, and she knew she loved him for it, no matter what his other failings. No matter what Hitler or Göring said. Damn them all for making her doubt him. Oh God! Why did she have to face this all on her own? What the hell was she doing?

But it was the right thing to say to Verina. The drugged woman nodded slowly with understanding, and the hand loosed its grip, moving to her cheek instead. The frail body lifted its way from the lounge, and the other arm was around her shoulders. "You have strength, Gallie." For the first time since they were reunited, Verina used her pet name. "Strength of the soul I never had. You survived. I never did. I died." The hand cupped her chin. "How did you live when I died?"

Galiena shook her head. "It was only once, Vee. Not like you. He had you for years."

"No Gallie. You had faith in your heart; faith that there was help for you. You stopped it," Verina whispered almost sibilantly.

She was going to tell Verina. She had to tell someone. "Vee, he's in prison, and tomorrow I am going to get him out. I have to for Riesa. For the Gessellschaft. I can't run it on my own, only Grandfather can. I have to do this for business." Galiena began to cry, the tears slipping silently from her eyes of their own volition. Now she felt it, the betrayal of herself, as Idalie put it. The betrayal of herself, and of Verina. The injustice of her own actions against this woman who had suffered. When had she become two entities? A body that ignored the soul, and a soul, mortally wounded by the actions of the body? "But he's going far away, Vee. Brazil. He won't get near you! I swear it! I'll protect you from him."

"Do you remember, Gallie, how you screamed when Mother pressed your hand into Father's coffin? Onto his face? I meekly did as she ordered. You screamed the house down, and help came. You were always so strong. You always did the correct thing. Do what you have to, Gallie. I trust you," Verina brushed the tears away, shaking her head slowly. "He can't hurt me anymore." There was a long silence as Verina sank back into her chaise. "If he came for me, I would be happy. I've been waiting for him for sixteen years. Leaving was the biggest mistake I ever made. I'm nothing without him."

The words chilled Galiena right to her core. "Please, Vee! Don't say that!"

Fog seemed to descend over Verina again. "Meta was our first. She was so beautiful. Like a little doll. But there was something terribly wrong with her, Gallie. I was so flawed I couldn't make a proper baby. He always said it was because I was too young. Poor little Meta. She's buried at Riesa, in the crypts. Meta Magdalena Sidonie Therese Pfalzgräfin von Steinberg zum Riesa. She visits me sometimes. I hear her crying on the wind and I feel her little breaths on my cheek."

Galiena's gorge rose and she swallowed back the bile. Her mouth filled with saliva and thankfully she managed to contain it. "Was she the only one?"

"My darling Rudi. That he should think that pathetic waste, Dieter von Taschen is his father. No. Rudi is Meinrad's. You will know when you see him. He is the very image of father." There was a hint of pain in the voice. "Or was the last time I saw him." Verina rubbed her chest.

It was the confirmation Galiena needed. "Vee, if I needed to, would you consent to me adopting Rudi? For Riesa? So that he could claim what's his by right of," Galiena choked again. "Right of blood?"

"You would make him Pfalzgraf von Steinberg, Gallie? You would do that for my Rudi?" Verina looked so hopeful.

Galiena certainly didn't think that would be doing the boy a great favour. "If I can, Verina. If I can."

The fog was growing greater. "Well that would be nice," Her sister was suddenly vague. "Very nice."

Her emptiness threatened to consume her. "Vee! Is there anything I can do for you?"

Before she could react, Verina launched herself at Galiena, her hands around Galiena's shoulders. Galiena grabbed at Verina's wrists, trying to protect her throat. "Get me out of this place! They're killing me, Gallie! I don't want to die here!" Spittle landed on her cheek, its wetness terrible. "Please, Gallie! Please!"

Galiena stared into the desperate eyes. "I will, Vee! I'll find somewhere else to get you better!" How could Verina not be getting better? She should be getting over her addiction by now! It made no sense!

The power of the sick woman overwhelmed Galiena and she was pushed backward into the chaise. "I don't want to be here! I don't like it!" The talons seemed to pierce Galiena's clothing.

"Are they hurting you, Vee?" Her sister's mad eyes were bare centimetres from her own. She didn't know if Verina meant to cause her pain or not.

"They make me have the shots! I don't want them, Gallie! I don't!" Verina climbed on top of Galiena, her eyes filling with confused tears. "I do, sometimes. Sometimes I need them, but I don't like it!"

It was so hard to breathe with Verina on her chest. "I will see what I can do, Vee! I promise!"

Verina's legs tangled in Galiena's as she collapsed down in hysterical sobs. "Don't let me die here!"

Galiena tried to wrap a comforting arm around Verina. Her sister's body was mere bones. Were they not feeding her? "I won't, Vee!" Those claws were worse than Emil's; pinning her down to the chaise like stakes.

"Send me to Meinrad! I want him!"

"Not to him! I will find another place for you!" Galiena exclaimed in horror at the thought. But they weren't the right words, for Verina started shaking her up and down violently.

"I want him! I want him!" The sick woman repeated over and over. "Take me to him!"

Galiena's head impacted the edge of the chaise and she saw stars. "Verina!" She shouted. "Stop this!"

Then Weber and a nurse were there, pulling Verina off of her. "Your Serene Highness! Are you all right?"

Galiena stared at him blankly, reeling from the attack. "I'm fine, thank you." Her head throbbed in time with her pulse.

The nurse dragged the kicking and clawing Verina away. "Promise me, Gallie! Promise me! Please!" Verina called out maniacally.

Galiena gasped for breath on the chaise, as Weber felt her pulse at her wrist. "Your heart rate is rather elevated, Your Serene Highness. Let me give you something to calm you!"

She stood up abruptly. "Every time I see you, Doctor Weber, you want to inject drugs into me," she inhaled. "Forgive me if drugs are the last thing I want at this time. Now leave me be."

Weber took a step back. "I was only concerned for your comfort, Madame."

"And I thank you, but the only assistance I require is to be returned to my car." Galiena managed to quell the shaking in her voice.

Weber said nothing but gestured towards the door. Galiena moved through the building and fled into the limousine. Von Schilling was there, waiting for her, a questioning expression on his face. "Cadet?" He asked softly.

"Sweet Jesus," Galiena breathed as her heart thudded in her chest.

When her gloved fist went into her thigh with all the strength she had, he said nothing, but when the second dropped, he grabbed it in his own, prohibiting the contact. "Now, now! Don't do that!"

Galiena cried out in frustration, wanting to make her pain external. Physical pain was so much easier to live with than this torment. "Let me go!"

"No!" He pulled her close, and pressed her head into his shoulder. In the absence of Hagen, he would do. More than do. She pressed herself into him and just huddled there.

The car started back towards Berlin and he held her for a long time. "So given your reaction, you had a very good time, and now you want to poke your eye out with a fork just to complete the adventure?" He asked dryly after a long while.

Galiena reached into her purse and pulled out a shiny silver flask. Calvados was a truly wonderful invention. She had a deep swig to get her bearings, and passed it to him in an effort to not be rude. "That would be an accurate assessment. Poke my eyeball out with a fork? Now that's a new one."

Von Schilling took a gulp from her flask, and corked it, stroking it against his knee absently. "Comes from a buddy of my in Fahnjunkerschule. They told us to go do fifty laps, and he was a lazy sort of fellow. He looked at me when the instructor was out of earshot, and whispered, "Sure. And if we have to so that every day, I think I'm going to poke my eye out with a fork, and get out of here."

She giggled against her will. "Did he matriculate from Fahnjunkerschule?"

Von Schilling laughed. "No. Washed out utterly. He's in the Kreigsmarine now, Kapitänleutnant on a U boat of all things, and happy as a clam. There's very little marching on a U boat." He leaned down, and his nose brushed that soft sensitive spot behind her ear. "There isn't the room."

Another laugh came burbling out of her throat as she drew away from him. "Hauptman Ritter von Schilling, are you flirting with me?" Galiena demanded, feeling the alcohol in her empty stomach.

He took another swig from her flask before handing it back to her. "I might be. Is that a crime in Hermann Göring's limousine?"

Galiena poked him in the shoulder. "I'm engaged to be married," She retorted, taking a sip from the flask. "I find myself telling you that over and over. In the words of the English, you seem a little thick on the subject and I can't quite understand how it is that you seem unfamiliar with the word.

This time it was his turn to laugh. "Thick?"

"Yes. Thick as an elephant sandwich, I would say." Galiena winked at von Schilling. "Engaged! I'm engaged! Or to be far more formal, I am engaged to be married. Betrothed if you like. Soon to be in a state of conjugal bliss." She glared at her companion sternly. "Engaged!"

The pilot shrugged gamely, stretching his arm across the back of the seat. "Engaged isn't married, Your Serene Highness. It's like the difference between a crash and a bad landing. A crash is with you forever, and you're pretty much hooped if you want to keep it a secret. The latter, well, it's really not such a big deal and it certainly isn't permanent. Guess which I consider you to be?"

Galiena frowned as she took the flask back. "I doubt Hagen would agree with you, Herr Hauptman."

Von Schilling leaned in. "And where is he, Your Serene Highness? Because I don't see him here to disagree with me."

"Isn't it dishonourable to tempt a woman away from the straight and narrow when her fiancé is away? There has to be something in some rulebook somewhere about that?"

"When the cat's away, the mice will play was always in my copybook." The man became a picture of boyish innocence.

"You were probably a very naughty little lad," Galiena admonished.

"I'm a pilot." His eyes sparkled. "We're all naughty. It goes with the wings."

"I love Hagen." It was unconvincing, and they both knew it. In this moment she was unable to dissimulate with him.

His eyelids dropped to half mast. "Allow me to convince you otherwise." His voice was low and silky.

She sobered slightly. "Stop this, Herr Ritter. Please." The stress was affecting her; the combination of Verina and the flirtatious onslaught was too much.

The pilot raised both brows with an all knowing expression. "I only seek to remind that you are lying to both of us."

"It's not your place to keep me honest," Galiena's tone was glacial.

Von Schilling laughed out loud. "Dear God, no! Certainly not in terms of your affianced."

"And if you turned me from him, what would keep you convinced that someone else wouldn't turn me from you?" she pressed him, suddenly curious for his answer.

"I don't leave my henhouse open to foxes."

How tiresomely arrogant the male could be. "You only managed to get this close to the hen because you are a fox with wings."

"Ergo, I know how to build a better coop," von Schilling chuckled. "I also wouldn't leave my hen alone."

Galiena poked him in the chest. "I do believe I find the implication that I'm a piece of poultry to be secured a tad insulting."

"I did not mean to offend," von Schilling smouldered in her ear. "Rather the contrary."

She didn't fall for his charm this time. Instead she chose to attack. "And if the doctors cleared you for flight, you would be back in Spain with the rest of the Condors faster than one could say 'reinstated for duty.'"

He looked completely torn between his desires. "Not, perhaps, if there was something more important to attend to back home."

"Now who isn't being honest?"

The pilot sighed and rolled his eyes. "Sometimes, you are entirely too pert."

361

"I know about Prussians and their duty." The words came out with far more bitterness than she intended.

Von Schilling put his arm around her and leaned back into the leather seats, undaunted by her choler. "Fine then. You might be right about me. But I'm not letting you drive off to Riesa without dinner to lighten this ever so serious mood of yours. Maybe some dancing. Yes. Or I might have to poke my eye out with a fork, and that would be a terrible shame for the Luftwaffe."

Chapter 26
March 4, 1938

Hagen felt a tap on his shoulder and was instantly awake. He expected to see Eugen standing over him, the familiar white head growling some condescension in his direction; but no. It was Alexander, Freffie's valet. The man was fully dressed, elegant as if it were the middle of the afternoon. His face was a mask of trepidation as his hand wavered over Hagen's right shoulder. "Herr Graf! Please wake up!"

Hagen rolled to face the man, the act of being awake not clearing away the cobwebs. God! He was so tired. "What is it?" His mouth was dry as a tomb, his tongue positively furry.

"Telephone call for you, Herr Graf," The man sounded afraid. "I would not have disturbed you, but the telephone operator insisted you be wakened."

A thousand things leapt to mind. Who would be calling? Would Himmler or Wolff risk calling him here? Of course, they knew where he was. Or Eugen? Had they been discovered? Von Ond compromised? Another bomb? "Who is it?" He asked, his ability to make articulate sentences slow to return to him.

"The Pfalzgräfin von Steinberg, Herr Graf! She instructed you be brought to the phone."

Hagen reached over and picked his watch up off the bedside table. It was four thirty in the morning. Why would Galiena call him here at four thirty in the morning? He leaned his head back and sighed. Then the brain started to work and his head flew back up. Unless she was in trouble? Hurt? Scared? What was she doing up at four thirty in the morning to call him?

"Where can I take the call?"

The man held up Hagen's black brocade robe. "In the library, Herr Graf."

The weight of the garment grounded him and he pulled it shut over his pyjamas. His feet found their way into his fur lined slippers quickly for the floor was cold. Hagen stopped by the bureau and poured himself a glass of water, gulping it back before following the man out of the room.

The house was dim, not unusual for this time of the morning, but Hagen thought he could hear music somewhere. Then it hit him, a cloud of smoke so different, and yet familiar. Harsh and odorous, like burnt coffee grounds with a hint of skunk spray. The stairwell reeked of it. As he crept down the stairs after Alexander, he could see the door to Freffie's study was open, and the man himself was sitting in a wing chair. Smoking from a large, ornate hookah, Freffie was listening to Zarah Leander. The man's eyes were closed, and he was keeping time with the mouth tip and hose. One two three four. One two three four.

Hagen passed the study and Alexander led him into the library. The fire had been brought up, as if for his arrival. The phone lay off the hook on the table beside a heavy leather chesterfield. He promptly sat and picked up the phone. "This is Hagen Kohl," he spoke quietly, yet crisply.

"Hagen?" Her voice was strained. Tired. Perhaps even breathless. "I'm sorry to disturb you in the middle of the night." Embarrassed.

"That's fine, darling." He looked at his watch. "I only went to bed about an hour and a half ago," he replied ruefully. "But what about you? What are you doing up at this hour of the morning?"

There was a laugh. He liked that sound. Suddenly he ached to be near her. It was a potent jolt to his person. He missed her. "I'm usually up now, these days. If I were at home, Idalie would be standing over me by now."

Too much information in that sentence to process. She wasn't at home? Where did she consider home, and why in God's name was she getting up at this time of the morning at home? "Where is home?" He asked stupidly.

Another laugh, this one amused, more than joyful. "Hasn't Freff told you? Home is where the servants are. In this case, Idalie is at Carinhall, so I suppose that is where home is at the moment."

"But you aren't at Carinhall?" Hagen questioned. Where the hell was she without Idalie? Galiena never went anywhere without Idalie!

Silence, or as silent as telephones ever were. "No. I'm at Riesa tonight."

Again, disturbing and not enlightening. "Galiena, why are you at Riesa alone?" That certainly explained the phone call.

"Oh, I'm not alone. Emil is here with me. It's just for the night. I came to pick something up. Would you like to talk to Emil?"

No. He did not want to talk to Emil. "Darling, I doubt there's much Emil would want to say to me!" Did she have no comprehension of how much telephone calls cost? He caught himself mid grumble. No. Probably not. "So why are you up at four thirty these days?"

"My new flight instructor, Hauptman von Schilling, insists upon it. He maintains that it will give me toughness and endurance. Uncle Hermann had him sent round from Berlin and he's terribly strict. I'm being treated like an officer cadet, which means lessons are at least eight hours starting from a truly ungodly time in the morning. Starting at five thirty usually gets me turned loose at two thirty or so, and then I can go to my appointments. It's killing me," Another quick pause, and then she continued. "Uncle Hermann sent me a plane and once I have one hundred hours in it with von Schilling, I can pilot it on my own."

New flight instructor? This didn't sound like a good thing to Hagen. On the other hand, Udet was a terrible old roué, and might encourage Galiena to acts of mischief Hagen wouldn't like. Perhaps this von Schilling was a more stable individual. "What happened to General Udet?"

"He's a little busy at the moment, so he and uncle Hermann knocked heads and found von Schilling. He's a Condor and was thrashed about a tad in Spain. He almost died and can't fly for the Luftwaffe until he's fit."

A Condor from Spain meant the man might be young. Not ideal in Hagen's estimation. "And what's this von Schilling like?"

"He's a positive Tartar during lessons. I work very hard not to let him know when he's made me cry." A self depreciating little giggle. "But he's almost as good a flyer as Udet. Less reckless." Her words seemed somewhat slurred to him and Hagen wondered why. Had Galiena been drinking?

With a decided mean-spiritedness of character, Hagen was glad this flight instructor made Galiena upset. Then she wouldn't like him, and he wouldn't need to worry. He yawned, so tired. "Less reckless I approve of."

Again silence. Long silence. Costly silence. "I went to see Vee today."

He clenched his teeth to stifle the expletive which flashed loudly through his mind. "Why did you go there?" He ground out.

She returned directly on the attack. "Why did you tell Doctor Weber I wouldn't be back?"

"I didn't tell him that." Denial was always a good tactic.

"Didn't you?" An icy pause. "No, Hagen Kohl. I don't think so. You might be able to lie to me, but he certainly doesn't have the skills to do so." Her tone turned silky. "I would hate to think you had interfered in my business with my sister."

His jaws were clenched so tightly together it hurt. He inhaled, trying to relax. "I have not interfered." Big lie, but necessary. Galiena would never understand why he had Verina committed to that place. Verina was a parasite, and her husband was a traitor. Hagen sent the man to Dachau himself.

"Why did you not tell me the sanatorium was an SS institution?" Galiena demanded. He could hear it in her voice. Suspicion. He had never heard it directed at him before.

"You didn't ask. I don't volunteer the names of all such places to you when you encounter them. I would constantly be about it." He tried to calm himself. "Our organisation is rather far flung."

She sighed. "I understand, Hagen."

"Why, Galiena? Why did you go there without me? I told you I would have taken you if you wanted to go," He asked gently. Getting angry was only going to make this situation worse.

"You weren't here, Hagen. I needed to confirm some information with Vee, which I did."

Those first three words were a dagger in his gut. "I'm sorry, Galiena. I hope you didn't go there alone. Did Frau Göring go with you?"

The swish of liquid in metal in the background and what sounded like a swallow. "No, I didn't go alone. I was fine. Vee was far more cooperative this visit, which was a relief."

But she didn't tell him who she went with. "What information did you need? Maybe I can help you instead of Frau von Taschen?"

"I needed to hear it straight from the proverbial horse, Hagen. I don't think you could have helped. God! I hate that place. Something absolutely needs to be done about it. The sooner, the better, I think," A pause. "Now I need to find my brother in law, or at least, one of my nephews."

DAMN! No! No! No! She couldn't go there! She would find out! "Your nephews? Why?"

She made a little humming noise. "I haven't met any of them, but I think it's time I took notice of their welfare. Lord knows! My sister has been in that ghastly place for months and those boys have had no mother."

This was his punishment from God for mocking Eugen's resurgence of religious faith. "You aren't responsible for them, Galiena. Why concern yourself with it now?"

"They are my blood, Doctor Kohl." There was that tone. He knew that tone. It wasn't a good tone. "And aren't you the one who rabbits on about clan?"

"That's SS dogma, Galiena. Your SS clan. It's a tad different."

"Well they are my blood. I'm sure that the Ritter von Taschen won't mind a visit from his sister in law."

There had to be a way to redirect this. "Your grandfather has not been kind to the Ritter. He might not appreciate an overture from your family. Did you pause to consider that?"

"Stuff and nonsense, Hagen. I'm not my grandfather. I don't have his tendencies." Again, she sounded so odd.

"Please tell me what this is about, darling? Talk to me," he entreated, feeling completely at a loss.

Silence, and then she laughed. "Are you interrogating me, Standartenführer Kohl? All these questions make me feel like you're going to stick me under a hot light bulb."

If only! "No, darling. It's just I'm worried about you. I haven't heard from you in weeks, and then you call me in the middle of the night." He decided to open up a tad. "I miss you, Galiena. Quite fiercely."

Her voice was raw, thick and constricted. "Oh Hagen! I miss you, too! I wish you were here. Tonight, I think I'm the loneliest woman in the world, and there's this terrible weight pressing down on me. But my duty is clear!"

"Darling, what is it?"

Another silence, and then careful words, as if she were weighing or choosing what she was going to say very carefully. "My nephew, Rudi, is also my uncle, Hagen. And I had a niece, or an aunt, who was born and died while I was at school." A quick gasp. She was crying. His Galiena was crying and he couldn't hold her. He couldn't make it better. "Her name was Meta. I went down into the crypt and there she was. I never knew."

"I'm sorry, Galiena."

She continued. "But I promised Vee I would see her son raised as a von Steinberg."

"Do you really think that's wise? He won't know the circumstance of his own birth, and how cruel would it be to tell him he was the product of incest. It's not your place, Galiena. Leave the boy alone. It's far kinder," he told her.

"Some part of all this is his by blood, Hagen. I am thinking to contact the boy's father and arrange a meeting. With proper education Rudi could become part of the Gessellschaft as a director. It's his right, even though Grandfather disinherited Verina and her line. I'm thinking to reestablish him as my heir in the event I have no children. With that on the table, I'm sure his father will agree to let aunt Gallie have a say in the boy's education."

"That's a little heavy handed, Galiena, don't you think?" Hagen exclaimed, feeling anger creeping up on him. While he had come to expect a certain degree of 'Lady of the Manor' out of his fiancée, this 'Konigen von Preussen'[16] voice was rubbing him more than a little raw.

"As the one potentially bestowing a fortune in excess of seventy five million pounds sterling, I think I'm entitled to some heavy handedness," Galiena muttered arrogantly. "I would say it gives me a fair amount of latitude, actually."

If he hadn't been sitting down, he'd have fallen. "What?"

---

[16] Queen of Prussia

"Something like that. That's a rough guess of von Kleist's, and the Grim Reaper doesn't know all the places that grandfather has hidden gold."

"Oh." Hagen was shell-shocked. He didn't think he could calculate that amount in his head. Seven marks to the pound was about the exchange he last heard. "You might be correct." He had to admit that; even to himself.

"At the moment, I'd rather like to chuck it. The whole sodding lot of it! It's hardly worth the torture," she whispered. "Oh! Excuse my language." He could hear her take a gulp of something. "I'm a little tired."

"You have a man of affairs, Galiena. Rely on him! Honestly, you shouldn't be allowing these people to wear you down like this," Hagen entreated her.

Galiena laughed thinly at him. "It's not them. But I am worn down. Down to the sodding nub." She had to be drunk to use that sort of slang. "I believe, were I to look in the dictionary, the entry for Pfalzgräfin would turn out to be pack mule."

And that made absolutely no sense to him either. "You are being a little vague, darling," he exhaled in frustration. What was she doing over there? "I don't think Riesa is a good place for you to be alone. Why are you there, Galiena?"

She started to laugh until she couldn't breathe. "You are half right. I don't want to go to any of the places I need to go, my betrothed. Yet still I do my accursed duty. I will always do my duty. I will marry and I will spawn heirs so that when I am gone, they can do their duty. I can enslave more to this accursed place and then it can be the millstone around their necks. Yes. Theirs and not mine." Towards the end, her sentences became quite slurred and he heard something shatter.

Hagen didn't know whether to be relieved or offended. "Shall I take it that you've decided that we can have a physical side to our relationship, Galiena?"

"Doctor Goebbels convinced me that I have no choice."

That didn't bode well either. That maggot would certainly gnaw at his brain in the morning. "You make physical intimacy sound like a trip before the firing squad, Galiena. I assure you, it will be pleasurable."

"I've heard that before," she hissed back into the phone.

"Darling, that's unfair," he protested heatedly. "I'm not the man who hurt you."

There was a long silence. "No. you are right. You aren't dear old Grandpapa."

"Please give me the opportunity to make it something other than a duty, Galiena. Our marital congeniality is of great importance to me. I don't want strife in our home. I crave your happiness." There was complete truth in that. He wanted her life to be as full as he could make it.

"That reminds me, Hagen! Some good news, or it is to me. I bought us a small house in Berlin. It's a bit of a fixer-upper, but I'm sure you will like it." Suddenly she sounded excited and less tired.

"You bought a house," he repeated, still reeling.

She laughed. It sounded forced. "A cottage, really. On the lake."

"The lake." Hagen rubbed the bridge of his nose between his thumb and forefinger. "A cottage on what lake?"

"Fine, then. Cottage might have been a slight underestimation. But it is beautiful. It's on Schwanenwerder, very close to Doctor and Frau Goebbels. It's sixty years old, a tiny bit overdone in the gilt department, but I think that you, Emil and I should be able to rattle around in there without bumping shoulders too much," her voice was much lighter.

"If you are pleased, then I am, Galiena. I hadn't precisely thought about our future living arrangements." He admitted, suddenly realising that they wouldn't all fit in his standard six room flat. Especially not if he included that damned lion. Oh yes. She was also going to require servants too.

"Only one of us had to." He could hear the smile in her voice. "I wanted a place for us to make our own memories, not one of the places owned by my grandfather. He has a place out in Potsdam, but I thought that would be a long drive. This was the best of both worlds. I take possession in a month and I was thinking of having Herr Speer and his men take a look into modernizing the place." Galiena yawned, obviously holding the phone away from her head. "So think about what colours you would like your apartment in. And your study! Oh! I think you will be quite entranced with the study. The inlay on the floors is of a workmanship one just doesn't see anymore."

A sickly feeling rose in the pit of his stomach. "I'm sure, darling. Might I ask how much this dream home cost?"

"Oh you scoundrel! You just made me lose a bet!" Galiena exclaimed accusingly.

"What?"

"Doctor Goebbels told me you would ask the tariff in the first five minutes of my telling you about the place. I told him it would take you at least twenty," she giggled again, and he could hear the alcohol in it for certain. "And if I bear up with the truth, it's going to cost me a fiver."

"I'm sure you can afford a fiver. So now will you tell me? Or are you keeping it a secret to spare my sensibilities?" Hagen scrunched his toes in the fur lining his slippers. He would have to clip his toenails; they felt overlong. She muttered a number, but it was inaudible. "I didn't quite catch that." He said.

"Two ninety."

It was a sum almost three times his carefully invested value. Spent on a villa! So completely casually! But what could he say, really? "I'm sure it's lovely. I can't wait to see it," Hagen choked, trying to contain his horror.

"Thank you, Hagen."

There was another silence, but he could hear her breathing. It made him miss her more. Her pain was a tangible thing and there was little he could do to help her. "Darling, is your hair up tonight, or down?"

A funny giggle. "Mostly down now. I look like I've been pulled through a haystack. Why?"

"I want you to bend your head down so that your chin is on your chest. Can you do that?"

"All right."

"Then I want you to lift up your hair, and touch the base of your neck. Right where you can feel your vertebrae," he whispered. He could imagine the place in his mind. He had touched it several times. "Is it warm when your fingers brush it?"

This time her voice was lower. "Yes."

"Now I want you to trace that vertebrae and imagine it's me doing that. I'm standing right behind you, Galiena. Can you feel me behind you? My arm around your waist, and the other tracing lazy circles on that place?" He didn't know about her, but he was definitely reacting to this conversation. He touched finger to his thumb and made that movement, imagining the feeling of her skin. His memory delighted him with her fragrance. "Can you feel my breath on that beautiful pile of hair?" Give her something to think about other than blasted Prussian duty.

Her voice sounded a great deal less sure of itself. "I can, Hagen."

Hagen had never been so overtly sexual with her, and it excited him. She was safe through her phone, he wasn't actually there. But all good things must come to an end and this was more than enough to leave a lingering effect in her mind for next time. "Now I am going to kiss you there, Galiena. Press my lips to that sweet, warm skin."

"Hagen, I--"

He interrupted her. "And now I am going to say goodnight, darling. I miss you and I wish I was there." Hagen wanted to say more, but his mouth wouldn't form those words.

"I miss you, too!" She sounded on the edge of tears.

"Only a couple more weeks and your Graf Hagen will be there to kiss you in person." He let the word slip easily over his tongue. The more he said it, the more he enjoyed the sound of it.

"Graf Hagen? Did you sign the papers?" Galiena was almost breathless to his ear.

"Just today."

"Oh Hagen! I'm so happy!" Galiena erupted into the receiver.

"I'm glad, darling. Now I must go to my bed. You must go to yours and I will see you soon."

"Good night, Your Illustrious Highness," she whispered.

"Good night, Your Serene Highness." Hagen hung up the phone. "I'm so glad you called," he said to the air, inhaling deeply, willing the blood to other parts of his body, rather than where it suddenly seemed to be congregating. There was too much to process from that phone call and he knew he would miss a great deal of it when he fell back asleep. He could still hear Zarah Leander quietly in the distance, and the smell of the Hashish was beginning to penetrate this room.

Sharp footfalls in the hall, caught his attention, and with some stealth Hagen moved to the doorway. He could see the entire hall from his vantage point, and there was Wills, swinging his cane diffidently, his bowtie undone, and top shirt studs missing. He appeared tired, but very satisfied. As Wills foot hit the steps, Freffie walked into the hall. "Well, well, well. The rambling knight returns." His voice was slurred with an edge sharper than a knife blade.

Wills turned on his heel. "Freff. I wasn't expecting you to still be awake. I was on my way up."

"Yes. I see that. You told me you would be finished two hours ago. I thought I would wait for you." Hagen was stunned at the bitterness in Freffie's tone; bitterness and suspicion. What Galiena served up to Hagen seemed to be rounding from Freffie onto Wills. Interesting. Hagen was momentarily happy to not be the only one in trouble.

"Things came up, Freff. You know how it is. You more than anyone should know that some things take slightly more time than others," Wills shrugged.

"Yes. Some things do take more time than others," Freffie repeated. "Like that new boy! Was that what took you two hours, Wills? Were you with that beautiful young boy?" Freffie took a step closer, his floor length robe swirling round his bare feet. "I've seen you looking at that von Ond!"

Wills just shook his head. "Don't do this, Freff. I'm going to bed now." He pivoted and resumed his journey to the second floor. "We finished what we went to do and then went to the club to have a few drinks. Nothing happened. The boy is untouched. Quit being so fucking jealous!"

Freffie drained his glass and then threw it at the stairs; the crystal flying past Wills head to explode on the wood near the runner. "Don't you turn your back on me! How could you do this, when I've tried to be everything you wanted me to be?"

The tableau was becoming embarrassing to Hagen, but he stood transfixed as Wills slowly turned back, fixing Freffie with a narrow-eyed glare. "Yes, Frederick. I can see that. Yet look how the prodigal Graf has returned. Drunk. Stoned. Just how I found you five years ago, in a perpetual fog, only at least five years ago you hung out with your betters and not with the enemy of your people." Wills took a step down. "Tell me, Frederick. Have you enjoyed your new boy yet? Are you enjoying your moment of trolling through the gutter? Are you enjoying some different but equally turgid version of the Nazi salute?"

Freffie threw his arm back. "What the hell are you talking about," he snarled viciously. "I've always been faithful."

Wills' voice turned silky as he approached his lover. "Come now, Freff. Your new son. You've spent ever so much time together. Should I be equally jealous?" He backhanded Freffie with a lightning fast hand. "How dare you give him your name! How dare you betray your class that way!"

Freffie touched a finger to his lip, looked at the blood on the tip, and reached over and rubbed the stain on Will's pristine shirt front. "Damn you, Herr Ritter! I did that to repay a debt," Freffie's voice became glacial. "And before you put on airs you don't deserve, von Glass, let me remind you that your title, knight, means nothing in the space of time of the von Reitersbachs. Why should you be any higher in my eyes than Herr Kohl? His Pater was a member of the Fugger. What was yours? He proved himself by being a butcher in the Franco-Prussian war! Your title means nothing to me. Titles in general mean nothing to me."

"Damn you, Herr Graf!" Wills spluttered with impotent fury. "I pulled you out of the gutter! There you were! Broke! Chasing after Galiena and Dickie's leavings like a dog! I made you a man!"

Freffie laughed; an ugly sound. "Au contraire, Herr Ritter." He shrugged off the top of his robe, and Hagen could see the most terrible mass of scar tissue on the man's back. The pain involved in the creation of that flesh! The torn and corded skin ran from shoulder to where the belt caught the fabric at the waist; the most horrible scars Hagen had ever seen, and he was no stranger to scars himself. Freffie pulled out a length of metal from his pocket. "My father made me a man the first time he beat me with a chain." He let the links fall from his fingers to dangle almost to the floor, a small golden weight on the end. Hagen could see that the links were stained with rust. "This chain."

Wills took a step back, the balance of power having shifted. "My God, Freffie, put that away!"

Freffie swung the chain in a slow arc. "Who raised who from the gutter, Herr Ritter! You have lived on my sufferance and I will be damned if I will let you cuckold me!"

"What about Kohl?" Wills spat back.

"He is Galiena's. That you could possibly think I would touch him disgusts me. He is hers. Her word is above all!" Freffie's eyes burned with an unholy light.

Wills fairly yelled. "And I haven't touched von Ond, or anyone else. You have my word." His outburst was controlled, as if he had seen that chain before. "But look at you! Freffie! You're drunk, and I can smell the drugs!"

Freffie caught the chain in his hands. "My knowledge of pharmaceuticals has been well served! It's served you, hasn't it?"

"Of course you have been a great help in my work," Wills took a step forward. "I won't deny it."

"Kohl was my decision and my name. I will do what she tells me. I will always do whatever she tells me."

"Damn it, Freff! I like Gallie. I always have, but I hardly see the source of your devotion! In the end, she's just a woman. Why would you be so loyal to her? She's very quick to betray herself with that Nazi! I thought she was something more, but in the end, women are all so terribly alike. They'll whore themselves to anything walking which catches their eye." Wills voice dropped. "Why would you be more loyal to her than you are to me?"

Freffie's face was a terrible thing. He swung out with the chain and it snapped around Wills' ankle. He jerked his arm back and Wills landed on the stairs in a twitching heap. "Gallie saved my life, you idiot. When she was seven, she came across my father beating me with this chain. I never screamed. Never! But trying to protect me, she got in between my father and I. Papa didn't stop. Her screams were fearsome when the chain wrapped around her; like an animal being tortured. Meinrad von Steinberg came, as he always did, pulled out the sword in his cane and ran my father through."

Wills stared at Freffie with horror. "I didn't know."

"The word was spread about that my father succumbed to wounds from the war. No one would have challenged Meinrad Pfalzgraf von Steinberg, bosom friend of Kaiser Wilhelm, with his actions. Not a man alive would have charged him with murder.

That is the power of the man." Freffie shook the chain and it uncoiled from Wills' foot. "The power of that family."

Wills scrambled to his knees, his pose that of the supplicant. "I didn't know, Freff. How could I? You never told me? I am not Rasputin. I can't read minds."

"I love you, Wilhelm, but never forget that you, too, were nothing before we met. Equally penniless. Absolutely, I was never sober before, and I've come a long way to become what you suggested I could be, but without me? You, too, would be nothing. Never forget that the money, the cars, the trips and the power are mine. Given to me because of who I am." Freffie held down his hand, gently.

Wills sighed and took the hand up. "I'm sorry, Freff. Perhaps I've been unfair."

"You may hate your Nazis, Wills. I hate them too. I understand that; but I hate bullies more." Freffie wrapped his arm around the other man. "Kohl has surprised me and he may surprise you too, if you gave him half the chance. The enemy of my enemy is my friend."

"How can he be their enemy when he's one of them?" Wills reached down and pulled up Freffie's robe, running his hand up the ruined flesh in a caress.

"They're not as monolithic as we might have thought. Some of them seem just as anxious to hurt him as hurt us. It's quite interesting, actually." Freffie shrugged into the sleeves of his garment.

"I can't trust him, Freff. You know I can't." Wills kissed Freffie, slowly catching the Graf's jaw with his hand. "Come, Freff. Let's go to bed. I'm not so tired that I don't want you."

Freff suddenly looked terribly insecure. "I thought you were done with me. I saw you with that boy. So young! So beautiful! I thought you were done with me! How could you want me after seeing him? I'm not the young man I once was. Not young like that."

Wills patted Freffie's cheek. "You silly thing! I love you and that's just the way it is. I would prefer it if you didn't use that blasted chain on me! I don't know why you carry it around and practise with it the way you do. It's ghastly."

Freffie rolled his shoulders as if to stretch his mangled flesh. "It's an old friend."

"No wonder you drink. Come. Let's to bed, Freff."

Freffie allowed himself to be lead up the stairs. "Never again call Galiena a whore, Wills. Don't even suggest it. She is Freya reborn; Queen of the Valkyries, in her golden chariot, pulled by two enormous cats. Crying out for the souls of the fallen. She is my Goddess. She will take me to Valhalla."

"I know, Freff. I'm sorry. I didn't mean it. I was jealous," Wills replied doggedly.

"I dreamed about Gallie tonight while I waited for you. About how special she is. About her and Dickie; Freya and Odin, King and Queen of Heaven. There I was behind them, basking in their glory." Freffie paused halfway up the stairs, examining his hands.

Wills stopped and wrapped his arms around the intoxicated Graf, nosing his ear. "And where was I, Love? Behind you?"

Agony slashed across Freffie's face. "You were in Valhalla, Wills. Freya embraced you and took you there, herself. It was terrible."

Wills chuckled and rolled his eyes. "I don't, for the life of me, understand why you persist in smoking that stuff, Freff. You always have the worst visions. I'm not going anywhere, sweetheart. Valhalla or otherwise."

"It will happen if you keep doing what you are doing."

"Ah, Fref! You are the mystic and I am the warrior! I'm not worried about Gallie taking me anywhere," the ritter replied and licked his companion's ear. "Damn! I want you." He ran his hands through Freffie's hair. "I always say to myself, 'never when he's stoned,' but then I always want you. I love you, Freff. There is a purity of my affection for you which no other boy will ever take away."

Freffie stared resolutely off into space. "You know, Wills, I knew it would happen. I think I knew what Meinrad intended for Gallie when he came to me two years ago. I didn't want to see it at the time, but deep down I am sure I knew. He kept talking about her perfection and her purity. Did I tell you about that?"

Wills sighed, a long suffering sound. "I remember you called him a perverted old bastard, but you were damn happy for the money."

"He told me his careful breeding had created a woman to resurrect the dynasty and how he'd be damned before he let my abomination soil her. I thought he meant with Dickie. I tried to tell myself it was Dickie he meant because Meinrad was so sure they were both of Atlantean stock and not the Aryan strain." Hagen lifted his nose like a hound as the Graf rambled on. Atlantean strain? This was the same nonsense as in that book Himmler had given him by that Blavatsky woman. Was the nobility bound up in all that folderol too? He tried to refocus as Freffie continued. "But how could he breed her to Dickie when they are first cousins and Dickie's been married for years?"

"I don't know, Fref. I can't believe he raped his own Granddaughter."

Freffie appeared consumed with guilt. "I'm going to write Dickie and tell him. I need to apologize. I should have told him at the time. I deserve to be punished for what I've done.

Wills shook Freffie sharply. "No. It's not your place to tell him, Fref, and you know what will happen if you do. Dickie will lose his composure and there will be a terrible incident of some kind. You know how Dickie's always looked upon Galiena as his precious baby sister."

"I failed her, Wills. I deserve to be punished," The drunken man reiterated brokenly.

"You know Dickie won't punish you, Fref. He never has before, no matter what stupid stunts you've pulled. Dickie loves you almost as much as he loves Gallie," Wills answered calmly.

"Because he is Odin, Wills. He's not a man; he's a God. Where was he to protect his Queen from Loki?"

The Ritter smirked sardonically. "Meinrad von Steinberg is not Loki, darling. Hitler is. You said it yourself. Come now! Leave your visions aside and let me pleasure you. The Warrior's blood is upon me tonight and you know what I crave."

Freffie rattled the chain in his pocket. "Yes. The priest-king and his warrior." Suddenly he kissed Wills passionately. "I love you, Wilhelm, my consort. Without you I am a pale shade screaming on the edge of the river Styx."

378

Wills pulled his companion along up the stairs. "And I, you, Frederick."

The men disappeared up the stairs, and Hagen leaned back against the door. This was proving to be a very interesting morning. So von Glass was a member of the NAO. He had to be. No wonder his hostility towards Hagen when he arrived.

What of Freffie? A new side of him, one far more dangerous than Hagen had anticipated. What did it mean, beyond that the man was highly unstable and a drug addict? This perverse blending of myth and reality confused and disgusted Hagen. He would have to think about it. Hagen wrapped his arms about his chest, thankful for Galiena's phone call. On the other hand, the display he had just seen made his skin crawl, and his need for a shower was strong. Suddenly he didn't like what he was about, here in Vienna. He wanted to go back home to Germany. He wanted to go home and lay his head in the lap of Freffie's queen of the Valkyries. Tonight he could even put up with the cat.

December 12, 1937
Dearest Poppet,

The pain is less, and I am feeling much better. Only two weeks, but the doctor is very optimistic. I should be out of bed and striding about by Christmas. Would that you had been here to hold my hand. Montrose is not the companion you are. I miss your laugh, and your music. Most of all, I miss your soul. Don't leave me here alone with the ghosts of the past. Come back to me!
Eternally yours,
Meinrad

Chapter 27
March 4, 1938

Jedem das Seine. Each to their own. The words consumed her vision as she waited in front of the wrought iron gate to the camp. The entrance to Konzentrationslager Buchenwald was not what she was expecting, reminding her more of a train station with its high entrance and clock tower. She had been expecting something far more ominous; dark clouds and lightning flashing, not this relatively benign exterior with carefully weeded gardens in front. It was only the long fence of barbed wire which reminded one this was a penal installation.

Her arms shook on the steering wheel as she contemplated the place, but that was more out of complete exhaustion than anything else. After her evening with von Schilling, Galiena had driven down to Riesa, arriving with Emil and Swanhilde at three in the morning. She had sent Swanhilde to bed while she and Emil went into the vault to move the gold. What a hell that had been! Her legs and shoulders still ached.

Galiena looked over her shoulder to the back seat of the car, where Emil was practically in a coma. She and Emil moved the gold last night! What a complete laugh. Emil had been no help, other than somewhat frisky company. She had tried to rig a sling to allow him to help her, but he made it patently obvious he wasn't a beast of burden and she'd almost been nipped for her efforts. The impudent wretch actually hissed at her for the first time in his life, and Galiena had loudly wished she had a pet dog instead. That comment earned her a second hiss. So on her own she moved the twenty-two gold bars from the vault to the office, and then from the office out to the car. One by one. Twenty-two times twenty-four pounds per bar was almost five hundred and fifty pounds, and Galiena was not a woman used to physical labour. It had taken two hours by the time all was said and done, and then she had sat with her hoard outside the car, looking for the best way to load it. Eight bars was the weight of a man, and as big a car as the Horsch was, could it carry the equivalent weight of three men in the trunk? So sixteen in the back foot well, and four more in the passenger's side foot well with von Klopfer's two in the glove compartment. Emil was another almost two hundred pounds in the back, but three men could sit in the back of the car, and she, well, she was over one hundred and seventy, but she certainly wasn't going to admit that to a soul.

Galiena should have gone to sleep, but instead she made her call to Hagen and then watched as Emil played with his ball, appropriately enough, in the Ballroom. There were now some scratches in the hardwood from his claws which would need fixing, but that was hardly her concern. A little football with the lion had been fun, and would have been more so were she not so tired from her labours. On the other hand, having Emil worn out would be a good thing for the day ahead. It was a three hour drive to Weimar on a good day, let alone when her car was filled with a ransom in gold. Thankfully, Emil was quite content in vehicles, having been moved about in them plenty as a cub. Yet still, how long would he be in the car before she could take him for a walk?

When Gebhardt knocked on the door to bring in coffee, she had been amazed at how fast the time had passed. She had known sleep would have eluded her anyway, but she didn't feel like she'd been up for twenty four hours. Fear, excitement, and resolution had taken over. Breakfast in the morning room had been wolfed down at a fast rate; Galiena hadn't eaten so much in years. A night's labour obviously had an effect on her appetite. Emil gorged himself on a raw large goose, brought up for him from the kitchen on a great wood block. Swanhilde rolled her eyes when she saw, but was otherwise silent. The sound of the lion crushing the bones in his teeth was cacophony enough.

They departed for Weimar at eight thirty. A maid helped Galiena with her hair, and she wore far more makeup than usual to cover her lack of sleep. All her knowledge of etiquette failed her in what was standard attire for visiting a prison, so she opted to wear something to boost her confidence. The scarlet suit with its matching hat complete with huge brim and ostrich tips was perhaps a bit much, but it made her feel good. Festive even. She felt she deserved the illusion. By the time she returned to the main hall, the maroon Rolls Royce sat waiting behind her car, Montrose beside it, and a Mercedes sedan in the rear to take Swanhilde and Emil back to the Carinhall should everything go to plan. If she succeeded then it wasn't fair to take Emil on the seven hour drive to Friedrichshaven to see the Pfalzgraf out of Germany. The lion would have more than done his duty at that point. If only hers were so easily discharged.

It was a good thing they left early, for traffic was terrible and the Horsch drove like a pig, weighted down as it was. They met the 'vons' at the Hotel Elefant in Weimar at noon, and Galiena conferred with them while Swanhilde walked Emil. All the necessary paperwork was pressed into her hands, and von Kleist took her aside to give her last minute advice. Don't get emotional. Never let them see if they've got you against the wall. Don't act like you want it too much. Let them walk into your trap, don't walk into theirs. Don't offer all the gold if you don't have to. Be vapid. When the enemy underestimates you, then they make mistakes. They will already have underestimated you, so it puts you into a position of power.

Just as she and Emil were to leave, von Kleist took her hand and kissed it. "I'm proud of you, Madame. This is not an easy thing you go to do. Right into the dragon's den, so to speak." The man, with his milky eyes, looked down with some embarrassment, then met her eyes again. "It will be my pleasure to serve you in the future."

Jedem das Seine. Each to their own. Galiena wondered what it was supposed to mean, in context to this place. She waited for the guard to return her identification papers and open the gate. Did everyone truly get what they deserved? Would she get her own, here, in this place?

The guard came to the door and saluted as he handed back her papers. "If you will follow me, Your Serene Highness, the Reichsführer is expecting you." The man in his grey uniform jogged at the front tires towards a large building where many cars were parked. She could see Himmler and Wolff coming across the parade ground as she came to a halt, quite separate from the others. Another glance over her shoulder confirming that Emil was still sawing logs like a good kitty, she felt confident to leave him in peace. Galiena picked up her folio and exited the car when the guard opened the door.

The parade ground was large, and all about there were people. The SS men, in their black uniforms, and the camp guards in their grey seemed drab on the sunny square. There were so many, trailing behind Himmler like a flock of crows. Galiena hated that analogy, but it seemed so appropriate. Here and there she saw people she assumed to be prisoners, in their black and white horizontal striped suits, and grotesquely shaved heads. They almost reminded her of larvae, their scalps so pale in the light. One man turned and stared at her, the bright splash of colour that she was, as if he couldn't believe his eyes. Then his face dropped back to his toiling in the black earth of the flowerbeds near the Administration building. The place was so dour. So grey. In her scarlet, echoed only in the swastika flag on the flag pole, she must look like a drop of blood on a piece of slate.

Himmler moved to intercept her, his eyes shining with something she couldn't define. In this place he was a thousand feet tall, and his knowledge of his power emanated from him in waves. The men trailing after him followed his every movement and gesture. When he smiled, so did they, when he laughed, they echoed, and the moment he stopped, there was silence behind him. Galiena had never seen this Himmler. This was the Reichsführer-SS, and his power was absolute. His eyes met hers as he clicked his heels and bowed his head before her. When the peak of his hat came up again, he was smiling; warmly and broadly. More the man of her acquaintance, but the look in his eyes seemed to mock her. This Himmler was a predator and he was in his lair with all his sycophants around to admire his magnificence.

"My very dear Pfalzgräfin von Steinberg! How pleased I am you could join us today, and how even more pleased I am that the weather is so beautiful for it." He took her hand and held it, before raising it deftly to his lips, almost as an afterthought. "My dear sister."

"I must thank you, Herr Reichsführer, for indulging me in my request." No fear. Faintly vapid. His reminder of their vow of family quite disquieting, especially in terms of what she came here today to do. Family. Galiena wanted to curse the very word. "It's very kind of you to do so. You are ever the gallant knight for a damsel in distress."

"Tis nothing, Madame. I was coming out here today anyway. One personally has to make sure the machinery is running properly, or be caught unawares when it decides to fall apart." Himmler gestured to Wolff. "You know Wolffschen, of course."

"Madame." Wolff bowed low, his eyes meeting hers long enough to convey his disapproval.

"Gruppenführer Wolff," Galiena replied, attempting to soften the man. She knew Wolff was Hagen's friend and didn't want him to think so badly of her. "It is nice to see you."

The sternness of his jaw relaxed, for Wolff knew he was trapped. He had to give the polite reply, and he knew it. "It is always a pleasure to see the Pfalzgräfin von Steinberg."

A small man moved up behind Wolff as if to attract attention and Himmler gave him a faintly amused look. "Ah, yes. Madame, might I present to you the Commandant, Standartenführer Karl Koch? Koch, this is Her Serene Highness, the Pfalzgräfin von Steinberg Zum Riesa."

Koch was a pudgy man of moderate height with thin lips and chipmunk sized jowls. His eyes were small, almost beady and he appraised both her and her car hotly. He was more than welcome to open the doors of the Horsch. Galiena was sure Emil wouldn't like this man either, and would make his feelings known. "Your Serene Highness."

"Standartenführer Koch," Galiena nodded coolly and did not offer her hand to this man. "Could I possibly trouble you for a favour?"

The lips parted in an indulgent smile. "What would that be, Madame?"

"If you would be so kind as to keep all and sundry away from my vehicle?" Considering Emil's mercurial temperament with strangers, it was probably a good idea. Galiena would hate to think of the lion's reaction to being awakened from his nap by a curious stranger.

Koch laughed outright and even Himmler looked mildly surprised. "Why, Your Serene Highness?" Koch asked condescendingly. "Is a Horsch so temperamental a car that an admirer can't go for a closer look?"

Galiena looked through her eyelashes at Koch, trying to mask her irritation. "A man or unwary dog might be truly surprised, perhaps dangerously so, at the temperament of my car."

Himmler stroked her hand with his own, apparently trying to soothe her. "By all means, Madame. We shall cordon off your vehicle."

She smiled at her host. "Thank you, Herr Reichsführer. I would rest much easier knowing it was done."

Himmler introduced her to so many more, all the way through his flock of admirers and to a man they were exquisitely polite. Then the Reichsführer led her to the administration building where Koch introduced her to his wife Ilsa; a petulant looking creature who fawned on Galiena while conspicuously assessing her every movement and gesture. This pair was so terribly common, and Galiena could tell they wanted to ape their betters. Grandfather once said that inwardly small people should never be put into positions of authority, and Galiena felt that way about these two. There was a cruelty about them and her flesh crawled in their presence.

The Reichsführer watched her very carefully; even protectively, and after a short amount of time sent the Kochs away with a dismissive hand. Himmler could be very languid in his movements and the Kochs needed no reminder of who truly ruled here. They left the room quickly and furtively at their master's gesture. Alone with Himmler and Wolff in Koch's rather bourgeois office, Galiena sat on the couch and the men across from her on stuffed chairs.

"You do not like my Commandant, Galiena," Himmler said softly as the door shut behind Koch.

Galiena addressed her host, wishing she could drop her guard. "It is not my place to like or dislike him, Heinrich. He's your commandant."

385

He smiled, his perfect white teeth flashing at her and Galiena was transfixed by how boyish he appeared. "No, but I would find your opinion interesting."

"He strikes me as the type who might have a deficiency of character," Galiena replied carefully, not knowing how much this Koch meant to the Reichsführer.

Himmler nodded, his face smoothing as he considered her words. "Yes. He might at that. He is very quick to put himself ahead of the rest." He turned to Wolff. "Why don't you see if you can hunt down the Pfalzgraf for our lady here." It was a blatant dismissal.

Wolff rose stiffly. "Certainly," He answered and left the room.

Himmler returned his blue eyes to her. "Wolffschen is most put out with me. He's very quick to make his displeasure known, and yet not so much as to actually irritate me."

"Gruppenführer Wolff is a very loyal man."

"He is, indeed. Loyal to all he considers to be his friend and he thinks I'm going behind Hagen's back by bringing you here." Himmler rubbed his hands together. "But he understands it's my prerogative to do so."

"Perhaps he should be mad at me for asking," Galiena supplied.

Himmler winked at her. "How could anyone be mad at you, my dear Pfalzgräfin? You are nobility itself. By your example we learn how we should be."

Galiena looked down at her purse, one gold bar in it. Was she really nobility? Or was she just one more desperate person trying to survive in a world where such things were increasingly falling by the wayside? She met his eyes, acutely embarrassed. "Please don't say that, Herr Himmler. I am certainly no example to follow."

Concern flickered up from the depths of those blue eyes, and the man who held her so carefully during the ambush was before her. "Are you troubled, Galiena? Is there aught I can do for you," he asked gently.

She smiled wanly at him; suddenly feeling every hour she had been awake and unable to make her move. "I am troubled,

Heinrich, but there is nothing you can do to alleviate it. You must agree this situation is awkward at best for me."

Himmler nodded slowly. "And you are bearing up to it with a superhuman grace, Madame."

There was a knock on the door before she could answer, then Wolff was striding into the room with a guard and her Grandfather. "The Pfalzgraf von Steinberg, Herr Reichsführer."

And SS man came into the room with Meinrad von Steinberg limping slowly after. His stiff legged gait almost tearing at her heart. When Hermann Göring shot Meinrad in January, the bullet must have shattered his knee, for her Grandfather had never walked like this before. He wore the black and white striped uniform as regally as any other garment, and his shoulders were completely unbowed. Galiena was pleased to see that he was only vaguely thinner, his face still as she remembered, but cleanly shaven, the elegant moustache gone. The colour in his skin was also normal; she had worried he would be grey with illness. All in all, his visage was almost unchanged from when she had seen him last. His eyes, those hooded blue eyes which haunted her dreams, caught hers in their snare, and while his expression was unchanged, his eyes were alight with pleasure. Galiena could read his mind in those eyes. They screamed to her, 'You came! You came! You came!'

Galiena rose, and when she did, Himmler followed suit. "Well, Pfalzgräfin. There he stands." Himmler gestured at Meinrad von Steinberg. The mocking had returned to his voice, but he wasn't mocking her. He was mocking his captive.

Again her eyes met her grandfather's and they communicated the man's amusement. The Pfalzgraf was certainly not afraid of Himmler and it showed. The very blandness of his expression was enough for her to know. He communicated his expectation to her: that she would do the right thing. She knew him so well, as he knew her so well. The knowledge that she could read his mind in this moment was a hard thing, for it meant he was reading hers too, and she didn't want him to know what she was thinking.

Galiena moved very close to Himmler's side, laying one hand on the top of his forearm, her fingers resting on the thick band of silver bullion ribbon decorating his sleeve. The other went

387

under his arm, almost near his elbow. There was an intimacy extended in the gesture, but more than that, the contact and the closeness allowed her greater power over him. She was right in his space, where she could bring her will to bear against his. Galiena was quiet a moment, allowing him to feel the warmth of her gloved hands through his sleeve, waiting until he turned to look down at her. "Heinrich, please! I beg of you! Will you allow the Pfalzgraf and I a moment of privacy while we talk? Things may be said of a highly personal nature, and I would prefer my shame to be mine and mine alone."

"Your Serene Highness, the lack of wisdom in such an action does not need to explored," Wolff retorted coldly.

Himmler frowned, but did not pull his hand away, and she knew she'd won. If he was going to reject her, he would have done so. He considered her a long moment. "I would not leave you alone with him, Pfalzgräfin. I would risk neither your safety," Himmler paused pointedly, "or his by such an action."

Wolff glowered at Himmler. "You aren't actually considering this, are you?"

Galiena gestured to the guard. "Then let the SS-Mann there stay. He can keep us both safe." She gave Himmler a sad, wide eyed look under the brim of her hat. "It would mean so much to me."

Himmler examined her, the SS-Mann, the Pfalzgraf and back; obviously considering. "I will acquiesce, provided you promise me that you will keep a civilized distance apart." He brushed the back of his index finger along her cheek. "I am inherently inclined to indulge you in all things, but I rather suspect you're aware of that."

She released him and moved back to the sofa. "Thank you, Heinrich. I promise that I shan't move from here."

Himmler acknowledged her promise with a bob of his head and crooked his finger at Wolff. "Come, Wolffschen. You can release your torrent at me in the other room." He moved to leave, and turned to the SS-Mann. "If the prisoner acts in anyway threatening to the Pfalzgräfin, I give you permission to use whatever means necessary to subdue him." He nodded again, before leaving the room; Wolff stalking out behind him.

388

Meinrad von Steinberg crossed the floor to sit in the chair Wolff vacated. He stared at her, his gaze travelling across her body. "Well, Poppet," he said in English at last.

"Grandfather." Galiena answered him in that language.

"That was very skilfully done, if somewhat unbecoming of a woman with your title." His voice was dry and so low. How she loved and hated the sound of it.

"Thank you." Her mouth was dust. Oh dear God! She couldn't do this! She couldn't! Why hadn't Himmler saved her from herself?

"You look tired, Galiena. Have you not been sleeping, Poppet?" Gentle concern. How many times had he said those words to her before? A thousand? Ten thousand? Dear God! Why hadn't he killed her that night?

"Not last night, no. I was busy." Galiena whispered, barely able to speak. "How is-" she stumbled. "How are you feeling? The surgery?"

The old man smiled slowly, a wonder in his face. It seemed like such a foreign expression on his face. "You went back. You found my letters."

"Yes. I went back." Could she not actually make a proper sentence?

"I knew you would return. Oh, Poppet! I knew you would. Just as I knew you would come to me here." Her grandfather sat expectantly and regally, waiting for her to give him the declaration he craved. She could see it in every line of his body.

The SS-Mann looked at them in consternation; obviously he spoke no English. It would be difficult for him to report to Himmler on their conversation. Galiena put him right out of her mind. "I didn't know, Grandfather, that you had been ill. The news did not reach me." She cast about for something to say, for her salvation. She had struggled to reclaim her sanity after the rape stole it from her, and now it threatened to leave again.

Meinrad von Steinberg cut the air sharply with his hand. "I forbid them to tell you. I knew you would come back eventually."

A part of her wanted to know how, but she supposed it was his arrogance. She had changed in the last months. He had changed her. The girl he could anticipate was dead. "I am sorry the cancer returned."

Meinrad von Steinberg's eyes gleamed with resolution. "My will is stronger than sickness, Poppet. I refuse to be brought low before my duty to Riesa is complete."

The word duty made her stomach churn. "If duty is your inspiration, Grandfather, I thank it for preserving your life."

"It reaps its own rewards," his lips curled up as he said it.

The churning turned into outright roiling. "This place cannot have made your recovery better."

A faint irritation passed over his face. "I had not expected this little sojourn into the baser aspects of Low German culture, but it's certainly not the worst place I've found myself over the years. No education is completely without merit. Yes. I've experienced worse."

Galiena decided to cut to the chase as there was no point in drawing this out any further. She pulled out her folder. "My reason for being here is twofold. First, it is my intention to ransom you from this place."

"As I had expected," Meinrad said approvingly.

"But you must leave Germany. We've made arrangements for you to go to Reino de Estrellas directly from here. We thought Brazil would be best for your health. The Reino is so beautiful this time of year, as I remember," Galiena told him. Thank God she had rehearsed this in the car on the way up here.

"I would prefer England," the Pfalzgraf commented absently; only the clutching of his fingers on his knees betraying how much he preferred that option.

"There are Nazis in England. For you to disappear out from under Hermann Göring's eye, you must go somewhere far away. You are absolute monarch at the Reino. I know you have been happy there. It wouldn't have to be for a long time," Galiena explained, searching for anything to say which would make him agree to go. Why did he have to be so difficult about this?

"Perhaps there is wisdom in that. I can run the Gessellschaft just as well from the Reino. I did it before," Meinrad considered, now smoothing his pants before folding his hands in his lap. "Yes. I will agree to go to the Reino for now."

She looked at his shoes. Rough, broken down things with thick cracks in the leather, they seemed so out of place on her

grandfather. "The second is that I wish your permission to wed."
Inwardly Galiena prepared for the blow.

"What?" The flat hiss of the word was feral. "I don't think
so, Poppet." He shook his head, the words grinding out from
between his teeth. "That does not suit me at all."

"And if one was conditional on the other?" She breathed,
praying to the heavens for a moment's respite.

"You wouldn't do that."

Galiena closed her eyes, smothering all the parts of her
which truly mattered. To get what she wanted, she had to lie, and
make him think she would give him what he craved. Her. She
knew from his letters how he wanted her to be. She had to shunt
away her soul and be that creature. One who wanted his touch.
When she opened her eyes and raised the brim of her hat, she
looked at the Pfalzgraf with a lover's gaze. The gaze she gave
Hagen when he proposed. "You don't understand, my darling," she
began, trying to make the words sound less mechanical. "I must do
this for legitimacy. The Graf von Reitersbach will be a suitably
docile husband, as I'm sure you are aware."

Confusion. "Von Reitersbach? But that would be a sham!
Frederick would never touch you. I rather doubt he could." The
hooded blue eyes fixed on her with a dreadful intensity.

"Frederick would never touch me," Galiena echoed as she
ran a dry tongue over parched lips. "Isn't that acceptable to you?"
She swallowed, cursing herself for eating, for the nausea
threatened to overcome her. "And should we visit the Reino and
leave expecting a child then who could possibly say a word as to
that child's origin."

"What are you saying, Galiena? Speak plainly, child!" The
man's eyelids opened and her grandfather's eyes burned with
basilisk's brightness. Dear God! He was killing her with his
expectations.

"Society will not accept me openly bearing your bastard,"
she whispered through numb lips.

"It would not be a bastard. We are wed in the eyes of God.
No child of mine upon your body would ever be-" he appeared
unable to say her word. "Illegitimate."

"The cruel minds of the outside world would disagree. Too
many people know of our past. They would talk. They would never

understand the nature of our world. How can they? They are peasants!" Galiena entreated him.

"Yes. The beasts of the field cannot understand the nature of the chosen." The Pfalzgraf studied her. "I see you have adjusted your thinking to our reality?"

"I was wrong. Terribly wrong." The flame of heat at saying the words! She broke out into a cold sweat across her torso. She was roasting and freezing at the same time. Sweat was pouring down her spine. "When I read your letters I knew what I had thrown away. I knew what you felt. I didn't understand. How could I? You hurt me that night." Hurt me? You very nearly destroyed me.

There was such pain in his face, the lines growing deeper in his cheeks. "That night! I have such remorse. It was not well done of me, Poppet. I was out of my mind with wanting you."

"I didn't understand," Galiena repeated, unable to think of anything else to say.

Meinrad moved to sit beside her and the guard froze. "No!" The man called in German. "You stay there!"

Galiena raised a hand. "It is fine, Mein Herr. The Pfalzgraf won't hurt me."

"The Reichsführer said apart," the uniformed man barked.

Meinrad sat on the end of the couch. "Here is not so close? She is my wife." The guard seemed fraught with indecision and then nodded his head curtly. Meinrad continued in English. "You are so beautiful now, Poppet." He seemed wistful as he drew in a deep breath. "You have become a woman while I've been away from you."

Her skin crawled and her eyes threatened tears. "Time has passed." Galiena fought to maintain control of her stomach.

"Perhaps only a woman could understand. Maybe that was my mistake. I was much younger when it happened to me. It was far easier to adjust my thinking, but then I am a man." An elegant hand lifted from his lap in a conceding, open gesture then descended between them onto the fabric of the cheap couch.

Galiena blinked. "Happened to you? What do you mean?"

The Pfalzgraf shook his head. "Now is not the time, Poppet. There will be plenty of other opportunities for that story. Let me look at you! My God! Only you would come to this place without a care in the world, dressed for an audience. Scarlet, my love? How appropriate!"

"Thank you." Why hadn't she worn black?

"What a treasure you are. What children we will make together." His words enveloped her and she felt imprisoned by them. Her grandfather watched her with a possessive gaze which made her feel like the convict. How could Verina wish to return to this madness?

Galiena didn't know how to answer. She reached into her folder and pulled out her prenuptial contract between her and a man written only as 'Graf von Reitersbach.' It wasn't a lie for Hagen had signed the paperwork. She passed it to the Pfalzgraf with a fountain pen. "Will you give your consent? Underneath is something von Kleist put together, to give me experience running the Gessellschaft. Everything from the Rhineland east has been broken off into a separate corporate entity, Von Steinberg Gesselschaft Ost, and I have 51% of the shares, becoming chief operating officer, and he will teach me how to administer it from here in Germany so that when I am the only von Steinberg, I have the tools to take over the rest. Everything in Western Europe, England, and the Americas is to be set up as Von Steinberg Gessellschaft Ausland, and the share division will remain as it is." She reached into her purse and took out a pair of his spectacles and put them atop the pile of papers.

The old man's eyes darted very sharply. "You would split up my company?"

"Not precisely. It all still exists as one company. The original Von Steinberg Gesselschaft is the umbrella company, and of that you are still 75% director as before. Under the umbrella are Ost and Ausland. I will report to you on all major decisions regarding Ost as the junior shareholder. As for the board of directors of the parent company, it will remain virtually the same, only I will join as vice chairman; a position which doesn't exist at this time. In terms of the board for Ausland, you may do as you please, provided I am a member to keep me aware of the progress of that company for the future. As for Ost, at this juncture I must maintain at least seventy-five percent of the present board; though it is my intention to retain all who are relevant to the new company for at least two years. After two years, I have more freedom over my board, but I cannot change more than one member per year. Those who leave through more natural forms of attrition, such as retirement or death are to be replaced at my discretion; but all in all, it retains the majority of your influence over the board for at least five years." So much easier a topic than the previous, and Galiena was content to rattle on about it for hours.

The hooded eyes gleamed back at her. "You will let me read this, of course." The glasses went on, and he took up the papers and went through, line by line, his finger tracing every word as he read. How many times had she watched him do this? He was so very thorough. It took some time, for von Kleist was nothing if exacting himself; but finally he put the papers down. "This would give you control over 40% of what I have spent my life trying to build. Why are you doing this, Poppet?"

"Because I need time to learn. When you came to this place, von Klopfer and von Kleist came to me for decisions, just like when you were sick. I wasn't equipped to make them, and you weren't around to consult with. One day, there won't be the option of ransoming you, for one can't ransom with the Ferryman, but until that time, this seems like a reasonable option to me. I will stay here in Germany for the time being to facilitate the changeover and spend time with von Kleist. Von Klopfer will go with you to the Reino and between the two of them the process should be seamless," Galiena explained calmly.

"That is far more reasonable than I would expect of your years. I see here that this agreement between you and von Reitersbach gives him no interest in the Gessellschaft unless both you and I are dead and he's in a custodial position for any children of your body." Meinrad nodded with approval. "He's forbidden to be a member of the board in your lifetime though it's not stated quite so baldly in this prenuptial. While he can be a member in the event of your death, should he be in a custodial position over your offspring, he is forbidden to be chairman," The Pfalzgraf chuckled gamely. "Ah! This reads of von Kleist and it's heartening to see. The man is a hawk and can be yours if he comes to respect you. There is no more agile business mind in Germany and Gustav Krupp has tried to steal him away for years." He sobered then. "But all that folderol about the board, Galiena. My board isn't like most. They only have the power you give them as the Gessellschaft is not a publicly traded company; and as long as I'm alive, will never be a publicly traded company. There are no shareholders and as such, you will answer to no one." There was a glitter in the bright eyes. "Other than me, of course. The board is advisory only; like the king's privy council. I retain my board because I look after them very well and give them a constant supply of fresh prey. Under no circumstances let them turn into carrion birds, for vultures will gnaw on you as you are a far closer meal than any corpse they can fly off to find."

Galiena took it all in without prejudice for these were the things she needed to know. This was why she was allowing this man to go free; so she could learn his secrets. "I shall remember that."

"No, Poppet. Learn? No. Learning is not the issue. Believing is the issue. Confidence is the issue. I've taught you all you need to know. You are more than a hawk. Like me, you are a dragon, and provided you remain a dragon, the hawks will follow you gladly. They do it because a dragon will find where the big game is; game too big for little hawks to tangle with on their own." Her Grandfather reread a section of the prenuptial agreement. "But it gladdens the heart to see your devotion to the family. Never forget that you are Riesa, as much as it is you. You are great, Galiena, but never forget that it is Riesa which gives you that greatness. The family must always prevail, Poppet!"

"What was built by the von Steinbergs stays in the hands of the von Steinbergs." He had said it so many times to her; it was easy to say it right back to him.

The blue eyes turned inward. "Frederick would never contravene my wishes. I know that." Meinrad tapped the folder and read the contract one last time. The pen lid twirled in his fingers and with only that one hand he twisted the pen and put the cap on the end. He always referred to the gesture as an affectation from his youth. "Frederick will never touch you. Promise me that." He tapped the pen against his lips. "And you give me your word that you will come to me at the Reino?"

It wouldn't be a lie, for the moment he was dead she would go to him, and bring his body back to Germany with all the honour it deserved. The Pfalzgraf would be buried at Riesa. "I will come to you at the Reino."

"You will wear the Eye of Riesa and lay with me under the stars. You will give yourself to me until you grow round with my child? Not once, but as many times as it takes." There was a long pause. "You will be my wife?"

Galiena leaned forward and took his hand. The guard said nothing. She raised the dry, veined limb to her lips, then at the last moment flipped his hand over and kissed his palm. The vassal's kiss of peace. "I am your wife already," she whispered, every word like a dagger in her body as she took his other palm and kissed it too, completing the medieval gesture which always pleased him so much. "I just needed time to understand, my husband. Understand what was right for Riesa."

The Pfalzgraf's hand cupped her face, and his thumb traced her lips, a smear of scarlet lipstick staining the pad. "So beautiful, my little Dragon. My perfect Poppet. I love you." Then he took his hand back and signed the papers, his hand firm and steady, so unlike her own being. "Now go! Haggle with that peasant and let us   leave   this   place."

December 19, 1937
Dearest Poppet,

I have come myself tonight. I am mobile again. I have had time to think, and have seen what I did wrong. It was wrong, Poppet. I am terribly ashamed. I should have had more control. I behaved like a green boy, and look what I did to you. How could I have done that? It torments me. You have to believe me that it will never be that way again. Never. I will make it up to you. I promise you I will. I love you.
Eternally yours,
Meinrad

Chapter 28
March 4, 1938

Meinrad von Steinberg Zum Riesa. There it was, in bold, black strokes on all the papers. It was over. Galiena picked up her folder and her heavy purse, moving towards the door, leaving her Grandfather behind without a second thought. The guard seemed racked with indecision and then he moved to open the portal for her. As Galiena passed him, she was so aware of the acrid smell of cheap cigarette smoke clinging to the man's uniform. Suddenly she couldn't breathe. She moved through the anteroom, passed a door through which Himmler, Wolff and Koch were sitting, and walked to the outside.

Aching with misery, coupled with anger for what she had done to herself, Galiena flipped open the folder and looked at the signature again. Please, Lord! Let it be worth what she just paid! Her eyes burned and a tear fell unbidden, searing a trail down her cheek. A puff of wind picked up the unstapled prenuptial agreement, like some kind of omen, lifting it into the air then swirling it into the courtyard. "Oh God in heaven!" Galiena cried, slamming the folder shut and leaping down the stairs after the papers.

The prisoner at the flowerbed looked up, his eyes glistening with fear, and glowing with something else. He brushed his dirty hands on his trousers and soared up from the soil. While Galiena chased after one piece which was proving damned elusive, he retrieved the other five. When she at last caught the first page, she turned to where he was standing. He put the papers together and handed them to her with his head bowed.

"My thanks, Mein Herr!" Galiena tried to smile at the man. "Many thanks, indeed."

The voice, so very educated yet rusty almost from disuse, spoke to her. "Do not cry, Fraulein! There are enough tears in this place."

Another guard ran forward, his rifle at the ready. "Back away, dog!" He shouted at the prisoner. "On your knees!"

Galiena turned to the guard in shock. "No! He helped me." She moved herself between the guard and the wretch before her. "He was kind to me. This man did nothing wrong."

"That is not for you to decide," the guard answered firmly.

Galiena threw up her hand in arrogant dismissal of the guard. "Stuff and nonsense. He did nothing wrong." She returned her gaze to the prisoner whose eyes stared with some terror at the guard. "Why? Why did you do it?"

The man brought his heels together. "Sometimes it's worth the risk of punishment to feel like a man again; if only for a short moment."

"What the devil is going on out here?" Koch bellowed arrogantly. He stood with Himmler in the doorway. Behind them was the blond head of Karl Wolff.

"My papers went flying. This gentleman," Galiena used the word very carefully, "helped me collect them. I am quite in his debt."

Himmler pushed past Koch, examining the tableau before fixing his attention back on Galiena. He nodded. "Go about your duties, all of you."

The prisoner's eyes darted up to Himmler; filled with indecision and then he shuffled back to the flowerbed. The guard returned to his post, and Galiena followed Himmler back into the building. "Herr Himmler, might I speak to you for a moment in private?"

The Reichsführer-SS turned, before gesturing to the room he had been sitting in with Wolff It was a small waiting room, but not uncomfortably appointed; faintly incongruous in this place. He shut the door behind them. "How can I be of service to you, Galiena?" He asked after they had both taken seats.

"My business advisors inform me that you have a Circle of Friends, as it were, who contribute to the SS," Galiena began, inhaling deeply when she finished speaking; trying to dispel the iron bands around her chest.

"Yes. My Freundkrais Reichsführer-SS," he answered slowly. "You are well informed."

Another calming breath. "It is a group I would like to join, Heinrich."

Himmler's lips curled up in gentle amusement. "My dear Galiena, you are already to be a member of my SS clan as the wife of Hagen Kohl, and by virtue of my special affection for you. Individuals aren't generally a part of my little circle of friends."

"I wasn't specifically thinking of me as Galiena, wife of Hagen Kohl; I was thinking of myself as CEO of Steinberg Gessellschaft Ost," she told him. She reached into her folder and pulled out a sealed envelope von Kleist had given to her this morning. "This is letter of introduction from a mutual acquaintance."

Himmler turned the letter over and ran his fingers over the very prominent seal of the Krupp von Bohlen und Halbach family. He cracked the letter and read the lines therein, before placing it on the table beside her. "Very impressive recommendation." Was it her imagination or had his face taken on a speculative air?

Galiena smiled as much as she could. "Thank you."

"Generally a modest donation comes with entry into the Freundkrais," Himmler spoke smoothly. "As well as other considerations," Himmler inhaled, his mind obviously churning. "But I don't want to burden a woman that I consider my family with such base concerns. Dear Galiena, surely you weren't thinking you need to join such a group to secure favours from me? I would move Heaven and Earth to secure the brightening of your day."

Disbelief covered her, and Galiena couldn't help giving him a stare which expressed her feelings. "Really, Herr Reichsführer!" Her use of his title was deliberate. "I didn't believe the SS to be so altruistic to grant favours to conglomerates without the slightest expectation in return."

There was a pensive expression crawling across he face of the Reichsführer-SS. "What do you want from me, Galiena? Speak plainly then, and I will see what I can do."

Galiena assumed a harshly businesslike mien. "I would be willing to make a sizable donation, directly to you, Herr Reichsführer, and allow a member of the SS onto my board, which is, I believe the other required consideration, in return for a consideration of my own."

"And that would be?" The man no longer seemed to breathe. He was so still it disquieted her.

"I request that you release the Pfalzgraf von Steinberg from this place provided he leaves Germany tonight, not to return during the term of this government," Galiena said finally.

Himmler turned his head, to stare out the window. "Galiena, you do understand that the Pfalzgraf is not my inmate, but that of Hermann Göring? You can hardly expect me to incur the wrath of your Uncle lightly, now can you?"

Galiena reached into her purse, pulling out the gold bar. It felt like lead in her hand, for all its value. "I wouldn't expect you to incur his wrath lightly at all. In fact, I don't expect you to tell him that you released the Pfalzgraf. I'm perfectly content to have him believe the Pfalzgraf is here. And I do guarantee that within eight hours of my Grandfather's release he would be on his way to Buenos Aires." She handed him the gold bar. As he took it, their fingers brushed.

He eyed the bar almost as if it were a snake. "This certainly is a sizable donation, Madame. I can only guess in the neighbourhood of fifty thousand marks. But I am not completely up to date on the price of gold." He put the bar on top of the letter, certainly not handing it back to her. "But what you are asking is a huge favour and what is my guarantee that the Pfalzgraf will leave? How can you promise that he will be out of Germany so quickly?

Galiena reached over and touched his arm. "Heinrich, what I've given you is merely a token of what the Gessellschaft is willing to donate to the SS for the release of the Pfalzgraf."

Himmler leaned forward, his body questioning and open. "What of you, Madame? I know what the Pfalzgraf did to you. Why are you doing this?"

Galiena raised a hand, shaking her head willing him not to ask her further. "That is personal. It's between my grandfather, the devil and myself. This is business, Heinrich. The two are completely separate. My personal feelings have no place in this transaction." Duty, pure and simple.

Himmler leaned back, tapping a small, pale finger on his cheek. "You are far more determined than I had imagined," he said quietly. "What would it be worth to your Gessellschaft for me to consider this?"

"Name me a price," Galiena answered, confident at last. Greed she was perfectly prepared for.

The Reichsführer-SS stroked the bar with his finger. "Nine more of these would be a good inducement."

"Herr Himmler, what if today, and today only, I was willing to find nineteen more of those? If, on delivery of twenty bars of gold, with a value of approximately 1,080,000 Reichsmarks, the SS would give me custody of the Pfalzgraf," Galiena pounced on him, praying he wouldn't desire a price more personal.

"Why is this offer only good today?" He asked suspiciously and she could see the gears spiralling in his head. It was an unimaginable sum. No. It was an imaginable sum. She had spent two hours last night moving it.

"Because it's a hard amount to leverage, and I'm paying by the hour to hold the Graf Zeppelin from flying until the Pfalzgraf arrives," Galiena told him honestly.

Himmler appeared disbelieving. Surely he knew such things were possible with enough money. "How much?"

"About five thousand per hour, whether he arrives or not," she supplied.

"Impressive. You have thought of everything," Himmler considered her very carefully. "Fine then, but here is my caveat. If you can deliver the gold within the hour, and provided you will allow one of my men to escort the Pfalzgraf to the Zeppelin so that he can confirm that the Pfalzgraf has left the Reich, then I will consent to this bargain." There was an air about him as if he had been set to an impossible task; one it would take Hercules to surmount. Yes. Heinrich Himmler had misjudged her, she could tell. Galiena doubted he would ever be so foolish again.

Galiena rose to her feet; knees weak and thighs trembling. "Come then, Herr Reichsführer, so that we can make the necessary arrangements. On delivery of the gold, I receive custody of the Pfalzgraf?" She held out her hand. "Though is it not proper to shake on a bargain first?"

He took her hand and shook it slowly. "It is proper. Yes. On delivery of the gold, within one hour." His voice was tinged with suspicion.

Galiena picked up the gold bar and handed it to him again. He cradled it in his arm like a baby. "Come then." She smiled. "Come with me." She simply couldn't help the glow of relief that Himmler had been bought off with mere gold.

"Where are we going?"

Galiena took his free hand. "Come, dearest Heinrich." She led him out of the room, and past where Wolff was standing close to the door with Koch. Wolff's eyes grew round when he saw Galiena and the Reichsführer almost arm and arm, and rounder still at the sight of the gold bar in Himmler's possession.

Himmler passed the bar to his subordinate. "Carry that, will you? And I would advise you to follow as well."

"Of course, Herr Reichsführer," Wolff answered smartly and Koch trailed along behind them.

Galiena proceeded to her car, which seemed to be bouncing on its springs. Emil must be awake now, for it had been well over an hour, closer to two. She prayed her upholstery was still in one piece, for the vehicle was brand new. One hazarded to think what a bored lion trapped in a car would do. She stopped several feet short of the vehicle. "You might want to wait here, Herr Himmler. Just to be on the safe side."

Both brows rose almost to the hairline. "The safe side?"

Galiena glanced around the compound with a careful glance. No dogs were visible. Swanhilde had warned her that Emil was apt to want to play with dogs and not in a healthy way for the dog. She approached the car, and called out "It's me, darling." Loud enough to be heard through the ragtop. The answering growl was enough to let her know that someone was quite displeased. She turned back to Himmler, who now had a very questioning expression on his face, his arms crossed over his chest. She smiled faintly and carefully opened the driver's side door.

402

Baleful amber eyes stared at her, crouched in between the seats below the level of the window. The growling rose in intensity and the ears were completely flat to his skull. Galiena met him glare for glare. "Don't you take that tone with me," she retorted sharply. The growling stopped abruptly; she was rarely firm with him, after all. Galiena placed her knee onto the driver's seat, never taking her eyes from his. "You did your job very well, darling, but now it's time to come out and play." She replied soothingly and the ears came up slightly. "I even have a ham for you if you're hungry." He hissed at her, but it was somewhat half hearted. She'd seen him really hiss before. Emil was more scared than anything else and obviously he was calming quickly with her here. "I love you," Galiena told him, slowly sliding a hand towards him. "I love my beautiful Emil. I shouldn't have left you." One ear came up. "And now we have to give these kind gentlemen their gold. It's not yours anymore, Sweetheart." The nose extended to sniff her glove and it took all her control to keep from shaking. Right now, more than any other time, she was aware that he was as big as she, with the temperament of a two year old. An angry toddler was a scary thing to face when it had ivory fangs and inch long claws.

The sniff turned to a snort, and then the lion butted her hand, rubbing it along his brow bone. Galiena reached the other hand over and scratched his head. The cub preened under her ministrations, and after a few minutes there was a hint of a purr. "Would you like to get out?" Galiena leaned over and kissed his head, and she was rewarded by a nose rub on her cheek. He must have been quite scared, for his nose was dry. She backed up, out of her door, smiled reassuring at Himmler, who was now looking rather mystified, and slowly opened the door as wide as it would go. She attached Emil's leash to his collar, under the slightly wilted red ribbon she tied around his neck this morning. It was hard to keep a lion looking festive when he rolled on his ribbon.

Galiena tugged faintly on the leash and Emil uncurled himself from the foot well. A paw came out of the car and then a nose. Behind her she heard Wolff whisper, "Jesu!"

Emil emerged from the car, returning to his defensive crouch, his body low to the ground. His tail lashed once and then was still. He assessed Himmler and Wolff with those eyes nature had so artfully rimmed with kohl, making a displeased sound in the back of his throat. Galiena crouched down beside him, her arms around his neck, and kissed his forehead. "Emil, those are Mommy's friends, Herr Himmler and Herr Wolff. You have to be nice to them."

"I sincerely hope you have your pet under control, Madame," Himmler snapped tightly, lines of fear appearing around his eyes. "I must tell you that I am not amused."

Galiena pulled the woollen blanket covering the gold in the back seat of the car away, and the shine of the sun on the bars was dazzling. "I'm sure even the Reichsführer-SS would understand that a girl might not want to drive around with one million marks worth of gold bullion in her car without protection she can trust," she replied coolly. As if to punctuate her words, Emil let out one of his little yowls, before lifting his paw to chew on the pad, his claws fanning open.

Himmler's jaw actually fell open. "You have it in the car? You drove here with a lion and a million in gold bullion in your car? You must be mad!" He exclaimed.

"The gold, the lion and I are here, Heinrich!" Half of her mouth rose up in a smile, before she chuckled against her better judgement. "Not mad, Herr Reichsführer, just very determined." She moved towards him hand extended, and Emil followed. "One hoard of gold for one inmate. I believe that was the arrangement?"

Himmler glanced at Emil before closing the distance between them. When the man came to close to his mistress, the lion moved forward, in a low protective stance. Himmler froze and then reached a hand towards the cat, to let the beast sniff him. Emil did so, slowly, before presenting an ear for Himmler to scratch. The Reichsführer's hand curled gently around the ear, then down Emil's head and neck. There was wonder on the man's face as his eyes met Galiena's. "What a remarkable creature he is! What did you say his name was?"

"Emil."

"Hello, Emil! Thank you for letting me stroke you." Himmler then addressed Galiena. "I love animals. I've never understood how man can hunt them, killing them for pleasure. Once upon a time, for sure, we had to hunt to survive, but now? It is such a waste. Who could shoot a creature like this?"

Galiena crouched down beside Himmler. "Only a monster. But I might be biased."

"Yes. I can tell that." He smiled with genuine pleasure as Emil began to purr. "Come Wolffschen! Come meet Emil."

Wolff was more reluctant, but he, too, introduced his hand to the cat. "Herr Emil."

Again Emil went through his ritual of sniffing the intruder before presenting his wedge shaped head for attention. Then the Gruppenführer was patting the lion with the rest of them. Emil, lover of attention that he was, flopped to his side, content to be friendly with Galiena close by. The men commented on his huge paws, and Wolff remarked that putting a red bow around the neck of a male lion had to be an affront to leonine honour. They all laughed and Galiena pulled the bow loose.

Suddenly Himmler took her hand in his. "We have an agreement, Galiena. You've more than adequately fulfilled the terms of our agreement."

She dropped her chin. "Thank you, Heinrich." Deep down, she realised she had been praying he would say no. In this place, she was safe from him, but out there, even in Brazil, he could get to her. One day he would. Grandfather was nothing but tenacious about the things he wanted. The wounded girl broke through the wall and her breath caught in her throat.

He must have heard her, for Himmler caught her chin in his hand, making it impossible to avoid his penetrating stare. "You are not as ambivalent to all of this as you would have me believe."

The pressure pushing down on her was almost more than she could bear, but she wouldn't break before him. She refused to lose her composure, for if she did, she would never get it back. Serene. I am serene. A serene highness. "I would do my duty, mein Herr." As she was born to do.

"You do not fool me, Galiena," he said, the words tinged with rebuke. Did he really think they were so close that she would use him as her father confessor?

"Then leave me what remains of my dignity," she whispered, so low she doubted he could hear her. It was an illusion she clung to and wrapped about herself with a cloak. Her dignity.

"As you wish." Himmler's hand ran down Emil's neck until it touched Galiena's, and he covered it with his own. She was struck by how small and white his hands were; almost like a woman's. All she wanted to do was throw herself into his embrace and beg for his protection. Still, her fingers twitched spasmodically under his, and he tightened his grip around the digits. It was some comfort. He knew how hard this was for her.

She looked up into his concerned blue eyes, her own shimmering with unshed tears. "Thank you, Heinrich." What exactly she was thanking him for, she didn't know.

Himmler's brow furrowed in thought. "Your devotion to duty moves me, Madame. This glorious beast of yours, your Emil, you will not drive with him down to Friedrichshaven, will you? That would be a long seven hours for this magnificently patient creature."

"No. He will return to Berlin with his keeper," Galiena replied, at a loss for where Himmler was going.

"Then take my Wolff for protection. A wolf is nearly as fearsome as a lion in some fairy stories. It was my intention to send an officer to ensure the Pfalzgraf boarded the Zeppelin as directed, anyhow, and while he may disapprove of this, he will protect you as his own." Himmler tilted his head to address Wolff. "Would you do that for me, Wolffschen?" A question, yes; but spoken as a command.

Wolff assessed Galiena and the hardness in his eyes softened. "Of course, Herr Reichsführer."

"Thank you, Herr Gruppenführer. You have my gratitude."

"It is my pleasure to be of assistance, Pfalzgräfin von Steinberg." The blond man bowed his head.

Galiena lifted her head and stared out at the compound. Now wasn't the time to grieve. It there was so much more to accomplish. She was not yet done with Buchenwald. "So, gentlemen? I believe that there are arrangements to be attended? I can't take up your entire day with my little problems."

December 24, 1937
Dearest Poppet,

Merry Christmas, sweet Poppet. I have a gift for you, but I won't leave it here. I want to watch your lovely eyes when you open it. I thought you would come home tonight. It is the only present I asked for. Wherever you are, know that I am thinking of you. Only of you. Your sweet voice, your silken hair, your warm body and your brilliant mind. No one will ever love you like I do.
Eternally yours,
Meinrad

Chapter 29
March 4, 1938

Emil rose back to his haunches and gave Galiena a plaintive stare. She knew that look. Distress. The poor creature had been in the car for a very long time and was probably desperately in need of a walk. "Herr Reichsführer, would there be anyone about who could take Emil for a stroll while the car is unloaded."

Himmler snapped his fingers. "Koch. See to it," he barked, standing.

Galiena and Wolff also stood. "Thank you!" She exclaimed with relief. "Emil thanks you too, I'm sure."

Himmler chuckled, his white teeth flashing. "I'm sure."

Galiena winked at him before addressing the lion. "Come on, Darling. Give me a hug." She tapped her shoulders as Swanhilde had taught her and the lion sprang up, his paws where her hands had been and his nose in her face.

"Jesu!" Wolff whispered again.

Galiena threw her head back, and Emil sniffed the column of her neck, his extremely rough tongue tasting the perspiration in the hollow of her throat. "I love you, Emil!" She wrapped her arms around his head and held the great skull to her cheek, before she lifted the paws from her shoulders and the cat dropped back to the parade square.

The Reichsführer was staring at her in awe. "You put a great deal of trust in your companion. He could crush your windpipe in a second."

She dipped her head. "I know, but equally I know he won't. I trust him and I've never abused him. I never intend to abuse him. He trusts me just as much."

Koch returned, the prisoner who had helped her earlier trailing after him, a guard with a shovel bringing up the rear. The prisoner's eyes were black with fear, Koch's eyes filled with amusement. "This one seemed so eager to help you before; I thought he should do so again." He turned to Himmler. "And if the lion gets hungry, it's no great loss," He smirked.

Himmler raised a brow. "Indeed, Koch," His tone was flat; not amused.

Emil crouched, eyeing the newcomers carefully, his tail lashing suddenly. He was affected by both Koch and the men behind him. The smell of fear made Emil's predatory instincts come alive. Galiena addressed the prisoner, intending to stem a potential problem. "What is your name, Mein Herr?" She asked gently.

"Doctor Roland Lammers, Madame."

Galiena reached out her hand to the man. "Don't be afraid, Doctor Lammers. Emil won't hurt you if you aren't afraid of him." Koch snorted and she rounded on him. "Herr Koch, are you trying to terrify this poor man?"

Koch's petulant face came alight with an ugly pleasure. "Me, Your Serene Highness? Heaven forbid."

Emil seemed to sense her anger, for he pushed past Galiena, placing his body between herself and Koch. A low growl menaced in his throat. He crouched and advanced, slow paw after slow paw. She held Emil's leash in her hand but it gave him enough room to get closer to Koch. The man needed to be taught a lesson.

The effect on the man was immediate. Suddenly he was the prey and he obviously didn't enjoy the feeling. "Madame! Control that animal."

Galiena took a step forward, giving Emil a little more lead. "Come now, Standartenführer! You intimated you wanted to see Emil predatory." She took another step forward, enjoying her humiliation of this abominable man. "Are you not enjoying it, Herr Koch?" She could feel her own eyes twisting with a perverse pleasure. Suddenly to be the one in control, the one who was causing the fear, thrilled her in a way she couldn't suppress. She supposed it was wrong, but she couldn't help herself. It was an abuse of her power and she wasn't disturbed by it one bit!

"Madame, this isn't what I meant," he squealed, his voice high and thready.

Himmler appeared at her elbow. "Pfalzgräfin von Steinberg?"

Koch's fear was almost intoxicating, but even Galiena knew that too much of a good thing could be detrimental. Emil's ears were right down and then he straightened and roared. It was almost an adult lion roar, and Koch turned as grey as his uniform. He jumped and took another lurching step back, stumbling as he did so. Galiena decided that Emil had enough fun, and she called his name sharply. He turned, and she patted her thigh. "Come here, darling. You've made your point. He's not worth getting choleric over."

The lion looked from his mistress to his prey and obviously decided that he should obey his mistress. With a spiteful hiss at Koch, he turned on his tail and moseyed back to Galiena, looking tremendously proud of himself. He chuffed at her, and Galiena crouched down, kissing him between the ears and singing his praises.

"Perhaps you should withdraw, Koch," Wolff suggested and the man scrambled away.

"Yes! Baby doesn't like the nasty commandant, does he?" Galiena kissed Emil's ears as he started to purr, leaving a scarlet lipstick mark.

"I would appreciate it if you didn't allow Emil to torment my officers," Himmler said mildly, standing at her shoulder. He didn't look overly fussed.

Galiena glanced up into his face and saw a twinkle in his eye. Had he enjoyed that too? "I'm sorry, Herr Himmler. Sometimes Emil just takes a dislike to people and acts accordingly." She grinned against her better judgement. "And so do I."

"God help your enemies." She could have sworn that Himmler winked at her as he spoke.

"Indeed." Galiena turned to the prisoner again. "Doctor Lammers, I assure you that fear is unnecessary. Emil really won't hurt you," she smiled at the man. He bowed his head, taking a slow step towards her, his hand outstretched. Emil turned and sniffed the limb with little interest, focussed on Galiena as he was. "This is Doctor Lammers, Emil, and he's going to take you for a walk. Just like Swanhilde does. You are going to obey him, just as you obey Swanhilde." Emil didn't look so impressed.

"Swanhilde?" Himmler inquired idly.

"His keeper," Galiena stood up and turned back to Lammers, handing him Emil's leash. "He will take you where he's interested in going. If it's somewhere you aren't supposed to go, pull gently, slap your thigh, and say 'come, Emil.' Sharply. He will obey you."

"Thank you." The man looked as dubious as the cat.

"And keep in mind that he's just a baby. If he seems to act like a goggly kitten, it's because he is," Galiena smiled warmly at Lammers. "Just a two hundred pound goggly kitten."

"Yes, Your Serene Highness."

Galiena gave Emil one last head rub and then turned to Himmler. "May I use a telephone while your men unload my car?"

Himmler met her eyes. "Of course. I shall escort you myself." He turned to his companion. "Wolffschen, if you would be so kind as to arrange a detail to load the gold into one of our cars."

"Of course."

Himmler offered Galiena his arm and she took it, allowing him to lead her back towards the building. A soft little yowl behind her tore at her heart, but she knew Emil would be fine and she didn't have time to see to his needs. The lion would go with Lammers eventually, and she needed to make a few phone calls.

Her first was to the Hotel Elefant, where she sent the message to von Kleist it was time for him to come. He assured her they would arrive inside fifteen minutes. The second was to Friedrichshaven where she informed the Deutsche Zeppelin-Reederei Company that the Pfalzgraf von Steinberg would be arriving in approximately ten hours. It was at least seven to

Friedrichshaven, two half hour stops, one full hour stop, and an hour until they left, for certain. That was fine, she was informed. The Zeppelin could leave in the night, and the airship would depart as soon as the Pfalzgraf arrived.

When her calls were done, she remained in the chair, taking a moment of quiet time. Ten hours to go, then she would drive back home to Carinhall. Or maybe only as far as Berlin. It was far more direct from Friedrichshaven to Berlin as from Weimar. Six hours. Seven and a half to Carinhall. Nine with a few breaks. Could she stay awake another nineteen hours? She'd already been up close to thirty, and she felt every single one of them at this moment. On the other hand, she wasn't worried about falling asleep. She had some pills in her purse to help with her endurance. Von Schilling had given them to her a week ago during her lessons to perk her up when they were flying. It had been like electricity running through her body, and she knew they would serve her well today. Yet she didn't want to take them unless she had too. They made her heart race at an almost unseemly speed.

Galiena stirred herself, feeling guilty at her inattention to her host, and moved outside again. Himmler and Wolff were supervising the gold and Emil was off in a far corner with his companion. At the sound of her heels on the stone steps, the lion perked his head up and came steadfastly in her direction; almost pulling Doctor Lammers from his feet. The man jogged behind the cat, trying to keep up. Emil almost pushed her over in his exuberance.

"Thank you, Herr Doctor," she said wearily, wrapping her arm around Emil's butting skull.

Lammers bowed his head. "Emil is a fine animal. He did what he needed to do," The hint of a smile curled at the man's lips. "And the guard is busy cleaning it up." He handed the leash back to her, obviously amused that the guard would rather clean up spoor than walk the lion.

Galiena examined the prisoner. He had kind eyes; noticeably kind, staring out of that stubble covered skull. There was a ragged pink scar just above the man's ear. An obviously fresh injury and Galiena couldn't help but stare at it. There was an acrid smell emanating from the prisoner's ill fitting uniform of black and white stripes; a combination of unwashed fabric

411

combined with fear. It seemed so desperately out of place with the man's cultured voice. "Why are you here?" The words slipped unbidden from her lips. "What is your crime?"

"I spoke unwisely about the Fuhrer," Lammers appeared undaunted, as if he would do it again. How old was he? It was hard to tell, shaven as the man was, but certainly not as old as Hagen.

Galiena blinked as the words permeated. "That's all?"

Lammers shook his head sadly. "It was enough."

"Is there anything I can do for you?" Surely he had done more, but then again, maybe not.

His face was troubled. "My family lives in Rostock. I have a wife and she is a fine woman. If you could please let her know that I am alive, and that no matter what happens, I will always love her?" He spoke with such simple dignity.

"Surely you will leave this place soon?" Galiena returned in disbelief.

Lammers shook his head. "No. I don't think so." The words were so soft she barely heard them. "Please tell my wife I love her."

Galiena ached at the man's devotion. "Of course I will!"

Himmler saw her, and moved towards them. Lammers promptly disappeared back to his flowerbed. "Galiena! That man did not upset you, did he? You appear distraught." Solicitous concern emanated from the Reichsführer.

"No. Not at all." Impulsively, Galiena took his hand, holding it between her own. "Please tell me he will go home one day? He took such fine care of Emil and was a complete gentleman."

Himmler's face shuttered abruptly. "He will return one day. Rest assured."

There was something in his expression which made her doubt. "Alive, Herr Himmler?"

He tilted his head, the glare reflecting off his pince-nez, obscuring his eyes. "You've already convinced me to release one inmate, Galiena. Are you pressing me for another?"

"If I was?" Galiena whispered, her being bent on a new course. What would it take to save that man?

Himmler sighed, a pained sound, then he raised his hand to touch her jaw line. His hand was warm on her skin and she realised how cold she was, standing outside without her overcoat. "You have a big heart. A gentle heart. A womanly heart. This is as it should be. Yet Madame, there are some times when a soft heart is not an asset. A jailor must have toughness, even when his own heart demands otherwise. He must do his duty, even when that duty is very difficult."

She reached up, touching his hand. "Please, Heinrich, don't seek to instruct me on duty today. I have done my duty." She watched as the maroon Rolls Royce entered the compound, her stomach tying in knots as it came closer. "I've discovered a toughness I never knew I had."

His hand spanned her cheek. "Indeed you have." Himmler turned, his arm dropping and followed her gaze. "You performed your duty admirably."

"Thank you." Galiena replied, her gaze drawn to the striped back at the flowerbed. "Though I fear no good will come of it, as far as I am concerned."

"That thought might have crossed my mind."

"Then let me do something good today. Something kind. I beg of you to release a man who was kind to me." She entreated with what was left in his soul to do so. "I'm sure he has learned his lesson. You run a most excellent camp here. I'm sure he's seen the error of his ways!"

"Pfalzgräfin von Steinberg, do you think I have ultimate authority in these matters?" Himmler exclaimed in consternation.

"I do."

Himmler was silent for an impossibly long moment, following her sight to where Doctor Lammers toiled in the dirt, unconscious of the brokering being made on his behalf. "Fine then. It is in the nature of princes to be merciful, and I would not be one to cast aside their example. I will remove him from this place, and upon your wedding, I will give him his parole as a gift to you. If he sticks to the straight and narrow, there is no reason he should not stay a free man."

Galiena threw her arms around him. "Thank you, Heinrich! Thank you so very much!"

"After you asked me so prettily, Madame, how could I possibly resist?" He flashed his perfect white teeth, before he kissed her on both cheeks. "But now you must leave my camp before you inveigle the freedom of every criminal in the place." He put his hands on her shoulders and took a step back. "And I believe that no doubt you could. I'm resolved to keep this in mind. You show amazing ability to wring concessions from me."

"Don't worry, Heinrich! I shall endeavour to use my powers for good," she exclaimed and he bowed his head, what looked to be a faint blush on his cheeks. "You are a true and parfait knight."

"Now it is you who honour me and the man will be yours unharmed. You have my word," Himmler's voice was firm. "Now introduce me to your advisors."

Galiena and Himmler walked down to the great English car, with the Mercedes sedan behind. She introduced Himmler to von Kleist and von Klopfer as Montrose scurried past, anxious to get to his master. Yet as he crossed by Galiena, he crouched down and pressed his lips to the hem of Galiena's skirt with reverence. She nodded in dismissal, fighting the urge to push the valet off with her shoe. Wolff escorted the rat-like man into the administration building. Himmler was fairly entranced by the appearance of Swanhilde, who towered over him with her perfect Nordic beauty. Emil was also happy to see his keeper, and he left Galiena to rub his ears on the other woman's thighs.

While von Klopfer pontificated to the Reichsführer, von Kleist came over and bowed to Galiena. "You did it, Your Serene Highness."

"Yes, Herr Ritter, it would appear I did," she answered him.

"You do not seem ecstatic, Madame," his voice seemed to mock her.

"I'm a little tired for ecstasy, Herr Ritter. I moved that pile of gold myself, last night," Galiena sighed and then plastered a wan smile on her face for his benefit.

"Of course. I'm sorry. I've taken the liberty of arranging accommodations for us both in Friedrichshaven for this evening. My car is meeting me there in the morning. Of course there is a suite for Your Serene Highness as well," The man intoned in his dusty, dry voice.

She shook her head. "Thank you, Herr Ritter, but I will return to Carinhall tonight. I'm on a short leash with Uncle

Hermann. He thinks I am at Riesa for two days, but I promised I would be home for Saturday." It was an easy lie and she couldn't bear an evening of congratulations on her triumph over the SS.

"Fine then." His cadaverous face beamed at her. "You have done extraordinarily well, Pfalzgräfin. You have most certainly proven yourself as a von Steinberg." Then von Kleist moved to confer with von Klopfer.

Galiena walked to Ishmael, giving her Grandfather's wide eyed chauffeur instructions for the route to take, and where to stop at the appointed times. He took careful notes in his book, made a few suggestions of his own, and eventually they hammered routing and times to Friedrichshaven. She would lead, for the Horsch was far faster than the Rolls, and he would halt where he saw her car parked. It was her intention to drive faster and rest a little longer than the others, for her need was greater.

Next she gave instructions to Swanhilde to go to Carinhall, not Berlin. Galiena wanted to go where she felt safest, and Hermann Göring's feudal estate in the Schorfeide was the place. As Galiena crouched down beside Emil, his great head against her chest, Swanhilde examined Galiena critically. "If I may be plain, Your Serene Highness?" The woman asked.

Galiena inhaled deeply. "Of course, Swanhilde," she responded wearily.

The beautiful blond stood with her hands on her trouser clad hips and leaned over Galiena. "You look like you've been pulled through a keyhole backwards."

She giggled at the image which came to mind and the men turned to look. "You might say that."

Swanhilde touched her shoulder. "I thought I just did. Take care, tonight." The lion tamer was never one to stand on ceremony and Galiena was not one to insist upon it. Frankness was such a comfort in her world.

"I intend to." Galiena found she didn't want to let Emil go. In fact, she wanted to set him upon the man she had come to save.

"Excellent. Emil would be very distraught if anything were to happen to you. He loves you," the blond woman told her with a magnificent smile.

Galiena kissed Emil's now wet nose and stroked between his eyes. He wuffled against her ear and purred loudly. "As I love him."

There was commotion on the steps, and Galiena turned to watch her Grandfather, a man transformed, coming down towards them. He was majestic in a navy pinstripe single breasted suit with a matching double breasted vest. His tie was the same navy against a pristine white shirt, a huge, blood red ruby tack in the middle. Draped on his shoulders was a navy coat, a massive black fox collar framing his face. On his head was a navy homburg. The Pfalzgraf surveyed all below him, his cane at rest in his hand and then took each step with care. His fathomless eyes fixed on Galiena and very slowly winked at her, before he turned his attention to the rest. He looked as if he were just leaving the spa, not a care in the world.

Gruppenführer Wolff followed; a shadow in his black leather trench coat and high peaked cap, so like Hagen's. Galiena could almost imagine him to be Hagen and it was such a comforting thought. Suddenly her mind drifted back to her conversation with her fiancé, so many hours ago. She could feel those imaginary lips on her neck, making her feel safe. She could get through this. There were only ten more hours and her Grandfather would be gone forever. There would be no need to fear.

Meinrad came to the bottom of the stairs and Galiena curtseyed in proper greeting; a salve to his ego. "Pfalzgraf von Steinberg Zum Riesa."

He offered her his arm. "Pfalzgräfin von Steinberg Zum Riesa. Come. Let us depart this place."

"Yes." The word was dry as dust as she rested her glove on his sleeve.

Meinrad turned to Himmler. "My thanks for your-" he paused. "Hospitality, Herr Himmler." He rolled the name about on his tongue, and the taste was not pleasant.

"My pleasure, Herr Pfalzgraf." Himmler was not intimidated. "If the Pfalzgräfin had not pleaded her case so well it would continue to remain my pleasure," the Reichsführer-SS narrowed his eyes. "Do not return to the Reich, Meinrad von

Steinberg, for I will be waiting for you the moment you step on German soil."

Meinrad smirked. "I'm sure." He moved past Himmler to his car; Montrose, von Klopfer and von Kleist trailing after him. When Galiena did not follow, he lifted his brows enquiringly. "Coming, Poppet?"

Galiena shook her head, quailing on the inside. "I must make a few stops on the way, Grandfather. I will not be able to travel the first leg with you." Nor the second, nor the third, she added in the vaults of her mind.

"I'm displeased, Poppet." Once those words would have cut her like a whip, but she found they had no power over her anymore.

"You won't even notice I'm not there, for Herr von Klopfer and the Ritter von Kleist have much to review with you," Galiena replied crisply.

Wolff grinned ferally at Meinrad. "And you have me to keep you company."

"How charming." The Pfalzgraf was swallowed up into his car.

Himmler came over and kissed both of Galiena's cheeks. "Until we meet again."

"Thank you, Heinrich. For everything." She let her head rest on his shoulder for a moment and then lifted it again. It was strange, her wary affection for this man. She wondered if she would ever understand it.

"You are my clan, Galiena. It is my duty to assist you."

"God speed back to Berlin." She nodded and with one last pat on Emil's head before he went off with Swanhilde, moved into her own car. Himmler himself shut the door, smiling at her as he did so. The top had been taken down, exposing her to the elements as she had requested. The air would keep her awake.

The Reichsführer reached into the car and picked up her hand, raising it to his lips to kiss it. "You are a very worthy woman, Galiena Pfalzgräfin von Steinberg. While I certainly don't agree with what we have done this day, your skill and determination to make it happen is formidable. You have earned your title, this day." He tapped the side of the car to let her know it was safe to drive away. "Now off with you, my dear Galiena. I will see you in Berlin soon."

Galiena smiled and turned the key in the ignition. The Horsch leapt to life, and she peeled away from where Himmler was standing. The maroon limousine trailed slowly behind her as she waited for the metal gate to be opened. The words stared back at her. *Jedem das Seine*. Each to their own. She had a word to finish it. Each to their own Hell. Today she had created a new hell. She had freed her Grandfather, as she had to, but it was a hollow victory. The first tear fell as the gate opened, and its fellows didn't stop for at least an hour.

Chapter 30
March 4, 1938

Hagen stepped out of Freffie's car and adjusted his cape on his shoulders. They were dressed to the proverbial nines, ready for what Freffie was calling the party of Hagen's young life. Hagen was more than fractionally dubious, but willing to keep an open mind. There was always a moment to experience something new, and as with Eugen praying in church, here in Austria the rules were different.

The ancient castle, a former convent from the mid twelfth century, was twenty minutes outside of Vienna and ablaze with light. Torches of sweet smelling smoke lined almost every foot of the drive and lanterns abounded. People were everywhere: in the windows, on the grounds and even on the drive. It was later in the evening, nearly midnight, and it appeared the booze had been flowing freely. Like himself, they all wore domino masks, in varying sizes. His own was simple black leather, covering the area around his eyes, matte and plain. Freffie's was an ornate half mask, white and silver, with paste diamond tear drops at the right eye. Wills' was matching black and silver with the tear drops on the left eye.

"Ah, Hagen, I should let you know that anything which happens tonight is completely off the copy book. No comments, no regrets. This particular group meets every month or so, sensualists, aesthetes and the like. Once initiated, one takes one's silence to the grave." His lips turned down under his mask. "I suppose such things will be verboten under Hitler when he comes. Has dirty fun been completely banned in the Reich?"

Hagen rolled his eyes at the irony. "Oh to be sure it has." His mind drifted back to Heydrich's debauches. If only.

"Well enjoy yourself," Freffie said with and elegant wave of his hand. "Do as you please for no one will tattle on you. Least of all me," he added, almost as an afterthought.

"I intend to be a spectator only."

Freffie nudged Wills with his elbow. "Oh where's the fun in that?"

Wills smiled lazily at Hagen; since the other night he had been far more pleasant. "None at all, but we shall see. There might be life in the old boy yet!"

Freffie gestured wildly; encompassing the entire façade of the castle, changing language from German to English with his usual facility. "Now as you might be aware, my son, this magnificent erection is the property of our young friend von Gazen, who, I must admit, has another magnificent erection, though not one that he has ever shared with me." The Graf had several drinks at the house before getting into the car, and was well on his way to his usual evening state of drunkenness.

"Oh Fref!" Wills laughed gamely, then pressed his lips to the corner of the Graf's mouth. "You are such a clown."

Freffie wound his way towards the drive. "What, Wills? You've seen that monster! I'm surprised he doesn't pass out when in a turgid state. Perhaps we should do a test, this evening. Once he's ploughing some lass, you sneak up behind him and demand he do his ten times table! See if there's blood flowing to the brain when his sceptre's engaged! It's brilliant!" The man lifted his head up like a hound, his top hat almost flying off. "Perhaps the boy could do it! You are a man of education, my dear son!" He pointed at Hagen with a gloved finger.

The thought was enough to make Hagen very uncomfortable. "I think I can live without the pleasure, Freffie."

"The thing is bloody enormous! Bigger than the one on that Nubian lad, Wills! You remember that Nubian lad in Paris?" The Graf continued as he breezed through the door of the castle.

Wills snorted, shaking his head. "How could I forget the Nubian lad, Freffie?"

"How indeed! How could anyone ever forget that masterful mahogany staff? But while I would look at the member in question with certain trepidation as regards my tender nether parts, the ladies seem to look upon it as a challenge, I daresay," Freffie blinked owlishly at Hagen. "Why do you suppose that is?"

Hagen handed his top hat, gloves and cloak to the footman who stood patiently waiting. "I couldn't hazard a guess, Freff." He wanted to escape this line of conversation desperately.

"It would be my guess, Love, that the nether parts of the female are more adroitly designed for such an invader, when your

420

nether parts are, shall we say, not specifically designed, merely manipulated to suit," Wills returned with a wink.

"Ah yes. There is a decided difference between the noble quim and the ignoble bunghole." Freffie gazed at his shoes for a time. "You know, I really hate to think of that part in that manner when it isn't engaged in its bungholery functions, but instead in a more quimly function. Perhaps we could adapt a more interesting name for the orifice when using it in a less standard way. A more quimly name."

"Oh for the love of God!" Hagen groaned as if in pain, for this was becoming intensely painful to him.

Wills picked up two champagne saucers from the tray of a passing footman, handing one to Hagen. "Throw that back and it won't hurt so much." The man said with a laugh.

"Why don't we just call it a manly quim?" Freffie liberated his own saucer from the man. "Cheers!"

They clinked glasses and the expensive champagne slid down Hagen's throat easily. He, too, had a glass of champagne at the house before he left, but knew he should keep his head about him. The stranger in a strange land was best served to be wary. He glanced around the hall, his mind taking in the ebullient, occasionally raucous laughter, the loud jazz music, the women whose gowns skirted the edges of propriety and the men in their evening dress. Above them was a giant chandelier with glittering crystals, afire not with electricity, but a multitude of flickering candles. Drops of wax fell onto the crowd from above, like water from a tree branch after a storm.

The air was a miasma of hot humanity, perfume, cologne, and over everything, a musky incense which burned from thuribles carried by beautiful young women dressed as Grecian nymphs. Hagen took a closer look as one such girl came closer; her tunic pinned at one shoulder with an ornate broach, coming to the waist to a metallic cord tie, leaving one breast exposed, her nipples and areolas covered in gold leaf. The tunic barely covered the girl's derriere and she wore sandals which tied up to her knees. Her silky hair was caught up in a coil on the top of her head, and her entire face was covered in the same gilt as her nipple, giving the girl an alien appearance.

"You know, Freff," Wills continued behind Hagen. "You could just refer to it as your M.Q. It has a particular caché, and everyone will want to use it; even if they don't know to what you are referring."

"M.Q.? M.Q.!" Freffie repeated with a chortle. "You know I like that? I do! M.Q. I do believe I will have all my monograms changed; and dashed if I won't have it put on my luggage!"

A man in unrelieved black, from his domino down came up to the trio. "Your Illustrious Highness!" The young man's voice was awash with pleasure, his German spoken with a clipped aristocratic accent. "Thank you for gracing my humble home with your presence."

"Albrecht, m'boy, I wouldn't miss it for all the tight assed Nazis to the North," Freffie winked at Hagen impudently. "Not that I'm sure I wouldn't enjoy the lot of them, but I highly doubt they would enjoy me. Though I digress! What a fabulous crush you have here, von Gazen. Fabulous. Makes von Hellenberg's wee soiree of last month seem like a child's tea party!" Freffie wrapped his arms about Albrecht von Gazen's shoulders in ready comradeship.

"Your approval is, of course, the benchmark for any humble host," von Gazen inclined his head. "Herr Ritter," he addressed Wills. "I suppose you are going to keep us all in line as usual?" There seemed to be an extra emphasis there, or was that merely Hagen's imagination?

"Bah, von Gazen, I'm in the mood for a little amusement and the night's still young. I doubt I'll be of a mind to be to responsible until at least two, perhaps even three," Wills grinned under his domino. "Even boring old Wilhelm likes to play from time to time, and I've been such a good boy!"

"Of course, mein Herr! Then let me tell you I have all manner of delights available for the connoisseur," von Gazen replied with an encompassing gesture, his face that of a barker at a fair. "In fact, I remembered a little conversation we all had about the Egyptians drinking pearls dissolved in vinegar, and lo, for my most esteemed guests, I have just such a treat."

Hagen's mind could not encompass such an extravagance. "You dissolved pearls in vinegar?"

Von Gazen's smile grew wider, almost speculative. "Of course, Your Illustrious Highness. How could I serve anything less to my most revered Graf von Reitersbach? Also I must outdo the very competitive Prinz of Zerbst. It's a very simple thing, mein Herr. What are a few pearls of wisdom to me? And my dear Graf Hagen! It absolutely raises the bar for the competition!"

"Oh yes! It completely does. Come, Albrecht! Take me to this delicacy! I must indulge before I destroy my palate with any more of this mundane Veuve Cliquot." Freffie took von Gazen's arm, gesturing for Hagen and Wills to follow along behind.

They were led into the Great Hall of the castle; the room ablaze with candlelight and torches. There was a twenty piece jazz orchestra playing at one end. A seething mass of humanity was dancing to it, their arms and legs flailing, sweat flying, bodies pressed against each other in a tangle. Many of the men on the dance floor had removed their tailcoats and were dancing in their vests and shirts; more than one woman was exposing far more than was decent as they writhed against their partners.

Interspersed about were large censers, and blocks of incense burned in them, creating a thick haze towards the ceiling. The smell of the incense seems familiar, reminiscent of Freffie's Hashish, but Hagen couldn't imagine that von Gazen would be polluting the air in quite such a fashion. After all! Hashish had to be smoked to be of any use to anyone; just having it in the air in a room of this size wouldn't have an intoxicating effect, would it?

A huge buffet ran along one wall, with every sort of delight imaginable, the food laid out around the bodies of more nymphs, both male and female, who lay very patiently in their poses. Hagen watched as one gentleman took the hand of his companion and pressed her hand into a salver of whipped cream, raising it to his face before his long tongue cleaned off the lady's limb. The man's eyes became obscene as they sucked each of the woman's fingers clean. When the couple moved off, an observant servant exchanged the contaminated bowl for another one.

The room was simply packed with people, the dark corners almost overflowing with revellers. There had to be hundreds of people here, and Hagen could hear half a dozen different languages. He saw a woman, who, from her posture was certainly not in the first flush of youth, using one of the male nymphs as a settee. The nymph was on his hands and knees while the lady perched on his back, her hands disappearing underneath his tunic to stroke his thighs and buttocks as she talked to another woman standing beside her.

All along the edges of the Great Hall were alcoves, shadowy places, some curtained partially, others completely unlit. Hagen could see the outline of writhing forms, and could hear the occasional moan of pleasure in those directions. To his other side, two women were locked in an embrace; one pouring champagne down the shoulders of the other and licking it from her partner's collarbones. Neither seemed to mind that their gowns became transparent in the act, their silk bodices plastered to teardrop shaped breasts in a way which left nothing to the imagination. So completely lost in each other as they were, the women didn't even seem to care that they were acquiring an audience.

Von Gazen led them towards a pyramid of champagne saucers which rose in a graceful tier at least fifteen feet. A frame had been built around it, a gilt edged catwalk behind the top glass; naked gilded bodies laying on the outside edge of the spindly railing. As Hagen got closer, he could see there was a small amount of liquid in each glass of the outer bottom edge of the pyramid and a medium sized pearl at rest in each one. He reckoned there had to be at least a hundred glasses with pearls in them, and his mind shrank in horror at the cost.

Freffie and von Gazen climbed the stairs of the frame, followed by two more gilded gentlemen. These nymphs' faces were gilded and their hairless bodies had been oiled to a high sheen. As Freffie crested the top of the frame, the band ceased their playing and struck up a jazz rendition of God save the King. Freffie flushed with pleasure and bowed his head regally; his hand modestly against his chest as if in surprise. Von Gazen marked each beat of the music like a flamboyant conductor as he waited for the musicians to finish.

"My lords and ladies; honourable guests; perverts and aesthetes all! Might I present to you our acknowledged sovereign, his Illustrious Highness, Frederick Graf von Reitersbach." Von Gazen began to clap, and the room took up the applause.

Freffie raised a hand to quieten the room down. "My gracious subjects, know that while I love you all, I cannot embrace you all," he leered down salaciously. "But I'll certainly give the attempt to those of you I find desirable." Then his expression became one of pious contemplation. "Politics being what they are, this might be the last of our gatherings here in Austria, though I pray one of you Frenchies or Flemmies picks up the torch soon. The Nazis are coming as I'm sure you are more than aware; my head's so damn fuddled with drink and all sorts of other things, but even I can see them knocking at the old front door," he winked down at the crowd, and then folded his hands as if in prayer. "If only it was the old back door, but I digress," he waited for the laugh like a true showman.

"But times are changing, as must we. Yes, my perverted companions, we must either go to war, lay back and take it, or flee like the rats we are. For some of you, I know that laying back and taking it will be the most pleasurable option, and all the power to you. Depending on the situation, write and let me know if it's true that Hitler only has one ball!" The laughter became quite raucous, and there was a spontaneous round of applause. "For those of you who want to go to war, let me remind you that whips and chains and a good spanking hand aren't going to do to well against the mighty Panzer legions of the Fuhrer, and his goose-stepping, firm buttocked soldiers. Might want to rethink that, what?" Then Freffie tapped his lips with a fingertip. "Then there's the option to flee. That's how people like us survive, my friends. How many of us are Austrians? Not many. I know of several dirty Hungarians, randy Italians, depraved Frenchmen; though for the record, the entire French nation is depraved; debauched Dutchmen, and their neighbours, the deviant Danes and even the odd stiff upper lipped, amongst other things, Englishman are out there amongst you. I say to you, after tonight, go back home. Go back home as fast as your two or three legs, as the case may be, can carry you. The Lady Freya only knows how much I'm thinking that summer in Gay Paris might suit this year. Take my rather uneducated advice, my loves. It's time to leave Austria."

There was silence in the room, and von Gazen threw up his hands. "But tonight! Eat! Drink! Be merry! For tomorrow we all may die!" He turned to Freffie. "As our esteemed leader, I beg of you to start our fountain." He reached down and picked up a litre of champagne and placed it in Freffie's hands. "Come on now, Herr Graf!"

Freffie bowed his head again and began to pour the champagne into the top glass. From there it poured into the ones below it and the ones below that; but like all things the bottle had to empty eventually. "Dear me, von Gazen! I usually last a damn sight longer than this! Just ask my dear von Glass!" He winked down at the crowd.

The younger man laughed merrily. "Come now, Herr Graf! Did you think I would expect you to use all your magnificence in one go? Why do you think I have these two Austrian Gods up here?" Von Gazen gestured to the two partially naked men. "To protect both your stamina and dignity!"

Freffie's eyes darted from man to man. "Dear me, yes, they are rather fine specimens, aren't they? Definitely one hundred percent to my tastes. But I must protest, von Gazen. I am not the one and only von Reitersbach anymore. There is another who is equally deserving of the honours you would bestow on my name." Freffie pointed down at Hagen where he stood in the crowd. "Come on, von Gazen! Get my son up here!"

Hagen felt a shaft of discomfort. He didn't want to be singled out this way; certainly not by Freffie, and not at a party like this. He raised a demurring hand to the men. "No, please!" He mouthed the words with a shake of his head.

"Come along, Son! This is a command performance!" Freffie cried out gamely, his eyes glistening in the torchlight.

Will's hand was on his arm, propelling him towards the catwalk and Hagen found he couldn't resist without making a terrible scene. Deftly he climbed the stairs to reach the top of the catwalk and was astounded by the sheer number of Nebuchadnezzars of Veuve Cliquot hidden amongst the nymphs' bodies. The two oiled men had begun to pour them into the top glass of the fountain, and the golden liquid fell like rain, the entire fountain ringing as successive layers of glasses overflowed to the ones beneath. The conspicuous consumption horrified Hagen, and yet it was beautiful to see.

As Hagen approached Freffie, he fixed the younger man with a steely glare. "Thank you, Daddy," he ground out from beneath his plastered grin.

Freffie thumped Hagen on the shoulder blades. "No father could be prouder!" He turned to the assemblage. "For those of you who don't know, this is my boy; the apple of my eye; the glorious progeny, Doctor Hagen Kohl Graf von Reitersbach. Soon perhaps to be the consort of my Glorious Goddess, the very pure Galiena Pfalzgräfin von Steinberg. I feel a touch of Pygmalion here, my friends, for when the boy here was sent to me, I could tell he was not one of us. I thought, what and who is this wolf in sheep's clothing? Or should I say sheep in wolf's clothing? But I took him under my wing, this friend from up North, and realised that perhaps there could be some good blood from that great black quagmire of mediocrity. You know!" Freffie waggled his brows at both Hagen and the crowd. "That quagmire of people who were born without a von! And I don't mean insult our brothers and sisters of the lower classes but it takes a great deal of practice and hard work to become an elegantly useless and self absorbed aristocrat. I dare say, I've been practising all my life, and I still don't think I have the same flair for it that Uncle Hugo had!" This time he patted Hagen on the cheek and Hagen wondered what this was in aid of. Was it more of Freffie's usual drunken rambling? "But no. The boy's done me proud. I think he's an exception to the rule and I want you all to treat him just exactly as you'd treat me; with nobility, honour, and discretion." Freffie turned and bowed to Hagen. "Say a few words, my boy, so that everyone knows you!"

Hagen turned out and faced the crowd; situated as he was, he was able to see the entire room and all the expectant faces beneath him. Then, from across the mass of humanity, almost at the end of the hall, he saw her. A woman stepped into a shaft of light in a glittering gown of metallic gold. She stood out like a sunbeam on a misty day and he was completely captivated. She wore a full domino, covering her entire face except for a cut-out for her perfect red lips. Under the lights, her hair flowed down in back in ringlets the colour of venous blood. The colour of his Galiena's hair, and she raised her hand to her throat in a perfect echo of his fiancée. She was the perfect size and shape to be his Galiena, and yet he knew it was impossible for her to be the same woman. Galiena was at Riesa, or at least she was last night. There was no way she could be here in Vienna at this party. Women like Galiena didn't come to functions like this. Not only would it be her reputation if it got out, his lady with her terrible fears of intimacy would bolt before she hit the castle entrance. To top it off, much to his eternal disappointment, Galiena would never wear a gown like that. But how could his brain have manifested the vision of his Pfalzgräfin at this party? So like the reality? If one thing was for sure, he was going to find the golden vision and find out for himself!

Chapter 31
March 4th, 1938

"Cat got your tongue, m'boy?" Freffie leaned over to him with an expectant expression.

"What?" Hagen asked, his eyes darting to Freffie with irritation. His mind was lost on the woman who so echoed his Galiena.

"You seem vacant, my son, and the entire room is hanging on your words of wisdom," the Graf drawled.

"To hell with them," Hagen muttered and scanning for the woman in the shaft of light. She was gone, as if she had never been there. What was this? He had most certainly not drunk enough to be experiencing figments of imagination.

"No, my son. These are my people, and as my boy you must address them. Come on now! Say a word or two!" Freffie cajoled, handing him an uncorked bottle of champagne.

Now was not the time to cut cards with the Devil, but Hagen felt as if he had no choice. He raised his voice to be heard about the room; his parade ground voice. "Yes. I am Hagen, newly of the von Reitersbach family. Why am I here? Obviously my new Papa felt I needed a more thorough education before I married his very pure Galiena. Whatever the reason, it will be my pleasure to meet you all later." Hagen carefully emptied the bottle into the top glass of the champagne fountain.

"Oh I bet it is, you dirty sod!" Freffie laughed crudely as he ran his hands up the oiled back of the male nymph. The servant's muscles were straining as he lifted the Nebuchadnezzar of Veuve Cliquot over his arm to continue the champagne fountain. "Who says that the apple never falls very far from the tree?"

Von Gazen leaned close with two champagne saucers on a tray, holding it still to avoid spilling. Hagen glanced down into it and noticed that unlike the rest of the pearls in the glasses, these ones were black. "Black pearls for the Prince of Darkness and his newborn son!"

Freffie took both glasses in his hands, looking into them and then back to von Gazen. "My very dear boy! My favourite!

How well you know me!" He handed one to Hagen. "Come on now, my lad! Before God and everyone! Drink! Drink!"

Hagen looked down at the pearl. Having a recent education in black pearls, this didn't look much like any black pearl he had purchased. It seemed more brownish than anything else. Still it was very round, perfectly round even. "Fref, I-" Hagen began.

"No buts, my son, unless you want to insult our host?" Freffie charged his glass to the crowd. "To you, our honoured guests!" He threw back the saucer and then stared at Hagen as if in a dare.

Hagen raised his glass to the crowd and there was a roar of approval. "To pearls in vinegar," he yelled and then poured the contents of the glass down his gullet. The mixture was incredibly bitter, possibly the vilest thing he had ever drunk, but he supposed that was the vinegar. It hit his stomach like TNT and he swallowed hard to resist tossing it back up again. He clamped his jaws together and prayed his mouth would produce more saliva, trying to get the taste from his mouth.

Then Freffie was taking the spent glass from his hand and replacing it with another. This one blessedly free of the pearl. "Have another sip of the old Widow, son. She'll cleanse your palate. I've had the previous treat before and I can attest that it sits poorly on the tongue. Trust von Gazen to get it wrong, but what can I say? The boy's but a pup and not very experienced in such things."

Hagen took the glass and had a momentary concern about his alcohol consumption so far. After this, he would take a small break from the booze. "Thank you." This time he sipped the drink, and it was the most beautiful champagne he had ever let slip down his throat.

Freffie smiled broadly at Hagen then enfolded him in his arms. "You have become my very own son this evening and I pledge to protect you as if you were my very own son!" He vowed fervently.

"Thank you," Hagen said lamely, for there was no amount of alcohol that would make him feel comfortable to be so clutched at by a man.

His adoptive father released him and returned to the rail as the two nymphs continued with their pouring of the champagne fountain. "My son!" He cried out. "I order you all! No harm shall come to him, other than that which I've deemed for him! So I demand of you all, so I entreat of you all! As your master and as your high priest!" Then the younger man picked up another large bottle of champagne and gave it a hearty shake before popping the cork and spraying the crowd, the golden wash soaking those closest to the fountain. "Let the games begin!" he screamed.

A purely juvenile urge came over Hagen, probably borne out of too much champagne, and he found himself echoing the Graf's movements. He sprayed the contents of his champagne primarily over Freffie, considering it a form of revenge for being called onto this catwalk. "Take that, Herr Graf." After all, everything that happened tonight was off the copybook.

Freffie laughed gamely when the Veuve Cliquot hit him and flashed his brilliant smile back at Hagen. "I knew you were my flesh and blood," he chortled as he took Hagen's hand and pointed towards the end of the hall where a huge swastika banner was unfurling. It floated down at least thirty feet from the ceiling to the heads of the revellers below. The banner dominated the entire back of the great hall. "Does it make you feel homesick?" He yelled in Hagen's ear as the crowd turned to look where he was pointing.

The banner hung with a heaviness which belied its texture. The entire thing seemed to shine in the strange light of the braziers. As Hagen looked at it, he almost wondered if this was some kind of a test. The banner interested him only to a point. What he really wanted to see was the golden woman he had seen earlier; discover if it was really his Galiena, and take her away from this place if it was. "Not particularly, no," he answered evenly. "I know I will see that flag again soon."

"Not like this, you won't," von Gazen murmured as he handed an old-fashioned cross bow to Freffie. The bolt on the end was far too fat to travel much distance and Hagen wondered what it was in aid of.

"This does me no good, von Gazen," Freffie moaned plaintively, as he examined the weapon. "Come on now, mein Herr! Give me what I need!"

"I've done that and a damn sight more!" Von Gazen laughed as he lit the bolt on fire with a lighter he produced from his pocket. The bolt erupted into ignition. The man began to cackle as the entire end glowed blue with flame.

"What the devil is that for, Fref?" Hagen growled as the weapon claimed more and more of his attention. It wasn't as old as he thought; definitely appearing to be of modern manufacture.

Freffie lifted the crossbow up to his shoulder and his face smoothed in concentration. "A peasant weapon with which to kill more peasants," he muttered as he tilted his head to kiss the stalk of the crossbow. "Now back away, my son, so as not to interfere with my aim. I would so hate to skewer one of my revellers instead. Praise be that I have so bloody big a target for I am a tad squiffy. I'm reduced to merely having the ability to hit the broad side of a barn, which would be all that's required tonight."

Hagen did as he was instructed and took a step back. Freffie shifted on his feet and there was a hush from below in expectation. Then the Graf pulled the trigger and the entire crossbow rang like a bell as the burning bolt arced through the air to hit the banner at the bottom of the white circle. The strange sheen Hagen had seen on the banner must have been kerosene or some other form of accelerant, for the silk exploded into blue flame which hungrily consumed the fabric. Tracing up and up, the banner turned into a sheet of blue fire. Hagen could feel the heat on his face, despite it being at least fifty feet away. The sight of it chilled Hagen to the very core of his soul, not only for the safety implications of having a flame like that in a room so crowded, but because the swastika symbolized so many of his personal beliefs. To see it defiled thusly caused him almost physical pain. So many times he had watched the banners blowing in the wind from his office in Berlin, their undulating movements calming him and to see this! This! It cut him right through to the soul.

"Nice, cheery blaze, what?" Freffie shouted into Hagen's ear, his handsome face becoming demonic in the firelight. The frenzied screaming of the revellers below become that of the damned as the orchestra struck up a perverted Jazz rendition of the Horst Wessel lied. Hell! Hagen was in Hell, and Freffie was Asmodeus himself!

It was then that Hagen began to feel the chill twisting in his belly. It was as if a knife of pure cold had been stabbed into him just below the ribcage and the nausea almost drove him to his knees. He was in the center of a maelstrom, his own anguish mixed with that terrible ice inside him. The heat of the burning banner, the screaming against the orchestra and the possessed revellers in his vision below made him shake. "No!" He raised a hand to his face, as if to shield his eyes from the abomination before him.

"Now Hagen! I'm quite crushed!" But Freffie didn't sound overly displeased in reality.

Hagen clenched his hands into fists, until his nails bit into his palms and he felt a measure of control returning. He reclaimed his posture and pulled his hands down. "Bit dangerous, don't you think, Freff? All that fire, all these people?" He tried to sound diffident and dry but his voice sounded terribly thready to his own ears. An image flashed to his mind of the bombing on the Wollzeile and the dying man he tried to help. Suddenly he was hit by a paralysing fear of the fire and what it could do to a man. With a terrifying certainty, he knew that one day he would burn, that fire would eat him away, and he would be destroyed by it.

"Nah, Hagen!" Freffie made a dismissive gesture. "Von Gazen's taken care of that. No need to worry."

Hagen nodded curtly, the cold knifing up into him again. "Then I won't worry about it. Not too much, at any rate," he added for good measure. Being responsible wasn't a skin that one was able to shed at a whim.

"I most certainly won't and I'm the one who lit the bloody thing on fire." Freffie took Hagen's arm and lead him to the stairs of the catwalk.

"Yes. You most certainly are." His foot on the first step, Hagen looked out into the crowd again. They were converging on the champagne fountain like locusts, the burning banner seemingly forgotten. What insignificant little gnats these people were! Like plebs at the coliseum, waiting for the next show the moment the last had lost its glitter. But there at the end of the room? Near the band? Was that her? The golden woman who so resembled his Galiena? What was she doing here? It was amazing how Galiena could have so true looking a doppelganger in this place. No. No. Or was she here? Was this some twisted game of Fref's? To bring Galiena to a place like this? Tear away the purity of his sainted Gallie?

Hagen descended the stairs and was swallowed by people, touching him, pulling at his clothing, congratulating him on being so honoured with the von Reitersbach name. He couldn't stand it, and the world took on a strange crystalline quality, like looking through a dark, clear amethyst. Dear God in heaven! Was he foxed? No. That couldn't be it. Three glasses of champagne, maybe four, wouldn't do this. He was a seasoned enough drinker to be sure, and he absolutely didn't have enough booze in him to explain this increasingly strange desire to throw up. He tried to move out of the throng of well wishers, backing up until his hip hit the buffet, and picked up a small plate. He hoped his inattention would make the throng disappear.

"Are you hungry, Herr Graf?" Hagen turned at the husky French accented contralto behind him. He was agog to see the blackest woman he had ever observed standing there, holding a perfect red strawberry, dripping with whipped cream in her ebony fingers. Her scarlet dress clung to her, leaving very little to the imagination. He could tell by the pertness of her stiff nipples that she was not wearing a thing underneath it. Her domino was also scarlet, just covering the area around her eyes; her lipstick matching perfectly.

Hagen eyed the strawberry and reached out to take it from her, but she curled her hand away from him. "Are you trying to torment me, Fraulein?" he asked her.

The woman leaned in with the berry, pressing it to his lips until he bit into it, before continuing in her broken German. "I would do more than just torment you, Herr Graf. Iphigenie would torture you until you cannot speak, but then the pleasure would be more than you could want." Her teeth were brilliantly white against her lips and skin; her mouth a black cavern which seemed bottomless.

The sweetness of the strawberry burst out across his palate in a way which surprised him. It was the best strawberry he had ever tasted, or so it felt. Hagen gripped the table wondering why things were becoming so much brighter now, tastes enhanced, senses on fire. There was an echo in his increasingly frantic mind. Back. So many years ago and he had a vision of his mother over him. 'Morpheus no more, Hagen,' she was saying.

"Iphigenie, my basalt goddess! I doubt that my good friend Hagen is quite up to your rather considerable talents." A voice. Familiar. Hagen swivelled his head to see the black pointed beard of his friend György Demeter at his elbow.

"I want Gallie." Hagen eyed his friend with no uncertain consternation before his stomach turned over again. "On the other hand, I might just be sick."

"And this isn't her, Hagen," György shook his head in disgust. "You poor leg shackled bastard."

"Come now, György!" The woman rubbed herself up against Hagen, her body hot against his. "Iphigenie wants the son of the Graf. While Iphigenie can't have one, she will have the other. Iphigenie is hungry too, just like him."

György moved a hand between them, his hand dipping into the woman's dress and squeezing her breast. "Nay, my black vixen. He doesn't want to play your games, even though you're the most lively fuck in France." Then he removed his hand and pushed back on her sternum, causing her to take a step back. "But I will play with you later."

The large lips twisted into a moist pout, and the dark finger traced its way up Hagen's shirtfront. "Go to Hell, György. Iphigenie will find your charming friend later and then he will scream." Abruptly she whirled and was gone like a shadow.

"Ah! The Algerian version of La Josephine; not nearly as sweet and twice as debauched." György shook his head sadly, his lip curling up in disgust. "And people who refer to themselves in the third person are so damned affected."

Hagen blinked as the colours became brighter still and he felt a blossoming euphoria in his chest instead; almost enough to counteract the frigid nausea. "There is something very wrong with me, György," Hagen pulled himself up to his feet. Again, he saw a vision of his mother against the wall, like a hazy form and her voice was in his ear. 'This will destroy you, my son.' He turned his head towards the charred banner, just an ember in the distance; barely any remained. "The fire will consume me," he whispered, lost in the embers.

"What have you had, my friend?" György's strong hands grasped Hagen's chin, tilting his head into the light of the torch.

"Don't bring me to the fire!" Hagen tried to jerk his head back as the brightness stung his eyes.

György's mouth opened with laughter, but the sound and the motion seemed disconnected somehow. "Now here is something I never thought I would see! Hagen Kohl absolutely gooned. What have you had? And don't tell me it's the hash in the air, because that shouldn't leave you like this." The Hungarian released Hagen's face and picked up a strawberry from the table. "Not that it doesn't take the edge off a man; but it's only enough to make you mildly intoxicated."

Hagen attempted to pull himself together, clenching his fists again. Where was his control? He knew it was in shreds, but he didn't know why. "Why are you here, György?" Where was the sword inside him? What was happening?

"I'm here for the fucking, Hagen. It's all about the fucking," György answered crudely. "Tonight's my night for pleasure, but then you know that about me. The eminent psychiatrist is a pervert." Then the man shrugged and a wry little smile crossed his lips. "And the drugs aren't so bad either. Which gets me back on track. What have you had, and maybe I can help you through it. You seem a little lost in yourself to have had cocaine, so what was it?"

Hagen shook his head. "No drugs. I don't use drugs." But somewhere he knew that was wrong. A little voice confirmed that György had to be right. Alcohol wouldn't fracture him like this. An image of himself in a shattered mirror flashed through his mind. "They've broken my mind."

"No, Hagen, my friend. Someone gave you something at some point, and now you are taking your first steps on a journey which will last a few hours. It's nothing to be afraid of Hagen, if only we can figure out what it is. Now I'm positive it wasn't injected, for you would have known it at the time. Did you feel a needle stick in you?"

Hagen thought about it, and became very lost in a couple along the wall. The woman was down on her knees before the man, and the man was clutching at her hair and moaning. "They really shouldn't be doing that here," Hagen whispered in consternation.

"By God's balls, Hagen! Of course they should. Now focus! Was there a needle?" György ground out in exasperation.

"No." Hagen ran his hands over his chest and was amazed at the sensation. The softness of his silk vest under his fingers was magical.

"I'm sure you know better than to take any white powder snuff." The psychiatrist tapped his lips with a fingertip

Hagen shook his head. "I'm not so gone that I wouldn't remember doing so. Snuff? No. I've never been one for snuff. It's ghastly."

"Speak for yourself, Hagen. Cocaine is quite magnificent in small doses. But as for your little problem, you ate or drank it. That's really the only method of consumption left." György slapped Hagen's face lightly. "Focus for a moment, and then I will let you do whatever you want. What have you had?"

"Dinner. Some champagne from the tray, and one of those pearls in vinegar," Hagen rattled off as a flicker of gold attracted his eye. "Galiena?"

"I seriously doubt you ate her tonight." György's frown was visible around the edges of his domino. "I had one of those pearls and they're just pearls. Very pretty, but the vinegar destroyed the champagne."

"I know. It was foul. Bitter black thing that it was." Where did that gold flash go? Where was Galiena?

György's green eyes met his own. "The pearls were white, Hagen."

"No. Mine was black. On the catwalk. I drank it with Fref."

"Oh." There was a world of understanding in that one word. "Oh. I see. Well then, Hagen, you are in for quite a night, and I'm almost envious, though not that stupid."

Hagen dropped his eyes down to those of his old friend, and felt a flash of his old self. "What is it? Freffie had the same thing."

"It would appear that the Graf inveigled you into sampling his substance Du jour. That wasn't a pearl at all, Hagen. That was a rather prodigiously sized dose of Mescaline."

437

Chapter 32
March 5, 1938

He was a fractured being. The intelligent, controlled man who was Hagen Kohl had floated away from the centre of his organism. That Hagen still had a voice in his head; the sober Hagen screamed at him to leave this devil's function and find Eugen for protection until his mind returned. The drugged Hagen, a languorous and curious creature, wanted to explore this strange new world of visions and sensations. It it left him feeling at once intrigued and bemused. Despite a disjointed rage deep in his chest at Freffie for drugging him, he couldn't bestir the will to act on the emotion. The anger was like a bee, a faintly distracting buzz on the edge of his consciousness.

"I'm fine." Hagen whispered to himself, his head becoming thicker as the nausea decreased. "It's like I'm on a boat." He refocused on György who was watching him; a half smile under his domino. "But we aren't on a boat, are we? But we could be? Couldn't we?"

His friend shook his head and laughed. "We could be to you, my friend, but we aren't. If you had forgotten, this is von Gazen's chateau."

Hagen nodded as he processed that information. "Yes. I know we aren't at sea, but the floor feels like it's rocking to me."

György patted Hagen on the shoulder. "Hagen, before you get too far along, I should let know you that you might see and hear things, like visions or hallucinations, but generally they won't hurt you. Some of my colleagues have experimented with mescaline on subjects at the university so I can say that you're fairly safe. Shamans in the Americas have been using it for centuries to commune with their Gods; they take several beads and then the Gods speak. It's fairly harmless, but it might encourage you to talk, and some people think it might make you tell the truth. But it isn't like morphine, opium or heroin and you don't need to be afraid. Do you understand me, Hagen? It's not addictive."

He rolled his eyes around in his skull; they felt so huge in their sockets. His vision fixated on a woman who was painting the exposed chest of her companion with chocolate before licking it off. The woman had discarded her mask and was attacking the man's chest with ferocious abandon. Her tongue seemed to be unnaturally long. Then he felt someone poking his arm and returned to György. "I suppose that makes sense now, György, but if you hadn't realised, I'm not exactly my normal self."

The doctor grinned back at him, his teeth glistening in the torchlight. "Yes. I had noticed that, Hagen. So does that mean we can get back to the reason we are here?"

The woman with the chocolate was busily removing the trousers of her partner, and pushing him back into the buffet. Brilliant silver bowls of fantastically hued fruit went spilled into the darkness under the table. A glowing ruby of an apple rolled to tap against Hagen's foot where it began to pulsate like a living human heart. "What are we here for again?" Hagen murmured as the blood pounding in his ears echoed the tempo of the fruit beside him.

"Fucking, Hagen. We're here for the fucking. Or at least I am here for the fucking; I haven't the foggiest notion why you are here," György answered him with a chortle.

That fascinated Hagen more than the couple having sex on the buffet table. The apple/heart had returned to being a simple piece of fruit. He frowned at György who was now rather absorbed by the intercourse going on a scant arm's length away. "And why are you here for the fucking, György? You're a psychiatrist, for God's sake?" A thought occurred to him. "Are you like Heydrich and need an adjutant to attract tail for you?"

"Heydrich?" Hagen could hear the confusion in György's voice. "I don't know who that is, but from what I can deduce, the answer would be no. I can get my own mistresses and I do have one, but she isn't like this. Not like tonight. I can sink myself into a dozen women here. and not have to buy them a bracelet in the morning. Somewhere in this museum of von Gazen's, he will have some who are really young, Hagen. I might get to pop a cherry or two and I might just buy one to take home later because a virgin can be ever so much fun for a while. Why am I here? Because it amuses me, and life is rather boring. I have to keep my cock attended to so that it doesn't disturb me when I'm busy in the real world. This is Central Europe's answer to the naughty Hellfire club and I'm just one more creatively inclined hound who knows that by being a member, I can walk into a room off this one and join into an orgy of ten or more." The smaller man winked at him, his eyes glowing with a burning hunger. "Because I've got the horns upon me and there's nothing I can't do at one of these things."

It was a lot for Hagen to take in, and the grunting of the woman beside them was becoming a distraction. "Orgy, you say? Eugen and I have shared women in the past. A long time ago we did that. Eugen's rather absorbed by the fucking," He used György's crude term. "It's not so consuming for me." He paused, lost again in a memory.

Galiena at Berchtesgarten telling him that he could never have her. Damn the woman! He would have her! She was his! Galiena was the only woman he really wanted. The realization astounded him. Then he thought about Eugen and the women they had shared. He had an incredibly graphic flash of Eugen on top of Galiena, the same way a nearby man was pushing himself into a woman on the settee. He felt himself transfixed by the thought. His woman crying out as his best friend took her. No. Eugen wouldn't do that. Would he? It was as if he was watching them in the flesh before him. Couldn't be. That wasn't Eugen and it certainly wasn't Galiena.

György shook his head, a mystified expression in his eyes. "Come now, Hagen! How can you say that? Heaven lays between a woman's thighs, if only for a moment or two."

A vision swirled around in his mind; Galiena sprawled on his desk at the Hauptamt in that billowing blue frothy thing she had worn back at Riesa. She was laid out before him, on top of his files, and calling his name while her fingers pulled that hem ever so slowly up her thighs. Those pale, white thighs. The effect on his body was immediate, both in his hallucination and in reality. "Galiena is here, György. I'm going to find her." Her perfect white feet were tracing the lip of his desk, and he just wanted to devour them. Yes. He could see her legs, bent at the knee; open and waiting for his touch.

"No, Hagen. I would stake my practice, education and reputation on the fact she's not here." György patted his arm in gentle consolation. "But we'll find someone else for you to fuck. It's not such a big deal."

Hagen pulled away from his friend suddenly, a man on a mission. He knew what he saw. "No. She's here. I saw her! I would know her anywhere." The sober, sane Hagen spoke up in the vaults of his mind. You're seeing what you want to see.

"Christos!" György swore in exasperation. "Hagen! She's not here. Now if it's blue-blooded pink that you want, there's plenty about. I'm sure I can find a Marquise at the very least for you. That should be good enough, given your new found desire for the finer things in life." The doctor inhaled deeply, his nostrils pinching as he did so. "That's not bad hashish von Gazen has burning, but watching you get higher and higher gives me the desire for something of more medicinal benefit."

Ignoring his friend, Hagen's eyes roamed around and he saw an empty chair not too far away. If he stood on it, he might spy Galiena in the crowd. She was all in gold, from her head to her feet, and that should be easy to spot. As he moved away from György, he felt the man following him. That was irrelevant to Hagen. He didn't particularly care whether or not György stayed around. "Where are you, my golden princess?" he whispered under his breath.

The psychiatrist clawed at his arm. "Don't be such a fool, Hagen."

There! There she was! On the catwalk around the champagne fountain! She stood there alone like the figurehead on the prow of a ship; still as if she was poured from molten metal. How could he get closer to her? He wanted to touch her! Taste her skin! Rip away that blank white mask and drink of her. His body was ready, and he knew once he touched her, she would be as well. "Galiena!" Hagen yelled, stretching his hand out to her, like a drowning man to a lifeboat offering salvation. He could feel his heart pounding in his chest; like the black pearl he had swallowed with Freffie. It seethed and pulsated like the red apple of earlier. He wanted to carve it out of his body. Yes. He would give it to her so that she could possess it and know she owned him. Then the worm turned in his brain. Then he would own her; never to let anyone touch her again. He would take her and then lock her up so she could exist only for him. Yes! There she was! Up on the catwalk; her arms cradling his dripping scarlet heart to her breast, her off hand beckoning to him.

"Who the hell is she, Hagen?" György yelled in his ear over the orchestra. "I don't know that woman from Adam?"

Hagen turned to György, a beatific smile on his face. "That's my Galiena, György! I told you she was here and there she stands! Now leave me be so that I can have her!"

György shrugged gamely, obviously giving up the fight. "All right, Hagen. If you think it's her, then best of luck to you! Find me after and let me know how it all went!" With that, the Hungarian melted away to search out his own pursuits.

Each foot moved of its own accord, lifting and falling with complete independence from his mind, taking him ever closer to his quarry. The black eyes in the white mask seemed to meet his own, and the blank face dropped as if in recognition. A white-gloved hand reached out to him in a beckoning gesture, calling him back to the catwalk before resting back on the rail again.

Hagen was jostled by something from behind and turned to see that the mass of dancers had swelled and moved in his direction. The frenzied swing dancing of earlier had mellowed, and the huddled forms just clung to one another, pressed into a single writhing mass. They had become a nightmare creature, all arms and legs, threatening to engulf him in their grasp. Hagen took a few steps away, tripped over an abandoned shoe, then his eyes found his destination again. The catwalk, with its painted golden nymphs hanging from the railings was empty of her. NO! She had to be there! He tore his eyes away only for a second and now she was gone. Hagen looked down at his hands and clenched them until they shook and the muscles knotted in his forearms, then he returned his vision to the catwalk. She was gone.

A spin on his heel told him she was not to be seen and Hagen sobbed in frustration. He threw his head back and forth, trying to spot anything of her, but the torches were guttering and the room's illumination was growing dimmer. The darkness itself was alive, roiling like a hot tar pit, spilling out to chip away at the monster on the dance floor. Something was touching him again; resting in his palm and Hagen curled his fingers around the stem of a glass. Champagne. The golden liquid was pure; there were no pearls in it. Hagen swallowed it down, realising that he had a powerful thirst.

442

"Thank you," he spoke to the person who gave it to him, his vision filling with a vision of green and gold velvet.

Pink lips; old and wrinkled with age, circling the peg-like teeth of an elderly woman, moved. "Let me help you, mein Herr! Come, my son!"

Fingers were plucking at his trousers and Hagen took a step back. "No. That's not for you! Not for you!" He repeated as he beat a hasty retreat, tripping and falling to his rump before springing back to his feet to look around.

There she was again! Over at the far side of the dance floor, her hands reaching out again, fingertips extended towards him. Hagen followed her, pushing through the revellers, fighting and shoving to get near her. He wanted his sword so that he could cut down everyone who stood between them. He would slay anything in his way! When he was almost close enough to touch her, she moved away again, leading him on a merry chase through the great hall. Galiena was the golden hind and he was going to capture her.

The vision led him out of the main room, fleeing down a hallway packed with people. How did she move so fast? Her head seemed to glide forward at an unseemly rate, never deviating, as if she flew high above the crowd. That made sense to Hagen. Galiena was an angel. His angel. So pure! He couldn't wait to cut his heart out of his chest to give it to her. He knew it was a present she would want! It wasn't black and withered, like the image fixating in his mind. No. His heart was an apple; bright red with a high sheen. No. His heart was the ancient, sacred swastika of Germany. The twisted cross and pagan sun wheel tattooed upon its pulsating surface. Was it burning? Why was his heart burning? Why was the swastika burning? His being was burning and the flames were carving their way up through his chest!

Hagen fell to his knees at the end of the hall where the area opened into a round room. He had lost her, and now he was burning alive. There was no salvation for him; no hope for him! He had lost her and was going to die! Hagen clawed at his collar, strangling inside his shirt, feeling the flames engulfing him. Why didn't she save him? Tears seared their way down his cheeks, the moisture spreading out under his mask. The only one who could offer him redemption was Galiena, and she had abandoned him forever. His sin was simply too great.

"Herr Graf?" The words were the barest whisper, as blessedly cool fingers plucked away his mask and gentle thumbs brushed his tears away.

She rose like a statue before him, a living, breathing goddess! Her cloth-of-gold dress gleamed in the candlelight of the room, a study in the nuances of the womanly form. Her perfume, Galiena's perfume, enveloped him in a cloud and Hagen inhaled in sheer delight. It didn't matter that she still wore that accursed blank white mask. His angel had come to him. Whatever she wanted, he would do. Whatever she craved, he would be. She owned him. She had to understand that, but how could he express the jumble of thoughts going through his head?

"Oh Galiena! Oh my Galiena! Please kiss me! Just kiss me once before I burn to death!" Hagen begged her brokenly.

Moist lips brushed his; then pressed into them ardently and aggressively. As she pulled away, she sucked his lower lip into her mouth, scoring it between her teeth. "Like this?"

Hagen climbed his way to his feet, using her body to steady himself. His penis was so hard in his trousers, he thought he was going to snap in two! The pressure was almost more than he could bear. "Tell me you aren't going to deny me! Tell me you won't say no, darling!" He kissed her back, driving his tongue into her mouth which tasted of champagne; but not, his normal mind screamed, of Galiena. "Don't deny me tonight! Please, Gallie! Please!"

"I'm for you here tonight and only for you!" Again, the words so softly spoken as to be inaudible, but they weren't right. There was something wrong. Her German was wrong. Why wasn't it her when it was her?

Hagen pulled off her mask, and felt a stab of pure unadulterated rage. She was Galiena, and yet she was not. The eyes were right, the hair was right, the face was so nearly right, and yet it was wrong. Dear God! She looked like Galiena; she acted like Galiena! She had all Galiena's mannerisms of movement, and yet, somehow it was just a doppelganger! "Who are you?"

"I am she," the perfect red lips worked out the words. "I am who you want me to be."

The visions melted and the Galiena and the not Galiena merged into one. "Please don't torment me!" Hagen growled, a maelstrom of hatred and lust rioting in his breast. "I want her!"

"Then take me!"

Hagen curled his fingers around her shoulders and drove her back into the wall. Galiena's head snapped back and her eyes unfocussed. He stalked forward and kissed her again brutally, in a way he would never touch his perfect Galiena. He punished her with his mouth, feeling her lips grinding against his teeth. "I don't want you!"

"I am who you want, Hagen Kohl." The woman shook her head as if to get her bearings, her hands rising to her shoulders to slip off the straps of her gown. Dear God! Her breasts were beautiful! Heavy and full with pink tips. "I want you to fuck me!"

Words Galiena would never say! Yet suddenly it didn't matter anymore! Hagen grabbed the woman by the neck and threw her down face first against a credenza. "Oh I am going to fuck you, make no doubt about it!"

She moaned in encouragement, sweeping off the decorations on the furniture with a wave of her hand. "Yes! Please!"

"Shut up!" Hagen pressed her down by the neck with one hand as he raised the skirt of her gown with the other. With that silky red hair running down her white back, it was Galiena again. "Don't talk to me in that voice which isn't hers!" That terrible German betrayed the doppelganger with every breath.

"Yes," the woman groaned as cold air hit her exposed derriere. She wore nothing under her dress, and her entire body was exposed for his perusal.

"Dear God!" Hagen breathed. It had been so long coming, this! Taking Galiena in a way he would never take her! All his fantasies coalesced in his head, and it was as if he wasn't having her at all, merely exploring another dream. As he kicked the woman's legs apart, opening her up further, he felt a perverse satisfaction. Hagen knew he had wanted Galiena since the State dinner last October. Maybe from the first moment he saw her, broken as she was from the brutal attentions of another man. Now she was his!

With a casual efficiency of movement, Hagen freed his straining organ from the confines of his trousers and thrust into his prey. Despite the complete lack of foreplay the woman was ready for him, wet enough that he slid into her with ease. She cried out

445

with an inhuman voice as he moved within her, bucking his hips as he took her with very little regard for her own pleasure. This wasn't about her. It was about him. It was about exorcising the ghost of a Galiena he might never have. Instead he took his frustration out on her doppelganger, ramming into her, over and over again; unable to crest into orgasm, yet unable to stop.

Her hair was a living thing, streaming across her back, and he twined his hand into it as his other hand reached around to fondle her breast. Suddenly he wanted to be merciful and attend to her needs. He wasn't a selfish man, and while he was resigned to be brutal, he wasn't resigned to be cruel. "What do you want from me?" he ground out as he rolled her hard nipple between his fingertips. He knew she wasn't completely averse to his methods by her frenzied panting.

"Hurt me! Please! I want it to hurt!"

More words Galiena would never say! Hagen dropped her breast and wrapped his arm around the woman's hips, bracing her as he rutted with abandon. He threw his entire body into his task and the doppelganger began to shriek her encouragement. Like an animal, he leaned over and bit the back of her shoulder until her scream became that of pain. Contrite, he licked the wound, but her voice had changed again. The pain set her free and she reached around with her arm, her claws grabbing at his tuxedo jacket in encouragement.

Hagen pulled the woman up by her hair until he could see her lips and attacked them, pulling her head back, straining to kiss and bite at her flesh. He rolled them off the credenza and they fell to the floor in a tangle of limbs. She was on her back and he picked up her legs, throwing them over his shoulders so he could take her as hard as he could. Then it began. He was almost there. The woman screamed before one last dizzying thrust and his seed erupted into her body. Hagen collapsed onto her torso, stinking of sex, too exhausted to move.

Afterwards, in that strange endless moment of afterglow, her fingers plucked at his hair, smoothing it away from his face gently. The way Galiena would, or so he dreamed on so many lonely nights. Dear God! He wanted this to be her so badly; but it wasn't and would never be. He had betrayed his Galiena with this succubus, and the pain cut him right through to the soul. Now she

446

wouldn't want his heart; wouldn't take his heart because it was fouled. It was that desiccated, burnt thing in his chest; still and lifeless, like a great lump of coal. He was empty. So terribly empty that it caused him physical pain.

He moved to roll off the woman, but she stayed his action by wrapping her arms and legs around him. "No. Stay for a moment. Please!"

"What have I done?" He asked himself aloud. It shouldn't matter to him; he was a man after all and such things weren't forbidden to him. But it did matter. It mattered very much.

"You did what you were supposed to do, Doctor Kohl," the woman whispered in her strange lilting German. "It probably saved your life. They want me to kill someone tonight, and most of them are insisting it be you!"

Hagen could feel her sweat against his cheek, where his head lay between her breasts. "Everyone wants to kill me. Lutz. His cronies. The Heer! So many." He rambled against her skin. The rational part of him was screaming to be quiet. This wasn't Galiena! Yet he could see them all, converging on him in marching ranks. Their eyes burned and they screamed out for his blood. Behind them came the bodies of all those he had killed, Kurt von Schleiser and his wife leading the pack; blood streaming from terrible gun shot wounds. He pulled away, trying to cover his eyes from the awful visions. No! They were dead. DEAD! They couldn't get him, not while he was alive; yet in this nightmare world, they could do as they pleased.

Hands were on his face. "Oh what have they done to you? He did this to save you, you know! He sent me to save you, the only way he knew how. The Warriors wanted you to be the Augury, but their blood is so high!" She slapped his cheek. "Doctor Kohl, you have to focus! You have to listen to me!"

He met her gaze, desperately trying to pull himself together, and ignore the blazing eyes which filled every corner of the room. The blazing eyes of the people he had killed. The blazing eyes of the people he would kill. They burned and flared in the darkness. "Who are you?"

"They call me Freya, but that isn't my name," her strange accent jarring in his ears.

"You aren't German! Who are you and what are you?" Hagen demanded, clutching at her jaw to look at her better. No. She wasn't Galiena. He could see that now, as the lust subsided. Her face was thinner, the cheekbones sharper, and her dark brown eyes had flecks of green in them that Galiena's didn't have. Most telling was that despite the fact she wore Galiena's perfume, underneath the scent she didn't smell like Galiena.

"My name is Gormghlaith. I'm Irish," the girl smiled down at him almost shyly.

Hagen tried to say the word again slowly, the pronunciation being very foreign. "Gor-em-lee?"

Her body shook with laughter at his poor pronunciation. "Good enough, I think. It's probably easier if you call me Freya like the rest of them," She sobered abruptly, the gentleness leaving her face. "They said it was astounding. Even my name was close to this Galiena's. They saw me singing in Galloway and brought me here years ago. I didn't mind. I was just a poor singer from the gutter, but now! Now it is changed, Doctor Kohl. It isn't fun anymore. People are getting hurt, and tonight, more than hurt."

Hagen pulled away, feeling around for a handkerchief to wipe himself clean before doing up his trousers. He felt so strange being completely dressed, his clothing barely disturbed while she lay there all akimbo, her dress just a ring of fabric rucked up about her waist. She was so pale except where her body was smeared with her own lipstick, most likely from his lips. "I don't understand?" he asked as he rubbed his lips on the back of his hand to remove any marks. The patterns on her body began to move of their own, like snakes under her skin. Hagen shook his head trying to dispel the hallucination. Another moment and he ripped off his tail coat to cover her with it.

Gormghlaith wrapped her arms around him, pulling his head back down against her chest. "I'm afraid, Doctor Kohl, but not so afraid as to go to the police because they won't believe me. Some of the men are very decent! You have to understand that. I like them very much for they have been very good to me! I live like a princess, and most of what I do is not objectionable. They are very gentle when they want me; the older ones often just hold me. I like that. The younger ones are more enthusiastic, but I'm not so bothered when I am in the mood. They are very courteous about it and being their Priestess was enjoyable until recently when things changed. The Priests just want to bring back their king, some man named Otto who lives in Belgium. It's the Warriors who want to start killing. I don't want any more blood on my hands." She drew in a deep breath. "And they are very afraid of you, Doctor Kohl. They know what you are and they want to make an example of you. The balance of power in the group is shifting to the Warriors, and they will kill you."

"Because I am a German?" Hagen furrowed his brow. Listen! The rational Hagen shouted. This is important! Listen to this woman!

"Because you are black. That's what the Warrior said. Because you are of the black. Something like that, I don't quite remember. He wants you to be the Augury, because you are important in Germany. The Warrior wants to use you to start the war," Tears glistened in the girl's eyes, and Hagen was struck by how young she was, certainly younger than Galiena.

"Why are you telling me this? Why don't you run away?" Hagen asked her, a strange moment of clarity from the fog. Did she know he was in Austria to hunt the NAO? Did they?

"I can't! They hold my papers, and I have been happy here. But I don't want to see anyone die, and I know that another is conflicted. He doesn't want you hurt. The Priest doesn't care if you live or die, but Freffie does, and the Priest will make me kill you if he finds you!" Gormghlaith traced a shaking hand up his cheek. "So I am going to hide you where they won't think to look. Right above them in God's bosom." She leapt to her feet, tugging impatiently at Hagen. "Come on! Get up! We don't have much time!"

December 26, 1937
Dearest Poppet,

Our usual night. You didn't come for Christmas. Will you come
with the New Year? I am so lonely. It is gnawing at me. I would
come to you, my sweet, but Göring has promised to shoot me if I
come near you. How dare he presume to threaten me! What lies is
he telling you? That monster! It makes me so angry to think of him
filling your mind with poison. I will come to you as soon as I am
better. I vow I will.
Eternally yours,
Meinrad

Chapter 33
March 5, 1938

    All her life Galiena had heard the phrase, 'the road to Hell
is paved with good intentions,' and by three a.m. when she pulled
into Deutsche Zeppelin-Reederei airfield, she had coined it instead
as 'the Road to Friedrichshaven is paved with recriminations.' She
had tortured herself the entire drive; what was she doing? Why was
she doing it? What purpose would it serve to let the monster
Meinrad von Steinberg go? Was it because she was weak? Was it
because she was stupid? Was it because she couldn't accept
responsibility? Was it because she had become his creature? Was it
because she loved Riesa? Was it because she loved him? Was it
because she wanted it to happen again?
    Round and round she went the entire drive along the
autobahn. In twenty-four hours, she had driven from one end of the
country to the other, which was an incredible distance in which to
contemplate one's actions. Yes. It was never good to be up too
long and alone with one's thoughts, Galiena decided, draining the
dregs of her mickey as she passed through the airfield gates. Just as
it was probably not beneficial to drink and drive, as she was doing,
or drink and take that magical little pill of von Schilling's, for the
effect was quite electric on the female body. Oh dear Heaven!
Galiena felt alive! Her entire body was on fire! Sleep? Who the

hell needed sleep? She was so awake; her arms were exploding with energy. Her fingers had been tapping their way across the steering wheel of their own accord since her last rest break; completely in step with the lecture she had given herself along the way.

Perhaps she shouldn't have taken two of von Schilling's little pills; but after her misery when she left Buchenwald, her energy reserves had been decimated. There had been nothing left, so at her only rest stop, she washed them down with two overdone wursts at the pension Kaiserschlaf in Aalen; her predetermined rest stop. She and Ishmael had agreed on Aalen because it was two thirds of the way to Friedrichshaven. What a difference the pills made. Now she knew why Dickie always cautioned her against Freffie's drugs; they made her feel like a God!

Unfortunately, released from her desperate need to concentrate on staying awake; Galiena was free to hate herself, and this evening, she did. Her mind, while covered in a veneer of exaggerated alertness, was doggedly focused on her mistakes and shortcomings. Dear God! She was so alone, and so lonely. What had happened to her soul and her strength? Was the only place where she found any strength at the bottom of a bottle?

Alone in her car, for Wolff was in the limousine with her grandfather, she had all the time she needed to run it over and over in her head. What in God's name had she just done? Had she turned into another Verina? Did she want the Pfalzgraf to get his hands on her again? Was that why she had brokered this hell spawned agreement with Himmler? Could that really be it? No. it couldn't be true. She had slain this demon well and truly two months ago. No. This was something else. Something different. It was business! How many times had she screamed that word out in the silence of the Horsch?Business! At the last petrol stop, she had even kicked her tire as she called out that word to the heavens.

The other word to torment her was Riesa. Tonight, she hated Riesa. What was Riesa anyway? A castle? A now defunct principality? A corporation? A dream? Perhaps that was it. Riesa was a golden dream; just as Germany was a golden dream, and a dream her father had been willing to die for. What was her sacrifice by comparison to his? Nothing. What had she asked of herself, really? A suspension of her own hatred for a man who victimized her. That was nothing by comparison to her father who had died to protect Riesa and Germany from their enemies. In terms of the present situation, the Pfalzgraf and his power were still needed to protect Riesa. Galiena's sacrifice was not so great in those terms. Still, every mile brought more accusations and justifications against herself, and now here she was, at the end of her journey, and no closer to any inner peace.

What a journey it had been, too! At the Buchenwald gate, Galiena had far outstripped the overburdened old Rolls Royce. She had informed Ishmael to stop as required for his passengers and to meet her at the Pension Kaiserschlaf, close to the A7. Galiena stayed at the small pension two years ago and had asked Swanhilde to phone and let them know she would be stopping there for a few hours rest sometime between nine and eleven in the evening. The Horsch made the drive easily in three and a half hours, and the innkeeper had been ecstatic to have the patronage of so distinguished a guest, no matter for how short a time. The three hours she spent curled up in a wingback chair in front of the parlor fire had been pure bliss, and the insistent slapping of her hand which returned her to wakefulness had been an unforgivable cruelty. With trepidation she had opened her eyes to meet those of Karl Wolff, who wore an expression of indefatigable resignation.

"Pfalzgrafin von Steinberg, you may wish to find your feet before the Pfalzgraf finds you," he had said, and not unkindly. At mention of her Grandfather, the man's eyes turned positively flinty.

"My thanks, Gruppenführer Wolff," Galiena spoke, stretching. He left before she could say more, heading off the Pfalzgraf before she could be cornered. It was a consideration on the part of Wolff, and she'd managed to choke down her pills and her wursts in some privacy before her grandfather appeared.

"Poppet! I will speak to you now," that beautiful voice surrounded her.

Galiena, defenceless, had pressed herself into the wall, feeling such apprehension at the situation. "There isn't time, Grandfather. I must get to Friedrichshaven to finish the arrangements for your departure. The Graf Zeppelin is waiting, as I am sure the Ritter von Kleist has told you."

"It can await my pleasure, Poppet. It is my money which is holding the airship, after all." Meinrad had walked ever closer, and Galiena could feel the wainscoting pressing into her back. "We have things to discuss. Important things. I am quite pleased with everything von Kleist has told me."

"We can talk at the airfield, Grandfather." Her tired voice had been in threads. Now she cursed her rest. If she had continued on her way, this could have been avoided.

A condescending glance from the old aristocrat had taken in the overly bourgeois hallway. "I don't think we should continue on tonight, my poppet. I think we should spend the balance of the evening here." The Pfalzgraf's eyes had taken on a lascivious gleam. "You and I should confer on the direction we intend to take the family holdings." His hand, with its crêpe-like skin had landed on her shoulder like a weight.

"I gave my word that we would hold the Zeppelin up no more than was absolutely necessary, Grandfather. I called in several favours in both your name and my own to make this happen," Galiena blustered, trying to make him see reason. It was all she could do to keep from screaming at his touch.

"That is little consequence in terms of my will, Poppet. I'm sure you realize that," the Pfalzgraf returned with a tiny smile playing about his lips.

"But it means much in terms of the Reichsführer-SS's will, Your Royal Highness," Wolff answered coldly, from where he stood in the doorway behind Meinrad. "We will depart now. You have a rendezvous with the border that, while I would be very pleased to see you miss, the Pfalzgräfn would not."

Her grandfather hadn't bothered to turn around to face Wolff; his face just took on an inexplicably cruel cast as he stared at Galiena. "You are one man, Herr Gruppenführer. Don't presume to threaten me like some arrogant little puppy."

"Am I?" The words were low and amused, as if Wolff was aware of something everyone else wasn't. "Do you honestly think the Reichsführer is so great a fool as to only send one man along when you have several with you? The SS didn't get to where it is by not understanding basic mathematics, Your Royal Highness, and your ostentatious English limousine is not hard to follow."

The Pfalzgraf moved his hand from Galiena's shoulder to cup the back of her head. In the car she had taken her hat off and undone the back of her hair, let it stream down her back like a young girl's, her locks dropping down past her shoulder blades. With his gnarled claw twining its way against her scalp she felt so unprotected. "The Pfalzgrafin von Steinberg is exhausted. We will stop for the night."

"Herr von Steinberg, you will go now to Friedrichshaven; if the lady chooses to remain here in Aalen that is her affair. I'm under very strict orders to see you to the Graf Zeppelin or in the event you do not reach it in time, back to Konzentrationslager Buchenwald," Wolff retorted, his omission of the Pfalzgraf's title an obvious insult. "Don't test me further, mein Herr. I'm neither impressed nor intimidated by you. I know your motivation is not as altruistic as you would make it."

Galiena knew this situation had to be defused, so she kissed her Grandfather on his cheek, and pulled out of his grip at the same time. "I'm fine, Grandfather," she whispered as her lips touched his skin, her body screaming out against the contact. "There will be plenty of time to talk before you board the airship. Now is not the time to argue with Gruppenführer Wolff. He is bound to obey his orders and you cannot expect less of a loyal soldier."

"I do not consider them to be soldiers of any stripe," the old man growled in her ear as he allowed her to precede him.

Galiena sent a grateful and apologetic glance at Wolff as she came abreast of him. "Then you would be in err, Your Royal Highness."

Wolff gestured towards the lobby of the pension. "Madame." He allowed her to pass him. "Will you be remaining here?"

"No thank you, Herr Gruppenführer. I will continue." Galiena moved towards the innkeeper who was waiting with her overcoat and small hamper. She hoped it had been refilled with food and brandy as she had requested on her arrival. She found that chewing kept her more alert. That combined with von Schilling's magic pills should keep her on the road.

Wolff came over, taking her scarlet coat from the innkeeper and held it patiently. "I assumed you would, Your Serene Highness." Again the resignation in his voice. He would never understand her actions of today; more appropriately, he would never understand her betrayal of his friend.

Galiena slipped her arms into the sleeves, all the while feeling her Grandfather's burning scrutiny. Where had she put her hair pins? Could she wind her hair up so he couldn't see it? Thankfully, the Ritter von Kleist emerged from the dining room, and claimed the Pfalzgraf's attention; giving Galiena a moment's breathing room. "Thank you again, Herr Gruppenführer."

"I but do my duty, Madame," Wolff inclined his head with a particular grace. Still his words were hard.

She turned, unable to help herself, and examined him from the brilliant silver bullion which piped the edges of his cap, the proud eagle below it. The disquieting skull with its grinning, peg-like teeth, polished leather visor, down to his flinty pale blue eyes and tight, thin lips. "But I understand, Gruppenführer Wolff, just how hard it is to do ones duty when one hates the duty being done."

His eyelids dropped, and Galiena was struck by how long his blond eyelashes were. "Pfalzgrafïn von Steinberg, I am a soldier. I do as I am commanded without question, which is as it should be. You are a civilian, which means you have the luxury of contemplation before you act upon your desires. I hope you made ample use of that luxury before you embarked on this course."

It was a rebuke, and it stung. Galiena took a step back from him and fumbled with buttoning her coat. "I did, Herr Gruppenführer. For many, agonizing hours. Do you think I did this blithely?" She snatched up the hamper that stood by his gleaming black boot. "I-" she stuttered stupidly. "I will meet you at the Zeppelin yards."

'Pfalzgrafïn von Steinberg," the black toe took a step towards her. "I misspoke. Please-"

Galiena cut him off as she fled towards the door. "You spoke as you intended, mein Herr and your words aren't without merit," she conceded. The door closed behind her, and she was in the freezing cold night. Did he really think her so inane? Perhaps. She had given him little reason to think otherwise.

The Horsch was near the door, as was the Rolls Royce, and a third car that carried her Grandfather and von Klopfer's luggage and Montrose. She dashed to the relative safety of her car and tossed the hamper in the passenger's seat, pulling her mickey out as she did so. A furtive glance back at the door to ensure her privacy and Galiena took a deep swig of the brandy, allowing the burn to roll across her tongue. Then something caught her eye; a flare across the street in the dark of the night. She examined the gloom to see a fourth car, a black Opel sedan parked in the shadows; the windows down and men inside. Another flare, as a second man lit his cigarette, and Galiena made out the shape of another visor cap. Wolff wasn't alone; he had his pack following at a discrete distance.

That thought had sent the spear of guilt back into her chest. She drove her forearm into the doorjamb of the car in her frustration. The pain was a balm, and bruises would fade. There was no time for self indulgent inner turmoil. Galiena threw the Horsch into gear and peeled away from the pension, the squeal of her tires loud in the silent night. Let the SS try and keep up with her. Only the devil traveled with her tonight.

So now here she was; the Deutsche Zeppelin-Reederei airfield. The mammoth craft was out of its hanger, a gigantic cigar bathed in the silver lights beneath it; ropes securing it to the ground while it waited for her Grandfather's arrival. The airship was a thing of incredible beauty, with its gleaming sides and graceful gondola. Far above, on the rudder fins, one could just make out the blood red of the swastika banner.

The gondola was awash with light, forms moving inside at cabin windows. Galiena suspected some of the passengers would be asleep by now, peacefully waiting to ghost into the sky. There were men all around the outside, holding ropes, double-checking and triple checking for safety, and loading last minute cargo. She manoeuvred the Horsch towards the main hanger, an equally huge building with several smaller buildings nearby, and parked clumsily, long having past caring about such things. The guard at the gate had telephoned ahead, or so it seemed, for the minute the Horsch came to a rest, a tired and harried looking man emerged from a block of offices.

"Your Serene Highness? I am Kurt Wessel, junior director of the Deutsch Zeppelin-Reederei. Let me welcome you to Friedrichshaven." Wessel was younger than she was expecting, mid thirties at the latest, in a rumpled suit jacket and shining new party pin at the lapel.

Galiena rose unsteadily to her feet, the blood or something else rushing to her head. A light breeze plucked at her hair and she raised a finger to pull a strand from her lipstick. "Thank you, Herr Wessel. My special thanks in return for being so accommodating to the Von Steinberg Gesselschaft in holding the Graf Zeppelin for us. It is most appreciated," she smiled at him.

Wessel bobbed his head as he came closer and a faint blush appeared to cross his face. "No. It is us who must remain grateful. That a gentleman of the Pfalzgraf's most high esteem would choose to fly on the Graf is of great importance to us."

She couldn't help but smile. "How can you say that, Herr Wessel? The Pfalzgraf and I have very fond memories of the Graf Zeppelin. It took no extra fortitude to book this passage on either of our parts."

The young man appeared very interested in his shoes. "After the unfortunate accident of last year, many of the more important people in the world would rather spend the nine days it takes to go to South America by ship, rather than the three it takes by us."

Galiena made a dismissive gesture with her hand. "A cousin of my mother's met his end on the Titanic, Herr Wessel, yet it has never stopped me from traveling by ocean liner. Why would the Hindenburg have more of an impact on my Grandfather or me?" Galiena winked at Wessel. "The von Steinbergs are nigh on invincible, mein Herr." She thought of her father. No. The good von Steinbergs died young. It was the bad ones who lasted.

The Rolls Royce was coming up the road towards them and Galiena had the urge to go diving into her car for what was left of her brandy bottle. The mickey might be empty, but there was always the bottle she had in the trunk, and another in the bar built into back seat of the saloon. No. She could make it through this without another sip, but she did reach into her bag for a candy to hide the smell on her breath. Her foot started tapping impatiently when her bag of mints became elusive, and Galiena couldn't believe how very jittery she was. Alive, awake, but jittery. Finally the bag materialized, and she popped the sweet between her lips with a sigh of relief. Her arms laced themselves around her waist in a self-protective gesture, as Ishmael let her Grandfather and the rest out of the car.

"Come, Herr Wessel, let me introduce you to my grandfather." Galiena manoeuvred the executive so that he was between her and the man she feared so much. The Pfalzgraf managed a few moments of polite conversation, then dismissed the man and limped over to speak to von Kleist. They drifted back to the hood of the Rolls Royce, where her Grandfather was signing a sheaf of papers; von Kleist making notes as the old man spoke. Von Klopfer claimed Wessel, taking him off to the office buildings and Montrose, carefully carrying a chest to his breast, was in the midst of a discussion with a porter. Karl Wolff stood slightly away from the Rolls Royce, making a gesture down the road with his hand, presumably at the men he had following. Would that she could just slip away now! Drive back home to Carinhall and be done with this! The last twenty-four hours had been nothing on these final moments of anxiety. The pressure was crushing her.

Galiena moved back to her own car and opened the passenger side door. She deftly slipped von Klopfer's two gold bars into her wicker hamper; a more discrete way of giving them away to the odious man. The seat of her car was too inviting, and a moment later she was sitting, trying to pull her scattered wits together. She had been up nearly forty-eight hours and despite her magical pills that kept her awake, the toll on her mental acuity was more than beginning to show.

Galiena didn't know how long she had been sitting when a commotion caught her attention and she rose from the car. Wolff had moved closer to the Rolls where he was talking to von Kleist, and a very apologetic Wessel was approaching them. Montrose and her grandfather were having some kind of an exchange beside one of several large trucks which must have pulled up from the other side of the airfield.

"I'm afraid our customs agent says these papers are not valid, Herr Ritter," the young man looked around furtively, his face taut and pale.

The grotesquely obese von Klopfer took that minute to round the end of the Horsch. "Pfalzgrafin, I do believe you and I have some unfinished business to discuss." There was a light in von Klopfer's eyes which disturbed Galiena.

458

'I do beg your pardon!" Von Kleist answered, taking the out stretched passport from Wessel. "They are indeed valid for I verified them myself with the customs authorities." He opened up the folder and leafed through the pages. "Of course they are valid. They are stamped until March 1st 1942."

Galiena held up a hand to von Klopfer. "One moment, mein Herr. I have what I promised you, but I would hear the right of this."

Karl Wolff leaned over von Kleist's arm, a golden brow completely disappearing under his uniform cap. "Might I see those?"

The passport was given to the SS General with all due deference. "Please be my guest."

Wolff examined the pages in detail, and then pulled a pen from his jacket to make a notation inside the book. "They are valid, and I have just signed for them. I'm sure your man will recognize my name. I'm not unknown in such circles. Take them back to your customs man and tell him who signed for the Pfalzgraf."

Wessel took the book back and disappeared into the building. Von Kleist and Wolff resumed their conversation so Galiena returned to von Klopfer. "Thank you for your patience, Herr von Klopfer. Yes. I have what I promised you," she repeated stupidly.

"Might I have a moment of Your Serene Highness' time? I would tell you how impressed I am by your skill and diplomacy in this situation with the Pfalzgraf. I must admit I didn't think you could do it and you have more than proved me wrong." Von Klopfer told her, a greasy sweat rolling down his temples. She found she could smell him; a thick, pungent aroma of body odor mixed with expensive, musky cologne. The two scents clashed with each other in such a way to surround him in a noxious cloud. "Please? A moment in private?" He offered her his arm.

Galiena glanced at Wolff but saw that he and von Kleist had the situation well in hand. Reluctantly she allowed von Klopfer to lead her over to the near the trucks, out of easy earshot of the Rolls Royce. "A moment, yes. What is it that you wanted?"

"Your Serene Highness has shown herself to be far less callow than I had thought. If I was difficult, then I apologize," von

Klopfer bowed his head and took a step towards her. "It wasn't my intention to add to your difficulties, Madame."

She narrowed her eyes, finding this sudden humility in von Klopfer a trifle false. She stepped backwards, trying to escape him and his despicable body odor. "Thank you, mein Herr."

Another motion at the doors of the building and Wessel was back, returning to Wolff and von Kleist. Galiena could just barely see them from where she was. "Excuse me, Mein Herren, but the agent says they aren't valid, and he just accused of me making this signature. I'm sorry, but until this is cleared up, I cannot let the Pfalzgraf board the zeppelin."

Wolff snorted derisively; disdain rolling with every word. "Oh, they're valid," he drawled dangerously.

"They were perfectly valid before," von Kleist replied, looking even more cadaverous in the gloom. "I had them validated at Gestapo Headquarters in Berlin."

Wolff glanced sharply at von Kleist. "Did you? Let me see those papers again." There was a strange suspicion in his voice as he retrieved the small book from Wessel.

The Ritter drew his head back indignantly. "If one wants something done right, one does it themselves, and I did this myself."

"I don't doubt you, Herr Ritter. At this moment, I'm doubting someone else, or more importantly, I'm worried someone else might have interfered." Wolff furrowed his brow under his cap. "But no. These appear to be in correct order."

Galiena stepped closer to von Klopfer, trying to see around the truck. "I should go see what that is all about."

Von Kleist shook his head slowly. "I'll go in and talk to the man. This to-ing and fro-ing is useless."

"See now! The Reaper's attending to it. You've done your part, Pfalzgrafin. Let us look after everything else," von Klopfer said soothingly, putting a hot, sweaty palm on her arm to keep her from passing him.

Wolff glanced in her direction with consternation and then nodded. "I'll come with you as I can supersede all this nonsense. For the Pfalzgrafin's sake, let's just get this over quickly."

Galiena sent Wolff a grateful smile and would have lifted her hand in recognition had it not been full of the hamper handles.

The forty-eight pounds of gold was starting to pull her arms from the sockets. "Yes. Thank heaven for the Ritter von Kleist," Galiena realized how close she was to von Klopfer and stepped back again. "I'm sorry, Herr von Klopfer if I didn't give you much choice about this trip to Brazil. I may have been overly heavy handed, but I know my Grandfather will need his indispensable private secretary at his side in the months to come."

"That is very gracious of you, Madame." The fat man took another step closer to her. "Very gracious indeed. No. I am resigned to the change of scenery, at least for a short time."

She couldn't help another few steps backwards and cursed herself, for she could no longer see the door of the building. "And your family, Herr von Klopfer? Will they be joining you in Brazil for the duration?"

"Yes, they intend to follow on a Hamburg-Amerika line ship next month. The Pfalzgraf has very graciously agreed to send them first class," von Klopfer spoke slowly, as if considering his words very carefully.

It was so dark between the two vehicles. It wasn't that it was that they were parked so close together, but the angle mixed with the height and the time of night, made it seem as black as pitch. "Then you shan't be lonely."

Von Klopfer's teeth flashed in the darkness. "No. I shan't be lonely." He gestured towards the hamper. "Isn't it a little late for a picnic, Madame?" He came closer to her.

Galiena backed up even farther and put the hamper down. "I believe this is the picnic I promised you, Herr von Klopfer."

The middle aged man leaned over with a surprising agility given his size and opened the basket. "Ah, yes. My picnic. Thank you very much, Your Serene Highness."

Her mouth was turning unnaturally dry. "A bargain is a bargain. Never let it be said that I don't keep my word."

"I'm glad to hear that, my very precious Poppet." Like lightning she was being pulled back against the black fox collar of her Grandfather's coat; his gloved hand around her throat. The pressure was just enough to keep her very still. "Very glad indeed." The words were silkily spoken, thick like syrup.

Chapter 34
March 5, 1938

Hagen watched as the fake Galiena repaired her dress and then covered her shoulders with his jacket again. "Why should I trust you?" Now that his lust was slaked, he felt the need to sleep. To focus on what she had to say was becoming increasingly more difficult.

Her hand came down towards his face. "Because I love Freffie, and would do anything for him. He's the one who brought me here in the first place. To the Devil with the Grandmaster and what he wants! The Grandmaster is losing control of himself and his original aims. He never wanted them to start killing in the beginning."

There was such desperation in her eyes that Hagen decided to believe her. He rose to his unsteady feet. "Then take me to this hiding place."

Gormghlaith took his hand and moved to a section of the wall, pulling it out to reveal a hidden passage. "I brought you to this room for a reason. I knew there was a way out from here." They disappeared into the gloom, and Hagen could smell cold, fresh air. It helped his head even more. Eventually she brought him to the back side of a door, pushed it open and they were outside.

Hagen couldn't orientate himself, as they were on the back side of the castle, and Gormghlaith was tugging him into the woods. It was cold out, and he shivered in his shirt and vest, drenched as they were with sweat. As they ran into the trees, he began to see things, more shapes moving. Wolves! It had to be wolves! Hungry wolves with pearly fangs which would rend them both. "They are going to eat us! The wolves!" He pulled back on her hand, causing her to stumble.

Her brown eyes caught his. "No. That's all in your mind. It's the mescaline. There aren't any wolves in this forest. Come on, now, Doctor Kohl! I know it seems bad and it's only going to get worse before it improves. Now that you aren't breathing the hash, you should feel better. They give it to me from time to time to give me visions, so I understand. Listen to me! There are no wolves near us."

462

He decided to believe her for what else could he do? "Where are you taking me?"

"There's an abandoned chapel that they use as a meeting place. That's why I know Herr von Gazen's castle so well. I live here occasionally when I am not living with one of the other Priests. They share me so that no one Priest is exalted over another. That is the Grandmaster's rule." Gormghlaith dove back into the night, almost too fast for him to follow. "They will be on the paths by now, rounding up the followers. They use these parties as an excuse to meet en masse. The rest of the time, the Grandmaster meets them in small groups." She paused and turned her face back over her shoulder to wink at him. "And because Warriors are such randy sods that they like to get their blood up before they come to chapel. They say it's what their ancestors did. I can't dispute it. My people, the Celts, did similar sorts of things too."

Out of the trees, they came to the edge of a clearing. Rising up above them was a small chapel, its roof a ruin and all the windows missing. Hooded and robed figures talked at the entrance holding torches. Their young men's voices were loud and raucous to Hagen's ears. Gormghlaith raised a finger to her lips, and pushed him back into the bushes, leading him around to the back of the building where there were no lights. With a furtive glance, she picked up her skirts and ran across the bare land to the walls of the building. Fumbling, his limbs not moving in sync with his brain, Hagen followed. He very carefully tried to focus his mind on what he was trying to do so that the hallucinations wouldn't affect him.

"Boost me up through the window," Gormghlaith ordered him and he did so. The window was about waist height, making the task not too difficult, but like his Galiena, the girl was no slender reed. When she was safely in, Hagen scrambled over the sill himself, into a room which had certainly seen better days. It was obviously the sacristy in its previous incarnation and the NAO seemed to use it for the same purpose. White and grey robes lay over a table, arranged with other strange regalia.

Without speaking, she took his hand and pulled him over to a rickety staircase. Very quietly the girl crept up them. Hagen followed, almost putting his foot through a hole in the stairs. She waited for him at the top. "Get down on your hands and knees and

463

crawl out into the gallery. The rail is spindly, so keep your back to the wall. Whatever you do, don't make a sound! They will kill you if they find you here." She looked just the tiniest bit afraid. "And they will probably know how you got here and who brought you. I would very much like for that not to happen."

Hagen nodded as he looked into the brightness below him. Several burning torches had been set up in a ring around a slab altar, each at the points of the pentacle star. Right beneath him he could see two thrones, one on a raised platform. The main doors to the church had opened and white and grey robed figures were filing in.

Gormghlaith patted his arm and returned down the spiral staircase. Hagen dropped to his knees and poked his head down to watch her. If he was careful he could just see into the room below. The fresh air had helped his head a great deal, and perhaps he was sobering in tiny increments. He hoped so. He didn't want to fall down into that maelstrom of insanity again. But to be cautious, he curled up into a ball, trying to watch the girl down in the room, and keep an eye on the main chapel at the same time.

Gormghlaith was stripping herself of her golden gown, when a grey robed man entered behind her. "Well, well, well!" Hagen knew that voice and it made him quite paranoid. He tightened himself up further. "Here's our little Goddess. And what have you been up to, Lady Freya?"

The girl spun, seemingly unconcerned about her nakedness and Hagen could see the mark of his bite on her shoulder blade. "I was at the party, mein Herr. It's allowed. You know that it is. What can I do for you? I must prepare."

The man threw back his hood, and Hagen recognized Wilhelm von Glass. "Yes. I can smell that you've been to the party, Lady Freya. I can smell man upon you. But who?" There was so much menace in those words. "If I were to taste you, who would you taste like?"

"You needn't worry, Warrior. It was one of the faithful." Gormghlaith turned her back on Wills and moved towards the table with her clothing on it. "Now leave me be." The dismissal was curt and direct.

Wills leapt forward and grabbed her by the hair, dragging her back against him. "I would very much like to believe you,

Freya," he bit out the words one at a time. "But someone is missing; someone very important."

Gormghlaith sneered, her teeth growing fantastically long in Hagen's mind. They became a maw of terrible fangs as her voice dropped furiously. "Then aren't you the fool for having left them alone? I haven't the foggiest notion what you are talking about, Warrior. Now leave me be, mein Herr. I command you."

Wills threw her forward and the girl careened into the table. "Freffie might think you're special, bitch, but don't forget that I know what you are. You're a whore. A low class little tramp from the Galway gutters. The only reason you are here is because you look like someone else. Never forget that with a snap of my fingers I can get rid of you, Freya," the word was spat out viciously. "You forget just how little influence you truly have, as compared to some."

"If you are this jealous of me, Ritter von Glass, what must you think of this Galiena who so commands Freffie's attentions?" The words came out with equal heat as the girl picked herself up and stared Wills in the face.

The Ritter stalked forward, his hand raised as if to backhand his victim. "You are unworthy to say her name!" Instead of hitting her, Wills slammed his hand into the table top. "You will do as I have told you, Freya; you will play your part as I have instructed! You will perform the Augury and you will start the war! By Heaven, if you had anything to do with Kohl disappearing, I will throttle the life from your little neck without so much as a second thought." The sleeves of his robe flapped like wings as he shook his fists, and Wills turned into a vicious devil. "In front of Freffie if I have to! You're nothing but a peasant, and peasants deserve to die!" His handsome face took on a satanic cast as he threatened the girl.

Another man entered the room, his silver hair a contrast to his pristine white robe and the strange length of chain that belted the garment closed. Hagen knew this man; he knew the face, but his poor brain wouldn't function enough to let him remember why. "What is going on in here?" The man asked quietly.

Wills abruptly moved away from the girl, as his face smoothed impassively. "Nothing. Nothing at all. I was just checking on Lady Freya." The words came out derisively.

The man's face hardened to a mask. "Out, Warrior. The Lady Freya is not your concern. Take your dirty grey robes and move along. You defile her purity by being too close."

"Oh yes! Priests and Warriors? What a joke, Herr Feldmarschall! More like those who are willing to do the fighting, and those who want to bankroll the operation while they sit at home at night with their brandy, dogs and slippers. I'm getting tired of all this childish inanity!" Wills turned and stormed from the room in a swirl of grey. "Mark my words, mein Herr, tonight things change."

The Feldmarschall moved over to the woman, clicked his heels together and bowed his head. "Apologies, my lady. I should have come sooner. He didn't hurt you, did he?" The man spoke kindly and with deference.

"I am fine." Once on her feet, the naked Gormghlaith patiently allowed him to rub oil into her skin. Her entire being turned glossy as the old man went about his work. But this was no impersonal massage. Hagen could see his hands dip between her thighs and knead her breasts. Gormghlaith moaned softly and bucked up against his hand. Her hands twisted in the Feldmarschall's hair as he brought her to a swift orgasm. When he was finished, he helped dress her in a white velvet robe. Then she sat as he ran a brush through her hair.

"So beautiful is our Lady Freya," the man crooned gently as the brush slid through the auburn mass. "I love your hair, Madame. Might I request, as your High Priest, to take you away from this place tonight. May I keep you with me in Vienna? You know how it soothes me to have you near. It keeps my mind at ease."

Hagen couldn't see the girl in the mirror, but her voice was not negative. "It entirely depends on the Grandmaster, mein Herr, but I am not averse to the idea." She raised her hand to rest it on the man's arm. "You know you are very special to me."

With that the old man nodded and offered her his arm again. "Let me escort you to the Grandmaster." Gormghlaith rose and walked with the man from the room.

Hagen turned around on his ledge and crawled along the gallery to resume his surveillance in the nave. Braziers of hashish had been set up and the nave was filling with that strange smoke. It made his eyeballs feel as large as hens' eggs inside his skull. The hooded figures were entering, so many in shades of grey and white. They came up the aisle and stood in a circle around the altar on the edge of the pentacle star. They were singing a song which Hagen didn't know, but which he thought sounded like an old Austro-Hungarian anthem. There seemed to be so many of the figures, tramping in with their cowls over their heads. Then Hagen saw the white velvet robe of Gormghlaith being escorted onto the throne on the platform.

"Make way! Make way for the Grandmaster!" A stentorian voice boomed from the entrance of the chapel.

Silence reigned in the room and Hagen craned to see the man who was his enemy. The individual wore a brilliant blue robe, and very unsteadily walked with a staff. Another white clad figure stood at the Grandmaster's elbow, carefully guiding the man forward. Hagen figured the Grandmaster must be very old, for he was stooped over and his movements were rather tentative. As the man came up the aisle, he seemed to diminish, curling over more and more as he came closer. Then he stumbled, careening to the side as grey arms reached out from the ranks to pick him up. The man said something that Hagen couldn't hear, and the men around him chuckled. With painfully slow steps, the man was mounted on the smaller throne below that of Freya.

"All hail the Grandmaster of the New Austrian Order! Long may we exist to guide our Fatherland!" The voice called out again.

"All hail the Order!" The men yelled in unison.

A grey figure came from the ranks and bowed before the altar and the thrones. "My Master! We all know why we are here. The Nazi scourge comes ever closer to our borders and the time for unimpeded conflict draws nigh. Von Schuschnigg is losing control of the populace and they don't realize what Hitler will do if we allow him into the country." It was Wills' voice, strident and proud.

A man in white limped forward; another who leaned heavily on a cane. "Unimpeded conflict, boy? Do you know what that means? I think not! While I have wholeheartedly agreed with our actions up until now, I will not condone the bringing of war into our country!"

The man who stood by Gormghlaith's throne raised his head. It was the one called the Feldmarschall. "I would countenance war if I thought it was a war we could win. I have no issue with slaughtering every bloody Nazi in our borders, if it meant that Hitler would not come, but he will come, and his brown shirted hordes will follow. Without international support, I will not agree to a war we cannot win. Perhaps if Italy was still our ally I would say differently, but that butcher Mussolini has apparently thrown his lot in with Hitler and left us on our own."

Wills crossed his arms in disgust. "Then what have we been doing, gentlemen? Can one of you answer that for me? Has this all been a lark for you? A few years entertainment before slinking off into the grave? One last hurrah?" There was an assent from the grey men behind him. "What broken, pitiable creatures you have become with age, gentlemen. Quite frankly, I would have expected better from men of your impeccable nobility."

The Feldmarschall pointed a long finger at Wills. "I was fighting wars for this country when your father was in leading strings, Boy. You would do very well to remember that we do not follow you, but the Grandmaster," The finger traced its way to the figure in blue. "Do not raise yourself to a position to which you do not belong."

"Who leads whom, mein Herr? While I am in service to the Grandmaster and have fought at his side, I lead the Warriors! What do you lead? A bunch of old men who lay about dreaming of days gone by and playing with their little doll Goddess! It's pathetic that you grant so much favour to your silly little games," Wills spat back, taking another step forward, his hand rising threateningly. "The time for play is over, meine Herren! The time for war has come to us all!"

The Priest who brought forward the Grandmaster spoke up. "As your host for this evening and one of the most moderate of you all, I find I must agree with the voice of the Warriors. There has been much talk of when this day might come, and when I read my morning paper, I see that it is here. As well as being a lover, our Goddess is a Valkyrie, and it is time she wore that face to lead us into the next phase of our plans. I say war."

"Then go join the Grey, von Gazen!" Another white robe growled. "What do you know about War? You play at the troubadour, but what do you really understand about politics?"

Still another voice dissented from the white clad men. "Meine Herren, I find that I-I-I-I m-m-must agree with the W-W-Warriors. It was my f-f-f-ire which burned on the W-W-W-Wollzeile and I-I-I will burn all of V-V-V-Vienna to save it from those b-b-b-bastards!"

This time, more of the white robes joined in the cry. The Grandmaster patted the Priest beside him on the arm and said something very quietly. The Priest stepped down a few steps towards Wills. "The Grandmaster says to bring forward the new recruits that they may be judged worthy by our Lady Freya."

Five men in sky blue cloaks were brought to the altar in single file. Down there! Hagen thought to himself. The young one. That was his little von Ond! Von Ond wouldn't let him get hurt! Von Ond would help him! Hagen stopped and thought about that for a moment. No. Then they would both be in danger. Hagen lay back down on the floor of the gallery and watched through the slats of the balcony. He was being smothered by the darkness, and the smoke from the braziers was making him almost dozy. He was floating above them all like God in Heaven.

The sky blue cloaks were removed and the men underneath were unclothed. Gormghlaith came down from her throne and removed her own robe, joining them in nakedness. Hagen saw her take the first one up to the altar; he screwed his eyes shut to avoid seeing what she would do to them. The men's moans of pleasure confirmed his dirtiest imaginings and he felt himself grow hard again at the sound. At the first moment of silence, he peeked and saw the girl on her knees before von Ond. NO! He couldn't watch. She was a demon! A demon Galiena! It was a complete abomination to him, and that they would do this in a church was a final sacrilege. How could she pleasure them in her mouth like that? The whole line of them?

It deepened in his mind as the moans increased in volume. This orgy of devils, screaming and shrieking in Hell which God had sent him to stop. He was an angel who had fallen into this abhorrence. He could feel his wings on his back, and as his hand crabbed about, it clenched around something. A sword? Yes! He was the Archangel Michael and he was going to swoop down there to smite the demons below him. Then he would ascend back into heaven and God would smile at him. God with his little moustache and pince-nez. The Reichsführer appeared before him in flowing robes and with one hand made a sign of benediction over him; lightning bolt in his other, ready to kill the heretics.

"Be careful, Hagen!" God ordered him in that calm, pleasant voice. "Remember what the girl said. Watch. Stay quiet. Learn and remember. Don't let them find you for we will return together and obliterate this perversity forever!" Then God faded back into the gloom at the back of the gallery.

Hagen pulled his sword up near his face and realized it was nothing more than an old wooden pole. What was happening to him? How much longer would it go on? He peeked back over the edge and realised that the 'ordination' of the recruits had finished. The five men, including von Ond, were being redressed in grey robes.

"Now that the new recruits have had their ritual initiation, shall we get back to the matter at hand?" Wills had pulled off his cowl and was standing there with an unflappable calm. "Captivating as this all has been, I thought we were going to examine the present situation. If it isn't then I will go back to the party and find something more entertaining to do," he drawled insultingly.

Gormghlaith had returned to her throne, sitting there in all her naked glory, the oil on her skin glistening in the torchlight. As she gazed at Wills, there was distaste in her eyes, yet she said nothing. Instead she touched the arm of the Feldmarschall, where it rested on the arm of her chair. Immediately, the man leapt into words. "We will not have you sit here and profane our sacred ceremonies, Warrior! You will withdraw, or you will contain yourself."

The Grandmaster spoke then, to his attendant, and there was a singsong quality to his words. Hagen couldn't hear or understand what was said, but then the Priest spoke. "Our Grandmaster has orders. He is ready for the Augury. Inside the enemy will he determine our course."

"About bloody time!" Wills snarled, and then clapped his hands. Two of his men disappeared into the gloom and returned, dragging with them a heavy-set, naked, young man in chains. The man's head swivelled around with a detached curiosity as he was led towards the altar. As Hagen saw the young man, something echoed in himself. This boy was drugged to the gills. What was going to happen now? Hagen knew for certain that whatever it was, it would be terrible.

They pushed the man down onto the altar and set him spread eagled atop it. The chains were pulled taut but the man didn't struggle or fight. He lay there like a baby. Wills walked up to the man, and stroked his forehead. "Behold, SA-Untersturmführer Ernst Gerger. He will tell us whether we go to war or not." With that, Wills turned to Gormghlaith, his hands clasped in front of his chest as if in prayer. "Come, mighty Freya!" There was just the faintest tinge of mocking in his voice. "Come and show the faithful your will! Show us the way! Prepare the Augury for our Grandmaster's reading!"

Again, Hagen felt as if he couldn't watch, but something held him anyway. Perhaps it was that pale white body, so much like his Galiena, walking around completely naked. Or perhaps the oblong score of his teeth marks on her skin. The Feldmarschall escorted her down towards the altar and gave her a boost, helping her up on top of it. No! Hagen prayed she wasn't going to have sex with this SA man! She couldn't! But as the girl straddled the chained man's hips and leaned forward to kiss him, that's exactly what seemed inevitable! Hagen slammed his eyelids together, trying to block out the sight, but perverse curiosity made him open them again.

Hagen knew he shouldn't believe what he saw, for Gormghlaith was raising a wickedly sharp knife over the prostrate man and lowering the point inexorably towards his sternum. On her face was a look of indescribable pain, yet underneath it all, resolution. Saliva welled in Hagen's mouth as the blade pierced the man's skin and the victim started screaming; a terrible, agonizing sound. The girl slowly sawed downwards using just the tip of her blade, and blood welled freely from the incision as she did so. Eventually she brought her blade down to where their pelvises met, and cast it away, the metal hitting the floor with a tremendous clatter in the otherwise silent room.

The young man's belly split open like a sausage, the blood pouring over the shrieking man and the girl who sat astride him. It was a grotesque image, and Hagen closed his eyes against it. Was he hallucinating again? He didn't know, but he prayed that he was. There was so much blood! Rivers of it, rolling in streams down the white stone of the altar. The girl threw her head back, her eyes closed and her arms wide apart. "Behold the enemy of the Faithful," Gormghlaith called out as arterial spray painted her white skin red.

The torchlight glistened over the man's innards, their multitude of textures and colours laid bare in the most obscene way. It was like looking into the guts of a freshly slaughtered sheep. The intestines swelling up to open the incision further, threatening to cover the girl and the altar with their miles and miles of length. The man's screaming reached a fever pitch; the terrible, piteous sound reaching every corner of the chapel and reverberating in Hagen's poor tortured mind.

When next Hagen peeked over the edge, the Grandmaster had been escorted down to the altar, his staff raised as if to spear the man. Instead, that end plunged into the open stomach cavity of the victim, stirring around and around while the SA man begged and pleaded for his life at the top of his lungs. Then with a massive flick of his staff, the Grand master sent the viscera out into the crowd of Warriors, flinging vast loops of the stuff. They landed on the men, making them appear as so many butchers. Not yet finished, the old man dropped the staff and reached in with both hands, pulling out hunks of blue and brown and red, throwing them to the stone floor. With a surprising deftness of movement, the Grandmaster moved around the altar to the other side, cowled head bent over the detritus for a very long time. The room was virtually silent now; the victim having long passed out.

Hagen wanted to vomit, yet found himself unable to. He couldn't understand the horror before his eyes, and decided it had to be another dream. Yes. It wasn't real! It wasn't real! It couldn't be real! He leaned out to survey the group and the Greys were on their knees before the Grandmaster. Slowly the blue clad man held his hands out in the manner of the Roman Emperors at the coliseum, thumb out and parallel to the ground. Slowly, ever so

472

slowly, he let it drop. The grays went wild and Wills leapt to pick up the blade discarded by Gormghlaith.

"War! It's war!" Wills shouted as he swung the long dagger in a flashing arc into the victim's throat. There was very little spray as Wills sawed the man's head off. When he was done, he held it aloft and then threw it down the aisle towards the door. "We go to war! Death to the Nazis! Death to Hitler! We will kill them all!"

There was a touch on Hagen's shoulder, and he whirled his head around. God was there, his face covered in disgust. "Come Hagen! Run! Run away and get help! You must survive to tell about this! Quiet as a mouse, Hagen!" Himmler's eyes glowed with a brilliant blue light, and it gave Hagen the strength to uncurl from his foetal ball.

He slithered down along the stairs on his belly, with Himmler floating up above him. "That was going to be me!" Hagen whispered in fear. What he had seen took him back to the war, but even in the war he had not seen such unbelievable brutality.

Himmler took his hand gently in his own. "I know, Hagen! You have to let someone know this happened. But quietly now, or they will hear you!" That soft hand was his lifeline to sanity. Yes. Himmler would protect him. The Reichsführer wouldn't leave him alone to die at the hand of these devils. He had served Himmler for so long.

The sacristy was empty and Hagen crawled on his hands and knees to the window. Carefully, he hoisted himself over the edge, only to fall head first into the ground. Completely dazed, he rolled like a wood bug into a ball again, trying to be just another rock in the ground. Afraid to walk, he clawed his way to the woods on his stomach, terrified someone would see him. The excited whooping inside the chapel spurred him on, and eventually he made it to the cover of the trees.

The woods were dark as a sepulchre and he didn't know which way to go. Trusting in God's mercy, Hagen set out forward, branches tearing at his body and face as he plunged headlong through the brush. He fell more times than he wanted to count, but each time Himmler was there urging him up, begging him to keep going. "Come along, Hagen! You can't give up! You must keep going." So he picked himself up again and pushed on.

The moon travelled across the sky, and it was so cold outside! His filthy shirt was torn and his vest offered very little protection against the temperature. Hagen was slowing down. God was no longer there to hold his hand and keep him safe. He stumbled and fell again, rolling pell mell down an embankment.

He simply couldn't keep fighting any longer. He was ripped apart and alone, his entire being a world of pain. Yet with one last burst of energy his hand splayed out and touched macadam. Road! He had found a road! No! It wasn't a road! It was a river! A river of pavement which he had to swim along. He didn't know if he had the strength to trudge down it. No. He would crawl instead! Hagen crabbed the length of the street, hand over hand, his palms turning bloody. The knees shredding out of his pants as he pushed himself forward with each breath.

"I have to get help! I have to get help!" Hagen repeated over and over again, yet the reason why was eluding him. Why was he crawling down this road in the predawn? Because demons were after him. Demon women and demon men, covered in blood and they were going to kill him too! They were going to butcher him like a hog if he didn't get away! And they were all dressed in red, and carried brilliant strawberries in their demon claws. No. They wanted to dance with him. That was it? He was crawling away because someone wanted to dance with him? Tears streamed down his face, mixing with the grime and sweat. He wanted the strawberry! Why couldn't he have the strawberry? He was so hungry! Where was the strawberry? So terribly hungry!

There was a sound near him. An engine? Hagen flopped prone to the pavement then stilled instantly, freezing like a statue. It wasn't so hard. He was freezing. Only the tears, which fell from his eyes, betrayed what he was. A man. Or was he a man? No. He was a ghost and he had escaped the chains of Tartarus.

There was the slam of a door, and footsteps. Oh God! They found him! The demons! They had him, and now he was going to die! He didn't want to die! Not like this! "Please God!" He whispered fervently. "Please God! Help me!"

"Hello?" A strange voice asked and Hagen flinched as he was bathed in the light of an electric torch.

"Dear sweet Jesus Christ!" Another voice swore in open disbelief. "That's Standartenführer Kohl!"

Hagen reared up to his knees. He wasn't going to die like a dog in the street! It would take more than this to kill him! He wouldn't be led like a lamb to the slaughter like- like- his brain kicked in. Like a lamb. Like an SA-man. Laying like a headless side of beef. He brought his own demon claws up to protect his face and neck. "You won't cut my head off! Not while I still breathe!" His talons were daggers, long and sharp blades of steel shooting from his nails. They would protect him from the demons. He growled, ready to slash at them and create his own rivers of blood on stone. White stone! Yes! If they tried to cut his head off they would learn he wasn't helpless!

"Herr Standartenführer! No! It's Rottenführer Braun! Kurt Braun? From the team? I'm von Ond's comrade!" Hands came into his vision slowly, palms upwards in submission. "From the department? We've been waiting for von Ond to reappear from that party. We're helping Herr Strohkeller tonight. Do you understand me, Herr Standartenführer? What's happened to you? We want to help you."

"What's wrong with him, Kurt?" The other man breathed in through his teeth with a hiss. "He's out of his mind!"

"Don't let Demon Galiena gut me!" Hagen raved, seeing it again. Her face as she was sawing into that meat.

"Dunno, Ulrich, but he's bleeding! Look at his hands!" The torch moved to illuminate the very young man's face. "It's me, Herr Standartenführer! You always say that von Ond and I should form a cabaret show! Rottenführer Braun! Come to us and we will take you to Hauptsturmführer Freisler? You know? Eugen Freisler?"

"She took von Ond in her mouth. I saw it." Hagen started to choke as it played over in his mind like a movie he couldn't get away from. "How could she do it? How could she do that in front of me!"

"Don't get too close, Kurt! Look at him! I think he's lost it! He's gone all barmy!"

Tears welled up in Hagen's eyes again. "You aren't going to cut my head off, are you? I have to find help! I don't know why anymore, but I have to find help!"

"We are help, Herr Standartenführer! Come with us and we will take you to Freisler! He will help you!" The one named Kurt crouched down and beckoned to him. "I don't want to cut your head off," then there was a rueful little pause. "If I did that, how could I get a promotion?"

"Eugen!" Hagen clung to that like a prayer, and forced himself to crawl forward. If these were demons, he didn't care anymore. He knew that the one named Eugen was the one he was looking for. The one named Eugen he could trust with his life.

"Yes, Herr Standartenführer! Eugen! We will take you to him and he will find out what is wrong with you!" Gentle hands wrapped around him. "Ulrich, get your coat off! He's like ice! Get a move on, man!"

Hagen pressed his cheek and shoulder around the man's hand. "Please take me to Eugen," he breathed, all the will going out of him. These men were sent by God to help him, he was sure! No! They weren't men, but angels! "Are you Gabriel? Will you protect me from the demons? Please don't let the demons butcher me!"

"No, Herr Standartenführer. I won't let anyone hurt you! But I'm Kurt, not Gabriel. Kurt Braun!" There was a commotion and then the man was wrapping him up in blessed warmth. "I don't know of a Gabriel in the department."

Hagen twined himself around the person in front of him, satisfied for now that the man wasn't a demon. He was so cold and so tired that he didn't think he could stay awake anymore. "Please help me!"

"Right away," the one named Kurt said and then Hagen heard   no   more.

December 31, 1937
Dearest Poppet,

Happy New Year! I vow for my resolution I will convince you to come back. I thought I could be patient, but I can't! Don't you understand how much I love and need you? My life is incomplete without you. Riesa is empty. I have such plans for us, my dear! I thought we would return to South America. We were happy when we were there. You were happy! I remember. Or perhaps we could go to Ceylon or Africa this time? Just the two of us. Anywhere you want, Galiena! I will do anything, everything! To have you back. I love you. Just give me a chance to make everything right.
Eternally yours,
Meinrad

Chapter 35
March 5, 1938

How could she not have seen this coming? Galiena had been so distracted by the issue with the passport, so distracted by what was in front of her, that she never saw the danger coming up from behind and obviously Wolff hadn't either! How had she been so stupid? "Grandfather! You startled me." The trembling began in the pit of her stomach and radiated outwards throughout her entire being.

"I would almost think that you were avoiding me, Poppet. Why would that be, when you were so ardent earlier?" The warm fingers splayed up; driving her chin skyward and exposing the long line of her neck to her shoulders. "I would hate to think you were playing me for a fool, Poppet."

Her eyes pleaded with von Klopfer to help her, but the terrible man just stared back, glowing with anticipation. "No, Grandfather. I haven't played you for a fool, but with the Gruppenführer around! My agreement with Herr Himmler was very explicit. I'm not to engage in unnatural conduct with you on German soil. His words. I have no choice. They assured me they would kill you if I did. If we did that act again. Why do you think Wolff is here?" The lie slipped so easily off her tongue.

The Pfalzgraf's nose traced the exposed skin of her throat and his tongue caught the lobe of her ear. "Unnatural conduct, indeed! It's sanctioned by the Pharaohs, Galiena. There's nothing unnatural about it." Then his lips were in her hair. "Dear God, I remember the smell of you, Poppet. In that place I would dream of it every time I closed my eyes. You intoxicate me." His hand tightened on her throat, making it hard to breathe. "Intoxicate me! You are so perfect, Galiena, so magical a creature, that I don't know whether to take you with me, or consign you to your father's care in the afterlife. I hazard to think what these Nazi brutes will do to you, once they know what you are. Even they should be able to detect the Atlantean blood." His other hand clutched at her belly. "That this is the Holy Grail."

Galiena closed her eyes, the blood pounding through her skull with her heartbeat. The world was turning hazy and indistinct, becoming a black tunnel before her eyes, her gorge rising with every breath. "Please!" She begged. "Please don't hurt me. I love you, Meinrad," It was the first and only time she had ever used his name. She didn't want to die here in Friedrichshaven. All she had to do was hold out until Wolff returned, but the way her knees were shaking, there was little hope of that.

Then she was released into the air. "Hold her, von Klopfer. Turn my angel to face me, and take her down to her knees," Then a tsking caveat. "But upon your soul, don't touch her throat. Only I control her breath. Only I control her life."

Those huge arms held her like bands of steel against the corpulent chest and she was eased down to the grass. Galiena remained still, with her head bowed and sucked oxygen back into her lungs. Above her, the Pfalzgraf made an abrupt gesture with his hands. "Get along with it, Montrose," he snapped with decided irritation. "We don't have all evening."

"My apologies, Master," the rat like man whispered. Galiena glanced up to see the little valet coming forward with the ancient chest in his arms. The top was open and her Grandfather was pulling out an ancient dagger she hadn't seen in years.

"Gentlemen of Riesa, I here present to you Galiena Marlis Therese Sabina Pfalzgräfin von Steinberg zum Riesa, your undoubted liege; wherefore all of you who stand witness this day, to swear your service and acknowledge her superiority. Will you spread the strength of her word and arm at the expense of your own life?"

"God save the Pfalzgräfin von Steinberg," Montrose intoned and von Klopfer echoed.

Galiena's head reeled. This was the coronation ceremony for Riesa, last used in 1787. Her Grandfather was crowning her? Crowning her for what purpose? Why? It didn't mean anything! She lifted her eyes to meet the Pfalzgraf's, and he smiled down at her benignly; almost encouragingly. "I-" she began.

The Pfalzgraf just shook his head. "Your Royal Highness, are you willing to take the oath?"

She wasn't royal, she was serene. She didn't rule at Riesa. He did; but the way he raised his eyebrows at her, compelled her to whisper the single word, "Yes." Anything to waste time until Wolff noticed she was gone.

"Will you solemnly swear to govern the peoples of Steinberg and Riesa with honour and resolution; thinking first only of the land and the peoples on it, so help you God?"

The ancient words hit her in waves and suddenly her grandfather was ten feet tall. They weren't in a strange airfield between two trucks, but in the great hall at the castle. Galiena knew the answers to these questions; had her entire life. The coronation oath had been a bedtime story to her. "I do solemnly swear."

"Will you use your power wisely; tempering your mercy with justice; yet punishing the enemies of Steinberg and Riesa with steadfastness and resolution? Will you be guided by the will of God and maintain his laws within your kingdom?"

"I will," Galiena breathed automatically to please him. It didn't matter that the entire concept was a joke.

Then her Grandfather was over her, unbuttoning her overcoat to where von Klopfer held her around the waist; then tore her suit jacket open violently, the buttons flying everywhere. It happened so quickly that she couldn't react, but to look down stupidly. Please Wolff! Galiena screamed in the vaults of her mind. Where are you? Where is everyone? When her Grandfather reached for her blouse, she began to struggle violently against von

Klopfer; her body thrashing in a quest for freedom. It was for naught, as she was held too tightly. The delicate silk blouse was ripped open, exposing her thin chemise and brassiere. "No!" she hissed.

"Montrose, put that down and hold her head," The Pfalzgraf ordered crisply, and his words were instantly obeyed. The valet's arms went about her head with one hand conveniently over her mouth. No matter how she flailed against the two men, she was rendered immobile.

"Sire, you may wish to speed this along," von Klopfer grunted, as he laid a calf over her ankles to keep her from kicking him somewhere sensitive.

The point of the dagger appeared in the hollow of her throat and Galiena froze, her eyes burning. "Will you give your blood, to the last drop, for the holy lands of Steinberg and Riesa? Will you tie your blood to that of the land, prospering as it prospers, and sacrificing when it is in need?" Her grandfather stared at her long and hard then made a sharp flicking motion at Montrose, who pulled his fingers away from her mouth.

A terrified tear broke from her eye. "Please don't kill me, Grandfather! Please! I don't want to die!"

His face twisted with tenderness and his other hand brushed the tear away; the moisture like a burn on her skin. "I don't seek to kill you, my beauty; I seek to exalt you over all others," Meinrad told her with uncharacteristic gentleness. "Now answer the question."

"I will," Galiena mouthed slowly; praying for salvation from a universe which didn't appear to give a damn.

With a deft stroke, the Pfalzgraf made a tiny cut in her neck; just enough to leave a crimson bubble on the blade. "Then with this first drop, given to Riesa, thus will it be one day followed by the last." Galiena couldn't help but cringe as he licked the blood from the blade before placing it in the abandoned chest. Then he retrieved an ampulla, raising it high. "Let her hands loose, gentlemen."

"Yes, Sire," von Klopfer dropped his arms, resting his hands on her hips to keep her from moving.

Off in the distance, she heard the door to the building slam. "I'm sorry, Gruppenführer Wolff. I don't know what that was in aide of, but I do appreciate your assistance, Herr Ritter."

Von Kleist spoke then. "Forgive my suspicion, Herr Gruppenführer, but that entire situation seemed a tad contrived. Didn't that abrupt reversal seem overly false to you? Or perhaps that it happened just a moment too soon?" Then there was a long pause. "Or does your name really carry that much authority?"

Galiena's head whipped around at the sound and Montrose clamped his hand over her mouth once more. The Pfalzgraf raised the ampulla over her outstretched palms. "Be thy Hands anointed with Holy Oil." Droplets of the heavily perfumed oil stained her from fingers to wrists; before the ampulla was moved, its contents poured from collarbone to collarbone, the oil running a trail down into her cleavage. "Be thy Breast anointed with Holy Oil." Lastly to her head, pouring with oppressive stickiness into her hair. "Be thy Head anointed with Holy Oil: as kings, priests, and prophets were anointed: And as Solomon was anointed king by Zadok the priest and Nathan the prophet, so be thou anointed, blessed, and consecrated Queen over the Peoples, whom the Lord thy God hath given thee to rule and govern. In the name of the Father, and of the Son, and of the Holy Ghost. Amen. Thou art Galiena Königin von Steinberg zum Riesa"

"One hates to be immodest; but in certain circles? Yes, my name does have a certain influence. On the other hand, I see your position, Herr Ritter," Wolff's voice took on a sick quality. "Where's the Pfalzgräfin?"

"She was over by her car. Perhaps she has escorted the Pfalzgraf to the Zeppelin?" Von Kleist remarked casually.

The cloyingly sweet oil enveloped her; it dripped down her scalp, behind her ears, between her breasts and ran between her fingers. She was drowning in it, or so it felt. Galiena stared at her convulsively shaking hands, the amber droplets falling to the grass at the motion. Very carefully, the Pfalzgraf dropped to one knee before her, the one which was shot, carefully folding beneath him. He took her palms very carefully in his two hands. "Let me be the first to swear allegiance to you, meine Königin. I do solemnly swear to offer up my life and limb for the preservation of your person and kingdom. I am your man in liege and fealty." Then he

481

gently pressed his face to her two palms, his lips sliding against the oil as he preformed the ancient kiss of peace as she had done so often for him.

"No. She's not there," Wolff sounded concerned.

"She must be around somewhere. They want to launch the airship in the next fifteen minutes," von Kleist's voice was questioning. "Maybe they boarded the airship?'

"No," Wolff said in a voice which oozed confidence. "I highly doubt that the Pfalzgrafin would board the vessel without me."

"Let her go and pledge yourselves to her service," Meinrad commanded of his men. The arms released her; von Klopfer and Montrose each repeating the pledge and brushing their lips against her palms. Galiena was still rendered mute and sat dumbly, staring at her Grandfather, shaking her head in the negative at him. When the men moved away, the Pfalzgraf enfolded her in his arms. "In your name I repudiate my oaths to my former Liege, the Prince of Prussia; turning my back on the treaty which stole the independence from our lands. In your name I declare Steinberg and Riesa independent kingdoms, as they always should have been. We withdraw from the Greater German Reich and the tyranny of the Fuhrer."

Shock robbed her of her senses and she spoke without speaking. "You're mad," Galiena repeated, the words dribbled in a slur from her lips.

"No, meine Königin, I'm not mad. I would give you the world, and this is only the beginning." Then the Pfalzgraf bent over her, claiming her lips with his own, his fingers tangling about her hair. Galiena raised her slippery hand in protest, her hands sliding across his face with an oily smear as she tried to push him away. It only served to increase his ardour, and he pushed her back into the snowy grass, his body covering her own, his tongue pressing against her teeth.

"I thought I heard voices over here?" Von Kleist's voice appeared between the two trucks. "What's this?" the older man's voice was tinged with shock as he took in the tableau. "Dear God."

Galiena screamed in the back of her throat and flailed her hand in the Ritter's direction; her jaw tightly clenched against her Grandfather's probing tongue. Von Klopfer chuckled and stood.

"Nothing you need concern yourself with, von Kleist. Business between the Pfalzgraf and the girl. Accept it or don't see it."

The Pfalzgraf licked Galiena's lips one more time and then his hand clamped around her throat again as he addressed the head of all his corporate interests. "Do not stare upon your Queen so, Herr Ritter. Not with shock, only with love. She will raise us all so above and beyond where we are now. On your knees before her." The fingers squeezed reflexively, cutting off her airway as her being exploded into desperate battle. She would be damned before he did this to her again. As if sensing her thoughts, her Grandfather looked into her eyes. "Calm yourself, meine Königin. Give yourself to me and I will take care of you."

"What?" von Kleist repeated in horror. "Dear God in Heaven! What are you doing to that poor girl?"

Then behind them came the metallic snick of a bullet being chambered. "Freeze," Wolff snarled viciously.

Galiena used the opportunity to break free of her Grandfather's powerful arms and dashed to her feet, pressing her back to the truck behind her. Her eyes rolled from Wolff to the Ritter von Kleist then von Klopfer and to her kneeling Grandfather. The cry came from deep in her chest, a sound of fear, disbelief and heartbreak. She opened her mouth and the sound came out in a wail. Then her hand clasped over her own mouth to stop the noise coming out.

How could this have almost happened again? It was all too much to bear. She clenched her shaking hands into tight fists, and ran over to stand by von Kleist; who from his obvious disgust, had no prior knowledge of this grotesque plan of her Grandfather's.

The Ritter stared at her torn clothing and oil smeared chest dumbfoundedly. Then he peered back to the kneeling Pfalzgraf. "What is going on here?" The man asked her, reaching out an arm in her direction, but pulling it back abruptly when she shrank away from him. Her arms came up to cover her chest and her modesty.

"Pfalzgrafin von Steinberg, are you injured?" Wolff called over from where he stood at the other end of the trucks with his gun drawn; his face bloodless.

Galiena reached a finger up to the tiny slice in her throat and then brought it away. There was just the barest smear of blood on her fingertip, not the flood that she feared. "I'm fine, Herr

Gruppenführer," she spoke so softly, she wondered if the words could be heard at all."

"Get up! You're all to Buchenwald, as far as I'm concerned," the Gruppenführer ground out through clenched teeth. "You have most certainly violated your parole. Herr von Steinberg! Up!"

The Pfalzgraf, obviously needing assistance to rise, held out his arm to Montrose. "Bah," he spat with condescension.

Galiena stepped closer to von Kleist, her shoulder passing behind his cadaverous body. Who would have thought she would ever hide behind the Grim Reaper? She forced her mouth to speak the lies which would suit the situation and made a negative gesture to Wolff. Dear God! Her mouth tasted of that rancid oil. "No, Herr Gruppenführer. The three of them will board the Zeppelin as before. I slipped and my grandfather was merely coming to my aid. No. The three of them will go straight to the Graf Zeppelin this moment and board it."

"Excuse me?" Wolff choked out, his disbelief palpable.

The Ritter von Kleist addressed her calmly. "That isn't what I saw, Madame." It was a heartening shift of alliance by this man who had been loyal to her Grandfather for so many years. "That certainly isn't what I saw." Von Kleist proved very readily that he was a hawk and not a vulture.

Galiena felt all the hatred in her soul for her Grandfather and let it shine out of her eyes. She pointed her hand in the direction of the huge airship with an imperious finger and took in a deep, calming breath. "Go!" She commanded, and then returned her gaze to the disbelieving eyes of Karl Wolff. "And you will let them go; out of Germany, never to return." The voice which spoke the terrible abjuration barely seemed to be hers. Who would have thought to powerful a sound could come from her?

"Pfalzgrafin von Steinberg, I must protest!" Wolff reiterated strongly, his narrowed eyes burning into her own.

"No, Herr Wolff. Please just let them go. I beg of you, just let them go. Don't make this all have been in vain." If the Pfalzgraf remained in Germany it would never be over for her, not even with a thousand SS men to separate them.

Von Klopfer slid his gaze over her with a sly expression and picked up the handles of the hamper, while Montrose reclaimed his chest. Meinrad von Steinberg brushed the snow from his knees, before offering his arm to Galiena in an elegant manner. "Meine Königin?" He spoke the word so damned easily.

Galiena quailed inwardly, staring at the limb; feeling the bitter cold on her exposed, thin camisole. She stared down at the ruins of her suit realizing just how much of her was exposed, then pulled the edges of her overcoat together, doing up the buttons with quiet dignity. Her hands shook with a geriatric palsy that she couldn't control and she bit the inside of her cheek to keep from crying. Von Kleist came to her aid as the silence seemed to stretch out interminably. "I shall escort Her Serene Highness."

"Her Majesty," The Pfalzgraf corrected the man sharply. "You are addressing the Königin von Steinberg."

"Come along!" The Gruppenführer shouted from behind them, coming up to place his gun against the Pfalzgraf's kidneys. "You will come now, or so help me God; I will irrigate you thoroughly with my Mauser!"

"He who saves a nation, violates no law." With another elegant shrug, her grandfather turned and allowed himself to be led away by Wolff. Galiena took the arm of von Kleist, and together they trailed a safe distance behind. The Ritter's eyes were laden with guilt as he stole glances at her from the corner of his eye, but Galiena had not the time to address either the man or the emotion. She watched in silence as the Pfalzgraf boarded the zeppelin, and marked the time dispassionately until the great silver airship lifted on its way to the New World.

Galiena found herself completely numb inside and when there was nothing more to see, she trudged her way back to the Horsch, leaving Wolff and von Kleist to follow behind her. It seemed so anticlimactic, and all she wanted was another drink to suspend her disbelief further.

Was it over now? With a terrible certainty, she knew it was not. The physical threat had sailed away, but now a different kind of game would begin. When it came to a battle of the will and the mind, Galiena knew she was David to Meinrad von Steinberg's Goliath; yet she took great comfort from the fact that in the Bible, David was victorious. Would she be so lucky? As Galiena liberated a large swig of brandy from the decanter in the Horsch, she realized that she doubted so.

"Madame, I," von Kleist began but she cut him off as she moved to replace the bottle of brandy in the bar.

Changing her mind, she passed the brandy bottle to the old man. He, too, took a drink straight from it; an action she never thought she would see. "Please don't, Herr Ritter. Now's not the time. If tonight needs to be discussed, then we can do it on another day. I have a long drive back home to make tonight; please don't press me further," Galiena protested as she reached into her purse to find her keys, curling her toes in her shoes at the electric tingle of the alcohol in her blood stream.

Wolff, the skin around his eyes dark and sunken, glared at her from von Kleist's side. "You are in no condition to drive back to Riesa or Berlin, Pfalzgrafin von Steinberg. It's a quarter to three in the morning, and no matter what you say, you've just been assaulted."

"Come, Pfalzgrafin! Let me take you to my hotel here in town. You can sleep for a few hours before you continue along. Please, Madame! I beg of you! Do not drive back to Berlin tonight," von Kleist entreated her, a surprising amount of emotion in his face; far more than she had expected existed in the older Prussian man. "The Gruppenführer has the right of it."

Her hands were icy cold without her gloves, and the sweetness of the oil; rancid with age, was causing her gorge to rise. Her useless hands rattled in front of her chest, palms up towards the heavens, keys clattering annoyingly. "Do either one of you have hanky? I-" she paused, unable to continue. "I-"

Wolff instantly produced one from his pocket, and took her hands in his own; deftly cleaning up the stinking smears. The thick amber syrup came off with relative ease, but the smell would take some scouring and a hot bath to eliminate. "There. That's somewhat improved," The SS man told her gently as he ran the soiled cloth between her fingers to finish his ministrations.

"Yes. Thank you." Unfortunately the oil was everywhere in her clothing and through her hair, but at least having it off her hands helped her feel a little more human. She reached into her purse and pulled out her own small lace handkerchief and very deliberately wiped off her mouth, scrubbing off the smeared lipstick and oil from her Grandfather's kiss. Her movements became obsessive, and her lips felt scrubbed raw by the time she

486

finished. Von Kleist and Wolff watched her in a strange, probing silence. Why didn't they just go away and leave her in peace?

"Please tell me this is all settled, Madame. Please tell me you will come back to my hotel for the balance of the evening," von Kleist inquired again, his face clouded with concern.

Galiena shook her head in positive denial. "No, mein Herr. No. While I appreciate the offer, I won't sleep tonight. I know I won't. The drive will be good for me. It will clear my head."

"This is just foolishness," Wolff sighed in consternation, and she heard the sigh all the way down to his boots. "I suppose you insist on driving?"

Galiena blinked at him. "Of course I am. Car's not going to levitate itself, now is it?" She yanked the door open herself, cursing her irrational temper. "I'm sorry, Herr Ritter, but I must go. Please come to me in a few days. I will call and let you know where I am. The urge to hide at Carinhall for a while is very strong, but I may be in Berlin."

The old man walked to the door and held it for her. "Tell me one thing, Your Royal Highness?" The use of her Grandfather's appellation caught her off guard. She searched his face for signs of mocking and found none.

Galiena sank into the driver's seat of her car, waiting to swing her legs into the foot well. "Yes?" As she said the word, it was like waiting for the hammer to fall.

"What I saw tonight? What I saw the Pfalzgraf do," The Ritter von Kleist paused in extreme discomfort. "It's happened before, hasn't it?"

Her eyes dropped to her shaking knees. "Yes." Trying to control herself, or at least appear so, Galiena swung her legs towards the pedals of the car.

Wolff opened the passenger side door and stepped onto the running board. "Why the devil do you think the Reichsführer had him at Buchenwald, Herr Ritter?" He slid into the car beside Galiena. "Ponder that for a moment."

"What the devil are you doing?" Galiena stole Wolff's phraseology as he settled into the passenger's seat.

"Please excuse my soldier's harshness, but Himmler would have my guts for his evening sausage if I let you drive back to

Berlin on your own," the Gruppenführer snapped back at her without missing a beat. "Let alone Eugen Freisler."

Von Kleist held the door for her. "Madame, I never would have asked you release the Pfalzgraf if I had known," His face was painted with regret.

Galiena took in the cadaverous man, and realized he wasn't so monolithic and uncaring as she thought. "I know, Herr Ritter, and I appreciate what you said this evening. I'm not leaving to spite you. I just need to get away from here. Please understand mein Herr!" It was her turn to do the entreating. "Please respect my need to flee and regroup."

Von Kleist slowly nodded his head. "God save Your Royal Highness," was all he said as he shut the door and stepped away from the car; head bowed and hands at his sides.

Her hands fumbled with her keys, trying to get them inserted into the ignition. The basic gesture seemed impossible to achieve. "You're sure you want to come with me?"

Wolff tried very hard to stifle a yawn, but in the end it got the better of him. "Yup," he said very informally into his glove.

"Fine then. When we get near Berlin, let me know where to drop you." Galiena bowed her head and turned on the car, letting it warm before throwing it into reverse and peeling out of the parking area with a truly juvenile amount of noise.

"Given the time we will get back, you might as well leave me at the Prince Albrecht Staße." She could feel his frown all the way across the car. "You know that is very hard on your tires, peeling around like that."

It was such a typical, masculine thing to say. "The wear on my tires hardly concerns me, Herr Gruppenführer," Galiena retorted with irritation. "I have people who look after those sorts of things for me."

Wolff grunted sourly in disgust. "That's no excuse to intentionally damage one's equipment. Perhaps you should care more about the little details and less unfortunate mishaps would come your way," the man said, hunkering into his seat.

Galiena took her eyes off the road long enough to look daggers at her passenger. "While I certainly appreciate your protection, Gruppenführer Wolff, the commentary on how I choose to handle my affairs is not required. I would prefer not to spend the next six and a half hours sniping at you. Quite frankly, I would have preferred it if you had your men, who could have been infinitely more useful earlier, drive you back to town. If you feel the need to criticize, please do so in the privacy of your own skull! Don't make me feel that letting you in my car was a mistake. I've made plenty enough today already."

Wolff crossed his arms over his chest, his leather trench coat squeaking. "Mistakes were made, Pfalzgrafin von Steinberg, most of them by me," the general stared resolutely out the window. "And   more   than   a   few   by   my   boss."

January 2, 1938
Dearest Poppet,

Von Blomberg stopped by today to invite me to his wedding and says he has invited you! It is a sign! He says you are well! Better than well! My heart almost bursts at the news! Soon I will be with you! Just ten days! And I am a whole man again, my Darling! Perhaps it was providence which kept you away. You didn't have to see me brought low again. I will please you, Galiena!
Eternally yours,
Meinrad

Chapter 36
March 5, 1938

They passed the drive in an almost frosty silence, for she chose not to respond to him. As the road to Friedrichshaven was paved with recriminations, the road to Berlin was paved with censure. How could she have been so foolish as to be taken in by von Klopfer? How much did the man know about the actions of her Grandfather? He must have known everything, for he and Montrose were very willing participants in- Galiena caught herself. In what? Her coronation? A coronation required a crown, and there was certainly no crown in that debacle. Königin? How could her grandfather even think such a ludicrous thing? As if Riesa could cede from either Prussia or the Greater German Reich? It would be impossible now! What was Riesa? Two hundred square kilometers? No. It was madness! Madness!

Beside her, a half snore alerted her that Karl Wolff had succumbed to exhaustion and Galiena glanced at her watch. It was just before six a.m. The Horsch was traveling very close to its maximum speed, nearly to one hundred miles per hour. She looked at the SS officer. His chin was down on his chest; his peaked cap crushed into the window. They had been on the road for two and a half hours already. He seemed deep enough asleep that he wouldn't be treated to the sight of some extremely unladylike behavior. She snaked a hand her to the brandy bottle in the bar behind the seat and brought it to her lap. Taking a queue from

Ernst Udet, she uncorked it with her teeth spitting the stopper into her lap and took a deep swig. The moment of contact with her stomach was electric, and combined with the pill from von Schilling, set her on fire. Another long swig and Galiena recorked it before tossing the bottle into the back with very little regard for its placement. Another snore from Wolff told that her terrible breach of etiquette had gone unnoticed. As her eyes unfocussed again, Galiena was pleased that the Autobahn was relatively empty. She was impaired enough that her perceptions were affected, but an empty road was no challenge to her abilities.

Galiena carefully navigated onto the A9 at Nuremberg and her mind drifted back to her Coronation. Of all the ill-brained lies! On a zeppelin field, between two trucks in the middle of the night, held down by a Prussian pervert and a rat-like Scotsman. Königin! Königin of what? Her Majesty? What Majesty? Galiena had no majesty! And then to hear her Grandfather quoting Napoleon Bonaparte! He who saves a nation violates no law! Dear sweet God in heaven! Riesa wasn't a nation! It hadn't been in almost a hundred and thirty years.

Still, there was von Kleist, now calling her 'Royal Highness', as if in his eyes, she was head of the family. The whole thing was just so incredibly ridiculous, and yet the Pfalzgraf seemed to believe it. How could he have built everything he had and not realized that the age of kingdoms was over? All this nonsense about blood and nobility was at an end! It had to be! But Himmler believed it too. Could she ever escape this insanity?

They were passing by the exits to Leipzig and Halle when Galiena realized she was going to be sick. Her hands shook on the steering wheel and there was so much pressure on her chest. She couldn't keep it in any more! Galiena was going to crack and soon; her carefully built up control was fading very fast. It was seven a.m. How could this be happening to her now? The world was still dark; the moon was bright in the sky!

They were traveling through a strange landscape of forests breaking into meadows and back again. The forest ahead of them thinned, and Galiena pulled the Horsch onto the shoulder of the road, coasting to a halt. Air. She just needed fresh air. She wouldn't actually be sick, would she?

491

Galiena exited the car, leaving the door open as not to disturb Wolff, and walked as calmly as she could to the small barrier at the edge of the autobahn. The air wasn't helping. She was going to be sick after all. Her dry mouth was filling with saliva faster than she could swallow it back, and her stomach was roiling violently. Galiena stepped over the barrier and tripped down the embankment which levelled the highway from the meadow before her. There was a thin layer of snow on the ground here, and she prayed she wouldn't step into a hole as she looked for a private place to disgrace herself. Running to a tree, half way across the meadow and falling to her knees, Galiena braced herself as her stomach heaved the bulk of its empty contents several times. Her hair was blowing in the faint breeze, and she attempted to wrap it around her hand as she threw up again.

Galiena was trying to crawl to a fresh place, sobbing as she did so when there was a gentle hand holding her forehead, and a glove holding her hair. "Just let it out, Pfalzgrafin," Wolff's sad voice floated down to her, and she could see his boot on the ground at her side.

"I don't want you to see me like this, Herr Wolff!" Galiena wailed as she leaned against his leg.

"Oh Christ, Madame! Accept help for just one bloody second, would you?" Wolff growled in exasperation, as he wrapped himself around her. "Just let it all out." His presence was so calming and comforting.

There was nothing left in her stomach, but her body went through the motions of vomiting anyway. "I'm so mortified!" Galiena whispered in one still moment, but there was no relief for her; the scent of the oil in her hair was enough to start the process over again. Soon she was spitting up yellowy green bile. Eventually though, as the sky lightened, the heaving stopped. Wolff hauled her a few feet away from the tree and sat with her.

"For God's sake, Pfalzgrafin! Why didn't you tell me you were sick?" Wolff said at last as he handed her another hanky. "My wife insists I carry two for emergencies," the man added somewhat sheepishly.

Galiena wiped her face and then reached into her purse, searching for one of her mints to kill the terrible taste in her mouth. Everyone knew mints helped settle the digestion. "Thank you," she answered him, not wanting to answer his other question. "Thank you so very much, Gruppenführer Wolff. I never would have survived today without you."

Galiena could feel the cold of the ground through the fabric of her coat, but she didn't care. She discovered her elusive mint and placed it between her lips, thrilled to have the taste of bile gone. She stole a glance at Wolff, who was sitting on his bottom, his elbows resting on his raised knees, leaning against the tree. He looked too young in this moment to be a general, and Galiena wondered how old he actually was. He also looked terribly tired. She didn't hazard a guess at how awful she looked.

The sun was rising in the horizon, the sky lightening in the distance. Soon the world would be awake again. Galiena leaned back against the tree and sighed, her body completely spent. There was nothing left in her, but thankfully Berlin wasn't that far away. She could feel the wetness of the tears against her face and brushed them away with her hand.

"Why didn't you scream?" Wolff asked her at last, his voice sounding as rusty as an ancient hinge.

"Pardon?" The question caught her completely off guard.

"Why didn't you scream when he touched you? My men would have heard if you had," the Gruppenführer leaned forward to peer into her eyes. "You didn't make a damn sound."

Galiena screwed her eyes up to block out the sight of his piercing blue gaze and to keep herself from crying again. "It didn't precisely occur to me," was the best she could come up with.

"Excuse me? You didn't think to scream? What does that mean?" The man's discord was palpable in the dawn light.

"I think I was afraid; I didn't want you to shoot him," she answered slowly, not particularly believing it herself.

"I can think of very few people more deserving of being shot, Your Serene Highness," Wolff ground out angrily. "Or perhaps I misunderstand the nature of your relationship with the man."

Galiena drew back again, stung to the core by his implication. "Please don't say that, Herr Gruppenführer. Dear God! Do you think I wanted him to touch me again? Do you think I wanted any of this?" She broke down, unmindful of her pride or dignity. "I think I didn't scream because last time I screamed myself raw and not a soul came to help. Why would I bother? Why would I try?" She wrapped her arms around her body protectively. "I thought he was going to kill me tonight. Maybe I wish he had."

"What?" Wolff exclaimed in shock.

She rounded on him, on the attack for the first time in hours. "Don't you know what today cost me, Herr Gruppenführer? I probably hate what I did more than you do! You think I betrayed Hagen? Well let me tell you something, mein Herr! I betrayed myself first. You simply have no idea!" Galiena's voice rose to a hysterical level. "And now I discover that the bloody man is mad! Mad! Mad as a bloody hatter! The things I promised him for the company; to save the company, and now I discover that his mind might be broken? You don't know what I did to myself and it might have all been for naught, except to let a god damn madman lose!" She had never sworn so much in her life.

Wolff's face twisted in puzzlement. "I don't understand? Then why did you do it?"

She buried her face in hands, finding a trace of comfort in hiding behind that wall of her own flesh. "I did it for Riesa. It was all for Riesa. It didn't take me very long to figure out that I don't have the experience to control the Gesselschaft. It made von Kleist so happy when I admitted I couldn't do it. I think more than anything, that cemented my plan to buy the Pfalzgraf out of prison. My personal feelings had nothing to do with it." Her breath sucked in noisily between her teeth as she struggled to breathe through her hysteria. "And now to realize he's mad. Cede Riesa from the Greater German Reich? Renounce his fealty to the Kaiser? There is no bloody Kaiser! While my acknowledged liege is the Prince of Prussia, it's a very empty thing these days!"

Wolff chuckled weakly. "He wants to cede your family lands from the Reich?" She heard him slap his hand against his thigh in amusement. "I highly doubt that is in the Fuhrer's plans."

Galiena dropped her useless fingers to her lap. "Don't you know what he did tonight, Herr Wolff?"

His chin jerked in a gesture to the negative. "No. All I saw was him holding you to the ground and you reaching for the Ritter von Kleist."

Galiena touched her head, fingers sliding through the noxious smelling oil. "What you saw was my coronation, Herr Wolff," she whispered brokenly as the strands of her hair caught under her nails. "This malodorous slime is the ancient coronation oil; probably not used since the late 1700's. He crowned me Königin von Steinberg zum Riesa. Prinzessin von Steinberg, yes; we don't use it, but the Hohenzollern do when they refer to us. Theoretically, one could call me the Fürstin Pfalzgrafin now, which von Kleist seems to have decided to acknowledge, as I've suddenly been elevated to the ruling Pfalzgrafin, instead of being an ancillary titled member of the family." She brought her hand down in front of her face before wiping it off on her jacket; the garment being ruined anyway. "But then why would he consent to impregnate someone less exalted than himself?" There was a world of bitterness in those words.

"Pfalzgrafin, I-" Wolff paused, obviously fumbling for his words. "How did it happen? Please tell me you didn't submit to all that willingly?" Wolff's brows drew together in consternation. "Please tell me that you didn't betray my friend."

"Von Klopfer lured me in between the trucks, wanting to talk about a promise I made him. He's never made me especially comfortable but I never suspected he would hold me down the way he did." Her gorge rose again and she rolled onto her knees as another dry heave hit her. "He knew about before; what my Grandfather did to me at Riesa. I think he wanted it to happen again! That sick bastard! Did he think he was going to get a taste too?" More bile emerged from the depths of her gut and she rolled over to be sick again. Why was it that now the entire situation made her so ill? Just talking about it made her roil and heave.

Wolff's arms were around her, holding up her head again. "Why didn't you say anything? You stupid girl! I would have sent the lot of them to prison!" He snarled again, clearly infuriated.

His insults didn't penetrate her illness and misery. "Never again! Never again! I will kill the next man who tries to hurt me! I swear to God I will!" She crawled out of Wolff's grasp, and climbed unsteadily to her feet.

"You let them go free, Pfalzgrafin!" Wolff also stood, dusting the snow off his jacket. "One word and I would have rounded them up and made them disappear! One bloody word!" He thrust his finger under her nose, the gloved digit shaking with barely contained rage.

"I wasn't thinking very clearly!" She screamed at him in impotent fury. "I've been up for," Galiena found herself looking at her watch. It was a hair off of eight a.m. "Fifty bloody hours! She clutched at her face, the nails biting into her skin; then lifted her face and let out a scream of pure frustration.

The Gruppenführer froze; his expression one of disbelief. "Excuse me?" He erupted again.

"Well I'm sure you've been up for twenty-four at least! You woke up last on Friday morning. I woke up last on Thursday morning; at four, no less! Cut me just the slightest bit of slack, Herr Gruppenführer! I'm not at my best." Galiena shouted back at him, balling her hands into fists until they, too, were shaking. "I've had a lot of Guernica energy pills," she said softly.

"Jesus Christ, you stupid woman! Are you an imbecile? What the hell are you doing?" Wolff barked; his temper strained to the very edges. "Of all the irresponsible behaviour! Of all the stark raving lunacy!" The man spluttered as his composure disintegrated to match hers.

Anger, combined with the pills she had taken, reacted like dynamite and Galiena flew into a rage unlike anything she had ever experienced. "Don't you take that tone with me, mein Herr! I didn't ask for you to come along today!"

As she fed from his fury, he fed from hers, his own loss of control escalating in tune. "Well you certainly seemed to need my help, woman, or was it your plan to let him rape again in between those two trucks?"

His words cut her off at the knees for how could she answer? Galiena felt her chin drop as she spluttered for some kind of answer, but the only one to emerge from her lips was "No."

"Because you didn't think!" Wolff wasn't finished yet though, as he raised his two balled fists in the air. "I'm so frustrated, I could just throttle you!"

Galiena tore open her overcoat; exposing her throat to the man. "Go right ahead, Gruppenführer Wolff! You wouldn't be the first to try today!" He stared at her in abject horror, both at her words and his own. "Would you please finish the job my Grandfather started?" Two large tears ran a trail from her left eye.

The words hung pregnant in the air; their breath coming out in white clouds as the combatants stared at each other. Then Wolff dropped his hands limply to his sides, and his face crumpled. "Dear God, Madame, I'm sorry."

Galiena's anger evaporated like a vapor. "No! Please! I'm the one who should apologize. I was unforgivably rude; especially after you were so kind to me."

"No. I won't accept your apology when I'm the one in the wrong." Wolff protested with a shake of his head. "I had no idea you had been up for so long. I should have been more understanding. I should never have used," he paused lamely. "What happened before as a weapon. That was conduct unbecoming a gentleman. I was completely out of line, Madame."

"No, Herr Gruppenführer!" She exclaimed with very real feeling. "I'm being completely irrational. You had every right to say the things you did. They were entirely valid. I was foolish. Have been foolish. If I could take today back and do it again, I would." Her eyelids dropped, obscuring everything but his glossy boots. "Please! Promise me you don't think badly of me!"

"No, Pfalzgräfin, I don't think badly of you. You're a very brave woman. I can't think of too many who could face down the Reichsführer-SS in his lair and their own personal Belial in the very same afternoon," the man conceded kindly after a quiet moment of thought.

Galiena laughed cynically; an ugly sound to her own ears. "Don't you mean Mephistopheles?"

"Did you sell your soul to him, Frau Doctor Faust?" Wolff countered her glibly, rising to his feet with a shy smile.

Galiena turned back towards the autobahn where the Horsch was parked, one foot in front of the other as he fell in step with her. "Not to him; I sold my soul for him, I suspect."

"I doubt it, Madame. Himmler is no Mephistopheles to want your soul. I can't say as I fathom your relationship with the Reichsführer. I know it will be a source of mystery to Hagen, but I don't think your soul is in any danger, provided you limit your contact with that monster we just sent to Rio de Janeiro." Wolff offered her his elbow politely.

She took his arm, grasping at the black wool of his overcoat under his fingers. "Please, Gruppenführer Wolff! Please promise me you won't tell Hagen about today? I don't want him to know about any of this. Please?"

His face read like a treatise on indecision. "You don't know what you are asking me, Pfalzgräfin von Steinberg. Hagen is one of my closest friends, and were the situations reversed, I would want to know."

"I don't want him to find out about it from someone else. I would rather tell him in my own time, at my own comfort." Galiena had told such a web of lies to so many different people in the last three days; she didn't think that one more was going to hurt. She knew she was going to hell anyway.

"I have very serious reservations that you will tell him at all, but in the interests of optimism, I will acquiesce to your request," The SS man conceded as he helped her over the barrier separating the highway from the meadow.

"You have my continued gratitude, Gruppenführer Wolff. Gratitude I am too dull to express properly, but let me say, I will never forget the assistance you rendered me today and the patience with which you did it. You are a true savior." She prayed that her words came out with the right amount of truly heartfelt sincerity, and not cloying or false.

The Gruppenführer snorted with uncharacteristic derision. "Yes. Saint Karl of the Wolves, patron of overtired princesses and Reichsführers everywhere. I can see the iconography now and it isn't a pretty thing," Wolff sighed, all the way down to his boots. "You don't know how responsible I feel for you now, and it's bad enough having to chase after Heinrich bloody Himmler all day long to keep him out of trouble."

"Heinrich bloody Himmler?" Galiena giggled against her better judgment. "Is that his official middle name? Or a Schutzstaffel cognomen?"

Galiena found herself on the receiving end of a truly hairy eyeball. "Very amusing, Madame. To be truthful, his middle name is Luitpold, but he never uses it. Unlike Heydrich who's always beating people about the head with his plethora of names," The man added, seemingly as an afterthought.

"There's nothing wrong with having an overabundance of nomenclature, Herr Gruppenführer. It lends one some individuality from the others on the family tree," Galiena said, thinking on her own four personal names.

"I hate to ponder what a poor, overburdened oak your family tree is." Wolff extended his palm upwards very deliberately. "Now Pfalzgräfin, your keys if you please."

"My car. I drive." It didn't help that she yawned as she said the words. Did he really expect she was going to give into his demands?

"You, Madame, are a road hazard and it would be a dereliction of duty if I let you drive," The man answered, tapping his fingers against his palm. "Keys. Please. Now." The choppy way he said it made each word its own sentence.

"Wait a moment, mein Herr. You've been awake a very long time too," she protested more out of principle than anything else.

"Half as long as certain other people an officer might name," Wolff paused a moment. "But I would never be so indiscreet as to tell anyone." The insistent tapping again, before the frown returned to his face. "How on earth have you done it, Madame?"

Galiena smirked at him, her wit a punchy thing. "Haven't you heard? Queens don't need sleep. It's part of our divine powers."

"It's the strangest thing, Your Majesty, but I find myself not believing you." The bright blue eyes, so tired around the edges, bored into her.

"Pure bloody panic. And the pharmaceuticals I mentioned," she admitted truthfully. "Ergo, I'm just as fresh as you are," she paused. "After a fashion."

"Yes. It's the fashion I'm worried about." Tap. Tap. Tap of his fingers against his palms. It was obvious he didn't think much of her taking the pills, for it showed in the rigid lines of his body.

Galiena dropped her key ring in his hands. "I won't sleep, mein Herr. I don't even know if I can."

Wolff escorted her to the passenger side door of the car. "Then I give you full permission to natter at me instead, Pfalzgräfin; just accept the help for a change." His fingers drummed on the roof of the vehicle. "Dear God! Just don't tell my wife I gave you permission to natter at me. She might think it applies in perpetuity to her; simply by association."

Galiena allowed him to seat her, and then she waited until he walked around the car to sit himself. "I really am thankful you came, Gruppenführer Wolff." It was honest and surprisingly heartfelt.

The exhausted officer heaved his shoulders as he put the keys in the ignition, then flashed her a boyish smile, so out of place on his wan face. "It certainly wasn't dull, Pfalzgräfin. I will give you that. It certainly wasn't dull."

Chapter 37
March 7, 1938

He first became aware of the pounding in his skull; a rhythmic, insistent tattoo of agony. Next was the ache in his bones, as if the joints of his body had been stretched beyond capacity. Lastly was the dry, pasty feeling in his mouth as if his tongue had adhered to his palate in a way that no amount of water could fix. He was agony personified. Everything in his body ached relentlessly.

As he groaned aloud, he became aware of a terrible odor; the acrid sweat of sickness. It was so close that he could only imagine it came from his own person. He could almost taste it. That was something rather surprising in itself for as he peeled his tongue into its normal position, the foul taste in his mouth was more than he could bear.

His mind rolled back, trying to account for this present state, but all was blank. It was as if nothing existed before this moment. No. That wasn't true. He was Standartenführer Doctor Hagen Luitpold Kohl. Yes. He had a name. Then an iota of memory flooded back. He had a past, like any other man and everything was as it should be. Except? His eyes rolled around under closed lids, feeling as if they had been rolled in grains of sand. What couldn't he remember? He drifted over his childhood, his time abroad, his time in the SS, and the last few months. Galiena. Yes. He most certainly remembered his Galiena.

Hagen opened his gummy eyelids to see he was in a dim room. He chilled as it registered in his mind that he had no memory of this place. Not only was there a terrible overabundance of chintz, the room was simply unfamiliar. The large cabbage roses in shades of purple, pink and teal were probably the most hideous thing he had ever seen, and Hagen was a man who had partaken of many visual horrors. He clenched his hands at the sight, and then winced as his finger pads touched his palm. It hurt! Aching arms lifted to show palms covered in scabs, as if his hands had been pressed into a sander. What truly terrified scared Hagen was that he didn't know how it had happened.

"So are you honestly awake this time?" The ruined voice floated above him, and Hagen turned his head to see gleaming eyes staring back at him from a chair beside the bed.

"Eugen," Hagen whispered, his own voice mere shreds from a throat which felt as raw as his palms. He felt such relief to see his friend, an unimaginable relief. He was safe from- What was he safe from? Hagen studied Eugen blankly. Whatever it was, it was horrific.

"You stupid, fucking bastard!" There was a measurable relief in those words. It had been years since Hagen had seen Eugen so haggard. His eyes were sunken into his skull and the skin of his face hung limply as the huge man grinned. Yet those magical, emerald eyes glittered with their usual amount of life.

"Where am I?" Hagen asked in confusion. His skin crawled and there was a revoltingly damp quality to the sheets he was laying in.

"Demeter's pension. The men brought you here to me, and you had best thank your lucky stars they did. Someone was watching over you the other night," Eugen paused and his face took on its usual ferocious scowl. "Now just what the hell were you doing, Hagen? Demeter told me they drugged you, and that he last saw you trailing after some girl. Then you disappeared and Kurt Kunz picked you up some four kilometers away from the castle at six a.m.; dangerously hypothermic, raving, and covered in blood."

"I don't know!" The words slipped out before Hagen could stop them and they shamed him to the core. He didn't know. He remembered going to the party; that was for certain. It was on the outskirts of the city in an old convent. Then in a flash, the image of the swastika engulfed in flames hit him; blue flames eating greedily at fabric. "It was a nightmare," he whispered brokenly.

"Come, Hagen! You have to remember some of it? How did they give you the drugs? What do you remember? The little shrink checked you over and assured me that no one koshed you over the head," his friend told him with an encouraging look. "It all has to be in there somewhere. You just have to think about it."

"Which is easier said than done, Eugen. It feels like the battle of the Somme is being waged in between my ears," But what was even more insistent was the terrible throbbing of his bladder.

When he thought about it, that might just have been what woke him up. "I need to pee," Hagen sat up, and the room began to rotate.

"Let me get you the pot. Just a moment." Eugen moved to reach under the bed.

"No. Not that!" Hagen interjected with haste, for using a chamberpot like some invalid felt like the final indignity. "I'd rather go to the bathroom if you don't mind."

"If you think you're up to it, sure! It's just down the hall." Eugen pulled the blankets off Hagen and held out an arm to his friend. "Can you stand on your own?"

Hagen glared up at the big man, the ferocity of expression causing the drumming in his skull to increase in intensity. The pain caused saliva to flow into his dry mouth, which didn't improve the taste any. "I think so." He swung his legs out and realized absently that the clammy garment he was wearing was one of Eugen's nightshirts. His muscles felt wobbly and it took a strong arm from his friend to keep his balance. "Jesus Christ! What's wrong with me?"

Eugen pulled Hagen's arm over his shoulders, his own going around Hagen's waist in support. "Well, you've not been so good, Hagen," The words came out with a small grunt as Eugen shifted most of Hagen's weight across the room. "In fact, you've been downright terrible."

"What is it? Saturday afternoon?" Hagen asked blankly. The party had been Friday, so it only made sense that today would be Saturday. He supposed if he had been on a four kilometer trek overland it might explain some of this, but he was an SS man! He was in better shape, even for a pencil pusher.

"It's actually Monday, my friend. As I said, you've been not yourself for a few days. I'm just glad you came around. Even Demeter was starting to get worried about you," Eugen told him, kicking the door open a little wider to let them pass.

They passed through the doorway and Hagen took a few minutes to digest this piece of information. He had lost two, almost three days. It seemed incomprehensible to him, and yet there was a hole in his mind. "Three days? You say it's Monday? What happened to me?" Hagen asked brokenly, his rubbery feet stumbling.

His friend kept him from careening into the wall. "You've been a mess. Had a terrible fever. Everything we tried to put in you, you spit back up like a fountain," Eugen rumbled a relieved sounding laugh. "Christ! What a mess. It's a good thing I like you, Hagen, because I'd kill any other man who puked on me as much as you have."

The hallway seemed to go on forever. Hagen's knees felt frozen, and his calves and thighs were shaking from the effort. He couldn't remember being sick. He couldn't remember past the swastika burning. A bitter frustration covered him, and he glanced over at Eugen's face. "I'm sorry for that. I don't remember doing it, but I'm sorry."

"Bah, Hagen! It's not the first time you've soaked me in vomit, and I'm sure it won't be the last! Remember? When I came to you in Augsburg? When you had the great flu? Now that was puking! It was everywhere! All your servants had fled after your parents' funeral? Hell! It was coming out of both ends of you then, and for a few weeks. I nursed you then, and I've nursed you now. No big trial for me." The big man pushed open a door, revealing the stark white bathroom with a large claw foot bathtub. "I wouldn't do it for anyone else, mind you, and if you tell anyone, I might have to kosh you one."

Hagen felt a humbling gratitude in his chest. "Thanks, Eugen. As usual, I owe you."

The Hauptsturmführer moved carefully to avoid jostling his friend, but still managed to drop him onto the toilet before leaning back against the wall. "It's nothing, Teufel. Nothing at all, really. Though I must say that I'm a little tired of putting up with your shit for one weekend,. Then a sly wink covered one emerald eye. "But come next weekend, I'll be right as rain again."

They were both silent as Hagen relieved himself; the noise of liquid hitting liquid filling the room. Such a basic task never felt like such a relief! As he flushed the toilet and washed his hands, he slanted an eye at the claw foot with undisguised longing. "I don't suppose you would consent to having our briefing in here, would you?"

Eugen smirked gamely. "More of a debriefing, hm? Why not? You smell like an SA locker room after a particularly debauched set of manoeuvres. Even my delicate sensitivities are insulted."

A flash. Breasts exposed and warm under his fingers. Galiena sprawled obscenely over a credenza, her hair trailing over the edge. Hagen closed his eyes, but the memory fled as fast as it appeared. Then the swastika again; consumed in electric blue flame with a heat that threatened to melt his flesh from his bones. "What happened to me?" He muttered as he clawed at his eyes with one hand.

A clamp at his wrist pulled the claw away. "I don't know, Hagen. You tell me! You've been raving for three days; completely out of your head! Kunz brought you in here like death itself, and all you said was 'God is Himmler, Eugen.' While quite the correct answer for organization to which you belong, it wasn't very helpful." His friend bent over and started the water in the bathtub then turned around and carefully pulled off Hagen's soiled nightshirt like an unabashed mother. "As I said, Demeter's been not much help. Took your vitals the next morning when he finally rolled in and muttered about some drug. Mescaline? Something like that. Said you would have one hell of a story when you woke up and dearly hoped you got laid by the doppelganger in the gold dress."

"Gormghlaith," Hagen breathed the name absently as he stepped into the steaming bathwater, then froze as he realised the mumbled word had significance.

"What's that? Some aristo slang this poor peasant wouldn't understand?" Eugen snorted under his breath as he stamped over to the linen closet and pulled out a towel. "Grom-lee?" He repeated with derision. "Sounds all frenchified to me, and you know how I feel about French things." A large finger was thrust in Hagen's direction. "Don't want 'em! Don't trust 'em!"

The water was a scalding balm against Hagen's confusion. "I thought you just skipped all the pleasantries and shot the bastards on sight." The familiar banter helped to focus him on the here and now. The nightmares would sort themselves out with any luck.

"If only you were so lucky. Kaiser taught me to kill them, but I have to say that anytime I get the opportunity-" The growl paused then flared in intensity. "Which is never, by the way,

505

Hagen! But where was I? Yes. It's still a great pleasure to shoot the bastards. The French are nothing but a crock full of slithering trouble."

"May I use that in my next report?" Hagen asked as an unconscious grin crawled across his face. He loved Eugen's use of language, for the man's turn of phrase could be absolutely delightful. "I think the Reichsführer would approve no end of that one." He had a mental image of Himmler tossing French soldiers into a butter churn and chortled quietly to himself.

Eugen rested his back against the wall and crossed his arms over his chest. "Be my guest, Hagen. I'm always willing to share my sunshine with the rest of the Order." One hand drifted to the big man's eyes and he knuckled them violently and yawned. "Dear Jesus, I'm tired."

Hagen reached for the soap and lathered himself with obsessive vigour. His mouth tasted so bad he was tempted to eat the bar when he was done. The froth covered his hairless chest and obscured his body from sight, the smell of lavender and mint strong in his nostrils. "Why so?"

The glare sent Hagen's way was positively withering. "You were sick, Hagen," The man said as if that it explained everything, but at Hagen's blank glance, he continued. "I wasn't going to let some Nancy-boy Rottenführer attend you! They might have killed you by accident, or even worse, told Heydrich that you can't handle your liquor. I'm certainly not going to let it get out that you were gooned out of your skull. No. I wasn't letting you out of my sight until I knew that you were out of the woods." His face took on a strangely possessive air. "I'm the only one who's going to clean up your vomit, thank you very much."

"I'm, uh, flattered, Eugen," Hagen stammered as he sunk under the water to his neck to wash off the soap. The water simply couldn't be hot enough.

"Don't get all uppity about it. I'll get my pound of flesh out of you in some other fashion." The growl was far more bark than bite.

Hagen raised himself up to a more normal posture and was about to soap again when he had the vision of a slice down his belly. His innards burst through his skin, but it wasn't his skin; he was so far above the image. There was so much blood; the crimson rivers showered like a waterfall over the block of stone to pour onto a stone floor. Hagen's hands began to shake and he clenched them, causing the bar of soap to shoot out of his grasp and across the bathroom. But it wasn't a bar of soap. It was a man's head; his expression one of surprise and unbearable agony. The head slid down the wall, the lips whispering at Hagen. "Remember me! Remember me!"

Hagen started throwing his head back and forth trying to dispel the terrible image from his mind when Eugen grabbed him by the shoulders and gave him a rough shake. "You've gone white as a sheet, man! What the hell's the matter with you?"

"Galiena!" Hagen gasped as his gorge rose. Galiena with a wicked knife raised over her head, a backdrop of robed figures in the darkness around her. "Oh, God!"

"What about her, Hagen? You've been calling out her name for three days now! What about Galiena?" Eugen leaned over with a terrible urgency written across his features.

The attack of shaking stilled, and Hagen bonelessly dropped his forehead against Eugen's bicep. "She killed a man, Eugen! I watched her kill a man. She was riding him and she pulled out a knife and slit him from groin to gizzard," the words tumbled out one after another like ice cubes from a glass. "Then she reached into his guts and pulled them out; snakes writhing in his belly falling off the altar. The Grandmaster, he flung them into the crowd and then Wills cut the man's head off with Galiena's knife. He looked so happy, Eugen-" He paused for a moment as the vision swam over him. "Then he threw the head away down the aisle and out the door. It was supposed to have been me."

Eugen stared down at him for a long moment before he blinked and heaved a tremendous sigh. "I knew you were too sick still to have a bath." He reached in to grab Hagen's chest. "Come on! Let's get you out of there."

Hagen refused to budge from his place, sitting like a dead weight in the bathtub. "I'm telling you the truth, Eugen!" The memory was like a millstone on his chest. "I saw Galiena give a French lesson17 to von Ond and four other boys," the proper term eluded him in his agony.

---

17 Early 20ᵗʰ C slang for fellatio

The brilliant green eyes were furious orbs just millimeters from his own. "If you were any other man, you would be swallowing your teeth right now, I swear before God and the Fuhrer!"

Words spilled from his lips without conscious thought as images flooded into his mind, and Hagen ignored his friend as he continued. "But I had already dishonored her. I threw her up onto a piece of furniture and I took her, Eugen." A terrible shame covered him as broken memories attacked him in a rush. "I was going to cut my heart out and give it to her; I could feel it beating in my palm." He flexed his hand, almost feeling the weight of the pulsating organ there. "Instead I hurt her and she encouraged me like a whore. 'I want you to fuck me, Herr Graf,' she said. 'I want you to make it hurt.'" He met his friend's terrifying gaze; finishing simply. "And I did."

The sound of Eugen's teeth grinding was audible as the man's entire jaw joint pulsed. "Do not, ever again, refer to our Pfalzgräfin as a whore!" He gave Hagen a second brisk shake then let go of him abruptly, dropping down to sit beside the bathtub. "Oh hell! It can't have been her. The Pfalzgräfin is in Berlin, or she was on Saturday morning. She arrived at Göring's Palais with Karl Wolff at nine a.m. or some such strange time. There has been some consternation in certain circles about that, but the Reichsführer seems to have known what they were doing together. That's what our reports from town said this morning and if she was with Wolff in Berlin at nine looking like someone who had been dragged through a keyhole backwards then I highly doubt she could have been murdering people at two a.m. outside of Vienna," Eugen paused again. "Though with a plane it could have been possible, and our people said that her appearance was practically a dog's breakfast but I don't believe that. I most certainly do not believe she was on the town with Wolff. Let alone the two of us, Himmler would have Wolff's tripe with his tea if Wolff dishonoured her. Besides, from what I hear, Wolff might have a little something else on the backburner."

Hagen barely registered the scope of his comrade's words as he tried to sort through the flashes in his head. "It wasn't our Galiena. You're right; but it was some sort of demon Galiena! I can't explain it, Eugen. It looked so much like her; they could have

508

been twins!" A thought struck him suddenly. "But her German had a strange accent, it's true, so it couldn't have been our Galiena."

"Demeter said you were chasing after a golden doppelganger!" Eugen rolled his shoulders and then grinned suddenly. "Oh well then! That's an entirely different matter to me! Good for you, Hagen! It's about time you crawled out of the monastery and joined the rest of us sinners," The grin widened, and Eugen's large, crooked teeth were completely in evidence. "How was it? How was this Succubus of our Pfalzgräfin?"

It was such an Eugen thing to say and Hagen couldn't help but chuckle. "Not as good as I imagine the real thing will be, but not bad at all!" He felt a flickering of guilt in the pit of his stomach, but he pushed it aside. He wasn't married, so it was hardly an affair; that coupled with the fact he had been drugged removed most of his culpability.

"Interesting. Interesting," the large man tapped the rim of the bathtub with a thick finger. "So if what you're saying is true, this Succubus Galiena killed a man in front of you? I can't say as I approve of that sort of thing being done by a woman."

Hagen thought about it; tried to process the things he had seen. "Gormghlaith. That was her name. I remember that. Gormghlaith from Galway. They call her the goddess Freya and the NAO consider her some sort of talisman," He buried his face in his sodden hands in frustration and groaned. "Christ, Eugen! I remember and I don't! I just don't understand this. It's maddening! There are these visions before my eyes; things I remember, but I don't know if they are real or something I dreamed up. I know I didn't cut my heart out, but I remember watching it pumping in my hand as I chased the Succubus down a hallway. I remember being in some dark place and Himmler talking to me looking like some renaissance vision of God. All flowing robes and hair and pince-nez, Eugen! When I was running through the forest he was flying at my shoulder like a glistening angel, urging me to keep running."

Eugen nodded slowly to himself as he took in Hagen's words, then he reached over and lightly punched Hagen in the shoulder. "Well I will believe whatever you tell me happened, my friend. I've never doubted you. While I doubt that the Reichsführer has become the Almighty, who can say? Maybe some part of Himmler's soul was there that night to watch over you. Lord knows, no one is ever going to see me in the guise of the Almighty and I have no special powers of the mind to be in two places at the same time. Himmler is grandmaster of the order, and I know all about his prayer sessions. Maybe he's cast a spell on you to protect you or some such thing. I don't know."

Hagen leaned back into the tub forlornly, taken somewhat aback by Eugen's words. "Himmler's not a warlock," He responded, rubbing a slick hand over his chest, feeling wrung out like a sponge. He still felt so filthy from head to toe. "He's no more a warlock than I am."

"You've never been ordinary, Standartenführer Doctor Hagen Kohl. You do things to men's minds unlike anything I've ever seen."

"That's not magic, that's manipulation. It's understanding how people think which gives me the ability to do that. Understanding what they want in an effort to get what I want." He slanted an apologetic look at his friend wishing he could explain better. "Could I trouble you to grab me the soap?"

"Next you're going to ask me to sing the SA lied, and then, Standartenführer Kohl, I am going to kosh you one!" But Eugen crawled over and picked up the glistening bar, depositing it in Hagen's outstretched hand. "So was someone really murdered? Or weren't they?"

The lye in the soap burned across the shredded skin on Hagen's knees and palms. "I swear to you that man was killed. They eviscerated him and screamed it was time for war. I don't know who he was, but I have this impression it was supposed to be me. Wills was furious they couldn't find me." It was like a light went on in Hagen's head; another thought struck him. "Wilhelm von Glass is one of the leaders of the NAO."

"I find that somewhat harder to believe than Himmler's spirit running around watching over his favorites, Hagen. That man is an undeniable fag." Eugen scoffed as he leaned back against the wall, his arms wrapped around his knees.

"Ass-banditry doesn't preclude militarism, my friend." Hagen soaped his face then carefully washed behind his ears and attended to his hair. "There have been many famous homosexual warriors; Alexander the Great for a start."

510

"I would say there is a huge difference between Wilhelm Ritter von Glass and Alexander the Great; Greek fashion18 or no. The man is a pouf." Eugen spoke through a giant yawn.

Hagen ran the water of the tap and dunked his head under it until the soap had run completely from his head. "I knew before the party that von Glass was a member; the other night just confirmed it for me. There are two divisions in the group. A group calls themselves priests and von Glass leads the warriors. The High Priest is someone who I think was familiar but I can't tell you who it was right now. If I heard his voice again, perhaps I could confirm it. The warriors are the ones who are perpetrating the violence against us; the bombings and the acts themselves, I mean. I don't know what the priests do beyond worship this Freya girl. I didn't see much. If what I remember is in anyway accurate, then it's not so much of an organization but a cult."

"So then we pick up von Glass and make him talk." The idea seemed to fill Eugen with a particular enthusiasm. "Him and that disgusting von Reitersbach."

"No. Freffie's not involved. I don't remember him as being there, and I remember the Succubus telling me that Freffie sent her to save me. I can't ignore that no matter how much I try." Besides, he had promised Galiena that he would do his best to protect Freffie.

"We can still make him talk." Eugen cracked his knuckles with a sharp pop, a sound Hagen had always found especially grating.

"Not that way. I would much prefer if Freffie told me what he knows on his own. Since I signed the papers of adoption, Freffie has taken me somewhat under his wing and I believe that I can convince him to tell me the truth. I think gentle coercion would be much better served than the physical alternative, no matter how much you prefer it."

The large man glanced up abruptly, his head nearly connecting with the wall. "Adoption?"

Hagen shrugged in acute embarrassment as he realized this might be the first time Eugen was hearing about the situation. "Didn't I tell you? Galiena wanted him to adopt me and he has. It

---

18 Old slang for anal sex

was official last week, but I'm not telling anyone and I'm certainly not changing my name. She needed done for some societal reason but I'm not giving it anymore attention than the damn thing deserves."

"So what's your name?" Eugen demanded in a tone which bordered on rudeness.

"According to the papers, Hagen Kohl Graf von Reitersbach."

Eugen blinked and his expression became a mystery to Hagen. "Graf von Reitersbach? You're a Graf now? A Graf?" He repeated somewhat dazedly.

"It doesn't mean anything, Eugen. Nothing at all. I would call it a gimmick for the nobility. As I said, I don't want anyone in the SS to know, even though Freffie has been shouting it from the rooftops. Perhaps I should rephrase and say I don't want it to become common knowledge," Hagen ordered sternly as inwardly he still cringed away from the concept. No matter what Freffie said, he wasn't going to pretend he was the man's toy son.

"Of course not, Your Illustrious Highness," Eugen replied in a saucy sing-song voice which grated on Hagen far more than the man cracking his knuckles.

Hagen pointed an angry finger at his comrade. "I swear to God, you do that again and I'm going to kosh you one!" He answered, stealing Eugen's favorite word.

"Whatever you say, Your Illustrious Highness."

The soap was a handy projectile and Hagen wasn't too weak to send it flying into Eugen's head. It caught his friend right over the ear and completely off guard. "Maybe that will teach you." Hagen muttered.

Eugen rubbed the offending place and affected a bruised expression. "Ow. That actually hurt. What an amazingly good pitch you have when you only have to throw something half a meter." Devilry still played at the corner of the man's lips. "So what is the plan now, Your Aristocratic Magnificence?"

Hagen decided to ignore that for if he made anymore comments, Eugen would never let up. "I return to Freffie's tonight. I will tell him that some tart took me back to Salzburg from the party and I'm just getting back now. He probably won't question it all that much. I want you to set up a meeting with Strohkeller for me on Wednesday morning. We might need to change our tactics. Talk to him and see if you can get someone closer to von Ond. I think our plant has passed his initiation and we need a more reliable way to get information from him. Faster too. This situation is escalating, but I don't want to talk to Strohkeller until I write down everything I can remember and come up with a solid plan of attack. My memories may solidify more with time and then I can give you something more definite than this garbage," For garbage was what it was. What person in their sane mind would believe him from what he had described?

"I don't want you going back to von Reitersbach's if von Glass wants to kill you. That's not exactly safe and I think you know that," Eugen protested with dreadful seriousness; all earlier jests aside.

"Don't worry about it, Eugen. I'm going to watch him very closely and I'm certainly not going to go anywhere alone with him. I will be safe enough," Hagen protested, raising his hands over his chest as if in defense.

The white head swiveled back and forth swiftly. "That's not good enough for me. He, or one of his people, could shank you at anytime, or slip something in your food."

"Freffie doing that to me once was enough. No. I will be careful and I'll keep to fruit and things which can't be tampered with. Freffie doesn't want me dead, so I doubt Wills will hurt me under their roof and I can watch Wills far better from the inside that we can from the outside." Hagen explained carefully feeling exhausted from the effort of talking. Throwing the soap at Eugen had drained his strength severely and his head was pounding. Now what he desperately yearned for was a toothbrush.

"I don't like it."

"I don't care."

This time it was Eugen's turn to ignore Hagen which he did with decided élan. "I will put an ear around if anyone is missing a follower; either the Austrian SA or SS. I can only imagine if there is a victim out there that he's one of ours."

Hagen nodded as he followed Eugen's logic. "Find out everything you can about von Gazen's estate. We might need to go on a field trip one night this week. I remember a building; a church, I think. That's where it happened if it did happen at all. It's hard to eviscerate someone and not leave a terrible mess. I don't think that the men of the NAO would take the time to do a very thorough clean up job; perhaps we can find something to prove what I think I saw." Doubt gnawed his intestines; a violent griping at his empty guts causing shivers to run through his body. Hagen hated being so unsure of himself; it only served to make him feel desperately helpless. Reliance on the powers of his mind had always been the route of his successes and now he couldn't rely on the fragments and hallucinations that swarmed like hornets inside his mind. "I just couldn't swear to anything at the moment."

"I will put some men on it." Eugen assured him, and Hagen was calmed to see that there was absolutely no doubt in the man's face. They had been crabbing around in the dark trying to discover their enemy, but now the New Austrian Order was revealed. Together they would hunt them down to a man.

January 9, 1938

Dearest Poppet,

I am so excited to see you! So much to talk about! So many plans to make! I am a whirl with it! You will find me a changed man! My love for you has exploded in size! You are the world. I worship you! I will make everything better. I will never be such a beast again! Three days! Three days! I cannot wait. Sweet Poppet, soon we will be together again! How I will show you how much I have missed you!

Eternally yours,
Meinrad

Pamphlet found outside of Vienna:

Brother Austrians;

Our revolution is at hand. This farce of a republic has failed. We of the New Austrian Order are determined to restore our beloved Arch Duke Otto and drive the slavering Nazi hoards from our lands.

To that end we have declared war on Adolf Hitler and his scurrilous minions. Be Aware, Nazis! If you come to our country, you will be thrashed. We pledge this in the blood of your own SA-Untersturmführer Ernst Gerger. He is but the first.

Join us, Austrians. You have moved away from our Teutonic roods and our present strife is proof of the Gods displeasure. The Goddess Freya is the side of those who would restore Austria's Natural sovereign. The Goddess Freya is on our side. We are the true faithful who will restore mighty Freya to her people.

Join us!

Grandmaster of the New Austrian Order

Wiener Zeitung
March 6, 1938

A night of unspeakable horrors was revealed when the body of a young man was discovered in a peaceful suburb of the city. SA-Untersturmführer Ernst Gerger, lately of Graz, was found hanging in a disgraceful fashion by the local constabulatory. Sources close to the investigation suggested that the young man was found in the image of Christ on the cross. He had also been subjected to the most inhuman mutilations.

Gentle readers, do you fear a monster lurking in our midst? This reporter has learned that the victim belonged to an organisation which is directly responsible for the present strife. Whether or not this was an act of murder or simple vigilantism is a matter for the constables, but in this reporter's mind, the city will not suffer for the loss of this person whose head was very much to the north. Those Nationalistic Austrians who are Loyal to the Fatherland Front have very little to fear.

As all things have a habit of growing, so too did The New Austrian Order. Look for the continuation and resolution in my next book, Anschluß.

Want to stay in the loop? Check out www.ldtowers.net and @L_D_Towers on twitter!

L.D.Towers

www.ingramcontent.com/pod-product-compliance
Lightning Source LLC
Chambersburg PA
CBHW070540030726
47505CB00001B/99